The Ariana Series

Be the Light

Becoming the Light

Fighting Darkness

Joan L. Scibienski

Flint Hills Publishing

Cover Design by Amy Albright

stonypointgraphics.weebly.com

Flint Hills Publishing
Topeka, Kansas U.S.A.

www.flinthillspublishing.com

Printed in the U.S.A.

ISBN: 978-1-7332035-5-5

The Ariana Series

Book 1

Be the Light

DEDICATION

This book is dedicated to the person whose help allowed it to manifest perfectly, Thea Rademacher. I would also like to thank my life partner, Chris Bellia, my loyal supporter, Elaine Johns, and of course the wonderful combined consciousness who channeled this material and so much more to me, Equinoxx.

Prologue

The wind rose in the west, forcing the waves to break fiercely against the rugged shore. Ariana stood absorbing the intense energy and smiled. She loved this small inlet that led to the sea. The energy she felt in this place filled her and elevated her mood. Today, however, Ariana's mood needed no improvement. She was excited, expectant. It was time.

Ariana turned and began her walk toward the spiral towers of Meria. How she loved this planet, this city, and especially her life! As she walked slowly toward her fate, she thought about her life. It had been a good one so far. Her abilities had manifested young and rapidly. She exhibited none of the struggles most of the younglings endured. Her path was clear to her from first sight. She would be a great healer and teacher. As her abilities began to appear, first empathy, then sight, her strengths became evident to the others as well. There was no hesitancy on Ariana's part, no confusion. Each new task was approached surely and well. Each new ability was mastered easily. Now in her 18th cycle of life, she was ready to be assigned her function, her purpose and path. She was sure she would be assigned to the healers and she was glad. This knowledge gave her joy as she clearly saw her life unfold in her mind. She would use her healing abilities to nurture and love her people and her planet. She would help those that were struggling to find their inner calling, their path. She would also help the younglings to learn to use their abilities. She would teach them to reach into their cores and discover their truth. She would help them define their abilities which would in turn, show them their path. There should be no struggle in this exploration of the self, only joy. She knew that she could teach them. This was her destiny. She felt wonderful because this was all she had ever wanted.

Ariana entered the red hall and breathed in the emotional substance of the building. Fear, excitement, anxiety, and happiness permeated the structure. The intense feelings did not surprise her. This is where all citizens of Meria came to hear what the Elders had decided would be their path, their fate. It was in this building where her planet's occupants learned who they would be and how they would contribute to their people and to the All.

Mother Tehan entered from the south corridor and smiled, "Ariana, we are glad you have come. You received your message that it was time, we presume?"

"Yes, Mother. It came as I was absorbing the storm."

"Ah, the Combined Mind has answered your desire then. You have been wishing to know your path?" Tehan asked.

"Yes, Mother," answered Ariana, "I am afraid that patience has not come to my inner being yet. Although I work at it, it eludes me."

"You are still young, little Ariana. Are you sure you are ready?"

"Mother, I have known my calling since I took first breath. I have learned all that the Teachers have to teach. It is time."

Mother Tehan looked closely at Ariana and asked, "Yes, but by your own words you have not learned patience. Could there be other things you have still to learn? Perhaps it would also be good to learn obedience, selflessness, and sacrifice? Remember our people have had to learn the hard lessons of ego, hubris, and too much desire, traits you have in abundance. If history has taught us anything, it is that these qualities begin to define a culture and that culture will become absorbed with greed and egotism which then wreak havoc and destruction. Our planet is only recently recovered from the devastation our ancestors brought upon it and each other. What will happen, Ariana, if your wishes are not the wishes of the Elders? Will you do your duty without understanding why? I wonder."

Embarrassed by the truth of the mother's remarks, Ariana bowed her head and said, "Then, Mother, I will have to work harder to overcome my faults and do what is necessary."

Mother nodded, "You have been blessed, child. I hope you will believe it. The Elders are ready for you now. Come this way."

Ariana could feel her stomach react to the Mother's words. *What's wrong with me?* she thought. *This is what I've been waiting for. This is what I desire. It is time to finally be a recognized healer, not just a student. It is time. I have to stop being a frightened youngling!*

Mother Tehan headed toward the north portal. As she and Ariana walked the hallway, it began to glow. Ariana knew the soft lighting was controlled by their body heat. She could feel the energy transfer creating the phosphorescence which lighted the walls. She knew that very few others could feel what she was experiencing. It was more proof that she was uniquely advanced as an energy empath.

"There's the ego again," Mother said. Ariana had forgotten that one of Mother Tehan's abilities was telepathy. "When will you learn to control it, as is customary of adults?"

Before Ariana could muster her answer, they reached the end of the hallway. The wall in front of her began to open upward. As she motioned Ariana forward, Mother Tehan said, "You must enter alone, Ariana."

Again, Ariana's stomach betrayed her outer calm. She breathed deeply, centered her mind, bowed deeply to Mother Tehan, and entered the circular room. Instantly, the door whooshed shut, taking with it Ariana's breath. Unreasonable fear gripped her. *Why?* she wondered, *What do I know that I am not allowing myself to see? I must still my thoughts so that I might have full access to them.* She forced herself to focus on the room. It appeared to be an ordinary room, no different than many she had entered throughout her life. She knew the ambient colors changed according to her energy, her aura. Right now it was a muddy blue. Fear was manifesting within her normally clear blue and violet aura. She adjusted her energy by focusing her attention on the peace and love within her center and was gratified to notice the room colors adjusting as well. It became a pale clear blue shifting at times into lavender. *Wonderful,* she thought, *perfectly appropriate colors for a healer.*

Ariana focused her attention to the other aspects of the room. The temperature was cool, but not cold. The light appeared to be natural lighting, though there were no windows. The walls were perfectly smooth with no apparent openings. The strangest thing about the room, however, was that it was completely empty. No furniture. She could feel no energy aside from her own. She wondered if she was in an antechamber. *Are they watching me right now?* she wondered. *Is that why I feel so anxious? Relax! Quiet yourself. Breathe and let go. . .* She began to focus on her breath. In. . . out. . . in. . . out. . . slowly. . . relax. . . in. . . out. . . slowly. . . relax. . . She continued to focus more deeply on her breath. In. . . out. . . in. . . out. . . slowly. . . relax. . . in. . . out. . . slowly. . . relax. . .

"ARIANA."

She jumped. The sound seemed to be coming from everywhere, but she soon realized the voice was really in her mind.

Yes, she thought.

Please sit, the voice instructed. She looked down, then around the room again. She still saw no furniture. Before she could ask where to sit, she received an overwhelming desire to sit on the floor right where she stood. She sat and immediately felt relaxed, her body and mind instantly at peace. She closed her eyes and smiled as she clearly saw and felt her memories, experiences, feelings, and desires run rapidly through her mind and body. She felt happy but somehow detached. It was as though she was reading about her life, not remembering it. The last memory, sitting on this floor, flashed in her mind and her consciousness was brought back to the present. Now she was not alone. Standing against the walls that surrounded her were the Twelve Wise Ones. She had not felt them enter or sensed their energies. This was very disturbing. She always felt shifts in energy.

Ariana, do not trouble yourself with worthless thoughts. You are here to receive your path, correct? questioned the eldest of the Wise Ones. None of them had names. They had no use for them. They were no longer individuals; they were one mind.

Yes, Elder, Ariana answered, centering her thoughts.

Sensing she was ready, the Wise Ones began. *Throughout the generations, since the Dark Times, we have been the guardians of the other humanoid planets. As we are the donors of the genetic material that seeded these planets, we feel this responsibility keenly. It is our greatest purpose, our ultimate mission, and Meria's Path. Only the most exceptional younglings are tasked with the responsibility of monitoring and helping these planets. Few of our people even know of this responsibility and connection, or that there are others like us in the Universes. Historically, all we did was observe these planets. Very occasionally we stepped in to help promote change. There are myths of our existence, but as time has progressed, they are considered to be stories without fact. We are glad of this as the less that is known of our existence, the better for our purposes. Those purposes are to allow these planets to evolve naturally toward consciousness, their own versions of consciousness and humanity, not ours. It has been hundreds of years since we were physically present on any of these worlds. However, it is now necessary again. Without our interventions, not only will the entities on this planet called Terra destroy their own home, but through their actions, there is a possibility that many other worlds will be destroyed. We cannot allow this. We must again have a presence on Terra and that presence will be you.*

Ariana gasped. She was astonished, appalled. *What of my dreams for my life here? I'm to be exiled from the planet I love? What is this new world? Is it primitive, violent?* She began to feel panic, an unknown emotion. There was nothing to fear on Meria. Panic never happened. She had no idea how to deal with it.

I will not be a healer? Tears filled Ariana's eyes.

Not on Meria, came the answer.

But I think that I am afraid. I want to disobey; to run away. Please reconsider. I am not the one for this assignment, she begged.

The Wise Ones filled Ariana's mind, *We do not make this decision without much work on our part. We have been observing you since you were conceived. We have been monitoring your gifts, your insights, and your grasp of energies that cannot be taught. You are not only a fine student, but also an instinctual savant. Many of your teachers have reported that you possess instincts far beyond any that they have seen since before the Dark Times. We believe that you are of the original stock. This is the original DNA used to seed these planets. As you know, we are changed. The Dark Times altered our DNA so that we only possess limited abilities, some more than others, but still greatly limited. Our original DNA was damaged irreparably. Yours, however, is not, giving you access to all the abilities the Ancestors possessed. You feel energies within the planet, through rock, water, and soil and also with humans and animals. But not only can you feel them, you have the power to manipulate them. You have the power to either destroy or bring them back to normalcy. We even believe that you may eventually have the ability to create from nothing but air and change what is normal to exceptional. You can access the corners and adjust the threads of all energy. You do these things naturally and without harm. You are not reckless, but you do what must be done almost without thought. You will do well. You must understand that the learning you have been doing on Meria has only been preparing you for what you must do to help Terra.*

The journey you are about to begin is your true path."

Ariana was amazed at what had just been said to her. She had never fully understood that her abilities were unusual; she just thought she was good at what she did. She understood that her dreams for her life on Meria would not come true now. She also understood that only in this way would she ever be able to completely realize her potential. She knew she was afraid. She also knew that she could do what was asked of her. She straightened her back and rose to her feet.

When do I leave?

Now.

⋨⋨⋨

"Push! Just one more push. I know you're tired, but we're almost there. I can already see the head. That's it, that's it! Congratulations Mrs. Abrams, you have a beautiful little girl."

The smiling nurse placed the blanket-wrapped baby into Anna Abrams's arms. "She weighs eight and a half pounds. She's 18 inches long. A beautiful, chubby little one. What are you naming her?"

Looking down at her new infant daughter, Anna replied, "She looks like an Ariana. Yes, Ariana Joanna Abrams."

The nurse smiled at the mother and child, "That's a beautiful name. It's too bad Mr. Abrams wasn't here with you."

"He'll be here later. He's working. He came to our older daughter's delivery but didn't see a need to be with us today. His business needs take priority," Anna said. "It might have been different if she was a boy, but as soon as we discovered she would be a girl, he lost interest."

"His loss," whispered the nurse. "You have a beautiful, healthy, very alert little girl and that is a blessing whether he realizes it or not."

Chapter 1

Ariana twirled her dark lock of hair around her finger. "When was the first time I thought about committing suicide? Well, that's kinda hard to answer. I can't remember feeling comfortable with my family, ever. I never felt like I fit in or was wanted. I always felt like an extra finger or toe, useless, but too hard to get rid of. The family already had a daughter, Lisa, my older sister. She and my mother were inseparable. She had been an only child for six years and my mother's constant focus for that long. My mom had no living family and my dad was never home, so Lisa became her life. I think the only reason Mom got pregnant again was to give my father a son, but whoops, no son, just me. The son came two years after me, so there was the complete family; the son for my father, Lisa for my mother, and oh, by the way, this other one, me."

"I can understand why you might feel lonely," the therapist stated.

"More than lonely, I felt unwanted, useless, and unnecessary. I wasn't the beautiful, talented one, which was my sister. I wasn't the namesake, the boy, every father's dream. No, I was the chubby one, the one that even my parents wondered about. I am not artistic or tall, lean and beautiful, nor have I ever done anything that my parents could brag about. How could I be one of the Abrams?"

The therapist said, "These things may be true to you, but you are highly intelligent, empathetic, perceptive, and caring. Those are wonderful traits."

"So you say," Ariana replied scornfully, "but no one else seemed to appreciate those qualities. This will probably sound weird or convince you I'm really crazy, but when I was a kid I was so lonely I had invisible friends. They weren't kids, but adult friends who played with me, loved me, and protected me. They taught me how to sense when my dad would be in a bad mood so that I could stay away from him. They helped me to understand the energies around me, like how to feel how the people around me were feeling, about me, life, whatever. They showed me how to modulate my own energy so that I blended into the environment and would not stand out." Ariana looked down at her feet and said, "Does that sound as weird as I think it does?"

"What do you think?" inquired the therapist.

"I think it does, especially because of how other people reacted when I told them."

"What other people did you tell?"

"When I was young, I tried to make friends with some of the kids in my neighborhood. It was hard because my family was Jewish. Everyone else in the neighborhood was Christian. That may not sound like a problem, but it was. Lots of people are still prejudiced. But there was one girl, Gloria. She was kind of an outcast like me. We got really close. I trusted her so much I told her my secret. But she betrayed me and told everyone else in the neighborhood. They laughed at me. They called me the Weirdo Witch. When my father found out he was incensed. How could I have embarrassed the family with such crazy nonsense? I got beaten real good that night. But the beating didn't hurt nearly as bad as the betrayal by a girl I thought was my friend. Once again, I was rejected and had no friends. Even my brother tormented me for years."

"Was there no one you could talk to?" asked the therapist.

Ariana smiled and seemed to be lost in thought for a moment. "My German grandmother, my oma. She lived with us for a while. She really loved me. When she heard about what had happened she came to my room and held me while I cried. She told me that in the old country many people had the ability to talk with spirits. She called these spirits guides or loved ones. She said that dead relatives often stay around to help those of us that are still alive. They protect us. She thought maybe that's what I was experiencing. Oma said she would help me to understand how to use my abilities better. Does this all sound nuts?"

"I think you loved your Grandmother and she was good to you and helped you to feel accepted. How did she help you with what she called 'your abilities?' "

"She told me that the Jews had a mystical heritage. That many Jews, especially the women, had special powers. These powers helped them survive. They even have a book called the Kabala that tells of some of these mysteries. She said that I should not be ashamed to be special, but that I should also not share this with anyone but her because most people just don't understand. Then she said we would play games that would help me to hone my powers."

"Games?"

"Yes. She taught me to use playing cards to see the future. She would ask me what I sensed from my environment or from people we met. She would give me clothing, jewelry, things, old things, to feel and tell what I saw or felt. Always, always, she was loving and encouraging."

"Your oma was kind to you," the therapist responded.

"She was the only one that was. I was so lonely, but also too shy and wary to even attempt to make new friends."

"Yes, it is hard to live in an environment where you feel you do not fit or are misunderstood," said the therapist. "All of us need to feel loved and accepted."

"You asked when I first thought seriously of suicide. The first conscious time was when I was 10. My Oma had just died and I was devastated. I was in my bedroom holding the stuffed elephant that she had given me for my birthday when I was called to dinner. I wasn't hungry so I begged my mother to please just leave me alone. That enraged my father. He came screaming into my room ordering me to get to the dinner table now! He grabbed the elephant out of my arms and ripped it into pieces. He grabbed me by the hair and dragged me into the hall. I was crying hard, not so much because of the pain, but for the destruction of Peanut, my elephant. It was the last tie I had to my oma.

'I'll give you a reason to cry!' my father screamed as he began to hit and kick me. 'Get up and sit at the table and eat everything or you'll really get it!'

With my mouth bleeding, one eye blackening, and a severe pain in my left ribs, I cleaned my plate, asked to be excused and went back to my room. I didn't know how to kill myself, but I really wanted to die. I decided I would find a way. You need to understand that this was not the first time my father beat me, it was a weekly, sometimes daily event, but it was the first time I didn't have Oma. There was no one who cared if I lived or died, so why should I live? The next night I crawled out my bedroom window and went to a house down the street that was under construction. It was a two-story house. I decided throwing myself out an upstairs window would accomplish what I desired. I was wrong. I succeeded in breaking my leg and drawing the attention of the neighbor, but failed miserably at killing myself. Hospitals in Indiana either didn't think a 10 year old would attempt suicide, or my dad made up some story that was awfully convincing, because they patched me up and sent me home. I was such a loser, I couldn't even die," Ariana exclaimed in obvious pain.

"How did your family respond?"

"It was strange. Dad didn't hit me or yell at me. Instead he took me to a child psychologist."

"How did that go?"

"Actually, it was great. My counselor befriended me. She listened to me and didn't judge. Back then I was into flowers. I wanted to plant a flower garden, but Dad wouldn't let me. Our house was professionally landscaped and maintained. What would the neighbors think if I wrecked its perfection? The counselor took me to a flower show, then to a nursery. There she bought me seeds and containers and showed me how to create a container garden. I loved it," Ariana explained, showing no emotion.

The therapist waited, but Ariana did not continue.

"What happened?" the therapist wondered out loud.

"It ended when the counselor asked to see my father during a session. She explained to him that the problem wasn't me. It was him and his violent behavior. He grabbed my hand and pulled me off the couch and out the door. When we got home, he emptied my garden into the garbage and never mentioned the counselor or counseling again."

The therapist raised one eyebrow but never changed her expression. "That must have hurt. Twice he destroyed something you loved. Was he violent with everyone in the family?"

"Yes."

"Did your mother ever attempt to stop the violence?"

"Not really," Ariana answered. "She was being beaten, too."

"Did the violence ever end?"

"The physical violence ended right before I came here to college because I threatened to report him to the police. After all, he was about to get rid of me soon and anyway, what would the neighbors think? The verbal violence continues, but I don't talk to my family much anymore. I don't think they mind very much. My father once told me that he wondered if his real child was switched with me at birth because there was no way I possessed his DNA." With a smile Ariana continued, "Actually, I hope he's right. I want nothing from them. My mother mostly ignored me and once I heard her admit to her best friend that she wished I'd never been born because she didn't need or want three kids and certainly didn't need another girl."

"That must have hurt."

"Not really. I think I knew that even before I heard it. I felt no loving emotions from my mother. No positive emotions anyway, just sort of an apathy toward me."

"What about your relationship with your sister and brother?"

"There really isn't much of one. My sister is six years older and pretty much had her own life. My brother is barely two years younger which is probably why we fought like cats and dogs. Probably to deal with the abuse in our family, he became angry and mean. He took that anger out on me and small animals. He knew no one would care. Going away to college was the best thing that has ever happened in my life."

"You like it here? You feel like you belong?"

"Before leaving for school, I thought about killing myself again. I was terrified of going to college. I saw it as just another big place with lots of kids who would be mean to me. It was another place I would probably fail and piss off my dad."

"What made you change your mind?"

"My invisible friends," answered Ariana, "they reminded me that no one knew me here and that gave me the opportunity to recreate myself, to become the person I've always wished I were."

"And who is that person?"

"She is smart, funny, and friendly. She has lots of friends, is involved in tons of activities and maybe even has a boyfriend."

"How's that working out? Do you have any friends yet?" the therapist asked.

"Here or at home?"

"Both, either."

"I was always shy, and after Gloria, distrustful. I didn't go out of my way to make friends. My parents probably wouldn't have wanted me to bring them home anyway, so I basically kept to myself. No one here either. I guess I should say, not yet."

"What about your roommate?"

"I think she hates me. She told me that I'm not her 'kind.' I'm not sure what her kind is: Christian, Arizonian, beautiful, dumb? All I know is she moves the furniture around when I'm in my night class so that I have something to trip over when I come to the room in the dark. She also told me she is going to torture me to get me to move out of the room. She's an amateur compared to my dad and brother. I can handle it," Ariana answered with a smirk. "Maybe *she'll* move out and I'll have the room all to myself."

The therapist nodded and asked, "Ariana, why did you begin counseling?"

"Because now I have the opportunity to begin the new life my invisible friends told me about, one that isn't about my family or my past. I'm scared and I know I need help," she said.

The therapist looked at Ariana deeply for a few moments before replying with a nod, "Making that kind of change takes hard work and is often very painful. Many people leave when the going gets hard. Are you a winner or a quitter? Are you willing to commit to the process no matter where it takes us and how difficult it may become?"

"Yes, definitely. I can't live my life anymore."

"I will need to see you twice a week, once a week for our private sessions and one weekly group session. Can you arrange that?"

"Yes," was Ariana's immediate reply.

"Group is Friday night at seven p.m. at Kiva Hall, Room 112. For our private session, is next Tuesday at two workable?"

"Like I said, I'll make it work."

Standing, the therapist smiled and walking Ariana through the door, repeated, "Friday at seven."

As Ariana walked back to her dormitory, she thought about this place she had chosen to make her new home. She wanted something very different from Indiana. Ariana had spent many days researching possible colleges and was actually surprised that her father had agreed to her final choice. However, no matter how much she had read about Arizona, she was not prepared for what she would find. The desert was so completely different. Instead of the green trees and flat fields, she was entranced by the rich browns and reds of the desert sands and tall mountains that surrounded the Valley of the Sun. Instead of the overcast, gray skies of fall, the Arizona sky was bright blue and sunny. Even though it was still a bit warm for fall, Ariana loved her wonderful new environment. Leaving Indiana, and hopefully the pain of her childhood behind her, Ariana's first in-person view of Arizona was as her plane approached Sky Harbor Airport for its final descent. She couldn't comprehend the scope of the city she was seeing out the window. It was huge and spread out in all directions, stopped only by the mountains that surrounded the valley.

After almost three months of living in Arizona, Ariana realized she had adjusted well. Maybe it was because she had isolated herself from the surrounding city. Arizona State University was a city within a city. Situated within the small town of Tempe, Arizona, everything seemed to revolve around the university. She liked the campus. It was so different from Indiana University which was huge, with old buildings, frat houses and an abundance of students. Where she lived now, the buff-colored buildings appeared to blend perfectly with the surrounding desert and mountains. Instead of looking out of place, they coordinated perfectly with the rock landscape. Even the atrocious "wedding cake" designed by Frank Lloyd Wright, in some weird way seemed to fit the landscape. Gammage Auditorium, large and round, is supposed to be Wright's attempt at outstretched arms welcoming students to A.S.U. Ariana just thought of it as the funny-looking building that was the center for all live performances at the University. It was a landmark; everyone knew where that building was, even those that didn't attend the university.

Somehow, Ariana did feel welcomed here—the only place she could remember ever feeling comfortable. She loved the variety of students that interacted easily with one another on campus and how friendly everyone seemed to be. There were no rows of exclusionary fraternity or sorority houses separating the Greeks from the dorm kids. Frat kids had dormitories just like everyone else. Comfortable for the first time in her life and having just committed to another person that she was going to create a new life—a new Ariana—she felt for the first time like her future was a positive one.

Humming to herself, Ariana entered her dorm.

Chapter 2

It was Friday, the day she had promised the therapist that she would go to group. Ariana was scared. She found it hard enough to talk to people one-on-one, but to open up to a bunch of kids her age seemed like an impossible task. What happened if they laughed at her like so many other people had done before? Would she have the strength to just sit there and take it? She remembered the therapist saying that therapy would get hard, and asking her if she thought she could take it. At the time she said she could, and perhaps she had really believed it then. But now, as the time grew near, all she wanted to do was back out.

I thought you wanted to begin a new life. She heard in her head.

Do I really? she wondered. *If I'm willing to give up this fast, without even giving group a try, what's going to happen when something really, really hard comes up?*

Determined not to give up before she even started, Arianna grabbed her backpack and ran out the door as fast as she could. *All I need to do is concentrate on the next minute. If I can just focus on getting there and not think about the 'what happens if,' I'll be okay,* she thought as she barreled across campus with her head down and a do-or-die look on her face.

She walked rapidly toward Room 112 in Kiva Hall trying to suppress her anxiety. She hated new experiences, especially those that involved other people her age. In the past, she had struggled to find friends. Ariana took a deep breath, squared her shoulders, and thought again, *I can do this. The past does not have to dictate the future.* She felt her resolve strengthen when she remembered how committed to changing her life she really was. *I will not continue the life I've been living,* she declared as she entered the building.

Ariana was early to the meeting. This was not unusual for her. Punctuality was essential for living in the Abram's household. She was expecting to be the first one there. That suited her well. It would give her time to orient herself to the meeting space and maybe relax a little. Room 112 was at the end of a long hall. As soon as she began the walk down the hall, her anxiety increased tenfold. Ariana had an overwhelming feeling that she had done this before, made this same walk, and that it had ended badly. She knew this was a ridiculous thought. She had been attending ASU almost three months yet had never been at this end of the campus before. She worked to convince herself that this was an ordinary hall in an ordinary building. There was nothing sinister here. All she was doing was trying to sabotage her commitment again. Even though the building was terra-cotta red, *a very stupid color for a building*, she thought, it was not an unusual color for buildings in Arizona. The walls inside the building were a pleasant blue, almost lavender. She knew those colors were used to relax people, *Nothing weird there.* So why did the strange unease persist? Her Oma would have called this déjà vu, the phenomenon of having a strong feeling that an event or experience has happened before. Ariana had felt this before, but never as strong and never so uncomfortably. She wondered, *Have I been here before? Perhaps in a past life?* Quickly tossing this idea away, she decided it was not possible because the building was only about 10 years old. *What the heck is going on?* Once again, she seriously thought about turning around, going back to the dorm and forgetting about starting her new life. *No, quit being such a baby. You made a commitment and you don't break commitments, especially ones that you made to yourself.*

Ariana continued walking down the hallway toward Room 112. As she drew near, the door suddenly opened, sending cold shivers up her spine. *Get a grip!* She blew out the breath she was holding and was startled when she saw a face staring at her from the open door. *Ah, now I see why the door opened! What an idiot scaredy-cat I am*, she thought. *I've got to get a grip!*

"Hey," said the girl who owned the face. "Whasup? You coming in or not? I'm Leesie, actually Leslie, but Leesie sounds so killer I changed it. Am I right ladies?" she said to no one in particular. The outgoing stranger continued, "Whoa girl, you look like a scared rabbit. Yeah, I've been told that I can be a bit overwhelming and sometimes a little cray-cray, but I'm not scary. I'm really rather harmless."

Ariana stared at the elf creature standing in front of her. *Wow*, she thought, *overwhelming is an understatement.*

The extroverted girl was tiny; she was just barely four feet tall with a face that seemed too small for her large brown eyes. Her nose and mouth, however, were as tiny as the rest of her. Her black hair was cut short with little fringes surrounding her long, thin face. Her skin tone was so pale she was almost translucent. The blue veins near her temples shone through her clear skin making her appear ill. Without discernable breasts or hips, she looked no older than 10. Her small frame weighed no more than 80 pounds. Ariana wondered, *Am I in the wrong room? She looked again at the number. Nope, 112. Do I have the wrong date?*

As if she read Ariana's mind, the pixie smiled, "Nothing wrong here babe, right time, right place; Friday night group therapy. And yes, I belong here, too. My looks are a type of camouflage, a defense mechanism to keep all the handsome hunks away. Looking prepubescent works well, don't you think? I'm actually just skinny, not young. I know I look 12, but I'm actually 15, precocious and in college early because I'm really, really smart," she said without taking a breath. "And because I'm 15 and in college and because I'm as weird as I am weird-looking and smart, I'm here now for group. Come on in," she said, opening the door wider.

Wow, Ariana thought. Instead of being completely creeped out, the huge word torrent from the tiny person behind the door had actually taken Ariana's mind off herself and helped her to relax. Ariana walked into the room and was relieved to see four ordinary walls and industrial blue carpet on the floor. Folding chairs were arranged in a circle. She wasn't sure what she had been expecting, but this was a relief.

Deciding she should say something, she replied to the elf, "Hi, I'm Ariana. I'm 18 and I'm also weird I guess, 'cause I'm here, too."

"Oh, you don't have to be weird to be here. You can be angry, suicidal, confused, psychotic, or just plain neurotic, too."

Well, that's comforting, Ariana thought sarcastically. Instead she asked, "How many kids come to group?"

"Counting you, 13. Creepy, huh?"

"No, actually 13 is a nice number," answered Ariana. "It represents structure and foundation, things that are solid and long lasting, like traditions. It was my grandmother's favorite."

"My favorite is three," stated Leesie. "I collect things in threes. My birthday is a three, I was born in March, the third month, and I'm the youngest child of six children, a multiple of three, of course. There are six guys in our group, three of whom are hunks, #reallyweird. There's one guy that's really screaming but you've probably got him locked seeing as you're pretty beaut yourself. Don't worry, I'm not leaning lez, but you will definitely draw his attention."

Ariana was shocked. She had never considered herself particularly attractive. Attractive was her sister, the perfect five foot eight, size two. She had thick auburn hair and long legs, a former Indiana 500 Festival Queen. Ariana never felt she could compete with her sister. At five foot five, she thought of herself as short and chubby though she was just a size six. She considered her mousy brown straight hair so awful she just left it alone rather that struggle to give it some style.

It was so confusing for Ariana to hear Leesie's compliments. She exclaimed to the tiny teenager, "What are you talking about?"

"You, girlfriend, who else is here? You, with the long, smooth, chestnut hair, big blue innocent eyes and that luscious Sofia Vergara body. What, you don't own a mirror? Or are you just one of those women who likes playing dumb?"

"I just don't spend a lot of time looking at myself in mirrors, or trying to look pretty. I don't even wear makeup," she exclaimed, truly flabbergasted. Never in her life would she have thought of herself as attractive.

"What? The dudes in high school didn't fall all over you?"

"I went to an all-girl private school. I really haven't had much to do with boys. I have a brother, but he didn't bring friends home, so my experience with boys is rather limited," she explained. "If I'm so hot, why is it no boys have noticed me since I started school here two months ago?"

"It's your vibe. It says, 'Stay away or I'll take off running!' I've seen you on campus. You walk with your head down and your hair covering your face. You're obviously intent on reaching your destination without being noticed and approached. That's it, you make yourself unapproachable," Leesie explained. "It's like you're scared or angry or something."

"You've been watching me?"

"Yup," smiled Leesie. "We have econ together. You wouldn't notice me, that head down thing, but you're hard to miss. You put out a really bizarre vibe. Anyway, I am an observer. I intend to be a writer one day, so I observe everything and everyone. There's nothing that goes on at this campus that I'm not aware of. I pride myself on that. And because I'm kinda hyper, I don't need much sleep. It gives me more time to do research about everything and everyone."

Ariana stood still, trying to ingest this new piece of information. "You know, that's kinda creepy. Like stalker creepy," she finally said.

"No, not really. I'm not fixated on one person or thing. I want to know something about everything," Leesie argued.

"Well, to me, it's a bit strange. But who am I to judge strangeness? That's definitely a definition that's been applied to me several times too," laughed Ariana.

"You'll fit in well in group then. That is, if you want to. By the way, if you have room in your intense, busy life for a friend, I could use one right now. Just sayin.'"

Ariana smiled back, "I'd like that. You'll have to teach me how, though. I've never really had a friend before."

"See, you are either really, really freaky, or a consummate liar," Leesie teased. "Let's grab a seat, it's almost time for the meeting. I think I hear the herd in the hall."

Ariana heard joking voices followed by rowdy laughter coming from the hall. As the door opened, she saw three guys laughing and punching each other.

"So, it's on?" asked the dark haired one. "After group, we adjourn to my room for the Assassin's Creed mega marathon where I'm gonna beat some serious ass."

"So you say," laughed the tall blond. "You said that about Call of Duty, too, but who holds the undefeated record of wins? It ain't you, bro."

The third boy stood looking intently at the girls, either that or his serious, old-guy glasses just made him look that way. Ariana thought, *He seems to be the odd man out, a bad match with the other two.*

Ariana smiled at the bespectacled boy and said, "Hey."

Instead it was Blondie who noticed Ariana. He smiled and said, "Hey back! And who might you be?"

Leesie leaned into Ariana's ear and whispered, "That's one of the hotties I was telling you about." Turning to the boys, Leesie answered,

"Hey, back at you. The newbie mental is Ariana. Ariana, this is Matthew, Zach, and Aiden; the Three Stooges."

"Hello," Matthew said, giving Ariana his most radiant smile. "What brings you to the loony bin?"

Ariana felt frazzled. She had never been this close to three boys before, especially being asked questions by a very hot, sexy one. She knew he was waiting for her to say something, but she was afraid that whatever came out of her mouth would be stupid. Luckily, Aiden jumped in and said, "You know, you don't look like you're cray-cray."

"Whoa, dude," Zach exclaimed, punching Aiden on the arm. "Talk about a lame come-on line!" He turned to Ariana displaying his own brilliant smile and said, "Pardon my uncouth friend Aiden. We don't let him out of his cage much so he doesn't know how to talk to a pretty girl. I'm Zach and the other lame-ass is Matthew. Please don't confuse us. I'm the cool one. Matt's the tall one, and Aiden's, well, Aiden can't be described in one sentence."

Ariana opened her aura by extending her inner energy outward. Now she could get a feeling for the boys' auras. Ariana felt herself relaxing. The energy coming from all three boys was not threatening. It was light and playful and put her at ease. Zach's energy was funny and sweet. Aiden's was more thoughtful. Matthew's was the most intense of the group. He was very complex, she noticed. She pushed deeper and discovered what was below the surface was very different than his assured outer façade. Matthew's smile faded a bit. Instantly, Ariana pulled back her energy.

"My Cheyenne grandpa says that probing someone without their permission is very rude," Matthew remarked, obviously irritated.

Ariana was shocked. He knew what she had been doing. That had never happened before.

"Oh, ah, I am so sorry! No one has ever said anything about that to me before. It's just something I do sometimes to help me become comfortable in a new environment. I didn't know it was noticeable," she stammered.

"It's an invasion of my privacy," Matthew replied. "Just because no one else has felt it, doesn't make it okay."

All Ariana wanted to do was run away and cry. Just then, Leesie exclaimed, "Hey, what's going on? Rude is having a private conversation when other people are standing right in front of you and don't have a clue what's happening."

"Never mind," Matthew said, walking away.

Zach looked at everyone and shrugged. "Our Matthew is also the moody one. Never can tell what will set him off." Taking Ariana's hand, he bent over, kissed her hand and said, "I apologize for my temperamental friend."

Calmed by Zach's kind gesture, Ariana replied, "No, he was right, I did invade his privacy. But so that I don't do it again, I'll let him tell you about it," Ariana stated as she turned to find two seats in the circle of chairs as far away from Matthew and out of his direct line of sight as possible.

Leesie followed behind Ariana, completely confused and perplexed. "What happened?"

Ariana said, "Maybe I'll tell you later, but not now, okay?"

Soon Ariana could hear other voices in the hall. Students began to trickle in two or three at a time. Shortly, everyone was seated and Ariana could feel the group sizing her up. She tried to ignore their looks by starting a conversation with Leesie.

"What now?" Ariana asked.

"Well, the therapist will probably ask you to introduce yourself and tell everyone why you're here."

"Oh great, just what I need right now. Forced to be the center of attention when all I want to do is be invisible," moaned Ariana.

"See, therapy is working already," Leesie teased.

"Okay everyone, let's settle down. It's time to begin," announced the therapist as she took her seat in the circle. "I'm glad to see that everyone is back and I assume, ready to do some work. As I'm sure you've already noticed we have someone new tonight. Try to be kind. Ariana, please introduce yourself and tell us what you hope to gain from the group."

Here we go, thought Ariana. Taking a deep breath, she began, "Hi, everyone. I'm a freshman who still doesn't know what or who I want to be when I grow-up. I'm from Carmel, Indiana. I'm not sure what I'm looking for from the group, but I know I hate what my life has been 'til now and I'm looking for change, direction, kind of a rebirth. So, I'm here, ready to work. I want to see where it takes me."

"So, being in a group of losers and mentals is your idea of change?" asked a Goth girl sitting across the circle.

Ariana thought a moment before answering, "Considering that except for classes, this is the largest group of other kids I've ever been with, yes, this is a change. I've never had friends," Ariana smiled at Leesie, "until now. I really can't judge what everyone in this group is or is not, nor would I, as I have experienced judgment and hate it. You don't feel like losers to me, maybe instead, we're all just a little lost."

"Bullshit," exclaimed Miss Goth. "You can't really expect us to believe that crap you just said, can you? Dafug!"

The therapist turned to the girl dressed head to toe in black and asked, "Wendy, where is all the anger coming from?"

"Why are you taking the new girl's side?" Wendy snapped back.

"There are no sides here," explained the therapist, "just observations. What's going on with you right now?"

"I hate liars!"

"I think we can all appreciate that, but that doesn't answer my question," responded the therapist.

"She just made me mad saying she's never had friends." Wendy continued, "A girl that looks like her has gotta have a lot of guy friends. Yeah, girls might be jealous, but the guys would wanna piece of that. It's just such an obvious lie it pissed me off."

"So, because she's pretty you assumed that she had to be lying?" questioned the therapist.

A plain, overweight boy sitting next to Matthew jumped in, "Yeah! You judge the new girl by her looks just like you say people judge you. What's up with that?"

Wendy extended her middle finger to him as she replied, "No one asked you, Josh. You've probably got the hots for her or something. Gonna protect the pretty new damsel in distress?"

"Or maybe you've got the hots for her yourself?" a girl sitting on the other side of Ariana suggested with an angry smirk on her face.

For Ariana, this intense level of anger usually accompanied a beating. The negativity in the room overwhelmed her. She tried protecting herself by pulling in her aura, but it was too late. Although she realized Matthew would feel what she was doing, she began to fill the room with the energy of peace and love. She visualized a tranquil scene in her mind; she imagined waves gently meeting the edge of a sandy shore. She sent this vision, with all its stillness, into everyone's minds. She extended safety and love by allowing her blue energy to surround the circle and especially surround the girl called Wendy. Ariana could feel the room calm.

"Okay," the therapist interjected, "this isn't accomplishing anything useful. Wendy, we were talking about your anger."

Wendy now appeared deflated, all the air taken out of her anger as she replied, "I really don't know what just happened, but I don't want to be mad anymore. I'm always mad, always jealous. Always feeling like life sucks and everyone hates me. So I guess I attack as some kinda pre-emptive strike."

"Yeah, like some strange kind of shock and awe. Act like a badass—no body's gonna mess with the badass," a pretty black girl with dreads agreed.

Wendy looked at Ariana and said, "You are just so like I could never be. What you said didn't make any sense. I just couldn't handle it. How can someone that looks like you, feel like me, alone and lonely?"

"Maybe Wendy, because sometimes everyone thinks the same way you are thinking," suggested Matthew.

"Why didn't you have friends?" one of the other girls asked Ariana.

Ariana wasn't sure what to say so she decided to be honest. "I grew up in a family that didn't want me and never let me forget it. My sister was truly beautiful; a beauty queen and a model. I was often reminded that I was lucky to be smart because, according to my parents, I was the fat and ugly one in the family. I threw myself into my education. Books became my friends," she said calmly. "When I was young, I tried to bring a friend home. She was a sweet, shy, black girl that was living in an all-white neighborhood. I was a shy, Jewish, white kid in a Christian neighborhood. We were a perfect match except for one thing, my parents. They informed me that having a black friend was out of the question. The next friend I made betrayed a confidence to everyone in my neighborhood. I became on outcast, continually teased and bullied. After that I decided having only books for friends was safer. As far as boys are concerned, I went to an all-girls school, no guys. Except for school and home, I went nowhere."

"Wow," Goth girl Wendy said. "That sucks. Sorry I called you a liar."

"What was the big secret that got betrayed?" Matthew asked.

Ariana looked at the therapist. The woman's voice expressed her kindness as she said, "It's up to you, Ariana. If it makes you uncomfortable, then don't, but holding back won't help you grow or learn to trust."

Ariana took a deep breath, "I told her about my invisible friends."

"That's not weird. A lot of kids have invisible friends. I had an invisible kitty," Leesie offered.

"My invisible friends were adults that protected me, taught me, and loved me," explained Ariana.

"Oh, okay, that *is* a little weird. But it's not like you told this girl that you murdered baby birds or anything," Leesie declared matter-of-factly.

"I guess a bunch of 10-year-old kids wanted a reason to hate and torture me. They used my secret and it worked. Throughout elementary and middle school I was called a looney and weirdo. It just reinforced what my family kept telling me; I was worthless, strange. I didn't belong anywhere. I withdrew. My safe place became my bedroom, away from anyone my own age," Ariana explained.

"I know exactly what you mean, not fitting in anywhere," a very feminine, Hispanic boy agreed. "People are accepting of gays and lesbians now, but those of us that believe we are in the wrong bodies, transgendered kids, aren't comfortable anywhere. My parents hate me. What kind of Mexican-Catholic family has a boy that wants to be a girl? They took me to the priest who tried to exorcise the demon out of me. When that didn't work, he molested me, to show me how to be a 'real man.' " Pausing to catch her breath, she continued, "I also secluded myself. What I didn't expect or plan to have happen was by having nothing else in my life but on-line school, I got great grades and a scholarship. Now I'm here working to transition to the woman that I am. Oh, I'm Tara and I'd love to be your friend, Ariana, if you aren't too creeped out."

"Thank you, Tara. I would love to be your friend and I could never be creeped out by someone wanting to be their authentic self," Ariana said.

"Anyone else want to comment on judgment?" the therapist asked.

"Yeah, I do," a girl named Gail piped up. "Everyone judges. You can't get through life without judging. Isn't it normal?"

Zach spoke up, "I think everyone has preconceived notions and opinions, that's just our society. Lots of those opinions aren't even ours from direct experience. Instead we accept whatever we've been taught. Some of those things are necessary, but many are hurtful and as we grow up we need to re-examine those beliefs, become a bit introspective. Then we can decide which of them we want to carry forward and which we want to leave behind."

Who is this guy? Ariana wondered. Her first impression of him was that he was the class clown: cute, but not a lot of depth. *Whoa, have I misjudged him?* She laughed to herself, realizing the irony of her thinking given the evening's conversation. *This guy deserves a closer look.*

"If we shouldn't use judgment to figure things out, what then?" a thin, caramel skinned boy to Ariana's left asked.

"How about discernment?" asked the therapist. "Discernment is a type of judgment but with understanding. It's the idea that we should really try to see a situation clearly by using our intelligence."

"But why do people hate anything different from themselves?" Wendy asked. "Like who decided that blue hair is weird? Or that tattoos and piercings are okay depending where on your body they are. On the face is bad, on the body okay. Everyone should be het and want to get married and have two kids and if you don't, then you are selfish, just to name a few things that have happened in my life."

The therapist waited to see if anyone in the group would answer. She broke the silence, "Sometimes it is as simple as fear. People are more comfortable with others that look and act like themselves."

"And share their beliefs, are in the same economic bracket, social group, and approximately the same level of intellect," offered Aiden. "As a matter of fact, people with superior intellect are often considered bizarre. Now they've labeled some of us with Asperger's Syndrome. Once we're labeled, others think they understand us and that makes them feel safe."

The therapist said, "It sounds like it bothers you to have a diagnosis. You see it as a label?"

Aiden just looked at her, offering no response.

"Isn't everyone labeled?" Ariana asked. "Tonight I've been labeled as 'killer.' Matthew and Zach might be labeled 'hotties' and Wendy is labeled 'Goth.' None of these terms does more than describe our outer appearance. None of them says anything real about us as people. Labels are used for identification, not for real information."

"Too true. But some labels create more problems than others. For instance, if someone is labeled as 'slow,' people will treat that person as inferior," Aiden answered.

"Sometimes I think this would be a better world if everyone was deaf and blind," Wendy grumbled.

"Our Wendy, always the bright ray of sunshine!" Matthew said sarcastically. "I'm really sick of listening to your negative attitude."

"And your empathy is remarkable," said the African American girl.

"Just sayin' what everyone's thinking," Matthew quipped.

"Please speak for yourself, Matthew. Everyone here will only talk about their own feelings and impressions, nobody else's. Remember the rules," said the therapist.

"I think he's right. I seem to live in a very dark place in my mind. Nothing looks good. I can't remember the last time I was happy," Wendy said as she started crying. "I'm just flat, all greys."

Sitting next to Wendy was Rhonda, a very tall girl with bright red hair. She put her arm around Wendy's shoulders. "I think I know how you feel. Nothing seems to change and every experience just reinforces all the past hurts and disappointments. I'm not going to tell you what to do, but what helps me is to write. I write down all my angry thoughts. I put all that pain on paper."

"I do that too," agreed Ariana, "then I burn the pages releasing all that negativity. It's quite cathartic."

Leesie who had been uncharacteristically restrained, chimed in, "I draw. I'm working on my own comic. It's sorta like Sin City, dark and violent. But working on it helps me release negative tension."

A very meek looking, quiet girl sitting next to Ariana spoke, "I wear long sleeves and long pants all year. It's not because I like sweltering in the Arizona heat," she said shaking her head. "It's because I'm a cutter. I used to cut myself to let the anger out. Now I design tattoos that represent my fear, anger, any significant experiences. I have them tattooed all over my body. It works for me and I think it's probably less destructive than cutting."

Wendy could understand the tattooed girl's pain, "I still cut and sometimes I purge. It helps me feel in control, if that makes any sense. I'm working on it with the therapist, though," she said hurriedly.

"I think all of us have done destructive things. Isn't that why we're here?" asked Matthew.

Ariana wondered what destructive thing Matthew could have done. His energy seemed so controlled and serene. Obviously, the deeper layer she had started to penetrate in his energy was much darker than what he presented on the surface. *I wonder what his real story is*, she thought.

"Group and talk therapy is a way to purge destructive thoughts in a constructive manner and to help teach new coping skills," advised the therapist. "Does anyone here feel they are having immediate problems coping?"

Wendy, who continued to seem so much more at ease than she had at the beginning of the meeting said, "A little, but group does help me vent, and that helps me cope. Sorry everyone for being such a whiner."

The therapist smiled at Wendy and then, making a point to look at everyone in the room said, "Between our meetings, some of you may find very raw feelings come to the surface. Because many of you have a lack of people in your lives that you trust with these feelings, you may become anxious and want to act out in an unhealthy manner. Most of you have been in group now for almost three months and seem to trust each other enough to release these feelings here. I'd like to make a suggestion for the in-between times; reach out to one another. Often when we are helping someone else, we help ourselves. That's one of the basic concepts of AA. They have used this approach successfully for almost 70 years. Get to know one another outside of group. I'm not talking about booty-calls, but using each other as support systems, friends. It's just a suggestion." Looking at her watch the therapist concluded, "Unfortunately, our time is up. I feel this session has left us a lot to think about and maybe even journal about," she said with a smile. "I know that journaling isn't everyone's favorite task, but like some of you said, it can be quite cathartic. Well, until we meet again, be safe."

The room exploded into motion as though someone had thrown open the cage doors in a zoo. Ariana was surprised to find herself surrounded by people. Their combined energy was almost too much for her. A whisper landed in her left ear. "You really should learn to shield."

Ariana turned her head toward the whisper. She found herself staring into Matthew's amazing aqua eyes. She was close enough to kiss him which disturbed her. She could see the mirth in his eyes. He was amused by her reaction to him, the smirk on his face revealing his feelings. Now Matthew was feeling *her* energy. Ariana found this exciting, both emotionally and physically. Even though she liked the feelings he was inspiring in her, she didn't like that he was controlling the situation.

"What do you mean by shielding?" she asked, effectively stopping Matthew's exploration.

"You've never learned how to shield yourself and your energy from other people? Boy, are you lucky your guides have been protecting you. Otherwise you never know what might have happened to you. You could have been having frequent mood shifts, like feeling happy, then driving for a few blocks and getting really depressed for no reason. Or feeling great physically then out of the blue you get a terrible stomach ache. Later you find out someone around you is feeling sick. Didn't any of that happen to you?" Matthew asked with genuine concern.

Matthew's words confused Ariana. Yes, she had episodes like what he described, but she thought it was because she was a sensitive person prone to mood swings. Her parents accused her of being a hypochondriac because of her frequent physical ailments that had no discernible medical cause. She was also sure that she had heard him say "guides." That was what Oma had called her invisible friends. A sense of relief flooded Ariana's body. He wasn't ridiculing her. Matthew was telling her he understood what she was talking about.

"I have had the experiences you just outlined, but doesn't every teenager? And did I hear you say 'guides?' " she asked. "That's what my grandmother called them. She told me they were my dead relatives."

"No, not everyone experiences what we're talking about. We need to talk later though," Matthew said quickly. "You really need to hear what I have to say, but there are too many ears right now and I don't want everyone hearing."

Ariana had been so intensely involved in their conversation that she had forgotten Leesie, Tara, Wendy, Zach, and Aiden were standing next to her, waiting to talk. *What kind of hold does this guy have on me?* she wondered.

"Hey, what about us?" Leesie whined. "It's not fair to have a private, whispered conversation in the middle of a crowd of friends, remember?"

Ariana smiled warmly, "Wow! Pardon my bad manners, but all this is really new to me. I know that sounds lame, but OMG, so many new people to get to know!"

"How about starting by finding out what dorms everyone is in?" suggested Tara.

"I'll go first," offered Leesie, "I'm in Barrett, and because my roommate was a duster and went home to Momma, I have a suite to myself."

"I'm in Manzanita," said Wendy.

"Me too," said Gail and Ariana simultaneously.

"Matt, Aiden, and I are in Palo Verde East," offered Zach.

Tara responded, "I have a condo right off Mill. No roommate either."

"Is this becoming a clique or can anybody join?" asked the black girl with the dreads. "I'm Teja, pronounced TE ja not Teeg."

"Don't be hella-crazy, girl, everyone's welcome," insisted Leesie.

"Even us?" asked a soft voice coming from the very thin girl lurking behind Rhonda.

"Well, 'us,' are you part of everyone?" Leesie asked. "If so, then join our new club." Without a second thought Leesie christened the newfound friends. "Let's call ourselves The Weirdxotics."

"I hope we're not leaving anyone out. I know I wouldn't want to be the one in our group that wasn't at least asked," mentioned Rhonda.

Leesie agreed. She stood on a nearby chair and screamed, "Anyone who wants to join our new friendship group, please come over here so that we can acknowledge you and dub you an official Weirdxotics. Really, we are getting everyone's phone number, e-mails, and dorms so we can keep in touch and get to know each other better. If you're interested great, if you're not, that's great too. No pressure, no judgment," she said with a smile.

None of the others chose to come forward.

"Oh well," Leesie said with a sigh. "It's just us. Where are we going to celebrate our new alliance?"

"Let's go to Fuzzies on Mill. They've got great fish tacos," suggested Zach.

"I've never eaten fish tacos," admitted Ariana.

"It's decided then," declared Zach. "Let's introduce the newbie to fish tacos and other really hot Tex-Mex food. Baptism by fire!"

There was agreement all around and a chant of "baptism by fire" as the new friends began their short walk to Fuzzies.

Ariana's head was spinning. She had friends! Here she was for the first time in her life laughing and bantering as though she was a regular person and now she was going to a place called Fuzzies for her first group celebration.

Chapter 3

Ariana's mind was buzzing with the thought of spending time with people who wanted to be her friend. Although she had been on campus for over two months, she had not ventured out to explore Tempe, the home of Arizona State University. The campus was large, but not huge like Indiana University. It had everything she needed. She had never really wondered what was beyond the boundaries of her new school.

The group began walking down University to Mill, the main hub of nightlife in Tempe and the gathering place for students, transients, musicians, and anyone interested in partying. Mill Avenue had a variety of restaurants, bars, and shops catering to the 72,000 students that attended A.S.U. The streets were crowded with all kinds of groups, including Rastafarians, older hippie-types some with their balding heads still sprouting ponytails, and every ethnic mix possible. Sidewalk musicians shared their talents and hoped for spare change. Leashed dogs led their owners through the maze of people. Couples flirted, walked hand-in-hand, and stole kisses in doorways. Music clubs lined the street. Happy hour and specialty drink signs helped entice people to come in for some food and a drink. *Everything feels so alive*, thought Ariana. The energy was dynamic, chaotic, but also fun.

Ariana absorbed the energy, breathing deeply of the life that swarmed around her. She had never missed this, friends, excitement, clubbing, because she had never experienced it. Now, however, she knew that if she were forced to return to her old life, her old self, she would be truly miserable. *You're doing it again,* she thought, *dwelling on negative events that haven't even happened. Enjoy! This is real life.*

Matthew was walking on Ariana's left, Zach was on her right.

"Okay, who is this?" Zach asked as he wiggled his eyebrows and leered at her suggestively.

"My lame friend trying to be funny," Matthew answered. "Dude, if you're trying to be sexy with that look, you're failing big time."

"Jeez, doesn't anyone but me watch old movies? Groucho Marx is one of the funniest dudes around and those guys got away with lots of innuendo back then. Like May West asking some guy if 'that's a pistol in your pocket or are you just glad to see me?' " Zach said as he imitated May West perfectly.

Zach continued to clown around, changing his voice to mimic other famous people and even the other kids. He playfully teased Leesie and Aiden. Matthew, however, became very quiet. He seemed oblivious to his surroundings. Ariana noticed that even his energy was difficult to distinguish from the others. *Such an enigma,* she thought. Matthew seemed to be lost in a world in his own head and didn't participate in anymore of the light-hearted banter. Ariana suddenly found herself wondering if she had done something else to anger him. *Get a grip,* she thought. *You're just not that important to him.*

With an exuberant wave of his arms Zach announced, "We're here! There's no place big enough for all of us inside, so Ariana, go grab some tables out front on the patio. Because this is your baptism by fire, I'm buying your food."

"Get me four tacos and some refried beans, bro," Matthew asked Zach. "I'll help hold the fort."

"Hey, dude," Zach said with a lopsided grin, "No use trying to move in on my babe. This charm is irresistible. But, yeah, it's probably not a great idea to leave her out here alone; too many other dudes strolling."

Matthew climbed over the low wall that separated the patio from the sidewalk and extended his hand to help Ariana onto the patio. They pulled tables together to provide seating for all eleven of them and then sat down themselves.

"Well, no one else can decide to sit out here, it seems," Ariana said. "Do you think the restaurant will mind that we have completely usurped and rearranged the patio?"

"I think the restaurant will be thrilled to have eleven hungry people eating here and that the kids that work here for minimum wage could give a hang what we do." Matthew's expression turned more serious, "There's a reason I wanted to be alone with you. On the walk over I was observing your energy and what you were doing with absorbing the energy of everyone and everything going on around you. That's why I became so quiet. It's obvious to me that you have some extreme raw psychic powers. I also think you don't know what you're doing or how to make sure that no harm comes to you or anyone else. You have no boundaries."

Ariana was shocked. *Psychic powers? No way!* Yes, she felt energy and sometimes was able to manipulate it, like when she calmed the energy of the group, but she couldn't read minds or tell the future. And what the hell were boundaries? She thought she was interacting, trying to fit in with the group. Did she do something wrong?

"I don't have psychic anything," Ariana quickly replied with a confidence she really didn't feel.

"It wasn't you I felt probing deep into my psyche? You didn't change the energy during group and calm everyone down? So just what do you think that is then?" Matthew asked, exasperated.

"I don't know," Ariana answered truthfully. "It's just something I've always been able to do. I thought it was a way to keep me safe, like a defense mechanism. I've never met anyone that could feel what I was doing."

"And this came naturally to you?" inquired Matthew.

"It's just always been there. I can't remember not being able to do it. The only other person who knew was my grandmother, but she died when I was ten."

"Well, I don't know a lot about these kinds of gifts," Matthew admitted, "but my edudi, my Cherokee grandfather, taught me how to use a white light visualization as a protective shield, a boundary. He also explained that the more psychic you become, the easier it is for you to be affected by what you pick up, other people's illnesses or emotions, for instance. Without shields or boundaries you will become overwhelmed. If you don't know that you are absorbing these things psychically, then you think it's you. Shielding will prevent you from picking up anything that you don't need to pick up. It really works. You just see yourself surrounded by this light and ask your God, or your invisible friends, to help keep you protected."

Ariana was intrigued. "Okay, I'll try it now," she said. Closing her eyes, Ariana concentrated on focusing her attention. She imagined a glowing white light surrounding her. She found herself thinking about her Oma and her invisible friends. She realized she was feeling very comfortable. The erratic energy of Mill Avenue was no longer bombarding her.

"Good," said Matthew approvingly. "I can tell it's working. You feel much more relaxed."

A huge smile spread over Ariana's face as she replied, "You're right. I am more relaxed than I think I've ever been in a crowd. I can still feel everyone else's energy, but it's muted, like background noise. It's not overwhelming like it usually feels to me. Wow! Thank you. This is wonderful," she said as she leaned forward and hugged him.

"Moving in on my girl, Matt?" Zach asked with a smile. "I leave you two alone for a couple of minutes and you just move on in?"

Matthew looked chagrined, shook his head and in typical fashion replied, "And you really think you've got a chance with this hottie?" he winked at Ariana. "She's got much better taste than that. Why would she want second best?"

Zach looked at Ariana, batted his very long eyelashes and said, "Could you really choose that pathetic creature over this wonderful hunk? How could you look into these puppy dog eyes and tell me that I'm not adorable and you want me desperately?"

Ariana was overwhelmed with this new-found attention. She enjoyed considering both guys, looking closely at one, then the other. "Well, you both look pretty equal to me, so, because I'm new to this, I think I'll just let the two of you fight over me. After all, no matter whichever one of you wins, I can't lose," she said with a smile.

"Okay, it's on! What do you say Matt, are you man enough to accept the challenge?"

"What challenge?" Wendy asked as she and the rest of the group approached the tables, their arms loaded with food.

"Oh, you know guys," sighed Ariana, attempting to look bored. "They're always trying to one-up each other. Ignore them, it only encourages them. Boy, does that food look awesome. Let's eat!"

With a mouth stinging from hot peppers and a stomach full of grease-soaked quesadillas, Ariana felt more satisfied by this meal than any she had ever shared. When they had all eaten more than they thought they could, the short walk back to the dorms was welcomed exercise.

When they reached Kiva Hall, Matthew pointed out, "We're all going different directions so I guess we should say goodnight until next week."

Zach didn't like the thought of waiting a whole week to see Ariana again. "The Arizona State Fair is happening right now," he said. "How about we go tomorrow night? We can use my Mustang to drive there. Anyone up for some fried Twinkies and scary rides?"

"Me, me, me," exclaimed Leesie, raising her hand in the air as she jumped up and down.

"Sorry, me and Lane already have plans," Rhonda begged off.

"I'm having dinner with my abuela," Tara said.

"I hate fairs. Too much noise, too many people," Aiden answered. "Count me out."

"Andrew, Ariana, Matt, Teja, Wendy, what about you guys? Up for it?" Zach asked. "Come on, what else do you have to do on a Saturday night?"

Deciding that Zach had a valid point, the other four conceded.

Leesie, always the hyper grasshopper, announced, "I don't really sleep much, so I'll send e-mail addies and phone numbers out tonight. We'll meet here tomorrow at what, six?"

"Sounds good to me," Andrew answered, seemingly for everyone as he immediately started walking south. "Laters."

Before she could turn in the direction of her dorm, Matthew said to Ariana, "Think about what we talked about, Ariana. It's important for the health of your psyche."

Zach looked from Matthew to Ariana with a puzzled expression, "Cryptic conversations are really rude, remember?"

"It's really nothing," Ariana apologized. "Matthew was just warning me about taking everything too fast and too seriously. He pointed out that I really don't have much experience dealing with other people and it's just safer to be choosey about how much I share with everyone." She smiled at Zach, "I don't think you need to worry about Matthew and me. He's acting more like a protective big brother than a potential romance."

"Not worried," Zach lied, "just a very curious individual."

As the two friends turned to leave, Ariana caught Matthew's eye and winked. He gave a slight nod in agreement, turned to Zach and said, "Come on dude, let's go 'cause you're coming on so strong I'm surprised she hasn't barfed. Lucky you. It's gotta be lack of experience on her part."

Even a block away, Wendy and Ariana could hear the banter

between the two friends. It was obvious that the two were not only roommates but best friends. Even though they were very different in both appearance and personalities, they complemented each other well.

"You've certainly made a hit with those two," said Wendy.

"Is that bad?" Ariana said with genuine concern. "I don't want to cause any problems for anyone."

"Not bad for you," Wendy declared sarcastically.

"You're not still mad at me, are you?"

Wendy's natural slouch became more pronounced, "I'm sorry. I don't know why I do that. I'm always so jealous of everyone and everything. I push everyone away and then I'm so lonely."

"Oh God, Wendy, I know exactly what you mean. Sometimes I feel as though I'm in a play where every other actor knows their lines and how to be their character and I don't even know which play we're in much less what character I'm supposed to be playing. Tonight was the first time in my life that I felt accepted by anyone. You're not alone now. You're part of a group. We might be a group of crazies and weirdos," Ariana said with a smile, "but we're your weirdos."

The girls had reached the elevator. Wendy's room was on the third floor, Ariana's the sixth floor of the 14-story, curved high-rise. The towering dorm is located on the north side of the campus near Sun Devil Stadium and the Wells Fargo Arena. Ariana was still growing accustomed to having a mountain outside her window and living among so many other, varied people. She knew that Mazie, the dorm's nickname, was a small city with over 1,000 residents. Even though it was close to midnight, the dorm was still a rowdy place. Room doors were open, and people were wandering in and out of their friend's rooms. Students milled about everywhere, often laughing and chatting. On Ariana's floor, the room that was four doors down from hers was especially busy tonight. She heard loud music and laughter through the open door. As she walked by, two people standing outside the open doorway invited her to join the party and several of the others said "hi." Ariana begged off, promising she'd be sure to attend the next party, all the time marveling at her new-found popularity. *What's changed?* she wondered. *Have the students always been this friendly? Why haven't I noticed before?*

Ariana opened the door to her room, praying that her roommate would be out for the night. Her luck was holding; the room was empty and she was ecstatic. Now she had some quiet time to think and journal about everything that had happened that day. She took her hair out of her familiar ponytail and let it fall naturally to her waist, pushing it behind both ears. She striped off her clothes and slipped into a loose tee and yoga pants. *Ahh*, she exhaled. *God, it feels good to relax*! Ariana sat on her bed cross legged and began her meditative process. Closing her eyes, she began to count down from 10 to one, allowing her body to relax completely and her mind to still its incessant chatter. She began to visualize going to her favorite mind place. She always envisioned a beautiful forest that she could walk through. Certain areas of the forest contained fields filled with soft grass and flowers. At other times, she would be sitting by a beautiful lake watching the sunlight glistening off its placid, aqua blue surface. Today, however, she found herself sitting on a high cliff towering over a black expanse of ocean. The waves were hitting hard on the rocky shore and Ariana could feel intense energy all around her. Even though she had never seen this place in her mind before, she had the overwhelming feeling that it was very familiar and safe.

Ariana heard in her mind, *Beautiful, isn't it?* She silently agreed.

You're starting to feel comfortable on Terra and allowing yourself to fit in, the voice spoke clearly in her head. *This is good.*

Ariana allowed her mind to ask, *Is that why I am making friends and being acknowledged by people who never knew or cared whether I existed?*

She felt a response. *Before, your aura was closed tightly around you. It announced energetically for others to stay away, so they did. Now it is different.*

Even though I am now protecting myself? Ariana asked, a bit confused.

The answer formed in her mind, *This is different, one way stops you from absorbing everything, the other repels.*

It didn't repel feelings like pain, she complained.

No, but it sent energetic information that said you were closed off. That can make you appear almost invisible or hostile to humans.

But aren't I human?

Yes, but you are also more. You have an ability to access energies on all levels of existence. This not only means that you can feel things that others overlook or just can't feel, but you can also heal or destroy with these energies. Because you have never felt secure in your environment, you have honed your clairvoyant abilities. You can sense what is good or bad in your environment and even perceive possible future events. As you become more comfortable with your abilities, they will grow and expand in new ways.

Ariana was very confused and uncomfortable with this new information. She felt that her life was too complicated now. How could she possibly become comfortable with these new abilities and still feel as though she fit in with normal people? She was tired of being isolated. She had just gotten a taste of friends and fun and wasn't willing to give them up. The thought of going back to her lonely life was appalling.

But what if I don't want these abilities? What if I just want to be a normal college student?

Unfortunately, it is not what you want at this moment that is of importance, the voice in her head explained. *It is our commitment to this planet that is of concern. Remember the purpose.*

How do I do that?

Begin recording your dreams.

Ariana's eyes opened suddenly as she realized that the voice had left her head. She was in pain. Her head hurt and she felt like crying. For the first time in her life she had begun to feel normal. She had allowed the hope that college would be the start of a new and wonderful life. She dreamed she would be like everyone else and could leave all the negativity in the past. She had felt hope. Now she felt crushed. It never occurred to her to doubt the voices in her head. They had always been her salvation. But now what they were telling her made no sense. What was the purpose of their message? Why did they refer to Earth as Terra and talk to her as though this was not her home or her people. Maybe she was insane. How would she know for sure? *I just can't deal with this right now,* she thought. So, as she had done for her entire life, she put her thoughts aside and decided she would talk things over with her therapist. *I will focus on normal, happy thoughts like Zach's wonderful humor and puppy dog eyes and Matthew's smoldering personality and intensity,* she thought. *I will think about silly things like what I'll wear tomorrow and about the fair.* A smile came to her face. *To hell with the negative voices in my head! I don't have time to be negative. It's the beginning of the rest of my life!*

Chapter 4

Ariana awakened the next day to the sun streaming in her window filling the room with crystal rainbows and exceedingly bright Arizona sunlight. She hadn't slept well the night before, excited about her first real outing with her new friends. She stretched and allowed herself to think about all the changes that had transpired in just 24 hours. She now had friends, both male and female. She had gone on her first group outing and eaten her first real Mexican food. Matthew knew about her and didn't seem appalled. He might even be able to help her figure out how to make things easier, how she could protect herself.

Ariana was amazed at the way some of the kids saw her. They thought she was hot! They thought her hair and body were pretty! She had always thought of herself as fat because both her brother and sister were tall and very slim. She looked up Sofia Vergara to see what her body looked like because Leesie had compared the two of them. She was shocked to think that anyone could think she looked that hot. And her hair, how she hated it, even though Leesie had commented on it saying she thought it was pretty. Ariana thought of it as just lank and shapeless. Sure, it was long, but only because it was so straight that any other style looked terrible, and unlike her sister who could do magic with hair and makeup, she was completely incapable of learning how to master either. She could never do anything with it because it refused to curl and just hung there. It lived in a boring ponytail or a single braid as those were the only hairstyles Ariana felt confident doing. Plus, they were fast and because she hated to fuss over herself, she rationalized they were good enough. Who cared anyway?

After wasting hours playing with her hair and wondering if she had stepped through the mirror into Narnia or maybe fallen down the rabbit hole, Ariana realized she was starving. She looked at the clock. *Darn, the cafeteria is closed.* She would have to go out and get some food. Sleeping in her yoga clothes had some advantages as all she needed to do was run a brush through her hair and she'd be good to go.

Ariana ran down the street to Starbucks and grabbed a mocha latte and an apple raisin muffin. *This will have to do,* she thought as she loped back to the dorm. It was already 4 o'clock and she was nowhere near ready to meet everyone in just two hours. She felt herself begin to panic. Instead, Ariana stopped in her tracks. She allowed herself three steadying breaths and slowed her pace as she walked back to her dorm.

When Ariana returned to her room, she discovered that her roommate was back. She was sitting at her desk, glaring at Ariana. Ariana chose to ignore the glare. Not even a cranky roommate would disturb her wonderful mood. Instead, Ariana smiled at her and said as nicely as she could, "Hi, Elaine. Did you have a good night last night?"

"Probably better than yours," Elaine smirked. "I'm being rushed by Alpha Chi Sorority."

"Congratulations," Ariana said sincerely.

"If I get in, it will solve both our problems because then I can move out."

"I know that will make you happier."

"Don't act like you won't be as thrilled as I will be. We're just way too different to ever be friends."

"I know you think that," Ariana answered, "but I'm not sure why. You've never seemed interested in getting to know me."

Elaine glared at Ariana, replying, "Me? You always seem so closed off, as though you prefer just being in your own space. You don't have any friends and seem to not care that you don't. You bury yourself in your books and barely acknowledge me. Do you have any other interests besides studying and that weird meditating thing you do? You don't drink, party, or seem to have any interest in guys, or for that matter, looking good. You live in T-shirts and jeans. No dresses, no makeup, not even any jewelry. It's as though you want to blend into the walls. And you seem to be angry a lot, too. Your vibe is really negative."

Okay, thought Ariana, *that's quite a list and not the first time this week I've heard that I block people out.* "Thank you for your honesty. I am working on myself and I will look at all the things you've told me, but you'll have to excuse me for now," Ariana said as she turned away. "I have to get dressed to go to the fair with some friends."

Ariana wanted so badly to turn around and relish the shock she knew was on Elaine's face, but she didn't want to be petty and anyway somehow the time had gotten away from her. She still had to take her shower, fix her hair, and walk to the meeting place. She knew she would have to hurry, but she wondered if she should try some makeup tonight, if for no other reason than to make a liar out of Elaine. She had some of course, she couldn't live with her family without wearing it to go out, but she rarely wore it when she was away from them. Maybe she'd try it out just for tonight.

Distracted by thoughts of what Elaine had said, Ariana didn't realize that she was lingering a bit too long in the shower. Elaine thought she was closed off, so had Leesie. Did she really push people away? Could her whole problem with making friends be her fear of driving them away, or was it just that she felt more comfortable around other misfits? Ariana realized that she had felt uncomfortable living with someone new to her. Perhaps it was her fault that Elaine and she had never clicked. Her fear had prevented her from even trying to know her roommate. *Fear,* she thought, *boy, can it screw up your life!*

As she finished her shower, Ariana realized she was back to her old problem; what to do with her hair. She thought about putting it in a braid or maybe piling it up on the top of her head somehow, but decided instead to just put it up in a high ponytail. She was very glad that she had picked out her clothing the night before, even if it was just black skinny jeans and a new ASU T-shirt. *Screw Elaine,* she thought and wondered whether she should take her bright pink hoody. Ariana decided that although it would be cold in her former home state of Indiana in late October, she doubted it would be below 90 degrees here in Arizona.

Coming back into the room with every intention to apologize to Elaine for not even trying to get to know her, Ariana was startled when she looked at the clock and realized she had only fifteen minutes to comb out her wet hair, get dressed, put on some makeup, leave the dorm and get to the meeting place. She hated to be late. Actually, she was obsessive about being on time. It was something that her father had literally beaten into her. Rushing to get ready, she decided that it was petty to put on makeup just to prove Elaine wrong and that her apology would have to wait for another time. *Shit,* she thought as she grabbed her money and cramming it into her back pocket yelled, "Laters" to Elaine and ran down the hall to the stairs. The elevators in the dorm were notoriously slow so taking one of them was out of the question.

Ariana arrived at Kiva Hall only five minutes late and began apologizing profusely.

"It's okay," Zach replied with a smile, "but now you'll have to sit on someone's lap as it appears my Mustang wasn't built to hold this many people."

Ariana looked into the car trying to determine whose lap she wanted to sit on.

"Just hop aboard," Andrew offered, "I've got room for two on this lap."

Ariana was relieved. She didn't think she would have been comfortable getting that intimate with Matthew just yet, and none of the girls looked big enough to hold her. Andrew, on the other hand, was the size of a linebacker and as unintimidating as a sheep dog. She crowded into the backseat and attempted to make herself as comfortable as she could in a space that at best was designed for three small dogs. It was already holding three normal sized females and a small giant. *I guess this is one way to get to know people*, she thought as she tried to figure out where exactly to place her bottom, then her arms, in the extremely cramped space of Zach's backseat.

"I call shotgun on the way back," announced Andrew working very hard to get comfortable. "No offense, you're hot and all, but this is damned uncomfortable and could even become a bit embarrassing if you keep moving like that."

Blushing a pretty shade of rose, Ariana replied, "No offense taken, I understand completely. I'm not used to sitting on strange men's laps. I just might fight you for the front seat later, though."

"I won't comment about you calling me strange," Andrew joked. "But no matter how hard my Mom raised me to be a gentleman, I already called shotgun first, so it's mine!"

"Well, whose lap am I going to sit on when we come back?" Ariana said playfully.

"I call sitting on Matt," Leesie squealed, "I called it, so his lap is mine!"

"Okay, sounds like a plan," Matthew agreed good-naturedly.

As they drove to the fairgrounds, Ariana only half-listened to the bantering of her friends. She was too busy looking out the window. The landscape was so different from Indiana. People said that the desert was brown and boring, but she thought it was beautiful. There was still green grass and leaves on the trees and all kinds of flowers blooming. In Indy, fall would already be striping the trees and a preview of winter would be in the wet, chilly air. And unlike Indiana, tornados never swept through Arizona. Ariana had had her fill of frightening weather. *There will be no snow to shovel here*, she thought, *only sunshine year-round!*

She had read extensively about Arizona before deciding it was the perfect state for new beginnings. She loved that it was a state of contrasts, from steep mountains covered in fir trees, to stony plateaus and vast deserts. *Even the deserts are unique*, she thought. Different from deserts in some countries, Arizona's deserts were not barren. They are filled with a vast variety of plants, wildflowers, animals, insects, and snakes. Even though rainfall is rare in the dessert, in the winter the mountains are covered in snow. Some of the mountains are desert. Others, however, reach as high as 9,000 feet. When the desert does receive rainfall, wildflowers bloom into an array of multiple colors and the cactus also sport magnificent blossoms. That's when the desert becomes obviously alive and even vibrant.

Even though she had not really minded the heat, she knew that Arizona's heat six months of the year could be a bit overwhelming, and that even though it is a very dry heat, it could feel like you were sticking your head in an oven. The answer of course was air conditioning; it was everywhere, and locals knew it was better to stay indoors during the heat of the day and do what has to be done either early in the morning or at night. Humans are excellent at adapting, and anyway, the other six months she knew were unparalleled in their beauty. Man-made irrigation systems have created grassy lawns in most of the cities. Many trees such as Fir, Pine, Mesquite, and Acacia provide ample shade for those who do wander out in the bright sunshine. Palo Verde trees bloom with fragrant yellow flowers every spring and roses are always in bloom. Citrus is so plentiful that Arizonans have problems even giving it away. Fields of white boles of cotton, looking like snow, and tall stalks of corn always dot the landscape because of the year-round growing season.

She loved Arizona; blue skies, the constant sunshine, and the excitement people exhibited when it rained. They seemed joyous, many going out and playing in it as though they were children. She never wanted to see the gray skies of Indianapolis again and even began to think of the skies above her former home as representations of the depressive life she suffered there.

Ariana found herself hoping that she would be able to experience all this wonderful state had to offer. Now that she had friends, she didn't want to spend her time cooped up on campus; she wanted to explore. She wanted to live! She felt a bit like the desert, realizing that the more she was watered with attention, companionship, and caring, the more beautiful the world and she became. She had begun to blossom and grow.

Ariana's thoughts of the beauty of Arizona were disturbed somewhat as she realized the Mustang had entered a seedier part of town. Tranquil visions were replaced with heavy traffic. They had arrived near the Fairgrounds.

"Anyone mind walking?" Zach asked. "Otherwise, we'll have to pay bizillians of dollars to park."

"No problem here," Andrew answered. "As soon as I get the blood flowing to my legs again, I'm good to go."

Leesie hit him hard on the arm for his teasing remark and the others agreed that walking was a good idea. Everyone needed a stretch after being stuffed into the tiny backseat. The group found a place to park on a residential street six blocks east of the fair grounds. The people who lived on these streets had either blocked off their property with signs saying "no parking" or were charging fair goers $5.00 to park on their lawns and in their driveways.

Walking will feel good after being cooped up in the car for the 30 minutes it took to get to the fair, Ariana thought. She hadn't realized how far the drive would be. She knew that Phoenix proper was a large city surrounded by many smaller ones, Tempe being one of those cities which was located adjacent to Phoenix on the east, whereas the fairgrounds were located on the west side, not too far from downtown.

As soon as they were out of the car Zach said, "We need a plan. We can't just go in without discussing what we're going to do. I vote that we throw out ideas as we're walking, then vote on what to do first."

"I want to eat a lot of crappy, unhealthy food," Andrew piped in with agreement from almost everyone.

Matthew and Zach said simultaneously that they thought the rides had to be the main focus of the evening.

"I really would like to see the animals and Wendy has promised to explain things about them, showing and winning ribbons," Ariana said. "If no one else is interested in this, we could meet you at the Midway later."

"I don't think splitting up is such a good idea," Matthew warned. "Saturday night is super crowded and we may never find each other."

"Duh, dweeb," Leesie exclaimed, "don't we all have phones?"

"Yeah, but why did we all come together if we're just going to split up?" asked Zach. "I vote we stay together and just see the whole fair."

"I'm up for that as long as I get my fried Twinkies and other assorted fried delicacies," Teja said agreeably. "I have to say that I have never spent much time around horses and cows, being a city girl and all. Not sure how I feel about them either, but I'm game to learn."

"Not being a city girl, I can assure you that they are sweet, harmless creatures. Some of my best friends are cows," Wendy said. "At least they don't judge me."

"Keep it light, Wendy," Matthew warned.

"Sorry," she mumbled under her breath.

Moving toward her, Ariana put her arm around Wendy's waist as a sign of encouragement, "So, Wendy, you're the expert here and I know I trust your opinion. What first?"

Appreciating Ariana's kindness, Wendy smiled at her and said, "Why don't we wait until we're through the gates and I'll point things out and we can all decide."

"Sounds like a plan," Zach exclaimed.

The weather was warm, but not uncomfortably so and Ariana was sure that would change as day became night. All the concrete of the city held in the warmth of day, but at night, the desert cooled off significantly.

There were lots of people walking toward the many gates into the grounds and long lines of people waiting to pay to get in. Ariana reached into her pocket and pulled out her money.

"Put it away," Zach whispered to her. "I've got a two-for-one ticket."

"I'm not sure that would be fair," Ariana objected.

"The others don't need to know, and if it bothers you, you don't need to feel like this is a date or anything."

Zach's comment took her by surprise. A date! She had never been on a date. It was exciting to think that he might want to date her, but because everything was still so new to her, she didn't feel that getting involved with one of her new friends right away was a great idea. She barely knew who she was becoming. How could she make such an important decision so rapidly? *Give me a break,* she chided herself. *He's offering to pay your way into the fair, not marry you!*

"I'll make a deal with you," Ariana said, "You can use your two-fer if you allow me to buy you something to eat or drink while we're here."

"That's a deal then. Follow me, my little chickadee," Zach said, wiggling his eyebrows suggestively.

As soon as they cleared the gate, the aroma of fair food filled their noses. Music blared from amplifiers inside a tent advertising a rock radio station. People were milling everywhere. Ariana noticed a large building to her right that was full of bright lights and noise. For Ariana, it was almost overwhelming. She visualized her bubble of protection becoming even thicker and stronger and everything became easier to withstand.

"That's either a demolition derby or a tractor pull," explained Wendy as she began to display her knowledge of the fair. "The demos can be kinda cool, but really noisy. If it was the Indian rodeo that would be rad to watch, but I'm not sure any of you would enjoy the tractor pull."

"I can't see us sitting again right now," Leesie commented, "Am I right ladies? My ass is sore and I'm stiff as an old lady."

There was yet another cavernous building directly to the group's left where a large crowd was standing, waiting to go in.

"What's that?" asked Ariana.

"That's the coliseum," answered Wendy. "There's some country band playing tonight and in the basement, there's a photography and art exhibit. I think the concert is what's causing the long crowds. Most Arizonians love their country music."

Andrew smiled, "I love my country music and I'm not from here. I'm from Ohio. I think country is universally loved now. It kinda bridges into rock a lot."

"You're right," Wendy admitted, "but do we want to wait in that crowd then sit for two hours?"

"So Wendy, because you seem to know your way around, why don't you tell us what's where and what order you'd suggest," Matthew advised, taking over as usual.

"Well, that's a big responsibility, but if I was here alone, I'd first go to the animal buildings. They're at the far left end. I checked online and rabbits, poultry, and cows are here now. There's also a petting zoo with ostriches, emus, llamas, sheep, piglets, petting zoo-type stuff. Next to that is the Dinosaur Exhibit. They're kinda chill cause they're animatronic and pretty lifelike. There are also other exhibit buildings like food, quilts, sewing, collectables, and all kinds of kid's crafts. Throughout the fair there are entertainment stages with magic shows, music, and other stuff. The Midway is in the middle of the fairgrounds. We'll have to walk through it to get to the animals. There's food throughout, so don't choose the first place you see. I'm pretty familiar with this fair because I spent about 12 years of my life here showing animals."

"Then it sounds like we have a plan. We'll see the animals first and then head in a circle until we stop to eat, then on to the Midway. Perfect plan; full stomachs and lots of sickening rides," Zach said with a lopsided grin, and because no one objected, they proceeded to the animal barns.

There was so much to see and smell. Many people were crowded into the barns. It was almost overwhelming. Ariana was glad that she had increased her shielding. With her new practice of mentally surrounding herself with white light, it was much easier to be among so many strangers. It also helped her to feel comfortable being close to her new friends. Yet despite her shield, Ariana was almost overpowered again by the noise as they neared the Midway. Different rock tunes blared from the rides and people were screaming or just talking loudly. Sideshow and game hawkers barked at passersby, attempting to lure them in. Children were yelling at their parents for attention. It was chaos. By taking her to the animals first, Ariana realized Wendy had done her a big favor. She could get used to all this commotion slowly. *I need to remember to thank her.*

By contrast, the animal barns were quieter and cool. Even though there was a definite earthy smell, the environment had a calming effect on Ariana. Perhaps it was the animals themselves; they seemed very content just standing in their pens eating. She noticed that some of the stalls had cots. Wendy explained that many of the 4-H and FFA kids actually slept here with their livestock because it helped the cattle, sheep or pigs adapt to the new location. She also explained that some animals had pets of their own. Because they are often nervous, racehorses, for example, will be given chickens to keep them company. Ariana wondered if having a pet would have made things easier for her. Her father would not allow her to have a pet because her sister was allergic to both dogs and cats. Once she had begged for a horse and swore to him that she would do whatever he wanted in order to earn one. Her father told her she had to do whatever he wanted her to do, horse or not, but he had eventually relented. That was the kindest thing he had ever done for her.

Ariana walked up to a cow and noticed how serene and placid the animal's eyes were, as though she didn't have a worry in the world. Yet in the future, the animal would be auctioned off for food.

"Do you think they know what's ahead for them?" Ariana asked Wendy.

"Yes, but I think they know that is their purpose. They are here to create other cattle, to give milk, and eventually become food. I know they understand."

"How do you know for sure?"

"Because they told me," Wendy said, looking embarrassed. "I know that sounds weirder than I usually sound, but I just get animals. I love them and they really know it."

"What? Like you hear their voices in your head or something?" asked Teja. "That's just crazy, girl."

Matthew responded quickly, "No actually, it's not. Among Native American tribes there are beliefs that shaman not only talk to animals but can actually become one. They are called Skinwalkers."

Andrew stepped backward, clearly disturbed, "You don't change into an animal, do you Wendy?"

Wendy blushed. "No, but you never know what will come next," she said with a twinkle in her eye.

Wow, thought Ariana, *she's really different from the girl in group. She's even joking!*

"So what's this cow saying now?" asked Leesie.

Wendy became quiet and looked deeply into the eyes of the cow in front of her. She moved forward, extending her hand. The cow moved toward her, nuzzling her palm. Wendy began to scratch her behind the ear while still looking deeply into the cow's brown eyes.

"She's wondering where her calf is. She says she calved this spring and the calf was brought with her, but was taken away. I told her I would try to find out what happened to her calf."

"How are you going to do that?" Zach wondered out loud.

"The boy who owns her is still here at the fair, somewhere, and his name is James. She says he is young, skinny, and light haired. I'll be right back. I think I know where he is." Wendy walked deeper into the interior of the building and disappeared.

"So now what?" said Teja, clearly unnerved by Wendy's actions. "Do we just wait forever for the nutcase?"

Before Ariana could comment, Leesie replied, "She isn't crazy, she's an animal whisperer. I've read about them. There's scientific proof that some people have special abilities, hers is talking to animals. It isn't kind to make fun of her. I thought we were all trying to be friends. That means not dissing each other."

"Sorry," said Teja. "This kind of thing creeps' me out. For as far back as I remember, my granny has been talking to things that aren't there. She says they're spirits and they are looking to her for help. She's done some really weird stuff. So, when I act like all snarky, it's just me being freaked."

"You know, Teja, medium abilities tend to run in families. Anyone else in your family talk to spirits?" Matthew wondered.

"When I was young," Teja admitted, "I thought I saw things and occasionally I heard whispers and tapping sounds. My mom, who is very religious, told me it was the devil and that when those things happened I should pray and ask God for help. It worked. I haven't seen or heard anything since I was about eight."

Matthew responded, "It doesn't mean you still couldn't do it if you wanted. I bet you just have to stop being scared."

"Why in the hell would I do that?"

"Because no matter what your mom said, it is not evil. It's a God-given gift to help those who need to be taken to the Other Side. You can use your ability to comfort those souls who are lost or scared and can't find The Light," proclaimed Matthew.

"What makes you such an expert on this?" Teja asked, somewhat angrily.

"Because I have been training to be a shaman for five years now," explained Matthew.

Everyone was dumbstruck by Matthew's statement, but before they could talk any further, Wendy approached with a teenage boy by her side.

"James, I assume," said Zach.

"Yeah, I'm James and that's Daisey," James stated, pointing to the cow. "I was just getting her some grain. Did you want something?"

Wendy smiled, "We were just wondering, did she have a calf with her yesterday?"

"Yeah, she did," James said, surprised by the question. "Got sold this morning to Morgan Rainey for her 4-H project."

"Great," exclaimed Wendy, "that means she will be well cared for. I'm sure that will make Daisey really happy."

"Cows ain't happy or sad, they's just cows. You get them fat and then sell them," James stated, looking at the group as though they were Martians. Under his breath he said, "City people," and walked away, shaking his head.

Laughing, Wendy stated, "He may be a bit of a cretin, but at least he seems to be good to Daisey. Don't trust all us farm kids by that one, please."

"No problem," Teja assured her, "but people, I'm not ready to ditch our conversation yet."

"What conversation?" Wendy asked.

"I promise we'll talk more when we stop to eat," Matthew answered. "Can you wait 'til then to get your answer, Wendy, Teja?"

"Sure, I guess," they both replied.

"Where to now?" Zach asked.

"The chicken barns!" Wendy, Ariana, and Leesie answered simultaneously.

The poultry area also held the rabbits and petting zoo. As soon as she entered the barn, Ariana loved what she found. The animals were exotic and beautiful. Some of the roosters looked like they were covered in downy fur instead of feathers, and the bunnies were adorable. She was astonished by the coloring of the pheasants and even of the more unique roosters and turkeys. She had never been so close to birds this large. She came face-to-face with a llama and noticed his eyes appeared so intelligent and soulful. *A little like Zach*, she thought. Baby goats nudged her hands looking for scraps of food and nibbled on her clothing. Tiny piglets squealed and played together. Everything here seemed to work in synchronicity. The energy in this large barn was vibrant yet calm. It all felt so natural. Here, among these animals, Ariana felt the rightness of the world. These creatures were not striving for power or control, for money or for greed. They were just being themselves and coexisting perfectly. Yes, they were in cages, but that had more to do with their owners. *Why do people worry about these sweet animals becoming violent?* she thought. What she would have given to be able to talk with them and understand what they were thinking. How she envied Wendy!

"The fuzzy chickens are called Silkies and the rabbits are Angora. The ones with the floppy ears are Lops and the beautiful roosters are called Polish," explained Zach.

"How did you get so smart?" Ariana questioned.

Zach blushed and said, "I read the tags."

"Ah, Mr. Sneaky!"

"Guilty," he admitted.

"I think we should join the rest of the group and figure out where we're going from here," Ariana said.

"Afraid to be alone with me? You never know what could happen in the middle of a poultry barn. Maybe it would bring out the animal in me. Grrrrrrrr," Zach said.

"Okay, quit messing with our girl, you horn dog," Leesie giggled. "Can't leave you alone for a minute. We have an important decision to make here. We're trying to decide whether it's time to eat or time to go see the other animals; the dinosaurs. The rest of us are split. Andrew says he's starving and won't be long for this world. Teja says that as long as she gets her fried Twinkie eventually, she's cool for dinosaurs. Matthew doesn't care, but thought we'd better rescue you from Zach, Ariana. Wendy's all for eating and I'd like to see the dinos. What do you guys think?"

Ariana shrugged, "I'm open for anything. What do you think Zach?"

"I think that I'd follow you anywhere," he smirked. "No really, dinos sound good to me. I can show Ariana how brave I am."

"Oh, gag me," exclaimed Leesie. "Dinos it is. Yeah!"

The group walked to the exhibition center next door to the animal barns. The path crossed the children's rides. Ariana stopped to watch the children with their parents. She felt a lump in her throat as she watched the children laughing and squealing with delight, the expressions on the parents' faces so filled with love and affection. She felt the start of tears as she thought about her own childhood. There were no memories of anything like this. No fair, no hugs and laughter, no rides, no feeling of family. Ariana opened her aura enough to let the energy of the young families enter just a little. The feeling of love and excitement was almost overwhelming. She quickly pulled her energy back in. Breathing deeply, she turned to find the group waiting for her in front of the dinosaur exhibit. She had no idea how long she had been standing there, observing the children. Ariana was grateful her friends had allowed her the time she had needed. She ran to them, ready to apologize.

Matthew put his hand up as though to stop her as he smiled and said, "Relax, no problems. Let's just go on in. We've bought the tickets."

"Who do I owe?"

"No one," was the answer.

The new friends walked into the exhibit to find their eyes adjusting to the darkened light. The interior of the building was cool and very humid. Ariana felt like she had entered another world. There were sounds too, bird noises and loud roars. Ariana was startled by the life-size dinosaurs. They were moving! She saw long-necked Borosaurus and Brontosaurus grazing with their young. A frightening Tyrannosaurus was roaring loudly. The Horned Triceratops was ready to battle the Armored Stegogsaurus as they both screamed in anger. Running throughout was the small bird-like creature, the Dryosaurus.

"Wow," all three males exclaimed.

"Yeah," agreed Ariana, "pretty neat."

"I knew the creatures were huge," Wendy stated, "but it's hard to conceptualize until you're standing among them. Whoa!"

Teja nodded, "Feels pretty Jurassic Park up in here. Hey, Wendy, do you think you could have talked to them?"

Leesie gave Teja a flabbergasted look as she stated pointedly, "You do know that they had tiny brains, don't you? That would mean that the extent of their thinking was probably limited to survival; eating, mating, defecating, and fighting.”

“Leesie, I was kidding,” Teja objected. “You know you don’t have to constantly prove how smart you are. The fact that you’re a sophomore at ASU is proof enough. Chill, girl!”

“Sorry,” Leesie mumbled, blushing, “I didn’t realize I was doing that.”

“Hey everyone, let’s all chill a bit here. We all have gifts it seems,” Matthew stated, “and I don’t think it’s an accident that we all landed in the same group. I think something or someone is at work here.”

“What do you mean?” Ariana asked, somewhat disturbed.

“Let’s grab something to eat,” Matthew said. “Then we can talk about what I mean. Everyone on board for food?”

It was unanimous and after conferring, the group decided to take the quieter route avoiding the Midway. Ariana noticed how eclectic the fair was as the group passed the Hispanic Quarter where everything Mexican was being sold. A vast array of spas and hot tubs came next. When they reached the food vendors, Ariana’s appetite approved of what she saw. There was a long row of trucks designed to serve as portable restaurants. So many choices! There was Chinese, Japanese, Greek, all types of American food including hotdogs, hamburgers, and barbecue, German brats, and of course the desserts: ice cream, cotton candy, caramel apples, fudge, and a variety of fried treats only to be found at the fair. *Wow*, Ariana thought, *how am I ever going to decide?*

“Wendy, is there anything here you’ve eaten and loved?” Ariana asked.

“That place has great burgers,” Wendy answered, pointing to a busy food truck to their left, “and that one has wicked sausage and ribbon fries. But I love that place best,” she said, pointing this time to a large stand with a huge pig statue out front and a wonderful aroma of roasting meat and corn on the cob.

“I’m going to assume that’s some kind of pork?”

“It’s not just pork, its barbecue. They have ribs, beef and pork, pulled pork sandwiches, brisket, delicious curly fries, and truly awesome roasted corn on the cob.”

“Sounds good to me. Want to split some?” Zach asked Ariana.

The rest of the group scattered like flies at a picnic, all going to find whatever sounded best to them. Wendy, Ariana, and Zach walked the short distance to the fake pig and ordered both beef and pork ribs, curly fries, ears of corn and Cokes to split.

"These are really good, but also really, really messy. Don't try to be lady-like," Wendy warned with a wink, "because they're too good to waste time trying to be prissy. Instead, pig out."

"Is that why you're not wearing your normal dark makeup?" Zach asked.

"No," Wendy replied, "I just decided that I didn't need to hide anymore."

Ariana smiled and hugged her. "Now that I can really see your face, I think you're very beautiful."

Wendy's shy smile and deep red blush suggested to Ariana that they shared the same trait, an inability to accept praise. *We're more alike than different,* Ariana thought. This realization comforted her.

Ariana turned to Zach and nodded as she said, "Let's go to it then! If we have to, there's a bathroom right over there to wash our faces and hands."

The three wasted no time taking large bites from their large, saucy ribs and as Zach moaned his approval, Wendy laughed and pointed to his face. A large glob of sauce had attached itself to his nose. Ariana and Wendy couldn't stop laughing as Zach covered his face in sauce.

"Hey, I'm a good eater and these are great," he said in his own defense, "anyway, you should see *your* faces."

Ariana looked at Wendy and they both began to giggle noticing that they had done no better than Zach at keeping their faces clean.

As the rest of the group reassembled at the table, there was much teasing and joking about their messy faces and the choices the others had made for their meals. Matthew and Leesie had chosen giant hamburgers loaded with everything conceivable. Teja had gotten her fried Twinkie as well as some chicken satay. Andrew seemed to have bought out the whole place. He had a hot dog, brat, hamburger, onion rings, and assorted fried foods.

"What the heck are those?" Zach asked, pointing at the fried things on Andrews's plate. "How can any one person eat all that?"

"You know what they say about growing boys," Andrew said, his mouth full of hot dog. "And for your information, those are crispy-fried pickles, deep-fried Snickers, beer-battered fried avocado, and onion rings."

"Dweeb, I know what onion rings are. The others look awful!"

"Hey, dude, don't diss my food without having tasted it. Here, have a pickle."

Zach took the pickle slice out of Andrew's hand, took a bite and passed the rest around.

"Not too bad," he admitted. "What's everyone else think?"

"I agree with you," Matthew said.

"Too salty and sour for me," Ariana said.

Wendy and Teja begged off, citing their reluctance to coat their mouths with grease. Leesie took a bite of the deep fried pickle but spit it out with a "yuck!"

Andrew looked at the girls, shook his head and announced, "It must be a guy thing. We're tougher."

"Yeah, right," Teja said.

"And your arteries aren't getting any cleaner eating that stuff either," warned Leesie.

"Okay, children," Matthew declared, "time to stop bickering and talk about a theory I have about why we've been brought together. I've been watching and listening to all of you. I can't help but use some of the shamanic powers my edudi, my grandfather, has taught me. I want to tell you what I am feeling." Matthew turned to Ariana. "It is clear to me that you have the ability to manipulate energy, even the energy of emotions. I also think you are a healer." Ariana felt her checks blush with Matthew's conclusion. Continuing his observations as though this were just a normal, everyday conversation, Matthew looked at each member of the group as he spoke, "Wendy, you have shown us today that you can communicate with animals. Leesie, you have monster brains and I suspect an eidetic memory, an ability to remember everything you've seen. Zach, whether you realize it or not, you can pick up past lives, especially of the people you live with, the people you spend the most time with. I think you have a significant connection to the history of our planet. Teja, though I know you probably don't want to hear it, I think you are a medium. Andrew, I'm still trying to figure you out, but you are wicked strong." Taking a deep breath Matthew concluded, "And me? I am connected to the planet and can use her energies for multiple things. I am still in training, but according to my edudi, I seem to learn rapidly and well."

The group sat quietly, digesting what Matthew was telling them. He continued, "I can't believe this was an accident, us becoming friends. I don't believe in accidents. Either the Universe or another person, or maybe both, instigated our coming together. I don't know why someone or something would want us to be together. I'm not sure yet. But if I were to guess, which is what I'm doing right now anyway, there's something we're supposed to do together. Well, what do you guys think?"

Teja was the first to talk, "I think I may understand what you're getting at. I've never felt like I fit in anywhere. I feel like I've been pretending my whole life. I never did fit in with the black folk in my hood, even if my grandmother would have let me hang with them. We moved here from Chicago when my dad died. In Chicago, we lived in an all-black neighborhood, but when we moved here, our area was almost all Latino. Didn't fit in with them either, even though my grams seemed to like them more. At least they were decent to me. When I started high school, there were some other African-American kids, but because they hated the Latinos, I kept pretty much to myself. I *have* had some weird experiences." Teja's eyes filled with tears as she trusted her new friends with an admission she had kept secret, "After my dad died, I saw him. I talked to him. I never tried to talk to my grams about this. I knew she would realize I could become more like her, develop the same skills she had to talk with the dead. But I am afraid. I don't want to be an outcast." Tears falling from her eyes, Teja smiled and said, "But here I am, with a group of people that I shouldn't feel at all comfortable with. Instead, I feel like I know and trust all of you completely. How weird is that? I also feel like I could tell all of you anything and you wouldn't really judge me or think I'm weird. For the first time in my life I feel like I fit in and heck, none of you are black!" she said, laughing.

Andrew shook his head in agreement, "You know, I have a weird thing, too. I can sorta feel places."

"What do you mean?" Zach asked.

"When I go somewhere, a new place, I can tell things about it. Like, if I go into someone's home, I can tell if the family living there is happy or not. I've had times when I've gone to a place and known something horrible has happened there. I don't know how I know, I just know."

"That's a form of psychometry, the ability to pick up information from a place, a person, or an object without obvious clues," Matthew explained. "I think that you could probably learn to expand your abilities to pick up feelings about more than just places."

"Well, if we're all going to do a show-and-tell," Zach said, "then I guess I should mention that I have that psychometry thing, but I see the past, not the present. Maybe I'm feeling the past life or lives involved with the place or thing? Which is really freaky because I'm Catholic and am told by my church not to believe in reincarnation. I just thought that I had a good imagination and should be a writer or something."

"I want to be more than just smart," Leesie pouted, her young age peeking through.

Rolling his eyes at Leesie's comment, Matthew offered, "One of the things I want to suggest is that we work together to enhance the skills we already have and maybe learn and develop other abilities and senses. I know it can be done because my edudi has done it with me." Lowering his voice Matthew concluded, "I think we should be very private about all this for now."

"What about the others in group," Ariana asked, "are they part of this?"

"I don't know," Matthew admitted. "I haven't been around most of them except in group. I have a suspicion about Tara. She's Hispanic and admits to being from a family connected to Santeria, which is a Latin American spiritual religious practice. Also, Native Americans believe that transgendered people are touched by God because they can identify and understand both sexes. But I'm not sure about the others."

"Anyone here able to move objects?" Zach asked, seemingly out of the blue.

No one answered.

"Oh, well," he said, "I was hoping one of us could rig the Midway games."

Everyone started laughing. It was a welcome change from the deep mood the group had fallen into.

"Let's go play on the Midway," Andrew said, jumping up and grabbing his trash.

As they all got up to go, Zach hung back. He grabbed Ariana's arm,

"I need to have some time with you alone," he said.

Ariana felt her heart quicken. "Why?" she asked.

"The fact that I want to get to know you better isn't enough?"

"And that takes being alone?" Ariana inquired, raising an eyebrow. "Actually, I think I exposed myself pretty well in group."

"Maybe what I really mean is that I want you to get to know *me* better," he claimed. "Somehow, I seem to be irresistibly drawn to you. I know that sounds like a bullshit line, but I mean it. As soon as I saw you at group, I was certain that I had met you before, not at group, but some other time I couldn't put my finger on. When you started talking about being from Indiana, I knew I couldn't have known you because I've never been there. But the feeling won't leave." The look that Zach gave Ariana was filled with sincerity, like he really felt she was someone he had known. "Do you feel anything weird about me?"

Ariana took a step back and said, "Everything has been going way too fast for me. I've been a loner my entire life, now I've got a bunch of new friends. I'm just trying to wrap my mind around having friends, much less a close relationship. And finding friends that seem to be as unusual as me is even harder to get my mind around. In the past, my abilities only caused rejection and trauma, now I don't have to hide them and may even be able to use them for some positive purpose. That's a lot to absorb in two days. I can say that I find you attractive, but I don't think that's what you are talking about. Give me a few days to digest everything and I'll get back to you. I'm not brushing you off, honestly, it's just so new. Everything is new. I am gorging on input and I feel like I'm overloaded. I haven't even allowed myself to think about individual people yet. Sounds like I'm rambling, doesn't it? That's how scattered I feel."

"I'm sorry that I'm pushing you. That's not like me, really," Zach said as he reached up and pushed the hair out of Ariana's eyes. His touch sent an electric shock through her. She jumped.

"What just happened?" Zach asked.

"I don't know," Ariana admitted.

"Well, something else to contemplate," he replied with his silly, lopsided grin.

"Hey you two, get a room!" Andrew taunted. "I thought this was about a group-thing here. You want to join us? We're moving on to our next adventure. Get a move on, you slackers!"

The rest of the night was just pure fun, riding all the rides, even those that Ariana thought would make her vomit all over herself, as well as the ones she worried could kill her. For the first time in her life, she felt like a normal teen.

The boys challenged each other to see who could win the most prizes for the girls. A hundred and fifty dollars later, each girl left with two stuffed animals of her choice. Ariana chose Carl, the one-eyed minion from *Despicable Me* and a giant blue and turquoise gorilla.

By the time they left the Fairgrounds, everyone was exhausted and not thinking clearly. It was only after they got back to the car that they realized there was no way they could all fit in the small vehicle with their newly acquired prizes.

"Oh, snap! What are we going to do now?" Wendy whined.

"We'll have to go back to campus in shifts," Matthew offered.

"I'm not hanging out here in the dark," Teja complained.

"What I meant to say," Matthew explained, "is that some of us will wait at the front gate on McDowell Street. It's well-lit so it's safer. Zach can drive a group back to campus. Then he can come back and get the rest of us."

"Sounds like a plan," said Zach. "Who stays and who goes?"

"I'll stay," Matthew offered.

"Me too," said Ariana. "After all, I've got the largest stuffed animal."

"I'll stay too," said Wendy.

"I think that will do it," Zach replied. "It may be a little tight again, but everyone can have an animal on their lap or in the trunk and that should work."

It was a tight fit in the car even though there were only four people this time. Ariana was glad to be waiting for the second round. She carried her Cyclops-like minion while Matthew carried the gorilla. Wendy had been more prudent in her choices and was able to carry her penguin and purple teddy bear herself. The trio sat down on a bench to wait for Zach. The girls were too tired to go back into the fair.

"Would either of you like me to go back into the fairgrounds and get you something to drink?" Matt asked.

"Aren't you too tired?" Ariana asked.

"Yeah, but I'm more thirsty. I think I can find something pretty close."

"Well, only if you're sure," Ariana answered.

Matthew got up and went back through the gate. Wendy, sitting beside Ariana, was almost asleep. Ariana found herself becoming very uncomfortable sitting there, virtually alone. She chided herself for letting her imagination get the better of her again when she suddenly noticed a feeling of prickles at the back of her neck. She thought of her shields and focused on making them stronger, tighter. Still the prickles wouldn't go away. She felt the tension around her increasing. Frightened, Ariana was tempted to wake Wendy and head back into the fair to find Matthew. Just as the tension became unbearable, she saw Matthew approaching with the drinks. He seemed to be rushing toward her. She stood up to move toward him, but he shook his head no. He got to her as quickly as he could and she felt her tension drain.

"What happened?" Matthew asked.

"I don't know," Ariana admitted. "I just felt this weird prickling sensation at the back of neck. I double shielded, but it kept getting worse. I got so tense and scared I almost woke Wendy so we could go find you. How did you know?"

"I felt your panic," he answered. "Let me send out my energy to see if I can I discover what you were feeling. Are you still feeling it?"

"Yes, but not as strongly," Ariana replied, still somewhat shaken.

Matthew seemed to zone out, as though his body was there but yet somewhat empty. Ariana was fascinated. She, too, opened her shields and sent a sliver of energy outward. Suddenly, she felt something very cold and dark. She jumped and withdrew her energy, double shielding again.

"What *was* that?" Ariana asked when she felt Matthew's energy return.

"I'm not sure. I have a suspicion, but I'd rather check with my edudi before I say," replied Matthew, trying to conceal his concern from Ariana.

"Give me a hint at least," pleaded Ariana.

"There are a lot of different possibilities. My edudi has talked with me about Asgina, a malevolent spirit, or Uya who is one of the evil Earth spirits who is opposed to anything of The Light. The Iroquois speak of

Sons of the Sky Woman. They talk of Bad Spirit who is one of their twin gods. Bad Spirit, in their belief, is the antagonist of humankind, creating natural disasters, disease, poisonous animals, and even death. I guess I'm talking about just plain evil spirits," Matthew concluded, his tone more serious than he meant it to be.

"But what do they want with us?" asked Ariana, fear creeping into her stomach.

Matthew hesitated, but seeing the concern on Ariana's face he confessed, "Again, I'm just guessing, but maybe we are here so we can work together to stop evil from destroying this world."

"Oh, is that all?" Ariana said sarcastically in an attempt to mask her fear. "And just how the heck are we supposed to do that?"

Matthew, who suddenly seemed much older than his years, replied, "I suppose that's yet to be seen."

Chapter 5

On her way to see the therapist, Ariana felt uncomfortable wondering how things would go with her second counseling session. So much had happened since her first session and she didn't know how much she wanted to confide right now. She wasn't sure she was ready to divulge to the therapist what her group of friends had been talking about or even if she should. Matthew had suggested that they keep their conversations private until they understood things better. Ariana thought maybe he had a point. She could always bring up more issues at other sessions. But wasn't therapy about talking over things that bothered you? Didn't the therapist have some kind of oath or obligation not to tell anyone anything that is said to her? All of these thoughts ran through her mind on her short walk to counseling, but by the time her session actually started, she still wasn't sure what she should or should not say.

Relax and just let things flow, she heard in her mind. Taking a deep breath, she waited for the therapist to begin.

"Good afternoon, Ariana. How have things been since I saw you last?" asked the therapist.

"Actually, it's been both amazing and perplexing," Ariana replied.

"Which would you prefer to talk about, the amazing or the perplexing?"

"I think I want to talk about the amazing part."

"All right."

"I've got friends," she exclaimed. "Real friends that aren't judging me for my weirdness, or my past. They seem to really accept me for me."

"It sounds like you're happy."

"Oh, I am, but scared, too. I keep thinking about my childhood experience with Gloria and how I really thought she was my friend. I think she was, at least until something better came along."

"You're afraid you'll be betrayed again, then alone," the therapist stated, summarizing Ariana's feelings perfectly.

"Yes," agreed Ariana. "Now that I've experienced being part of a group of friends, going to the fair together, laughing and teasing each other without anyone being mean, I just know I couldn't go back to the way things were before."

"The loneliness?"

Ariana nodded. "Before, I didn't really know what I was missing. Never having experienced being a normal teenager with friends, I could rationalize that my life was fine. At least I wasn't getting drunk, arrested, or tempted to use drugs. I was doing well in school and was interested in my classes, especially writing. I thought that was all I needed. But I guess that was just denial. I couldn't face the reality of my life so I denied how bad it really was. I can't do that anymore."

"What are you afraid of?"

"Losing what I've found, I guess. Finding out my new group of friends is all a big lie and that they're all really just laughing at me."

The therapist sat quietly looking at Ariana, waiting for her to continue. *Is there more that she isn't even admitting to herself?* the therapist wondered.

"Maybe my real fear is that what I thought I wanted, to have a real life, a change from my past, will become overwhelming for me," Ariana said. "Really, I just don't know. Everything is so new. It's strange. On the one hand, everything feels so good and exciting, but on the other, everything feels so frightening."

"Change is always frightening."

"Yeah," Ariana agreed, "but there seems more here than just regular, run-of-the-mill change."

"What do you mean?"

Ariana thought deeply before she ventured a reply, "Like there's more here than gaining friendships. I think there could be some sort of deeper reason the group of us are coming together."

"Hmm, any idea what that might be?"

Smiling, Ariana replied, "Would it seem like delusions of grandeur if I said to save the world?"

"The world you were so eager to leave only four months ago?"

"Yeah, weird isn't it? Four months ago, before my guides told me I could change my life, all I wanted to do was die. Now all I want to do is live! It's like I haven't really been living until now. I think I was in limbo, gathering knowledge, waiting for the time that everything would come together."

"And the time is now?"

"That's the other bizarre thing. Now I feel that we have to hurry, like it's past time."

"You seem to be someone who puts a lot of pressure on herself."

"Yes, I take responsibility very seriously," Ariana admitted.

"And you feel responsible to whom and for what right now?"

Embarrassed, Ariana spoke softly, "For everyone and everything, the whole planet."

"Well, it appears that you've bitten off quite a bit wouldn't you say? Is it possible that focusing on this great plan might be a way to distance yourself from others and also a way of creating an opportunity for you to feel terrible about yourself and your life again?"

"Yes, I guess so. But it really doesn't feel like that. It feels like for the first time in my life, I care about this world more than I care about myself. It's as though I've been so busy feeling sorry for myself that I couldn't allow anyone or anything in. Now I've stepped out. I've felt and seen the world which is really filled with wonderful things, not the dark existence I had created."

"It does sound like we are making some progress here," encouraged the therapist. "But I would like for you to take the time until our next session to really analyze your motivation. Take a serious look at where you think you're going, why, how, and all the things, good and bad, that could happen. Can you detach from yourself and your desires long enough to see clearly? I believe in you, Ariana. Do you believe in yourself?"

Ariana smiled, grabbed her backpack from the couch next to her and stood, "Thank you for all your advice. I do promise that I will think, journal, and meditate on everything we discussed today. I don't know if I can separate myself from my desires, but I'll do my best."

The therapist walked Ariana to the door. The door closed with a thud; it matched the therapist's mood. She turned to face her desk, dread clouded her mind. *It's happening.* She had been waiting so long for this. But there was concern too, concern for this fragile young woman, a woman so blessed with ability. But were her abilities strong enough to do what she had been sent here to do? The therapist had concern for the other younglings involved as well. *They have no idea how large the stakes are.* She sighed and thought, *What next?*

We wait, was the reply.

Chapter 6

Walking back to her dorm room, Ariana felt she needed to contact the others. The meeting with the therapist had made her realize how close she felt to her new friends. She had their contact information, so communicating with everyone at once would be easy. But who should she include? After the first group meeting, Leesie had loudly invited everyone to join their new group. The Weirdxotics was open to anyone who wanted to belong. *Do I talk with everyone about what I'm feeling? Should I include everyone in helping with this work?* Ariana decided she would only reach out to the six others that had been at the fair because they were the ones with which she felt most comfortable and were definitely part of the plan, whatever that was. She decided to let the group decide if they thought anyone else should be included.

"Can we get together to talk?" Ariana texted everyone. Instantly, Leesie answered, "Where and when?" Within 15 seconds everyone except Andrew had answered, "OK."

The friends agreed they would meet at Dash Inn on Rural Road, about eight blocks from her dorm, a reasonable walk from campus. Matthew promised to make sure Andrew knew of their plans.

Ariana had never been to Dash Inn or Rural Road for that matter, but she was confident she could find it. Meanwhile, she would use the time to compile information including her thoughts and Matthew's observations. *I want to tell everyone what happened to me while I waited for Zach to come get us from the fair. They need to know.*

When she finally got to her room, the stillness helped Ariana realize how scattered her thoughts were. She knew she needed to center herself so she would be clear when talking with her friends. It was time to meditate and ask her guides for help in understanding what had happened in her life over the last few days. They had never let her down before, and right now, she knew that she needed their help.

Ariana made herself comfortable on her bed, legs crossed, spine straight, hands on her knees with her palms up. Allowing her body to relax, she began to breathe very deeply through her nose and exhaled very slowly through her mouth, seeing each breath allowing her to release and relax even more. Still breathing deeply, she started to visualize numbers, beginning with the number ten. The number ten was the only thing that was in Ariana's mind. When there was no room for another thought other than the next number, her mind turned to the number nine. She felt herself grow more relaxed. She was going more deeply within her own mind, free from any other thoughts from the outside world or the noise within her mind. With another deep breath, she thought of the number eight, then seven, each descending number sending her into a deeper state of relaxation, then six. . . five. . . even more deeply relaxed . . .four. . .three. . .two. . . one. . . She had entered her perfect mind space for relaxation. Feeling only peace, she noticed she was standing in a beautiful field. Yellow and green grasses waved gently around her, extending a warm greeting. Flowers of every color shimmered in the sun. The cloudless sky was an unusual shade of pale violet. It held two suns, neither of which was as bright as the marvelous sun that shone in Arizona. There were mountains on one side of the field and a forest on the other. The subdued light made it difficult for Ariana to see clearly in the distance. The air was cool and slightly damp, but not uncomfortably so. There was a scent in the air containing a fragrance that was somehow familiar to her but she couldn't identify it. She tried to retrieve a memory that might tell her where she was, but nothing seemed to fit anything she could remember from her own life. She didn't recognize the flowers or grasses and seeing two suns surprised her. Yet everything was still somehow familiar. Perhaps she had dreamed of this place? It didn't matter to her. What mattered was how calm she felt. Feeling as though she was actually in the field, Ariana found a soft patch of grass and sat down. She closed her eyes. She felt ready to call to her guides. Ariana felt a breeze blow over her skin. She heard a rustling sound come from the forest to her left. Ariana continued to breathe deeply, waiting to hear the voice.

"Open your eyes, Ariana."

Standing before her were three people, each of them seemingly weathered by time. They were dressed in different shades of pastel blue robes that perfectly matched their eyes. The deep lines on their faces made them look ancient. The energy emanating from their bodies was immense, all encompassing. Ariana could see this force rippling off them in continuous waves of violet, the highest form of spiritual energy. This energy, their auras, was mesmerizing. It even appeared to create sound. A high-pitched hum came from them. Ariana was speechless. She knew she had never seen these beings before. Yet, she felt a burst of recognition, that she somehow knew the entities standing in front of her. She felt another burst of feeling she instantly knew came from them. Calmness flooded her body. She realized she had never felt such joy, such peace. In her mind she called out, *Are you my guides?*

"No, we are the Elders."

Hearing the voice out loud instead of in her head shocked her. That had never happened before. She was very confused now. Wasn't she still meditating?

"Yes, Ariana, your body is back on Terra in its relaxed mode, but your essence is here with us. That is how we can speak with you face-to-face."

"But you can also hear what I'm thinking?"

"Yes."

"And you can talk with me in my head, like we have before?"

"Yes."

"Then why are we communicating like this? It is so different from the other times."

"It was determined that our last communication was disturbing to you and that we need to begin to refresh parts of your memory. We decided that we would begin this way, face-to-face, in order to make you more comfortable."

Ariana's mind was racing with questions. Trying to sort out what was happening she asked, "What are Elders?"

"Elders are the ruling consciousness of our planet. We hold the memories of the past of our people, our triumphs, and our failures. We determine our planet's destiny and thus its future. We determine those things that must be done in order to keep the balance in the Universe. We are the watchers, and when essential, we are the saviors or the destroyers. This is the penance of our people."

"You were the ones that spoke of a path for me?"

"Yes."

"I'm not even sure what a path is. Is it my destiny?"

"Your path is not your destiny; it is the road you must walk to reach your destiny. Our people begin to train from conception to walk a path that will utilize their abilities in the best way. The training is rigorous but also defining. It helps us ascertain strength, weaknesses, and how their abilities have manifested. Usually, the individual excels in only two areas, perhaps healing and energy work. If the person is a healer, they must walk the path of a healer. Their destiny is the totality of that life and the use of those gifts."

"You led me to believe that I was not human and that Earth is not my home, that Earth is my 'path.' What do you mean?"

"You were born upon Terra just as everyone is born there, but you were not conceived the same way. You were implanted. Your DNA is slightly different from a normal human's. This difference enables you to have abilities that humans do not possess to the degree you do. You have knowledge of many things, energy being primary. You can use this knowledge to make much needed change. Much of what you know is still dormant. Until now, you did not have a need for that knowledge. The situation is changing rapidly and you need to be at full power. Consequently, we are beginning the activation process. This process will be difficult initially on many levels. You will be challenged physically, emotionally, spiritually, and energetically. We assure you that it will become easier as you gain strength and recapture all of your abilities. Additionally, you are not alone in this endeavor. You have already met some that will be of assistance. Know that we will always be here for you. Help those others to grow in their abilities; you have the tools."

"What if I am not capable of accomplishing the things you desire of me? I can't conceive of myself doing anything important and frankly, I'm kind of freaked that you claim I am not really a part of this world. How different am I? Am I Mr. Spock different? Frankenstein's monster different? Or just different like that energy thing I can do? You know, manipulating energy and feeling it."

"You are no different in your base physical self, only slightly modified so that your body does not accept disease; it heals itself and can regrow damaged parts. You have a deep empathetic ability that allows you to understand and manipulate matter and energy by entering into those things and altering them without damaging yourself. This gives you an ability to help initiate healing in all forms, including the planet itself."

"What if I don't want this assignment?"

"Then you will allow Terra to be destroyed," the Elders stated flatly.

"Whoa," Ariana exclaimed, "how?"

"There are many ways it could happen, but the most logical would be that the residents of the beautiful blue planet destroy themselves and take her, the planet, with them."

Ariana sat silently trying to absorb all she had just heard. The deep calm she had felt was now replaced with fear. She just wanted to run away, but how do you run away from yourself? She thought about what the therapist had said to her, "I believe in you, Ariana. Do you believe in yourself?" Clearly, now was the time to figure that out.

Looking to the Elders for help, Ariana said, "Something happened the other night that was quite disturbing to me. I felt an energy that was cold and dark and somehow malevolent. I panicked, and if it hadn't been for the return of my friend Matthew, I don't know what I would have done. If I can't handle a little feeling, how can I do what you say I must? What was that thing?"

"As we said, you are only now beginning to be activated. You have much to learn in a very short time and many abilities to hone. When you are at full power, this energy will be manageable."

"But **what was** it?"

"Where there are watchers, there are things to watch. Where there is light, there is darkness and darkness has a voracious appetite. It feeds on fear and pain and Terra is filled with these emotions right now."

"How does a person fight darkness?" Ariana asked.

"By becoming one of The Lights. All it takes to begin to dispel The Dark is to light one candle."

Suddenly, Ariana awoke. She was sitting on the bed in her dorm. She grabbed her journal and began to write. She wrote everything she could remember, word-for-word. She recorded her feelings, what she smelled, sensed, and saw. She wrote down every thought she could remember. She would share these things with her friends at dinner. Maybe, with their help, she could get a grip on herself. *I've got to figure this out! Am I going nuts, or is there something to all of this? Matt said maybe we are here to save the world. Could he be right?*

How can I possibly do or be what they think? I have proven my whole life that I run when the going gets rough. I never faced down my father or brother, the kids in the neighborhood or at school. Instead, I ducked my head and retreated into my books. I chose to live a life of a hermit; no one forced me, and I did that because I was too scared to do anything else. Maybe I am crazy. If not me, then those Elders if they really think I have some crazy superior genes and untapped knowledge. Yeah, you can certainly tell that by the past 18 years of my life. They think I'm Wonder Woman and I know I'm just a weak little nobody.

Huge, deep sobs erupted from the depth of her being along with a torrent of tears. Her body shook as her mind filled with loathing for her weakness. All she felt was desperation and hatred—for the task she had been given, for the Elders, but especially for herself. "This isn't fair!" she screamed out loud, but heard no answering voices. Maybe they had deserted her realizing she was not the one for this job. Hadn't she been told all her life she was worthless?

Deep in her mind she thought she had a memory of another disappointment and failure, perhaps long ago, but as she searched for the information, nothing came.

Realizing the light had changed and that her body had grown cold, Ariana decided it was past time to end her pity party. She would meet with her friends and tell them she couldn't do this. She would apologize and hope they would still consider being her friends, but if not, she really didn't blame them. She would continue as she always had before allowing this fantasy of friendship and even love to enter her mind. She had done fine without them in the past. She would survive without them now.

Time to take a shower, she thought as she grabbed her towel. Looking into the mirror as she entered the bathroom she noticed how puffy her face had become from crying, her eyes and nose red and raw. *Oh, yeah, you sure look like a hottie now.*

The cascade of heated water that engulfed her created a dense fog. She hoped it would reduce the bone-numbing chill that had invaded her body. Ariana blanked her mind. She succumbed to the calming, relaxing sensation, letting the water cleanse her body, mind, and spirit. She filled herself with fresh, clean, white-light energy, and breathing as deeply as she could, she became peaceful. Letting go of the sadness and self-loathing, she stepped from the tub.

Wow! It's cold in here. How is that possible? This is Arizona not Indiana.

Her bedroom not only felt very cold, but also appeared quite dark. There was sunshine outside, she could see it at the windows, but it didn't seem to penetrate the room. *OMG! Could I have been experiencing The Darkness or the desperation of others in the world or even just this dorm? Was that why I was feeling so hopeless?* Tightening her shields, Ariana screamed, "Leave here Darkness! You no longer control me or my thoughts. By the power of the White Light and God, I demand that you go!" Almost instantly the room grew warm and became filled with light. *It worked! I did it!*

"This was a test," she heard the Elders say. "You did well. We could not help you because you brought The Darkness to yourself through your doubt and fear. Now you know how easy it is to be deceived and forget The Light. Teach the others and be proud of how well you allowed your inner-knowing to guide you. Blessings."

Chapter 7

Ariana looked at her phone to see if there were any more texts and discovered it was 5:55 in the evening. She was going to be late again! Feeling slightly panicked, she looked up Dash Inn and ascertained it would take at least nine minutes to get there. Shoving her journal in her backpack, she raced to the stairway. *What is happening to me*? Is it The Darkness adding all this chaos so that we will be too scattered to succeed? She was never late. Everything in her life seemed to be full of chaos and anxiety. *I need to get a grip if I'm going to have a chance-in-hell of being the savior of the world*! When Ariana realized what she had just thought she couldn't stop laughing. Laughing and running didn't work well together so she quieted her thinking and concentrated on making the nine-minute run happen in less than eight.

It took Ariana just four minutes, thirty-two seconds flat to get to The Dash Inn. She was the first one there. She chose a table on the patio where she hoped they would be alone. The inside of the restaurant was already crammed with students. The place was a popular and rowdy hangout for the University students, serving beer and Mexican food. *These Arizonians do love their Mexican food,* she thought.

Waiting for the others to arrive, Ariana found herself wondering how she had gotten there so rapidly. She wasn't even winded. *Maybe Google Maps aren't always accurate*? Just then Ariana heard a familiar voice. "Hi there," said Matthew, "it took me a minute to wade through the crowd and find you. That's why I'm late, but it seems that everyone is."

"Hi back. I've got a question for you that has me a little confused. You know the campus and area around it pretty well, right?"

"Yeah, I explored everything when I first got here. Why?"

"How long do you think it should take someone to run here from Manzanita?"

"Even if you got all the lights, umm, probably about 10 minutes."

"Somehow I made it here in just a little over four minutes."

Matthew's expression changed. "What were you thinking as you were heading here?"

"That I would be late and I'd better hurry. I was thinking because I'd been late last time, I had to get here on time this time. I hate being late," Ariana admitted.

Lowering his voice, Matthew said, "I think what happened is that you bent time."

"What on earth is that?"

Matthew answered, "A lot of scientists believe time does not really exist as we perceive it, that it's just a manifestation of man's desire to put order in the Universe. Time is more accurately seen as fluid, elastic. Because it doesn't really exist, it is mutable. You can work with it, speed it up, or slow it down. You must have been so intensely concerned about being late that you slowed time down, preventing you from being late. Ariana, that is pretty amazing. You can really manipulate energy in powerful ways."

"Is our girl discovering more exciting things about herself?" Zach asked with a grin as he and Andrew sat down. "The others are almost here. We saw them as we were driving up."

"Yeah, she can manipulate time," Matthew answered, downplaying his excitement.

Ariana felt embarrassed by the attention and had some doubts as to whether or not what Matthew thought was true. "We don't really know that's what happened. We don't really know anything yet. That's why I wanted to get together and talk. Please, let's wait until everyone else is here so that I don't need to explain things twice," she said.

It took only a few minutes for everyone else to show up. Filling hungry stomachs became the focus. Guacamole, tacos, enchiladas, beans and rice satisfied their appetites. The conversation with dinner had been jovial but now that the plates were cleared, the group looked to Ariana for an explanation as to why the meeting was called.

"Okay," Ariana said, "besides enjoying our time together at the fair and wanting to see everyone again, I want to discuss what Matthew brought up the last time we were together. I have been thinking a lot about what he said and have some questions for each of you." Ariana turned and spoke to Leesie, "Leesie, you're a math wizard, aren't you?"

"I've always loved math and seem to be good at it, but I'm good at a lot of things. Why?"

"And the name you chose for the group, the Weirdxotic, where did that name come from? How did you decide on it?"

"I don't know. It just kinda showed up in my brain."

Ariana looked around at her new friends. "Has anyone here ever heard of numerology?"

"Isn't it kinda like astrology, except with numbers?" asked Wendy.

Ariana nodded, "Yes, it's an ancient science. In Judaism, there is a book of mysticism called the Kabala that has a vast amount of information on the meaning of the numbers and how to determine all kinds of information from them. I tried to study it once, but it was way too complex for me. However, I did find a great book about numerology that was easy to understand and I studied it a little. The interesting thing about the name you chose for us Leesie, is that it is comprised of Master Numbers, numbers that have a spiritual and karmic meaning." Taking out her journal, Ariana turned to a page she had prepared earlier. "Here, let me show you. Each letter of the alphabet is represented by a number, one through nine. The number one is tied to the letters A, J, and S. Number two is connected to B, K, and T. Number three is C, L, U. Four is D, M, and V. Five is E, N and W. Six is F, O, and X. Seven is G, P, and Y. Eight is H, Q, Z. Nine is I and R.

Each number has some very specific meanings. I can't really go into detail, that takes a book or three, but essentially, the number one represents self and independence, two means others and sharing, three means balance and harmony, four means structure and stability, five means freedom and fun, six is family and responsibility, seven is spirituality, eight is power and control, while nine is endings and karma."

Ariana had the group's attention. "The next step is to take the letters in a name. For example, I can use the name that Leesie chose for the group. From that name and the corresponding numbers, I can figure out what destiny, heart's desire, and personality is represented in the name." Turning the page of her journal, Ariana had written:

W e i r d x o t i c

Vowels   5 9 6 9 = 29/11/2

Consonants   5 9 4 6 2 3 = 29/11/2

2 2 / 4 DESTINY

"The numbers are added across, for example $5 + 9 + 6 + 9 = 29 = 2 + 9 = 11 = 2$."

"The doubled numbers, like 1 and 1 in 11, also the 22/4, are Master Numbers that are not decreased to a single digit like all other numbers. Their meanings are much more important than the number as a single digit. The Master Number has a meaning that has more to do with the world than with any individual."

Ariana's friends seem captivated by her knowledge which encouraged her to continue. "Additionally, we met on October 3rd, 2014. October is the 10th month so if you add $1 + 0 + 3 + 2 + 0 + 1 + 4$, you get 11/2 again. A coincidence? I don't believe in them." Ariana became quiet waiting for the others to digest what she had just said. She expected questions but everyone remained silent. *Have I thoroughly confused everyone*, she wondered.

Finally, Leesie stammered, "How'd I do that?"

"My suspicion," offered Matthew, "is that you have some untapped knowledge inside that smart little head of yours."

Ariana smiled, and nodding in agreement said, "That's what I was thinking, too, but I don't think Leesie is the only one. I think we all have hidden knowledge. I called this meeting to see if we can figure out the what, the why, and how we can help one another. I also need to share with all of you an experience that happened to Matt and me last Saturday night while we were waiting to be picked up from the fair." Lowering her voice, she continued, "I also need to tell you about a meditation I had just before coming here tonight and what happened right after it."

"Sounds like a long night," Zach interjected. "Do you think we should continue to talk here or adjourn to someone's room?"

"I don't have a roommate," Leesie offered, "and my dorm's not far."

The group was quiet as they walked the short distance to Barrett Hall. They were each lost in their own thoughts. Barrett Hall, a residential complex for the Honors College, is composed of nine buildings with open courtyards. None of the others had ever been in this set of dorms and Leesie endured some half-hearted ribbing about being in the "smart dorms."

After entering Lessie's suite Andrew exclaimed, "Boy, not only are you in the smart dorm, you have two bedrooms and a living room.

How'd you rate, you little shrimp. And look how clean this place is! Do you have maid service too?"

Ariana was surprised to see the usually quick-tongued Leesie not only embarrassed but also mute.

"Duster," Teja scolded, coming to Leesie's rescue, "don't you remember her telling us her roommate moved out and went home? Don't you listen?"

"I listen, I just thought I'd lighten the mood around here by saying something lame," Andrew said, smiling shyly. "Did it work?"

Everyone laughed, breaking the morose mood.

"Leesie, your room is really nice. You've made it feel really homey. I could get very comfortable here. Great energy," Ariana commented. "Let's all of us get comfortable and see what we can figure out."

Leesie went into her mini-kitchen which was a perk for those students lucky enough to have a suite. "Anyone want a Coke before we get started?" she asked as the others took their places on the floor and the bed. After passing out the drinks, Leesie sat at her desk, her computer in front of her.

"I'll take notes," Leesie announced.

"Good idea," Matthew agreed. "So Ariana, how do we proceed?"

"I think we should talk about what happened while we were waiting for Zach to come back Saturday night," she suggested. Seeing Matthew nod his head in agreement, she began, "After you guys left us, Matthew, Wendy, and I walked to the front gate on McDowell Street and sat on a bench. Wendy promptly fell asleep and Matthew decided to go back into the fair and get something for us to drink while we were waiting. While I was sitting watching Wendy sleep, she looked so sweet, I started feeling a very strange feeling on the back of my neck, like a prickling sensation. At first it was only slightly annoying, but very quickly it began to scare me. It felt creepy and dark. The feeling became more and more sinister. Just as I was about to wake Wendy so we could go find Matt, I saw him coming back out. Matt, can you finish?"

The group's attention instantly turned to Matthew, "While I was inside paying for the drinks, I got an overwhelming feeling that something was wrong. I felt compelled to rush to the girls. I didn't even wait for my change, just ran out. As soon as I got through the gate, it was as though I had hit an evil wall of dark energy. It really scared me. When

I got to the girls, Ariana told me what she was feeling. I extended my energy to see what I could feel. I felt cold, hostile, dark energy. Thankfully, once it knew that we had recognized it, I guess you could call it a force, it seemed to dissipate rapidly."

"I slept through all that?" Wendy asked incredulous.

"I don't think it wanted you awake," Ariana replied.

"It?" Leesie asked with a tremor in her voice.

Matthew shrugged, "There are many religions and cultures that believe in evil energy. My people believe in an energy that thrives on fear, sadness, and pain."

"Like the devil?" asked Teja.

Matthew responded, "Well, probably not that extreme. I'm not talking about a being, like a fallen angel, and it doesn't run around trying to turn people bad or get them to sin. What I felt was an energy that is the opposite of love or joy or peace. Everything on Earth has an opposite, a polarity: good-bad, male-female, up-down, like that. Think about it. Would we know happiness without sadness? The problem right now is that there seems to be a lot more sadness than happiness and a lot more fear. Because negative energy grows under those conditions, the scarier the world gets, the scarier it will become. The energy feeds off those feelings and grows."

"Kind of like terrorism," Zach offered. "Are you saying that one of the ways it works is by keeping people in fear so that they become reactive and things fall apart?"

"Not quite," Matthew responded, "because the energy does not create the negative, it just feeds on it. And like all energy, if you feed it, it grows."

"But what's this all about?" asked Andrew. "Why is this energy around you guys? What is it looking for?"

Ariana broke her silence. "That's one of the things we need to talk about especially because I think it paid me a visit today, too. The last time we were together we discussed the idea that we each seem to have some, well, special abilities. I'm really starting to think the reason we have all come together is to grow these abilities in some way." With a confidence that seemed to be expanding by the minute, Ariana continued, "I think we are here to grow so that we can do something good for the planet. I have the ability, at least in a small way, to change hostile energy to calm energy. Remember in group when everyone became so angry, so confrontational? Well, I'm embarrassed to admit it, and I would understand if you didn't believe it, but I mellowed out the energy so that the hostility would dissipate. I focused my attention on changing the energy so that a healthy dialogue could take place."

"You took away my anger?" Wendy asked.

"I'm sorry, Wendy, but I can't handle hostility or raised voices. I know it was wrong, to intervene the way I did, but I did it without thinking. Please forgive me," Ariana pleaded.

"Of course I'm not mad at you," Wendy said, tears forming in her eyes. "I'm grateful. I hate being angry and hurt and envious about everything. Ever since that meeting, I've felt much better. I'm feeling good about my life and my need to hide has almost disappeared. Without your intervention, I would still be alone and wanting to die."

"And maybe the fact that Ariana can dissipate negative energy is why it was there. Ariana represents a threat," suggested Matthew.

"Okay, we think that one of Ariana's super powers can piss off evil guys 'cause she'll be taking away all their fun, but how do the rest of us come into this? My 'ability' to sense past lives, how can that help?" Zach questioned.

"I don't know yet. We're just brainstorming," Matthew said, scolding his friend.

Andrew looked disturbed as did Teja. Both of them seemed to be sinking into their own thoughts. Finally, Andrew asked, "What happens if you don't want to be part of this thing?"

Teja nodded her head in agreement, "Yeah, I have been dodging this creepy stuff my whole life. Why would I want to get involved now, especially if there's something nasty lurking about?"

Matthew responded, "No matter whether you become involved with this or not, your abilities will not go away, nor will this energy. I think it's ancient and probably has been a part of this planet from inception. Teja, I think your abilities may even begin to increase now that you are fully aware of them. Being in a group that understands and might even be able to help seems like a smart idea."

Ariana sensed the growing discomfort among the group. "Leesie, you're awfully quiet. Whassup?"

"Just thinking. Letting my brain put things together. I've been researching paranormal abilities. There's actual research out there and our government was and might still be studying it. One of the things that the government accomplished was training people who were psychic-sensitive to do something called far or distance seeing. There was a movie made about ten years ago called *The Men Who Stare at Goats*. I streamed it last night. It was really weird. But my point is, abilities can be worked with and expanded."

"I saw that movie," exclaimed Zach, "that was true?"

"I'm sure Hollywood added its thing to it," Leesie offered, "but it really did happen. I think everyone should download it."

The conversation made Ariana feel closer to everyone present. She decided to just keep sharing her thoughts, "More things have happened. I know some of you are really overloaded, maybe thinking about running for the hills, but I feel that no matter what, we should always be honest and tell everything. So here goes. Today when I was meditating, I wanted to ask my guides about that nasty energy I experienced at the fair. My mediation was far different from anything I'd experienced before." Determined to continue no matter what the others might think of her, Ariana explained, "This time I felt that I was taken somewhere that was obviously not Earth. I wasn't scared. Even though I knew something very different was happening to me, I felt calm. There appeared before me three elderly people I had never seen before. They imparted some pretty disturbing information. When I came back from the meditation, I wrote down everything I could remember. I think it would be best if everyone read it, then we can talk about it. Here." Ariana handed her journal to the others.

Ariana watched as the group read her journal. She was anxious, afraid that they would all freak and take a hike. Then she would be alone again. She wouldn't blame them for running, though. *It's as though we've all been thrown down the rabbit hole and we're trying to survive the Mad Hatter's tea party.* Not only were they discovering new things about themselves that could put them in danger, but they were reading Ariana's intimate experience. *Everyone's going to see first-hand just how other-worldly, or maybe just plain crazy I really am. Stop it! It's these kinds of negative, fearful thoughts that feed the thing. I will need to work harder to monitor my thinking,* she vowed.

Leesie was the first one done. She looked at Ariana, blinked and said, "Wow! That's a lot to absorb. How are you feeling about all this?"

"I was really freaked and needed to talk with my friends. I'm really afraid that I might have tipped over the edge or something. Maybe I'm trying to sabotage the good life that has begun. I don't know, but my own fear and negativity drew the thing to me again. I became so negative and fearful right after I finished writing down what happened. I felt defeated before we even began and started thinking about ways to run away. I was more depressed than I had been in years," Ariana confessed.

"What did you do?" Wendy asked obviously frightened.

"I took a shower and while the water was washing over me, I found myself becoming calm, peaceful. I filled myself with light. When I got out I felt better and I noticed the room was both dark and cold even though there should have been sunlight streaming through the windows. That's when I knew that it had been The Darkness intensifying my fear and doubt, turning it into despair. I deepened my White Light shield and ordered it to leave. It did."

"Wow," Teja said for the group.

"How do you feel now about what the Elders said? Are you still scared? Do you believe any of it, or think it's just that thing messing with you?" Zach asked.

"I really don't know. I know that somehow I knew how to dispel the thing and the Elders told me I had called to it and that was why it came. They also said it was a test so I would know that I know what to do to get rid of it at least temporarily, but that could have been all part of my delusion, too." Shaking her head and looking very uncertain she continued, "I just don't know how we'll ever be able to figure it all out. Maybe the therapist will finally diagnose me with Schizophrenia or something."

"There is one way to find out if some of it is true," offered Matthew. He looked straight at Ariana and said, "We could injure you and see if you can heal yourself."

Zach was shocked. "Oh, yeah. Let's just cut off her finger and see if it will grow back. Wow, are you ever a heartless son-of-a-dog!"

Matthew calmly looked at Zach, "No valuable body parts need to be harmed, just cut her and see if she can heal it."

"Are you nuts?" blurted Wendy. "What happens if it isn't true, or it takes time? We could really hurt her."

"But we'd know for sure if what Ariana experienced in her mediation is true," Matthew replied. "Then we could talk about the other information she was told. Otherwise, we are talking about things that may just be a delusion, not facts. What do you say Ariana? It's your body."

"If it's the only way, I'm game. I can't spend the rest of my life thinking that I may be crazy, and if this works, then I'll know for sure."

"Well, if we're going to do this stupid thing," answered Wendy, "we need first aid supplies. Got anything, Leesie?"

Leesie went into the bathroom and came back with a professional looking first aid kit. "I'm a little paranoid about accidents, and also more than a little accident prone. I seem to cut myself a lot, so I make sure I have everything I could ever need," she admitted as though she were ashamed.

Andrew patted her on the shoulder as he said, "Don't be upset about being prepared, it's smart. So what do we use to cut her?"

Blushing, Leesie also admitted that she had a very sharp Swiss Army knife.

"Again, smart girl. It's always good to be prepared for anything," Wendy assured her.

Ariana put out her right hand waiting for someone to cut her palm.

"Aren't you right handed?" asked Leesie.

"Yes."

"Probably best to use your left hand, then. Not that I think you can't do it. I believe in you, but just in case," Leesie suggested.

Ariana placed her left hand on the desk, palm up. Closing her eyes, she nodded her head to signal she was ready. She took a deep breath and waited.

"Ouch, that hurt!"

"Sorry, sorry, I didn't mean to cut you so deeply!" Leesie's panicked voice said. "Don't look, just use your mind and heal it quickly."

What the heck am I to do? Ariana could feel the blood dripping from her hand onto the desk. The wound throbbed so badly that she could think of nothing else. *No,* she told herself, *breathe and concentrate, see the blood slowing down and the skin healing.* As she breathed deeply, Ariana allowed the calm energy to envelope her just like in the shower.

She concentrated on changing her aura to a healing blue and sent that energy into her hand. *My hand is not wounded. It is only whole and complete.*

"OMG," screamed Teja, "she's doing it!"

Although Ariana could hear Teja, it was as though she was hearing from within a cotton cocoon. The sound was muffled and muted and of no importance. Eventually, Ariana's hand began to feel cool and she felt that was her cue to open her eyes. When she did, she didn't bother to look at her hand, she knew it was whole. She was instead overwhelmed by the expressions of awe on everyone's faces.

"I guess that answers our questions," mumbled Andrew. "Dang! It's all real. So where do we go from here?"

Ariana looked at her palm. She wiggled her fingers. No pain and no evidence that there had been anything wrong. Her hand was still streaked with blood and there was wet blood on the desk, lots of it. But there was no sign the blood was from her. She looked to Matthew. She wanted an alternative explanation. She didn't want to know that she could be a monster, a freak, an alien species. She had spent her whole life as an outsider, now that she had finally found people she could relate to and even befriend, she was deeply afraid that they would reject her, too. *I don't want to be alone again.* Ariana felt a stabbing pain deep within her. She could not contain the loud moan that escaped from her body.

Zach walked over to Ariana and taking her into his arms said, "Don't worry, I for one won't abandon you." It was as though he had read her mind. Looking around at everyone else he asked, "What about the rest of you?"

Leesie wrapped her arms around the two of them saying, "If you can handle all our weirdness, then we can handle yours. Can I get an amen?" she asked, looking at the others.

"I have to admit that I'm pretty creeped out here," Teja replied, "but unless you intend to suck out my brain or implant me with an alien baby, I'll stick around, too."

"Andrew, Wendy, Matt, what are you guys feeling?" asked Leesie.

"If I can embrace shamanism as my path," Matthew said, "then I must explore the unexplorable and embrace all life. Nothing's changed for me here."

"I don't abandon my friends. You guys didn't reject me, and I seem to have gotten rid of a lot of anger thanks to Ariana's abilities. I'm not going back to that ever, so come here, girl," Wendy said, opening her arms.

Ariana felt a rush of relief. Yet one member of the group had remained silent. "That leaves you, Andrew," said Ariana. "I wouldn't blame you if you needed to run out of here screaming. If it wasn't me that all this was about, **I'd** be outta here. Please don't feel like any of us will look down on you if you don't want to stay."

Andrew remained silent, but did not leave. Finally, he approached Ariana and looking directly into her eyes said, "You scare the pants off me. Every instinct I have says get the hell away. But my brain, such as it is, reminds me that all I've ever seen from you is kindness and caring. I'm not going to be like that girlfriend you had that rejected you for being you. I'm going to get a grip and take all this stuff as it comes, until I can't. Okay?"

Ariana smiled, "May I hug you?"

"Group hug!" exclaimed Leesie enthusiastically. And as they hugged, the ice and fear broke, and only deep friendship remained.

Chapter 8

Matthew interrupted the hug shared by the new group of friends. "Hate to put a damper on this Hallmark moment," he announced more sarcastically than he intended, "but we still have work to do. I think we should start by listing what our abilities are." Taking a pen off the desk, he turned to a new page in Ariana's journal and wrote:

Ariana: healer, energy worker, Darkness slayer

Matthew: skin walker, healer, energy worker

Andrew: place psychometry

Zach: psychometry, past lives

Wendy: animal communicator

Leesie: numerology

Teja: medium

"Anything I've missed?" Matthew asked.

No one added anything.

Matthew continued, "I realize we may not know what else we can do, yet. We may have more abilities. The Elders said Ariana could train us, but I'll bet she doesn't think she knows how. Right?"

Ariana nodded her head in agreement.

"Shouldn't we discuss what the Elders said about what might happen to our planet and how we can do something about it?" asked Zach.

"I can research the training techniques used by the government," Leesie offered, "then Ariana will have something to work with."

"You know, my grandmother used to play games with me that I think was her way of helping my abilities develop. We could try that," offered Ariana.

Andrew smiled, "Games; I can handle that. I'm good at games."

"I've been thinking about what Zach asked." Wendy said, "We have many serious issues facing our planet. Besides the environmental problems, we have hatred in the form of terrorism. Gun violence is so extreme that every year, thousands of people in our country are hurt or killed. There is violence against innocent children and the economy has declined so drastically there is almost no middle class left. Poverty is increasing and the divide between the rich and everyone else is expanding yearly. I'm sure I've missed some things, too. However, I can't for the life of me figure out how we can do anything about any of it. Anyone have any suggestions?"

"I think the energy on the planet has gotten way out of whack," stated Matthew. "That will cause people to begin to act strangely, too. It's like an irritating, low pitch hum that you don't recognize, constantly playing in the background. As the pitch changes to something more irritating, then your nervous system becomes disturbed. This causes you to feel on edge until some event sends you into a violent frenzy. As the climate continues to change, more violent Earth activity is possible. And as communities become disrupted by lack of normal necessities like electricity, water, police and medical assistance, fear will increase creating more violence. To me it is obvious; we need to work to rebalance the energy and help alleviate fear."

"I know that I can balance energy in small groups, but I have **no** idea how to extend that to encompass the entire planet," Ariana said.

Matthew said to Ariana, "You won't have to do it alone. You can teach us. We can help. I believe that there will come a time very soon when we will have help throughout the world. I know the Native people have been working on this, as have the Buddhists. All we have to do is find a way to make others aware that we exist and are also working on this problem. We need to be the hub in the wheel, and the others, the radiating spokes. The problem has been that everyone was working individually or just among their own cultures." Leaning toward Ariana, Matthew concluded, "Now you're here to lead the way."

"I think he's right," declared Leesie. "We all know that people are afraid. One way to get rid of fear is to educate and help people to feel empowered rather than impotent. We make a plan, announce the plan, work the plan, and I think we will be The Lights the Elders mentioned. We must bring the other lights together with ours if we're going to banish The Darkness and create balance again."

"Not to appear contrary, but how do we get started?" Andrew asked.

"How many of you meditate?" inquired Ariana, fully expecting no one to raise their hands. She was not disappointed. "Okay, just as I thought. Most people think it's hard or that you have to do transcendental meditation and completely clear your mind, but that's not true. All you have to do is allow your body to relax as completely as possible and then focus your attention on something: counting down, a chant, or your place of deep relaxation, for example. This won't be natural at first. Your body might try to sabotage you and your mind will race, but with practice it gets easier and very pleasurable. I think our first step is helping everyone learn to meditate. I'll lead you through a guided meditation and then we can discuss how it went. I'd suggest that you record it on your phones to play when you meditate at home."

Ariana sat on Leesie's bed, crossed her legs and said, "First, make yourselves as comfortable as you can. I suggest sitting straight with your hands, palms up, on your knees. Now, close your eyes and take a deep breath through your nose, as deep as possible, hold it, now release the breath through your mouth and relax. . . relax. . . relax your body and your mind. Take another deep breath and focusing on this breath, feel yourself relax. Breathing deeply, think 'relax,' and as you exhale, think 'deeper and deeper.' Deeply relaxing now, just listening to my voice, breathing, relaxing, and going deeper and deeper. Continue relaxing now. Feel how good it is to relax, your body feeling wonderful, lighter and lighter as you go deeper and deeper within. You want to relax completely now. You love relaxing deeply now, so with the next exhalation of breath allow yourself to go ten times deeper, deeply, deeply asleep. Listening to my voice only makes you more relaxed. Any sound you hear will only send you more deeply within. Deeper, deeper, relax. I'm going to count down now from ten to one. With each descending number, allow yourself to relax even more and go deeper and deeper and deeper. Ten, going deeper and deeper, relaxing deeply, visualizing the number 10 and go deeper. Nine, visualizing the number 9, feel yourself going even deeper. Eight, see the number 8 and go deeper still. When we reach the number one you will be completely relaxed, completely at peace. Relax now and go deeper. Number 7, going even deeper, 6, deeply relaxed and deeply at peace, 5, when we reach the number 1 you will be 10 times deeper or 100 times deeper if you so desire. Relax and go even more deeply within, 4, breathe and go deeper, 3, even more deeply relaxed, relax as completely as you can, much deeper than before,

2, almost there now, relax, 1, as completely relaxed as you can be now concentrating only on my voice. Now I want you to visualize a wonderful place, a place that is absolutely beautiful, serene, and safe. It could be a forest of tall green trees in which the sunlight barely penetrates except for occasional streaks of light with dust motes dancing within it. Notice the damp smell of the forest and the coolness of the air. Make this place your own, your ideal place of relaxation. Or perhaps it is a field of green grass waving in the breeze dotted with yellow, white, and blue wildflowers, or a wonderful white sand beach stretching for miles completely undisturbed. The ocean is tranquil with small waves rolling silently in and leaving small shells behind. Create your perfect place of relaxation no matter where it is. It is your place, the place you can come back to whenever you want to gain knowledge, talk with your guides, or just relax. I am going to allow you to explore this place for a bit, and when next you hear my voice, an hour of time will have elapsed at this level of the mind."

Becoming quiet, Ariana observed the others. Everyone, including the usually hyper Leesie, seemed to be meditating. She looked at their auras and was amazed at how well they blended with one another. Even though she could distinguish each individual aura, they also seemed to create a group aura of gold. It made her feel good to look at them, her new family, each so special in their individuality, but so powerful and good as a group. She had the overwhelming feeling that they could do this, they could save the world. She looked at her watch. It had been almost 15 minutes. It was time to bring them back.

"It is time to come back from this beautiful place, your beautiful place that you can return to anytime you enter this level of the mind. Take another deep breath. I'm going to begin to count up from one to five. When I reach five, you will be back with me in this room, wide awake, feeling wonderful. 1, 2, begin to feel your body start to awaken, a tingling in your hands and feet, 3, feel a cool breeze over your face realizing that when I reach the number 5 you will be wide awake feeling better than before, 4, almost awake now, 5, wide awake feeling great."

Immediately, everyone opened their eyes and smiles stretched across almost everyone's face.

"Wow, that was great," Wendy exclaimed. "I really didn't think I'd be able to do that, but it was easy."

"Yeah, for me too," agreed Andrew.

"I don't think I've ever seen you so still, Leesie," Ariana teased.

"I don't think I've ever been that relaxed. I was totally killing my place of relaxation," Leesie claimed. "It was really dead!"

Zach seemed troubled. The others noticed he was unusually quiet.

"What's happening bro?" Matthew asked. "You okay?"

"I'm not sure," Zach stated. "I don't think I stayed on this planet. The place I went was like what Ariana described, two suns and a violet sky, but it wasn't beautiful. It looked like it had been destroyed. I was so overwhelmed with guilt. I knew it was my fault somehow. It was horrible."

Ariana walked over to him and took him into her arms this time. "I am so sorry, Zach. Was there anything else that you saw?"

"No, there was nothing else to see. There was only a deep feeling that if we don't succeed with our plan, then what I was looking at would happen to Earth. I was terrified that somehow that it would be my fault, too."

"Sounds like a past life memory to me," Matthew speculated. "Now we know what Zach has to offer—his memories of what went wrong before."

Zach looked devastated, his face white. Ariana just held him wondering if he had seen what had happened on her planet or whether he had truly lived through the cataclysms that the Elders claimed happened on her planet. She turned to Matthew and asked, "Is it possible that he was picking up what happened to my planet because I was leading the meditation, not because he had actually lived it?"

"Yes, I would think that's possible."

Ariana hugged Zach harder as she tried to reassure him. "See, you might not have done anything terrible."

Matthew continued, "Even if he did, it doesn't have anything to do with Zach as he is now. That wasn't even Zach; that was the soul contemplating what it had observed before."

"Okay, now I'm really confused," Teja complained.

"That's because you're thinking like most Western religions think, that the soul and you are one. I believe that the soul is connected to the Source, the Creator, God, and never leaves. But because the Source wants to grow in knowledge, the soul writes a play and the ego, the actor, acts it out. You are no more your soul than William Shatner is Captain Kirk in *Star Trek*. You are just an actor playing a role that the soul wrote and directed. You have freewill only as long as you follow the script. You can improvise a little, but you can't completely rewrite the play. If the soul intent in a lifetime is to learn prosperity, then you might prosper, but if you are meant to learn the lesson of lack, then you may struggle. Where the learning takes place is the attitude toward the experience. For example, there are people who grow from loss and actually help their world in some way, or those that become victims and add to the negativity. Consequently, it was not Zach that created the destruction, it was his soul remembering."

"That was a bit deep," complained Zach, "but I'll think about it. It sure did feel like my memory and my guilt, though."

"I think we all have a lot to think about," offered Ariana. "I don't know about everyone else, but I'm exhausted. Is it time to go home?"

"Yes," answered Wendy. The rest of the group nodded. "I know we have a lot to do, so I feel kinda guilty. But I couldn't absorb anything else right now, no matter what."

Leesie turned from her computer. "I recorded the whole session. I'll send everyone everything I feel is pertinent, as well as the recording. Meanwhile Ariana, why don't you put together some games that will help us develop. Matthew, research what others are doing to help the planet and what the Native people are saying about what's going on. And Zach, you have the hardest assignment; meditate and see if you can get a clearer picture of why you were shown that other planet. Everyone down with that?"

There was a general agreement from the group and they began to split into smaller groups. Ariana watched Teja and Andrew leave together, talking quietly. Wendy was talking with Leesie, which left Matthew, Zach, and Ariana standing together. Ariana wondered if they would be able to hold onto everyone in the group, or if things would get too difficult for some. She couldn't blame them if they left. This was not what she had in mind when she decided to begin a new life.

"Can I walk you back to your dorm?" Zach asked. "I would really like to talk with you, if you're not too tired."

Hearing the conversation, Matthew turned to the two and said, "It's okay, don't worry about me. Go on. I've got some stuff to do anyway. I think you two should talk alone."

Ariana and Zach left the dorm and began their walk across the campus. There was only silence between them. Ariana let Zach take his time, knowing that he had to sort through a lot of thoughts and emotions before he could put them into words.

"Can we sit here under this tree a moment?" he asked.

They sat facing each other, his head down. Ariana took his hands in hers and when he looked up, she smiled, hoping to put him at ease. He sat staring into her eyes for what felt like hours, took a deep breath and said, "What does that make us?"

"What do you mean?" Ariana asked, confused.

"I mean, from the moment I saw you, I felt a strong connection to you. I wanted to know you and to help and protect you. I felt like we were meant to be together in some way. Now I'm wondering if I am your father or something."

Ariana began to laugh, almost uncontrollably. This was definitely not what she had expected. Seeing the hurt look on Zach's face, she began to feel guilty and immediately stopped laughing. "I'm so sorry that I laughed," she stammered. "I'm not laughing at you. I'm laughing at what you said about being my dad. Even if you were my father in the past, you certainly aren't now. I feel no familial bond at all. What we might have been in some distant life has nothing to do with who we are now. The memories, if they rise up, are just to show us what to do or not to do this lifetime."

"But wouldn't you feel weird being with me?"

"Like dating?" she inquired, feeling an excitement build within her. She had never had a boyfriend and she did really like Zach. He was so sweet in a completely innocent and caring way and very hot. His Italian heritage was evident in his curly, dark brown hair, puppy dog brown eyes and olive complexion. He even had the perfect Roman profile, complete with the aquiline nose. Tall, at least six feet and very well built, he was a complete package, a total hunk. His mouth was sensual and full and she found herself wondering what it would be like to kiss. She blushed and he noticed.

"Did I embarrass you somehow?"

"No, it's just that this is new to me. I've never had a boyfriend or a date for that matter. I've been pretty much a loner, you know."

"Yeah, but you have to jump in sometime and I'm pretty harmless," he said with the signature twinkle in his eyes.

"Why do you use humor to hide your feelings?"

It was Zach's turn to be embarrassed. "Enough heavy talk for today," he replied. "I'll bare my soul on our third date, how's that?"

Smiling, Ariana answered, "It's a deal then."

"So you will go out with me? Alone, not with everyone else?"

"When?"

"Saturday night at seven?"

"Sounds great. How should I dress?"

"You're perfect just like you are," Zach said, his smile beaming and his aura bright orange.

"Time to get me back to the dorm," Ariana insisted. "You know you left your car at Barrett."

"Oh, darn, I was so messed up when we began our walk, scared you'd reject me, that I forgot all about it. I'll still walk you to your place and then go back for it, okay?"

"Okay," Ariana responded.

Zach stood and reaching down, pulled Ariana to her feet. As they started walking, he continued to hold her hand. She smiled to herself, *I could get very used to this*. Ariana was disappointed the walk was so short. When they reached Manzanita, she turned to face him, "I'd invite you in, but I really don't know if my roommate is there or not and believe me, you don't want to meet her."

Zach smiled his incredible smile and asked, "Already afraid of me?"

Ariana blushed and stepping even closer, put her arms around his neck and planted a soft kiss on his lips. "Do I act afraid?" she said.

Holding her closely Zach replied, "Now you'll never get rid of me. I'm like a stray cat, once you started feeding me, I never go away."

"Don't want you to go away, just leave for today," was her response.

He looked down at her, and then moved her hair from her face, his fingers leaving little trails of shivers. "Did anyone ever tell you that you're short? Beautiful, but short."

"Great way to break the mood," she exclaimed, hitting him in the chest with both hands. "Go."

He smiled, tipped an imaginary hat as he said, "Until group Friday, au revoir." Wiggling his eyebrows, he turned and began to walk back to his car.

Smiling, she stood watching him walk away, somehow unable to stop staring at his cute butt.

Chapter 9

Ariana spent the rest of the week trying not to think about her date on Saturday, her studies suffering from the lack of attention. She was very frustrated with herself because **all** she wanted to do was think about Zach, not about her path or her schoolwork. She had even avoided her daily meditation. Working hard to figure out what was going on with her, she found her mind exploring two different possibilities. *Am I afraid of what is expected of me? Is this why I'm avoiding my meditations? Why am I afraid to think about my path? Or is it because I never really experienced adolescence like other girls? I never dated, never fell in love or even talked to any boys, never had to deal with boys at all. That's why I'm acting like a 12-year-old instead of a grown woman.*

Ariana's thoughts raced. Finally, she came upon an answer to the many questions she was pondering. She realized she was afraid of everyone's expectations of her and that it was much more pleasant thinking about Zach. *Oh, that kiss!* That was certainly easier to think about than negative energy and the end of the world.

She had also been thinking about their Friday night group therapy session. She wondered if the therapist would realize that something was different. Would the other kids notice something and feel left out? Should they ask anyone else to join them? She wished that she had talked to the others about this. Maybe she should send them an e-mail.

To: Weidxomics

Question for tomorrow re: group. I vote no discussion yet about what we're doing. Any others we should include? How should we approach them? Think about it tonight. Be early to meeting tomorrow and we'll decide.

Ariana hit send. It was only eight in the evening, too early to go to bed. *I don't feel like studying, even though I really should. I guess it's time to meditate. Can't put it off any longer.*

When she got to her place of relaxation, they were waiting for her. *What awful piece of information do you have for me tonight?*

Elder Number Two responded, "It is not productive for you to act like a pouting youngling. We are not here to punish, but to inform, educate, and train. We listened as the group postulated as to the purpose. The group is on point; you are here to adjust and balance the planet's energies, to re-establish the polarities. Somehow, Terra has become completely fear-based. It is fear that creates greed, anger, jealousy, revenge, and negative judgments. It is fear that allows selfishness and rationalization. Originally, Terra was a rich and beautiful world. There was enough of everything and all creatures lived in harmony. The memory of this place has remained among the religions, although it has been perverted to create shame and judgment. This place was known as Eden. In religious texts, it is implied that humanity was forced from Eden due to the female's trickery. This is not so; man walked away with his eyes wide open and has been walking away ever since. If anything was the villain, it was man's ego convincing him there was something better elsewhere. After leaving this paradise, man discovered a world that was often hostile and hard to survive in. He lost his memory of Eden and it disappeared into myth. Humanity convinced itself that its continuation was all that mattered and it started to destroy the very planet it needed for survival. Soon these entities began to experience loss and then fear. Once fear had a foothold, it grew. We know that you experienced the dark energies which were awakened by the fear. Fear breeds superstitions, which create religions, which create sin and punishment. It allowed men who crave power to rise and trample those weaker than them. It created an environment where man could rationalize all types of brutal behavior and destruction to everything around them, including the planet. People began to see variations among them and to separate from those they considered different. Different became bad and created an excuse to do harm. It is a circle that grows as greed grows. Man began to war in earnest, using bigger and more violent tools, until with a simple push of a button he can destroy thousands of years of life. But that is not the true problem, for even if the bomb had been launched, some part of Terra would have persisted and begun again. However, now it is the planet herself that is in danger. Man's destructive power has truly done her damage and as negative energy grows, her polarities shift, causing extreme disruption in her core. Her oceans, which adjust the climate and were filled with such wondrous life, are dying. Water, which is the source of all life on Terra, is so filled with chemicals that even the rainwater is toxic to life, as is the soil. Disease, starvation, and wars are the result of this negatively disruptive energy. If your group can fix even a little of this energy, there is a chance of creating a shift in consciousness that will take Terra from a fear-based planet to the Eden she truly is."

How do we do that? Ariana asked.

Elder Number One replied, "You already know how to manipulate energy. You were born exceptional, but you also had training. We will replant the memories of that training and the life you lived on Meria, our planet, the fifth star in the belt of Orion. From these memories and from the techniques your oma used, you will train the others. There will be more that join you, some from very far away. But the initial eight are the center, the power. Each of you has a polarity within the group. One has yet to join, but will within the next three days. You will see the polarities begin to pair. When they link, they are at their strongest. Some have already been drawn to their pair. The pair does not have to be a love bonding, although this works best. The pairing can be two kindred souls that work well together. Triangles will also form, as will circles within circles, what is called Sacred Geometry. All of these forms have uses that you will employ to make the energy bow to the group will. Record all conversations you have with us, whether through your meditations, dreams, or voices. Pay attention to the planet. She too will direct you. Matthew and Andrew are good at that."

Elder Number Three added, "Find each individual's strength and weakness before they are discovered by the forces arrayed against you, as they can be exploited as almost happened with you. Each of you must watch for your own fear-based, self-defeating thinking as these things are footholds for darkness. Find the strength and weaknesses of the group, those will be different. These also can be exploited. Two of your weaknesses, Ariana, are perfection and discouragement. Commitment will overcome them."

"It is time for you to sleep now," said Elder Two. "You will sleep deeply and when you awaken, you will remember this conversation, record it, and share it with the others."

Chapter 10

The sun was high in the sky, streaming through Ariana's open curtains as she awakened for the day. The mourning doves were cooing in a way that sounded more like owls, and the air had taken on a crisp, autumn feel. Ariana stretched and looking at her roommate's bed, realized it had been days since she had seen her. *What a wonderful, good omen. Maybe she has moved out!* Rising from her bed, Ariana's curiosity led her to investigate Elaine's side of their room. To Ariana's disappointment, Elaine's belongings were still on her desk. *Oh well, one can hope.* Ariana immediately felt guilty about being so nasty, but the beauty of the day quickly changed her mood. She would be seeing Zach in just a few hours and that made everything else inconsequential.

Gosh, I feel lazy. Like a fat Persian cat, all Ariana wanted to do was lie down, bask in the sunlight and daydream about Zach. *What's happening to me? I've got to get a grip*! Ariana grabbed her towel and headed into the bathroom. *Maybe a hot shower will energize me.* The water cascading over her head and body felt so good, almost as good as the caress of Zach's fingertips on her face. She blushed remembering how wonderful the energy had felt as he touched her. Suddenly the memory felt real. She physically felt his soft lips on hers. Ariana was so startled she jumped backwards and almost slipped on the wet shower tiles. *What just happened*? It felt as though Zach was in the shower with her, kissing her. *Mind link,* she heard plainly in her brain. It was a thought from the Elders. They had said they would be with her. *That felt a lot creepy*, she thought to herself and the Elders, if they were listening. *I need to know what happened.* A response became clear in her mind, *Finish your shower and then we will talk.*

Ariana rinsed the shampoo from her hair and got out of the shower as quickly as she could. Wrapping a towel around her wet head and putting on her robe, she prepared to meditate. To her surprise, the Elders instantly began to communicate with her. Their voices were more than thoughts now; she could clearly hear what was being said to her.

"Meditation is not necessary now to reach us. Meditation is only necessary when you need to relax. We are available to educate whenever there is a need, as there is now. A mind link is a connection between two polarities. Two minds can connect and work as a team, two parts of one whole, the yin and the yang. Both of you were thinking of the kiss, which created it in the third dimension."

"We actually kissed again?"

"Yes."

"He was in the shower with me?" This was more than Ariana wanted to hear!

"Only his mind, his thoughts. Not his eyes."

"I guess that's better, sort of. He was thinking of me, too?" Ariana exclaimed, afraid her excitement would be obvious.

"Again, you are responding as a youngling. It is not important that the two of you are attracted as male and female. What is important is that you have the beginning of a telepathic bond. Now you can work on improving it so that you can do more than kiss. It will make your teaching him easier as the bond will allow a knowing rather than a learning. You must write now. Write what you were told last night and what you have learned now."

Ariana sat at her computer and wrote everything that happened and e-mailed the group. She left out the kiss but did mention what a mind link was and how it helped connect people. *The kiss is private.* Something for her to think about, then treasure. If Zach was in her mind, did he know that she was thinking intimately about him? *Oh no, I hope he doesn't know how obsessed I'm getting about him*! Ariana shielded and hoped that would keep things more private. Her thoughts turned to what had transpired in the shower. *Did the kiss happen only because we were both thinking about it, or just because I was? The Elders said both of us were, so maybe he is as excited about me as I am about him?* Ariana realized she was panicking over nothing. *Deep breaths,* she reminded herself. *Think this through.* She realized Zach couldn't know what she was thinking because she didn't know what he was thinking. *If it is a polarity as the Elders mentioned, it goes both ways, right?* That made sense, but she was still a bit anxious now about seeing Zach.

Ariana could tell by the quality of the light coming through the window that it was already late morning. She had missed her Intro to Psychology class and if she didn't hurry, she would miss American Lit, too. *Crap! I have to try and do something with my hair and get dressed!* Her life was definitely spinning out of control. Brushing out her hair as she simultaneously put on her jeans was hard enough. But trying to pull her T-shirt over her head at the same time was impossible. Ariana found herself lying in a lump on the floor. *What a mess I am*, she thought. *Super Hero Ariana is going to change the world. Yup, I can see it now.* Slowing down, she grabbed her backpack—made sure her lit and trig books were in it—and left for class.

The day was as beautiful as she thought it would be. Ariana knew that she would never take the wonderful weather and bright blue skies of Arizona for granted. Recent rains had caused the temperatures to fall well below normal. A slight breeze caressed her and ruffled her hair. She noticed a crispness in the air, a rare event for an Arizona October.

Although the campus was located in a desert, there were many green areas. Today, students filled the grassy knolls, taking advantage of the weather. As Ariana walked, she observed her surroundings, marveling at the beauty and diversity of this planet. Even in something as brutal as the desert where temperatures could reach over 120 degrees, a variety of beautiful plants and wildlife could be found. In fact, seemingly against all odds, creatures continue to thrive. Ariana was struck with the power of the planet. *No matter what humans do to destroy our environment, the planet fights to survive. It's almost inconceivable to believe that this world could be destroyed. But obviously, that's one of man's worst traits—denial; the ability to see what's right in front of you and still think that it will work out somehow.* Weren't there people who still believed the Earth was flat?

Ariana had always seen herself as a realist. She had read the warnings about climate change. Like most other people, however, she rationalized that someone else would find some way to solve it, or that what scientists were predicting was really just extremism, an effort to create unnecessary panic. Ariana was beginning to understand that she, like so many others, was willing to close her eyes and let someone else take care of the problem. Suddenly, she was seeing the planet differently, seeing its beauty and realizing how fragile the balance really is. This was a desert, but everywhere she looked was grass, flowers, and trees. The

West was suffering one of the worst droughts in history, but people were still watering their plants, filling their swimming pools, and washing their cars. There were artificial lakes and fountains spewing water into the sky as though water was an unlimited commodity. *Why haven't I noticed this before and understood the implications?* she wondered. A small thought began to rapidly grow in her mind. Could it be that now that she knew her path, she would no longer be able to close her eyes to what was happening around her? That now she would feel the planet's need and notice what had to be changed?

Boy, class will be like a vacation from these heavy speculations, Ariana thought as she entered the language and literature building. The cold air from the air conditioning hit her hard as she entered. *Air conditioning? It isn't hot outside. What happened to opening windows?* A few feet from the door to her classroom, she heard her name called. Turning, she saw Zach. Ariana found herself becoming very excited at seeing him here, but she was confused too.

"What are you doing here and how did you find me?"

"Well, hello to you too," Zach teased. "I went to your dorm first and then saw you walking across campus. By the time I parked my car, I thought I'd lost you. But lucky for me, there you were, entering this building. I had to run to catch up with you."

"Okay," Ariana said quizzically, "and?"

"Oh, sorry. I had a weird experience earlier and needed to talk to you about it." Stepping closer to Ariana, Zach said, "I was getting ready for class this morning and thinking about seeing you later. Suddenly, it felt like we were kissing. I could **feel** your lips on mine, as though you were really there. It was nice, actually wonderful, but really freaky, too. Do you have any idea what that was about? It really kind of freaked me out."

Ariana felt her face turn bright red as the blood rushed to it. "It happened to me, too," she admitted. "I asked the Elders what happened and they said it was a mind link. When someone is the other's polarity they can create this mind link thing and if both people are thinking about something at the same time, they feel it, or see it, or get the same thing at the same time."

"You were thinking of our kiss?" Zach asked with his traditional smirk.

"Yeah, and so were you it seems," Ariana replied with a smirk of her own.

Zach took some of her hair in his hand. "I really like your hair down like this. You look so darn hot! I'll never be able to think of anything but you in my trig class."

Ariana smiled coyly, and wiggling her eyebrows in imitation of his signature move replied, "Well, we could both skip class." *Did I really just say that?*

"Let's go."

Walking across campus hand-in-hand toward Zach's car, Ariana was again wondering what was happening to her. She had never cut a class in her life, nor had she ever considered herself irresponsible. But here she was, cutting class with a guy she'd only known a week! *Sure, he's adorable, that little dimple that only shows when he really smiles; it's so cute! But what am I thinking? Skipping class?*

Shaking off her thoughts, Ariana asked, "Where are we going?"

"Hadn't really thought beyond picking up my car," Zach admitted.

"How about just going back to my room," Ariana surprised herself by the suggestion. "My roommate hasn't been there in days, so we'll have some privacy."

With the lopsided smirk back on his handsome face, Zach stopped to look at her, "What shenanigans are you suggesting, girl?"

Dang, he can embarrass me. "I only meant that we'd have some privacy to talk about what's been happening," Ariana stammered. "And maybe we can work on developing our mind link. Shenanigans? What are you, 80?"

Taking her face in his hands, Zach smiled and bent forward to kiss her. Ariana thought about moving backward, but realized she wanted this kiss. It was soft at first, like a gentle wind brushing her lips, but it soon became stronger, more passionate, as though he was taking possession of her. She found herself responding as deeply.

"Whew," Ariana said as their lips finally parted. "That's better than what romance novels describe."

Zach took her hand as they began walking again. "Now we'll have something else to think about when we are working on our mind link."

"You think?" Ariana said, laughing. "That may be **all** I can think about for a while."

The couple rode silently in the elevator to the sixth floor. *The dormitory seems so quiet,* Ariana thought before realizing most of the students would be in class at this hour. She began to wonder if being alone with Zach in her room was a great idea. All she wanted to do was kiss him again. *Probably not the smartest idea.*

Arriving at the door to her room, Ariana was surprised to find it open. *Oh heck, did I forget to lock it? This just proves how screwed up I am right now.* Looking at Zach she said, "I don't remember specifically if I locked it or not, but I always lock my door."

"Let me go first then," Zach said.

Entering the room, neither of them noticed anything odd. Guiding her back toward the door with a sweep of his arm, Zach checked the bathroom and the closets, but discovered nothing unusual.

"I guess I was in such hurry to get to class, you know the lit class I ended up skipping, that I just forgot to lock it. I've been really scattered this last week," Ariana said with a slight smile.

"Is anything different from when you left?"

"I don't think so, but somehow, the energy feels different. I can't explain how, just different."

"Maybe you're just a little freaked. Wouldn't that make the energy feel different to you?"

"I guess," she admitted, even though she felt there was something more. Something else was different. She hated not understanding her feelings. Shutting the door, Ariana stood in the center of the room. She closed her eyes and began to breathe deeply.

"What are you doing?"

"Shush. I'm trying to figure out what's off," she replied. "Come here and take my hands. Let's see if our polarity will help me get clear."

As soon as they touched, Ariana could feel their energies link. She felt as though they were surrounded in each other's aura, creating a dimension where they were separate from all other energies. *Is this what it feels like to stand detached?* she thought. Ariana began to observe the room and the objects in it. Immediately she became aware that the objects themselves had color and vibration surrounding them. Yet somehow they were different than normal. Ariana wondered if this was a true energy field or a transfer of her energy to the objects. She also noticed that even though the room was bathed in sunlight shining from the windows, there was an area near her bed that was shrouded in darkness. *That's not normal*, she thought.

"Zach, are you seeing anything?"

"Yeah, I see light surrounding everything. I also feel as though the room and everything in it is vibrating, like it has its own frequency."

"Look over at the bed," Ariana insisted. "What do you see there?"

"Well, nothing. It's as though there's an energy void or something with no discernable vibration. It doesn't feel like the rest of the room. It doesn't feel like it belongs here. There's something about it that feels empty. It's weird, because everything else feels so alive."

Ariana sighed. This is not what she wanted to hear. Doing her best to remain calm, she said, "I think The Dark energy has found me again. Zach, protect yourself with a white light. Think of creating a force field of good that is impenetrable." Instantly, Ariana felt Zach do what she had asked. Ariana could feel that when they both concentrated on light, the dark was shrinking. She increased the volume of love contained within her energy field and felt the room grow warm and even brighter.

"What are you doing?" Zach asked, impressed by what was happening.

"I'm increasing the vibration of the energy by thinking about love," she responded. "I've got an idea. Let's think about our last kiss and how good it made us feel."

"Why don't we just kiss again?"

"No, I want the loving, close feelings the kiss produced, not the sexual feelings."

Holding hands and locking their eyes, both Ariana and Zach released intense feelings of connection, safety, and love. Instantly, the room became vibrant, calm, and soothing. They could see the shadow decrease. The dark hues dispersed, becoming lighter until finally, it was gone.

"We killed it!" Zach exclaimed.

"No, energy can't be destroyed. We just got rid of it for now." Realizing the danger that she and Zach had been able to avoid, Ariana continued, "We need to make sure that the others know about protections and are on the lookout for this thing. We all need to remember to monitor our thoughts, too. No negativity or fear as that seems to draw it."

"I feel wonderful now, though," Zach claimed, unable to contain his smile.

"Yes, tapping into the energy of the Source, of God, always makes you feel wonderful. It's a little addicting."

"It's a little like having great sex, but on steroids," Zach blurted.

"I really wouldn't know," admitted Ariana. *Time to change the conversation*, she thought. "Looks like I was right when I said that the room felt different."

"How did you know what to do? I mean, how did you know connecting our energies in that way would drive that thing, that bad energy, away?"

"I just knew. Maybe it was what the Elders were talking about. They said that the training I already have would become activated."

"I guess that will teach me to question you," Zach said, smiling. "So, what do we do now?"

"I was going to try to explain to you what I mean when I talk about energy, but I guess I don't need to now. Maybe we can pretend like we're just normal college students getting to know each other. Things seem to be moving pretty rapidly between us and I really don't know anything about your life. Tell me about yourself."

"Let's sit down first and I'll give you the story of my life even though there's not much to tell." Zach sat at the desk chair and Ariana made herself comfortable on the floor. She wanted to avoid sitting on the bed.

Zach began, "I'm the youngest of four, two brothers and an older sister. I was born in Detroit, but am so glad to be out of the dark skies, snow, and the desperate depression of that city. I am my mom's favorite and she spoiled me horribly. I was raised Catholic, but don't believe in much of anything right now."

"There's got to be more than that," Ariana said impatiently. "What about your dad?"

Ariana felt Zach's energy change immediately. He became irritated and hostile.

"I don't want to discuss him."

"Okay," Ariana said, quickly trying to change the subject. "What do you do when you're not in class or with me?"

"I draw, read. I also collect things."

"What do you collect?"

"That's more important than my artwork?" Zach said, his mood improved enough to start teasing again. "I collect comics, art books, World of Warcraft figures, games. A ton of things."

"Sounds like you're pretty serious about art. Why are you an engineering major instead of art?"

"Because two of my favorite things are eating and amassing money, neither of which happens easily in the world of art. I chose not to starve. But I do love to draw."

"Are you drawn to any particular type of art: Renaissance, Modern, Classical, Impressionist? Who's your favorite artist?"

"A German engraver named Albrecht Durer is my favorite artist and Renaissance art is my passion. Impressionism is just mall art, in my humble opinion."

"Anything scare you?"

"Yeah, everything we're involved with right now," Zach admitted.

"Me too," Ariana agreed with a shiver.

"Come here," Zach said as he stood, holding out his arms. "I think we both can use a hug."

Ariana went into his arms and leaning in, closed her eyes. She concentrated on breathing in his scent. She recognized shaving cream, soap, and some underlying spicy aroma she couldn't identify. Everything about him helped to make her feel calm and secure. *Is this what love feels like?*

"Your hair smells good and is so soft," Zach said, running his hand over the smooth thick strands that flowed down her back. "I love it like this, loose and wild. Do you have any idea how beautiful you are?"

"Is that a line?" Ariana asked honestly.

"No, I mean it."

"Thank you, but I don't know how to respond to that. I'm just me."

"I can't understand why you would choose me over Matt. He's tall, blond, and handsome, right? I'm just this dweeby little dude."

"Wow, both of us have a very skewed self-image, don't we?" Ariana turned Zach toward the bathroom mirror. "What I see is a very sexy, handsome hunk with broad shoulders and great abs, nice butt, too. Your eyes are so expressive, soft and loving, and your mouth, um, oh heck, I'd better not go there," she said, growing uncomfortable with how forward she had been.

"So, what's going on in here?" Elaine's voice interrupted from the doorway. "Little Miss Prissy was just an act?"

Zach and Ariana separated and looked toward the door. "How long have you been standing there?" Ariana demanded.

"Oh, I just got here." Staring at Zach, Elaine said, "Why don't you introduce me to your killer friend?"

"Zach, this is my roommate, Elaine. Elaine, this is my friend Zach."

With a look that swept from Zach's head to his feet, Elaine replied, "Not her roommate for long. I'm moving out, roomy. Moving to Adelphi Commons." Looking at Zach she said, "So, hotty, come look me up when you get bored with her."

"Thank you for the invitation, but I'm quite happy with Ariana," Zach said, containing his irritation.

"Well, your loss," Elaine replied, as she moved toward her desk. "I'll be packing for the rest of the night, but don't let me get in your way. Just pretend no one's here."

Rolling his eyes, Zach looked at Ariana and said, "It's getting late. Let's go have dinner."

"Yeah, I think it's time to leave, too. For some reason, it feels crowded in here. Hope you enjoy sorority life, Elaine. Please lock up when you leave. Oh, and leave your key."

When they got to the elevator, Zach started laughing. "Boy, I can see why you had a problem living with her! What a bitch."

"Not my problem now!" Ariana replied happily. "Now I have a whole room to myself. Yeah! And we have another room our group can meet in."

The elevator arrived and as they stepped on, Ariana said, "It's really too early to go to dinner, why don't we go to the coffee house next door and talk about what to do in group tonight."

Zach replied, "I was really enjoying being alone with you, but since your now ex-roommate removed that option, I guess the coffee house will have to do."

The coffee house was a national chain that was always crowded, but it did have an outside patio. After getting their drinks, the couple luckily escaped the noise, finding seats under a huge eucalyptus tree. The tall tree formed a pleasant canopy above them, creating shade from the sun which was now low in the sky. The pleasant smell of coffee and pastries escaped the interior of the store, adding an additional pleasure to an already perfect environment.

Ariana sat with her eyes closed and her head tilted back, a smile covering her face. Zach watched her for several minutes, marveling in the thought that this beautiful, sweet person could be attracted to him.

"What are you thinking about?" Zach asked, hoping he wouldn't break the exquisite mood.

"How happy I am," Ariana said, opening her eyes and looking into his. "Isn't it wonderful here? We could almost convince ourselves that everything is normal."

Zach took her hand and ran his thumb over her wrist, noting how much smaller her hand was than his. Her skin was so soft and unblemished; it seemed to have its own illumination. She was glowing.

"Are you glowing because you're happy, or is that normal?"

"I'm glowing?"

"Yeah. It's pretty amazing. I see a halo of purple light surrounding you."

Ariana suspected something and said, "Okay, I want you to look at that guy over there. Stare at him like you were staring at me. Let your eyes become unfocused if they want to. What do you see?"

"Killer! He's got one, too. Not as bright and it's a different color, but I see it. It's like the energy that was in your room. What am I seeing?"

"That's the energy that I can manipulate. Everything has it. It's called the aura. The colors are supposed to mean something and you can tell if the energy is healthy or not by how it looks: clear and vibrant or smoky and dull."

"Why can I see it so easily now when I've never been able to before?"

"I don't know, but maybe because we are polarities our link helps us to share abilities."

"Way cool," Zach exclaimed. "Will I be able to do what you can, manipulate it?"

"I don't know," Ariana admitted. Changing the subject, she said, "What do you think about our weekly group meeting? How do we handle things tonight?"

"Act exactly like you would if none of this ever happened. Group isn't about psychic stuff. It's about handling our lives and dealing with our issues."

Ariana nodded in agreement and asked, "Is there anyone in the group that you think belongs in Weirdxotic?"

"I haven't thought about it. Ask me after the meeting. I'll see what their auras look like," Zach said proudly.

"You're puffed up like a peacock," Ariana laughed.

With growing confidence, Zach asked, "Hey, do you think I could teach you what I can do?"

"The past life stuff?"

"Yeah, and the psychometry."

"Let's try. How do we begin?" Ariana inquired.

"I know just what to do. Come on." Zach said, grabbing Ariana's hand.

"Where are we going?"

"Right now? To my car, then dinner.

I never knew skipping class could be so much fun, thought Ariana as she and Zach walked together in the Arizona sunshine.

Chapter 11

Ariana enjoyed being with Zach in his car for the long drive to the restaurant they had agreed on, The Oyster House. The restaurant was in a charming bungalow with a courtyard in front containing small tables covered by umbrellas. The building was made of intentionally weathered gray wood, an attempt to mimic a typical Cape Cod cottage. The smell of fish and beer permeated the interior. Ariana assumed they would be eating outside because that seemed to be what Zach preferred. The interior was much darker than the bright sunlight outside and it took Ariana a few moments for her eyes to adjust. She felt an uncomfortable chill, but chalked it up to walking into the air conditioned interior. As she had suspected, the motif of the interior was typical of most fish restaurants. Nets stuffed with all types of sea life were suspended from the walls and rafters. She saw anchors, buoys, and even a harpoon. The place, however, did not feel welcoming. *Something is off*, she noted to herself.

It was obvious Zach had been here before. He asked the hostess to be seated upstairs. They had the entire space to themselves.

"I hope this is okay," Zach said.

"As long as they have something other than oysters," Ariana replied, wrinkling her nose.

The waitress came over and took their drink order as Ariana looked over the menu. She couldn't shake the feeling that someone or something was behind her. She felt a cold chill at her back and really wanted to turn around and look but she was sure she and Zach were the only ones seated upstairs. Finally, she couldn't stand it anymore and turned around.

"Looking for the waitress?" Zach asked, taking Ariana's hand. "Kinda nice eating in candlelight isn't it?"

"No, I'm not looking for the waitress," Ariana said. "I keep feeling like someone is behind me, watching. Downstairs I felt a chill, but I thought it was the air conditioning. Now the chill is more intense and I smell a very strong odor of gardenia perfume. Did you take me to a haunted restaurant?"

Zach's smile was huge as he said, "You did it. You felt the place and you knew what you were feeling. That's great. Did you come to the conclusion that the presence was a female before you smelled the perfume?"

"I think so. I felt uncomfortable, as though someone was boring holes in my back with their eyes. The energy felt like Elaine, my roommate. It was like she hated me for no reason. It was a very female feeling. The perfume was the capper."

"What does the place feel like to you?"

"Not particularly inviting, but not hostile until we got up here. I wasn't thrilled about the place almost from the moment we pulled up. The feeling was one of foreboding or something."

"Are you too uncomfortable to eat?"

"No, but I'd prefer to eat outside if you don't mind. She won't follow us, will she?"

"I don't think so."

When the waitress came with their drinks, Zach apologized and asked if they could move to the outside area to be seated. The waitress did not seem surprised by the request. She turned them over to the hostess to be reseated.

"I don't blame you," the hostess confided to the pair. "Couples aren't usually very comfortable upstairs. Groups are fine, but lovers usually don't stay long. Here, is this table better?"

Curious, Ariana asked the server, "Has anyone ever seen anything weird upstairs."

Glancing behind her before speaking and looking very embarrassed, the waitress whispered, "This may sound cray cray, but once I thought I saw a woman. She was dressed strangely, in a 50's-looking dress, not the usual shorts and shirts most of our clients wear, and one moment she was there, and the next gone. I went downstairs to look for her, but only me and the owner were here because the restaurant hadn't opened for the day yet. I asked him if he'd seen her and he told me not to talk nonsense, but really, I think it freaked him out some. There are rumors that the restaurant is haunted, but before I saw her, I didn't believe in ghosts. Don't say anything to anyone though, please, it will get me in trouble."

"No worries," Zach assured her winking at Ariana.

While they waited for their food, Ariana wondered out loud whether there were a lot of people with abilities who either ignored them or didn't realize they had them yet.

"Well, didn't the Elders tell you that there were others that would come to help us? Sounds to me that they were telling you that we aren't the only ones to be coming into our abilities—we're just the lucky ones."

"Lucky?"

"Ya, we're not alone and we have you to teach us."

They ate slowly, relaxing and talking about anything but metaphysics. Ariana had to admit the food was good, even the oysters that Zach had forced her to try. There was a nice breeze and the temperature was perfect. *Boy, I love Arizona.* It was very easy to forget about the hot summers when fall came.

Ariana found it easy to talk with Zach. She learned that Zach had known Matthew since high school and even though their backgrounds were very different, they had developed a deep bond. Zach said he was used to being overlooked when Matthew was around. Matthew seemed to be a chick magnet. This had never really bothered him until he met Ariana. Zach shared with her that he had known immediately that they were connected. This knowledge, which he admitted was almost an obsession, had caused him to panic. He was sure Ariana would be attracted to Matthew. His fear worsened as the group developed and it became obvious that Ariana and Matthew were the leaders. Revealing his deepest insecurities, Zach confided in Ariana that he was completely confused as to why he had been chosen to be Ariana's polarity.

"I think it's because of your inner sweetness," Ariana explained. "I'm used to cruel men. My father was violent and angry, always taking that anger out on me and the rest of my family. He was a terrible role model for my brother who became cruel as well. He would tease me in malicious ways. When I entered Matthew's energy before my first group meeting, I think I felt this same anger. Matt had it under control, but it was definitely right under his calm exterior. It scared me and it upset him that I had invaded his privacy. It set up a wall between us. I can respect him, but I don't think I would ever be completely comfortable with him."

Relieved, Zach replied, "So, it wasn't my swarthy good looks?" his humor lightening the mood.

"Someday, you'll have to tell me why you use humor to prevent yourself from dealing with anything emotional. But it's quarter after six. I think we'd better get to group. I told our friends to be there early so we could catch up and be prepared for the meeting."

As they left, Ariana, noticed that Zach automatically took her hand. She felt like he was laying claim to her. She liked it, this feeling that she belonged to someone. She felt safe and wanted, as though she belonged. *It feels really, really good.*

When they got to Kiva, all the others were already there waiting outside. Ariana was still holding Zach's hand and fully expected the teasing to come. Instead, everyone else had paired too. *What the heck*, she thought. Leesie was next to Teja, Andrew and Wendy seemed to be a couple. Only Matthew was standing alone.

"Hi everyone," Ariana said. "Is there a reason most of you are paired?"

The others looked around as though they hadn't realized what was happening.

"I think they've found their polarities within the group," Matthew offered. "That leads me to believe someone else needs to be asked to join us as I have yet to establish a connection."

"That's what I think, too," Ariana agreed. "Any idea who?"

"I'm leaving it to Spirit," Matthew answered. "My kindred will find me."

"Okay," said Ariana, no longer surprised by the serious way Matthew spoke. Turning to the other four she asked, "Have any of you noticed anything different since you've come together?"

"I didn't even know we'd come together, until you said something. Good grief, I'm confused again. I'm straight. Why am I paired with a girl?" Teja asked.

"Polarities have nothing to do with sexuality," explained Matthew. "It has to do with finding your complement, the person that adds to your strength and fills in where you are weakest. If you are shy, they will probably be bold. If you are too bold, they will be more cautious. Or if you are hyper, they will be calm. Some of us function from anger; their compliment would be someone that functions from love. And those that function from fear will form a polarity with someone who is brave. Understand?"

They all agreed that they did indeed understand.

"However," Matthew said, a rare smile interrupting his usually serious tone, "sexual energy is a strong force and can make the two people even stronger."

As the group continued to talk, the others began to arrive for the large group meeting. Matthew motioned them to move away from the doorway. Everyone arriving said "hi," but no one joined them.

"Anyone experience a mind link?" Ariana asked, "Have any of you had a mental connection with your partner that you were aware of?"

"Yes," said Andrew, anxious to share an experience that had unnerved him. "Last night I was thinking about calling Wendy to see how she was doing. For some reason, I really felt she needed me to call her. As I was looking up her phone number, she called **me**. She said that she was freaked out about some dreams she was having. We met to talk and discovered we were having the same dreams, but different parts of them. She would see a destroyed landscape, like Zach did, and I had seen fighting and explosions. When we talked about it, it made both of us feel better."

Teja got excited and looked at Leesie, "Yeah, for some reason I decided that I wanted to research the stuff Leesie was working on, like the numerology. I found out that she was wishing for someone to help her and maybe explain some of the things she wasn't sure if she understood or not. We've been getting together and working on it and we've gotten really far."

"Hi everyone. Is this a private conversation, or am I still a Weirdxotic?" said a voice the group instantly recognized as Tara's.

"Hello, Tara. Everyone who wants to be a part of our group is still welcome," Ariana assured her.

Tara nodded and immediately turned to Matthew, "I've been thinking about you all weekend. Has something weird been going on with you?"

Ariana smiled at Zach, both of them thinking that Matthew might have found his polarity.

"Yes," Matthew responded. "I have a lot to tell you. I think we should talk after group."

"Sounds good," Tara said.

Winking at Matthew, Ariana said to the group, "Time to go in. Zach has suggested we keep our comments in our weekly meeting just like any normal therapy group. Let's not discuss anything we Weirdxotics are doing, okay?"

Everyone agreed and proceeded to group. Ariana, Zach, Tara, and Matthew hung back, letting the others go in first. Matthew said, "Zach, hang with me. Ariana and Tara can walk in together. We don't want the session to be about everyone pairing up and the others feeling separate."

"Good idea," agreed Ariana.

Zach leaned in toward Ariana, giving her a quick kiss on the lips. "I'll miss holding your hand," he whispered as he walked away.

Tara turned to Ariana, "Wow, looks like I did miss a lot. So, you two have hooked up?"

Grinning, Ariana admitted, "Looks that way. Ain't it grand!"

It was hard for Ariana to sit through group. She missed not sitting next to Zach. She missed touching him. *He looks so cute sitting there with that stupid, adorable grin.* Every so often Zach would look over at her and wink or wiggle his eyebrows. Ariana had to work very hard not to laugh at the wrong times. She knew she should be listening and offering more, especially because this was only her second group meeting. Her mind just wasn't on listening to people's troubles. *Am I becoming selfish?* She vowed to listen more.

"Ariana, how was your week?" asked the therapist.

It took Ariana a moment to realize the question was directed at her. "Um, it was pretty good. I've been getting to know people and am feeling much more comfortable having friends. And my horrible roommate moved out today."

"How do you feel about living alone for the first time?"

"Right now, it feels great! But she just moved out today. Ask me next week, I guess."

"Hey, maybe I could be your roommate?" offered Wendy. "After all, we do live in the same dorm."

"Right now I think Ariana should experiment with what it feels like to be completely on her own for the first time," suggested the therapist.

Ariana welcomed the therapist's remark, but it was something to think about. She was concerned the dorm administrators could move someone else in, someone she didn't know. It would be nice to have a roommate that was a part of her group. *I will definitely think about it,* she admitted to herself.

"I didn't mean to be pushy," Wendy mumbled, obviously hurt.

"We'll talk later," Ariana said. "It might not be a bad idea. I'd much rather live with someone I already know then let the administrators give me another new person."

Matthew nodded, "I agree. There are lots of reasons like-minded people should share space. Each can grow through the other." He turned to the therapist, "Like what you said last week about AA. Also, it can prepare you for marriage."

Everyone in the group laughed, breaking the tension.

"Well," said the therapist, "looks like we are at the end of another fruitful meeting. Thank you for sharing and participating tonight. See everyone next week."

The group broke up quickly, as though everyone had some place more important to be. Only the eight Weirdxotics remained. Walking out together, they immediately drifted back into their pairs. When they got outside, Ariana waved them over to the side of the building, away from the normal flow of students.

"We have a lot to talk about, but I'm just too tired to think about anything else tonight. I think we should go home and rest up. Let's meet again Sunday at my room. I'm in Manzanita Room 618. I'll order pizza for all of us. How about meeting at around five?" Ariana suggested.

The group was in unanimous agreement. As they said their goodbyes, everyone seemed to drift off two at a time, leaving only Ariana and Zach. "Come on, stumpy, I'll drive you home and put you to bed," offered Zach.

"Yeah, like that's going to happen. There's no way you're putting me to bed. You'll never leave. Just a second," she said, then yelled, "Wendy!"

Wendy and Andrew turned around.

"Come back. Zach will drive you home."

Zach looked at Ariana quizzically, "Chasing me away already?"

"No, but I know if you come up to my room neither of us will want you to leave, so I'll use Wendy as protection. You won't have to walk me to my room because you're worried something might be there, I'll have Wendy with me. I also want to talk to her about her earlier offer to be roommates. It might actually be a good idea."

"I know you're right, but it will be hard to say goodnight. Don't forget we have a date tomorrow night."

"Of course I haven't forgotten, but you've got to promise me that you won't take me to anymore haunted restaurants."

"Haunted restaurants?" inquired Andrew, walking up to them with Wendy.

"An experiment Ariana and I tried earlier. I'll tell you when we're driving home and Ariana can tell Wendy when they get up to their room."

"Their room?" Wendy asked hopefully. "Really, you'd have me as a roommate?"

"If we can arrange it, yes."

"That's just so chill," she exclaimed, hugging Ariana. "You won't be sorry, I promise."

Chapter 12

Matthew was silent and withdrawn as he and Tara began walking. The campus was quiet, most of the students didn't come to this part of campus at night unless something was going on at the Gammage and there was no entertainment scheduled there tonight.

There was a chill in the air which made Matthew happy. He was glad winter was finally coming. Arizona heat depressed him. He was different than most people at ASU; he actually liked snow and cold. He was, however, concerned about Tara.

"Is it too cold for you out here?" he asked her.

"No," Tara said, "I like the cold. That's why I go to Flagstaff and ski and snowboard every winter."

Matthew smiled to himself. *Maybe we are polarities.*

"Then would you mind if we sat here on this bench to talk. I don't really want to go to a brightly lit, crowded restaurant," Matthew explained.

"I wouldn't mind at all," said Tara. "It's beautiful out here tonight and it would be a shame not to enjoy it."

They sat on a wood bench on a little hill with a view of the cars driving by on University Street.

"I have quite a bit to go over with you, so I would prefer if you'd just let me talk till I'm done, then ask questions. Is that okay with you?" Matthew asked Tara.

"Whatever you think is best."

"This has been an eventful week. I'm sure there are things even I don't know yet that have been happening with the others. I guess we'll have to wait until Sunday to get their stories, assuming you don't decide to run away after you hear what's going on." Tara simply smiled and Matthew continued. "I want to tell you about myself. I am half Cherokee and even though it is a half my mother would like me to forget about, I've always been drawn to the Native way. At age ten, I finally got my mother to allow me to get to know my grandfather, my father's father, who is a Cheyenne Medicine person, what white people call Shaman. We became very close because my father had abandoned his family and his heritage whereas I wanted to leave white society and all the pain it produced and join my grandfather. I spend every summer with him in Montana where I am learning many things about living in harmony with Spirit and Elohi, Earth. I am also learning to harness those things within me that can call to Waya, wolf—my spirit animal—and harness his knowledge, power, and body to my will. I have gained certain abilities. Yet I am nowhere near what I can become. It was with some of this knowledge that I realized Ariana had the ability to manipulate and change energy as well as enter into another and feel their inner-self. I also understood that she had no real training and was potentially in danger. I decided I would help her."

Taking a deep breath, Matthew continued, "When we went to the fair Saturday night, we discovered that the rest of the group also had talents that they had kept hidden or tried to rid themselves of. Wendy communicates with animals, Zach and Andrew can pick up information by being in a place or touching objects and people. Teja is a medium. And later we realized that Leesie has an inner knowledge of numbers. Numerology comes naturally to her."

Matthew told Tara all the events from the group's trip to the fair. He was careful not to leave out any details. Tara deserved to know about the negative energy they had encountered and the messages Ariana received from her guides. Handing a stack of papers to Tara, Matthew concluded, "Leesie typed up all Ariana's notes for us. Here's your copy. I'll be quiet and let you read it."

After several minutes, Tara looked at Matthew and said, "This is amazing and frankly, very hard to believe. If I didn't already trust you, I would think you'd flipped. It's new to me too, trusting someone right away. People are usually cruel to me, especially when they find out what I am. But somehow, I just don't feel uncomfortable with you." Tara hesitated then said, "Weird huh?"

Matthew smiled at Tara and said, "Not really, because that's another part of the story that I need to tell you. The world is made up of polarities. Most people think of them as opposites, but that's not quite true. They are complements, two ends of the same string. To me it is more like they enhance and balance each other. It was apparent tonight that the others had found their polarities within the group. I was the only one that hadn't. We decided to wait to see who of the therapy group would come to us while we waited outside and who would just walk into the building without stopping. That was the way we thought we could determine who else belonged in the group. You were the only one to stop. I believe you are my polarity." He looked at Tara, wondering how she would react to his statement

"Why do you think that? Is it because I'm the only other single?" Tara questioned.

"Well, that would be an obvious conclusion," Matthew conceded, "but I think you are what I need." Matthew looked at the floor, his voice grew quiet. "I'm going to share something with you now that I have only shared with very few other people. I have a lot of rage and hatred toward women. That's why I'm in group and in therapy. When I was three, my mother began molesting me. At first it wasn't an obvious molestation, just some fondling and stuff. As I grew older, it became more sexual. She made me sleep with her. Her excuse was that boys needed to be taught how to treat a woman. It devastated me and eventually my helplessness and confusion turned to anger and violence."

"That's horrible! Why didn't you tell anyone?"

"When I was six, I tried telling my father, but he didn't believe me. He was too busy working or escaping into his bourbon to care. Eventually I told Zach, who told his mom and they took me in."

"How old were you?"

"15."

"Oh, God. What happened to you mother?"

"It was hell. I felt really conflicted so I begged Zach and his family not to tell anyone. I just made sure I was never alone with her."

"But what if she does it to someone else?" Tara asked frantically.

"Not possible. I'm an only child and she has no connection with children. I've been watching." Matthew clearly needed to change the conversation. "I want to talk about why I believe you are my polarity. You are feminine in every way, apparently a girl. But you aren't. You've lived as a male, too. I believe you are a hybrid. You are not just a woman or a man, but something much more valuable; a being that can bridge the two. In that way, you can help me heal the two halves of myself so that I can be in balance."

"That's quite a responsibility. What do I get out of the deal?" inquired Tara.

"Total acceptance and being part of a group that will help you grow. It will be an adventure."

"I don't know why I feel that this is something I must at least attempt," Tara said. "My life is complicated enough without adding this, but I just feel in my gut that if I walk away, I would regret it for the rest of my life. So, I'll say yes for now, but reserve the right to back out at any time if it all becomes too much for me. Agreed?"

"I agree. And Tara, thank you for understanding and keeping my past a secret."

Opening her arms, Tara asked, "Do you think it would be okay to give me a hug? I think we could both use one right now."

Tara held Matthew close for several minutes. Matthew had no desire to pull away, nor did she. It just felt right. Tara had never felt this comfortable with anyone except her grandmother. This day had given her so much to think about, but for now, she would just allow herself to feel the rightness of this moment and think about everything else later.

Chapter 13

Ariana's date with Zach had gone wonderfully. He had found a delicious little pizza place in downtown Phoenix with a beautiful outdoor patio. It had grapevines, pretty Venetian glass lights and even though it was very crowded, it still felt intimate and romantic. After dinner, they went to a movie theater not far away and watched a romantic comedy. She teased him about being willing to go to a chick-flick, but was very appreciative of his kindness in letting her pick the film.

What made the evening even more wonderful, though, was the drive to the top of South Mountain. It was a beautiful spot where they could see all of the Phoenix Metro Area spread out to the north, east, and west and the Indian Reservation and towns growing toward Tucson in the south. Once again, Ariana was in awe at how large this city really was and how beautiful. She loved that she was surrounded by a vast desert as well as different types of mountains. It was amazing to her that within just a two-hour drive, there were ski resorts carved out of thick pine forests. Standing on this mountain with Zach, her eyes looking outward, she became overwhelmed with the sheer beauty and wonder of this planet the Elders called Terra. *I will do whatever I can to protect this planet. I promise I will do what it is that I have been put here to do. I will help save this beautiful world.*

Somehow, Zach felt the swelling of emotions within Ariana. He put his arms around her and holding her close, whispered, "We will do this. Don't worry, you're not alone."

They kissed deeply, sealing their pact. Zach stood behind Ariana holding her close and breathing in the dreamsicle smell of her hair, thanking God that he had found her.

⇦⇦⇦

It was Sunday, and Wendy and Ariana were busy tidying up their room to prepare for the rest of the group's arrival. Text books had been shoved aside to make room on a desk for pizzas; two cheese, two pepperoni and two supreme. Ariana's mind was racing. *Gosh, I hope this is enough!* She had also bought a side of breadsticks and wings. *You can never tell with guys.* She took a deep breath, attempting to relax. *Why am I so nervous?*

When Ariana heard familiar voices in the hall outside her door, she ordered herself to calm down. *These are my friends!* She realized that she wasn't used to that yet. She was still waiting to be rejected and ridiculed.

Andrew was the first in the door, probably wanting to see Wendy in the same way she couldn't wait to see Zach. But as soon as he found the food, he pounced on it like a lion attacking a zebra. "Yum," he announced with a mouthful of pepperoni.

"Yuck, close your mouth," Teja complained as she headed to the desk as well to scoop up a piece of pizza and some wings.

Ariana had the perfect amount of food and when everyone was settled, she began. "We have to start working on increasing the abilities we each already have and then explore how to develop new ones. The Elders seem to think I have the information within me, that I can teach you what I already know how to do." Feeling her confidence rise, Ariana continued, "I want to show you how I can manipulate and feel energy. If you are not already sitting with your polarity, please sit across from them with your knees touching. It's fine if you have to sit on the floor."

When everyone was seated across from their other half, Ariana continued. "Put your palms together as though you are praying, then begin to rub them together briskly. Separate them by about an inch and see if you can feel a current going between them. Now separate them by six inches and then move them very slowly together again. Stop when you begin to feel a resistance. It might feel very tingly or as though you are coming up against a kind of spongy force. When you feel it, then you are feeling your own energy, your aura." Ariana looked around the room at her new students. "Anyone have a problem feeling that?"

Each person in the room shook their head no. Ariana smiled and continued. "Good! Let's see if you can feel your partner's energy. One of you put your palms up while the other rubs theirs briskly again. Now, one partner place their palms about ten inches above the palms of the other person. Bring them together very slowly until you begin to feel your partner's energy."

"Wow!" exclaimed Teja, "Leesie's is much stronger than mine. It seems to throb or vibrate or something."

"I don't know why you seem surprised," said Zach. "We all know she's the Energizer Bunny."

Ariana wanted to get the group back on track with the exercise. She continued, "Now, reverse your hands so that each of you has a chance to feel the energy." She waited and when she saw that everyone had taken a turn she asked, "Anyone having any trouble or feel uncomfortable?" Again, every head shook their heads. Pleased, Ariana continued, "Separate your hands again. Okay, those of you that were feeling the energy, I want you to think of a scene in your mind. It can be a pleasant scene or a negative scene, but it should be an intensely emotional one. Try to see the scene in your mind as clearly as you can. Really visualize it, but also feel the feelings. If you can't get a clear picture in your mind, then just feel the feelings associated with the event as intensely as possible." Ariana waited patiently for several seconds then spoke, "Partners, put your hands over the other's hands again. If it's easier for you to touch, then go ahead and lay your hand on top of, instead of over, their hands." As Ariana watched and waited, she saw that Tara had begun to cry.

"Tara, are you okay?" Ariana asked.

Tara, reaching out and taking Matthew into her arms, began to tell him it was all right, she was there now to share his pain. Tara rocked him as she would a child, continuing to reassure him. The others fell silent.

After a few minutes Wendy asked, "What just happened?"

Ariana's voice was barely above a whisper. "It looks like Tara is an empath, a person who can feel the emotions and physical pains of others. It's a good guess that Matthew shared a particularly difficult memory." Wanting to turn attention away from Tara and Matthew out of respect for their privacy, Ariana said, "Tell me what the rest of you felt."

Wendy spoke first, "I tasted chocolate cake then I smelled candle wax. I just knew that it was a birthday party and everyone was having fun." She looked at Andrew, "Was I right?"

"Perfect," he replied, a big smile on his face.

"Wonderful!" Ariana said. "You just displayed other abilities that not everyone has: smell and taste. Good job!"

Looking at Teja, Leesie said, "I felt very comfortable and content. I had the feeling that I was being held and I could almost hear something."

"Right on, girl. I was remembering cuddling with my gram while she read to me," Teja said.

"I am seriously impressed," admitted Ariana. Turning to Tara and Matthew, she asked, "Are you all right now or do you need more time?" When they assured her they were doing fine, Ariana asked, "Do you want to share your experience? Or Matt, will it make you too uncomfortable?"

Matthew thought for a split second and replied, "I know it's important for all of us to be completely transparent with each other if we are going to completely trust each other, but I'm not really ready yet. What Tara picked up was a very difficult memory, but it was not the one I was sending." Perplexed, Matthew turned to Ariana, "Why do you think that happened?"

"I can't know for sure," Ariana offered, "but I would think it was because this memory was much stronger than the one you were sending and it needed to be shared." Ariana out of concern for Matthew asked, "Do you want to continue, or do you need to take a break?"

"I'll continue," Matthew replied, determined to address his pain.

"Time to change places again. Do the same thing; send and receive."

This time everything went smoothly. Each person was able to pick up the essence of their partner's memory.

Ariana was pleased with the group's progress and was ready to continue. "I want each of you to try and **see** energy. Like I've said before, the energy of things can be seen as well as felt. This energy is called the aura. It usually has a color and a vibration or tone. Sometimes there are multiple colors. You can tell the health of a person by the quality of their aura. Dark or muddy auras can show illness or negativity. The more brilliant and pretty the aura, usually the healthier and happier the person. Sometimes the sound or vibration of the aura is chaotic or disharmonic. That can also be a bad sign. Not everyone can hear the energy, though. That ability is rare." Ariana walked over to one of the plain white walls of the room and instructed the group to focus their attention about a foot above her head. "Just stare at that place on the wall." After a couple of minutes, she asked, "Do you see anything?"

"I'm not sure," volunteered Leesie. "It looks like you're surrounded by a white glow, but I don't see any color."

"Often the color is subtle at first," Ariana offered, "but as you continue you'll. . . " Ariana's comment was interrupted by a loud yell.

"Whoopee, I see it!" shouted Leesie. "It's blue and purple and it's way out. Way past a foot. That's probably why I didn't see the colors at first—I was looking too close to your head or something. How mad chill is this?"

"I still don't see any color," grumbled Andrew.

Wendy took his hand and said, "Look just above Ariana's right shoulder. Unfocus your eyes. That's it. Relax. Do you see it?"

"Yeah. I think I do. It's moving sort of, isn't it?"

Matthew agreed, "I see it shimmering, too."

Ariana broke her pose against the wall and spoke, "Sometimes people see things in an aura, like deceased loved ones, objects or holes in the aura. The holes could mean a physical problem, or that a body part is missing. I've never seen anything but color and movement but that doesn't mean someone else might not experience more. Does anyone hear anything?"

"Sort of, I think," Leesie answered again. "I hear a high-pitched hum, like you sometimes hear with electricity in the wires."

"Very good again, Leesie," Ariana responded. "All of you will experience an increase of your abilities to see and hear auras and energies of all kinds the more you practice and work with them. This will be particularly true when working with your polarities." Pleased at how well their session had gone, Ariana said, "Now I'm going to show you one last thing. Keep looking at the wall as I walk away from it."

"The energy's still there. There's still an Ariana imprint!" Leesie exclaimed. "This is so killer!"

Ariana explained, "Energy cannot be destroyed. Energy can only be changed. So when you imprint on any object, a person or a place, it never completely leaves. The energy will fade so as to be almost unnoticeable, but those of us that are sensitive to energy will always pick it up. That's what psychometry is about, feeling the leftover energy." Ariana's knowledge impressed her group members. They nodded their heads in agreement when she said, "Make sure you guys get together regularly and practice these exercises with each other. If you find there are other talents that start to come up, let the rest of us know. If you get frightened, or have any problem, immediately text the rest of us."

The group began to talk about their experiences and all the new things they had felt. Ariana's attention drifted away from the chatter and turned instead to Matthew and Tara. *Their auras combine beautifully, as though they have been together for years*, she thought. She was glad that Matthew had finally found someone he trusted enough to share the immense anger and pain she had felt in him the first time they met.

The group began to disperse. Ariana found herself in her room with just Zach, Matthew, and Tara, Wendy having gone out to be alone with Andrew for a while. "Are you all right Matt?" Zach asked his friend.

"Yeah, I guess."

Ariana was struck with how different it was to see the usually confident and aloof Matthew now so vulnerable. *Whatever darkness he is hiding must be pretty awful*, she thought.

"You know, Matt," Ariana said, "all of us must rid ourselves of the darkness we are still enduring from our childhoods, otherwise the dark energy can gain a foothold."

"Yes, I know you're right," Matthew said, scrubbing his hands over his face as though he was cleaning away dirt. "But it's really hard. I've been working with therapists for years on this pain I feel, but it's still there, seething." Sitting on Ariana's bed hunched over, head in his hands, Matthew looked utterly defeated

"Have you ever tried to scream it away?" Ariana asked to everyone's surprise.

Matthew raised his head and asked, "Scream it away? What's that even mean?"

"Going somewhere quiet and screaming out your pain, your anger, and also what you fear."

"No," Matthew admitted, "that's one I've never even heard of."

"I suspect there's a scared, angry child inside you that didn't get heard," Ariana offered. "This will give him back his voice."

Zach wanted more than anything to be able to help his best friend. "Come on, I've got an idea." Pulling Matthew up by his arm and dragging him toward the door, Zach turned and said, "Both of you, too."

The two couples climbed into Zach's car, no one but the car's driver knowing where they were going. "What's the plan?" Ariana asked.

"That's my usual question," Zach objected. "Guess you **are** my other half."

"No, really. Where are we going?" Matthew asked, his voice like his energy, sounding diminished.

Flashing his beautiful smile, Zach said, "You'll see. Just enjoy the ride."

With no knowledge of where they were going or why, the three passengers did enjoy the nighttime drive. The autumn moon shone brightly on the road's dark asphalt, providing a comforting glow. Ariana relaxed to the soothing hum of the engine. She sat back in her seat, closed her eyes, and let her energy calm. She sent a tendril of loving energy toward the backseat and was amazed to feel how linked the energy of their two passengers was. *It's as though Tara is using her natural sweetness to bring peace to Matthew's darkness.*

Ariana was not surprised when Zach stopped the car at the same place she and Zach had shared alone the night before. *I will always think of this as our special spot.* The two young couples got out of the car, greeted by a soft breeze coming off the mountain.

"Okay, we're on a mountain. Now what?" Matthew asked, his tone skeptical.

Zach looked at his dear friend with complete seriousness, "Now you howl."

"I do what?"

"You howl! Let your wolf scream your pain. Howl! The moon is full. There is no one but us to hear. Let it all out!"

"Do it, babe," Tara encouraged. "See if it helps. Let your mind remember, then respond with the depth of your pain and anger."

Matthew closed his eyes and as the three watched, they felt his energy going darker and darker, as though he was gathering a storm within himself.

Suddenly, the night was shattered by a gut-wrenching howl, a howl that split the quiet into tiny shards. The howl wanted to go on forever but lack of breath brought it to an end. Matthew was now quiet but still the sound continued. Matthew had not been alone. The coyotes of the mountain were joining him in his release. He breathed deeply and howled again and again, until his voice was raw and still he continued. With his voice nearly gone, the three friends took him in their arms and howled his pain for him.

Chapter 14

Ariana announced to the group gathered in her dorm room, "Tonight we will be working with psychometry." It had been a week since the group had gotten together to work on their growth. The individual partners had been working on combining their energies and increasing their connection to each other, but the group had decided not to get together as a whole until Sunday. They needed time to absorb all they had already learned and to catch up on their school work.

"As I'm sure you remember," Ariana continued, "psychometry involves sensing the energy that's left on an object or place by anyone that had contact with it. The longer or more intense the contact, the deeper the imprint will be. It is also possible through psychometry to pick up past lives and information about the lives of those that have imprinted on it. It is often through psychometry that psychics connect with murdered or lost persons and help the police find them. The psychic is given a piece of clothing or another personal item and then tells the detectives what he or she is sensing. I need to warn you. If you do have some empathic abilities, this can be quite painful because you could feel whatever happened to the person. Occasionally this will happen with a place like a concentration camp or a battlefield, for instance." Looking to the two to whom psychometry came naturally, Ariana asked, "Zach or Andrew, do you have anything to add?"

Zach explained his process, "What I do is relax and let whatever enters my mind just play out, like in pictures or feelings, sensations or whatever. If nothing enters, then I begin asking questions like, does this belong to a woman? Do I feel loving energy or hostile energy? Where is this from?"

"I concentrate on the feeling I get in my hand. Is it hot, cold, tingly, feel empty?" added Andrew. "These feelings sometimes bring other things into my mind. I also sometimes feel things in my body or smell or hear things."

"So, you **are** using the object for a focus, allowing all your senses to receive information. I also think that like Tara, you are an empath because as you described your process you kept using the word 'feel', instead of the word 'see.' That's really good," said Ariana.

"Lots of psychics use focuses. I've been doing a ton of reading," Leesie explained. "Even the ancient seers used them. Some used bones, some smoke, and others the entrails of animals. Current seers prefer Tarot cards, crystals, bowls of water, pendulums, or palms of the hand."

"What's a pendulum?" Wendy asked.

Leesie continued, "It's usually a weight connected to a cord or chain that the seer asks questions of, and depending on how it swings, gets answers to the questions. It's like dowsing—what the old-timers used to do to find water except they used a Y-shaped stick. Some pendulums have crystals on the bottom, others use pointer shaped metal. But any necklace will work. Here, I'll show you." Taking off her necklace, a peace symbol on a silver chain, Leesie braced her elbow on the desk to hold her arm steady while holding the necklace between her thumb and index finger, allowing it to dangle just above the top of the desk. She asked, "Are we going to succeed in helping our planet?" The group waited. The necklace just hung there, doing nothing. Suddenly, it began to rotate in a circle.

"You moved it," Andrew said suspiciously.

"No I didn't," Leesie denied. "At least I don't think I did and definitely not on purpose, you duster."

"What's that movement mean?" Ariana wondered.

"I think the book said that moving in a circle means the answer is uncertain," Leesie said.

"Well, that certainly makes sense," Matthew replied.

"Should we keep asking questions or wait and finish what you are teaching us?" Leesie asked. "My arm's getting tired."

"I think we should continue with what we started. We can work with pendulums when we all have one," suggested Ariana. "I've actually come prepared with some things to test our psychometry skills on." Opening a small paper sack, she moved through the room asking everyone to take an object out of the bag without looking at it. Ariana explained that looking at the object would allow your logical brain to take over. You might see a man's ring and assume the owner had been male. From there you might create a story to match that assumption instead of letting your psychic sense tell you what its history actually was. When everyone had received their object, she instructed them to close their eyes and focus their inner sensing on their hand, the one that contained the object. Was the hand tingling? Warm? Cold? What was the feeling from their hand? She advised them not to try to figure out what the object was. That was not relevant and would create the same thinking as looking at it. Ariana concluded, "Now, begin to ask the object questions, especially if you have not gotten any impressions from it. If you are a person that is visual, you might see a scene play out in your mind, like a memory. If you are an empath, you might feel physical things including what the person that imprinted on it looked like. Just allow your inner knowing to take over."

Ariana became quiet. She let her eyes drift to each of her students, watching the others find their ability. Like she did during the meditation last time, she watched their auras. The colors told her who was afraid. She could distinguish those using their left, logical brain from those that automatically went to their center, the still place within their minds that allowed the information to flow. Usually when someone resisted, it was because of fear implanted early in life. Ariana knew some of the fear came from religious training as many religions consider anything psychic or metaphysical to be evil. Other times, fear could be caused by seeing spirits or events that were terrifying to a youngster that might not understand what they were seeing. When this happens, it is usually to older children. Very young ones make no judgment about good or bad. If the older children, kids above age three, for example, tell anyone about what they had seen or felt, the usual response would be negative. Consequently, at an age when children desire love and acceptance, they abandon their abilities and believe they do not exist at all. Reopening them later can become very frightening. It can bring back the old fear that was not dealt with effectively at the time the young child first saw a spirit. Sometimes making the person aware of why they were blocking helps to remove the block. At other times, it is much more difficult. Ariana hoped that none of her group would struggle with doubt. She realized now that doubt creates negativity and anger, feelings which attract dark energies. These emotions would sabotage their efforts to free the planet of this darkness and even help to increase it. *If someone is blocked like that I hope they are paired with a polarity that was not, that way their partner can perhaps decrease the fear and help the blockage be removed. One can only hope,* she thought. She hated watching other's struggles. It made her want to jump in and take it all away somehow, but she also knew that fighting through your own battles made you stronger and more sensitive to others. *What a conundrum!*

"Anyone want to tell the rest of us what they're feeling?" Ariana asked, breaking the silence.

Andrew was anxious to speak, "I'm pretty sure this is a ring. I feel the color blue and a clear stone, like a diamond. I also feel both an old lady and a young girl. There's love here, lots of love and safety and understanding too. This is a keepsake of a very dear love and not worn real regularly. It's become almost a lucky charm or something." He held up a small sapphire and diamond ring. "So, how'd I do?"

"Amazingly," Ariana replied. "That ring was given to me by my oma when I was six. She said that she had filled it with love and it would always remind me of how much I was loved by her. She also suggested that love, real love, the kind that is given without strings or expectation, was the energy of God, and when you have God with you, you are always safe. It became my talisman. I never wear it, but I keep it with me always," Ariana said as Andrew handed the ring back to her.

"No fair," complained Leesie. "We already know that psychometry is one of his abilities."

Zach who had been impressed with Andrew's success said, "Don't compare abilities. That's just a way to create fear of failure, which only increases the chance you'll fail. Andrew just showed us what to work toward and how it's done. You don't have to be an expert at everything, nor do you have to be perfect your first time." Zach's face gave way to a smile, "There are lots of other things that Andrew and I will struggle with, I'm sure. Why don't you go next, Leesie, and just say whatever pops into that huge brain of yours?"

Leesie looked uncomfortable but proceeded. "I see a field and it feels really peaceful, but also very free. My stomach rumbled like I was hungry, but I'm not. Also, I feel love, but a very simplistic type of thinking, too. Oh, I don't know. I'm probably way off."

"What do you have?" asked Ariana.

Leesie turned over her hands and produced a photograph of a horse.

"See, I'm wrong," she said, disappointed.

"No, actually you are right. That's my horse, the only friend I had as a child. Being with her was the only time I felt at peace and free. She and I used to run through the fields. That always made me feel wonderful," Ariana acknowledged. "My horse was always hungry and certainly she thought much more simplistically than we do."

Leesie's face lit up, "You mean I actually did it? Wow, killer!"

"And see, you almost sabotaged yourself, too. You didn't trust what you got and if you didn't trust us as friends, you probably wouldn't have even told us you got anything. You would have let your fear of failure or ridicule stop you from believing in yourself. That's what being in your left brain, logical mind can do," Zach warned.

Happy for Leesie, but still concerned about her need to be precise and analytical, Ariana also cautioned, "One of the worst things you can do when you are working with your inner knowing is to doubt it and try to analyze. That never works. If you doubt, then you won't mention what you're getting and perhaps then you'll convince yourself you're no good at it and stop using it altogether. I'm glad you went with your gut and mentioned your stomach growling. Good going!"

"I've got to admit that I have some real problems with this," declared Teja. "I know I keep getting in my own way, doubting. Then I try to figure it out with my brain, not my inner voice. I really feel frustrated right now. Also, how do you know it's your inner voice and not just me making things up?"

"I was waiting for someone to ask that question," acknowledged Ariana. "When we first talked about all this, you told us that your mother was quite religious and condemning of your grandmother and anything metaphysical. I'm sure that created a conflict within you. Even though you had been seeing spirits for years, you were so deeply into denial you never acknowledge your abilities. You'll need to take more time with yourself now and work through the fears that have blocked you for so long. Additionally, all of us will doubt our inner voices until we get used to trusting them. I know one way I resolved that it wasn't me making things up was seeing how different the thoughts I got from the voices were from my own. Often, they would talk to me about things I wasn't even consciously concerned about. When they would help me with those things, or give me warnings about things that hadn't happened yet, I began to realize it couldn't be me. Also, the way they talk is different from the way I talk," Ariana added.

"But how do I work through the fear?" Teja asked.

"I'm not sure, but I think your polarity will be able to help. I'll try asking the Elders," Ariana offered. "You might also try examining the fears. Look at them from all sides. Are they reasonable and logical? Is it something your mother warned you about that is based on more than just religious superstitions? Let's remember we are all new to most of this. I predict that at some point we'll all run into a roadblock or two. If anyone thinks of any ideas about how we can help each other to work on this, write them down and let the rest of us know. After all, we're a group so that we can help one another, right?"

"I have an idea," Matthew stated. "Many cultures believe that Halloween has a special significance. That it's the time that the veil between the dimensions thins and ghosts walk free. Seems like a good time for Teja to teach the rest of us her abilities. How about it Teja, will you conduct a séance?"

"Wait a minute!" Teja objected. "What makes you think I can do that if I block even doing psychometry? There's no way I'll be rid of my fears by then!"

"Because I believe in you," Matthew answered. "Talk to your grandmother. I think she'll be able to help you. She might even help alleviate some of the fear by explaining what she has learned and help you to separate truth from superstition and fear."

"Halloween is on a Friday this year," Leesie reminded everyone. "What about our therapy group?"

"That doesn't take the whole evening," Matthew pointed out. "We'll just make it a late night. We can handle it."

Ariana looked troubled before she replied to Matthew's suggestion. "I think you've just identified one of **my** blocks," she admitted. "I really don't want to be calling ghosts to my room."

"I'll ask Gran if we can do it at her house, that way she can help us," Teja offered. "That might make me feel safer too. That is, unless any of you object to her being there."

Everyone admitted they would actually be relieved to have someone with them who knew more than they did about talking to ghosts. *It will be comforting to have a grandmother there who has lots of experience talking to the dead*, thought Ariana.

Teja said, "Okay, I'll talk to my Gran and ask her for help. How much should I tell her about us?"

"Tell her as much as you feel comfortable with," was Ariana's reply.

Chapter 15

Even though it was a little chilly, the day was beautiful. Azure blue sky, brilliant green winter grass, and vibrant orange Birds of Paradise plants showing off their exotic, other-worldly blooms dotted the campus landscape. A faint smell of wetness escaped from the sprinklers, adding much needed moisture to the very dry air and sustenance to the varied plant life. It was very early and the campus was still empty. Pumpkins, skeletons, and harvest displays decorated the campus as students welcomed Halloween and brought a little of their own flare to their surroundings. Faint laughter and wonderful aromas were coming from the coffee shop. It was a perfect day to be alive.

Ariana loved the fall in Arizona. With the changing intensity of the sunlight, the cooler, yet mild temperatures, and the excitement of the approaching holiday season, everything felt welcoming and alive. She still marveled over having friends and for the first time thinking about what to get everyone for the holidays she had never celebrated before. Being Jewish meant no Christmas, but this year she was already thinking about what to get each of her new friends; her new family. She hadn't ever felt this much joy for her future. She was bursting with happiness!

Warm winters in Arizona provided the luxury of special grass planted just for the colder months. Walking on the winter grass, Ariana took off her shoes and let her toes caress the softness of the bright green blades. As a young girl, she had rejoiced in the spring season. Watching the new growth come to life was always exciting and energizing for her. In a way, Arizona's fall and winter were like Indiana's spring. The temperature was cool, but not cold. There was more of a chance for rain, and the new young plants were everywhere. Feeling invigorated and very happy, Ariana allowed herself the time to luxuriate and expand the happiness she was feeling as she closed her eyes, reached her arms toward the sky, and filled herself with the healing energy of the planet.

There were some deciduous trees on campus, the change of seasons causing their leaves to fall from branches. Most trees on campus, however, kept their leaves. Well attached to their branches, these leaves rustled confidently in the morning's breeze. Their sound created a harmonious song that combined perfectly with the song Ariana could hear from the planet's energy. She heard the planet's song whenever she turned her focus to the earth. Ariana found herself humming in response and adjusted her energies to harmonize with the planet's energy, sending it the joy and love that she felt. She allowed the blended song to become a focus for her inner being and began to combine her energies with all the living things that surrounded her, too. She could feel her energy swell. The feeling of wellbeing that followed was amazing. Ariana realized something, *This must be why so many Chinese people practice the art of Tai Chi. It balances their energy with that of the planet and all other living things. No wonder many of them live far longer and happier lives and don't use as many over-the-counter prescription drugs as we Americans do.*

The sun, now lower in the sky, was beginning to heat the day. The former stillness of the campus made way for conversations and the normal sounds of campus life. Ariana had no idea how long she had been standing in this deep meditative state, but she did know she had to get to her first class! Grabbing her backpack, she prepared to head to her nine o'clock American Lit class.

"Hi," a male voice said from directly behind her, startling her out of her reverie. Ariana hadn't even felt him there which made her very uncomfortable. She usually felt people before they got this close.

"Hi, back," Ariana replied, wondering what he wanted. The young man was cute in a mysterious kind of way. It wasn't that his face was beautiful or that he had a fabulous body, though he did have the trim build of a runner or biker. He was medium height and very lanky, with light brown hair that kept falling into his eyes obscuring them somewhat. Ariana noticed that there was something very alluring about him, but she couldn't explain what. There didn't seem to be anything unusual about his aura, it was actually sort of a pretty shade of green. She decided he was probably harmless, at least for now.

"I was watching you back there. What were you doing?" the young man asked.

"Meditating," Ariana answered.

"You know you glowed a bright purple," he stated matter-of-factly.

Oh, heck! He can see auras! Better to act dumb, Ariana thought. "I did?" she said, feigning surprise, but realizing there was more here than was easily apparent. *Be cautious,* she warned herself.

"Yeah, and you were completely still for over 45 minutes. I've never seen anyone do that before."

"Ah, well, I've been practicing martial arts and meditation for ten years," she lied. "That's why I can do that."

"Oh, sorry. I didn't mean to intrude. I'm Josh. Josh Rogan. I just haven't ever seen anything like that before," he said shaking his head.

"I'm Ariana Abrams."

"What dorm are you in, pretty Miss Abrams?"

Feeling a little flustered, Ariana wasn't sure she should answer him. Not fully trusting him, and not knowing how much she was ready to share, she decided to let him know she wasn't available.

"I need to tell you, I have a boyfriend that I'm very fond of. I'm really not needing anyone else in my life right now."

"I wasn't asking you for a date, just trying to get to know you. Is he the jealous type?"

Boy, did that embarrass Ariana. She had made an assumption and that was really stupid. "Sorry," she muttered. "No, he isn't jealous. It's just that I would feel uncomfortable getting to know another guy without checking with him first."

"Whatever," he replied, sounding annoyed. Waving goodbye, he walked away. "Maybe I'll see you around, Miss Abrams."

Why did that whole thing make me feel so uncomfortable? Ariana wondered. Was there really something wrong or was it just because relationships were still uncertain territory? *Am I becoming too paranoid about the simplest things?* Vowing to ask Zach and maybe one of the girls, she proceeded to her class.

At the conclusion of class, Ariana headed to the cafeteria for some lunch, then finally, she would continue on to her room to do some studying. However, while walking back to the dorm, she had the uncomfortable feeling that she was being watched and with what had happened that morning with the guy called Josh, this made her very uneasy. She stopped, looked around, but did not see anyone. Ariana took a deep breath, quieted her mind, and opened her shield. She sent out a sliver of energy to look for the source of the discomfort. Suddenly, she became even more disturbed. *There is some dark energy that is paying close attention to me.* Ariana tightened her shields again and walked more rapidly. Despite what she had felt, she chided herself for being freaked, especially because the campus was so crowded. She was by no means alone. Still, Ariana felt a panic begin to arise within her. She remembered what she had told the others, *If anything weird occurs, let's contact each other immediately.* She stopped, pulled out her phone and texted the group to tell them of her dilemma. Immediately her phone dinged with a reply. "Where are you?" it read. The text was from Matthew.

"I'm outside the science building," she texted back.

Matthew responded, "Stay put. I'll be right there."

Now she was really scared. If Matthew was leaving class to rush to her aid, he must think something dangerous is happening. Ariana looked around but saw nothing out of the ordinary. The hairs on the back of her neck, however, began to tingle, a sign that contradicted what her eyes were telling her. There was something here and it was very close and very malevolent.

Within minutes, Ariana saw Matthew heading her way.

"Are you all right?" he asked as he came running up.

"Yes, just feeling really creepy. How and why did you answer so fast," she asked confused.

"I was waiting for something like this to happen to someone," he answered. "Zach and I started having some disturbing feelings in the last week, and rather than freak everyone out, we decided to be ready for anything. We are taking shifts when we aren't in class. It's my three hours now."

"I guess I should be grateful, but I'm a little freaked out that I needed rescuing," Ariana admitted.

"Let's deal with that later," Matthew insisted. "What happened?"

Ariana felt a little stupid now that Matthew was with her. She wondered if she just panicked over nothing. Deciding it would be better to discuss it, she told him what had happened.

"Are you feeling anything now?" Matthew asked her.

"Let me check." Sending out her energy again, Ariana realized that she did still feel something. It was more subtle, but definitely still present. "Yes, it's still there, but it's as though it's hiding."

"Let me walk you back to your room."

Ariana and Matthew were quiet as they walked, both attempting to see if they could sense what was going on. She noticed that even though the sun was still high above them, they were surrounded by deep shadows. Ariana intentionally peered into one; she felt that it had substance. Attempting to mask her concern, she stopped and pretended to tie her Nikes. She hoped Matthew would get the hint that something was wrong. He did. Bending down, Matthew whispered, "What's up?"

"Have you noticed all the shadows?" Ariana said, trying to calm her concern. "The one to our right near the ag building has substance. It's not just a shadow."

Matthew also concentrated on remaining calm. Slowly, he turned his gaze to the shadow. "You're right. What the hell is going on?" Grabbing Ariana's arm, he said, "Let's keep going."

The shadows followed the two friends all the way to Ariana's dorm. Though the shadows were present during the entire walk, the ominous darkness made no attempt to move closer to them. Walking into her dorm room, Ariana was overcome with relief to see there were no shadows that did not belong.

Matthew looked around, smiled, and said, "They worked. Good."

"What worked?"

"When we were cleaning up after the meeting last Sunday, Zach and I cleansed your room and protected it with sea salt in all the corners and the doorways. We also placed crystals around the room. Both represent the White Light and are wonderful protections. It appears they worked. We should probably do this to everyone's room and we should all carry a crystal as well."

"Where did you put the crystals? I haven't even noticed them."

Matthew led her to the windows where Ariana saw each windowsill held a clear quartz crystal.

"They're over the door, too," he stated.

Picking one up, she immediately felt a strong pulse of energy emanating from it. Looking closely, she noticed that the crystal in her hand contained a beautiful rainbow, seemingly coming from a triangle within it.

"Oh, I love the triangle with the rainbow," she exclaimed.

"That's a record keeper. They are rare and only people who are attuned to the energy of crystal can see them or work with them. They are said to hold information for the person who is tuned to their special frequency. Sometimes the triangles will multiply. That usually means that there is information for a whole group. We'll have to watch this crystal. It can tell you many things if you listen."

Ariana was impressed with Matthew's knowledge and was surprised by what he said next. "Obviously, one of your talents is working with crystals, which isn't surprising as they are thought to be pure white light energy. There are those that believe crystals are the seeds that were planted to create the formation of this planet. They believe they are alien in nature. Sort of fits with your history, doesn't it?"

Fascinated by what Matthew had to say and thrilled with his knowledge of the subject, she asked, "Will it mess up the protection of my room if I choose this one as the one I carry on me?" she said, still clutching the beautiful object in her hand.

"Not if we replace it with another one. How long do you have until your next class?"

"About an hour."

"Well then, let's go get you a crystal. The shop's not far and should only take you a few minutes to find the right one. Meanwhile, I want you to leave that one here."

"What about the shadows?" The thought of leaving the room unprotected scared her.

"I don't think anything will happen, especially with us together. It seemed to be observing you, not trying anything. When we got together, it really backed off. Trust me, okay?"

"Any idea how long it might have been watching me?" she wondered.

"Why?" Matthew inquired. "Did something else happen?"

"Sort of," she admitted. "I may just be paranoid, but this morning I was meditating outside and this guy named Josh went out of his way to talk to me."

"That doesn't sound odd to me. After all, you are kind of a hottie."

"No, the weird thing about my interaction with him was that he told me I glowed purple. He could see my aura. He also claimed I was perfectly still for 45 minutes. That means he was watching me for that long. Why would someone do that when usually everyone is rushing to class? He also seemed really eager to know more about me."

"Well, that doesn't seem terribly sinister. I could see myself doing something like that. Let's not worry about this guy Josh unless we need to. Okay?

"Yeah, but with everything else that's been happening, it's gotta make you wonder," she declared. "As a wise Bodhisattva once pointed out—there are no accidents."

Matthew thought about what had been going on the past two weeks, but realized that like everything else, they didn't have enough information to make any conclusions. "I guess we'll just have to wait and see. Meanwhile, let's go get a crystal."

Disturbed about how frequently she was feeling fear and jumping to unreasonably negative thinking, Ariana thought about what the Elders had said about one candle being enough to stamp out darkness. She decided **she** would be the candle. *I will not let The Darkness create the negative energy that it needs to feed and grow. I will not let the Darkness use me as a source for its own growth especially by worrying about things that don't really amount to anything*! Ariana felt an immediate change in her mind and body as a peaceful vibration ran through her from head to toe. She was overwhelmed with feelings of love and strength. Calmness rose up in her mind, pushing out any fear she had felt before. Perhaps it was the crystal, or maybe just the awareness of her personal power, but she felt positive and strong.

"Let's go!" she said, heading toward the door with newfound confidence.

ৡৡৡ

The crystal shop was almost too much for Ariana. Crystal held an abundance of energy. Being in a small space that contained hundreds of crystals was actually painful to her. She strengthened her shields and allowed the one that wanted to be hers to call to her. On the way to the shop, Matthew had educated her some more about crystals. He suggested that she run her hands over any that she was interested in and allow her inner knowing to tell her if it was the right one for the intent she had in mind. If her intent was protection, a different one might draw her than one used to help with focus. However, when they started the process it became clear using her hands to feel the energy wasn't necessary; a particular crystal spoke to her and drew her to it, as though it had been waiting for her. It was a wonderful clear crystal that already hung from a setting and a chain. She could wear it around her neck. The silver setting was shaped into a Goddess symbol. The body was the clear crystal. The head of the symbol held a deep blue, perfectly smooth Lapis Lazuli stone. She loved it and knew it was made just for her.

Ariana held the necklace up for Matthew to see and asked, "What do you think?"

Matthew smiled, "It's a channeling crystal and another record keeper, I think. It's perfect."

"What's a channeling crystal?" she asked.

"A channeling crystal teaches you to use your inner wisdom to connect to the spirit world or to channel your inner light outward," Matthew explained.

Ariana stared at her crystal. "That's a tall order, but I think this crystal is meant for me, and that together, we can accomplish all that," she responded as though it had already imbued her with some deep inner resolve.

Matthew nodded and said, "Yeah, they say that the crystal picks the person, not the other way around."

"Does the blue stone at the top mean anything?"

Matthew looked closely at the stone that represented the head of the goddess, "I think it's a Lapis, which is a very ancient stone prized by Egyptian royalty. It is believed to be the symbol of truth and wisdom and stimulates your desire to learn and understand everything. It can help you learn and brings up your mental blocks so you can deal with them."

"This is one powerful necklace," Ariana stated as she admired the Goddess symbol. "The Goddess represents fertility, right?"

"The Goddess symbol means many things in different cultures, fertility being one. She can represent regeneration. She is also considered the keeper of wisdom. It is believed that she is the spirit of both Earth and the heavens."

Holding the necklace, Ariana began to prowl the store. "There's something else I want to do," Ariana announced as she walked toward a tray of crystal points. Holding her hand over the tray, she thought specifically of each person in the group. As she thought about Leesie, the energy of one of the crystals seemed to brighten, as did six other crystals as she thought the names of each friend. Ariana decided she needed to find a crystal to represent the group. She tried holding her hand over the tray, thinking of the Weirdxotics, but nothing happened. She closed her eyes and let the crystal tell her where it was. She was drawn to a shelf at the back of the room. Sitting among dozens of other crystals was a large blue crystal. It had sharp looking points that grew from its base.

Standing behind her, Matthew said, "It's called a fairy cluster crystal. It's often thought of as representing a family and reaching into other realms, like the realm of the fairies."

Perfect, Ariana thought, announcing "I want this one, too."

"You know, this isn't going to be cheap," Matthew cautioned her.

"I don't care. It's what I need to do."

As they walked back to the campus, Ariana drank in the energy of the crystals she was carrying, each one representing one of her friends and the group. She had already given Matthew his which he immediately placed in the medicine bag he always wore around his neck. Ariana noticed how there were no shadows near them. She believed that because the crystals represented light and knowledge, The Darkness would be scared of them and would stay far away. *They are like millions of little lights penetrating The Darkness. The crystals are doing exactly what I hoped they would do*, she thought. The day looked and felt brilliant and she felt great.

Chapter 16

Leesie had become obsessed. She was reading every metaphysical book she could get her hands on. She'd already mastered numerology. Leesie loved numbers and anything to do with them was so easy for her. Now she was learning all she could about séances. The modern history of them was very interesting. Séances actually became popular in the United States and England in the mid-1930s. However, she had found a much older book written in England in 1760, but was really surprised that she couldn't find much from earlier in history. The book purported to have quotes from famous deceased people. A hundred years later, after Abraham Lincoln's mother and son died, séances were performed frequently in the White House. Lincoln himself claimed to see a ghost there. He had a premonition about his death. To a close friend, he described in great detail a dream he'd had about his death. Up until President Truman left office, world dignitaries who visited the White House often reported seeing the ghost of Lincoln himself. Leesie was surprised by how many famous people in recent history believed in mediums and spirit communication.

Leesie learned that there are several different ways that séances can be done. Some employ specialized tools such as spirit trumpets which are horn-shaped speaking tubes. People claim to have witnessed floating above the gatherings, from which spirit voices can be heard. Others include light-weight spirit tables that also may levitate, rotate, or float. Ouija boards—made popular as a board game—have been used, as well as spirit cabinets that confine the medium so that she cannot manipulate anything. Other mediums darken the room and use a candle to answer questions from the people holding hands around the table.

Excited, she couldn't wait to hear how Teja's Gram would be conducting their séance. She wondered if she should bring her protection crystal. When Ariana gave it to her, she suggested that Leesie wear it all the time. *Will it discourage the spirits from contacting us?* Leesie decided to keep it with her. From the minute she held the crystal, it felt like it belonged to her. As strange as it sounded even to her, Leesie felt that the crystal talked to her. It calmed her and helped her sleep better, an amazing benefit because even sleeping pills hadn't helped much. Leesie had used the crystal to meditate. Some days, just holding it allowed her to enter her calm place. At other times, she would stare into its center and feel as though she was entering a cavern of white light. It allowed her to go much deeper. She had even met some of her own guides. She particularly liked the child who said her name was Sara.

She had become completely fascinated with crystals and had spent almost the entire night researching them. She learned that there are a variety of types, shapes, and colors. She learned that many believe crystals not only have their own healing abilities, but that they can also help open the psychic and energy centers known as chakras.

Staring into her crystal, she allowed it to transport her deeply within her mind. It was amazing how much she learned this way. It was awesome how much knowledge appeared to be contained within it. All she had to do to get answers to many of her questions was to just listen. She realized it wasn't really the crystal that contained the knowledge, but she surmised instead that it was a doorway or an avenue to connect with the Cosmic Mind. Carl Jung, a famous Swiss psychiatrist, spoke of a collective unconscious, a consciousness that all living things share. Leesie preferred to think of this shared consciousness as tapping into the mind of God, the Cosmic Mind, a place where all things are known.

Leesie had made a goal for her current meditation—an intention. She wanted to look into the Cosmic Mind to see if any of the group had been connected in past lives. She was not doing this without the group's knowledge. She had asked everyone's permission the last time they met, because she never wanted to invade anyone's privacy and create the potential for anger or negative karma. Despite her best efforts, nothing had come to her yet. During her meditation she became frustrated, causing her to lose her connection. She found herself coming back to the outer world.

Failing to reach her meditation goal, Leesie found her mind thinking instead about polarities. She immediately thought of Teja. She was very happy they had formed a polarity. Leesie acknowledged to herself that she wasn't ready to get that close to a guy. Even though she was 15, she was smart enough to realize she had the emotional maturity of a 12-year-old. Her parents had sheltered her because she was the baby in the family. They were concerned that it would be hard for her to adapt and fit in with anyone her own age. They had been right. When Leesie came to the University, she was isolated there as well. But now she had a twin soul in Teja. They were the other side of the same coin. Teja was black and you couldn't get much lighter than Leesie whose skin was almost transparent. Teja was an only child, Leesie had four siblings. Leesie was part of a big, close family where education and intellect was God. Teja was raised a strict Baptist by a single mother and a spiritual grandmother. Teja was the first to go to college, a step her mother thought was a waste of time. Everyone in Leesie's family was educated, both parents having earned doctorates. Teja struggled with her studies, while Leesie sailed through school. Leesie was shy, even though she used a barrage of words to hide it. She was emotionally immature. She was sure she could learn a lot about dealing with all types of people from her strong, assured, and fearless new friend. All-in-all, Leesie thought she and Teja complimented each other well. Except for Ariana, she couldn't see herself being as comfortable with anyone else in the group.

Yet Leesie did have a fear she had not shared with anyone; she worried that she was the weak link in the group. Unlike the rest, she didn't have any discernible psychic abilities. Yes, she could do the numerology, keep notes and post them to the group and do research for them. She had had a little luck with psychometry, but really, any of them could do that. Thinking about this, Leesie became determined that she would find her special ability no matter what. That was one of the reasons she was looking so deeply within herself and getting to know her guides. Maybe she could find help through them.

Feeling a vibration in her lap, Leesie realized her crystal had fallen. She picked it up to find that it was vibrating and very warm. *This is new*, she thought. *What does this mean?* Holding the crystal in her hand, she concentrated on that question. Thinking about what she had been doing before the vibration, she realized she had made a commitment to find her power. Had it been telling her she had some kind of power with crystals? Her crystal grew warmer and vibrated harder. *Unbelievable!* She thought, *I've found my ability, but what can I do with it?* Closing her eyes, Leesie concentrated completely on attuning her energy to the crystal's. *Do I have the power to manipulate you?* she asked the crystal, feeling just a little silly talking to a rock. It moved in her hand. *Can I use you for more than answering questions?* It moved again. *Wow! It's working like a pendulum without a string.* Now if only she could think of what questions to ask it. *Will I be able to amplify the energy within us?* It moved even more strongly. *Will I be able to extend the energy to protect the whole group when we're together?* It traveled up her arm. *Okay, what does that mean?* She knew she wouldn't receive an answer; it wasn't a yes or no question. *Was that your no?* she asked, trying to learn to communicate with her crystal. It didn't move. *Is that your no?* It wiggled. *So, movement is yes, lack of movement is no?* It wiggled again. *Traveling up my arm, does that mean an emphatic yes?* The crystal wiggled even more.

Leesie was so fascinated by her new discovery that she forgot to sleep that night. Instead, she talked with her crystal, learning its nature and the extent of their combined power. When the sun rose the following morning, she had typed everyone a synopsis of what she learned. Finally, she felt like an important part of the group.

Chapter 17

Running a brush through her coarse, thick, shoulder-length hair always allowed Tara to relax and think. Her life had taken on so many new dimensions in the past month. It was hard for her to comprehend the complexity of what was happening. Before she had met her new friends, all she focused on was finding her place in a world that so often rejected her. She lived in a society that couldn't imagine her desire to make her body into what her mind perceived herself to be, not fully committing to her feminine or masculine self, but living somewhere in-between. She had never felt like a boy. As young as three years old, she could remember dreaming of growing up to be a mommy, wearing pretty dresses, and having breasts. When her family corrected her and told her she would have strong muscles and grow up to be a daddy, she had cried for days.

Living in a culture that valued males over females, and expected their men to be macho, Tara's desires received nothing but resistance. At age 10, her mother dragged her to their priest. She asked the priest to try and rid her little boy of his desire to be a girl. When that failed, her family tried beating the idea out of her. She realized she could never be the person her family wanted her to be. Instead she would continue to embarrass them. She begged her parents to let her go to Arizona and live with her abuela. They relented. There she let her hair grow long and began to wear a little makeup, eventually dressing more feminine. That got her thrown out of Catholic school.

In high school, Tara found that only a few people understood her. Most of the kids thought she was gay, which really did not describe her. She got bullied and even beaten often. She finally convinced her abuela to let her finish school online. That was absolutely the right decision. She made straight As and completed high school in just three years.

As a gift for receiving a full scholarship to ASU, Tara's grandmother bought her a condominium. Tara loved it and decorated it herself in shades of rose. The condo had very high ceilings and large north-facing windows with sheer drapes that moved with the cool breezes and was filled with the beautiful Arizona sunshine more than 340 days out of the year. She had decorated the walls with original Native and Mexican American art. The floors were terracotta tile. Hand woven Navajo rugs accented the floor in colors of mauve, pale red, and brown. There were always fresh flowers on the large dining table and blooming plants on the balcony. It was feminine and very much her.

Tara's feline roommate, Diablo, was an exotic black Persian cat with large gold eyes. He had an affinity for dryers and made them his home whenever he could. He loved to lie in one right after Tara removed the laundry. It was warm and cozy and just his size. His collar was a brilliant red with rhinestones and a large heart that had his name engraved on it. Just recently Tara had added a beautiful crystal to the collar. Diablo knew that he was beautiful and had a way of strutting with his tail held high. Acting as though he ran the house, anyone who entered had to pass inspection, receiving a large quantity of fine black fur. If you didn't like cats or Diablo didn't like you, you weren't welcome in Tara's home. Along with her grandmother, her cat had been her only friend.

In her mind, Tara could picture Matthew's face. She could feel the pain of the memory she had experienced. Both she and Matthew were damaged. *Is that why I've been designated his polarity?* she thought. She still didn't understand exactly what that meant or what was expected, but she did feel closer to him than she had ever felt with anyone but her abuela and Diablo, much closer than her family. Matthew had a sweetness hidden under all that pain and armor. She could relate to that. *If you're betrayed or hurt enough, I know how easy it is to become very aloof and controlled. There have been times I've felt so bitter and angry.* Tara suddenly realized that her friendship with Matthew was different. She felt she could share anything with him and he'd understand or at least not condemn her. He really seemed to see her for who she was, a woman.

Belonging to this new group of people was both wonderful and frightening. They all seemed to accept her as she appeared; a girl. No one questioned her or treated her differently. Matthew didn't seem at all uncomfortable. When she held him, he didn't pull away. That was a completely new experience for her and it felt wonderful. The group allowed her to be herself, not what her betraying body tried to make her. She was luck. Her body was naturally feminine looking. Tara was not very hairy, that came from the Indian side of the family. Any unwanted hair could be removed by electrolysis. She was seriously considering starting hormones. Then she would never get hairy. But Tara was concerned that the large amount of hormones could cause breast and other types of cancer. Tara tortured herself daily about whether to have the sexual reassignment surgery so that her body would be what she needed it to be, but she was scared. She had no one to discuss these things with. But maybe, eventually, she could really open up to Matthew and get his advice. For now, she would begin to dress more and more feminine so that she would at least look the part even though she wouldn't fully be a woman until she could make her body fit the vision she saw in her mind.

Isn't it funny, she thought, *our group is working to save the world and all I can think about is myself.* The metaphysical practices the group was learning scared her. She was sure the fear began when her mother had taken her to a curanduro, a healer, who claimed that Tara was "cursed," the result of a sin the family had committed. Tara's mother had spent several thousand dollars to have the curanduro burn candles to "remove" the curse. When she did not change the way her mother wanted, her mother could barely look at her. Tara, according to her mother, was a reminder of the sin the family must pay for. She knew her family was glad when she left and went to live with her abuela.

Examining what she knew about herself, she wasn't sure whether she had any other abilities besides empathy and she didn't even know whether that worked with anyone other than Matthew. Regardless, she decided that she would continue to be a part of the group. They accepted her and made her feel welcome. But deep down, she worried about whether she would ever be able to get past the fear that perhaps she really was cursed. *I only want to help the group. The last thing I would ever want to do is bring harm to these people who have accepted me for who I am.*

Tara's thoughts still lingered with gratitude for her new friends as she pulled her crystal out of her pocket. She had kept it with her ever since Ariana had given it to her. She didn't think the crystal held any particular power. She just kept it in her pocket because Ariana asked her to and it was so kind of her to give her this gift. It was pretty. Holding it up to the light from the window caused a rainbow to appear on the wall. The crystal acted like a prism, magnifying the light. While still holding the crystal, she began to stare at the rainbow. She thought she saw it pulsing. There was some kind of movement. Tara realized she couldn't take her eyes away from it. It was as though she was becoming hypnotized. Her eyes became very heavy. She closed them. A scene began to play behind her eyes as though she was watching a movie. There were two people who appeared to be in their late teens, a girl and a boy, standing on a riverbank. She saw a village, a dense forest behind it. The female was obviously Native American even though she was not dressed like one from a Southwestern tribe. She had long, loose black hair and dark red skin. She wore a simple skin shift and no shoes. The male may have been a settler. He had on black pants, a dirty white shirt, and suspenders. He also wore a hat and scuffed black boots. He looked the way Tara imagined a Puritan or Pilgrim might look. They were arguing, the girl was crying. The boy was telling her that life together was impossible. Somehow Tara knew the girl was pregnant and the young man was the father. She watched him walk away. She could feel the pain of the girl's broken dreams. The girl could not go back to her tribe; they would never accept her now. Tara watched as the girl walked into the trees, knowing she was going to her death. She could feel the tears for this stranger streaming from her eyes. *How can I be crying this hard for someone I don't even know? How can I be feeling this overwhelming pain so acutely?*

Tara's eyes flew open. It took her a moment to realize she had returned to her living room and her own couch. She could still smell the cooking fires from the village and hear the sound of the river. She could also still feel all the emotions the girl was feeling. Somehow, she knew that she had just experienced a past life—her past life with Matthew. Looking down at her hand, she found the crystal firmly held there. She now understood what having a focus object could do and it hadn't scared her at all.

Chapter 18

Three days. She had only three days to get ready for the séance! Teja was terrified. She had no idea how she was going to actually make this work. Her Gram had begged off, saying she was not feeling well. Attempting a séance required a level of energy Teja's Gram did not currently have. Gram did give Teja instructions about how to set things up and the basics of what to do. Still, Teja was nervous. She had never even attended a séance, much less run one. Her Gram had tried to assure her that she could do it. She told Teja that she would never encourage her if she wasn't sure that she would be all right. But Teja was still very doubtful and afraid.

Matthew claimed she was a medium, but truth be told, Teja had no idea why he'd come up with that shit. In the past, she had run from anything her Gram had tried to teach her. *Maybe that's the real reason Gram had said she couldn't do it*, Teja thought. *She wants me to find my own abilities, not rely on hers.* She had never really had any experience with psychic stuff except for thinking she'd seen her Dad. She was a little kid then. *What do kids know? Hell, they believe in the Easter Bunny and Santa Claus, too.*

But Teja was no longer a child and she did not want to disappoint the group. *What if I fail miserably? Then the group will think I'm a fraud.* Failure had always been one of Teja's biggest fears. She decided to do two things; she would meet with Ariana and confess her fear and she would research séances until she had read everything that was written about them. She realized that her polarity, Leesie, was a walking computer. She would ask her to learn everything she could from the internet. Then they could work together. *Duh, my fear of failure almost stopped me from using my greatest resources.* Now she had first-hand proof of how negative fear was. It could defeat you before you even tried. Teja e-mailed Leesie with a request for help, and then called Ariana. It felt good to take these steps. She was a woman of action, not a coward.

Ariana answered on the third ring. "Hey there Ariana, can we get together today?"

"Sure," Ariana answered. "What's up?"

"Just having some doubts and need someone to talk to."

"Okay, I don't know what I can do, but sure, let's meet. Where?"

"How about the coffee shop right next to your dorm," Teja suggested, not wanting to inconvenience her.

"That'll work. What time were you thinking?"

"Will in half-an-hour work for you?"

"Perfect," answered Ariana.

Twenty minutes later, Teja was waiting outside the coffee shop for Ariana. She was nervous, not wanting her new friend to think less of her. She really needed to sort through this irrational fear with someone. Ariana seemed like the most knowledgeable and approachable of the group. Teja was sure Ariana was the perfect choice. She spotted Ariana about a block before she arrived and headed to meet her. Admiring how confident Ariana always looked, so in control, so assured, she determined that she wanted to be more like her friend. *I wonder if she really feels like that way or if it is something she learned to do to make her feel less vulnerable to bullies. Whatever she's doing*, Teja thought, *it works. Fake it till you make it.*

"Hey, girl," Teja said to her as she opened her arms for a hug. "Thanks for doing this for me."

Ariana smiled, "You actually did me a favor. I've been studying since I got back from class four hours ago. I needed a break and something to eat. Would you mind terribly if we went around the block to the pizza place?"

"No prob. The bus ride made me realize I'm hungry, too." She realized that she had been so uncomfortable about both the séance and talking with Ariana she had forgotten about eating. *I must **really** be upset*, she thought.

Ariana waited for Teja to begin talking about what was troubling her, but it was not until after they finished eating that she began.

Taking a drink of her soda and thinking how kind it was for Ariana to wait her out without probing, Teja began, "I'm panicked about Friday. My Gram won't be with us, she says she's not feeling well enough to participate. That means I've got to do this myself. I've never even gone to a séance. What happens if I can't do it?" Shoving her plate away, Teja confided in her new friend, "I'm totally freaked!"

Ariana smiled at her friend and said in a comforting voice, "Well, if it doesn't work, it doesn't work. We're all learning here. You're not in this alone."

"But what if something goes wrong? I'm really scared. All the stuff my mom has shoved down my throat about the Bible and sin is coming up and it's gagging me."

Ariana looked calmly at Teja and said, "Do you believe in God?"

"Of course," Teja said.

"Then you know that the Source's energy is the most powerful, right? Do you believe in a loving God, one that sees you as perfect, or a wrathful God that hates and punishes?"

"I want to believe in a loving God."

"Then believe. Look around you. Would God create all this beauty, or create love and kindness, then hurt you for being a part of it? Would he give you abilities and then punish you for using them, especially if those abilities helped others instead of hurt them? That sounds like evil to me, not love," Ariana offered. "If what you are doing is coming from a pure heart, one that only wants to be of service, God would never punish you. Why would you want to believe the opposite and punish yourself?"

"What you're saying makes sense," agreed Teja, "and my mother's religion does not seem to help her feel better or act loving. In fact, it's just the opposite. So, until something happens to prove otherwise, I'm going to listen to you and keep trying to help this planet and focus on all the good that we are trying to do. It's just hard to block the fear, but I'll keep working on it."

"Good! You have to keep trusting in yourself and in the Source's love. If you don't, you are giving your power to The Darkness. You know that negativity feeds on fear and distrust. Having faith that God's power will always protect you will keep you safe. You must believe that." Ariana paused, smiled again and said, "So, are we still having the séance at your Gram's or do we need to find another place or do something else?"

"She's letting us use her place. Gram said she would be going over to Mom's house, and I still want to give it a try, I guess."

"Okay. I'll come over early and you and I will set things up. I'll bring some smudge to clear the energy. I'll also bring crystals. They are a natural protection."

Just being with Ariana had calmed Teja's fear. She felt much better. Ariana looked at Teja with genuine compassion and asked, "Do you think you can get a handle on your fear?"

"I think so," Teja said, though despite Ariana's reassurances, she still felt some concern.

"Remember Teja, it isn't all on you. Also, right down to the absolute last minute, if you don't want to participate in the séance, we won't have one. No big deal. We can always work with our crystals, okay?"

Teja nodded her agreement. She wrote her Gram's address on a napkin and gave it to Ariana. She really did feel better. After giving Ariana a long hug and telling her how much she appreciated her and was glad she was her friend, she walked to the bus stop. She would spend the time on the bus ride home reading about séances and protection. She knew knowledge would help her feel more comfortable.

The history of séances was really interesting. Teja was surprised to find out that a religion evolved out of them. It is called the Spiritualist Church and was founded in the 1840s. She was relieved at what she discovered on Wikipedia, "The Spiritualists may also focus on the tenets of their chosen religion to help them attain a higher existence. These may include standard prayers (Hail Mary, Shema Yisrael, or Salat etc.) focusing on the name of God (Jesus, YHWH, or Allah etc.) or other aspects of a holy nature." *How can that be evil?* she thought. Learning that there were lots of famous people who believed in spiritualism and participated in séances also relieved some of her anxiety. Among the adherents were Abraham Lincoln and his wife Mary Todd Lincoln, the writer Sir Arthur Conan Doyle, abolitionist Horace Greely, and Edvard Munch, the artist who painted The Scream. *Wow! If one of our presidents, especially one so revered as Lincoln could be involved in séances, surely it can't be evil or demonic.*

As Teja looked out the window of the moving bus, she began to relax. She decided that if she had a moment before Friday, she would talk further with Gram. She loved and trusted her. Gram was the one person who was always kind and loving to her and Teja had never seen her do an unkind thing. That was certainly not true of her mother who used her religion to scare and to judge. Understanding why her mother was bitter didn't seem to help much either, because it sure didn't seem very Christ-like to her. *Gosh this world is screwy*, Teja thought. *It's so easy to condemn anyone that doesn't think or look like you. Then you can rationalize that it's all right to hate or hurt them. After all, they think they have God on their side. Look at all the terrible things that have been done by people who thought they had a monopoly on God!*

Sitting on the well-worn bus seat, Teja felt a surge of love run through her body. A wonderful feeling came to rest in her mind. She knew she had uncovered an understanding about the world that would forever be a part of her. *The **real** God was pure love. He would never want evil, pain, or violence perpetrated for any reason. I will never again believe in a hateful God. I will choose to believe in the Source, the God of love and all things good. I will give no power to hatred, pain or fear*. Nearing home, she knew what she had to do.

Chapter 19

The streets were filled with ghosts, ghouls, skeletons, and super heroes and not all of them were children. High pitched squeals and laughter and shouts of trick-or-treat could be heard on every street. Even the shop owners on Mill were passing out candy to anyone in costume. It was Halloween and college students and children were roaming the streets, many looking for mischief.

Ariana's dorm was decorated in black and orange crepe paper. There were cutouts of witches and skeletons, black cats and mummies. Crime scene tape covered many doorways and the outlines of corpses were traced in chalk on floors. There were parties on every floor. Liquor disguised as "witch's brew" flowed freely. Ariana's neighbors hosted a party as well, complete with ice cubes shaped and decorated to look like eyeballs floating in a smoking caldron of purple-colored beer. The room's occupants, Bill and Stephen, had also made a cake decorated to look like a cat litter box, complete with Tootsie Roll poop! It was almost too realistic. Ariana was amazed at how much the students in her dorm got into Halloween. They had even changed the lights in the hallways to orange bulbs. *How did they get all this done and keep up with their studies?* Ariana wished she could stay. She had never been to a Halloween party and it really looked like everyone was having a lot of fun. But she had made a commitment to go to her group meeting and she would not miss it, even though the severed finger sandwiches her neighbors had made did look delicious!

Saying goodbye to Stephen and Bill, and some of the other kids that lived on her floor, Ariana headed outside. She was sure it would be quieter, but boy, was she wrong! Many of the revelers had taken the party to the streets creating their own Zombie Apocalypse. Ariana had to fight a whole group of them off who were determined to 'turn' her. *Their makeup looks amazing! If I were a stranger who didn't know about Halloween, I'd think the end of the world was here!* As Ariana was deep in thought about how much fun people could have on Halloween, Dracula jumped out from a bush near the sidewalk. He was accompanied by the Joker from Batman and a mummy. Despite their hastily made costumes, their sudden appearance gave her quite a scare.

"I vont to bite your neck," said Dracula as he bent Ariana backward and began nibbling on her neck, his plastic fangs refusing to stay in his mouth.

"Yuck!" she said, pushing the cheaply dressed Dracula away. "You're slobbering all over me, you nut!"

Zach looked at the beautiful girl he had come to feel so close to and feigning hurt said, "What? You knew it was me?"

"You're lucky I wasn't carrying my wooden stake. Oh, if you don't own a cross, would a Star of David or a Mezuzah work as well? Or maybe my goddess crystal?"

"Only if it's a Jewish or metaphysical vampire, so you're out of luck, I'm Catholic. Come here wench and give me a kiss."

"I don't think so," Ariana replied, wrinkling her nose in mock disgust. "You're wearing more makeup than me." Turning to the others she asked, "Why are you dressed up to go to group? And then we have the séance."

Andrew, torn strips of bed sheet barely clinging to his white T-shirt, looked at Ariana like she was an alien. "We're trick-or-treating. See?" he said, holding out a pillowcase nearly full of candy.

"People actually gave you fools candy?" Ariana laughed. "Arizona is definitely different from Indiana! We stop trick-or-treating at 12."

"You're never too old to rot your teeth," replied Matthew, his white makeup beginning to run down his handsome face.

"Hey, bro, you look less like the joker and more like some creepy, evil clown," Zach teased. "The makeup around your mouth has melted and it looks like you've been eating children, not candy. You'll have every mommy and daddy out here fearful for their little kiddies."

"Oh great! Now I've got visions of the villagers attacking Frankenstein," Matthew exclaimed, wiping his mouth on his sleeve, only making himself look even crazier.

Remembering what they had planned for tonight, Ariana interrupted, "You know guys, Teja is already afraid about tonight. Your get-ups might make things worse."

"That's why we did it," Zach explained, "to lighten the mood. Halloween was first invented to chase fear away. People lit bonfires and played games. The focus was on fun, not fear."

Walking to Kiva Hall, the four friends ate candy and discussed Halloween, monsters, and fear. Ariana filled them in on her visit with Teja and her subsequent visit to Gram's house to help cleanse it. She told the boys about smudging the house with sage while Teja put sea salt in all the corners of the room they would be using for the séance. On the dining table, they lit a pure white pillar candle that had been placed inside a crystal bowl of water infused with sea salt. The girls also surrounded the room with crystals. Ariana placed her large crystal cluster on the dining table. When the group gathered at the table later that evening, she would suggest that each person put their personal crystal in front of them. As an extra precaution, Teja placed an open Bible on the hutch, a ritual she had read about while doing her research on the bus. The girls agreed that no room could possibly be better protected.

"How did you know about smudge?" asked Matthew.

"The web," replied Ariana. "I've been doing research all week. When I discovered that Native Americans used smudge before their ancient rituals, I decided that we should do the same."

"What is smudge?" Andrew asked.

Ariana answered, "Smudging involves lighting a stick, made up of some kind of dried herbs or dried grasses. I used a bundle of dried sage. You then blow it out. The sage continues to smoke and then you can pass an object through the smoke or fan the smoke around a person or a place. It's supposed to cleanse the space of any negative objects, spirits—well, I guess one might say—evil influences."

"Does Teja feel less afraid now?" asked Zach.

"Yes, I think so. But after seeing you guys tonight, who knows," Ariana teased.

"Well, we're about to find out. There are the others," Matthew said, pointing ahead.

Ariana was surprised to see that the boys weren't the only ones who had dressed up. Leesie was Minnie Mouse, complete with ears and whiskers. Teja was a gypsy. *Very appropriate*, Ariana thought. Wendy was dressed as a Greek goddess. But the most spectacular costume was worn by Tara. She was dressed as a beautiful woman, her hair curled and falling to her shoulders in waves. Her makeup was perfect and her brilliant red, very short dress was striking on her slender body. She looked exactly like the woman she felt like on the inside, the woman she so wanted to completely become.

"Wow!" said the guys, almost simultaneously.

"Look at those legs and f-me heels," Andrew exclaimed, causing Tara to spin around, showing off everything to its greatest effect.

"You like?" Tara asked coyly in a soft, feminine voice.

"I like," Matthew stated truthfully, taking her arm to walk with her into group.

Ariana felt a little uncomfortable being the only one not in costume. She wondered why no one had said anything about dressing up. It made her feel left out. *Get over it*, she thought. *I always seem to find some reason to feel excluded.*

"I feel like you're upset," Zach said to her. "Is something wrong?"

"Oh, I'm just being petty. I feel bad that I'm the only one not dressed in a costume. I'm wondering why no one said anything about dressing up."

"Probably because no one thought to," Zach stated matter-of-factly. "It's just something that people do on Halloween. I'm sure everyone thought you'd just know. Anyway, you **are** dressed up."

"As what?"

"An alien from planet Meria!"

Ariana liked that idea and smiled broadly. None of the other kids in group except her friends would get the joke she shared with Zach. And that, she thought, was all that really mattered to her right now. Hoping that didn't make her selfish and exclusionary, she followed Zach inside.

Ariana and Zach were the last ones into the meeting room. By now Ariana wasn't that surprised to see that even the therapist was dressed up. She was pretending to be Sigmund Freud, German accent and all.

The room was decorated with cobwebs and giant spiders. There were bats hanging from the ceiling and the table was covered with food. The food actually followed the room's motif; there was a spider cake and bat-shaped sandwiches. Finger-shaped ice cubes floated in the bright green punch. Dry-ice hidden in the punch caused it to bubble and smoke. Spooky sounds played on someone's iPod and the lighting was low. "Pretty cool atmosphere," said Zach.

"I guess we're having a party instead of therapy tonight," Ariana observed.

"Very astute observation, Fraulein," the therapist answered in a terrible German accent. "Sometimes fun is the best therapy. And vhat is your costume?"

"I'm an undercover alien. Nan Nu, Nan Nu," Ariana replied, pulling on her ears. Walking away she raised her right hand, separated her fingers and said, "Live long and prosper."

Chapter 20

The group was subdued as they rode in Zach's Mustang to Teja's grandmother's house. Again, it was a tight fit, but they managed. Ariana could tell that they were all taking the upcoming event seriously. This would be the first time they would attempt something as an entire group. It was also something that created a natural fear in most responsible people. Opening contact with another dimension was not something to take lightly. Just because they intended to reach out to deceased loved ones did not mean that they might not open the way for something much less safe. After all, none of them really had any experience. During her research, Ariana had come across stories of kids playing with Ouija boards. Some of them had really disturbing experiences. There were reports of poltergeists having been called through the board, resulting in some very violent hauntings. Ariana really didn't like the idea of children playing with Ouija boards as though they were playing a harmless game. She knew how important protections were. She and Teja had cleansed the house and filled it with white light, but even that didn't guarantee safety. *How can children who think they are playing a game be* safe?

Teja had left all the lights on in the house, trying to make the home look more inviting. As they walked through the front door, Ariana could still smell the sage she had used to smudge the house, and the candle—a large round white pillar—was still burning. The house felt safe and nurturing. It was obvious that Teja's grandmother had decorated this house with love. There were pictures of Teja from birth to the present. Her high school graduation picture was displayed prominently above the fireplace. There were also lots of pictures of a handsome black man that Ariana assumed was Teja's father or grandfather. She didn't want to ask, aware that Teja was sensitive about her dead father.

"Should we sit and talk awhile, or just go ahead and get started?" asked Teja, still uncomfortable with what lay ahead.

"It's already well after nine," Wendy remarked. "I'm not sure I'll be able to stay awake if we wait a lot longer. I'm usually asleep by 11."

"Hey, maybe we should wait till the witching hour," Zach teased.

"No way," insisted Leesie.

Putting her arm around Teja's shoulders, Ariana led her to the dining room. "It will be okay," she said. "If you don't want to run things, maybe Matthew or I can."

"No," Teja said, "I can do this." She called out, "Everyone, come in here and take a seat around the table. I'll sit at one end and Leesie, because you're my polarity, I think you should sit at the other end. Maybe it would be a good idea for all the polarities to sit across from each other."

Everyone found their appropriate seats, and at Ariana's suggestion, placed their crystals in front of them.

"I'm going to turn off all the lights. We will have all the light we need from the candle. I also think we should hold hands and say a prayer," Teja offered.

The candle glowing brightly, the friends put their clasped hands on the table. The flickering of the candle caused eerie moving images on the wall and ceiling. Even Ariana felt slightly creeped out. She took a deep breath and relaxed.

Encouraged by Ariana, Teja said, "Take a deep breath and close your eyes. Breathe deeply and allow yourself to relax. Visualize the room filled with white light, God's White Light of love and protection. Fill the entire house with this wonderful energy. Hold the thought of God's mercy and goodness firmly in your mind. Breathe and relax. Ask your guides and angels to surround our group as an additional circle of protection. Now, bring to mind any loved ones who have passed to the Other Side that you want to talk to. Allow yourself to feel your loving connection to them. When you are ready, you may open your eyes but continue holding hands."

Ariana opened her eyes. She immediately saw a brilliant white glow surrounding the circle of friends. But outside this glow, there was a deep blackness. The blackness was so thick it seemed to have substance and texture. It felt oily and crawled with erratic energy. *Take your mind off the evil*, a voice said in her head. *Stare at the candle and focus on the Light.*

Ariana quickly repeated this instruction to her friends, adding, "See it expanding and creating a secure bubble around all of us."

The light around the candle began to expand and the temperature in the room felt warmer. *Energy,* Ariana thought, *that's why it feels warmer.*

"Oh, my!" Leesie said, her voice catching in her throat. "I think I see something. There's a man behind you Teja. He has his hand on your right shoulder. Can you feel him?"

"I think so," Teja said cautiously. "It feels very cold behind me. What does he look like?"

"He's tall and athletic. He's wearing some kind of uniform, but I can't tell what kind. He's black, but real light-skinned. He feels really loving. I can feel how much he loves you. He wants me to tell you that he is sorry. He's holding a stuffed animal, a rabbit with floppy ears. He says he's taking care of it for you."

"That's Flopsie," Teja explained, tears welling up in her eyes. "I lost him the day my dad died."

Leesie continued, "He wants me to tell you he didn't do what everyone thinks. He would have never done anything to hurt you or your mom."

Tears spilled from Teja's eyes. The group sat silent, each one feeling love and empathy for their friend. When she could compose herself, Teja explained, "My dad was a cop in Chicago. Other cops said that they found my father in his cruiser with a bullet in his head, his gun lying at his side. An inquest said suicide. They said he was a dirty cop. We had to leave Chicago in disgrace. My mother has never forgiven him. That's why she's so bitter. That's why I have been so screwed up. My Gram never believed what the inquest said. She claimed that my father's energy was too honest to ever be dirty and that he loved me too much to leave me. Maybe she was right. Can this be real? Please tell him I'm sorry for hating him and being so angry that he left us."

"It's true," Leesie assured her. "I can see his aura and it's beautiful. There is no way he was guilty of any crime. I think he was set-up. He says he understands why you felt the way you did. You don't need to feel guilty or ask him to forgive you. He wants you to know that he is with you a lot. He loves how well you've turned out and he's so very proud of you. Can anyone else see him?"

"I see something," Wendy said. "It's like a clear, wavy energy next to Teja. Is that what you're seeing, Leesie?"

"I can see him more clearly than that," Leesie explained. "He's not solid, but he's clearly visible to me. I can make out his features and even his expressions. When he talks to me, I hear his voice in my mind."

"I can see him, too," Zach admitted. "At first I thought I was seeing things, but as I tried unfocusing my eyes, he became visible. Now I don't even have to unfocus and I still see him. Maybe everyone should try that."

When the others tried what Zach suggested, each of them could see something. Other spirits standing around the table became visible. Zach's grandmother, Wendy's German shepherd, and Andrew's best friend from high school who had died senior year in a car accident, could be seen clearly.

"I see three old people standing behind you, Ariana," Zach said. "Are those the Elders?"

"I'm not sure, probably. Anyone else see anything behind me?"

"There are four," Teja said. The other one is an older woman. She's shorter and standing to the side. Her hair is white, very thin, and held back with mother-of-pearl combs. She has a sweet, loving smile."

A radiant smile appeared on Ariana's face as tears formed in her eyes, "That's my oma!" Continuing to speak out loud, Ariana said, "Thank you for coming. I've been missing you so much!"

Teja answered for Ariana's beloved grandmother, "She says that she's never left you, nor will she. Ich liebe dich, mein Mäuschen. Du fehlst mir," Teja said in a perfect German accent. *She even sounds like my oma,* Ariana thought.

Ariana had read about this, mediums or channels that left their bodies and allowed the dead to speak through them. Even Teja's aura had changed. It was no longer its usual pale yellow. Now it was a radiant blue.

"Sei vorsichtig, du bist nicht sicher," Teja exclaimed.

"What is she saying?" Wendy said, beginning to panic from Teja's seeming transformation.

"It's my oma talking through Teja." Ariana explained, comforting Wendy. "First she said that she loved me." Taking a breath, Ariana continued, "Then she said be careful. She said I am not safe."

Trying to comprehend all that was happening, Leesie blurted out, "I didn't even know she spoke German!"

"She probably doesn't," Ariana explained, trying to suppress the fear rising in her stomach. "That's not Teja. My oma has taken over her body."

Matthew nodded in agreement and added, "That's what a trance medium does." Looking toward Teja he said, "Oma, do you have anything else to tell us?"

"Vorsicht, das Böse ist im Raum!"

All the color went out of Ariana's face. Was the dark shadow she had felt and seen just beyond their table evil? *We have done so many protections. How could this happen*? The fear she felt in her stomach began to boil.

"Is there anything we can do?" Ariana asked her grandmother.

"Bau deine Schutzmauern auf, befrei Dich von deiner Angst und glaube völlig an Gott und an deine eigene Kraft!"

"She said tighten your shields, rid yourself of fear, and believe completely in God. Believe in your own power," Ariana quickly translated.

The energy in the periphery of the room became even darker and denser. Ariana felt that The Darkness had a life of its own, even a personality. It was pure evil. Discomfort plagued Ariana's body. She raised the volume of her voice to almost a shout, "Everyone, expand your White Light shields! Focus your thoughts on love, joy, and all things good. Don't let yourself feel fear, anger, or any other negative emotion." Feeling the fear in her own body starting to ebb away she continued, "If you have to, think about something wonderful. It can be from your past when you felt loved and secure, or think of something that creates those feelings." Her voice growing even louder, Ariana pleaded, "Oma, release Teja. Tell her what to do. Saturate this room with God and his love."

"She says someone in the room is filled with old anger that they haven't released. This is what The Dark is feeding on," Teja responded. "She also said that we are still afraid. We must feel the White Light and trust completely in its ability to protect us."

Ariana and the others felt the room begin to vibrate. The Light was fighting the Dark. Suddenly Ariana's thoughts of God and love were interrupted by what felt like a hand closing around her shoulder, pulling her backward. *No*! She thought with all her might. *I am stronger than you. You don't scare me and you won't succeed.*

The air in the room began to suffocate her. Breathing was becoming very difficult. There was a horrible stench of rotting meat. Ariana thought she heard voices whispering and people screaming in agony. She retched, choking down her vomit. In her mind the Elders were telling her that everything she sensed was only an illusion. *It certainly feels real to me,* she screamed at them. *Help me!*

Ariana tried to believe the words from the Elders, but now she felt a crawling sensation on her legs. She felt thousands of small insects under her pant leg. Looking at her arm she saw spiders, hundreds of them. Spiders horrified her. There were black widows with long spindly legs, tiny brown recluses, and small light-brown scorpions. The creatures were all over her body. Ariana was afraid to move. She was sure she would be stung over and over by these venomous pests. Knowing that their stings were neurotoxins that would send her nervous system into excruciating pain, Ariana became paralyzed with fright. As her fear turned to full-on panic, she felt teeth cut through the skin on her arm. She screamed, trying to pull away, the thought of spiders temporarily forgotten as the teeth from some unknown source dug in deeper, gnawing on the soft flesh of her upper arm.

The Elders spoke to Ariana's, *Ariana, none of this is real. You are safe. Nothing here can hurt you unless* **you** *let it. The Dark can only harm you when you forget that* **you are The Light**. *Fight the illusion. It will vanish like smoke if you try.* **Be The Light. Fight it!**

There was another voice in Ariana's mind, a more seductive voice, telling her she would fail. Though she did not know the source of the voice, she heard it clearly. *You are weak, Ariana. Fragile, a pathetic creature that no one will ever love. You can never out run The Dark. It will always be waiting here to lure you back to the truth—***you can never win***. You are pitiful. Even your own parents couldn't love or believe in you. Other people abhor you, no friends, no roommates, no family, ever. You are a fool and fools always fail. The power of darkness will only continue to grow as humanity becomes greedier and meaner. You puny few that are working for The Light, as you call it, can never succeed against us. We have been here since the birth of man. We drove you from the garden. Humanity needs us and The Dark will grow with each new convert to fear and apathy. The Light will shrink until this planet cannot* *survive*!

Ariana began to see visions of times past: the black plague of Europe with thousands of corpses lying in the streets, the Spanish inquisition and its brutal torture devices. She saw the blood-soaked battle fields of all the wars humanity had waged against each other. She saw horrors from the present: thousands of dead whales beached on a coastal shore, tropical rain forests full of life being deforested for lumber, people dying or new, strange diseases or being tortured by extremist groups in the name of religion, all the different wars that were still raging on Earth.

You think you have found your strength with these others, the voice of The Darkness taunted. *You think that the eight will become the thousands, but like Jesus, there is a Judas among you, one that holds The Darkness through hate and fear. This will be your betrayer!*

Ariana found herself tumbling deeper into despair. *How can we ever defeat this?* The Darkness began to over shadow her belief. Doubt and confusion clouded her thinking. *How can I ever fight against anything so powerful?* Ariana thought of her planet and all the beauty and kindness that filled her home world. As soon as she began to remember Meria, she could hear the Elders again. Their voices now clear, Ariana heard them say, *Ariana, remember we found our way out of The Dark before. It was entities such as you that saved us. It can happen again, this time for Terra. Find your strength, Ariana. Fight!*

At that instant, Ariana felt strong arms around her and heard Zach's loving voice telling her, "It's all right, Ariana. You are safe. We all love you. You have the power and the strength to fight!"

Though to Ariana it only sounded like a whisper, she was sure she heard Matthew say, "Come back to us. Take back your power and come back to us. You can do it, Ariana."

Feeling someone stroking her hair and someone else holding her hand, she focused on the love she felt. Wrapped in the love of her friends, she began to realize that all The Dark had were lies and illusions. It played on anything that could make you uncomfortable to produce strong negative feelings, like pain, hurt, and self-doubt. There were no spiders or teeth. The Darkness was the great deceiver; it had no real substance. It needed help from others to form its illusions. All the group needed to do to fight The Darkness was to refuse to give it the ammunition supplied by fear, doubt, hatred, and any other negative emotion.

Ariana opened her eyes and smiled. The lights in the room had been turned on and she was surrounded by people who really loved her. This was her family of choice and the only family that made a difference.

"I have a lot to tell you," Ariana said to everyone.

"What happened?" Zach asked. "You really scared us! You were sitting in your chair with your eyes closed, moaning and twitching. You even screamed once. I was so scared. But instead of allowing negative emotions to overwhelm me, I kept remembering our kiss and sending you that memory, too."

Looking at Zach and then around the room at her dear friends, Ariana said, "The Darkness tried to take me and I think it almost succeeded. It created doubt in me. Then I felt physical pain. I felt emotional pain. It found a memory of my childhood fears and used that to paralyze me. It creates illusions of whatever will cause you to forget about The Light. I found myself falling into such deep despair. I didn't think I could find my way back to you. The Elders came and worked to make me aware that it was all an illusion. Zach, when I felt your hug and all the love everyone extended to me, it broke the doubt and allowed me to escape the despair. You guys saved me. **Now I know how to fight it**. The Dark is the great deceiver. It can only be successful in destruction if you believe that it can and you allow it to destroy you by planting doubt and taking away your personal power. It can only hurt you if you choose to be hurt. We have each other to live for. Together we are strong and if we trust in each other and in our individual power we can't be stopped."

Standing from her chair, her voice growing stronger with each word, Ariana said, "We've got a lot of work to do. We've got to continue to build our abilities and our power. We have to work to combine our minds and learn everything we are capable of doing. We have to become a force of love." Reaching for Zach's hand, the others followed suit, creating an unbroken circle between the new family of friends. Smiling, Ariana proclaimed, "First and foremost, however, we have to know that we can do this and that The Dark's only real power is through our own doubt and fear." Ariana felt a surge of love run through her body. Sending the power of that love to her friends she said, "Am I right, ladies? Can I get an amen?"

The Ariana Series

Book 2

Becoming the Light

Chapter 1

"Ariana, you almost died," a frightened Leesie exclaimed. "Even with all the cleansing, clearing, and protecting we did, The Dark still almost got you."

"That's only how it appeared from your end. I was in no real danger," Ariana lied. "As long as I have the Elders of Meria, you guys and God, I'm invulnerable. The only reason it got as far as it did is because we're so new at this and some of us were still afraid. Fear is what The Darkness uses to get in and what it used on me tonight."

The group was quiet, each thinking their own thoughts about what they had just witnessed and wondering what they feared enough to draw The Darkness into this protected room. *I've got to get them talking or I'll lose them,* Ariana thought. "Do I get an amen? Are we all still in this, or did The Dark win?"

"I've got to admit that I'm really shaken up," Teja said. "I felt so vulnerable and frightened when we seemed to be losing you, Ariana. But I'm not giving up. I don't want to spend the rest of my life afraid. This was the first time The Dark tried to defeat us and we beat it. We aren't even as strong as we will be and we beat it. I vote we work harder, that we take this really seriously. This is not a game and now I believe we can win. The Dark is gonna be very sorry it pissed off this sista!"

"I agree," said Matthew, "but I think we need to know what it did to you Ariana and what you did to drive it away."

Ariana responded, "It attacks you through all your senses. It brings up any fears or insecurities you have. There were smells, touches, stinging sensations, voices. I'm afraid of spiders and it made me feel as though my body was covered in them. I felt like I was being stung and suffocated. I felt either human—or maybe it was some kind of animal teeth—biting my upper arm and ripping away my flesh. The pain was terrible. The Elders and guides were in my mind too, constantly reminding me that this was an illusion, that The Dark had no real power, only what I gave it. The Dark was also talking to me. At times it sounded like my father, at other times it sounded like my inner voice. It told me I would fail, that I was weak and unlovable and that I would be betrayed and laughed at again. It showed me scenes from history of violent, horrible events, and told me that this is humanity. I found myself sinking into a pit of despair, doubt, and confusion. At that moment I felt Zach put his arms around me. I felt his love. It allowed me to remember who I am and that I had a choice. I could fight and win or I could give in to an illusion. I could lose all that I have gained or I could believe in us. Those thoughts shattered the illusion and brought me back."

Zach continued to hold Ariana. Quite shaken himself, he confided, "I felt it. I felt your pain and doubt. I became scared that I would lose you. Then I heard in my mind, *Your love will give her the power to drive The Dark illusion away.* Was that the Elders, those old ones from your planet?"

"I think as my polarity you picked up my pain and fear. You know we have a mind link—the ability to feel what is going on with our other half. Polarities bring balance to one another, so balance to fear is bravery. I was feeling unlovable, so you gave me love. That's what a polarity would do, right?" Ariana asked, looking at Matthew for confirmation. He seemed to know more about these subjects than she did.

"I think you're right," Matthew agreed, "but to answer Zach's question, it could have been Ariana's Elders, but it also could have been your shared guardian angels, your guides. Ariana still doesn't remember much about her past life on Meria or those three old people she calls the Elders, but I think they are probably with both of you most of the time. They did say Ariana would continue to learn what she had been taught on her world. Maybe with their help she'll remember how they fought The Darkness and won permanently."

Always the outspoken one in the group, Leesie asked, "Okay everyone, are we in or out? We're all cray-cray already, so I'm ready for anything. I'm in."

"Spoken just like the genius, hyperactive 15 year old that you are," stated Leesie's polarity, Teja. "You're crazy enough to jump into anything. But like I said before, I'm pissed, so I'm in."

The girls shared a high five and turned to the rest of the group.

"Wassup with the rest of you?" Leesie asked again.

"I'm still pretty spooked," Andrew admitted, "but I don't like feeling helpless. And like Teja, I don't want to be scared for the rest of my life. I'm in too."

"Can't let my polarity go it alone," stated Wendy. "YOLO, or maybe more! But no matter what, I'm in."

"You've forgotten the most important thing," Tara said anxiously. "We can't run away. What this event proved to me is that if The Darkness is real, then all the rest must be too. If we don't fight, the planet will be destroyed, remember? We have no choice. We've been chosen because we have the best chance of success. How could we go on knowing what's to come if we don't try to protect our planet? You think this episode was scary? Imagine what it will be like if all the possibilities for the destruction of this world begin. That's really scary."

"Any suggestions as to our next step?" Matthew asked.

"I need to go back to my room and rest," Ariana answered. "I'm burnt."

"Should we still get together for our normal lesson on Sunday?" inquired Wendy.

Ariana responded, "Yes, meet in my room at six and we'll work on strengthening the group bond and the mind links between the polarities. Who wants to bring the food this time?"

Tara smiled, "I'll cook us something special. Can we meet at my condo, though? If I'm cooking, it will be easier for me to serve everyone at my place."

The group agreed to meet in two days at Tara's condominium off Mill Avenue. With that, the séance broke up, each polarity going their own way.

Matthew turned to Teja, "Will you be okay here alone?"

"Wendy's staying here with me until Gram comes home," she answered.

"Do you need us to help clean up?" asked Ariana.

Teja looked at Ariana as though she had lost her mind. "Go, girl. You look really wasted. Go home and let your man make you feel better," she said.

Ariana smiled and taking Zach's hand, headed outside to his Mustang. Zach opened the car door for her and she smiled at him. *I must really look beat if he's opening doors for me,* she thought. Ariana put her head against the window and closed her eyes. She awakened when Zach opened the door.

"OMG! Did I fall asleep?"

"You said you were burnt. Let's get you up to your room." Zach took Ariana's hand and helped her out of the car. "We have a bit of a walk," he said, putting his arm around her waist. "You can just lean on me."

The couple walked three blocks to Ariana's dorm. She did have to lean on him a little. Ariana was surprised at how tired she felt. It was as though someone had pulled a plug and all her energy had drained out. She even tripped a couple of times. Thank God Zach kept her from falling. His arm around her waist made her feel safe. Even though her ability to think was as blurred as her energy, she recognized how good it felt to be walking next to him. Zach felt so solid, so there for her. She trusted him completely. Yet she remembered something she had been told while The Darkness griped her: *Someone in the group will betray you.* If it were Zach, she'd die. *No,* Ariana declared to herself, *nothing will cause me to break my commitment and let doubt win. There is no room for fear. No matter what, we must win!*

The dorm was a riot of activity. Ariana had completely forgotten that it was Halloween. She had been so tired on their walk back to the dorm that she hadn't even noticed the people passing by wearing costumes. *Boy, I need to be more attentive to what's happening around me. It could be dangerous if The Darkness realized how depleted my energy is right now.* Zach and the others had removed their costumes when they got to Teja's grandmother's house for the séance. Given her state of mind, it was easy for Ariana to forget what day it was. She felt as though weeks had gone by. *How could it have been only hours?*

As usual, students on Ariana's floor were friendly. She and Zach were invited to join the 6th floor party. Ariana declined. It made her feel guilty as this was not the first time she had refused an invitation, but she knew that her dorm mates could see how wiped out she was.

Zach took Ariana's keys and opened the door to her room. "Let me go in first and check things out. You wouldn't be of much use if it's in there waiting for you."

Ariana knew Zach was right. She stayed in the hallway leaning against the wall. She seriously considered sitting on the floor, but she was afraid she would fall asleep again.

"Okay, it looks like the crystals and sage have done their jobs," Zach assured Ariana. "Do you want me to carry you in?"

"Thanks, but I think I got this," Ariana replied, her fatigue making her voice sound testier than she meant. "You can head home now."

"No way. I'm not leaving you alone while you're this vulnerable. I'm sleeping here tonight. You've got two beds. I'll use your ex-roommate's."

Ariana started to protest, but rapidly realized she didn't have the energy to argue. Anyway, she liked the idea of Zach staying to protect her.

"You've got to promise to be good," she warned.

Zach gave Ariana one of his signature smirks, arched an eyebrow and said, "I'm always good, but tonight I'll leave you alone. I know you're beat and need to replenish your energy."

Ariana nodded her head and replied, "Because you're going to behave yourself, I'd rather you sleep in my bed with me. I'll feel safer, but we should probably stay dressed. Okay?"

"You got it."

"I'm going to wash up and brush my teeth. I have an extra toothbrush you can use."

"Oh, you're prepared for overnight guests?"

"Absolutely," Ariana teased. "I have dozens each week. No, I like using a new toothbrush every three months, so I buy several at a time. Boring, I know."

They each took a turn in the bathroom then lay down in the single bed. They spooned, Zach behind Ariana, his nose in her hair. He breathed in the smell of dreamsicle shampoo and thought about how much he loved her smile. He tried not to notice the feel of her body against his, but it was difficult. So instead, he began going over the events of the evening. When Teja spoke German, allowing Ariana's deceased grandmother to talk through her, he was totally amazed. He had never been to a séance before or seen a medium at work. It was fascinating. Zach fought not to think of the fear he had felt when The Dark began to take over Ariana. The idea of losing her had caused him to freeze in fear. It was then that he heard the voice in his mind telling him he could counter The Dark with his love. He thought about how wonderful it felt when he held her. He thought about kissing her and all the love he felt for her. It worked. When Zach first put his arms around her, he immediately felt The Dark retreat. That had given him confidence. He poured every ounce of their shared love and connection into her. Now as he lay in her bed, listening to her breathing deeply, his love for her filled him and so did a strong desire to keep her safe forever. Every molecule of his body felt the bond he shared with her. They would not fail because the love they felt for each other could conquer anything. He was sure of it. With that final thought, Zach drifted into his own deep sleep.

Chapter 2

Rain, she heard rain. Ariana was startled from her sleep. *It doesn't rain in Arizona*, she thought. Had she dreamt the past month? She knew she wasn't dreaming when she felt the warm body holding her from behind. Zach had spent the night and nothing bad had happened. He had been a perfect gentleman, loving and protective, but not sexual in any way. And The Darkness had left them alone.

Ariana lifted Zach's arm, rolled over and found herself staring into his beautiful, puppy-dog eyes.

"What are you doing?" she asked.

"I'm watching you sleep," Zach said. "You looked so beautiful and calm and very peaceful. I'm sorry if I woke you."

"You didn't. I thought I heard rain." Ariana listened a moment, looked at Zach and said, "I did hear rain. It's raining in the desert!"

"Yeah," Zach said, as he smiled and kissed her nose. "Even in the desert it sometimes rains. But the problem with rain here is that it puddles. Sometimes there are very deep puddles and then floods. The ground doesn't absorb well if there's a lot of rain at one time. And it's been raining hard for hours."

"How long have you been watching me and why didn't you wake me up? What time is it?"

"It's about 10 and I didn't wake you because you needed the sleep after last night. You were completely drained and fell asleep almost before you got into bed," Zach explained.

"Oh no," Ariana exclaimed. "I'm missing my lit class again. At this rate I'll have to kill myself making up what I've missed."

"Don't worry, we have a very smart little friend that's a sophomore here, remember? Leesie's already taken that class and she'll help you, no problem. I really don't think you need to worry."

"I can't ask Leesie to help me just because I keep skipping my classes. And don't tell me not to worry, grades are important," Ariana protested.

"You can ditch when you are exhausted. Leesie was there last night. She'll understand and want to help you. But, no worries, it's Saturday, we don't have classes. Oh, and by the way, your phone has been buzzing a lot."

Ariana looked puzzled. "OMG! Am I that confused that I don't know what day it is? What's going on with my brain?" she wondered out loud. "Hey, and instead of telling me first thing that it was Saturday, you tortured me! Now I know what a beast you really are. Oh, did you also say my phone's been buzzing? No one calls me. The group always texts and my family doesn't usually call. I wonder what's up."

"Well, you could try to divine it, or you could just pick up your phone and check," Zach said with his usual smirk.

"Always the smartass," Ariana teased as she picked up her phone. "Wow, Leesie called five times starting this morning at 3:19." Ariana felt a wave of panic as she called her friend. "Leesie, it's me, are you okay?"

Zach listened intently, but he couldn't hear anything but hysterical screaming on the other end of the phone.

"Okay, okay, we'll be right there. Hang tight. Zach's with me and it shouldn't take longer than 10 minutes for us to get there. Just breathe. Bye." She turned to Zach. "Leesie's freaking out and needs us to come over right now. I'll tell you what happened on the way. Let's take the stairs, it'll be faster."

Hurrying down the stairs at breakneck speed, Ariana and Zach ran out of the dorm and into the first rainy day Ariana had experienced since coming to Arizona. Shocked, she stopped dead in her tracks. Zach ran into her. "OMG, I completely forgot it was raining. Oh well, let's try to run between the raindrops."

"Is that a real thing?" Zach asked doubtfully.

"Who knows? And who cares? We'll just get a little wet. Leesie really needs us. Move it," Ariana said, tugging on Zach's arm.

"We'll get the car seats all wet," Zach protested.

"Which is more important?" Ariana asked. "Your car seats or a good friend who's very scared?"

"Okay, okay, let's go. Maybe if we run real fast we won't get as wet," Zach said as they began their three block run to his car.

There were very few students on the sidewalk so they raced to the car easily. But Zach and Ariana were drenched and cold when they finally climbed into the Mustang. The drive to Barrett Hall seemed to take forever as the rain made the drivers more cautious on the road. Ariana's anxiety grew. It had been almost 15 minutes since she had talked with Leesie. Finding a parking spot in the rain proved to be impossible so Zach dropped Ariana off in front of the dormitory and went looking for a spot somewhere else.

Ariana arrived at Leesie's door dripping water and shivering. The door opened before she could knock, revealing a disheveled and frantic Leesie. The tiny girl, just over four and a half feet tall, looked more like a hobbit than a sophomore in college. The fact that she was only 15 was probably why she looked so young and vulnerable. Leesie, however, made up for her young age and diminutive size with a giant IQ. She was a genius with an eidetic memory; she forgot nothing. She was also one of the bravest people Ariana knew. If Leesie was this shaken, Ariana was scared too.

"I'm so glad you're here," Leesie said, wrapping her arms around Ariana. "Where's Zach? Ick, you're wet, really wet," she exclaimed, dropping her arms.

"It's raining like hell out there. Zach is trying to find a place to park. What exactly happened?"

"It tried to get me," Leesie squealed.

"Do you mean The Dark tried to get you?"

"Yes, yes! What else?"

"Okay, let's sit down. You need to relax. Breathe. Tell me from the beginning what you mean 'It' tried to get you," ordered Ariana.

"You're not sitting on my furniture dripping wet. Wait here. Don't move," Leesie said, walking toward the bathroom. She came out carrying several plush towels and a bathrobe. "Here, dry off and put this on."

"That will never fit me. You're six sizes smaller than me and at least 20 pounds lighter. I'll wrap a couple towels around myself and sit on the others. How's that?"

Leesie agreed and Ariana sat on the desk chair as Leesie went into her tiny kitchen. "I'll make you some hot tea. Then we'll talk. Maybe by that time Zach will be here and I'll only have to tell it once. Taking care of you is helping me pull myself together, but I still can't stop babbling. When I'm nervous I babble. Actually, I don't shut up most of the time even if I'm not upset. I think it's my ADHD or my manic stuff. Who knows, but it does help me feel better to have something else to think about and something to do. Oh, thanks for coming over so fast. Hey, what took you so long to answer my calls? I started calling late last night and called at least a bazillion times."

"I fell asleep on the ride home last night, and when we got back to my room, I fell into bed with all my clothes on and passed out. I never heard the phone. I slept like the dead until almost 10 this morning. As soon as Zach told me my phone had been buzzing, I checked and then called you."

There was a knock on the door and a completely-soaked Zach entered.

"Eck! My rug!" shrieked Leesie. "You're ruining my authentic Navaho rug. Off!"

Zach jumped off the rug, glaring at Leesie. "You're looking fine now. What was so important that we had to rush over and I had to drown getting here?"

"Sorry," Leesie replied, obviously embarrassed, "but that rug is important to me. I really did need you two and I'm still freaked. Want some tea?"

Zach shook his head in disbelief and answered, "No tea, but do you have any coffee? How about some eggs or cereal? We didn't even take time to brush our teeth much less eat anything."

"Oh, yeah, sorry." Leesie replied, "I've been up since sometime around three this morning. Which do you want—cereal or eggs?"

"Got any oatmeal?" Zach asked hopefully.

While Leesie busied herself making the instant oatmeal, Zach used some of the towels to dry off as well as he could, then seated himself on the floor.

Leesie brought over the bowl of oatmeal and placed it on the floor next to Zach. She handed Ariana her tea and a banana in case she was hungry and sat down on the bed. Breathing deeply, she closed her eyes, opened them and said, "Okay, here's what happened. When I got home after the séance, I was hyped. I sat down at the computer and typed up everything that happened so that I could send everyone a copy. At about two in the morning, I finally felt sleepy and went to bed. I had a dream. At least I think it was a dream, but it seemed so real. I think I was on your planet, Ariana. It looked like Zach described it: desolate, burned, and smoking. The smell was awful. I knew I was smelling burning flesh and hair, even rotting corpses. I could feel the planet's pain and the terror and agony of the people that had lived there. As I watched, the land began to tremble and split into pieces, giant landmasses and cliffs crumbling. The sky was obliterated by smoke and ash. There were volcanic eruptions and the sea was boiling. The shores were covered in the dead, both animals and humans. There was no longer any vegetation. The planet was in ruins. I was in so much pain, both emotionally and physically.

Then I heard the laughing, the evil, vile laughing. A voice began to taunt me. It told me that I was weak and pathetic. It told me to look closely and feel everything thoroughly because soon this would happen to Earth and it would be my fault.

I have no real fears, at least no fear of spiders, heights, falling, dying, things like that, but I do fear failure and causing harm to anyone or anything. The voice kept telling me that I would be the one that harmed the group. That because of me, all of you would die horribly.

Somehow I realized I was dreaming and that I could wake up if I wanted to. But when I woke up, The Dark was smothering me. It was everywhere. The room was full of such negativity. I actually felt it on top of me, spreading the stench of death and filling me with every negative emotion there is. I screamed and screamed and screamed and then I noticed I was loose from its grip on my body and mind. I grabbed my crystal and filled myself full of the love I feel for my family and all of you. I thought of my crazy little dog Harley and how much he loves me and then the horrible energy vanished. I jumped up and began calling you. That's everything, the whole story."

Ariana sat horrified at what Leesie had just recounted to them. She was also very angry, angry at The Darkness, and also at herself. Why hadn't she realized that Leesie needed more protection than the rest of the members of the group? Leesie was the youngest, the least mature and most naïve. She also lived alone which meant she had no one to help her if anything happened.

"I am so sorry," Ariana said. "I want you to know how unbelievably proud I am of you. You fought it off alone! When I was attacked, I had the rest of you to help. But you did it all by yourself. I always thought of you as special, but now I know you are also amazingly brave and resourceful."

Ariana walked over to Leesie and put her arms around her. Holding her close and stroking her hair, she said, "Everything you did was perfect. The Darkness chose you because it underestimated you. It thought your youth and innocence made you the weak link. Boy, was it wrong. You haven't been tarnished. You still absolutely believe in the goodness of all things. You were raised in a loving, nurturing family which taught you to love and trust. Because of all of these things, you are probably the strongest of us all. I am so glad you are my friend."

Zach walked to the girls and held them both. He hated feeling helpless, but there was nothing more to do but hold them. "Leesie, I'm not sure I could have held up as well as you did," he admitted.

Leesie smiled broadly up at her two friends, "I just kept thinking that we were stronger than this. Not me, we. That's why the Universe brought us together, because each of us had been loners forever and wanted badly to belong to something. Our pasts make us stronger because we are driven not to go back to our lonely existences."

Ariana was always amazed by Leesie's intellect, "You're right. I never thought of that. We're stronger because we had to go it alone for so long. We each had to privately fight our own demons and we won because we're all still alive and in college. Any of us could have given up, and instead of moving ahead, just wallowed in depression or given up all together and committed suicide. Each of us is stronger alone than most people, but together, we're a force to reckon with."

"So, what now?" asked Zach. "We need to let the others know what happened and how Leesie triumphed. Should we text everyone or call a meeting?"

Ariana asked Leesie, "How do you want to handle this? After all, it's your story to tell, not ours."

"I want to call a meeting," Leesie declared. "This is too important to try to convey through texting or email."

Chapter 3

It was four in the afternoon and everyone was sitting in Leesie's room waiting to find out why the meeting was called. Ariana noticed that each of them was sitting with their polarity. She wondered if that was always a good idea. This was a group, not a bunch of couples.

"Hey people, before Leesie explains why we're all together again so soon, I'd like to suggest something," Ariana began. "I notice that now we automatically break into our pairs whenever we're together. For some reason, that's bothering me. I'm not clear why. Maybe it's because in some way that can separate us. I'll have to meditate on it later, but for now, can we form a group of eight without the pairs?"

"That seems a little strange because I thought the polarity thing was what we wanted," Andrew said.

"Yes," agreed Ariana, "but it can become exclusionary, too. What happens if I have a disagreement with Wendy? Will you be mad at me, too? If both of you become angry, then will Zach take my side whether I am right or wrong because he's my polarity, causing a rift between the four of us? I can see how we could be pushed apart if The Darkness decides that we are too powerful together. Beyond anything else, we must remain united as a group."

"I agree," said Matthew. "Maybe we should find a mediator, someone outside the eight of us who could act as a referee."

"Then won't that person have to know what we're doing?" asked Teja.

"Probably, but eventually we will need others to join forces with us anyway. We can't do this alone," Matthew reminded the group. "Any suggestions?"

Ariana knew who needed to be their mediator. It was more than a mental knowing, she knew in her gut. "It needs to be the therapist," she announced. "I'm sure of it. She knows all of us individually better than anyone else in the world. She's also trained to mediate and we all already trust her."

There was no debate over Ariana's suggestion. Everyone in the group knew that she was right. They had all shared their deepest secrets with the therapist. She was the catalyst that brought them together.

"Well, now that we have come to an agreement about that," Leesie stated, "I need to explain why I called this facetime." Leesie proceeded to explain the events of the night and morning. "Anyway, my conclusion is that part of our strength lies in always thinking as a group, knowing that we have each other's backs and that our love and trust of each other can defeat The Darkness. If the group shatters into individual splinters for any reason, then I think The Dark will win. Am I right ladies, whoops, and gentlemen?"

Teja was obviously upset. "I'm your polarity. Why didn't I feel any of this and why didn't you call me?"

"I knew that you were safe," answered Leesie. "Somehow, I just knew. I didn't call you because I knew you were still at your Gram's and that the buses stopped running at midnight. There was no way you could get to me."

"Okay, I'll accept that reasoning, but that still doesn't explain why I didn't feel anything." Turning to Ariana, Teja asked, "Shouldn't I have felt her fear or something?"

"What did you do after we left?" Ariana asked.

"I finished cleaning everything up, then I waited for Gram. When she got home we talked about what had happened. She explained some things to me. I'll have to catch everyone up on that later. Then we went to bed. I slept with her because it helped me feel safer."

"There's your answer," Ariana replied. "Your gram has been a medium for many years. She would have been a formidable opponent for The Darkness. Additionally, the two of you together would have been harder to defeat. The Darkness is a coward. It chose instead to attack what it thought was the weakest link; the youngest and most naïve. What a mistake that was! Leesie's a fighter. I also think the Universe's intent was for all of us, including Leesie, to realize her strength and understand that even the smallest of us can at least temporarily defeat The Darkness. The brilliance of a light is not in its size, but in its wattage."

"So, do you think it will attack the rest of us in our dreams, too?" asked Wendy, obviously alarmed. "I'm not sure I can be as smart or as brave as Leesie."

"I don't know, but we all now know how Leesie defeated it. We can all do the same things she did," answered Ariana.

"The Dark uses the same themes: fear, disaster, and creating self-doubt. But it seems to change how it interacts with us," offered Tara. "It uses shadows, séances, and dreams. The crystals have warded off the shadows, now we all have to work on protecting our dreams. But what if it finds a new way to turn one or all of us next time? It wants at least some of us to lose faith in The Source and join the 'Dark Side.' "

"I think you're right, Tara," Matthew agreed. "If the Dark keeps altering its approach, it might succeed. If it keeps doing what it's been doing, it will fail because we are now prepared."

"So what do we do to counter its next move?" wondered Zach.

Andrew was growing worried. "Yeah, I'm feeling a little freaked right now. What should we do?"

"Well, one thing would be to go to sleep while meditating and ask your guides to awaken you if The Darkness tries to enter through your dreams," said Ariana.

"I think the most useful thing to do would be to find someone, a professional, to teach and help us," said Zach.

"A professional what? Ghost buster?" asked Andrew.

"No, a professional psychic medium," said Zach.

"How are we supposed to find that?" Wendy wondered.

Teja suggested, "I'll ask my gram."

They all agreed with Teja's idea. The group decided to forgo their usual Sunday training. Ariana, who was teaching the group metaphysical skills, decided that what the group really needed was to get together for a picnic and relaxation. The entire group agreed, and with that decision made, the meeting was adjourned.

"I can't leave you alone," Teja announced. "Don't even try to argue. It's obvious the school isn't going to give you another roommate, so why not me? I live between my mom's house and my gram's anyway, depending on how negative my mother is being, so this would work our even better 'cause I wouldn't be takin' that damn bus anymore. What do you think? Could ya handle me full time?"

Grabbing Teja around the waist and squeezing as hard as she could, Leesie squealed, "Thank you, thank you! I was afraid to ask you knowing that you are awfully proud. I was worried that you would think I thought you needed charity or help to get through the semester. I know money is tight, but really, you would be helping me not the other way around."

Ariana was relieved. She was confident that Leesie could take care of herself, but having Teja stay with her would probably help both of them feel more secure. It sure helped Ariana feel better.

Feeling that everything was working out well, Ariana and Zach headed to his car, holding hands as usual. The rain had stopped and the sky was filled with stars. A fingernail moon glowed from behind a remaining cloud and the air felt clean and crisp. Ariana was sure the temperature had dropped several degrees since the rain stopped and the sun set. *It finally feels like fall and I'm even a little cold.* She shivered and he put his arm around her shoulders to help keep her warm. Ariana felt a little guilty. She was content and connected to Zach as they walked so close to each other. With all that was going on, and all that she knew might come, it seemed almost sinful to feel this good. She knew that any one of her friends could be under assault at any minute, but for **this** minute, life was good.

<h1 style="text-align:center">Chapter 4</h1>

Matthew was alone. Zach was with Ariana, and Tara had gone to meet her grandmother. He really didn't like being alone. Since moving in with Zach and his mom, Matthew was almost never alone. Being alone meant that Matthew had too much time to brood and remember. He still felt guilty about his relationship with his mother, Marley. Often he was torn between the wrongness of it and how much his mother needed him. She had no one. Marley's parents had died when she was eight. With no living relative, she became a ward of the state and went into the foster care system. That system was very hard for a grieving eight-year-old. Marley was at an age where adoption was unlikely. Living in a foster care home could be difficult. Children in the homes often fought with other foster children for privilege, love, or even survival. Sadly, many foster families were abusive or uncaring. Marley's first foster mother was nice, but it was only a temporary placement. The next family found Marley's grief and anger too hard to deal with. Finally, at age nine, Marley found herself in a home with six other foster children and foster parents who were only fostering for the money. There were four boys ranging in age from three to thirteen, and two other girls, ages five and six. They all shared one large dormitory-like room. Eventually, the thirteen-year-old began to sexually abuse Marley.

The social work agency responsible for Marley was so understaffed and overworked that Marley only saw her social worker every year or so. Her foster family didn't care what went on between the children as long as they weren't bothered. They didn't want to raise a problem that would cause the agency to take a closer look at them. So when Marley told them what her foster brother was doing to her, they called her a liar and told her to be quiet or she might not have a home at all. They warned Marley that if she became a problem child, no foster family would take her and she would be forced to live in an orphanage. This frightened her into silence.

Eventually, Marley grew accustomed to her situation. The sex was the only affection she received and her abuser did protect her. This arrangement continued for three years until he ran away. Again, she grieved. This was the third major loss in her young life. Her abuser had abandoned her too, and she had thought he loved her.

The loneliness was unbearable until a new boy was brought into the home. He was nine, the same age she had been when she came to this home. He had also lost his parents. She brought him to her bed and they soothed each other.

When Marley aged-out of foster care and had to make it on her own at age eighteen, she was frightened and bitter and completely unprepared. She had not been a good student, nor did she have any skills that would land her a good job. Marley's social worker arranged for her to become a server at a local restaurant chain and also helped her to get an apartment with three roommates. The apartment was a dump and the roommates were no different than the other messed up foster kids. But it was all she had and she knew she could cope.

Marley hated her job and her living arrangements, so when Matthew's father asked her to marry him after only one month of dating, she accepted, hoping to finally find love, security, and a home and family of her own.

Until Matthew was born, all Marley found was abuse and alcoholism. Her new baby Matthew was her savior. He would always love her and never leave her. What others called abuse, she saw as a way of showing love and affection. Her life had taught her that.

As soon as she became pregnant, Marley had thrown her husband out of the bedroom. Matthew could not remember having a bed of his own. He always slept in her bed. His father slept in the spare bedroom. Finally, when Matthew was six, his father left them. Matthew became the man of the house in every way. He took care of his grieving mother and became her only source of affection and love. She never stopped telling him how much she needed him and how afraid she was that he would abandon her, too. At age 15 he fulfilled that prophecy when he left her and moved in with Zach and Zach's mom. But on nights like this one, Matthew's guilt was almost impossible to bear.

Matthew knew that dwelling on his pain only increased it, and that he should do something to stop this obsessing. He thought about calling the therapist, but it was Saturday night and he didn't want to bother her. He tried playing video games and watching TV, but nothing held his interest. Matthew felt lost in despair, guilt, and pain. How could he have hurt his mother like that? He began pacing.

At times like this, being alone and having too much time with nothing to do usually created problems for Matthew. When he was lonely all he could think about were the good times they shared. She loved to bake. They would often bake cookies for his entire class. They liked to go to the park together and lie in the sun, telling stories about the little people that lived in the trees. Or they would just sit together watching a movie. Recalling all these memories, Matthew doubled over in pain.

Matthew began to cry. Gut wrenching sobs, sobs of confusion and hatred for himself. That's when he heard the voice. It was seductive and sweet, telling him that it was not too late. He could still make amends to his mother. He just had to realize that it was the world that was corrupt and dirty, not his mother. She had loved him enough to sacrifice her marriage for him. She had loved him more than anything or anyone. Yes, people said what she had done to show this love was sick and abusive, but until he was told that it was bad and wrong, he had felt loved. The voice told him that those people didn't know what love was. They were jealous of the closeness the two shared. Those people were the ones that made everything bad and dirty, the churches filling people's minds with judgments and lies, the police and the courts losing sight of the people involved and focusing only on their vision of right and wrong. What about people as a whole who jump from one relationship to another, looking for what he had all along and hating he and his mother for having found it? The worst of these offenders, the seven people that called him friend, would probably also be the first to condemn him for his thoughts. They didn't know him at all. He thought about each of them: the self-righteous, all-knowing Ariana who always acted as though she was better and smarter than him. His supposed best friend Zach who abandoned him as soon as a hot babe smiled at him. Leesie, the brain that never shut up. Teja the bitch that thought she was the only one that ever suffered a loss. Andrew, who was too dumb to see that he was being led around by the nose by people who thought he was as stupid as a brick. And Andrew's new squeeze, Wendy, who was just a down-and-out pathetic loser. Then there was Tara. What kind of dude would want to be a girl? That had to be major league crazy. He heard the voice laughing as it said, *And these are the losers who intend to save the world?*

Matthew began to feel his anger growing, not at himself anymore, but toward the seven others. His thoughts pounded in his head. *These losers want to be my friends? I'm way too good for these emo freaks. I'm the powerful one. I'm the one with the training. I should be the leader. I'll show them what real power looks like.*

Opening his shield, Matthew sent his inner self in search of Wendy's energy. She was easy to find. She was in her dorm room reading. *How lame is that on a Saturday night? I thought she and Andrew were a thing, and even he doesn't even want to be with her.* She wasn't shielded, either. Her only protection, her crystal, was on the dresser several feet away. Matthew smiled. He knew she was vulnerable. He sent a tendril of his energy into Wendy's mind, searching for her fears. He found several memories of rejection and knew this was a very deep fear—that she would be alone and sad forever. The past month had eased these fears considerably, and the work that the skank Ariana had done on her had helped, but the fear was still there, buried. He began unearthing it. First he planted a thought: *I wonder why Ariana hasn't said anymore about us sharing her room.* Then a doubt: *Maybe she doesn't really like me and is only pretending, laughing behind my back like everyone else. Using me. WTF! Why would she be any different than anyone else?*

Matthew decided to leave Wendy to stew as he went looking for someone else.

Andrew was asleep, snoring like a wild ox. Matthew noticed that he wasn't in Andrew's mind like he had been with Wendy. Instead, he had astral projected to Andrew's room. His spirit had left his physical body and was now standing next to Andrew, watching him sleep. How cool was that! *See how powerful I am,* he thought.

Matthew had read about astral projection and he knew his grandfather, the Cheyenne medicine man, did it often. But this was a first for him. He wasn't sure what he could do exactly, and decided to experiment. Reaching out, Matthew attempted to pick up Andrew's phone. No luck. He tried pushing it with his finger, still with no luck. Finally, he used his energy to move the phone. It moved, almost falling off the desk. *Wow!* Walking to the sleeping form on the bed, he bent over and whispered, "Andrew." Andrew snorted loudly and turned over. *Holy crap, he can hear me!* Again, he bent toward Andrew's ear, "She doesn't love you man, she's using you. Ariana convinced her to act like she liked you so the group would keep your muscle as protection. They're all laughing at how stupid you are."* Andrew snorted again and mumbled something unintelligible. *That's enough for now,* Matthew decided.

Next he searched for Teja and found her talking with Leesie. *That's a trick, I didn't think Leesie ever stopped talking.* He decided that it would be way too hard to do anything with both of them wide awake and together. *Later*, he thought.

Tara was sitting at her dressing table combing out her long, blue-black hair. She was wearing no makeup and was dressed in a silky top and panties. *She really is too feminine and pretty to be a guy.* Matthew continued watching. Tara looked around the room. Matthew had an uncomfortable feeling that Tara had felt or perhaps seen him. But no, she was looking for something. She left the room calling, "Here pretty kitty."

Tara re-entered the bedroom with a large black cat in her arms. Just then, the cat hissed loudly, scratching Tara and jumping from her arms. Hissing and spitting, its hairs on end with its back arched, the cat stood in front of Matthew's spirit. *OMG, it can see me!*

"Diablo, what's wrong?" asked an alarmed Tara. "Come to me. There's nothing there." The cat would not budge. It continued to hiss and screech loudly.

Tara pulled a chain from around her neck and Matthew could see that there was a crystal suspended from it. Tara held it in front of her. She turned toward Matthew, focusing her attention on the area around her spitting cat. "I can see your energy," she claimed, apparently not frightened at all. "I am surrounded by God's White Light of protection, my guides and angels, too, so you cannot penetrate my shields to harm me. If you are not of God, I demand that you leave!"

Matthew was shocked. Not only was Tara not frightened, but he felt her power sending him back to his body. His energy could not remain in the room. Tara's protection was causing his energy to shrink. Matthew knew that if he tried to remain, his energy would never be able to return to his body. He fled.

Matthew re-entered his body violently with a jerk. *My God!* he thought as he reoriented himself to being physical again. *How did Tara do that?* He was amazed not just that Tara handled the situation so well, but that she had the power to repel his energy so completely and easily.

For the power of darkness to overpower light, there must be some strong emotion present: fear, hatred, anger. Tara had none of these emotions. Instead, she had faith and trust in The Light, her crystal and her personal power, Matthew heard a voice in his head explain.

So how do we overcome that?

The voice didn't answer, leaving Matthew feeling confused, powerless, and vulnerable once again.

Chapter 5

Ariana received a text from Tara first thing the next morning. "Received a visit last night and chased it away," was what it read. She showed the text to Wendy who had come by at eight and awakened her.

"I wonder what happened," said Wendy.

"I guess it wasn't that bad or she would have told us. I'm sure she'll tell all of us at the picnic."

"What are you thinking about doing for food for today?" Wendy asked.

"I hadn't thought about it," Ariana admitted. "Any ideas?"

"There's a deli at the Safeway that has lots of things. You want to walk down there and see what we can find?"

"Okay," Ariana answered.

"I want to talk to you anyway. I guess you figured that out because I don't usually stop by so early in the morning and uninvited."

"Yeah, I kinda wondered what was going on," Ariana confessed. "But I figured when you were ready you'd tell me. Give me a sec to get presentable enough to go out and we can talk as we walk. Okay?"

Wendy was quiet until they reached the sidewalk. "I've been wondering about something," she said. "Why haven't you said anything more about me rooming with you?"

"Honestly, with all that's been going on, I hadn't even thought about it. Why?"

Wendy seemed embarrassed but she answered honestly anyway. "I was wondering if you'd decided you really didn't want me as a roommate and if somehow you didn't like me anymore."

Ariana stopped walking and said, "OMG girl, nothing's changed. When do you want to move in? I've got to warn you though, Zach may be around a lot."

Wendy seemed elated. "Wow, that's wonderful! You really still want me to move in? How about today, or am I pushing it? Oh, and it's okay if Zach's around. I'm hoping Andrew will be, too. That is, if you don't mind," she added hastily.

"Today is fine if you think we have the time, but what brought all this up so early this morning?" inquired Ariana. "We could have talked at the picnic."

"Last night I started having one of my paranoid episodes. I haven't had one since the group got together and you did that thing the first time we met. You know, where you balanced my energy. I just kept thinking that maybe you didn't really like me and that you never intended for me to move in."

"Was there anything I did to make you feel insecure?"

"No, actually I had been feeling really upbeat. I was so proud of Leesie. Andrew and I are getting closer, and for the first time in my life, things just seemed to be going really well. I was relaxing in bed reading, and all of a sudden, I was sure that you were lying to me. I couldn't stop obsessing about it. I barely slept last night thinking all kinds of negative thoughts. Finally, around six this morning I decided to meditate. I calmed myself and my mind began to look at things more logically. That's when I decided to talk with you. Usually I would have withdrawn and become angry and depressed, but this time my meditation showed me how this wouldn't help me accomplish what I really wanted, to continue to have friends and a life. I waited until I thought you might be up and came to you."

Ariana took a moment to think before saying, "You know Wendy, you've made an amazing personality shift since I adjusted you. Maybe you just had a slight set-back last night."

"You think I was just having one of my old depressive episodes?"

"It makes sense," Ariana offered. "You haven't had a problem with self-doubt since I adjusted you, but I don't know how long an adjustment lasts."

"Yeah, it was kinda weird. It just came out of the blue and was so intense. The thoughts just wouldn't leave me alone. Wow, how weird. Did I do okay coming to you?"

Ariana gave Wendy a big hug, "Yes sweetie, you did. You didn't brood. Instead you came and talked to me. You didn't cut yourself or withdraw or go back into any of your old negative behaviors. I'm really proud of you," she said smiling broadly. "If you want, I could do some rebalancing before we figure out what to take to the picnic. Okay?"

Standing still and facing Wendy, Ariana allowed her mind to see Wendy clearly, physically and energetically. Sending soothing blue energy to her, Ariana observed Wendy's aura smoothing out and becoming vibrant again.

"Done. Are you feeling better?"

"I feel great," Wendy said enthusiastically.

"So, what do you think we should get for the picnic?" Ariana asked.

"Fried chicken and coleslaw of course," Wendy said.

Ariana agreed and when they arrived at the grocery store they selected an 18-piece mixed bucket and a pound of coleslaw.

"Do you think this is enough? I think Andrew could finish this by himself," Ariana said.

Wendy giggled. "Yeah, you're right, but we're not the only ones bringing food. Do you think maybe we should get some munchies for our room, too?" Wendy asked, happy to think of the room as theirs.

"Yes, that's a great idea," agreed Ariana.

The girls spent the next half hour discussing what was safe to keep in their room. They weren't lucky enough to have a mini kitchen like Leesie, so their food would have to be non-perishable and precooked. That was mostly chips and cookies. This was appropriate fare for Wendy who seemed to have no problems gaining even an ounce of weight, but Ariana had struggled most of her life to keep her weight down. They decided on popcorn, apples, Cutey's mandarin oranges, and a small box of Oreos, a concession to Wendy's sweet tooth.

Walking back to their dorm, Ariana and Wendy discussed the moving process and debated whether to talk to the housing office first. Wendy didn't want to wait for housing to okay the move. Ariana, who usually followed every rule, worried that if they didn't check first, they could get in trouble. But when Ariana realized Wendy wasn't as secure as she had claimed, she agreed that they would immediately go forward with the move.

Wendy was ecstatic. When they arrived at their dormitory she parted ways with Ariana to go to her room and start packing. Ariana headed toward her room contemplating what The Dark's next move might be. *I think I'll begin making a list.* But the list would have to wait. Arriving at her room she discovered Tara outside her door waiting to talk to her.

"Hey," said Ariana, "are you okay? I knew you wanted to talk, but I thought we could do it at the picnic. Must be important if you came all the way over here."

Tara nodded her head, "Yeah, the more I thought about it, the more I figured we should talk alone first. Hope that's not a problem."

"No, no problem. We'll be alone until Wendy starts bringing her stuff over."

"So, you're really going to do it, have Wendy move in with you?" Tara asked. "You are braver than me. She seems to have changed recently. But before you came, she was really hard to be around. Hope she keeps improving, not going back to her old ways."

Ariana thought about what Tara had said. "You know, I'm not worried. I think we've seen the last of the angry, depressed Wendy. She feels she belongs to something important and she also feels loved and accepted by more than animals."

"I can understand that," Tara confessed, "everyone makes me feel very comfortable, too. But I have to tell you what happened last night."

Ariana opened the door to her room and they both sat down to talk.

"Last night as I was getting ready for bed, I felt an odd vibration. I ignored it and went looking for my cat, Diablo, who was enthroned on a chair in the living room. He sleeps with me at night. I was carrying him into my room when he went completely crazy. He scratched me, leaped out of my arms, stood in front of me with his back arched, all his hair standing on end and began hissing and spitting at nothing. The odd feeling grew, whether from my reaction to the cat or from an actual increase in a vibration, I'm really not sure. I pulled my crystal out—I wear it on a chain around my neck—and focused my sight on it. I was holding it in front of me. The crystal seemed to illuminate the room, all except one spot directly in front of me. That was the spot the cat was attacking. That area was different, kind of misty and gray. I just knew something or someone was there. I told it to get out. I called upon the White Light, God and my guides and told it very forcefully and without fear to go. It seemed to shrink in on itself and snuff out. As soon as it disappeared, the cat jumped back into my arms and everything was back to normal."

"Wow!"

"Do you think I was just imagining something, or do you think the Dark came to call?"

"Well, I don't think you were imagining something," declared Ariana, "but if it was The Dark, it sure was acting differently. You didn't feel fear, cold, or darkness?"

"No, just weird and it looked kind of smoky or something."

"It still might have been the Dark, I guess, using a new tack. And when it didn't create fear in you, it became powerless. That would make some sense with what the Elders told me at the séance; it has no power of its own, only what you give it. You didn't feed it your power. Wow! You really are amazing," Ariana proclaimed.

"No, I just have always had a deep faith in the goodness and love of God. No matter what things were done to me in his name, I never thought that God was a party to it. I've always had a deep spirituality. I see that as different from religion," explained Tara. "Spirituality is a search for truth and meaning in the Universe, and the truth that I have come to is that God loves us equally. It's man that screws things up."

Ariana smiled at Tara and said, "You know, I think you have a vast amount of wisdom that I would love to tap. Religion was not something practiced much in my family. I think I only went to Temple a handful of times. But absolute belief in a higher power was always part of me. I know something besides myself sustained me through some of my darker times."

"Hey girls, wassup?" Wendy asked from the doorway. Her arms were laden with boxes and clothes so that without the voice, Ariana and Tara would have had a hard time figuring out who was behind the massive bundle. They each jumped up to help lighten Wendy's load. "Must have been worse than the text made it sound, or you wouldn't be here. Right?" Wendy said to Tara.

"Not exactly horrible," Tara answered, "just perplexing."

Ariana laughed, "Perplexing for Tara because she handled everything amazingly, but it would have been very scary for the rest of us, I'm sure."

"What happened?"

Tara recounted her story to Wendy, this time with Ariana stopping her to clarify some points she was unsure about. When the story ended for the second time, the room became quiet as each girl thought about what had happened.

Wendy was astonished by Tara. She couldn't believe how composed and assured she had been. Wendy was sure if any of that had happened to her, she would have run to Ariana screaming her head off. She thought about how insecure she had been that very morning and how she had to find Ariana immediately. She thought she had gotten past that much insecurity. Wendy had been feeling loved and safe and befriended for the past month. *Odd to have had such a severe panic attack out of the clear blue sky,* she thought. She had been content in her bed reading a novel about a young girl with cancer who finds the love of her life. She found the book really inspiring and the love story reminded her of the closeness she was developing with Andrew. So why had any of that turned to panic and paranoia? Even in her darkest past, there had to be a trigger event. Something Ariana said a moment ago made her start thinking and she turned to Ariana to ask, "You know how you said that The Dark is finding new ways to harass us?"

Ariana shook her head yes.

"Is it possible that The Dark planted thoughts in my head last night without alerting me to its presence?"

"You'll have to explain what happened before I can even try to answer you," Arianna said.

Wendy began, "You know how I showed up here bright and early this morning? Well, it wasn't a random decision. I was up all night stewing and growing angry and sad. Oh, heck, I already told you all that. Let me start at the beginning," she said exasperated. "When I got home yesterday I was in a great mood. I felt as if I was a real part of our group and that you were all my good friends. Because Andrew had to study, we decided to each go our own way. I got into my PJ's, grabbed a really good book I'm reading, and was all snuggled in for the night. Nothing changed, but all of a sudden I started thinking that you, Ariana, were messing with me, that you never intended for me to become your roommate and that you were laughing at me behind my back. I became obsessed with whether you really liked me or not. A voice in my brain kept telling me I wasn't likable and that all of you hated me. I started thinking about cutting again. I even had a razor out when I stopped myself. I meditated and began to think logically instead of emotionally and I decided that I would talk to you first thing in the morning and find out for sure. Until then, I would come to no decisions or retreat into past negative behavior. And that's what I did. Do you think I'm still too cray-cray for the group, or was it The Dark?"

"No, I don't think you're crazy, but I can't answer your question about The Dark either. My instincts say yes, but my logic says there's not enough data. God, I sound like Spock!" said Ariana.

Both Wendy and Tara started laughing.

"It is puzzling," Tara said. "It attacks in so many, varied ways. I suggest that anything unusual be considered The Dark until we know better. Not to get paranoid or anything, but it seems safer that way."

Both Ariana and Wendy agreed and the three girls began a discussion on how to find help from someone with more experience in things like The Darkness and the psychic realm.

Chapter 6

"What an incredible day for a picnic," Teja rejoiced, as she plopped herself in the grass. "The temperature is perfect, warmer than usual, but still wonderful. I like that there is a smattering, might I say, a small scattering of cloud cover, too," she said with a badly faked British accent and a silly smile.

"Why are you so happy today?" asked Zach.

"I'm with my great, bright, beautiful friends. We survived the séance intact. And life is good!"

"If you're feeling that good, you can help Matthew and me unpack the car and set everything up to eat," Zach suggested.

"Me too, me too," Leesie squealed as she ran toward Zach's Mustang.

"You're looking a little worse for wear, Andrew," Tara said.

"You sure would too if you had slept like I did last night," Andrew replied. "You're kind of a smartass today, **little boy**."

Wendy, Ariana, and Tara looked at one another. It was obvious that the three were wondering the same thing: what had Andrew endured last night that had created this monster?

"What happened?" Wendy asked. "I thought your roommate was going home and you had the whole room to yourself. You seemed happy to have the quiet so you could get some studying done."

Andrew looked at Wendy, but not with his usual sensitive and caring expression. "Yeah, he's gone, but I don't know, my sleep was rough. I finally got up around three and just spent some time thinking. I almost didn't come today. Didn't really want to picnic. I'm getting kinda sick of always being with all of you."

"Because you didn't sleep?" asked Ariana.

"Nah, just didn't see a reason to come. I'm not really sure why I got mixed up with you guys. I realized last night that I normally wouldn't have chosen any of you as friends. All we have in common is group and this stupid idea that Matthew and Ariana came up with. It's all bull and I'm sick of playing along with all this weird shit," Andrew responded.

Wendy felt like she'd been punched in the gut. "Didn't you want to see me today?" she asked.

"Why?" Andrew responded.

"What's wrong with you, Andrew? I thought you liked me. I thought you were glad to be friends with everyone else. What's changed?" asked Wendy, barely containing tears. She wiped her face on her sleeve, hoping that no one saw how hurt she was. She really cared for Andrew. She trusted him, felt comfortable with him. But today, she wasn't sure who he was. Had she really ever known him? "What did I do to make you not like me anymore?" she asked.

Andrew looked from Wendy to the other two girls. He could see the concern on their faces. He thought he felt genuine unhappiness from Wendy. *Look at their auras,* he heard a voice say in his head. *That should tell you if they're lying.* Even though he had come to the conclusion last night that this stuff was all garbage, Andrew looked anyway. He looked first at Ariana. Her aura was brilliant purple, no hint of the gray or black he associated with deception. Next he looked at Tara and noticed that hers was a beautiful pastel blue. He knew it would be hard for him to look closely at Wendy without feeling her pain, but he had to. He unfocused his eyes before staring in her direction, hoping to avoid really seeing her. *Maybe then I won't have to look at her face.* He couldn't see her aura at all—he had drawn it so closely around herself that it was barely perceptible. *Why would she do that unless she was really feeling hurt?* Andrew began to feel very bad. Sadness and loss overwhelmed him. Standing there in the bright sunlight of this beautiful autumn day, even he couldn't make sense of his behavior. His distrust and anger were so different from his normal easy-going personality. *What's going on with me? I have a sweet, cute girl that doesn't act like she thinks I'm stupid and actually seems to be attracted to me for me and I am getting ready to throw her away? I've never been more comfortable with anyone in my life. What the hell am I doing?*

"Andrew," said Ariana, putting her hand on his arm, "has something happened? This is so not like you. You're sweet and you have a really good thing going with Wendy. Please don't blow it. We all care about you and want only what makes you happy. Think! Did this anger just come from nowhere? Did someone do something that caused it? Or could The Darkness be messing with you, too?"

Wendy looked at Andrew with hope in her eyes. She said, "The Dark screwed with Tara and me last night. It convinced me that Ariana was a liar and was laughing at me behind my back. We're not even sure what it was trying to do to Tara. Could it have put unreasonable anger in you?"

"Use your logic, Andrew. Have any of us done anything that should have you all riled up?" asked Ariana.

Zach and Matthew walked over to the girls. "What's going on?" Matthew asked.

"We're trying to talk to Andrew," Ariana said. "For some reason, he's in a bad mood. Can you guys give us a few minutes, please?"

"Sure," Zach replied, taking Matt's arm and heading back to Teja, Leesie, and the food.

Having taken a moment to decompress, Andrew scrubbed his face with his hands. Again he looked at the girls. The only thing that seemed to have changed was the deep concern on all their faces. He let the guilt come up from deep within him. He didn't want to hurt his relationships with his friends. *Ariana's right,* he thought. *I don't act like this.* "Could The Dark really have manipulated my feelings like that?" he asked.

"It looks like it to me," Ariana responded.

"Last night I became another person, too. If I hadn't had a chance to talk to Ariana this morning, I don't know what state I would've been in by this afternoon," Wendy assured him.

"Because we've become so good at repelling it, I think The Dark is using new tactics, like implanting disturbing thoughts that fester and grow in our subconscious. If it hadn't been for my cat Diablo, I wouldn't even have known it was there and then I bet it could have played sick games with my head, too," Tara proclaimed.

Andrew looked tired and sheepish. He didn't know how to apologize for being so incredibly nasty.

"There's nothing to feel ashamed about," said Ariana feeling his guilt. "It could have been any of us."

Looking at Wendy, Andrew asked, "Can you forgive me? I know I hurt you really bad. I could see it. I am so sorry."

Even though Wendy still felt the pain of his rejection, she wanted a relationship with Andrew. "I'll forgive you this time, but it gives me a get-out-of-jail free card that I get to use next time I'm PMSing. Okay?" she asked, tentatively.

Andrew moved toward Wendy and held out his arms. He held her for several minutes, thinking, *This is where she belongs. How could I have ever doubted her? How could I have hurt her?*

Turning around while fanning her face, Tara announced to the remaining members of the group, "Feed me or I'll faint."

"Come and get it then, you hosers. It's been ready for hours," Leesie exaggerated.

While the group gathered their food and sat down around the picnic table, Zach grabbed Ariana's arm and pulled her backward. "What was that all about with Andrew?"

"It's complicated. I guess The Darkness was busy screwing with Wendy, Andrew, and Tara last night. It activated Wendy's and Andrew's insecurity, making both of them doubt the group's loyalty. Tara's cat alerted her that there was something in her room and she forced it away before it could do anything to her. I've been putting out fires all day. Anything new with you?"

"Not really. But Matthew has been more quiet and moody all day. It probably didn't help when you didn't answer his question about what was going on with Andrew and instead told us to leave all of you alone."

"I wasn't trying to be rude. You guys just came over at a bad time. Do you think The Dark got to him, too?"

"How can I answer that until I know what happened?" Zach asked Ariana, sounding very frustrated. "Were you planning to discuss what happened with everyone?"

Annoyed, Ariana said, "Of course. Why wouldn't I warn the others of what The Dark is trying now?"

"Whoa! Just asking. Maybe while we're discussing it, Matthew will open up. That is, if anything did happen to him."

"Are you guys going to eat or not?" Leesie yelled.

Ariana and Zach joined the group and after everyone had eaten their fill of the assorted picnic food, Tara, Wendy, and Andrew told the others about what had happened the night before. Ariana asked Leesie, Teja, and Matthew how their nights were.

"I can't remember," admitted Leesie, "I slept like the dead until 10 this morning! I can't tell you how rare that is for me. I **never** sleep."

"That's the truth," Teja agreed. "That girl loves her computer and is usually doing something on it most nights. Thank God nothing can stop me from my sleep or wake me once I'm out."

Ariana looked at Matthew and asked, "What about you, Matthew? Sleep well?"

Did she know something? Is that why everyone is having secret meetings today? Matthew put on his most glorious smile and replied, "Actually, I had a pretty good night. Had the place to myself for once," he stated, taking a poke at Zach. "Didn't have to listen to Zach's snoring, so I fell asleep easily. I must have fallen asleep before he came in. Nothing wakes me once I'm asleep."

What's really going on? Ariana wondered. *His aura looks weird. It's not clear like usual. It looks a little smoky. Smoky? Isn't that how Tara described the energy that scared the cat?* She decided to let her thought lie for now and talk to Zach about it later. But her thought continued to bother her throughout the picnic. Matthew's energy was way off and he seemed to be too friendly and outgoing, not himself at all. Finally, she couldn't take it anymore and pulled Zach aside.

"What's with Matthew? You said he seemed more quiet and moody earlier, but look how he's been all afternoon. I've never seen him so animated." Ariana asked Zach.

"What do you mean?"

"Something's off. His aura is weird and he's acting like someone else. Don't you feel it?"

"You know Matt," Zach argued, "always the moody one. Maybe today his mood has changed to good."

"When you got home last night, was he asleep?"

"He was in bed with his eyes closed, so I assume he was. I didn't go over and examine him. Why?" Zach asked.

"An idea I'm working on. I just have an uneasy feeling about Matthew today. The Dark has been very active in the past 24 hours. It could have filled me with some paranoia about him, I guess. We'll talk later."

"We'd better," Zach announced. "Remember, Matthew is my best friend. I'm pretty protective of him."

"I'm not attacking him. I'm worried. If he weren't your BFF you'd see it too," Ariana said defending herself. *Is this going to be our first fight?* "Zach, I don't want you to be mad at me. Once you think about what all went down last night, maybe you'll understand my concern. Until we're completely alone and can talk, please observe Matt with an open mind."

"Okay, I don't want to be mad at you," he said, kissing the tip of her nose.

When they returned to the rest of the group, Leesie started chanting, "Zach and Ariana, sitting in a tree, K-I-S-S-I-N-G."

Zach looked at Leesie with disgust. "You know, sometimes you act your age," he said.

"Okay, okay, children," Teja interjected. "Let's play some games!"

"Yeah, let's leave the girls to clean up and us guys can play some touch football. There's a ball in Zach's car," Andrew said.

"Whoa, I'm not getting stuck doing 'women's work.' I can play touch football as well as any guy," challenged Teja.

"Why don't we have a boys-against-girls game then?" Zach suggested.

"Sorry, but who's side does that put me on?" asked Tara.

"The girls' side," said Leesie. The other girls agreed.

"Okay, seeing as it will take all of you to even come close to competing with us, we'll agree to that," conceded Andrew.

Late into the afternoon, the eight friends laughed, played, and teased one another with no one actually keeping score. For that short while, Ariana actually forgot her concerns.

♊♊♊

On her way to see the therapist, Ariana felt uncomfortable wondering how things would go with her second counseling session. So much had happened since her first session, and she didn't know how much she wanted to confide right now. She wasn't sure she was ready to divulge to the therapist what her group of friends had been talking about or even if she should. Matthew had suggested that they keep their conversations private until they understood things better. Ariana thought maybe he had a point. She could always bring up more issues at other sessions. But wasn't therapy about talking over things that bothered you? Didn't the therapist have some kind of oath or obligation not to tell anyone anything that is said to her? All of these thoughts ran through her mind on her short walk to counseling, but by the time her session actually started, she still wasn't sure what she should or should not say.

Relax and just let things flow, she heard in her mind. Taking a deep breath, she waited for the therapist to begin.

"Good afternoon, Ariana. How have things been since I saw you last?" asked the therapist.

"Actually, it's been both amazing and perplexing," Ariana replied.

"Which would you prefer to talk about, the amazing or the perplexing?"

"I think I want to talk about the amazing part."

"All right."

"I've got friends," she exclaimed. "Real friends that aren't judging me for my weirdness, or my past. They seem to really accept me for me."

"It sounds like you're happy."

"Oh, I am, but scared, too. I keep thinking about my childhood experience with Gloria and how I really thought she was my friend. I think she was, at least until something better came along."

"You're afraid you'll be betrayed again, then alone," the therapist stated, summarizing Ariana's feelings perfectly.

"Yes," agreed Ariana. "Now that I've experienced being part of a group of friends, going to the fair together, laughing and teasing each other without anyone being mean, I just know I couldn't go back to the way things were before."

"The loneliness?"

Ariana nodded. "Before, I didn't really know what I was missing. Never having experienced being a normal teenager with friends, I could rationalize that my life was fine. At least I wasn't getting drunk, arrested, or tempted to use drugs. I was doing well in school and was interested in my classes, especially writing. I thought that was all I needed. But I guess that was just denial. I couldn't face the reality of my life so I denied how bad it really was. I can't do that anymore."

"What are you afraid of?"

"Losing what I've found, I guess. Finding out my new group of friends is all a big lie and that they're all really just laughing at me."

The therapist sat quietly looking at Ariana, waiting for her to continue. *Is there more that she isn't even admitting to herself?* the therapist wondered.

"Maybe my real fear is that what I thought I wanted, to have a real life, a change from my past, will become overwhelming for me," Ariana said. "Really, I just don't know. Everything is so new. It's strange. On the one hand, everything feels so good and exciting, but on the other, everything feels so frightening."

"Change is always frightening."

"Yeah," Ariana agreed, "but there seems more here than just regular, run-of-the-mill change."

"What do you mean?"

Ariana thought deeply before she ventured a reply, "Like there's more here than gaining friendships. I think there could be some sort of deeper reason the group of us are coming together."

"Hmm, any idea what that might be?"

Smiling, Ariana replied, "Would it seem like delusions of grandeur if I said to save the world?"

"The world you were so eager to leave only four months ago?

"Yeah, weird isn't it? Four months ago, before my guides told me I could change my life, all I wanted to do was die. Now all I want to do is live! It's like I haven't really been living until now. I think I was in limbo, gathering knowledge, waiting for the time that everything would come together."

"And the time is now?"

"That's the other bizarre thing. Now I feel that we have to hurry, like it's past time."

"You seem to be someone who puts a lot of pressure on herself."

"Yes, I take responsibility very seriously," Ariana admitted.

"And you feel responsible to whom and for what right now?"

Embarrassed, Ariana spoke softly, "For everyone and everything, the whole planet."

"Well, it appears that you've bitten off quite a bit, wouldn't you say? Is it possible that focusing on this great plan might be a way to distance yourself from others and also a way of creating an opportunity for you to feel terrible about yourself and your life again?"

"Yes, I guess so. But it really doesn't feel like that. It feels like for the first time in my life, I care about this world more than I care about myself. It's as though I've been so busy feeling sorry for myself that I couldn't allow anyone or anything in. Now I've stepped out. I've felt and seen the world which is really filled with wonderful things, not the dark existence I had created."

"It does sound like we are making some progress here," encouraged the therapist. "But I would like for you to take the time until our next session to really analyze your motivation. Take a serious look at where you think you're going, why, how, and all the things, good and bad, that could happen. Can you detach from yourself and your desires long enough to see clearly? I believe in you, Ariana. Do you believe in yourself?"

Ariana smiled, grabbed her backpack from the couch next to her, and stood, "Thank you for all your advice. I do promise that I will think, journal, and meditate on everything we discussed today. I don't know if I can separate myself from my desires, but I'll do my best."

The therapist walked Ariana to the door. The door closed with a thud. It matched the therapist's mood. She turned to face her desk, dread clouded her mind. *It's happening.* She had been waiting so long for this. But there was concern, too. Concern for this fragile young woman, a woman so blessed with ability. But were her abilities strong enough to do what she had been sent here to do? The therapist had concern for the other younglings involved as well. *They have no idea how large the stakes are.* She sighed and thought, *What next?*

We wait, was the reply.

Chapter 7

Finally alone with Ariana at their special spot, the top of South Mountain, Zach asked, "So what was going on with you and Matthew?"

"I don't want to make you mad at me, but his aura was very smoky today. Tara's crystal showed her the same thing last night. I can't stop thinking about the warning I got during the séance, that one of us who held deep anger would become our betrayer. None of the girls hold deep anger, only emotional pain. Andrew had anger today, but he's not an angry guy." Blushing, Ariana admitted, "I don't want to even consider that you have deep anger, cause then it could be you and I don't want to think that's possible."

"Well, I do." Zach countered. "I've never really dealt with what my dad did to my mom and me. I pretend to work on it in group, but I usually only go because of Matthew."

"Be honest." Ariana probed. "Whose anger is worse, yours or Matt's?"

"I think Matt's is complex. He was so young when it started. It's a mix of pain, love, anger, distrust, and confusion. He's really a damaged person."

"What did you do after you left me last night?"

"Went back to the room and slept."

"Any strange dreams? Did you wake up feeling rested? Anything happen that was unusual?"

"No, why?

"I don't think you could have been doing the things that happened last night without having some clue. I also think I would have felt something."

"Well, couldn't I have been like, sleepwalking or something?" asked Zach. "And why don't you think it could have just been The Dark?"

"It didn't act like The Darkness and I don't think Tara could have gotten rid of it as rapidly and easily as she did if it had been. No, I think when we had the séance, The Dark deepened the anger and doubt in Matthew and used him to do its evil deeds. I think it helped him to astral project and implant negative thoughts. That wouldn't work with Tara for two reasons; she's his polarity, he cares about her. And her cat alerted her."

"Why don't you just accept that the Dark may have changed tactics?"

"I do accept that, but that doesn't stop me from thinking the new tactic is to use one of us. We trust each other. What's more perfect than using that trust to defeat us?"

"Maybe the Dark planted this idea in you?" Zach questioned.

"Maybe it did," Ariana agreed. "Why don't we try to see if that's the case?"

"How?"

"Hold my hands and sit facing me. That's it. Now, stare above me. Is my aura any different?"

"No, it's still that bright purple color and clear," Zach assured her.

"And yours is still soft pastel blue like Tara's. But yours also has some purple," said Ariana. "Now close your eyes and try to feel me. Do you feel any anger or darkness?"

"You don't feel any different to me. But couldn't you be masking your feelings?"

"I don't think I could mask from my polarity. And I think you would feel The Dark since we are both weary of it. Understand?"

"I think so," Zach answered. "But why didn't I feel it with Matthew? And how do we find out if you're just being paranoid or if something really has happened with him?"

"Well, you weren't looking for anything today and I don't think he'd try what he might have done with the others with either of us. He might think it's more likely we'd know it was him. Maybe next time we're doing a teaching exercise we can make sure one of us is paired with him."

"But that won't be for another week. What do I do till then?"

"Be yourself, but observe him. See if you feel anything different. If you can figure out how, check to see if he still has the crystal I gave him. He put it in his medicine bag."

Zach was quiet for a moment. "I can't think of a time he takes the medicine bag off. It was a present from his grandfather."

"What about when he showers? I can't imagine him wearing a suede bag into the shower."

"You're probably right. If he doesn't lock the door next time, I'll check." Changing the subject he asked, "Can we have some love talk now?"

Ariana slid closer to Zach, nuzzling her head on his shoulder. "Love talk?" she said teasingly. "I'm not sure I know what that is. Care to show me?"

Zach put his nose in Ariana's hair and breathed deeply, "I love the smell and feel of your hair. Your smile is so beautiful and your eyes light up when you're happy. They change color, too. They match the color of your aura. Your laugh sounds like wind chimes in a gentle breeze, and I love the feel of your body in my arms."

"Wow! I think I like love talk."

"Want more?"

Slightly embarrassed, Ariana smiled and nodded. She did not want him to stop.

"When I think of your lips, my whole body becomes alive with the memory of our kisses. Your lips brushing mine so gently, like butterfly wings, then growing in intensity as your passion grows to match mine. It's the most wonderful thing I've ever endured."

"Endured?" she asked quizzically.

"Yes, endured, because the agony of the pleasure it causes is amazing and so difficult to absorb. My desire for you is torturous."

"Then maybe we should avoid kissing," Ariana teased.

"That would be worse than torture. Don't tease."

Taking his face in her hands, Ariana ran her thumbs over his lips and face. They both felt the electric tingling that always accompanied their touches. Zach shivered and kissed her deeply, feeling as though he was melting into their kiss. "Oh, sweet torture," he moaned.

"Does it bother you that I want to take the intimacy slow?" she asked after their kiss. "You are the first boy I've ever dated. I'd like to savor every little piece before moving ahead."

"First, I'm not a boy, and second, because I am a man, I can restrain myself until you want me as badly as I want you."

Ariana kissed Zach and snuggled against him, looking out the window at the beautiful landscape around them. "I love how wonderful I feel when I'm with you. With your arms around me, I feel safe and wanted. These are new experiences for me and I'm enjoying them so much. Every time we're together I feel like we're melding more and more. One day, the rest will happen naturally and easily. Maybe I'm being immature, but that's what I hope for."

"Then that's when it will happen. I will never push you. Until you are comfortable and pursue me, you are safe," Zach said, holding her closer. "I'm sorry I was so sensitive about Matthew. But since he and I first met, I've felt somehow responsible for him. He was so alone and confused when he came to live with my family. He didn't even understand how terrible his situation was. He hadn't known anything else, so to him it was normal."

"I know he is very private, but do you feel comfortable telling me what happened to him?"

"Please don't ever let him or anyone else know what I'm about to tell you, okay?"

"I swear. No matter what happens, I will not divulge anything unless you tell me to."

"Matthew and I became good friends when he was twelve. He had no other friends and was never allowed to go to anyone else's house or to bring anyone home to his. His mother knew that if people understood what she was doing to him, he would be removed. Having never been around other kids and their families, he had no idea what they were like. He thought his life was normal. His dad left them when he was six. Matt's dad hadn't been much of a father anyway. He was a drunk. So, with just him and his mom in the house, Matthew became the man in the family."

"Lots of little boys are put in that position," Ariana said. "How was this different?

"Zach was quiet for many minutes as he thought about betraying his friend and telling Ariana everything. He also wasn't sure how to tell it. "Ariana, understand this is hard for me. I feel like I am betraying Matt."

"But if he needs help, I won't know how to help if I don't know where all his anger is coming from," Ariana protested, hoping this would make things easier for Zach. "You aren't betraying Matt if I can help him."

"His mother sexually abused him."

"Oh, God. Now I understand why he hates her."

"No! That's the problem. He doesn't hate her. He's completely conflicted. He's been told that he should hate her and that what she did was horrible, but until someone told him it was wrong, he thought that his life with his mom was normal. I know he still feels extremely guilty for what he sees as abandoning her. The person Matthew hates is himself."

At first Ariana was shocked, but the more she thought about Matthew's early life, the more she could see his conflict. The only love he received was from his mom. How was he to know at a very young age that the love she was giving was a love shared only between adults? All children love to be cuddled and held, and because he was a child, he would have no knowledge of sexuality or natural sexual urges. He would see what they were doing as an extension of cuddling and showing love. By the time he was thirteen, real sexual feelings would have begun, no wonder that was the time things began to be discovered. Thank God he reached out and allowed Zach to enter his life.

"How did you find out what was happening?"

"You know how teenage boys are. Oh, maybe you don't. A group of us boys were looking at a Playboy magazine at school one day, acting like we knew something about women and sex. Matthew kept correcting us, obviously much more comfortable and familiar with female anatomy and pleasure than the rest of us. Everyone else assumed that he must have a girlfriend that taught him everything, but I knew better. I knew that he wasn't allowed to socialize and had to go home right after school. I knew he wasn't allowed to go anywhere on weekends either. So how would he know so much? What he knew wasn't something families would go into with their sons when they told them about the birds and bees. I knew his mom didn't work, she got alimony and child support, so it was hard to think it could have been a babysitter. The only other place he went was to his grandfather's, but when I asked Matt if he had a girlfriend there he said no and I believed him.

I found myself having a really uncomfortable feeling. Not sure where it came from or what it was exactly, I became scared for Matt. I told my mom. We have a really close relationship, my dad being an asshole and my asthma drawing us close, but nothing of course like Matt and his mom," Zach said hurriedly, blushing.

Ariana smiled at Zach. "I'm listening," she said.

"My mom went to Matt's house one day while we were at school. She had a talk with his mother and concluded that maybe we were misinterpreting things. We decided to watch and wait. Throughout that school year, Matt seemed more moody and kinda pushed away from me and the other guys. I knew that I wouldn't be seeing him over the summer, but I also knew he would be spending the summer at his Cheyenne grandfather's house. He had been spending entire summers there since he was ten. So I thought he'd be safe. Being pubescent myself, I didn't spend much time that summer thinking about Matt— girls seemed more important. When he came back, he seemed fine, and again, I let things slide. It wasn't until right before his fifteenth birthday that I became very concerned.

There was this girl, Heather O'Brien. She had the hots for him. At first he ignored her, but when the guys started teasing him about being gay, he asked her out. He never told us what happened, but he alluded to her being a cold fish. I had known Heather since the fourth grade and knew she was a nice girl, definitely not cold or mean. So I asked her what happened. She told me that as long as they were around other kids, Matthew was sweet and charming. She had been having a really nice time. But when he walked her home, Heather said Matt became mean and angry. He scared her. At one point, he grabbed her arm roughly and forced a very demanding kiss. When she pulled away, he called her names and left her standing there, alone, several blocks from her home.

After that Matthew became a real player, never without some babe on his arm, but no one girl for any long period of time. The other guys were envious of him but I didn't think he was happy.

Eventually, one of the girls, Thea, came clean and confided in me that Matt was all talk and no action. Everything was for appearances, they barely even kissed. It wasn't him that was leaving the girls, it was them getting bored with his lack of intimacy and connection. They were calling him a poser behind his back and laughing at him.

It was time to do something. It was time to ask him directly what was going on with him and his mom. He caved, actually falling apart when I asked him. I think he felt he'd hidden everything pretty well, but when I asked him if his mother was doing him, he knew he couldn't lie to me.

The two of us went to talk to my mom. All three of us went to Matthew's house to confront his mother. She tried to lie, but Matthew wouldn't let her. He became hysterical, screaming at her, telling her that she had ruined him. He couldn't stop crying. His mother just stood there helpless. My mom told her that we were taking Matt with us and that he would never be alone with her again. He and I gathered up his personal stuff and he moved in with us. When he lived with his mom he didn't even have his own room. He was sleeping in the master bedroom with her. It was creepy as hell."

"How did he adjust to leaving her?" asked Ariana, obviously touched by what Zach had shared with her.

"Not very well. He worried about her and constantly said he had abandoned her like she said he would. He was miserable and spent a lot of time very quiet and obviously depressed. My mom suggested counseling to him, but he refused. Eventually she had to threaten him in order to get him to go."

Ariana looked puzzled, "Threaten him?"

"Yeah, my mom told him that she would call the police on his mom if he didn't start counseling and actually work to get a handle on what had happened to him. He couldn't stand the idea of his mother going to jail, so he went. After that, he had good days and bad, often very bad. The confusion and guilt were destroying him, so the counselor encouraged him to express his anger as a way of dealing. There were times he would rage over the littlest thing. Eventually, he learned to control that, too, but I never really felt that the rage or guilt were gone. I think working with his grandfather actually did more for him than the counselor he went to."

"I don't doubt that," agreed Ariana. "Often people in trauma find solace in spirituality or religion. In Matthew's case, what his granddad is teaching him is both. It is also giving him an identity and a purpose."

"So why would he muck that up?"

"I don't think he means to, but remember how convincing The Darkness is. It knows exactly where we are most vulnerable and makes sure it utilizes that vulnerability for its purposes."

"If it was Matthew that tried to do harm last night, how do we help him?"

"I don't know. Everything seems to be pointing to the fact that we need more help from someone who is a professional in all this."

Zach looked doubtful. "Where are we ever going to find someone who is both metaphysical and a counselor?"

"Research, I guess. Leesie's good at that and she has an additional resource, Teja's grandmother."

Chapter 8

"You really scared me this afternoon," Wendy admitted to Andrew. "I was so afraid that you were kicking me to the curb. I don't know if I could have handled that. I guess I'm still weak when I really want to be strong."

Andrew looked forlorn, "Yeah, I was a real jerk. The last thing I want to do is make you sad or feel weak and scared. You mean a lot to me and I guess that's why The Dark decided to make me think you were only using me."

Andrew kissed Wendy's nose. "When you first came to group, I really didn't like you. You were so mean and looked really angry and scary," he said truthfully. "But under all that dark, scary makeup was a beautiful, sweet woman. I am so glad Ariana helped her find her way out."

"You have no idea how glad I am. I know now that I chased everyone away. I was so sure that everyone hated me that I made myself awful and then everyone did hate me. It was as though I thought that if I pushed people away before I needed them in my life, they couldn't hurt me. Unfortunately, it was me hurting me. I was so lonely and depressed that I couldn't even see the top of the hole I'd dug for myself. When Ariana adjusted my energy, my self-loathing seemed to back away enough so that I could begin to see much more clearly. I could actually stand back and observe my behavior. That allowed me to change it. I owe Ariana everything good in my life. I'm so glad she's my roomy. And I am really glad you're my polarity."

"Can I be more than that?"

"Like what?"

Andrew smiled at Wendy and said, "How about your main man?"

"I'd love that," Wendy admitted, "but you'll need to help me get used to completely trusting you. That's really hard for me. And I can't guarantee that I won't have some bitchy moments."

Pulling Wendy into his arms, Andrew said, "I'll just have to find a way to make you laugh when you're bitchy. I promise I'll work really hard at keeping your trust and hopefully earning your love."

Wendy had never felt better. This big bear of a gentle man actually wanted her. How great was that! Just as she was getting ready to tell him he wouldn't have to work too hard to earn that, they heard a key in the door.

"Hey there," said Ariana. "Did Andrew help you get all moved in?"

"Yup, and guess what, he bought us as a housewarming present?" Before Ariana could answer, Wendy continued, "A mini fridge and microwave!"

"That makes sense," replied Zach who had followed Ariana in, "after all, he is the one that likes eating the most. Right, big guy?"

"Absolutely," Andrew answered. "Want some popcorn? I could eat some popcorn."

As soon as the popcorn was prepared, the group sat down to talk. It felt very comfortable for Ariana to be sharing her space with the other three. She felt that having Wendy here would be good for all of them.

"We got the popcorn, how about watching a movie?" Andrew asked.

Ariana blushed as she replied, "I don't own a television."

"Who needs a television when we have computers?" Zach said. "There's lots of stuff to download. I belong to a streaming service anyway. What does everyone want to watch?"

"I picked the movie when we went out. It's your turn," Ariana offered.

Both guys screamed simultaneously, "Bloodshot!"

The movie was light and a bit stupid, just what the four of them needed. They laughed and joked and teased one another. It was the perfect beginning the two new roommates needed. When the movie was over the boys left together, Zach driving Andrew to his dorm. Wendy and Ariana were alone for the first time as roommates.

"I don't think I snore," Wendy said, "but if I do, just put a pillow over my face."

"Do you think that will work?"

"Well, I'm not as smart as Leesie, but I think if you cut off my oxygen, that should do the trick. Oh, do you shower at night or in the morning?"

"Usually the morning. Why?" Ariana asked.

"So we don't get in each other's way, I'll shower at night. Do you have a morning class?"

"Yes, on Monday, Wednesday, and Friday at 9:00."

"I've got a nine every day. I'll try not to wake you."

"Don't worry; I'm not a light sleeper. Anyway, on Tuesday and Thursday I have a 10. What's an hour between friends?" Ariana offered. "The only thing that might be a problem is that I meditate for 20 minutes every day. It's important for me that it be quiet then."

"When do you meditate?"

"In the morning, but not always."

"Well, if we could decide on a good time for both of us, I'd like to start meditating regularly too," said Wendy. "I was also thinking that maybe we can work on some of the psychic stuff together. You said we should be practicing with other people besides our polarity."

"Sounds like a really good idea," agreed Ariana. "How about we meditate from 7:30 to about 8 in the morning every day and work together Wednesday evenings? Zach has a class so we don't usual see each other on Wednesday."

"That works for me," Wendy said, trying to cover a yawn. "I'll go take a quick shower and then I'm going to bed."

When Wendy was done with her shower, Ariana brushed her teeth and combed her hair out. Putting on her yoga pants and T-shirt, she came back into the bedroom. Wendy was brushing her hair, wearing a pair of red flannel pajamas with feet and a drop seat.

"What on earth are you wearing?"

Wendy laughed, "I guess I do look kind of ridiculous, but they're really comfortable and my feet are always cold."

Laughing with her, Ariana said, "Well, if you ever want to make sure Andrew doesn't get too frisky, wear those."

"Well, girl, you're not looking real sexy yourself," Wendy said, climbing into her bed.

Ariana noticed Wendy slept with the stuffed penguin she got from the Fair. Ariana tried to remember who won it. She bet it was Andrew. She smiled to herself looking over at the four-foot-tall purple gorilla Zach had won for her. Feeling very happy as she got into bed, she hugged her pillow and breathed in the peace and tranquility filling the room. Life was so different now from her existence in Indiana. She fell asleep thinking how grateful she was for her new life.

Chapter 9

Leesie was busy thinking, which was not unusual for this brilliant fifteen-year-old. This time her thinking was about a person; she was worried about Matthew. Leesie never worried. She was the eternal optimist. But Matt's aura today was truly disturbing. Ever since Ariana taught the group to see auras, Leesie practiced constantly. She had noticed, for example, how nicely Tara's, Wendy's, and Ariana's auras had blended yesterday. She knew they had spent the morning together and it was obvious that their bond was getting tighter. Leesie felt that Tara was finally feeling as though she belonged.

Seeing the transformation in Teja's aura had been amazing. Since getting the messages from her dad at the séance, all her hurt and anger had disappeared. Leesie was happy that Teja was spending most of her time here in her room at the dorm. She was sure that being away from her hate-filled mother was helping Teja's changed mood continue and she really enjoyed having Teja as a roommate. Truth be told, Leesie didn't really like living alone. She was used to her rowdy, active family, and since her first roommate moved out, she had been really lonely and even a little scared.

But there was something that was weighing on Leesie's mind. Matthew's aura seemed as though it was getting dark and muddy. She knew this wasn't a good sign. Something had to be wrong. Leesie wondered if Teja had noticed anything. Maybe she was just being an alarmist.

"Hey girl," Leesie said. "I've been pondering something that I need to ask you about."

Teja looked up from her psychology book and said, "Yeah, I've noticed something was eating at you. You haven't been at your computer or said a word for the last hour. That has to be an all-time record! I intend to record the event for posterity."

"Yeah, yeah, yeah," Leesie replied. "This is some serious stuff I've been pondering. Did you notice anything weird about Matthew today?"

"Something felt off with him, but I couldn't get why. Maybe he's PMSing," Teja suggested with a silly smile.

Still serious, Leesie said, "His aura was way off. He was oddballing today, acting more like a creeper than one of the group."

"Girl, you don't have to be smack talkin' just cause he was having a bad day."

"I'm not putting him down. I'm really worried," Leesie said, defending herself. "His aura was really ugly and dark. I just wondered if you'd noticed."

"I really wasn't paying attention. Sorry I bitched at you," Teja apologized. "It's just that I want all of us to continue being as close as we have been. I'm worried that if we start talking 'bout each other behind everyone's backs, then the group will go straight to that place-that shall-go-unnamed because it's probably where that thing-that-shall-go unnamed lives."

"I think I'll call Ariana and see if she noticed anything or if it's just me," Leesie decided.

Picking up her cell phone, she dialed Ariana's number. *This is too important to text,* she thought, but the phone went to voicemail. *Hey call me,* she texted.

When Ariana didn't text right back or call like usual, Leesie became insecure and began to worry. *What's going on with me?* she wondered. *I never worry, but now I'm worrying about both Matt and Ariana. Maybe it's me The Dark has infected.* Becoming alarmed at that thought, she turned to Teja.

"Hey, would you do me a favor?"

"Wassup?"

"I need you to check out my aura and make sure I'm all right," Leesie said.

"Yeah, you are acting kinda weird. I'm not as good at it as you are, though, so you'll have to go over and stand in front of the wall or door or something."

Leesie got out of bed and walked to the door. Standing with her back against it, she closed her eyes so that she wouldn't be staring right at Teja and maybe make her uncomfortable. "Anything weird?" asked Leesie.

"I don't see anything weird. It's a little closer to you and not as orangey as usual, but it's still clear with nothing strange in it. Does that make you feel better?"

"Lots, thanks. Maybe I just need to meditate and get a grip," Leesie admitted as she walked back to her bed.

Leesie closed her eyes and began her slow breathing technique. Soon she found herself in her ideal place of relaxation. *I think I'll pimp it out even more.* She created a wall in her perfect room that was glass. It gave her a view of a beautiful tropical landscape complete with a shimmering waterfall and a cerulean blue pool of water. There were exotic orchids and other rare and wonderful plants and flowers everywhere. She walked to the wall and it opened upward. She stepped out into her self-created paradise.

You have a remembrance of Eden, came a voice from her left.

Even though Leesie was startled, she wasn't afraid. She knew who was talking to her. She turned toward the voice and said, "You are one of Ariana's Elders, right?"

"I am," was the reply.

"May I ask which one?"

"It doesn't really matter because we are of one mind, but you may call me Lysheara if that makes you more comfortable."

"Lysheara, that's a very beautiful name."

"It is typical of Meria."

"Why are you here in my meditation? I thought you were working only with Ariana."

"We go where we feel we must. You have been troubled and began to doubt your inner knowing. I am here to assure you that you did not imagine what you felt or saw. Matthew is very troubled and in much pain. These are doorways for The Darkness to use. It has taken a foothold within his mind. We think he is somewhat aware, but is also in denial. Ariana is concerned like you are, but Zach will not doubt his friend. You must speak with Ariana tonight when she returns from her encounter with Zach. She, too, doubts herself and could begin to believe in Zach's explanations for Matthew's new behaviors."

"I intend to talk to her, so I'll make sure it's tonight. Is there anything we can do for Matthew?" asked Leesie.

"There may be, but he must want to accept what you do even if he doesn't know he is being treated. You must gather the women in your group. Each of you must blend your energies and enter a meditative state as one mind. Then you must attempt to enter Matthews's deep consciousness, his inner being, and begin healing his guilt and pain. You must fill his being with deep love and trust. Healing the pain within will allow him to accept what you are giving. Beware, though. If The Darkness senses what is being done, it will attack. Whether it chooses to attack the group or Matthew is not known."

"Why just the women?"

"There is intense power in combining female energy. Females are the creators and the nurturers on Terra; this is the energy Matthew needs. He must learn to accept healthy female energy. It is time for you to contact Ariana. She is in her room with Wendy."

"Wait!" begged Leesie. "Why did you call this place Eden?"

"Eden was created by our people as a perfection of Meria. Terrans chose to leave it and began to destroy this home. Only those that were there in the beginning can remember. You are one of those."

"What's that even mean?"

"For a later time," Lysheara said as she turned and vanished.

Chapter 10

Leesie immediately called Ariana. "Hey, girl, you got Skype?"

"Hi, Leesie," Ariana replied laughing. "Good to hear from you at what, 10:30 at night, with such an important question," she teased. "Yes, I have Skype."

"The important stuff comes after I get all of you together on Skype. I'll call Tara and then I'll get us all on a group call. Log on," Leesie said. "Oh, is Wendy there? She needs to be in on this, too."

"Yes, she's here and I'll be awaiting your call with baited breath," Ariana continued to tease.

"Okay, but this is really important, so get ready to change your attitude, okay?" Leesie responded. "In a minute, bye."

Leesie immediately made a second call. "Hey Tara, are you near your computer? Oh, this is Leesie."

"Hi, Leesie. I can be by my computer if you want," Tara answered.

"You got Skype?"

"Yup."

"Okay, get on. I'm going to get a conversation going between Ariana, Wendy, you, Teja, and me. Hold tight, I'll be calling in a minute."

After succeeding in getting the group together on Skype, Leesie began. "I called this meeting tonight because of something that has been going on all day and then got mad chill during a meditation this evening."

"Why only us?" Wendy interjected.

"Because that's what I was told to do," Leesie replied a bit angrily. "If you let me go on, everything will make sense. No interruptions, please." She continued, "Since yesterday's picnic, I've been very disturbed by some things I felt and saw around Matthew. His energy seemed off, he seemed to be oddballing or something, so I decided to observe his aura and see what I could get from that. It was really weird, kinda smoky and unclear. I didn't think that he was acting real, and his aura seemed to confirm it. I've been thinking about it all day and the more I thought, the more worried I became. You know me, I don't worry. It's a waste of time when you can just figure it out or move on to something you can deal with. But I couldn't get this feeling out of my mind. I asked Teja if she'd seen anything unusual and she said she thought he was a little off but attributed it to his normal moodiness. But it felt like something worse to me. Getting nowhere, and with Ariana not answering her phone, I decided to meditate. I went to this really killer place. It was all tropical and beautiful and here's the crazy part; one of Ariana's Elders was there. She said her name was Lysheara and she would come to any of us if needed. She assured me that what I was feeling was real. Matthew is filled with anger and pain which allowed The Darkness to enter and take root. According to Lysheara, Ariana noticed something too, but Zach tried to convince her she was wrong.

Lysheara said we have to do something as soon as possible. She instructed me to inform all the females right away. Then she said we had to get together and I'll quote her now cause you guys know I never forget anything. I asked, 'Is there anything we can do for Matthew?'

She answered, 'There may be, but he must want to accept what you do even if he doesn't know he is being treated. You must gather the women in your group. Each of you must blend your energies and enter a meditative state as one mind. Then you must attempt to enter Matthews's deep consciousness, his inner being, and begin healing his guilt and pain. You must fill his being with deep love and trust. Healing the pain within will allow him to accept what you are giving. Beware, though. If The Darkness senses what is being done, it will attack. Whether it chooses to attack the group or Matthew is not known.'

I asked her, 'Why just the women?'

'There is intense power in combining female energy. Females are the creators and the nurturers on Terra. This is the energy Matthew needs. He must learn to accept healthy female energy. It is time for you to contact Ariana. She is in her room with Wendy.' "

Leesie concluded, "So that was the urgency for my 10:30 call. Whew, now I feel better."

"But I don't," replied Tara. "Matthew's my polarity and I didn't even notice. What's wrong with me?"

Ariana answered immediately, "It's not you, it's The Darkness. I bet it's blocking your connection. Have you tried reaching him through your mind link?"

"No."

"Give it a try right now. We'll wait."

Pulling her crystal from around her neck, Tara began concentrating deeply on Matthew. Focusing on the center of the crystal, she felt encased in white light. But when she tried to reach Matthew, she felt like she was banging against an obstruction, as though Matthew had closed the door to his mind.

"I'm blocked by something. I can't reach him," Tara said, distraught.

"I figured that," answered Ariana. "That's why Lysheara wanted us working together. With our combined energy, maybe we can break through the obstruction The Dark has put in the way. Hum, I wonder. I'm having a kinda 'aha moment' right now. Do you think it could have been Matthew doing that stuff to Wendy, Andrew, and you, Tara? You all trust him and would not reject his energy. Also, the crystals would not keep him away."

"Wow, that makes sense to me," Wendy said. "Tara, what do you think?"

Tara felt great sadness. She responded, "It makes sense. I didn't feel threatened and if it hadn't been for the way Diablo acted, I wouldn't have noticed anything. Yeah, I can see that it could have been Matthew."

Ariana replied, "And if it was Matthew, maybe that's why it was so easy for you to get that force to leave you alone. He cares about you and doesn't want to hurt you."

"Where do we go from here?" Teja asked. "I don't want anything to happen to our group and anyone in it. I've found a new family and I'm fighting for it. Am I right, ladies?"

Ariana smiled as she said, "You sound like Leesie, but yes, you are right. If the way The Dark is choosing to fight is by pitting us against each other or hurting one of us, then we must fight it with everything we've got."

Tara was still worried, "What happens if we fail? I don't want to get scared and freak out or anything because I know that's exactly what The Darkness wants, but this is my polarity we're talking about. What might that mean for me directly? If he's lost to The Dark, will I be, too?"

"Truly, I don't know," admitted Ariana. "Please understand that just because I'm supposed to have some extra knowledge doesn't mean I know everything or that I even know how to access what I'm supposed to know. But, and I'm making a guess here, because we all have free will I think you would have to choose to let The Darkness in. It can't just take you over because of Matthew's choices."

"We need to get together in person, just the females of the group and start doing the work Leesie was told to do," Teja said. "So when?"

"As soon as possible," answered Tara.

"What's everyone's class schedule tomorrow. Any breaks?" asked Leesie.

After a discussion of their schedules, it was discovered each of them had a three-hour block of time with no classes starting at two. Leesie felt they should gather at Tara's condo because she was Matthew's polarity. The others agreed and decided they would meet at 2:30 the following day to begin their work on Matthew.

Chapter 11

After disconnecting from the call with the girls, Tara was very troubled. She couldn't sleep. She appreciated Ariana's explanation, but couldn't help but feel she'd let Matthew down. He had shared his story with her. She had held him after he howled his pain into the sky. Tara alone knew the depth of that pain. As an empath, she had felt it all. She had experienced a memory so excruciating she had almost doubled over in pain. Tara's own life had been filled with trauma, but nothing like the kind Matthew lived. It was as though he was split in two. One part, the innocent child, felt responsible for his mother. He loved her deeply and needed to be there to protect her. The other part, the adult male, was angry, guilty, and filled with self-loathing. He blamed himself for letting his mother down, for leaving her. Yet he also hated her and the world for what had been done to him. Tara knew all this, but still she hadn't realized how vulnerable to The Dark he was. *How could I have been so stupid and self-centered*, she thought. *Should I call him, to see how he's doing?*

No! she heard plainly in her mind.

Was that my inner voice, The Darkness or who? she wondered.

Again, Tara heard clearly, *We are the Elders. Do not contact Matthew. It will only alert him that you suspect something is wrong. When he suspects, The Darkness will know and take action against you.*

I can hold my own, Tara thought.

But can all your sisters? Do you really want to be responsible for something happening to one of them? the Elders said, responding as one mind.

What do I do then? I can't stand how this is making me feel!

Use your crystal as a focus of love and light and send these energies to Matthew. Because he still possesses free will, he has the choice to accept this love and light or he can reject it and walk this path. You can do no more than offer help and love, the Elders answered.

Tara pulled out her crystal and held it up so she could stare at it. Thinking of Matthew, she began to feel her connection to him. He was asleep and dreaming. Tara began to concentrate on every feeling of love and security she had ever experienced. She filled herself with feelings of being and receiving love. Thinking of her deep belief in a Source of all kindness and light, she also sent that. Bathing Matthew in feelings of completeness, clarity, and calm, she whispered, "You are loved." She held these thoughts until she was sure he had received them. She closed her eyes and slept deeply.

The next morning, Tara awakened feeling especially refreshed. She stretched, completed her morning grooming rituals, and then sat down to see if she could feel Matthew. She pulled out her crystal from its chain around her neck and focused her thoughts through it to Matthew. At first she felt nothing which alarmed her. *Did I do something last night that caused him to shut down our connection?* Clearing her mind of this negative, fearful thought, she tried again and this time she found herself standing in his room observing him. He seemed to be arguing with Zach. Now she was really concerned. Should she eavesdrop on their conversation or disconnect? *How am I doing this anyway?* she wondered. *Maybe this is how Matt's energy got in my condo. Maybe I can do it because we are polarities?* Tara concluded that observing what was going on between Matthew and Zach might provide a way to help Matthew later, so she decided to stay.

"How would you know if I was acting weird?" Matthew asked Zach. "You're never around anymore. Now that you've got a girlfriend you don't have time for me."

"Whoa, dude. You sound jealous," Zach exclaimed.

"Not jealous, just stating a fact," Matthew replied.

"My relationship with Ariana has nothing to do with us. In high school you had babes all the time, but I still knew you were my friend. Now the shoe's on the other foot and you're pouting? Is that what's going on?"

"You're never here anymore. What happened to our Assassins Creed mega marathon? Since we got together with this group, we've let everything else slide. When was the last time we even spoke to Aiden?"

"Since when did you start worrying about Aiden?" Zach asked. "You know that if he wanted to get together he'd let us know, and if you were so stoked to have the marathon, you could have called Aiden, told me when, and it woulda happened."

"Just saying," Matthew pouted.

Zach was pissed. "And what do you mean since we got together with the group we've let everything slide? It looked to me as though you were one of the leaders of the group. If you didn't want to be part of it, why did you start the thing to begin with?"

"Just trying to help out your damsel in distress. But now that she's got you, she doesn't need my help."

"Wow, you should hear yourself! She was right, there is something wrong with you," Zach answered.

With a sarcastic smile, Matthew replied, "Oh, so she's trying to turn you against me? Filling your head with a lot of bullshit about me?"

"No! She's worried about you and cares about you and wants to see if you need anything. She just mentioned it to me because she knows how close we are," defended Zach.

"Yeah, dude, believe what you want. She's got you too blinded to see anything but what she tells you anyway. That beaut has you seriously whipped. When are you going to get what women really are? They're all manipulative skanks looking to make a score."

"What could she possibly want from me? What's wrong with you? What happened to the Shamanic Way you've been practicing? I've never seen you act so negative and mean."

"Not negative, just realistic. I have lots more experience than you do. She's trying to pull our friendship apart. If she can do that, then she's got the power and can do anything she wants with you and the rest of us."

"Holy crap! What do you think she wants?"

"The power to control all of us."

"To what end?"

"I don't know yet, but I'll figure it out. Meanwhile, watch your back, buddy," Matthew said as he left for class.

Standing alone in the dorm room he shared with Matthew, Zach felt completely lost and helpless. This was not the person he had been so close to for the past six years. *Or was it? Maybe I wanted to see a different Matt, not the one that was so damaged that he hates women.* There had been signs, though, like the way he treated women in high school and the fact that he hadn't even looked at women since coming to ASU. Zach had never seen this jealousy before, but he hadn't really given Matthew any reason to be jealous. Zach hadn't dated much in high school. He often just went out with friends of the girls Matthew was with at the time. He hadn't found anyone that really meant anything to him, so the situations were always very temporary. Maybe Zach had been waiting for the time he and Ariana would find each other.

How am I going to deal with this? Zach thought. *I don't want to lose either Matthew or Ariana.* Zach was worried about what would happen to the group, too. There was so much at stake. He felt physically sick to his stomach. *What am I going to do?* Looking at the clock, Zach realized he had better get to class. He'd think about this tonight when he had the time. Taking a deep breath, Zach closed his eyes and whispered, *Ariana, Elders, Guides, and God, whoever is out there, help me know what to do!*

 క్రీ క్రీ క్రీ

Tara was freaked. Now she knew for sure that Ariana and Leesie had been right. *Holy Mother of God, have we got a lot of work to do,* she thought. Trying not to think about what this would mean for her situation within the group, and how these changes in Matthew might affect her, Tara began planning the afternoon ahead.

Chapter 12

The four girls arrived together at Tara's condo. Tara gave them the grand tour because none of them had been there before.

"This is really wonderful," Teja declared. "Did you do all the decorating?

"That's one of my passions. I'd even thought about becoming an interior decorator but decided that counseling is more my calling. I still love doing it though, so it was fun to have a whole place of my own to experiment with," Tara explained.

"Well, sista, you definitely have a knack. You even got yourself a cat that matches perfectly. Look at those giant, orange eyes," Teja exclaimed as Diablo plopped himself on the couch next to her. "Hey, this cat doesn't have a nose. Wassup with that?"

Leesie started laughing, "Teja, haven't you ever seen a purebred Persian cat before? They breed them for those flat faces. There is a nose there, honest. It's just flattened."

Wendy walked over to Diablo and immediately the cat jumped into her arms. They cooed at one another for a moment before Wendy said, "He really loves it here."

Teja looked astounded. "I've never seen him jump into anyone's arms but mine. He's usually more standoffish. How do you know he likes it here?"

"Wendy has an affinity with animals. They talk to her and she can understand them and talk back," Ariana answered. "Ask him about what happened here the other night, Wendy."

Wendy cuddled Diablo and scratched his neck just where he loved it the most. That was all the others saw. Neither the cat nor Wendy appeared to be making a sound. After a minute or so, Wendy said, "Okay, I think I got it. Correct me if I misinterpret anything, please."

"Who are you talking to?" Tara asked.

Wendy explained, "The cat, of course. Here is what he said

happened. He heard some strange sounds, then he saw the air waiver and the energy felt different. The shifting air took on a somewhat human form, not solid, but discernible. It was a tall male that had no scent. He knew it didn't belong and it felt bad, so he chased it away to protect the human that he is bonded to. He's proud of himself. His human and he worked together and put back the right energy by chasing away the wrong one."

"Well, that's pretty much what happened," Tara said. "You can really talk to him?"

"Yes, it's actually easy," Wendy stated.

Teja looked at Wendy as though she had grown horns. "Yeah, maybe for you, but some of us can't even understand each other, much less things that don't say words."

"Seriously, how do you do it?" asked Tara.

"First you believe you can," she said, looking directly at Teja. "Then you send feelings of safety and understanding. Animals do better with pictures, so if you visualize things to them they get what you want more easily. After you send an image, you listen to what pops into your head. Animals think much more simplistically and more straight forward than people. They get right to the point."

"Well," said Tara, "I'm seriously impressed and would love to work with you so that I can talk to Diablo."

"He says he would love that. You frustrate him sometimes because it takes you so long to understand what he wants," Wendy replied. "So I guess it's a go. Just let me know when you want to begin."

"Hey you two, we're here for other purposes today," Ariana reminded them, "and we don't have a lot of time."

"You're right, Ariana. I have something to tell everyone about Matthew," said Tara. "Last night I was worrying about him and I heard the Elders tell me to send love and light to him, so I did. When I got up this morning, I decided to check on him and see how it had worked. This time was different. Instead of me being in his mind, I was standing in the room watching. Do you know what that is?"

Leesie answered, "It's called astral projection. Your spirit left your body and went to Matt. From what the cat told us, that's what he did with you, Wendy, and Andrew."

"That was Matthew putting all that shit in my mind?" Wendy

exclaimed angrily.

"We'll deal with that later," said Ariana. "Was there more, Tara?"

"Yes. He and Zach were arguing. Matt was mean, jealous, and really nasty. I'd never seen him like that, even in group, and I don't think Zach had either. He said some awful things, especially about you and your relationship with Zach. He was really hateful. I think you guys are right, The Darkness has him. What does that mean for me? I don't want to be petty and only think about myself, but he's my polarity. If he gets turned, will I? I remember what you said about this, Ariana, but if I continue being scared, won't it create a foothold?"

"I don't think so. Polarities are not exactly opposites, they're more like complements. So although you have both been traumatized, your reactions were very different. You decided to become strong, loving, and more connected to God. Matthew, on the other hand, withdrew into anger, guilt, and himself. The Darkness needs a crack to enter. Fear, anger and guilt are prime cracks. Release the fear of what might happen and go back to your strong, trusting belief in the Source." Ariana answered.

"Will I still have a place with the group? I don't want to lose any of you. You're my family now," said Tara.

"We aren't lettin' you go girl. Once in, in for life, kinda like a gang," Teja stated. "Can I get an amen, ladies?"

Ariana turned to Tara, "You are more valuable now than ever. Your connection to Matthew is the key to us helping fight The Darkness within him. He seems to really care about you, and to be a little indelicate, because you are not yet fully female, he doesn't hate you like he does most women."

"In a crazy way, that makes me feel better. I feel very connected to the Matthew I know is really in there. He's as lost as I was, and like I said before, helping people is my real mission," Tara said.

"Or to put it the way the Elders did: healing bodies, minds, and spirits is your path," said Ariana.

"Okay, what do we do to get this going?" Wendy asked.

"I think we should form a circle again, holding hands, with our crystals in front of us as our focus objects. We should focus our attention completely on our crystal and think of Matthew. Think good thoughts of him. No fear, anger, or anything that would draw The Darkness. Tara, you can tell us where he is so that we can see him in our minds. You can also tell us if he is feeling anything. Does everyone agree with this plan?" Ariana asked.

Everyone was in agreement.

As they assembled around the dining room table, the girls noticed the white pillar candle sitting in a crystal bowl of salt water. Tara said, "I protected the house completely in preparation for our gathering. I think it's as safe as it can be."

"Very smart of you, Tara. Thank you," replied Ariana. "Let's start by holding hands and breathing deeply. Allow yourself to relax completely. Relaxing your jaw, your shoulders, and your back, go deeply into your center. Breathing and counting down from ten to one, enter your perfect place of relaxation and protection. When you are completely relaxed, open your eyes and focus on your crystal." Ariana was silent for a moment. "Now that everyone is focused on their crystals, begin to think of Matthew as Tara connects with his energy and tells us where he is. Keep thinking loving thoughts."

Within seconds Tara said, "He's sitting outside, under a tree. He doesn't want to go back to his dorm room in case Zach's there. He's feeling bad about what happened earlier. He's conflicted."

"Is there anything around him that can help us figure out where on campus he is?" Ariana asked.

Tara was quiet a little longer than before as she searched Matt's surroundings, "I know where he is," she exclaimed, "he's at the place he first talked to me about all this. He's by Gammage, the Mill Avenue side."

The group concentrated even harder on including Matthew in their circle of love and trust. Each of them was thinking about their personal loving memories of Matthew and each was allowing their concern and protectiveness to be part of their love. They held him in their minds as though they were holding him in their arms, like lovers.

Several minutes later Ariana announced, "It's time to come back now. Release your connection to Matthew slowly and lovingly. Now release your focus and come back to this room and to this time," Ariana instructed. "Well, Tara, how'd we do?"

"I'm not sure. I know he was conflicted before we began and he was still confused when we left. I suggest that each of us hold him in our thoughts tonight, too. He might be more receptive when he's asleep. Protect yourselves and do what we did here, but see him asleep," Tara suggested.

"Sounds like a good idea. Please let us know tomorrow if we did any good," said Wendy.

"Leesie, you've been awfully quiet," Ariana said. "Is everything all right?"

"Been thinking a lot. I am convinced of two things; we need to see if we can enlist the therapist somehow because she knows all of us better than any of us know ourselves and we **have** to find someone who knows more about this than us."

"I'll ask Gram. Now that I'm living at Leesie's, I keep forgetting. I'll call her as we're walking home," Teja promised.

"What else have you been thinking, Leesie?" asked Ariana.

"You know me, I'm usually real positive, especially if I can get information about something. But this is so much more. I can't even get my head around it. I'm not wanting us to mess something up that's this important. We can't make any mistakes or this planet is going to be one really terrible place to live," Leesie said, her eyes brimming with tears. "If we can't even keep our group together, how are we going to save our planet?"

"Okay, I've got a name," announced Teja on their walk home. "The only problem is that she lives in Glendale, which is in the West Valley. Zach will have to drive us."

Leesie asked, "Does she have a website we can look at and see how we all feel about her? It is a woman, right?"

"Yes, it's a woman," answered Teja, "and I don't know about a website because my gram doesn't like computers, but she says this woman is the real thing. We can google her if you're worried."

"What did your grandmother say about her?" Ariana asked.

"Just that Gram's known her a long time and really trusts her abilities. She does readings, channeling, and teaches classes."

"Okay," said Leesie. "I'll google her and see what I can find out."

The group split up and headed to their respective dorms or to class, everyone feeling both concerned and hopeful about the coming days. Wendy and Ariana headed to their dorm.

"Do you think there's anything else we can do?" Wendy asked. "I'm feeling kind of helpless here."

"I know what you mean. I'm going to try meditating and talking with the Elders. You could try that too," Ariana offered.

"Do you think they'd talk to me?"

"They've been talking with everyone else, I'm sure you'd be no different," Ariana assured her.

"Then I guess when we get back, I'll try it. Hey, are you hungry? I think I need to eat something before I do anything else. How about you?" Wendy inquired.

"Sounds like a really good idea," Ariana agreed.

They walked the rest of the way to their dorm in silence. Working to distract herself, Ariana decided to focus on the beauty of the day. She liked filling her soul with the wonders of this place. The weather was perfect, 74 degrees and very sunny. There was a slight breeze and the sidewalks were filled with happy, laughing students. It was easy to be in a good mood in a state that rarely experienced overcast skies or inclement weather. Every day reaffirmed to her that she had made the right choice moving to Arizona.

Ariana decided she wanted to explore the state more. Maybe she could coax Zach into driving into the high country this weekend. She had heard that the Red Rock country of Sedona was beautiful. Or if they really wanted to have an adventure, they could drive a little farther to Flagstaff or Pinetop and go skiing. She had never attempted skiing. She had vowed to create a new life for herself here, so why not give it a try? She'd love to stay in a log cabin with a fireplace burning and cuddle with Zach. Being in snow was tolerable as long as she could leave it and come back to the warmth of Tempe. Indiana winters were often brutal and treacherous. Snow and black ice were a sure prescription for a lot of disasters. She did miss ice skating, though. That and horseback riding were the two physical activities that had kept her sane growing up. She still wasn't sure why her father had relented and bought her horse, Modesty Blaze, for her twelfth birthday. Her father had always been indifferent or violent to her, so this great gift was very uncharacteristic of him. Maybe he was hoping that she would become a champion equestrian and finally make the family proud of her. Unfortunately, that was not interesting to Ariana. She liked the freedom of riding either bareback or Western. Those styles were much less complicated than the traditional English with the posting and proper seat. She missed Modesty. Before she moved to Arizona, Modesty had been Ariana's only friend. Ariana hoped the little girl that now owned the horse loved her as much as she did. She initially wanted to bring her horse to Arizona, but was immediately told by her father that was not in the cards. He was willing to pay for her education, but not for any luxuries: no car, no horse, and no apartment. Originally, Ariana assumed she'd be going home for Christmas, spring and summer breaks, and could spend time with Modesty then. But now she knew that unless she was forced for some reason, she was never going back to Indiana. Her summers could be filled with school. She thought that her father would not object to her staying for that. But breaks were more problematic. Although her family treated her like she didn't belong with them, she wondered if there was an expectation that she be in Indiana on the holidays. Despite any guilt her family might try to lay on her, Ariana had no interest in returning home. Thanksgiving was easy. She only had three days off from school and no one would fly all the way back to Indiana for what would essentially be one day. But Christmas break was a lot longer. She might be expected to return home then. She hadn't broached the subject with her parents yet. She was waiting to see if they would. Christmas was only a little over a month and a half away and nothing had been said. Even the thought of spending time with her horse didn't tempt her. *I wonder what Zach is planning for Thanksgiving and Christmas?*

Arriving at Manzanita Hall, Ariana was surprised to see both Zach and Andrew waiting at the front door.

"Where have you girls been?" Andrew asked. "We've been worried about you."

"Why? Were we supposed to get together tonight?" Wendy asked, confused.

"No, but none of you have been answering your cell phones for hours," Andrew replied.

The girls had turned off their phones while working on helping Matthew and forgot to turn them back on. Ariana knew the guys were making themselves available in shifts in case anything happened to anyone, so she understood why they would worry.

"Has something happened?" asked Ariana.

"Matthew has vanished," Zach answered. "He and I had a blowout this morning. Matt didn't come back from class or show up to take over my shift. I called Andrew to see if he'd seen him, then we tried to call the rest of you. No one answered. It really freaked us out. Where have you been and why aren't you answering your phones?"

"We had a girl's day at Tara's and we all turned off our phones. I guess we just forgot to turn them back on. I'm sorry. Did you find Matthew?" Ariana asked.

"No, and I think you may be right about him. I told Andrew what you thought. Did you tell Wendy?" said Zach.

"Yes, but what happened that makes you think my concern about Matthew is right when you didn't last night?"

"I tried to talk to him this morning. He went crazy on me. He said that I was dumping him for you and even implied you had some sort of plan to make that happen. He was really different. He was acting so nasty and spiteful. I've never seen Matt behave like that before, so it started me thinking. Maybe that's not Matt, but The Darkness talking through him or something."

"Yes, that's possible," Ariana agreed. "But the anger had to have been there for The Darkness to gain a foothold. Obviously the counseling hasn't helped him enough. Do you think we should try talking to the therapist? I know she has a confidentiality thing, but if we tell her he's disappeared and we're worried what he might do, maybe she'll help us."

"We could try asking Tara to find him," Wendy said. Grabbing her phone, she dialed Tara's number. "Damn, still not answering!"

"I'm going to call the therapist and see if she'll talk to us," Ariana said.

"You don't think we should look for Matt or something?" Andrew asked. "We don't want to cause him any trouble. Let's try his phone again."

Zach tried calling, no answer. He texted, but after five minutes, he decided it was no use. Zach looked beaten and Ariana could feel his guilt, pain, and worry.

"You didn't do anything wrong, Zach. You were talking to Matt because you care about him and don't want to hurt him. You also can't be blamed for our relationship. Are you sorry that we're together? Does that make you feel like you abandoned him?" questioned Ariana.

"No, yes, oh I just don't know. I haven't been this happy in ages and it's because of us, you and me. The group is important to me too, because I really feel that this is what I'm supposed to be doing. But that doesn't mean that I don't feel guilty that I'm letting Matt down somehow. He's been like my bro, BFF, and confidant for six years. We've lived together for the last three. I know what he's been through. I feel helpless and it hurts," said Zach.

"The Dark's new tactic is working, isn't it?" asked Wendy, obviously alarmed. "It's tearing the group apart, filling us with pain and fear so that it can get a foothold."

"No, it's not winning," Ariana exclaimed emphatically. "The Dark only wins if we let it. Okay, things are a little rough right now, but it can bring us closer. Look, four of us are together trying to work this out right now. Let's contact as many of the others as we can and stop being helpless. Let's make a plan and follow it."

They reached Leesie and Teja immediately and decided they would all go to Tara's apartment to see if Tara was there. Leesie had all the girl's schedules because she coordinated the activity at Tara's earlier. She knew Tara did not have a class. The four piled in Zach's Mustang and headed to Barrett Hall to pick up Teja and Leesie. The girls were waiting out front for them and with a little work, all six were in the car and on their way.

The lights were on in Tara's condo, giving the group some hope. But when they knocked, there was no answer. They tried calling again, still no answer. Ariana could see the worry emanating from everyone's energy. *I've got to mellow out the energy.* She concentrated on sending positive, hopeful energy to the group. Ariana thought it had worked as the energy around the group appeared to grow lighter.

"Sorta weird, don't you think? Both of them missing?" said Leesie. "Do you think they could be together?"

"I sure hope so," Zach answered. "That would make me feel better. Tara's so stable. What do we do now?"

"Look for Matt, I guess. Let's start at your dorm room, Zach," Ariana suggested. "I'll keep trying to reach both of them on their cells."

No one was in Zach's room. They checked with Aiden who said he hadn't seen Matthew all day.

"Where now?" Zach asked.

"Let's go to Gammage, street side. That's where he and Tara meet to talk."

They decided it would be easier to walk than to try to find parking in that area. Walking the short distance to the auditorium gave the entire group a feeling of positive action. That, along with the change in energy Ariana provided, seemed to be helping everyone cope.

As they approached a small hill, they thought they heard sobbing. Zach began to run toward the sound. The others followed. When they got to the top of the rise, they found Tara sitting alone, crying.

"Tara, what's happened?" asked Zach. "Did something happen to Matthew?"

Looking up and noticing all her friends made Tara cry harder. She got a hold of herself and replied, "He's in so much pain and he won't let me talk to him. He's shut me out. I came here hoping I could convince him to come to me and talk, but instead he closed his shields completely.

I have no idea where he is or what's happening. I feel so useless and empty!"

Ariana kneeled down by Tara. Taking both of Tara's hands in her own, Ariana concentrated on relaxing Tara and filling her with peaceful, loving energy. When she felt she had succeeded, Ariana asked, "Did you talk with him or just connect telepathically?"

"Just through our mind link," Tara replied. "Why?"

"Because if he shut you out of his mind it could mean that he cares enough not to cause you pain. That's really important. It means the old Matthew is still in there."

Zach needed to do something, anything, to help his friend. He said, "I'm going to text Matt again. Let's all send caring energy his way. Envelop him in a cloud of our group energy. Is that possible, Ariana?"

"Yes, I think it is. It's definitely worth a try."

Forming a circle and holding hands, the seven friends began growing their energies by concentrating on God's White Light and unqualified love. Each member of the group began feeling a well of power growing in the center of their being and expanding upward and outward, finally merging with the energies of each of the others. Ariana could see their individual energies as they joined to become one. Their combined energy was a brilliant gold with wonderful streaks of violet. Concentrating as hard as she could, Ariana released this vibrant energy toward Matthew. Suddenly it was as though a bubble burst and the energy began to flow outward in a dynamic column that Ariana knew was being absorbed by Matt.

"It's working," Ariana exclaimed. "Keep it flowing. Visualize Matthew standing here with us, holding Tara's and Zach's hands. Visualize the love and caring we all feel. Hold that love."

Watching the energy that the group was producing was amazing. It felt like a complete force of love. Its frequency was so pure. Ariana imagined the sound she heard must be like angels singing. The sound relaxed her. It soothed and filled her with delight. The colors she saw swirled like oil in water: blues, violets, and golds. The color began to shift and Ariana thought she saw the outline of a man.

"Oh my God," Ariana exclaimed. "I think Matthew has joined us."

Immediately, the others opened their eyes. Standing in the middle of their energy circle was the faint energy imprint of a person.

Leesie turned to Tara and asked, "Is it him?"

Tears rolling down her face, Tara said, "Yes, yes it is Matthew. He responded to our love."

Zach, who was also tearing up, spoke to the figure, "We love you man, all of us. We want you with us. We want you to know that with all of us working on it, we can release you from the guilt and pain that The Darkness is using to pull you away from us."

The energy in the middle of their circle became brighter and each of them could see Matthew much more clearly. Then he vanished.

"What happened?" Andrew asked. "Where'd he go?"

"I think he did as much as he could to show us he had felt our love, but it is very difficult to do what he did, much less do it that long," Ariana explained. "Unless you are very well trained and experienced in spirit walking, it will exhaust you."

"What is spirit walking?" wondered Andrew.

"It's also called astral projection. You need to understand that our energy is not the same as our body. The body is like a container that our energy uses to get around on this three-dimensional plane of existence. It is not us. We are energy and energy cannot be destroyed, only changed. It is possible to learn to leave the container, your body, and move around. As I understand it, you can't do much but observe in your spirit form; you have no substance. But if you are really powerful, you can be seen. Matthew used a lot of energy to be here with us. He must be very powerful," Ariana told the group.

Leesie responded, "I read something on the net that some people get so good at astral projection that they can manipulate things. People can hear them and they can touch and move things. But you know how the web is, there's a lot of BS among a little truth."

"Do you think he's all right?" worried Tara. "Can using up all the energy he did doing the astral projecting cause him harm?"

"No, I don't think so," responded Ariana, "I think he'll just have to rest."

Zach's cell phone buzzed. Pulling it out of his pocket he announced, "It's a text from Matt!"

"What does it say?" Tara asked.

"On my way to Lame Deer," read Zach.

"What the heck is Lame Deer?" Leesie asked.

"That's where Matt's Cheyenne grandfather lives. It's in Montana. I'm sure he's going to his grandfather for help. His grandfather is a medicine man. He's been working with Matt every summer since Matt was ten years old. He's been teaching Matt the path of the medicine man," said Zach. "Matt must realize what's happening and is trying to fight it."

"Text him back that we are all supporting him and that no matter what, we love him," Ariana insisted.

They waited, hoping that Matthew would text Zach back, but after several long minutes, they realized they were not going to hear anything else from him. At least they knew Matthew was safe and on his way to find help that he trusted. They had done all they could do for now.

No one was surprised when Andrew exclaimed, "I'm starving! Let's go eat!"

Wendy smacked Andrew on the arm as though he was out of line, but Ariana assured them that eating was an excellent idea. "When you build and send out that much energy," she informed them, "it takes a lot out of you. Besides resting, food is a wonderful way to replenish the energy we expended. Let's go get a big, gooey pizza."

Chapter 14

Matthew looked out the window of the Greyhound bus, watching the world pass by in the darkness. He was trying to clear his mind and just be, but his mind would not shut off. He knew he would be on the bus for at least 20 hours. Lots of time to think, whether he wanted to or not.

Heading for Lame Deer was almost a reflex for Matthew. Since he was ten, whenever he was confused or scared, he went to his namee'me', his grandfather. Talking with his grandfather always made Matthew feel better.

Namee'me' was a Cheyenne—shaman—a medicine man. He was wise and knowledgeable in so many areas especially spirituality, healing, and living in balance with the planet. Matthew had been working with him over the past eight years on how to return his energy to a proper balance of love and calm. His grandfather was teaching him how to allow peace and forgiveness to flow through him instead of anger, guilt, and pain. Matthew knew he needed his grandfather's help more now than ever. In the past 72 hours, The Darkness had consumed him and had actually convinced him of things that his higher self knew were lies. He felt as though there were two beings fighting for control of his soul. The Darkness and the Matthew he had worked so hard to become. Approximately four hours ago, he realized The Darkness was winning. He decided then that he had only two choices. He could go to his namee'me' or he could commit suicide. Already guilt ridden, he could not hurt Zach or Tara, so suicide was out. The way he had treated Zach earlier had sent him into such a whirlwind of despair that he had blocked Tara from feeling what was going on within him. He knew he had hurt both his friends deeply and when he felt their outpouring of love, he knew he had made the right decision. He would fight for his life, his soul, and his group. That's when he had bought the ticket to Lame Deer, Montana where the Northern Cheyenne reservation and his grandfather were.

Even though the bus was heated, Matthew could feel the cold as the vehicle drove through the mountains near Flagstaff, Arizona. He leaned against the icy window, fogging it with his breath. He saw snow at the side of the road. Leaving in such a great hurry, he didn't think to bring his coat. All he was wearing was his gray hoodie. He knew that would not provide enough warmth. Living in Tempe, Arizona with its mild climate made it hard to remember it was winter almost everywhere else. As he neared Montana, Matthew would have to call his grandfather and ask him to pick him up at the bus station. If he tried to hitchhike, he would freeze.

The other thing Matthew forgot to bring was money. After paying for his ticket, he only had 14 dollars and some change left. He had a debit card, but he didn't want to spend any of his scholarship or student loan money unless he absolutely had to. *Oh well, depending on how much time I miss, I may not be in school for long anyway,* he thought.

Pulling out his phone, Matthew decided to watch a movie to try and prevent his mind from thinking depressive thoughts. *Son of a bitch, no signal. WTF!* Realizing he was feeling annoyed, Matthew took several deep breaths and willed himself to relax. He thought about meditating but was afraid that might let The Dark take over. *I guess I'll play a game, one that doesn't need the internet. Angry Birds maybe?* Three hours later, he fell asleep.

Matthew awakened only when the bus stopped for a restroom and food break. Stepping off the bus to stretch his legs, he noticed he was starving. There was a McDonald's inside the rest stop. After gulping down a cup of coffee and two Sausage McMuffins, Matthew went into the bathroom to wash his face and use the facility.

"Hey, guy, you wouldn't have some spare change would you?" a rough voice asked.

Matthew turned to say no, sorry, when he was overwhelmed by the stench of imminent death. He gagged. *Oh, shit. I yell at Ariana for not double shielding, and here I am, wide open,* he admonished himself.

The man before Matthew was ragged and obviously in bad shape.

"What happened to you?" Matthew asked, clearly disturbed by what he felt and saw from this man.

"Been on the road a long time," he answered. "Ever since I got back from Afghanistan, I can't stand being indoors for long or around people much. Was camping outside Zion. Some bikers came to my hidey-hole and decided to hassle me for my stash. They took exception to me fighting back and did me over real good. I think I got a broken rib or two."

"I'm no expert," Matthew advised, "but I think you might have some internal bleeding. You need a hospital, man."

"No money and no VA anywhere close. I just need some food. Can you help me out?"

Matthew was torn. The guy really needed an ambulance. Matt was sure something was very wrong, but didn't know how to convince him. *Maybe if I buy him some food, I can talk him into going to the hospital.*

"Okay, let's get you some food," Matthew said.

Matthew bought the stranger breakfast. They sat down together in a booth near a window overlooking the parking lot. Matthew watched as the stranger gulped down two Egg McMuffins and coffee. His left eye was almost closed now, purple bruising extending down his cheek. There appeared to be a deep cut on the right side of his jaw and there was blood on his forehead, possibly from a scalp wound. The stranger winced every time he moved. He looked considerably worse in the bright sunshine than he had in the bathroom.

"Wow man, you look terrible," Matthew exclaimed. "Those guys really did a number on you."

"Yeah, the SOBs didn't want to leave their work poorly done."

"But why?" Matt asked.

"Nobody needs a reason anymore," the stranger said. "People are just shit. See a dude on hard times, bash his skull in. Humanity doesn't deserve to survive. Look what we're doing to each other: wars, starvation, rape, and what we're doing to the planet. People are worse than locust, we're a plague!"

"There are some good folks out there, too. Not everyone is bad," Matthew protested.

The stranger looked at Matthew like he was completely naïve. "Listen, man, I've been to war. If you'd seen what I have, you'd give up too. What's the use? The best thing for this planet would be to wipe it clean and start over."

Matthew didn't want to give up that easily. "Don't you have some friends, family?"

"Family's the first ones to let ya down and friends," he snorted, "when the goin' gets rough, the friends ditch ship. Nah, it's better to just go it alone."

See? This guy knows. Your friends will let you down now that they see you as weak, said a voice in Matthew's mind.

"When I came back from Afghanistan," the stranger continued, "I was shot up both mentally and physically. Even the VA let me down. My family, what a joke, wanted me to be the man I was before I went away." He looked at Matthew with haunted eyes and said, "Humans can do some horrible things to each other. How do you forget that and just go on?"

This man needs your support. Are you going to let him down like you did your mother? You don't need to go to your grandfather's. He doesn't even know you're coming, the voice reminded him. Matthew felt himself becoming depressed and disillusioned. *Listen to the stranger. He's seen it, what the world is really like. There's nothing you can do to change it.*

Even though the sun was shining brightly, Matthew felt a dark cloud obscuring everything. His mood continued to darken as he absorbed The Darkness inside the stranger and allowed it to add to his own.

"If I had my gun," the stranger said, "I'd blow away some people. I'd hunt down the bastards that did this to me and show them who the hell they're dealing with!" Racking coughs began to shake the man's entire body and when he took his hand from his mouth, there were flecks of blood on the napkin.

It alarmed Matthew more that this stranger was bleeding than that he was thinking about killing people. *Yeah,* Matthew thought, *why shouldn't we hunt them down and blow them away?* He heard the voice in his head say, *While we're at it, let's just take out everyone who's hurt us.* Terrified, Matthew responded to the voice, *No, I don't think like this!*

Answering the stranger Matthew said, "I have some really good friends that are always there for me, one in particular, Zach, never lets me down. There are good people out there."

"Yeah, until he meets a babe, then you're toast. If she doesn't like you, see how fast he finds excuses to dump your ass."

You know that's true, said the voice in his head, *it's already happening.* Matthew thought about the past few days and how badly he had felt. He thought about his friends and immediately he felt their love. He felt torn, ripped in two like the old cartoons with the devil on one shoulder and an angel on the other. *Listen to the stranger. Can't you see he needs you?* the voice said again, taking his mind away from the feeling of love and back to the guilt and pain. *The others don't need you. They have each other. There's no place for you. If the rest of the group knew who you really are and what you've done, they'd run screaming.* The Darkness inside him was creating a feeling of deep isolation, separation, and despair.

Looking out the window, Matthew noticed that snow had started falling. Big, fluffy snowflakes had begun to turn the world outside white. It was magical. He felt his inner warrior begin to reawaken. *I will fight this darkness. This world is beautiful and worth fighting for even if there are some f'd-up people in it,* he thought.

Matthew began to surround himself with a blanket of white light. He envisioned himself lying in the snow creating snow angels with his friends, laughing. As soon as he thought of his friends, their love bombarded him. He knew they were all sending him love, clarity, and healing. He breathed it in. With each breath he felt more renewed and whole. *I can do this!*

Turning to the stranger he said, "I have to get on my bus now, but before I go, I'm calling 911. You can stay and let them help you, or you can leave. Your choice. You have filled yourself with so much darkness that you cannot even see The Light anymore. I was there for you and I'm just another dude with pain and fear and disillusionment, but the difference between us is that I still believe in having hope and fighting for this world. I still believe in The Light. Later."

"You'll be sorry dude," the stranger said hatefully, "the Dark doesn't let go real easily. It's already in there and sooner or later, you'll turn, just like everyone else."

Matthew kept walking. *The difference between him and me,* he thought, *is that I know The Light is still there, too. Between my namee'me' and my friends, I'll give the Dark one hell of a fight.*

Chapter 15

"Have you noticed the garbage that is all over the place?" Wendy asked Ariana.

"All over where and what garbage?"

"You know, the news: radio, TV, social media, media of every sort. All they can talk about is what's wrong or bad. It used to be around the holidays people became happy and there were all kinds of stories about the good people were doing in the world. Now all you hear is war, terrorism, flu, Ebola, shootings, politics, and internet hacking. No wonder people are irritable!"

"You know you have choices," Ariana reminded Wendy. "You can watch something else, not listen to the junk and focus on what you are seeing around you, or you can let it get to you. How are things going with your classes? Do you feel loved by Andrew, your friends or your family? Is the weather beautiful? Even if the answer to all those questions is no, if you look hard enough you'll find something to be grateful for. What you focus on grows. You know that. If you focus on what's negative, you become more negative and see everything from darkness. That way everything seems ominous and ugly. You make up stupid stories in your head about things that aren't even real, like maybe Andrew's found someone else. Then you become miserable about that and it's not even reality. But if you fill yourself with gratitude for what is working in your life, then everything seems easier and good things just keep coming. Wendy, please don't fall back into old habits. Focusing on what you think may be wrong or fearful is a path that you have walked unsuccessfully before, remember?"

"Yeah, you're right. Been there, done that. Maybe you need to adjust my energy again?"

Ariana gave Wendy's aura, the energy that surrounds all things, a quick look then added some blue energy into Wendy's already orange aura. Blue was calming and healing so she thought that would help

Wendy be in better balance.

Wendy took a deep breath and smiled. "Yup, that's what I needed. When's Zach coming to pick you up and take you to the psychic?"

"He'll be here in about 20 minutes."

"You sure you don't want me to go with you, like for moral support or something?"

Ariana laughed. "I think I'll be all right. What do you think she's going to do to me anyway?"

Wendy looked embarrassed when she replied, "Sorry, some of my old religious programming coming through. I guess I'm letting myself worry that you'll be cursed or something."

"Curses aren't real. God is the one with all the power, anything else needs the power you give it to thrive. I won't give up any power to anything negative. I believe in love, light, and us," Ariana answered passionately.

"And I believe in us," Zach said as he walked into their room.

Ariana walked toward Zach to give him a welcoming hug. "And anyway, I'm well protected. I'll have Zach, the Elders, my oma, and my guides. Nothing can get through that force field. I'm also triple-shielded with God's White Light of protection."

"Protected from what?" Zach asked.

"Oh, Wendy's in the mood to be worried about everything. Old habits die hard," said Ariana.

"Sorry," Wendy apologized, "I'll focus on all the good that will come out of this, what, session? Reading? What's it called?"

Ariana thought a moment and said, "Let's call it help or enlightenment."

As they walked to the car Zach asked Ariana, "So, you're not scared at all? Not even a little nervous?"

"No, actually I'm feeling very hopeful. We need some help and after reading the psychic's website, I think this is the person that can give it. I meditated this morning too, and the Elders are feeling confident as well."

"We have about a half hour's drive," Zach told her. "When we get there do you want me to come in or wait in the car?"

"I think I'd prefer if you waited in the car, that way we aren't feeding her any information. I want her to know nothing about me. Not even that I have a boyfriend."

Zach nodded then asked, "What did she ask you when you called to make an appointment?"

"She asked whether I needed a day or night appointment. She wanted my first name and phone number."

"That's it? Well, she can't get much from that, I don't think. Are you going to ask any questions?"

Ariana answered, "No, at least not at first. I want to see what she tells me. If I think she's for real, then maybe I'll ask some things."

"Like about Matthew?"

"Yes," Ariana replied, "but other things, too. Stop quizzing me. You're making me nervous. Let's enjoy the ride, the beautiful day, and us being together. Okay?"

Ariana turned on the radio and the two of them sang along to songs, talked about classes, and how well the group seemed to be doing even after the problem with Matthew. Everyone still seemed to be positive and confident that he would be back. They both relaxed and enjoyed the ride.

"There it is," Zach announced, "6919 West Wren Court. The house doesn't even look haunted," he said with a smile. "We're right on time. Give me a kiss goodbye and I'll see you in an hour."

Ariana gave him a quick kiss on the nose.

"Oh, no you don't," Zach exclaimed. "You're not getting out of here without giving me something wonderful to think about."

The kiss was warm, the embrace warmer. Ariana breathed in Zach's scent and held him for as long as she thought wise. When they parted, he stroked her cheek and looked deeply into her eyes. Ariana knew he was worried for her, but she was feeling happy and optimistic. Kissing his nose again she smiled and said, "Be back real soon."

Jumping out of the car, she walked the short distance to the front door. The house looked like any other tract home in any American city. It was two stories, painted a pale blue with lots of blooming bottlebrush bushes and other flowering plants lining the walkway. The front door was painted a slightly darker shade of blue and had a beautiful stained glass window panel on one side. Ringing the doorbell, Ariana waited for a response. When the door opened, Ariana was slightly surprised by what she saw. She shouldn't have been. She had seen the woman's picture on her website. But subconsciously, Ariana had been expecting a weirder looking individual. The woman who answered the door, however, was an average looking grandmother holding a small furry dog.

"Hi, I'm Lydia, come on in," the psychic offered, holding the door wide. "If I don't stop the dog, he'll take off. You don't mind dogs, do you? Of course you don't, I can tell by how you're responding. He'll leave us alone as soon as we begin, but he has to sniff everyone that comes into the house to make sure they're acceptable."

"He's adorable. What kind of dog is he?" Ariana asked, reaching out to pet the squirmy little creature.

"It's debatable. He was found on the street. We're going this way, but watch your step as there's a step down here that's not easy to see when you're coming in from the bright sunlight," she said as she put the dog down and led the way through the living room to an office. It was a perfectly ordinary office, containing a desk, book shelves, two chairs, and two computers. There were angel and fairy figurines, books, as well as Venetian glass on the book shelves.

"Have a seat," the psychic instructed. "There are a few things I like to go over with people the first time they come to me. Okay?"

"Absolutely," replied Ariana.

"I'm going to be contacting your guides. Do you know what guides are?"

Ariana answered, "No," not wanting to divulge anything useful about herself.

"The easiest way to describe them is they are like guardian angels. They are not loved ones who have passed. You guides are with you from birth. I believe you knew your guides in past lives. They're the little voices you hear when you're about to do something stupid and you hear 'stop!' or the voice you hear that says, 'be careful of this person' when you meet someone. Because I believe they always have your best interests at heart, I will tell you everything they show me. I will censor nothing. They won't show you anything you absolutely can't handle unless you ask them a question you really don't want the answer to. No question is trivial. They usually begin by going over your physical body to warn you about anything you might need to pay closer attention to. Then they'll go into what's happening in your life right now, followed by the potential for the future. I say potential because the gift and curse we were given by God at birth is free will. This allows you to change anything I tell you today, good or bad.

Now, I need your full name as it appears on your birth certificate. Then I will say a prayer out loud, which opens me to your guides and the Akashic records, the records of all you've been in past lives and all you may become in the future. When I get to the end of the prayer, I will tell you what they're showing me. Okay?"

Ariana nodded yes.

"May I have your full name, please?"

"Ariana Joanna Abrams."

"Okay, bear with me a moment," the psychic said, closing her eyes and taking a very deep breath.

Ariana watched the psychic's aura. It extended out from her body and began to encompass the two of them. Ariana was now within the psychic's aura. It was amazingly alive and vibrant. It contained all of the visible color range and as she listened, she realized that the two auras were blending, creating a wonderful, harmonious sound. Ariana felt fantastic. Continuing to watch the psychic, Ariana became aware that within her aura were people she assumed were the psychic's guides. There were so many and they were all smiling at her. After about a minute, the psychic began the prayer out loud.

"I ask God if he will have his shield of love and truth around Ariana Joanna Abrams so only love and truth exists and only love and truth exists between me and Ariana. I ask that the guides and loved ones of Ariana Joanna Abrams channel to me and give me whatever information they see fit. I open myself to the Lords of the Akashic records so that I may look into her records and remove whatever information I am allowed." Opening her eyes, the psychic looked at Ariana's left shoulder. "There's a dead woman behind you. A grandmother?"

"Both my grandmothers are dead," Ariana answered.

"This one loves you very much. She is also saying that she is very proud of you and the work you and your friends are doing. She thinks that you are a good leader and with you, the group has the best chance of success. Does any of that make sense to you?"

"Yes."

"Do you believe in reincarnation?" asked the psychic and when Ariana nodded, continued. "First, you need to understand that this is not the only inhabited planet or even dimension. I don't believe that you are originally from Earth. As a matter of fact, I think you may have only been here once before, at the very inception of this planet. Consequently, this planet and its people may seem very strange to you. I believe that you are an original Lemurian."

"I'm not familiar with that term. What does that mean?" inquired Ariana.

"The Lemurians were a race of aliens that seeded this planet. They terraformed it like in that Star Trek movie. The majority of them left after doing this, but a few beings were left behind to monitor the survival of the inhabitants they had created. I believe you were one of these. These aliens were very long lived. The myths of them continue in many cultures including the Old Testament. When you were younger, did you feel as though you were lost and didn't belong here?"

"Yes," Ariana admitted.

"Often those people who are not from this planet have thoughts like they don't belong here or that they want to go home. Many can't relate to members of their families, nor do their families relate to them. It is often hard on them until they understand why. I can tell that you had a very difficult home life. You have a lot of old hurt inside that you must rid yourself of. It will do damage to your body if you don't. There is a saying I like in regard to this, 'Resentment and anger are as though you have taken poison and expect the other person to die.' Those who hurt you have moved on even though you haven't. These feelings of resentment and anger then begin to destroy your thinking and your body. You are too smart to allow anything to take your power. You are an old soul even though your lifetimes have been elsewhere."

Darn! I thought I had rid myself of all the old hurt and anger. More work to do, I guess.

The psychic continued, "I also feel a male around you. Do you have a new love interest?"

Ariana shook her head yes.

"He was with you the first time you lived on Earth, but he was Atlantian, not from Lemuria. He owes the planet because of the destruction he caused when he was here then. You are here also to help prevent a repeat of that life. You have a lot of work ahead of you, but you also have some extreme psychic abilities to help you accomplish your purpose and help you have from other realms. Am I scaring you?"

"No, you are answering some important questions for me. Are you saying Zach and I are meant to be together to accomplish some big deed?" asked Ariana.

"That is your soul's intent. Remember, I spoke of free will earlier? In most cases, humanity has a great deal of latitude in each life. As long as the soul is learning, it lets the ego do its own thing. Of course the ego must be working according to the soul's script, but there's still a lot of leeway. In your case, however, that is not true. Your soul has one mission: to save our planet, anything else is unacceptable. There will be times when you will feel driven, almost obsessed, but at other times you will feel unequal to the task. You are not. You have help all around you, on this planet, dimension and plane, as well as on others. Your guides and teachers and even the people of your planet are teaching, observing, and sending energy. You are not alone in this endeavor.

I feel an adult who is not a family member. Are you seeing a counselor?"

"Yes, why?" asked Ariana.

"Because she is here to help you, too. It is no accident that you ended up here in Arizona, or with this counselor, or for that matter, your current friendships. All this was put in motion, in case it was ever needed, centuries ago. I, too, have been waiting for you even though I didn't realize it till now."

Ariana was shocked. All this was preordained? She felt like a token in a game, perhaps the old shoe in Monopoly. Was the psychic telling her she had no free will of her own? That she was just following a destiny written for her with no way out? So Zach didn't like her for herself? He was programmed, too?

The psychic continued, "This disturbs you. I understand why you are feeling this way. It does not mean that the people in your life do not really care about you. On the contrary, because they still have free will, they can choose not to follow you. They may even choose to work against you. This is a problem you are concerned with now, right? You are worried about a member of your group leaving? Remember, each ego must work through soul lessons in their own way. Some will succeed, others may not. There is nothing you can do to help their growth. I realize I've just given you an overload of information, much of which you probably didn't want to hear, correct?"

Ariana responded, "I want to hear everything. Burying my head won't accomplish my goals. I need stark reality. How do I do this? How do I fight The Darkness with only six or seven other people?"

"You enlist the aid of the thousands of others out there that are waiting to be activated. You learn about your enemy and techniques that have worked in the past to defeat it and you develop new ones for the future."

"There is so much we need to learn. Do you teach classes?"

"Yes, as a matter of fact, I have one starting a week from Sunday. They're from one to four in the afternoon. You might also want to consider coming to my first Friday channeling sessions. I think you could learn a lot there, too," the psychic suggested.

"Friday night is when we have group therapy. I don't think we could attend," Ariana said.

"If your counselor doesn't think it is a good idea to miss group once a month, then perhaps we can figure something else out," offered the psychic.

"My friend, the one that's gone missing, will he be able to fight off The Darkness?"

"Let me see if your guides know," Lydia replied. She became quiet for several seconds then she asked out loud, "Equinoxx, can you access this person or her guides to see if they will answer that question?" Turning back to Ariana she explained, "Equinoxx are the entities I channel once a month. I don't usually use them except for channelings and occasional private readings, but because this is the week I'll be channeling, I know they are around. Okay, what I am hearing is that your friend is fighting hard. He has just passed one hurdle and he is on his way to find expert help. He knows he's fighting and he knows he needs help and is seeking it. Sounds like a good strategy to me."

Ariana felt considerably better and decided to ask about some of the others in the group. "He has a polarity, Tara. Will she be all right while he is fighting or will she be sucked into the fight? What happens if he doesn't succeed, will she be damaged?"

"She is the one in the most danger. If The Darkness can't get to him, it will try to get to her. The group must keep her close and insist that she alert all of you if anything uncomfortable happens," Lydia answered. "Tara is not her real name, is it?"

That took Ariana by surprise. "I don't know. I would think not, but I don't know her by any other name."

"Like your lost one, she has had a lot of pain in this life. Neither person is fully understood by anyone. Both feel separate from all other people. You and your other friends are the closest relationships these two have ever had. Both have had family members injure them in ways that children should never be hurt. And both feel guilty and blame themselves. The Dark can use that guilt and pain."

Ariana said, "We have a very young one in the group. She is only 15. I am worried about including her in this fight. She is so young and naïve."

"But she is a very old soul who is extremely brilliant. She is the one you should be worried about the least. She is very resilient, partially because she is naïve, but also, she had a solid family upbringing. She absolutely believes she's safe and trusts in all of you, her family, and God," Lydia assured her. "Again, don't worry about her. Isn't there another male involved?"

"Yes," agreed Ariana.

"He is also vulnerable. He sees himself as the protector of the group. That is a huge under taking. Because you are a group, no one person should have all the responsibility for anything. Think of how exposed that makes the group. If anything happens to the sole person responsible, then everyone will be out of luck."

"How do I help him to realize it isn't all on him?"

"By discussing with your group the concept of teamwork. Each of you has personal abilities and strengths, but all should be ready to fill in for any of the others if needed. That includes you, Ariana; you are also vulnerable. As long as you believe success or failure is all your responsibility, you can be attacked, too. It is not preordained what will happen. You understand, don't you, that a majority of people alive on the planet also have to agree with what you aim to do. Actually, I don't have any idea what the exact number is. Equinoxx calls it the hundredth monkey. Are you familiar with the term?"

"No," Ariana admitted.

"The hundredth monkey effect is a phenomenon in which a new behavior or idea spreads rapidly from one group to all related groups once a critical number of members of one group exhibit the new behavior or acknowledge the new idea. Essentially, when there are enough of us that believe The Light is stronger than The Darkness and allow ourselves to change the current paradigm that says that mankind must be controlled by fear, lack, pain, loss, greed, then this planet will stop being fear based. There are others, many in the media, who are also working on helping with this enlightenment. You are not alone in this. Do you have any more questions?"

"Is there something I'm forgetting to do, or something really important I need to be considering?"

"Keep everyone communicating, especially Tara and the other male I felt. Additionally, let your new man know that it is not his job to take care of you. He is a caretaker, so it will be hard for him to understand that, but if you allow yourself to acquiesce to his directions or demands then you will not be the leader you are supposed to be. You worry too much about hurting him. Speak honestly. Also, there is more danger around Tara. Warn her."

"Thank you. Is it possible for you to read for the group of us all at the same time?"

"I've never tried that before," Lydia admitted. "I am also concerned about only having one hour to work with an entire group. I think perhaps coming to the channeling might work best first. If not the public one, maybe I can figure out something else. I'll be sending you a link to download the recording I've made for you of our session today. Maybe for now, if you are comfortable doing it, you can let everyone listen to it."

At the front door, the two women hugged. Ariana had not felt this comfortable with anyone besides the group since her grandmother died. She knew she would be back. She was convinced they had found their teacher.

Chapter 16

"Did everybody listen to the recording?" Ariana asked the group. Seeing everyone nod she continued, "What do you guys think?"

"I've got to admit, what she said about me really has me feeling freaked," Tara said. "Twice she repeated that I was in danger. What kind?"

"I'm sorry I didn't ask, but I don't think she knew precisely what kind of danger, only that you are more vulnerable than the rest of us. If Matthew gets himself together, The Darkness may try for you in an effort to weaken Matt again. Or if he doesn't get it together, The Dark could come for you because it thinks you are weaker now."

"So what do I do? I'm using all the protections I know about," replied Tara.

Ariana thought a moment then said, "First off, I don't think you should be alone in your condo. Do you have a spare bedroom?"

"You know she does," Leesie spoke up. "It's the rose colored one with the beautiful flowers. Don't you remember?"

"Oh yes, sorry. I'm not thinking as clearly tonight as I should. Anyway, if it's okay, I think one of us should stay with you. And Andrew, until Matthew returns, I think you should move in with Zach."

"Me, why?" Andrew asked, clearly disturbed. "I don't need a babysitter."

"I don't think any of us should be alone while Matthew is fighting this thing," Ariana explained.

"But if someone moves in with Tara, then one of us will be alone," Teja objected.

"That's why it will be both Wendy and me. If we both don't fit in the bed, then one of us will sleep on the couch. Okay, Tara?" asked Ariana.

"Won't that be hard on you two?" Tara questioned.

"Heck no," Wendy said excitedly. "It will be like a slumber party. I think it will be awesome!"

"Well, if you're sure it won't put you out, then I think I'd really like that," Tara admitted.

"Don't you think Matt might get mad if he comes home suddenly and finds someone else in his bed?" wondered Zach.

"Yeah, I don't want to take over the dude's space or anything," Andrew agreed.

"Zach, you can text him what we're doing and explain that we are trying to make sure that The Dark doesn't make things worse for him by his worrying about us," suggested Leesie.

"Hey, why don't I just move in here with Wendy?" Andrew asked.

"Whoa, boy," said Wendy, blushing. "I'm enjoying our relationship, but isn't it just a little too soon to move to the next level?"

Andrew smiled broadly as he said, "Well, you can't blame a guy for trying."

Ariana turned to Zach, "Go ahead and see if you can reach Matt. Ask him if he's at his grandfather's place yet and if he's okay."

As Zach texted, the rest of the group discussed what the psychic said. They all agreed that she seemed to have gotten to the point pretty rapidly and had been right on the money about everything she'd said. There was some concern about how many people it would take to create the hundredth monkey effect, but Leesie assured everyone that getting the word out through Twitter, Facebook, and several other websites and blogs was sure to enlist helpers from all over the globe.

"We could even make some videos and put them on YouTube. If they go viral, we're all set," Andrew said.

"Yeah, like that's easy," Teja chided.

"You never know," Tara offered. "In the last five years, more people have learned about transgendered kids via media than in the last 1,000. It's amazing what is possible now if you know how. We're all pretty smart. I think we can come up with lots of ways to get people talking."

"Maybe they'll even make a movie about us," Leesie dreamed. "I call dibs on Jennifer Lawrence playing me."

"Yeah, right," Andrew laughed, "and Zach Efron can play me."

"Has Matt texted back yet?" Ariana asked.

"No," Zach answered her, "but it's only been a couple of minutes.

Give him a chance."

"It's been two days since he left," Wendy said, "he'd be there by now, wouldn't he?"

Zach replied, "I would think so. Wait! Okay, he says he's there and do what we need to do."

"I hate texting," Leesie announced. "You can't tell if he's okay with it or if the 'do what we need to do' is him being snarky."

"Ask him if we can call him," Ariana suggested.

Zach's sent the message. "He says it's a bad time. He'll call later tonight. I'll make sure everything's good then. Anything else we need to ask him?"

"Just find out how he's doing, what he's doing, and when he's coming back to us," Ariana said.

"Yeah, and tell him we all miss his face a lot," Leesie interjected.

"Are we going to talk to the therapist about group Friday night?" asked Teja. "I'd really like to go to that channeling thing so I can see the whole thing from the other side. You know, when it isn't me speaking German and being someone's grandmother."

"I'd like to go, too," Tara said. "I'm really curious about this psychic."

"How many people usually go?" Zach asked.

"I don't know. I didn't ask her," admitted Ariana.

"Do we really want a whole group of people hearing what we're talking about?" asked Andrew.

"You doofus. We want people to know what we're doing so they'll join us," Leesie declared.

"Duh, I meant our confusion and lack of knowledge about this stuff," Andrew answered.

"Okay children, take a break," Teja cautioned. "We need to at least appear as though we are a together group of people."

Andrew looked hurt when he replied, "We were just playing. Somebody's got to lighten things up now and then."

"I have my regular session tomorrow with the therapist so I'll ask her if she minds if we go. I'll also try to explain where Matthew is," offered Ariana.

"Sounds like we've decided to go," Zach said. "Are we sure?"

"I am," said Leesie.

Zach glared at Leesie. "We haven't really discussed what she told Ariana or what we expect to get out of this channeling."

"What's bothering you, Zach?" Ariana asked.

Ariana could tell Zach was feeling troubled. When they drove home from Lydia's yesterday, Ariana had told him everything she could remember about what Lydia had told her. He was quiet then, too, but she assumed he was thinking about all the information she had gotten. But all through this meeting, Zach had seemed a little off. *Maybe he's still really worried about Matthew,* she thought.

"I don't know what's bothering me. I just feel uncomfortable with all this," Zach said.

Ariana was confused. "Uncomfortable with all what?" she asked.

Zach replied, "The stuff she told you. This channeling shit. We seem to be giving this psychic a lot of power and none of us know anything about her. How do we know she's not part of The Darkness?"

"My Gram has known her for like, 30 years. She really respects and trusts her. We researched her on the web, too. Ariana felt good with her and even claimed her aura was wonderful. What more do you need?" Teja asked.

"Zach, what's really going on here?" said Ariana.

"What do you mean? Now you don't believe me?"

"No, but it just feels like there's something you're not looking at," Ariana replied. Like a flash of deep insight, Ariana suddenly knew what was bothering him. "It's the past life thing, isn't it? The idea that you did something in a past life that created this whole situation. Oh Zach, that wasn't you. Remember what Matt said. You are not that person. You're the person that will repair the damage, but **you** didn't cause it!"

"That's not how Lydia made it sound," he argued.

"You weren't there. I know what I felt and observed when she talked about it. It was our souls not us. We are the actors in **this** play not that one. I know it's confusing because we see things linearly, in a straight line, and we think we are our souls. But it's so much more complicated than that. That's what I'm hoping this Equinoxx can shed some light on. Please just go this once with us. Keep an open mind. Meet Lydia, and if you're still uncomfortable, we don't have to go back. There are other teachers in Arizona."

"Okay, just one time," Zach conceded.

Chapter 17

For the most part, Lame Deer isn't much of a town, even though it is the tribal and governmental headquarters of the Northern Cheyenne Indian Reservation. A lot of the businesses are boarded up and the town consists of plain brown or metal buildings, trailers and forlorn looking houses. The hills that surround it are green with sparse pine forests. There are slightly over 2,000 people who live here and most of them are poor. Matthew's grandfather is the spiritual elder of the tribe. He and his family have been well thought of for many generations, producing a continual series of shamans.

Even though it was not yet Thanksgiving, the weather was cold and bleak as the bus entered Lame Deer. A deep blanket of snow covered the ground and gritty slush remained in the streets. The dark sky promised more cold weather to come.

Matthew had not called his grandfather before he made the decision to come to Lame Deer. He hoped that he wouldn't mind or be angry. Matthew knew his grandfather was proud that he was going to college and would probably not be happy he was missing classes. *Why didn't I talk to him before I decided to jump on a bus and head here? Because I was too scared to think straight? Well, it's too late now,* he thought as the bus pulled into the station.

As he was getting off the bus, Matthew was surprised to see his grandfather sitting patiently on a bench outside the station. He rose as he saw Matthew, waved and smiled. Matthew had never felt so much relief; he was so glad to see him. They hugged briefly, Matthew feeling the safety he always felt when he was near his grandfather.

"How did you know I was coming? Did Zach call you?" Matthew asked suspiciously.

Matthew's grandfather looked at him through his black eyes now clouded with the blue of cataracts and said patiently, "Would I be a decent Medicine Man if the Elders and ancestors did not talk to me? I have been following your journey since I was alerted that the time for you and your friends had begun. I, too, have battled The Darkness. All on the path of the Shaman have. It is not unexpected that The Dark would be drawn to your ancient energy first. Our people are of the original seed. We are the protectors of this planet. All Native people were chosen to walk between the worlds to keep the energies on Earth in balance. Unfortunately, there are many white men and few of us, so the work has been hard and often we have failed. Do you not feel a brotherly kinship to the one called Ariana? Placed here on our reservation, would she not almost blend in? She, too, is of the original seed."

Matthew was so grateful that his grandfather was not going to condemn him for running away from The Darkness that he almost forgot about the biting cold. But soon he began to shiver and his grandfather placed an old leather coat on his shoulders. They walked to the truck in silence, Matthew trying to absorb this new information. His sleep-starved brain could make no sense of it all.

"Namee'me', if Ariana looks like our people, why do I look so different?"

"Like the white buffalo, a few among us look much like you, but it is the light in their soul that proclaims them Tsitsistas, the people, not their physical appearance. When the covenant was made with Maheo'o, the creator, we promised to be a peaceful people and care for this planet. But shortly after this was done, a new group of aliens came to exploit our earth mother. You are a mixture of these two races, the product of their two ideals: creation and exploitation. That is why there is a war within you. Maheo'o and the Thunder beings fight. They are unhappy with what has been done to this beautiful place. It will be destroyed if the balance is not righted. You contain the balance between these two opposite forces, just as your polarity contains the balance between male and female."

"I thought that I had released my past," Matthew said, "but all I did was bury it and by burying it I created a path for The Darkness to enter. If I can't even keep myself balanced how will I help the planet to succeed?"

"It is what is often done, burying the pain. People believe that not paying attention to a thing will make it vanish, but what they don't realize is that it actually empowers it because it can now be working in the background, unobserved. That is why a good Shaman knows what is happening in the observable world and also those levels that are most often unobserved, even those levels within ourselves. Now that you know what holds you back, you can face it, fight it, and perhaps eradicate it permanently. That is what a true warrior does—fights the battles within himself, not those outside himself that he projects his pain upon.

There is a wise man, a psychologist that spoke at the Grandmother Council gathering. His name is Eduardo Duran. He has come to the Native people to help us release the demons from our past. The people came to him with the usual challenges of Native peoples: substance abuse, health issues, domestic violence. But they told him these were not the real issues. The issue was soul loss. They told him if the parts of the missing soul were returned, then these problems would drop away. At first he was mystified, but soon he came to see what they said was true.

Duran shared with the attendees his discovery that a perpetrator committing an intended act of violence shoots a part of their own soul into the victim, almost like shooting them with an arrow. With this action he also removes a piece of his victim. He called it 'an act of sorcery.' It is for this reason that so many victims feel guilty, why so many feel like part of them has gone missing, that they are no longer whole. If the victim is an introvert, they turn their pain onto themselves, abusing substances to escape, harming themselves or, in the worst cases, committing suicide. If the victim is an extrovert, they turn their pain onto others, becoming abusers themselves in the illusion that this is killing off their own perpetrator. This may continue for generations, abused becoming abusers and so forth."

"How do we go about healing this?" asked Matthew.

His grandfather responded immediately, "Tomorrow we do a cleansing ritual called a sweat lodge."

"I've heard about those. Isn't it just a bunch of guys sitting in a hut, sweating and chanting?" Matthew said, though he knew it was much more than this.

"That is the white man's way. Our way is a ritual of cleansing and pulling together the lost parts of your soul. It is a sacred ritual practiced by all Native people for centuries. After you have completed this ritual you will go on your first vision quest."

Although Matthew had not participated in a sweat lodge ceremony, he did understand what it was meant to do and knew what a sacred event this was. It frightened him. He knew the experience was meant to allow him to know his spirit helpers and his power animals and to explore and rid himself of The Darkness that was hiding within. *What if the Great Spirit refuses me? How will I face my grandfather?*

"It is nothing to worry over. You are one of my family. You will do well," Grandfather said. "It is past time for this, but I was waiting for you to be called. Most people do their vision quest to figure out their path. You have already been chosen. You will do it to face your demons and learn to work with your personal spirits, ancestors, and animals. It is time to stop talking of your wolf and know him."

"Yes, Grandfather," Matthew replied, "I will succeed for you and the planet."

"No," his grandfather said angrily. "You will do this for yourself. It is your path and you must understand it. I have my own path, part of which is to be your teacher, but you must do this for yourself so that you will be fully committed to this path. Understand?"

"Yes, Grandfather, I **will** do this for myself and I **will** be brave."

"That is better. Now, you must prepare. You must fast from now on, not even water will touch your lips. Until the morning you must pray. This is your prayer:

> The most important thing is my relationship and my dependence upon the Creator and the spirits. Everything they show me is for my spiritual growth and the peoples' welfare. I know that with the help of the spirits I can do and I will do. Oh, Grandfather, I am so weak and pitiful. Help me for the sake of your people."

"Yes, Grandfather."

"If you feel like adding anything to the prayer from your heart, do it, but make sure you include those exact words I just said," Matthew's grandfather warned.

"Thank you, Grandfather."

"We've got to stop meeting like this," Zach said to the seven people crowding his Ford Mustang. "Really, one of you has got to buy a car. Aren't you a little tight back there?"

"Ha ha," said Andrew sarcastically. "Why don't you let me drive and you can hold two women on your lap at the same time."

"You've got the right size lap for that, man," teased Zach.

"How long are we going to be like this?" Wendy asked. "I don't like sharing my man, not even with my roomy."

Ariana answered, "Unfortunately, a while yet. Lydia lives on the other side of town in Glendale."

"I don't hear Tara bitching," Zach said. "She's smaller and is still holding Leesie on her lap."

"Leesie weighs less than a small dog," Andrew whined.

"Hey," chided Leesie. "Don't make fun of me cause I'm short. I'm still young, I could grow more!"

"Okay, children, we have to be on our best behavior because we want this woman to consider teaching us," Ariana reminded her friends. "We also want to learn as much as we can from this channeled entity. Did you guys write down some questions?"

"I wrote down a zillion of them and am having a very hard time deciding which ones to ask. Anyone need any extra questions?" Leesie asked.

"I might," Tara said. "I'm a pretty private person, so I don't think I'll be asking much for myself."

"I'm with you," Zach agreed, surprising Ariana. Obviously he was still uncomfortable about going tonight. *That's why all the silly banter,* she thought. *Everyone is uncomfortable. Duh!*

Ariana decided to try to ease their fears. "You know, guys, no one has to say anything. We could just listen. I don't think we'll be forced to do anything tonight. She didn't force me to talk during my session with her. She was kind, comforting, and easy to be around. I don't think things will be different tonight. Maybe you could practice your aura watching skills if you don't want to ask questions."

Leesie looked dumbfounded. "How can you dweebs actually be thinking about letting this opportunity get past you? We have a chance to ask all those questions we've been wondering about. We potentially have the source of infinite knowledge in these beings and you're afraid to ask questions? Whoa, dude! I'll ask for everyone then."

Teja gave Leesie a high five and stated, "Me, too. My Gram told me that this would be a great experience for me and I believe her. I plan to watch, listen, and ask all kinds of things."

"Me too," Wendy said. "Why not?"

"I'll decide after I've watched awhile," said Andrew.

"Let's try something," Ariana suggested. "Let's all think about what we would like to happen tonight. Call on your guides to be in attendance with you and ask them to help you know what you should ask. So breathe deeply, close your eyes, and just relax. Everyone except you, Zach," she added.

They rode in silence the rest of the way, each concentrating on what they wanted the evening to be like and what they wanted to learn. Each of them relaxed and allowed their fearful thoughts to dissipate as they fantasized a positive, insightful evening.

Ariana sent calm and serenity to Zach. She reached in and sent him the sensation of being held by her and kissed.

"You keep that up and we'll never get there," he whispered.

"Sorry."

"The calm was nice," he continued to whisper. "Just send that."

Ariana allowed herself to feel as though she was floating on a beautiful river. The sun was warm on her skin, but there was a wonderful cool breeze, too. The smell of honeysuckle was heavy in the air and the gentle sound of wind chimes was also present. She let her fingers trail in the cool water and watched the sunlight sparkle on its surface. Small fish darted toward her fingers then swam by rapidly. The boat she was riding in ran ashore and Ariana perceived herself walking on soft green grass. She was barefoot. She loved the feel of the cool tender shoots under her feet. There was a field with beautiful flowers. She walked into the field. The flowers were huge and fragrant and she drank in their pungent aromas. She felt almost intoxicated. Allowing the peace of this place to fill her mind and Zach's, she absorbed the amazing energy of this place until she knew they had turned into Lydia's cul-de-sac.

"Good thing we're early," Zach said. "There's no place to park on her street. We'll have to park on 70th Avenue somewhere. Either her neighbors have lots of cars, or there are going to be a lot of people attending."

"Great," Andrew moaned.

Leesie hit him hard in the arm. "Get a grip! You're not going to your funeral. You're going to a class. I bet your classes at school are a lot bigger than this. Are you scared to go to those, too?

"You'd better quit punching me, sprout. I'm getting really sick of it. I'll cope, so leave me alone," Andrew answered her testily.

"Someone's going to have to help me out of the car," Tara claimed. "My legs are asleep."

"Yeah, girl, amen! My butt's asleep, too," Teja announced. "Let's get going. A walk sounds great!"

The group walked the two blocks to the cul-de-sac, chatting and teasing each other. The neighborhood seemed normal with children playing and parents watching them from open doorways and chairs setup on their lawns. They could smell meat roasting on a backyard barbeque and heard a television and music playing somewhere. Shortly they came to Lydia's house. It glowed with light and they could hear laughter coming from inside. Climbing the three steps to the front door, each of them was wondering what would happen once they were inside.

Ariana rang the doorbell and heard several voices yell, "It's open, come on in." She opened the door to discover that the living room had been transformed into a small lecture hall. There were folding chairs setup in five rows facing the couch. There were several people seated in the chairs already and three on the couch. An attractive woman came into the foyer from the kitchen and said, "Hi, I'm Elaine. Welcome. Have any of you been to the channeling before? No, okay, let me go over some things. There are two bathrooms, one straight up the stairs and one down those two stairs and through the laundry room. I need to collect some money from you, then I will be giving you a ticket stub, you will use that for your second question. Don't lose it. In the kitchen are water, coffee, and tea if you want some. If you don't know how to use the coffee maker, I'll show you. It's not hard. Later there will be dessert. There's also a sign-in sheet for those of you that have never been here before. Lydia won't spam you or anything, but she would like to have your email address so she can tell you about upcoming classes or any changes. You may sit anywhere you want except the first row or the couch. Any questions?"

They found an empty row with four chairs and a row right behind the first that had three empty seats together. Everyone that was already seated seemed to know each other. They were having an animated conversation about the Iraqi Dinar, money from Iraq.

"Equinoxx doesn't believe that will ever happen, you know," one of the women stated.

"Yes, I know, but I'm not going to give up hope," a bald man with a German accent claimed. "If there are enough of us that believe, we can make it happen."

"Hi," said a woman standing next to Wendy. "I'm playing ambassador tonight. Are you new to this channeling?"

"Yes, we all are."

"You'll love it. I've been coming for almost three years now and it's my favorite thing I look forward to all month. I'm Wendy and if you have any questions, most of us here would love to help you."

"Did you say your name is Wendy?" Wendy asked.

"Yes, why?"

"Because that's my name, too. My mom was a Peter Pan fan."

"Well, now there will be three of us. I'm Wendy Two. The pretty blond is Wendy One, and I guess you'll be Wendy Three," the woman said amiably.

"I've never met another Wendy," Wendy confessed, "and now I've met two. Wow!"

"Wendy, who called me?" Wendy One said from her seat on the couch.

Wendy Two answered her, "We have another Wendy here, Wendy Three."

"That's weird. Can the world handle three of us?" Wendy One teased.

Zach was watching this exchange and whispered to Ariana, "They seem friendly and normal enough."

Ariana smiled and nodded.

Wendy Two introduced herself to the rest of the group and then introduced Wendy One, Victoria, Bernie, Len, and Holly. As everyone was saying hello, new people kept entering and taking seats. Even though there were many that seemed like regulars, Ariana noticed there seemed to be other newbies too.

"Where's Lydia?" Ariana asked Wendy Two.

"Oh, she's upstairs meditating. She'll be down at 7:30."

"Is it always this crowded?"

"This is about average. Somewhere between 15 and 20 is usual. It's been much bigger and much smaller, you can never tell," Wendy Two said. "I'm going to sit down because it's almost 7:30, but make sure you hang around after to talk. You'll enjoy it."

"You guys feeling more relaxed now?" Ariana asked the group. Everyone nodded yes. "It's almost time. Breathe! And remember what you programmed on the way over here."

Lydia came down the stairs and sat on the couch between the girls named Elaine and Wendy One. They spent the next ten minutes putting everyone at ease by explaining what they would be participating in and the sequence of the evening.

Lydia began, "I want to explain a little about what channeling is and how I will be doing it. There are two ways people channel. They can be awake and alert and be repeating what they are hearing said to them in their mind by a discarnate entity or person like a guide or loved one. This is what is often seen in readings or séances. Or their energy can be gone from their bodies and another energy, that of the entity or person that will be channeled, takes over. That is the kind of channel I am. Equinoxx explains this by calling me the vehicle. They claim it is similar to driving a car. If you have the key and the car runs, anyone can drive it. I will be gone and they will be controlling my body. Those of you that can see auras, I am told it will change often and is very interesting to watch. They use my left hand, I am completely right-handed. And they will speak very differently than I do. I am also told my face changes. They have a special greeting they use—it is Myama. It is like saying blessings, aloha, peace, an all-encompassing greeting. We suggest when you address them you say, 'Myama, Equinoxx. My name is…' Anyone have any questions about this? Good. The last thing, Elaine has transcribed some of the answers to old general questions and has put them on our Yahoo group. You must join the group to read them, but you can also use the group to email some general questions to be asked at future channelings, too. The group's name is transcendentjourney. Does anyone have any questions about any of this?"

"I do," Leesie said, raising her hand. "How do you know what happens while you are gone?"

"I don't. I have to rely on these people around me to tell me what has been said. We used to record the sessions but I can't listen or watch myself channel. It completely freaks me out. So either Elaine transcribes it for me, or people tell me what they think I should know."

"That sucks," Leesie exclaimed out loud. The room burst into laughter.

Lydia laughed too then said, "Don't be sad for me. I've had access to them anytime I want for 34 years."

"You can talk to them whenever you want?" Leesie asked. "How totally killer!"

Lydia laughed again and continued. "Now I'm going to ask all of you to do the hardest thing you will do all evening, create an unbroken circle by standing up and combining hands. If you can't reach someone's hand, touch their arm or shoulder. There, you got it. Now please just follow along with me and do as I ask. I would like you to feel a warm, tingling sensation in your left hand. Feel this warmth growing and fill your left hand with this wonderful white light energy, God's energy of healing and protection filling your left hand. Fill that hand so full of this beautiful, vibrant energy that it must begin to fill the entirety of your body. Fill your entire body with God's healing and love. Fill yourself so full of this light that it must spill out your right hand, thus connecting us in God's White Light of protection, healing, and energy. Fill the house, the country, the planet with this wonderful healing energy. Send this energy to everything and everyone that might need it and send clarity and peace to our world leaders. Keep building The Light." More quietly Lydia prayed, "I open myself to the entities known as Equinoxx and all other risen entities of the White Light and of God. I ask that my ego not be present tonight and all that comes through me be of God, be of Light, and be of truth. Okay, you can sit down now. Bear with me while I leave."

Ariana watched closely as Lydia's aura began to shimmer and change from the lavender blue that was her natural color to a vibrant array of shifting rainbow hues. Lydia's eyes were closed and her face had momentarily gone slack. Suddenly, the aura settled into a glittering golden light and her face became very animated. "Myama," said a voice that was energized and very different from Lydia's. "We are Equinoxx, and yes, we are of God. What is the group needing this wondrous evening?"

Elaine responded, "Thank you, Equinoxx. As usual we would like to know what we need to know right now, The Message for the World."

"It is of utmost importance for all of you to realize that the energy on Terra is shifting due to seismic activity, nuclear testing, volcanic activity and meteor activity, as well as a shifting of the poles. If you are familiar with the constellations and planets of your star system, you will have noticed that they are no longer in the exact positions they were even one of your years ago. The Inuit people have been warning your leaders of this change, but they have been ignored. The reason we are telling you of this phenomenon is that the shift is creating very erratic energies. Persons who are susceptible to changing energies will find themselves especially vulnerable to changing moods, health problems, and irritability. This can create extremes in behavior and those persons who are emotionally unstable may become volatile if they do not get help. It is imperative that you shield yourselves continually, even in your own homes. Keep your bodies and minds in balance through meditation, exercise, and right eating and thinking, but don't forget to help the others that have not been warned and do not know about energy. Do you understand us?"

There was a general acknowledgement.

"We also have some general questions for you, Equinoxx," Elaine explained. "Bernie, you're first."

"Myama, Equinoxx," he said. "Can you explain why humans decided to learn through suffering?"

Equinoxx replied, "Humans did not **decide** to suffer, they learned to. Originally this planet was a paradise for all that lived on or in it. The planet and all its inhabitants lived in balance with all things and each other. Your books speak of the planet then; they call it Eden. But this Eden had many more inhabitants than two. It was filled with people both from the seeding and from Lemuria. Eventually it drew the notice of another alien race. They came to explore and then exploit. They set themselves up as gods and lived on mountaintops. You have many myths of them as well. Because of their alien technologies, they were revered. Because of their demands and excesses, they were feared. They used this fear to create action from the humans much like one might train a dog: punishment and reward. Terra became fear-based and because of this indoctrination, humans began to believe the only way to be rewarded was to first be punished. Once a populace believes in a vicious superior being or beings, there must be those that are given the task of negotiating for humanity with this 'god' to bargain for the people. Thus, religions began and priests, ministers, rabbis, imams, and priestesses were created, taking away most human's ability to negotiate with this god themselves. They had to go through an intermediary. These religious leaders were given unprecedented power which continues today. We believe one of your wise men proclaimed, 'power corrupts and absolute power corrupts absolutely.' It was to their benefit to continue to teach that suffering is what is needed by God to allow a soul to progress to a better place than this one. Man walked out of Eden and has continued to walk away ever since. God would never want humanity to suffer. The Source is complete, boundless love. There is no judgment within this absolute love and no need to create suffering. Do you understand?"

"Yes, thank you, Equinoxx. Anyone else have any questions on this general question?" Elaine asked.

Ariana spoke, "Equinoxx, will you please explain what you mean by the seeding and Lemuria."

"Lemuria is the name given to the first settlement on Terra. It was founded by a group of alien scientists from the fifth star in Orion's belt. They created land from magma, planted seeds for plant, animal, and humankind. Theirs is the original DNA, the seed of humanity. They were hoping to create a perfect environment for the growth of creativity, imagination, and love."

"Who were the second group?" Wendy asked.

"They were also scientists, but this time from the star group the Pleiades. They wanted to experiment by altering the DNA, but were completely fascinated by humanity and the power that race gave to them. Their downfall was their egos. They now have karma with your planet and must attempt to right the wrong that they caused not only with the alterations they made which exterminated many of the plants and wildlife that had once thrived here, but also with humanity. Due to their intervention your planet is near extinction."

"So you're saying that there are alien beings on the planet now trying to fix things?" asked Ariana.

"Yes," answered Equinoxx.

"Are they all from the Pleiades?"

"No, some are from Meria, the founders of Lemuria."

"Anything else on this topic?" Elaine asked when everyone had become quiet. "Okay, I think maybe we should go to some personal questions now and then if there is time, we'll ask some more of these general questions. Wendy One, why don't we start with you?"

The group began asking questions about everything from boyfriend and children problems to health scans, spiritual paths, and personal karma. They followed the rows and each person in the row would ask their question or pass. The first of their group to be in the queue was Zach. Ariana was sure he wouldn't ask anything.

"Myama, Equinoxx. My name is Zach," he began. "Am I from the Pleiades?"

"Myama, Zach. You are correct. You worked very hard to stop what was happening, but you did not succeed. To this day you hold the guilt for your entire species. That is not necessary. You are doing the work and that is all that is required. Do you understand?"

"Yes, thank you Equinoxx."

Ariana could feel Zach's energy lift. She wanted to say something to him, but it was now her turn.

"Myama. I am Ariana and it is a pleasure to be here. What do you see as my soul path in this lifetime?"

"Myama, Ariana. It is our pleasure. We believe that you have been told your path, but we will also tell you that you are here to heal this planet and its people and animals. You will be the leader of a movement that we hope will create the hundredth monkey that will transport Terra from a fear-based, dying planet back to the Eden she is. You will open humanity's eyes to the wonders of Terra and their unlimited power so that their consciousness will be lifted and they will walk from the illusion that has prevented their growth. You are an original seed and were on

Terra during the first destruction. Do you understand?"

"I do. Thank you."

Other than Ariana's friends, everyone in the room seemed stunned by what they had just heard. Ariana could hear whispering all around her. People in the rows in front of her turned around to look. She began to feel uncomfortable.

Elaine seemed to sense that Ariana was feeling exposed and said, "Okay, who's next?"

Wendy answered, "Me, sorry. Myama, Equinoxx. I am another Wendy. What is my part in this grand plan?"

"You must communicate your group's intent to the animal kingdom to prepare them. They can also help your group accomplish your task. You will shortly be capable of communication at great distances with these creatures and they can tell you what they are doing and what is happening in their part of Terra. Your help will be invaluable."

"Wow, thank you. That's really, really wonderful!"

"Me, too, me, too!" Leesie exclaimed. "Not to sound redundant, but how about me? Oh, sorry, hi there, Myama. I am Leesie."

A very large smile appeared on Lydia's face and her aura became huge and bright violet. A new voice answered her, "Myama, friend Leesie. Your energy is wonderful. You are the generator. You will keep the momentum and be the holder of the memories. You will plan the approach to the calling of the others throughout the world that must be a part of the work. You will keep the group together, even when it involves thousands."

"Okay, I can do that," Leesie replied confidently.

"Myama. My name is Andrew. I don't really care what I'm here to do for the group, I'll do whatever needs to be done. But what I want to know is, do we have any chance at all of success?"

Equinoxx answered, "Many have been activated already. Many others will be soon. They are waiting for direction. Many humans desire change desperately. The timing is much better now than it ever has been. We cannot see if you will succeed, but we do know it is extremely important that you try."

Confused, Andrew asked, "Sorry, I don't want to ask two questions, but I don't understand what you mean by being activated."

"Being activated means awakened. Just as you have begun to

discover abilities you had very little awareness you possessed, others are finding these also. They are now being downloaded with information about the planet and the purpose for their incarnation at this time. Unfortunately, many do not have a group of friends that understand, so the activation in addition to the energy changes is creating unnatural behaviors like extreme violence, suicides, and insanity. That is why your group must work to let the world know what is happening. This is especially important for the young that are being activated because many of them feel lost and powerless."

"Thanks. Now I understand."

"Good evening, Equinoxx. It's a pleasure to be here listening. What do you have to tell me?" Teja asked.

"Your father is at your left shoulder. He will not leave you. Also, you must know that you have the power to talk to and for the dead. This is very important. You must enlist help from the Other Side and also help those that are lost to cross over. This is the legacy of the females of your family even though your mother has refused her responsibility."

"I understand. Thank you."

"Myama, Equinoxx. My name is Tara. What am I doing in this group?"

"You and your polarity have the power to walk between the worlds, dimensions, and planes of existence. Both of you are original to this planet. You contain the unaltered DNA of the original seed. Your tribes have a debt to care for this planet, and for this responsibility, Native people have many understandings and powers other races do not. Additionally, you walk between the sexes, neither male nor female. Do not alter your body; you must remain as you are to teach others to appreciate the fact that we are not our bodies, but we are instead the energy that inhabits that body. Your energy is female, but your body presents as male. Being allowed to live as both gives a perspective that others do not have. Originally there were three sexes, male, female, and the balance, people like you. Your job was as a bridge to bring together these opposites. You must still do that."

"It is very hard to do in the world as it is now," Tara replied.

"Yes, but hopefully not for long."

"Thank you."

There was a second round of questions, but the Weirdxotic group decided that they would give their question to Ariana to ask for all of them.

"Myama, this is Ariana again. I know we were told not to ask anything about someone else without their permission, but I don't think this is breaking the rules. Please tell us if it is. We have a friend that should be with us right now, but he is going through a hard time. We will not ask you what is happening with him. What we hope you will answer is, what can we do as a group and as individuals to help him through this?"

"What you have already been doing is wonderful. The only additional thing we would suggest is that you do not allow yourselves to even consider that he will fail. See him complete and taking his necessary role of co-leader of the group. Hold that thought in your minds no matter what the illusion attempts to make you believe. Remember, The Darkness only has the power you give it. There is nothing greater nor lesser than you. This is true of all souls. We are all a piece of the Source. As such, we are all creators. What do you want to create?"

"Harmony and beauty out of the chaos," Ariana answered.

Chapter 19

After the channeling, the group was overwhelmed with all the information they had gotten and needed some time to talk and decompress. They made their apologies to Lydia and Wendy Two for leaving early and promised they would stay later next time.

Everyone, even Leesie, was very quiet as they walked to Zach's car. Ariana was allowing herself to feel the good remnants left over from the channeling. Somehow the channeling had energized her. Her energy felt very full and light. She loved looking upward at the stars and planets. The immenseness of the sky never failed to make her feel humble, but tonight it reminded her that she was not in this fight alone. There were others living on this planet, on Meria and the Pleiades that were committed also. Even if many on Earth did not realize it yet, they would soon. She knew she could count on Leesie to find ways to contact those that were activated. Wendy will reach the animal realm and Tara and Matthew will do their jobs, too. Andrew, Teja, and Zach will do whatever they must to protect and support the group and with the help of the Source, Ariana knew she would do what she must to make sure everyone succeeds and that this planet not only survives but thrives.

"Well, what did you think?" Ariana asked once they were all stuffed into the car. "Zach, why don't you start?"

"I have a lot to think about, but for now, I feel a lot better. Even though we have so much to do, I'm feeling hopeful," Zach answered.

"Amen," Teja added. "I feel so much better about my role. I have Gram and my dad to help me. How could I ever be defeated?"

"Don't get cocky," warned Leesie. "This will be a fight and The Darkness has a lot of energy out there to feed off of. I believe we can do this, too. I know I'll be able to do my job, but if we get too sure of ourselves, we'll miss some important things, I know it. I'm really glad I went. Not just because of the information we received about us, but those general questions and their answers were mad chill! The one about animals and how they are here to teach us unqualified love really was beautiful. I have the greatest dog and cat at home, and when Equinoxx was talking about all the things animals do for humanity, it made me feel guilty that since I've been at school, I haven't bothered to go home and see them. I talk to my family at least once a week, but I just disregarded my pets. How horrible is that?"

"That one got me, too. Animals have always been my best friends and there were times when I was going through my super emo stuff that they helped me cope," Wendy said. "I never thought of it as them trying to heal me and that their love was sending me good energy—just like we're trying to do with Matthew. I can remember once when I was sick my dog broke out of his run and raced to my bedroom. He jumped on the bed and lay next to me. He refused to leave until I was well. Drove my mom nuts, but helped me feel so much better. I'm glad I'm going to be helping the animals. Instead of majoring in agriculture, I think I'm going to be a vet."

Ariana replied, "I feel like both of you about the animal answer. When I was at my lowest point, my dad bought me a horse. Every time I was with her I felt hopeful and free. I think she was healing my energy. Isn't it interesting, animals give us so much, companionship, love, healing, they die so we can eat, they guard our flocks, businesses and houses, they provide transportation, they do so much to balance the planet and we take it all for granted. Equinoxx really opened my eyes, too."

"You all know how I feel about Diablo. That cat has been my lifesaver way too many times," said Tara.

"I definitely have a lot to think about. That stuff about ego and soul, I think some of it went way over my head," Andrew admitted. "Anyone understand it?"

Tara said, "I think I do. The soul is the connection to the source. It doesn't leave, but instead creates a fantasy."

Ariana chimed in, "Matthew called it a play."

"Yeah, that's a good analogy," Tara agreed. "The soul writes a play and then it creates the characters that will act out the play. Those are the egos, us. The reason the soul does that is to learn and have experiences. Those experiences can be completions of past lives, new experiences, or a combination of both. The egos don't remember that they are actors because that would ruin the learning. When we are acting out the play as written, things go smoothly. It's when we attempt to completely rewrite the play that everything goes wrong. Now, even if we are following the play perfectly, it doesn't mean our lives will be easy. If the play is about living in poverty or learning about loss, then there will be pain, but the struggle won't necessarily be there or at least not as intensely. At least that's what I got from the discussion."

"That helped, thanks," Andrew stated.

"There's more, though. The more scripted a life is, the less free will," Ariana added.

"What do you mean?" asked Andrew.

"Remember in my reading Lydia said that I had to do this work," Ariana answered.

"Yes, I remember that," said Tara, "but you still have the free will to choose not to. Unfortunately, if you do that, Earth will be destroyed and you will probably doom yourself and your home planet to a hell of a lot of bad karma."

"Yeah, some free will that is," moaned Leesie.

"Next time let's ask how you get rid of karma," Wendy said.

"Already making plans to fail, Doodle Bunny?" Andrew asked.

"Doodle Bunny!" Leesie exclaimed, laughing.

Wendy blushed and said, "I think it's really sweet." She wiggled around enough to kiss Andrew's forehead. "He's my Sweet Baboo."

"You stole that from the Peanuts comic strip didn't you? You're not allowed to do that," admonished Leesie.

Ariana shifted the subject, "What did everyone think about what they told us to do for Matthew?"

"I think it might work," Zach said. "Ariana, remember during the séance when The Darkness was trying to defeat you and you said you heard me saying 'I love you?' You said it brought you out of the despair and made you fight. We can do that for Matthew. We can constantly show him how important he is to all of us."

Tara revealed, "I'm working on astral projecting to him. I hope he won't see me. Instead, I want to see how he's doing and also to give him support. I'll let everyone know what I pick-up."

"Tara, what did you think about what they said about you and your body?" Ariana asked. "If it's too personal a question, you don't have to answer."

"It is very personal, but I've needed someone besides the counselor to talk to about it. I've been agonizing for the past year because soon I will be old enough to make the decision about whether I should go on hormones and eventually have the surgery," Tara admitted.

"Okay, Tara, I do love you, but thinking about cutting off parts of my body, especially that part, is seriously creeping me out," Andrew objected.

Tara laughed, "Yeah, me too. It's a huge step and obviously irreversible. But I don't feel right in this body. It really is as though I'm wearing a costume. When I dress up and really look like me, the girl, I feel authentic, real.

Hormones can cause some pretty bad problems, too. Trans people have to take massive doses. Massive doses of hormones can cause all kinds of cancers. But if I don't take them, I'll become more masculine facial hair grows, Adam's apples enlarge, and my voice deepens."

"Close your ears, Andrew," Leesie warned, "I've been doing some reading. You don't have to remove the whole thing, you can just have an orchidectomy, surgical removal of the balls," she explained. "That way, you won't be producing testosterone. That would help you stay more feminine."

"It sounded to me as though Equinoxx was saying to stay exactly as I am now, though," Tara replied.

"That's what I heard, too," Wendy said.

"Sounds like we need further information about a lot of things, so I'm going to call Lydia tomorrow and make another appointment. I would like to make it for the whole group and see if she'll channel for just the seven of us," Ariana stated.

"I agree," Zach said. "And while we're waiting for the appointment, we need to write down a bunch of questions. Let's get together at Tara's on Sunday to hash that out."

"Why Tara's?" Andrew asked.

Zach replied, "Because I haven't been there and I'd like to see it and meet this awesome cat that saves lives and because Wendy and Ariana are moving in with her for a while, remember?"

"I'm jealous," Leesie pouted, "I want to stay there, too!"

"Okay," Tara offered. "We'll do it tomorrow night and make it a proper slumber party. Everyone bring pillows, sleeping bags or blankets, pajamas, and anything else you need for the night. You guys, bring something to sleep in even if you usually sleep bare. Okay? Don't bother bringing food or anything to drink, I'll have more than enough for dinner, snacks, and breakfast.

"That sounds wonderful," Teja exclaimed. "But are you sure we can't bring anything?"

"No thanks, I've got it all covered."

Chapter 20

When Matthew awoke the next morning, his stomach rumbled loudly, reminding him that he hadn't eaten in over 24 hours. At first he was disoriented trying to remember where he was. As soon as the frigid temperatures hit him, he remembered. He threw the old leather jacket over his T-shirt and padded barefoot, shivering all the way to the old wood stove his grandfather used to heat his small frame home. He put some kindling in the stove and lit it, then added a few small branches. Once the branches were on fire, he put on a log. The stove quickly filled the room with heat. Matthew soaked in the warmth of the fire as he stood next to the stove. He wondered what time it was. Looking out a small window, he saw that the weather was overcast and bleak. He could only guess that it was some time in the morning. He was sure his grandfather would be able to tell, but he hadn't learned how to read the energy of the planet that well, yet.

Matthew's stomach growled loudly again, but instead of reminding him of food, this time it reminded him of what was to happen today. This was the day he would participate in his first sweat lodge followed by his vision quest. He knew that the Elders and helpers of the tribe built a new lodge every spring by a creek on the outskirts of town. They used young willow saplings and bent them into a dome shape that they covered with blankets and canvas. The door always faced east, signifying where all things begin. What went on inside, though, was still a mystery to Matthew. The thought of what lay ahead of him made him feel unsure and frightened.

Just as Matthew's worries began to grow, his grandfather came through the front door of the house, carrying a beautiful carved pipe. It was obviously quite old. The bowl was red pipestone and the stem was carved from wood. The two pieces of the pipe represented the merging of male and female energy, the male energy in the stem, the female energy in the bowl. The feathers and bear claws that adorned the pipe represented the animal and spirit realms.

Grandfather went to a cupboard in the main room and removed a small pouch filled with tobacco. Handing it to Matthew he said, "You must present this gift to the medicine person who will be leading this sweat lodge."

"Namee'me', you won't be the leader?"

"No, Matthew. It is better for me to be a participant and support you in your journey, not lead. You must do certain things in this ritual. You must gift the leader and state your intention for the ritual. You must be sincere in this intention so that Great Spirit will recognize and accept your plea for cleansing and renewal. Follow these instructions and all will go well."

"Thank you, Grandfather."

"It is time to go."

Matthew and his grandfather walked to the sweat lodge following several of the other residents of Lame Deer. When they arrived, Matthew noticed two Elders waiting out front. He asked his grandfather which was the leader and was told the one on the right. His grandfather acknowledged the Elders and introduced Matthew. Matthew presented the Elder on the right with his pouch of tobacco. It was wrapped in a red prayer cloth representing the South and the red people. The Elder accepted the gift and motioned for the other Elder to smudge the two. Matthew and his grandfather stepped to the side and allowed the second Elder to pass the smoke of a sage smudge stick through their auras and over their bodies to cleanse any negativity before they entered the lodge. They remained at the side of the sweat lodge as each of the participants was smudged. When everyone was present and cleansed, the Elders entered through the eastern door and seated themselves in front of the western door. Next, the women participants entered, moving clockwise around the center pit. They sat in the north, facing south. The rest of the male participants entered next, Matthew bringing up the rear. They sat south facing the women. At the end, the grandfathers entered and seated themselves around the pit. As soon as the last grandfather was seated, five stones, which had been heating in a fire pit for 24 hours, were brought in from outside, one at a time, on a forked stick. As the first stone was brought in and placed in the middle of the lodge, the lead Elder told Matthew that each stone represented something. The first one represented the Creator. The second stone was placed in the east touching the first stone. Matthew was informed it represented the eagle which carries the prayers to the Great Spirit. The third stone was coyote, the spirit keeper or wolf stone, and was placed in the south. It represented love, emotion, and community. The fourth stone, brown bear, represented medicine, physical strength, and healing. It was placed in the west. Finally, Matthew learned the fifth stone was placed at the north point and was the white buffalo or salmon which represents wisdom and sacrifice. The hot stones were sprinkled with healing herbs: sweat grass, sage, and cedar. A wonderful smell filled the lodge along with the smoke. The door was now closed. Four pinches of tobacco were placed in the bowl of the pipe and the lead Elder asked, "Matthew, what is your intention today?"

"My intention is to connect with my purpose and heal the darkness, pain, and guilt that is trying to devour me."

"This is a good intention," the lead Elder proclaimed, drawing deeply on the pipe and passing it to Matthew who inhaled the acrid tobacco. Trying hard not to cough, he passed the pipe to the person next to him. Matthew noticed that only the men smoked. The women were touched on the brow to send their intent to the Great Spirit. After the pipe made a complete circle, one of the grandfathers began to chant, singing a song of release to the Great Spirit. After the song, the lead Elder praised the Wise One above and asked for all in attendance to be honored by the spirits and totem animals. Stories were told of the greatness of Maheo who created the Earth out of the void.

After the creation story was told, a second round of stones were brought in. The leader explained that the first round was creation, the female attribute. The second round represented the male aspect. The pipe was passed again, prayers were said, and the life and death of Sweet Arrow Boy and the story of the four arrows was told. Matthew was familiar with these stories but they were told with so much feeling it almost caused him to cry.

When the stones were brought again for the third round, it was time for healing. There was singing and chanting, rattling and drumming, and as the heat brought the sweat, illness leached out of the body. Matthew felt dizzy but also more alive than he had in weeks. His entire body felt as though it was vibrating, and this time when the pipe came to him, he didn't feel like coughing at all.

The fourth round of stone placement was for the group attending the sweat lodge. Stories were told of community and praise was given for ancestors known for their selfless service. The grandfathers and Elders were honored and the pipe smoked again. The sweat lodge closed with a prayer to the wise one above for strength and wisdom and the preservation of Grandmother Earth. All but two stones were removed and everyone filed out. When they exited the lodge, the participants immediately submerged themselves in the creek. The air was cold, the water was frigid, but Matthew felt innervated. His whole body was alive with energy. He didn't feel the cold at all.

When they had gotten out of the creek and dressed, Matthew's grandfather said, "Matthew, you must go now."

"Go where?"

"It is time for your vision quest," Grandfather said, handing him a rolled blanket, a flannel shirt, and the leather jacket. "This is all you may take. You are not allowed food or water for four days and nights. You must walk to the top of that hill. Find a spot where the land will accept you and sit. Pray for the Great Spirit to honor your vision quest. Ask the ancestors, your personal spirits, and totem animals to be present and guide your quest. If your intent is true, you will return in four days a different person. You will be a man and a warrior."

Chapter 21

After stopping at their dorm to pick up the personal items they would need for their stay at Tara's, Zach dropped Tara, Wendy, and Ariana off at Tara's condo. From out of the darkness of the living room, Diablo sprang at Tara as soon as she entered the condo. Although Tara seemed used to this welcome, both Ariana and Wendy were blindsided. Wendy let out a shriek which startled the cat and all three girls burst into hysterical laughter.

"Wow, are we ever paranoid!" Wendy said, laughing. "Poor Diablo. We scared him so bad he won't even tell me where he is."

"Oh, don't worry about that. He always goes to the same place when he's scared—under the couch. Come on in and we'll sooth his fragile ego," Tara said, walking toward the living room.

"I've never had a house pet," Ariana admitted. "You seem to be really bonded to each other. Your auras even blend."

"What does that even mean?" Wendy asked.

Ariana answered, "When two people, or in this case Tara and Diablo are connected, and the connection is harmonious, their auras blend together. Like, let's say that Tara's aura is blue, which it is and Diablo's is pink. When they are together they will appear to have one aura which will be lavender."

"What happens if he's mad at her?" asked Wendy.

"It will still blend, but may be slightly cloudy or less distinct."

"What happens if there's a problem with our relationship?" asked Tara.

"The auras won't blend and may even have sharp edges."

"What if someone has a red aura and their partner has an aura that clashes with that, what happens then?" Wendy inquired.

"I've never seen that," admitted Ariana, "but I'll bet they wouldn't have been attracted to each other to begin with."

"Well, will you tell me if Andrew's aura changes toward me?"

asked Wendy. "I don't want to be the last person to know if he's gonna dump me. Okay?"

"There's that negative thinking and fear again," Ariana said, warning Wendy.

"Sorry," Wendy said, embarrassed.

"I don't think you have anything to worry about," Tara offered. "It looks to me like he's got it bad for you, Wendy."

Wendy blushed, "Me, too. I've never had a real boyfriend before, only guys that wanted something from me, but didn't want to get to know me first. Because of the way I looked I guess they thought that made me easy or something. There was one boy, Chris. hH was Goth, too. He and I had a kinda thing, but I think it was more about saying we had someone than really liking each other. This is the first time I've really liked someone and he's liked me back. It feels wonderful. I don't want to lose Andrew, but I'm always worried that I will."

"No need to worry. You guys are good together and I think he knows it," Ariana assured her.

"Anyone hungry?" Tara asked. "I have salsa and chips, homemade chocolate chip cookies with pecans, all kinds of fruit, and peanut butter filled pretzels."

"Yeah! Let's just pig out and have a little of everything," Wendy suggested enthusiastically.

"Well, that proves you and Andrew are made for each other," Tara laughed. "You both seem to like to eat."

The three girls walked into the kitchen and watched Tara pull out plates of food and bowls of fruit and salsa. Her kitchen was fully stocked with beautiful ceramic plates, hand painted with a flowered Mexican pattern. She had Martha Stewart cookware and every conceivable electric appliance.

"I love to cook," Tara informed the two. "The salsa is fresh and so are the cookies."

Wendy piled on the chips and salsa first, followed by the pretzels and cookies.

"Oh wow," she exclaimed, "this salsa is to die for!"

Tara blushed and said, "Thank you," as Wendy took a bite of the cookie.

"I lied," Wendy squealed. "I couldn't possibly die before having more of these amazing cookies. These are melt-in-your-mouth soft and alarmingly tasty. Yum! Ariana, it's time for some all-out feastiality here. Dig in. Oh, but we've got to save some of these for the group sleepover. The guys have got to taste this stuff," Wendy added.

"Don't worry. You can eat as much as you want. I can easily make more," Tara responded.

"You don't have to tell me twice," Wendy answered, taking two more cookies. "What's wrong with you Ariana? Eat up."

"Sorry," Ariana said. "My family didn't allow me to have cookies and chips. That's why I haven't eaten any of your Oreos."

"What the heck?" Wendy said. "Why not?"

"Everyone else in my family was skinny without trying to be. I, on the other hand, had a weight problem almost forever," explained Ariana.

"You, nena, are not fat," Tara announced. "The only thing wrong with you is your hairstyle. I hope that doesn't offend you, but just wearing it in a ponytail all the time must get boring."

"Boy, does it," Ariana answered, "but it's so straight it won't do anything else."

"That's because it's so long. If we cut it shorter and in layers, I think we could get it to curl and look really pretty," Tara offered.

Ariana responded, "Unfortunately, Zach really likes my hair long."

"He hasn't seen it any other way," objected Tara. "Anyway, we're only going to trim it and layer it. It will still be long."

Wendy said excitedly, "Come on Ariana, let her try. Then if you look good, I'll have her give me a makeover, too. Please."

"I'm as good with hair and makeup as I am with food," Tara wheedled. "At least you pluck your eyebrows. What's with yours, Wendy?"

"If I take off my glasses I can't see anything, so I've never tried."

"I'll do them for you then," Tara stated. "What do you say, Ariana?"

"Okay, but if Zach hates it, you can explain that you two forced me," Ariana said.

The girls adjourned to the master bath. It was huge with a double sink and a very large jetted bathtub. The tiles were white with one small row of iridescent blue tiles running around the room at waist level. The floor, also white, had the blue tiles intermixed in a pattern that accented the blue towels and small rugs.

"This is really beautiful. Aren't you afraid we'll make a big mess?" Ariana asked.

"Everything is cleanable. You're not backing out that easily," Tara responded. Pulling out a small stool covered in plush blue fabric, Tara ordered, "Sit!"

Approximately an hour later, Tara turned Ariana back toward the vanity mirror. "Well, what do you think?"

Ariana couldn't believe the transformation. Her usually lifeless hair fell in soft waves just below her shoulders. It was feathered around her face making her already big eyes look huge. The layering not only seemed to give her hair style, but also made it appear very thick. It was beautiful.

"Oh Tara, I love it. But will I be able to make it look this good?"

"I'll show you how. The right product to give it curl and texture, a little blow drying with a large round brush, and you're done. It's really easy," Tara responded.

"Me next," Wendy pleaded. "Can you help me to look even a third as good as her?"

"Sure, but because you have a long face, I think we should do a short cut, maybe like Jennifer Lawrence. Someday I'd like to add high lights too, but don't have the stuff right now. First I'm going to pluck your eyebrows. This may hurt, but it goes numb pretty fast. If you're blind without your glasses, why haven't you gotten contacts?"

"I couldn't get used to them. I had a real problem putting them in and they bothered me all day so I just gave up," Wendy explained. "Will the plucking really hurt?"

"Only a little," Ariana answered. "My sister sat on me when I was twelve and plucked mine. Just relax and it will be over soon."

Wendy's transformation took a bit longer than Ariana's. Wendy wouldn't stop squirming when her eyebrows were tweezed and as she watched all the hair being cut from her head. Her dark brown hair fell in piles at her feet. Ariana was aware of how frightening it probably looked to her. But when Tara was done, Ariana was astonished at the transformation. Wendy looked younger and fresher. The short cut accentuated her high cheekbones and slim pretty nose. With her eyebrows tweezed, Wendy's eyes appeared more almond-shaped.

Before Tara could turn Wendy around to see her transformation,

Ariana exclaimed, "Wendy, you look beautiful. I love what Tara's done to you."

Tara waited as Wendy stared into the mirror at her reflection. It was a full two minutes before Wendy said anything. "Is that really me?" she asked. "I look pretty, don't I? I never thought I'd look pretty."

Tara said, "Wendy you've always been pretty, but you didn't bring out your best features, especially when you wore all that black makeup and let your hair hang."

"Tara's right, but boy, do you look great now," Ariana commented. "I think Andrew will be blown away."

"Now if I only had some sexy clothes," Wendy said wistfully. "All I have are old jeans and hoodies. I never needed much else and I threw away all my Goth stuff. It wasn't real sexy anyway."

"Let's see what I've got. Your hips are broader because you're a real girl," Tara said smiling, "but I might have some things that will work for you. Not for Ariana, unfortunately, she's too voluptuous. No put down, I'm envious."

"No offense taken," Ariana assured her.

After going through most of the clothes in Tara's full closet they found a short brown skirt and stretchy top. The skirt came to about mid-thigh and showed off Wendy's long legs. The top had a scooped neckline, three-quarter length sleeves and was a scene of leaves in various colors of brown, beige, and green with multi-colored bling on the front. It was very unusual for Wendy, but the colors brought out the golds and reds in her brown hair.

"Well, I think that looks pretty good. What do you think?" Tara asked Ariana.

"She looks great," Ariana responded.

"If only we had nicer shoes," Tara said, "but my feet will be way bigger. Maybe tomorrow the three of us can go shopping for shoes, hair products, and more decent clothes for both of you."

"It's a deal," Wendy replied enthusiastically, "but money is tight in my family."

"No worries," Ariana answered. "I can buy you both some Christmas presents tomorrow. I know it's still over a month off, but I wanted to buy you both something anyway and this would be perfect."

"But I haven't even thought about Christmas yet," Wendy objected, "and I really don't have money to spend either."

"Please don't think I'm angling for a gift from you. I want to do this because it makes me feel good, not because I expect something back. My Oma used to tell me that if you give something with an open hand, with no expectations, the Universe will give back 10 fold. See, you'd be doing me a favor. And Tara, what you've done for me today is the best gift I could have asked for."

"But we're not done," Tara said. "Both of you need new clothes and makeup, too. I know just where to go to get a free makeover."

"It had better be right down the street or we'll have a very long walk," Ariana replied.

Tara responded, "It's at Scottsdale Fashion Square and I'll borrow my abuela's car. Now it's time to get some rest. Will the two of you be comfortable sleeping together on the queen bed in the guest bedroom?"

"I don't want to mess up my new look by sleeping on it," Wendy complained.

Ariana said, "Me either. I'll never get my hair to look this good again."

"That will be a great teaching experience. I'll show both of you step-by-step what I did so you can repeat it," Tara assured them. "It will be easy."

The girls parted, Tara going to find Diablo and Wendy and Ariana going into the spare bedroom.

"Hey, where do you think you're going?" Wendy and Ariana heard Tara say from the living room when a large puff of black came sauntering in the guest room door. "Diablo, come back here!"

Diablo didn't even look back toward Tara's voice, instead he made himself at home on the guest bed and waited for the two girls to join him.

"What's up with him?" Tara asked. "He always sleeps with me."

Wendy laughed and replied, "He's mad because you ignored him all evening and even forgot to feed him."

"OMG, I forgot to feed him. I never do that." Tara rapidly crossed the room to Diablo, picked him up and started cooing to him. "Mommy's sorry. I'll give you something special, I promise," Tara said as she carried him out of the room."

"He knows just how to play her," laughed Wendy.

"That's what you can give me for Christmas," Ariana suggested, "you can teach me to communicate with animals. We could go to your parent's house and practice talking with the animals. Okay?"

Wendy seemed uncertain but eventually agreed she would give it a try.

The girls could still hear Tara talking to the cat as they fell asleep.

Chapter 22

Zach was dreaming. He was standing on a small rise overlooking a lush green landscape. There were grapevines, olive trees, and fields of fragrant flowers. Standing next to him was a man. He felt he knew this man well, but Zach could not think of his name. Zach felt uncomfortable being so near to him, as though this was a person that was supposed to be a friend, but he was no longer trustworthy. It was very irritating to Zach to know that he had forgotten so much that was important, but then he realized he wasn't being the other man, he was watching the two men interact. This feeling of both being one of the men and watching them was very disorienting. He began to feel dizzy. Zach decided to just allow himself to be an observer of the scene, not a participant.

"This world is beautiful as it is. Why do you want to meddle with it?" the man Zach thought of as himself asked.

The other man responded, "Ares, that is what we do. We experiment and alter worlds in order to make our world better. If we did these tests on Alcyone we could cause a disaster. Experimenting on other planets is our way."

"A history lesson is not what I need today, Hephaestus. Just because this is how it has always been done does not mean it is right. The evidence is everywhere in our history. Remember what we did to the red planet of this solar system? In attempting to create a breeding ground for our crystal forms, we destroyed a viable planet and its natural inhabitants. We have done this on so many solar systems maybe it is time to return to the Seven Sisters and reevaluate our science."

"You must admit," Hephaestus answered, "there are many benefits to this small world. The people revere us and will do whatever we want. That is incentive enough. But this place is rich with crystal, and with just a small adjustment, it can be altered to a hundred times its natural strength."

"What about the risks?" Ares objected. "The chances of doing extreme damage to this environment and the species that inhabit it are huge."

Hephaestus frowned at his colleague, "What has happened to you? You know our mandate is to our own people. A world that is beautiful but far inferior to our own shouldn't matter to you. Did our fathers and grandfathers worry when they were testing viruses to develop a cure for the epidemic that almost wiped out our world? No! Where would we be if they had? If we still existed at all, we would be little more than instinctual creatures just attempting to survive. But because of their work, we are superior beings. We have conquered illness, we have expanded our brain power, and we teach other worlds to become civilized."

Ares objected, "On this world we are doing harm to the indigenous peoples. It is as though we have enslaved them instead of bringing them knowledge. Many of our kind have become heady with the power we have been given and are using it wrongly. We are mating with these beings and altering their DNA. We have created chaos not peace."

"But this, too, can be research," Hephaestus argued.

"In many cases, enhancing their DNA has led to disease like the one that eats their cells."

"In the interest of science and helping our civilization, a few deaths are nothing. It also allows us to try out our laser knives and pulses."

Unconvinced, Ares responded, "And the pulses have created disharmony in the atmosphere and disruption in the tectonic plates. We are not sure what that may do to the planet itself. The Lemurians have attempted to warn us of the possible destruction this could cause. How can we in good conscience continue on this track?"

"Ares, you have always been the worrier of our crew. We will continue with our work until it is done," Hephaestus declared. "Meanwhile, why don't you speak with the Leader, perhaps he will help you to release these morbid fears and remind you why you are here." Shaking his head, Hephaestus walked back to the labs.

Standing on the same spot, Ares turned to watch the sunset. He decided he would talk with the Leader. *Maybe my concerns will resonate with the Leader as well, and a decision will be made to take these fears to the Alcyone council.*

As Ares walked toward the Center, the mountaintop fortress the

Atlanteans had created as their home and work space here on Terra, he began to formulate his arguments. He had to convince the Leader that their current plans were too dangerous. If they kept up their experiments, Ares was sure damage would be done to the planet itself. That would only invite disaster. Any major change to a planet in this solar system would cause havoc to the other planets and then possibly to other solar systems. All things are linked throughout the Universe, of this he was sure. Now to convince the Leader that he was not being an alarmist. He could not mention the Lemurian female who had been talking to him about her observations. It was forbidden for Atlantians to spend time with the other aliens on this planet. It was also forbidden to interact with the humans, but many did. This, too, was creating problems. Mixed race children were being born, changing the purity of this species and causing genetic anomalies. Eventually his people would leave and these children would be without one parent. This was not a problem for his people, they did not attach to their young. But humans bonded with theirs. Within the units they called tribes or communities it was not acceptable to be without a mate. Yet his people would not remain here after their work was complete.

The Lemurian female had been the one who alerted him to the potential for planetary damage. She had pointed out that many of the more unique species of animals were either migrating far away from the Center or had seemed to vanish all together. He had not seen a unicorn, Pegasus or dragon for many months. When he had first come to Terra it had been filled with all manner of animals and reptiles. Now, however, the herds seemed smaller, the seasons more erratic, and the planet less stable. He had felt some of the seismic activity and had assumed that it was part of the planet's natural process. The Lemurian informed him that it was not so. The planet had been stable for generations until they had come and begun their experiments. She had thought they would not stay long, but now it had been many cycles of the sun, one hundred by her reckoning, and they did not appear to have any intention of leaving. That is why she had sought him out, to bring them her warnings. She claimed she had been watching him. She had noticed over the past three sun cycles that he also had noted the changes and was beginning to question the wisdom of their actions. That is why she had chosen him. She had been one of the original seeders of Terra who had been tasked to be left behind to observe and oversee. Consequently, she knew the system and could tell when it was off balance. She had observed the first seismic wave after their second attempt at harnessing the master crystals. After the third attempt, the seismic activity increased exponentially. Now she claimed the rumbles were almost constant and increasing in magnitude. She stated that she was afraid of a massive land shift if this was not controlled. At first Ares did not take her warnings seriously, but as they continued to increase the intensity of the crystal waves, the seismic activity became easily felt. No longer was it a slight shift of energy occasionally, instead it was actual rumbling of the planet at its core and upward. He had seen minor crystals shake on their pedestal and overhead lighting sway. Today he had actually thought he felt the earth beneath his feet move. He could ignore her pleas no longer. His attempt to bring attention to these concerns had been dismissed by Hephaestus; he was too focused on proving his theories to worry about the potential for harm. Hephaestus was too ambitious to think of anything but what he considered success. His goals were to ignite the Master Crystals, producing enough power to propel their ships indefinitely. He wanted to cleanse their home planet and mine new planets for the riches their planetary system devoured. He realized now there would be no help from Hephaestus. Ares's only hope was to be heard by the Leader. He was supposed to be the manager of the mission, the person in whom the responsibility of success or failure lay. If they destroyed this planet, it would most definitely be failure. Ares **had** to convince the Leader of how dire their current situation was.

When Ares arrived at the Center he was surprised to find that the Leader was expecting him. He was led to his private cell. The Leader was not alone. Ares was dismayed to see that Hephaestus was waiting with him.

"Hephaestus has told me of your fears," the Leader began. "He also assures me that they are unfounded. Present your case."

Ares explained his observation of the seismic activity and the vanishing animals. He also mentioned the mixed race children and the DNA anomalies he had observed in the laboratory. "I don't believe this can continue without the planet sustaining immense damage, and you know what would happen if this planet was no longer in its current position. As I observe all the possibilities, if the current seismic conditions continue to accelerate, I can see no eventuality that would be beneficial to the planet or ourselves," Ares concluded.

"And you have been observing this phenomenon for how long?" asked the Leader.

"120 days, 4 hours, and 33 minutes thus far."

"You believe that is a long enough span in which to make such a dire prediction?" Hephaestus scoffed.

"I do because it is accelerating exponentially. Consequently, we have no time to debate," Ares warned.

The Leader was quiet then asked, "Are there others that have also made these observations?"

"Not our scientists," said Ares.

Hephaestus looked at Ares suspiciously, "Then who?"

"I was first made aware of this problem by one of the Lemurian overseers."

"This from the man complaining about some of us involving ourselves with the humans?" Hephaestus laughed. "You know they don't want us here and still you believe her. What a fool you are."

"Enough, Hephaestus," the Leader warned. "Ares, why do you believe this person?"

"Phanes, my Leader, I have checked her data and made my own observations. The information about the mutated DNA is my own. When was the last time you saw a dragon or unicorn? They have vanished from this place. I have been watching herds of animals and even birds leaving this area. I believe they are sensitive to the seismic activity and are fleeing before the land begins its collapse."

"It is only a seasonal migration," countered Hephaestus.

Phanes waved his hand dismissively in Hephaestus' direction. "I will consult some of the other researchers before making my decisions. You may both leave now."

Out of hearing distance from the Leader, Ares complained to Hephaestus, "I cannot believe you felt the need to run to Phanes."

"Well, you were on your way to see him. Why should I not also state my case?" Hephaestus retorted.

"This is not a competition between us. This is a matter of preservation. Why do you not want to see what is right before you?"

"One more activation and the Master Crystals will be empowered. If you cause this process to be stopped now, all the work that we have done will be for nothing. My entire life's research and work wasted for your fear and the allure of an attractive woman," Hephaestus answered.

"Why do you refuse to see reality?" Ares exclaimed. "You are so blinded by your desires you have forfeited objectivity. I will no longer defend my view to you as you are unwilling to alter your course. I pray that your ego does not destroy what our entire civilization has worked to become." Ares said as he walked away briskly.

Zach woke up shaking. He had just watched his first fight for Earth, the one that failed.

Chapter 23

It was getting dark and Matthew still had not found the spot where the land would accept him. He had walked, feeling the energy of this place. He tried to find the exact area where this energy would embrace him. Now he was at the very top of a hill looking down at the town below. The spot where he stood was barren dirt with no wind breaks. He was sure that the temperature had dropped considerably since he began his hike. He knew that by midnight the temperature could be 30 degrees lower. Even with the leather coat and flannel shirt he wore under it, he shivered.

The stars are very bright up here, Matthew thought. *It's really quite beautiful. The contrast between the land and the sky is amazing. I could just stand here and stare at this for hours. I think I've found the place,* he thought jubilantly. *What was it that Grandfather wanted me to do first?*

Pray for the Great Spirit to honor your vision quest. Ask the ancestors, your personal spirits, and totem animals to be present and guide your quest. If your intent is true you will return in four days a different person: a man and a warrior, he heard clearly in his mind.

Matthew dropped his bundle into the dirt and began to carry fallen leaves and pine boughs toward his spot. He placed them together forming a soft circle to sit upon. He opened his blanket roll and placed the heavy wool blanket over his shoulders for warmth. Standing tall, he raised both arms to the sky and prayed aloud, "Great Spirit, I ask for your help today as I begin my vision quest. Ancestors, guides, and totem animals, I also ask that you bless me with your help. Animals of the forest be with me in this place of honor and help guide my way. Animals of the sky, be with me in this place of honor so that I may use your eyes to clearly see my path. Great Spirit, guide me to become a man and a peaceful warrior. Rid me of my pain and anger and help me in my battle with The Darkness so that I may help with the commitment my tribe has made and walk the path of my ancestors and my soul as a healer and protector of this planet, our mother."

Sitting on his seat of plants, Matthew awaited Great Spirit's answer. He stared at the stars and watched as the beautiful full moon rose in the sky. Letting his thoughts wander, he attempted to become one with the environment. He opened his shields and, for the first time since he was small, allowed himself to feel completely. Now totally aware and alive, he felt the life in the forest, its plants, and its animals. He knew that he was now either protected by the Great Spirit, his ancestors, and totem animals or they had rejected his plea and found his quest and his commitment to growth lacking. If he was wide open and unprotected, The Darkness would take him completely. If he was protected, The Darkness might try, but with the help of his protectors he would fight and vanquish it once and for all. It would never again have a foothold. His soul would be whole again, no guilt, no anger, just knowledge of his path and an understanding and acceptance of his past.

Breathing deeply of the fragrance of the night and the earth caused Matthew to feel almost intoxicated. Closing his eyes, he continued to breathe until he became aware that there were new aromas in the air. He opened his eyes. Directly in front of him stood an enormous silver wolf. Its eyes were golden and intelligent looking. It had a huge ruff of fur around its neck in anticipation of an especially cold winter. Matthew felt no fear, only curiosity. Was this his totem animal or was it the form the Great Spirit had chosen to assist with his quest? Matthew had always hoped that his totem animal would be a wolf. He loved the look of this animal. He also liked that they were social animals with a defined hierarchy and loyalty to the pack. He realized that by wanting this animal to be his totem, he was expressing his need to be a leader and to have a close-knit family and friends. This was a new revelation for Matthew who had always considered himself a loner. The wolf sniffed the air and howled. Matthew didn't know what this meant or whether he was supposed to respond in some way. He sat waiting for some sign. To his left he felt another presence. When he turned to see who was there, nothing was visible. The wolf growled. Matthew turned back to him, but the wolf was gone and in its place stood a very old Indian man. His hair was white and very long, adorned with feathers, leaves, and seashells. He was dressed only in a skin loincloth and a buffalo hide draped his shoulders. In one hand he held a rattle made from a carved gourd. A white raven perched on his other arm. Even though he appeared ancient, his eyes were clear and bright. "You have called me," the man stated without question.

"Great Spirit, I have need of your direction. I have allowed The Darkness to take root in my soul. I need to reclaim the piece that it took and shut the door forever. But there is still so much anger, pain, and guilt within me that I know I must release. I ask you for help purging my soul of all of this."

A great wind arose around Matthew. It buffeted him, scattering the dried leaves and dust into a spiral like a small tornado. Pebbles and dirt began to cut at his skin, entering his eyes and his mouth. He could see or hear nothing except the cacophony around him. Abruptly the wind stopped and Matthew noticed a sickening odor and the sound of laughter. The stars and the moon were gone, replaced by absolute blackness. An all-encompassing fear took hold of Matthew. His mind was racing. The only thought in his mind was that he was lost; the Great Spirit had rejected his pleas and had thrown him into a dark pit where he would remain forever. He had been rejected, just as he had rejected his mother. He was overcome with guilt and sorrow. The laughter stopped. Now it was not only pitch black, but absolutely soundless as well. Matthew couldn't even hear his own breathing. When he tried to make a sound, he couldn't. He didn't know if he had become mute or if any sound was absorbed by the void before it could be heard. Even the stench was gone. *Oh my God, I am lost,* he cried in despair, the sound unheard. Matthew felt tears on his cheeks and realized he was crying. He sat and cried his pain into the void.

What seemed like hours later, Matthew thought he heard a sound. It was the sound of something slithering, crawling along the dirt. He still could see nothing but blackness. He should have been afraid, but instead he was so glad to hear a sound he forgot about fear.

"Why have you come?" the voice hissed in the darkness.

"I have lost my way and can't find it again in the dark," Matthew answered.

"You live in the dark," the voice hissed. "You allow the darkness of your past to color the light of your future. Is this not true?"

"I am trying to stop that," Matthew objected.

"But trying is not doing. You can never succeed by trying. Have you tried to walk? You either walk or you don't. You identify with what was done to you instead of what was done for you. You allow your soul to be shattered instead of stitching the edges with the light of those who have shown you real love. You identify as the victim not the victor. You are always busy punishing yourself or expecting to be punished. You refuse to see the love that surrounds you. If you desire punishment, then it is time to be punished," the entity in the darkness said as it struck outward, biting Matthew on the thigh. "If you survive this, then you can choose The Light once again. If not, you are truly of The Darkness and will remain here forever."

Matthew heard the sound of slithering and then complete silence returned. He was alone again. The only input in the silence and darkness was the throbbing of the wound in his thigh. It burned terribly. The pain pulsed with his heartbeat. When he tried to stand, his leg gave out and Matthew found himself sprawled on his side in the dirt. What had bitten him? If it was a rattlesnake, he was doomed. But because he couldn't see it, he wasn't sure. If he allowed himself to panic, it would cause the poison to kill him faster and what would that accomplish? Instead, he decided to assume that this was a trick and the lesson was to believe in his strength, not succumb to his fear.

Matthew turned over onto his back and stared into the darkness above. He saw and heard nothing. With his thigh screaming in pain he kept finding his thoughts turning back to what had happened. Was he holding The Darkness to him by dwelling on his guilt instead of on all the people in his life that had helped and encouraged him? Was his father's abandonment going to continue to fill him with the fear that he was unworthy of love and that others would find out and abandon him, too? He realized clearly now that he had believed that so much, he had given no one but Zach a chance to get close. He had driven away every girl that had shown interest in him in high school and recently tried to push the group and Zach away. He understood now that he used his psychic abilities to shield himself so completely that, just like Ariana, he pushed people away. Through his bitterness, anger, and negative beliefs about himself he had created a world in his mind where people were angry and bitter. He had projected all his fears and hatreds on the world around him and believed that he was the only real and honest person left. He saw danger and negativity everywhere. No wonder The Darkness had chosen him and he had fallen into its trap so easily.

Matthew began to shiver. He was freezing and hot all at the same time. He reached down to touch the wound on his thigh and found his leg swollen to twice its normal size. It was hot to the touch. He attempted to stand again and immediately fell over, his leg refusing to hold him. *I think I might panic now. Is this how and where I am going to die?* He lay on his back, consciously trying to breathe deeply and relax. *I guess if the Great Spirit has refused my quest, being dead is not such a bad thing. At least The Darkness won't be able to use me.*

A soft feminine voice in the dark said, "The Darkness can still use the dead if they are not cleansed and have not forgiven themselves and others before they die. You must decide who you want to be, Matthew."

Matthew's head pounded so badly now he couldn't lift it. It hurt worse than his thigh and that felt as though it had been dipped in scalding water and electrocuted both at the same time. *I can't even find peace in death,* he mused. *Who am I now? Don't I need to know that before I can decide who I want to be?*

"No," he heard the voice in the dark reply. "Who do you want to be? Once you know that, becoming him is easy."

Matthew realized that the voice was speaking in his head and also reading his thoughts. Was she with him on the hillside or somewhere else? Why did that matter? She knew what he was thinking no matter what. *I want to be free,* he thought. *I want my past to be but a memory with no power to control my world now.*

"We are all a sum of our pasts. We can use our pasts, good or bad, to help us to understand and treat others better, or our pasts can use us to destroy ourselves. Even those things you might find good, someone else may find bad and vice versa. Everyone has the opportunity in each life to decide what they want to believe. You could see your past as that which gave you the strength and gifts that you now have, or you can see it as something that has taken your power.

Who are you and what do you want to be? You have free will—choose."

Trying to think was becoming more difficult for Matthew. He felt as though the skin all over his body was burning off. His head and neck throbbed in matching rhythm with his thigh, and his tongue felt swollen. He longed for a drink of water to quench his thirst.

"Matthew, the time to decide is now. You are very close. If you do not decide now, it will be too late," a voice that sounded like Tara's said into his left ear.

Oh, she is here with me, Matthew thought. *At least I won't die alone. Am I dying? If I die, do I want to feel this unresolved? God, my head hurts! How can I think? Is that you Tara?*

"The poison from your past is destroying your body. Heal yourself!"

How? Matthew thought but received no answer. *The poison from my past? Then this pain is not real? I just have to see my past for what it really was.* He began to replay memories of his childhood as though he was observing a play. He saw how lonely and afraid his mother was. He saw his father, too, a man trying to live in a world he didn't understand. Having grown up on the reservation it wasn't an easy task for his father to leave and attempt a life in the city where he had no friends or family for support. That is why he had sought out a wife. He needed someone to love him and support him in his new life. His mother was the wrong choice. She needed someone to lean on, someone she could trust completely, not someone who needed to lean on her. They were two, scared, wounded people looking for anything to help them feel all right. Eventually, his father turned to alcohol and his mother turned to him. Neither person was trying to hurt anyone, both were so wounded they couldn't see beyond their own fear and pain. He had allowed them to infect him by growing up to be just like them. *The difference is that I now know I have a choice. I don't need to choose pain, anger, or hatred for myself or for either of my parents. We're all just fragile creatures trying our best to find our way. Some of us succeed and others don't. I can choose to be strong, loved, and valuable. I have friends and loved ones who are fighting for me right now. They believe in me. They see me as strong, a leader.* A realization hit him hard, *I **am** strong and valuable, and I am a leader. That's who I am. Now I want to be a wise leader, a Shaman, a good friend and a warrior for peace. I want to continue my tribe's commission to help our Mother Earth and fight The Darkness that is consuming her people. I choose freedom and I take back my power from The Darkness. I am the wolf.*

Matthew could see the sun rising in the east, just as it had every day for millennia. He didn't feel feverish any longer and when he looked at his thigh, he realized it had all been a hallucination. He had completely forgotten that he was wearing jeans. His leg couldn't have swelled to twice its size confined within the denim of his pants. Matthew felt wonderful and renewed. His head no longer hurt and he was no longer shivering. In fact, he had never felt better! He had no idea how long he had been gone, but he knew it was time to go back to his grandfather's home. He rolled his blanket, gathered up his things and began his walk back. As he walked, he noticed a hawk keeping pace from the sky. A silver wolf walked with him on an adjacent path.

Hawk as a totem animal would help him use the power of vision and intuition in his daily life. The hawk totem provides wisdom about seeing situations from a higher perspective, using the power of observation and focusing on the task at hand. The hawk would help him keep his focus on the present moment.

Unlike the hawk which is a singular creature, the wolf is a social animal. Even though living in close knit packs provides wolves with a strong sense of family, they are still able to maintain their individuality. Wolf totems represent the spirit of freedom, but they realize that having individual freedom requires having responsibilities, so wolf can also teach how to balance the responsibility of family needs and not to lose one's personal identity. He teaches developing strength and confidence in our decisions. He shows us we will learn to trust our insights once we learn how to value our inner voice and then we may become teachers ourselves.

Matthew knew all of this and would not forget who had chosen to walk with him on this day. For the first time in his life, he felt confident he was ready for this path, the one chosen for him by his ancestors. He trusted that the Great Spirit guided him and that with the help of his friends, they would succeed.

"Thank you Great Spirit, ancestors, guides, wolf, and hawk for guiding me to my path and staying beside me as I fulfill my life's mission," Matthew called to the sky.

Chapter 24

What a wonderful meditation! Tara was sure she had really been with Matthew, helping him at his time of greatest need. She had felt the pull somewhere around 11:00 that night. She knew she had to meditate and try to reach Matt. He needed her.

At first Tara was too nervous, she couldn't relax. She was sitting on her couch trying to breathe deeply and go within, but it just wasn't working. Her mind wouldn't stop betraying her. Her thoughts wandered from counting down to all the things she needed to do to get ready for tomorrow. She was about to give up when she felt a strong desire to hold her crystal. She grabbed it off the coffee table and just held it. Diablo jumped onto her lap. Immediately, she felt the energies around her increase, whether from Diablo or her crystal or both, she wasn't sure. She closed her eyes again and breathed in the combined energy of the three of them. Her crystal grew warm and she sensed that it was glowing. Diablo's loud purring also helped Tara relax. Suddenly she felt that she was in a forest. She could smell the pine trees. She thought she heard voices ahead of her and began walking toward the sound. Tara came to a clearing where Matthew stood staring at a wolf. He turned toward her as though he somehow knew she was there, but he didn't seem to be able to see her. He turned back to the wolf who now appeared to be a man. She could not hear what they were saying and without warning, a wind began to blow and stir up dust and debris in the area. It became impossible for her to see what was happening. The wind stopped as suddenly as it began and when Tara could see again, Matthew was sitting on the ground. The old man and the wolf were gone and she was sure Matt couldn't see her. She watched him, walking even closer and noticed he was crying. *Was he hurt?* she wondered. But looking as closely as she could, she saw nothing apparent on his body. She sat in the dirt near him and just watched.

After what felt like hours, Matthew stood, straightened his posture and appeared to become more alert. He seemed to be talking to something, but Tara saw nothing at all. She got up and walked around the clearing trying to hear or see who Matthew was talking with. Again, she saw nothing. Had he been given a drug? Was he hallucinating? What was he doing up here on this freezing mountain with just his clothes and blanket, not even a fire? Had he been abandoned by his grandfather? Tara decided that if she could find Matthew by thinking about him, maybe she could find his grandfather. She focused all her energy on Matthew's grandfather.

Tara felt very warm. She realized her spirit was now standing in a small living room that was heated by a roaring fire in a potbellied stove. An old man sat in a chair in front of the fire smoking a pipe. He was staring deeply into the fire and chanting. She could barely make out the words, but believed he was asking the Great Spirit to protect and help Matthew in his quest.

"You have come to help my Matthew," the old man said.

Tara looked around the small room expecting to see that someone had entered, but she was alone with the old man.

"You girl, I am talking to you," Matthew's grandfather said. "You, two-spirit."

"Me?" Tara asked, confused.

"Yes."

"How can you see me?"

"I am a Cheyenne Medicine man and skin-walker. I walk between the dimensions. You are walking between the dimensions now. You are not fully in the third or fourth, but between the two. I am familiar with this place as I walk there often. That is why you are visible to me. But even if I couldn't see you with my third eye, I would have sensed the energy shift caused by you entering my home."

"What is a two-spirit?"

"You are two-spirit, not woman nor man, but a little of both. You are Matthew's polarity," the grandfather stated.

"Yes, I am," Tara agreed.

"The Great Spirit has answered my prayer. The Darkness has convinced Matthew that it has killed him. He will begin to think all is lost and give himself to The Darkness for eternity. You are here to stop this."

"Me? How?" Tara asked confused and afraid.

"You must enter his dream and speak to him of truth. Help him to feel the love that is all around him. Help him feel his power."

"How do I enter his dream?"

"Sit with him and open your mind to his. Allow yourself to become Matthew so that you may see the illusion that has been placed there by The Darkness. You are his polarity which means you already have a mind link with him. It will be very easy to enter his illusion. Just do not get caught up in what you are seeing. Keep reminding yourself that it is an illusion created by The Darkness, nothing more. Nothing in it is real. It is exactly like what your popular magicians do, all smoke and mirrors."

"Thank you, Grandfather," Tara said. "I will take care of our Matthew."

"I know," he replied, "I have known you in many lives and know you to be a woman of your word. Matthew is in good hands now."

Tara began to think about Matthew again and found herself back in the clearing. Matthew was lying on his side in obvious pain. He was sweating and his face was twisted in agony. He was moaning and shivering. Quickly she entered his illusion and found herself in total blackness. There was nothing, no sound, no light, no smells, just blackness. Then she heard Matthew think that maybe it would be good if he died. She kneeled next to him and whispered that The Darkness could still claim him in death. She tried to cover him with the blanket, but she had no power in this realm. But she thought he had heard her. She kept listening to his thoughts and answering his questions. He was growing stronger and surer of himself as they talked. *Maybe he is absorbing some of my energy. I'll focus on him being well and strong and realizing how much we love him,* she thought.

Tara kept answering Matthew's questions and planting ideas in his mind so that he would stop focusing on the illusion The Darkness had created. Instead, he needed to absorb the light she was sending to him. She thought that she had tapped into the energy of their group because she was sure she felt both Ariana and Zach with her here. That combined energy allowed her to whisper in Matt's ear and be heard. "Matthew, the time to decide is now. You are very close. If you do not decide now it will be too late." Now that she had his attention, she added with all her strength, "The poison from your past is destroying your body. Heal yourself!" She could feel it working. Now she knew their entire group had felt the pull and joined with her to reach and heal Matthew. She sent Leesie's positive energy, Wendy's connection to the animal world, Andrew's gentle strength, Ariana's healing abilities, Zach's love for his friend, and Teja's passion along with her own love and his grandfather's love, too. It was enough. She felt him break free just as the sun rose on the fourth day.

Chapter 25

Ariana had awakened from a sound sleep realizing that she and the rest of the group were needed. She woke Wendy and the two tip-toed into the living room looking for Tara. They found her in a deep trance state on the couch, Diablo protecting her.

"We need to contact the others. She needs us to help her save Matthew. We all need to be sending love and light to both of them. Let's call everyone."

After reaching the last of the group, Wendy and Ariana sat across from Tara. They each held their own crystal and willed themselves into a deep meditative state. Reaching out with her energy, Ariana worked to expand her power so that she could reach into the rest of the group's auras, combining them into a group energy which she used to surround Tara in their combined love and light. Tara immediately grabbed and absorbed this additional force. Ariana concentrated on building the energy they were sending and filling it with love. Feeling Zach's love for her, and Matthew as pure white energy, she visualized Matt accepting it easily. Ariana could feel all the force in the room. The room was becoming very warm and there was an electric current in the air.

Ariana saw Matthew clearly in her mind. She saw him as healthy, smiling, lovable, and accepting of their love. Visualizing all negative energy flying off of him like smoke flowing upward from a fire, she sent the feeling of freedom. A burden lifted. Ariana filled this force with the wonderful sensations she felt when she was on the back of her horse running free. She sensed Wendy's warm memories of the innocence and deep loving natures of the animals that shared the world with humans and sent those, too.

Reaching out to Andrew, Ariana felt his gentleness and feelings of deep responsibility to the group. She sent those feelings along with Leesie's respect and admiration and Teja's spunk. The energy in the room was feeling so powerful now it was almost overwhelming. *Dial it down a little,* she thought. *We don't want to swamp him with too much feeling.*

Breathing even more deeply, Ariana allowed herself to relax and send calm as well as love. She filled herself with memories that seemed to flow from nowhere. She realized the Elders were sending her calming memories of Meria, her home planet. The lavender colors and muted light were so beautiful. She was standing at her favorite spot overlooking the sea. The wind was blowing her hair and she absorbed the vitality it sent her. The air was crisp but not cold and smelled of the sea and the lives it nurtured. Everything about her planet was soothing. There was no chaos. All energy was in balance and all the people lived in harmony. It felt so different from Earth, but she wanted to believe, she needed to believe, that this could be Earth someday. She sent these thoughts and feelings through Tara to Matthew. If he could see it as she was seeing, if he could believe as she did, then he would survive to fight the battle that they had to win.

Ariana would not allow herself to think that they would fail tonight or any other night they chose to fight The Darkness. If just one candle can drive away the Dark, then eight will eradicate it. And if they could do the work correctly, there would eventually be thousands fighting the fight. How could they lose?

Tara's breathing changed and Ariana realized she was back. Opening her eyes, she observed Tara's aura. It looked beautiful. It was healthy, vibrant, and very alive. Seeing this, Ariana knew that they had won. Matthew was healed and would be coming home.

Wendy opened her eyes. She also felt the energy shift. "Well, what happened?" she asked.

Tara's smile was huge on her pretty face as she said, "We won. He's free. Thank you so much for all the help. But how did you know?"

Ariana responded, "I felt your need and called the others so we could help. We are all mind linked now, I think. If any of us are in trouble, all of us will know. But Tara, what was amazing was how you instinctually knew what to do. The amount of energy it took for you to project yourself there and be able to talk with Matthew was astounding. All we really did was send waves of love to Matthew. You handled all your own energy and even channeled extra energy to him so that the illusion would vanish."

"It wasn't just me," Tara confessed. "Matthew's grandfather called to the Great Spirit for help and he sent me."

"His grandfather was there, too?" Ariana asked, shocked by what Tara had said. "I didn't feel him."

"No, he was at his home. I went there to see why he wasn't helping Matthew. He said he had prayed and the Great Spirit had answered his prayer by sending me. He could see me. He said I was walking between the third and fourth dimensions. He also claimed he had known me in previous lives. He explained to me what I had to do to help Matthew and how to do it. I don't think I would have succeeded without his help," Tara claimed.

The phone rang and it was Zach. After assuring him that they had succeeded and he would be hearing from Matthew soon, Ariana called the others and shared with them the good news as well as the news about the mind link. After disconnecting from her friends, Ariana realized she was exhausted. Kissing Tara on the forehead, she turned to Wendy and announced she was going back to bed. When she hit the covers, she immediately fell asleep.

Chapter 26

The following evening the others arrived for the slumber party. Andrew and Zach had not seen Wendy or Ariana since Tara had transformed them. Their responses were everything both girls had hoped for.

"Wow! Just wow," Zach said, running his hands through Ariana's newly-styled hair. "You look different, even more beautiful, enhanced somehow. I really like that outfit, too. It shows off your pretty legs and curvaceous figure."

Blushing, Ariana gave all the credit for her transformation to Tara's handiwork and tutelage. "Without her dressing me and showing me how to style my hair, I'd still be plain old Ariana," she said.

"You've never been plain, just toned down some. But now I'll have to worry about some stud out there on campus taking you away from me."

"I doubt that," Ariana assured him, "unless of course you don't take exceptional care of me."

"No one's getting near my Wendy," Andrew announced. "Anyone tries, they'll be sorry. Just because she's the greatest looking girl on campus, doesn't mean it's open season. You're still my main squeeze, right Wendy?"

Snuggling closer to Andrew, Wendy replied, "Always, big guy. No worries. You really like my new look?"

"You're always beautiful because I know the real you. That loving, caring girl is who I'm in love with, not this hot babe on my lap here," Andrew said with a big teasing smile.

"We need to stop this BS and get down to business before I puke," said Teja. "So anyone hear anything from Matthew?"

"He called me first thing this morning," Zach announced to the group. "He sounded great: optimistic and happy. He's going to spend a couple of days with his grandfather and then he'll be home. He will have missed about a week's worth of classes but Matt's smart. He'll make them up easily. He'll be fine."

Tara told the group about Matthew's call to her that morning. "He wanted to thank me for helping him last night. He said that he knew it was me and somehow that made him feel safer. He also said that through me, he felt everyone else's love. Because it was me bringing your love, he allowed himself to accept it. He told me we saved him and allowed him to escape the illusion. He also said he would never let us down again. I assured him he had not let us down and that we all knew he would succeed. I think that made him feel really good. It will be wonderful to have him back with us again," she said with tears in her eyes. Embarrassed, she wiped them away.

"Well, I think it was sick how we combined our energies last night," Leesie exclaimed. "And now having a mind link with everyone in the group, not just my polarity, how really awesome is that!"

"Will we really get to listen to everyone's thoughts?" Andrew asked.

"It's not that simple. I think the other person has to be in great need or thinking about you before it happens," explained Ariana. "If I'm wrong, I'm sure the Elders will let us know."

"Hey, yum, these cookies are to die for," Teja said, stuffing a third cookie into her mouth.

"Save some for the rest of us," Andrew chided her, taking two.

"Slow down people," Tara said, "we have a lot to do this afternoon and there's tons of food. We won't run out of anything, I promise. So why don't we think of questions to ask Lydia? Oh, Ariana, did you get an appointment scheduled?"

"Not yet. I was thinking it might be better to wait till Matthew comes home so the whole group will be together for this."

"You're right," Zach agreed. "We should all be together. Also, Matt might have some questions that we haven't thought of."

"Should we still write some down?" Teja asked. "Isn't that one of the things we were going to do tonight?"

"We could, but I'd like to suggest that we each write down what we think are our most important subjects or items to be discussed, then we will compare them and pick out what we think the top 10 or so are. Kinda like what they did with the general questions at the channeling," suggested Tara.

"Do that now or on our own time?" Wendy asked.

Tara shook her head. "I'm not sure, what's everyone else think?"

"I'd rather do some strategizing about how we are going to recruit other people," Leesie suggested.

"You're the computer whiz. Shouldn't it be done on the computer?" Andrew asked.

"That's one way. Let's brainstorm some others," Leesie responded.

Zach answered, "I think first we need to research to see if anyone else is working on this."

"Fighting The Darkness or ecology?" asked Leesie.

"Probably both. I'm afraid, though, that if we look at 'fighting The Darkness' we'll get a lot of religious fanatics talking about Hell and demons. Do we really want that?" Zach asked.

Leesie began clicking away on her phone. "Okay, for keywords, 'fighting the darkness,' I get a song by Primal Fear and blogs on depression. For 'the darkness,' I get a rock group, comic book, and a video game. When I use just the word 'darkness' a horror movie comes up. 'Evil' brings definitions on Wiki and a Catholic dictionary. The word 'fear' brings up lots of interesting articles, but nothing really helpful for us. Any keyword suggestions?" When no one answered she asked, "Any suggestions, period?"

"Has anyone looked to see if there are any clubs or groups on campus working to help the planet?" asked Wendy.

"That's a really good idea, Wendy," Ariana said. "Starting closer to home may help the rest of us feel like we can be more involved. The computer work should really be one or two people. What do you think, Leesie?"

"Whatever works," Leesie said testily.

"Are you pissed?" Teja asked.

"Sorry, but I feel like I'm being relegated to a back room somewhere to work alone."

"I didn't mean it to seem like that," argued Ariana. "I just don't know much about what you do and think we should leave that to people who have a clue, that's all. Sorry if I made you think I didn't appreciate how much hard work you will be doing."

"That's okay. I just don't want to have the whole responsibility for something this important," Leesie admitted.

"I'll help, too," offered Zach. "I'm pretty good with computers and so is Matthew. You won't have to do this alone. Okay?"

Feeling much better, Leesie smiled and said, "You've got a deal, dude," and gave Zach a high five.

Wendy asked, "How do we find out what clubs and groups are on campus?"

"By using the computer, of course," Leesie answered. "Whoa, there's a lot of them, but obviously many won't work for our purposes. We'll probably have to go to a meeting to know what they are really about, but I can tell you what they claim they do. Okay, here they are. We can look them over together."

After reading pages of material, the group decided on four clubs to begin with. Zach and Matt would check out the Arizona Science Outreach that claimed to work with middle school and elementary students to promote independent thinking and problem solving through math and science skills and teaching. Andrew and Wendy would look into the Global Sustainability Students' Initiative, a research and educational project. Leesie would check into Barrett Sustainability Club because it was only open to Barrett students and Teja and Leesie would also check out the Student Interactive Global Network Service that made videos about solutions for global problems. Finally, Ariana and Tara were to investigate Greenlight Solutions, a consulting group on sustainability projects.

"Through these clubs," Ariana said, "maybe we can find some that are more focused on what we are trying to do. If not, we can start one I guess. Anyone know how?"

"We'll figure it out," Leesie assured her. "No biggy. I've just discovered that there are a bazillion 'how to save our planet' sites. I'll start getting to know them better and see who I think might be on the same page as us."

"Sounds like a plan," Ariana agreed. "After we check into all these clubs, what do we do next?"

"Let's ask Lydia if she has any suggestions," Tara said. "I'm sure that there are other ways, ancient ways, we can fight. Maybe she knows some."

"Okay, we've been working long enough. I vote we eat now. I need more than cookies to keep this great body going," Andrew claimed.

"I second that," both Zach and Teja said almost at the same time.

For the rest of the evening and throughout the night, the group acted like any other group of college friends. All thoughts of negativity and The Darkness left for another day as they laughed, teased, and gorged themselves on Tara's wonderful food. No one noticed as the sun set and the room filled with shadows. No one noticed that The Darkness was inside, watching and waiting to attack the next weak link.

Chapter 27

Wendy sat on the couch in the therapist's office. She had never paid much attention to the décor of the office before. She had been too depressed to care. But as she waited for the therapist to attend to an emergency, she found herself looking around. The office was decorated in brown tones. A large, cherry wood desk dominated the center back of the medium-sized room. There was a beige ultrasuede couch on the left wall and two ultrasuede chairs sat in front of the desk. The therapist's chair was a plain brown desk chair. The pictures on the walls were pastoral scenes of farms and forests with no personal photographs. Wendy didn't see any signs of a computer. She realized that although the office was comfortable, it was in no way comforting, and it told her nothing about the therapist.

The door opened and the therapist entered. "I'm very sorry, Wendy. I didn't mean to take any of your time. I am glad to see you today. I wasn't sure you would be coming."

"Why not?" Wendy asked. "I've been coming every Thursday for four months now."

"You've made such a wonderful transformation in the last six weeks I'm not even sure you need these sessions anymore. What do you think?" the therapist asked.

Wendy thought about the question for a moment then answered, "You're right, I am much better. The anger against the world is gone, but I'm not one hundred percent sure the anger against myself is. I'm afraid it's just hidden and will create an opening for something horrible to enter."

"Something horrible?"

"Yeah," Wendy answered, not sure she wanted to go into details about The Darkness even though Lydia had said the therapist was meant to help them in their work.

"What do you worry is horrible?"

Wendy decided to go for it. "The Darkness."

The therapist looked at Wendy for several minutes as though she was trying to decide what to say herself. Finally, she asked, "Why do you think The Darkness can use your pain?"

"Because it used Matthew's," she replied.

"Tell me what you mean, Wendy."

"Because of Matthew's self-hate The Darkness got in. Matthew started acting really weird: mean, negative, and even suicidal."

The therapist was disturbed by this news. "Why didn't any of you call me?"

"We didn't know whether we could trust you. We were afraid you would have him institutionalized," Wendy admitted.

"I understand why you might think that," the therapist acknowledged, "but I want you to hear me now—I am here to assist you and your group. You must understand that I will do everything I can to help you achieve your goals. Tell me how Matthew is now."

"He went to Lame Deer, where his grandfather lives and got help. We think he's fine now, but he's not home yet. Didn't you wonder why he wasn't in group or his private session?"

"Yes, I did, but I wasn't alerted by the Elders that I should be concerned," the therapist admitted.

Wendy was shocked. The therapist had mentioned the Elders. "You know about the Elders?" she asked.

"Yes, Wendy, I have been waiting for the eight of you to come together. Like I said, I am here to help your group succeed any way I can. That is my path. So talk to me about why you are so worried The Darkness can find a foothold in you when you are doing so well."

"I've been having dreams about my brother," Wendy said quietly.

"Dreams or are they the nightmares again?" the therapist inquired.

"Some feel kinda like nightmares, but not as bad as they were. Others just feel like I am really talking to him," replied Wendy.

The therapist continued to explore, "With all you have been learning, I am wondering why you do not want to consider that you really are talking to him? You know death is just another dimension, an energy dimension."

"Yes, I believe that. But he doesn't seem to hate me and he seems so happy."

"From what I have learned, the Other Side is wonderful, a place filled with unqualified and unfiltered love. Why wouldn't he be happy and why would he hate you?"

Almost too quiet to be heard, Wendy whispered, "Because he was so young and I killed him."

"Wendy, we've discussed this before. You know that's not true. He died in an accident that wasn't your fault," the therapist sternly replied. "You know that when it's someone's time to die, nothing can prevent it. He was kicked in the head by a horse. How could you have prevented that?"

"If I'd paid closer attention, I would have seen him."

"You told me you were in the barn saddling your horse and he was in the pasture," the therapist said.

"Yes, but it was my job to keep an eye on him. I resented that. I was sick of being his babysitter. Maybe I wanted him dead. Could I have killed him by wanting him dead?" Wendy moaned. She was crying.

"No," the therapist stated.

"But if thoughts can manifest, why couldn't I have caused him to die?"

"Because you weren't focused on doing evil. You were only eleven years old, only a child. Children often think angry thoughts. If they could manifest everything they think, the world would be filled with winged pink ponies," the therapist declared.

"What do I do to forgive myself?" Wendy asked, still in obvious pain.

"If Ariana told you she had caused something terrible to happen to someone, what would you say to her?"

"I'd ask her what she had done," replied Wendy.

The therapist continued, "And if Ariana said that she had been driving and her attention had wandered for a few minutes and she had an accident that killed someone?"

"I would ask her if she meant to hurt anyone and then, because I know she could never be malicious, I would ask her if she had learned to pay attention when she was driving."

"If she said that she never wanted to drive again and would never forgive herself, how would you respond?"

"I would try to help her to understand that sometimes you can't control everything and that she needed to be realistic. Someday she would have to drive again and if she determined that she would not take her attention off the road, nothing like that would ever happen again. And as far as never forgiving herself, that's just downright screwy. Accidents happen, it's just too bad this one had such a difficult lesson attached. Then I'd tell her how special she was, hug her, and hope that helped," Wendy explained.

"So you'd treat Ariana differently than you'd treat yourself?" the therapist asked.

"What do you mean?"

"You said that not forgiving herself was 'downright screwy' and you knew she wasn't a malicious person and never planned to hurt anyone. Accidents happen," the therapist reminded Wendy.

"Yeah, but my situation was different. He was my responsibility!"

"Wendy, your mother was home. You thought your brother was inside with her. How was it your responsibility?" asked the therapist.

"Am I thinking like a victim?"

"You are thinking like someone who treats others better than she treats herself. To be a good friend you must love yourself enough to be worth befriending. You must understand that each soul has an agenda that the ego often doesn't understand. You don't know what your brother's soul intended. For that matter, you don't know what your soul's agreement with your brother's soul was. Perhaps you needed the experience of losing him so early to prepare you for things you might encounter on your path. Also, because he has started communicating with you, it is possible that you will begin to develop the ability to talk with the dead."

"Like a medium?"

"Not necessarily. Mediums usually go into trance in order to communicate. The trance can be light, almost unobservable, but still a trance. Whereas you seem to communicate through dreams. You might find that eventually you will not need to be asleep to hear and talk with them. Did you ask you brother for his forgiveness?"

"No, I've been too afraid," replied Wendy.

"Ask his forgiveness and then forgive yourself. That way you won't need to worry about The Darkness gaining a foothold. I would also suggest that you tell the rest of the group about your vulnerability. They will not judge you, I am sure of that, and they can help you release this guilt and shame. Each of you must become completely transparent to one another. If anyone is holding secrets that can be exploited by The Darkness, the entire group is at risk. If any of you has a deep fear of anything, the group must know."

"I am really glad I came today," Wendy admitted. "I had been thinking I didn't need counseling anymore, but when I dreamed of my brother last night, I decided to come. I feel much better now and I have a lot to tell the group that will help us to get better, including that you are one of us. That's really awesome!"

Chapter 28

The whole group was waiting in downtown Phoenix for Matthews's bus to arrive. Everyone was feeling excited and they couldn't wait for Matthew to tell them about his trip and what he had learned and experienced.

For Phoenix, the weather was chilly, around 55 degrees. Ariana could feel winter in the air. The downtown hotels, restaurants, and shops had already begun decorating for Christmas and everything seemed more festive and bright, adding to the excitement of the season. It was only three days until Thanksgiving. The group had made some wonderful plans for their own private celebration. Although those who lived in Arizona had responsibilities to attend family events, everyone arranged to have the evening available for what the group had planned. They were excited to see how Matthew would respond.

Tara was subdued as she waited, hoping the ordeal Matthew had survived had made him better, not injured him in any way. She hadn't told anyone in the group of her fears as she didn't want anyone to think she was being negative. Since she had helped him survive his quest she had felt so connected to him. She couldn't imagine how she could remain in the group if he was no longer the person who accepted her for who she was. If he had grown as much as Zach felt he had, would he reject her now that he wasn't as wounded as she? She had let these thoughts consume her for the past few days as she played the happy Tara for Wendy and Ariana and the rest of the group. It had been hard to pretend to Ariana and Wendy because they were living with her, but also because she genuinely cared about them. She knew they completely accepted her as a female. That was amazing to Tara especially because she was still trying to come to grips with staying exactly as she was, no physical modifications. She prayed that Matthew would feel okay with that, too.

"I think this is his bus," Zach said excitedly. "It's only been a little over a week. Why am I acting like I haven't seen him in months?"

Ariana put her arm around his waist and answered him, "Because you love him and worry about him. Because he's your best friend and you missed him a lot."

Zach kissed the top of Ariana's head, "And that's why I love you so much you understand me and don't think I'm a dweeb."

The bus pulled in and parked. It took a few minutes for people to start to disembark. Everyone had cases, backpacks, and boxes they had to retrieve from the overhead racks. Leesie was impatiently hoping from one foot to the other when she said, "Do you see him yet? Are you sure this is his bus? Where **is** he?"

"There he is," said Andrew. "He's wearing a brown leather jacket. See him?"

Matthew had just gotten to the bus door and started down the stairs. His hair was mussed, which was unusual. But other than that, it was still him, their Matthew.

Zach rushed over to Matthew and scooped him up in a giant bear hug. Messing his hair even more, Zach held Matthew at arm's length and just looked at him. "How you doing, bro? You're looking good."

Matthew laughed, "I've only been gone a week, dude."

"Yeah, well it's been a very long week for us," said Zach.

Matthew nodded, "For me, too. It was a week that lasted 10 years. But I think I'm fully whole now, no more missing pieces."

Leesie couldn't wait anymore. Running up to Matthew she said, "Hey Zach, save some of him for the rest of us." Hugging Matthew, she said, "What's that mean, 'no more missing pieces?' "

"I'll tell all of you my story after we get something to eat. I'm starving. All I had to eat in the last 24 hours was a couple of stale doughnuts I got at a 7-Eleven. But first—Tara, don't stand over there—come here," Matthew said, holding out his arms.

Tara walked into Matthew's embrace. He held her for several minutes. Tara felt no holding back, no resistance, just real feeling.

"Thank you," Matthew whispered, tears in his voice. "You saved my life. Everything I've become, I owe to your intervention. You are my blessing and I am so happy that we are polarities. Namee'me' wants me to tell you that you are now one of the Cheyenne and he looks forward to performing your first sweat lodge."

"It wasn't just me," Tara objected, "the entire group worked with me. They fed me energy and light. Without them I wouldn't have succeeded."

Holding his arms open as wide as possible, Matthew yelled, "Come here everyone, I need to give you all a hug."

"Group hug!" Leesie screamed, grabbing the rest of the group and herding them into the hug. "This is as it should be. The circle is complete. Can I have an amen?"

"Amen," Matt agreed. "Now, can we please get some food?"

As they had often done before, everyone piled into Zach's car. This time Tara sat on Matthew's lap in the front seat, Teja and Wendy sat on Andrew with Leesie beside them in the backseat and Ariana sat on the console between Zach and Matthew. They ended up at a Chinese restaurant on Madison Street not far from the bus station.

The group ordered a variety of food to share and after Zach showed everyone how to use chopsticks, they dug in. Matthew and Andrew proved just how much food 18 year old men can eat.

"Hey you two, slow down. This isn't the last food on the planet," Wendy warned.

"It is amazing how much men can eat," Teja stated, eating her fourth egg roll.

Leesie shook her head in agreement while picking all the chicken out of the vegetables.

"What are you doing?" Teja asked her.

"I've decided to become a vegetarian," Leesie explained. "I figure if Wendy's going to teach us how to talk to animals, I don't want to feel guilty for just having eaten one."

Wendy looked at her blankly, "Why?"

"What do you mean 'why'? " Leesie asked.

Wendy finished chewing and answered, "What's talking to them got to do with eating them?"

"It just seems really creepy weird to eat something that you've had a conversation with," Leesie explained.

"Growing up on a farm gives you a very different perspective on eating things. Do you think that plants don't have a consciousness? Are you going to stop eating them, too? Then what are you going to live on?"

"Oh, shit! Plants have a consciousness, too?" said Leesie.

"That's what some scientists believe. There's been research done that claims they've recorded plants screaming when they or another plant near them is hurt," Tara replied.

Leesie became very quiet thinking about what her diet choices might be. Finally, she said, "I guess seeds are out too, right, because they are baby plants? If I take the seeds out, can I eat fruit that has already fallen to the ground?"

"Leesie, relax," Wendy answered. "The animals we eat, at least the ones treated humanely, are aware of what they are giving us. They have been bred for it. Same with plants. It's only when they are treated badly, put in cages where they can't even lay down, or hurt in other ways, that they fight it. You can even taste the difference. Until I went to ASU, I only ate what we raised or grew. The food was much tastier. It's really hard to explain until you've actually tasted the difference. Hey, I've got a great idea. How about if I bring the turkey and some veggies from our farm for Thanksgiving? Then you'll taste the difference yourself. Will that be okay Tara, or have you already bought everything?"

"I can always freeze the turkey I have and use it for Christmas and we'll eat the veggies during the week. I think I'd like to taste the difference."

"Then I'll go to the farm tomorrow and get a good bird along with some stuff from the garden," Wendy committed.

"You girls are having Thanksgiving together?" Matthew asked.

"We all are," several of the group said in unison.

Zach explained to Matt, "I wanted to keep it a secret until we got back to our dorm, but we're having dinner at Tara's and mom's flying in to be with us. Tara's Abuela and Teja's Gram will be coming, too."

"It will be great to see your mom and to celebrate this holiday with my real family. I have a lot to be thankful for this year," Matthew replied.

"We were a little concerned that you might not want to be around so many people so soon after your experience," Ariana said. "I am very happy that you're okay with all this."

Matthew smiled and said, "Whenever there is good, plentiful food shared with friends, you can always count me in."

"So, when are you going to tell us about your awesome adventure?" Leesie asked.

"Let's go back to Ariana's dorm room and I'll tell you everything that happened."

"You mean go to Tara's then," Leesie informed him. "Ariana and Wendy are living over there right now to make sure she was okay while you fought your fight."

"Sounds like a lot's changed in one week," Matthew replied.

"Not to mention that you missed at least four tests this week, too," said Andrew.

"Thanks, Andrew. I needed to hear that right now," Matt said, punching Andrew's arm.

"Hey," Andrew objected, "what's with everyone hitting me on the arm? Do I look like a punching bag?"

"No, Sweet Baboo, it's just that you are so big and look like you can take it," Wendy explained. "They just don't realize how sweet and squishy you really are."

"Okay, it's obvious we won't need dessert now. That was so sticky sweet it's gonna make me hurl," Teja teased. "Let's head to Tara's."

The group squeezed themselves into Zach's car again and headed down Van Buren to Mill Avenue. As they drove, Ariana noticed that this area of town had seen better days. There were several motels, many of them closed and boarded up, others looked like they charged by the hour. There were people on the street, some pushing shopping carts, others lounging in doorways, a few passed out on benches, and some just standing in front of small bars talking. Several seedy looking car dealerships and pawn shops also dotted the area. There were very few chain restaurants or fast food places, probably because the people in this area spent their money on drugs, alcohol, and sex, not food. The area was depressing looking and made Ariana think about the beautiful desert that was destroyed to create this area which was once probably a thriving center for a much younger Phoenix. *So many things need changing,* she thought, feeling her mood sinking.

"Look," exclaimed Leesie, "look in that park!"

Ariana followed the pointing finger and saw a group of people stringing colored lights, picking up trash, handing out food, and decorating a Christmas tree. Children were laughing and helping.

"See, even in the midst of all this poverty and pain," Leesie said, "people are still helping one another and finding reasons to be joyful."

Ariana thought about what she had just been pondering in her mind.

Stop it! Stop being negative. Leesie's right. Even in the middle of the worst of mankind, the best of mankind exists and is fighting for change.

"Did Tara tell everyone her part of the story?" Matthew asked. When there was a general acknowledgment that she had, he continued. "I guess I'll start with the night I invaded everyone's privacy.

I hadn't realized how alone I was feeling. I had been used to having Zach around for the last few years, and when he and Ariana hooked up he just wasn't around very much. I didn't realize it then, but I became jealous, not of their relationship, but that it had taken him away from me. I now know it triggered unresolved abandonment issues. I thought I'd gotten rid of these issues with help from my counselors years ago. I started thinking about my mother. Some of you don't know, but from about age six to when Zach and his mom rescued me, I was being sexually abused by my mother. The fact that it started so young made it difficult for me to understand that it was a bad thing. I just thought she was showing me love. She kept telling me that someday I would abandon her like her parents and my dad had, so when I went to live with Zach, I started feeling extremely guilty that I had done just that—abandoned her. Because everyone else thought that I should be angry with my mother, I never told anyone that what I was really feeling was hatred toward myself for letting her down.

The Darkness entered at the depth of my guilt and despair and convinced me everything I had experienced from the moment I left my mother was the Universe and people as a whole conspiring to hurt the two of us, my mom and me. I became really angry at Ariana for what I perceived as her purposely taking Zach away from me. She became an evil force in my mind. I'm sorry, Ariana. Generalizing from her to the group, I began to see the group and each individual person in the group as sinister and negative, that you all wanted to hurt me. My anger grew. The only one I was conflicted about was Tara. Our link was too strong for me to believe that she was truly out to hurt me. That's when I discovered my ability to astral project. I was able to leave my physical body and let my energy go to other places. I projected to where each of you were. I planted negative thoughts and fears or brought out the old ones that still lurked in your minds. Everything worked until I went to Tara's. The cat noticed me and reacted and Tara wasn't afraid, maybe because deep down she sensed it was me, or maybe it's her nature to calmly assess a situation then take action. Regardless, she did everything right and I was pulled back into my body. It was weird and very uncomfortable.

The next day at the park, I was still filled with negativity and rage. I worked very hard to act normal, but I knew some of you felt what was really happening. That made you an even bigger threat.

When Zach came to me the next day telling me that you, Ariana, had sensed a problem, The Darkness made me want to fight back as hatefully and as hurtfully as I could. That's why I said those things, Zach. At the time, part of me really believed them. All I wanted to do was to put doubt and confusion out there to all of you so that the group would implode. I guess The Darkness realized that as long as you worked together, it could not block the love that you were sending me. That love reached the part of me that craved love and acceptance. It helped me override the self-loathing I felt.

What you seven did at Gammage saved my life. That's what pushed me over the edge and made me head for Lame Deer. Before you did that, I thought my only alternatives were to turn completely dark or to commit suicide. You guys made me want to live and beat this thing. I'm still not sure how I materialized in the middle of your circle, but if I had to guess I'd say Namee'me' had something to do with it. Your actions crystallized my commitment and kept The Darkness at bay for my trip to Lame Deer. I had only one episode along the way that could have turned out very badly for me, but somehow I saw through it and kept going."

"Not to interrupt, although that's what I just did," Ariana said with a smile, "but you need to tell us everything. The more we know about how The Darkness works, the better prepared we are to fight it. What was the episode that happened along the way?"

Matthew told them about meeting the battered man at the rest stop and how this poor soul's story began to resonate with his own anger, but that something, and he still wasn't sure what, had set off alarms within him that had loosened the grip the stranger had begun to get on his brain.

"I think I know what eventually turned you off to the guy," Zach offered. "I think it was two things. First, you are not violent toward others, only toward yourself. And him talking about blowing people away would have freaked you out on some level. Secondly, it seems like all he did was whine. You don't like people who whine. You have always kept your troubles to yourself, never complained about them to other people. Not that keeping your troubles to yourself is a particularly good idea for you, but whining is not your style."

"I think you are right, on this level of consciousness. But since the sweat lodge and vision quest, I now believe we are protected and helped from several dimensions and worlds. They weren't going to let me be turned so easily," Matthew shared.

"What happened next?" Leesie asked.

"When the bus was nearing Lame Deer, I was concerned about reaching my grandfather. I hadn't told him I was coming and wasn't even sure he would be home. He doesn't usually go far, but he could have been gone for the day. It was cold there, around 30 degrees. All I had on was my hoodie, jeans, and Nikes, no jacket. There was snow and the sky looked like it wasn't done yet. If I had to walk from the bus station, I'd freeze. But when I got off the bus, Namee'me' was waiting for me, just as though I'd called to tell him I was on the way. He said that he knew I was coming and had been waiting. He also claimed to know what had been happening to me and had already arranged a sweat lodge ceremony for the next day. Namee'me' explained that these were sacred ceremonies to our people and are most often performed when our people are younger. But because of my past, he had been waiting for the best time. The sweat lodge is a purification ritual, and in my case, was used to purify and cleanse me for the vision quest I would be undertaking. The vision quest's purpose was to ask the Great Spirit to guide me on my path, to ask the ancestors and totem animals for their assistance in walking this path, and to completely drive out The Darkness by eradicating my personal demons.

I was allowed no food or water until I returned from my quest four days later. If the Great Spirit honored me, I would return whole, no pieces of my soul missing. If not, I would be dead and lost in the spirit world forever."

"What do you mean, 'no pieces of my soul missing'?" Andrew

asked.

"My people believe that if a person is injured by another person, the person doing the injury takes a piece of your soul and replaces it with a piece of theirs. That is why even though I had been the victim, I felt hatred toward myself and guilt at abandoning my mother. Others might experience this differently. They may take the perpetrator's anger and inflict it outward and want to hurt others, as the man at the rest stop wanted to do. It depends on what personality type you are," Matthew answered.

"But all of us have been injured," Tara responded. "Are you saying that potential is within all of us?"

"Yes," Matthew replied. "I believe that is why to be a spiritual person you must practice forgiveness. You must not let pain consume your life. Forgiveness is not forgiving the deed. You must allow yourself to release the injury within yourself."

"I read a quote once that I think works here," Leesie said. "It goes, 'Hatred and resentment are as though you have taken poison and you expect the other person to die.' Holding onto all that pain only sickens and weakens you and allows The Darkness in, it does nothing to the one that caused the pain."

"Lydia said that same quote to me," Ariana remembered.

"I like that quote," Matthew acknowledged, "and you're right Leesie, holding on to pain only continues to victimize you. What most people don't know is that whatever happens to us is part of a greater plan. I know many will find that a disturbing thought, that somehow our lives are being manipulated, but that is too simplistic. In the wheel of life, all experience will happen and then be undone. I know that sounds a little cryptic so I'll try to explain a knowledge I now seem to possess on a visceral level, not a logical one. I'll try an example—but first you must believe in the concept of reincarnation for any of this to make sense. Also, you must believe in a loving God, not a punishing one. The punishing God model is what causes people to think that things are done to you because you deserve pain for the sins you have performed and that this world is made up of pain so that you can receive the blessings of Heaven or a multitude of virgins for your sacrifices on Earth, for example. Or you could believe that God is testing you, like Job from the Old Testament.

The reincarnation model that I believe is that the soul creates lifetimes to live so that it can gain knowledge and experience to give the Source, the Creator, God. If one lifetime is filled with bounty and the soul has learned enough about bounty for a while, it will next create a lifetime of lack. It is not punishing, it is gaining new knowledge. How the ego responds to these different scenarios determines what kind of knowledge the soul receives. For instance, if you are living in a third world country and barely surviving, you have several choices. One might be to endure as your family before you has, another might be to leave and attempt to find better conditions, another might be to become bitter and hateful and envy those with more, or share the little you have because that makes you feel better, or become a nun or priest and give your life to service. Do you see where I'm going? For every situation, there are thousands of things you can do and hundreds of ways you can perceive the situation. Even something as horrible as the loss of a child can be turned into something great like John Walsh did after the death of his son Adam. He created a change within our world that might not have happened if he had turned in on himself and just became bitter in his mourning. There are many examples of people having the same types of experiences. Some grow strong and make positive changes that help others and there are those that do the opposite and even go on to hurt others. Those that go on to hurt others are then giving those people that are hurt the opportunity to grow strong and good or keep the abuse going. It is the ego's free will, not God that determines which direction a person will go. God will always see you as perfect. After all, you are a reflection of God. If you believe that God is a loving God, then you must believe that God would never judge you. Judgment has no place in unconditional love.

Now back to Tara's question. It is this anger, pain, and resentment that The Darkness feeds on. It is imperative to release it through the understanding that you have no idea what the soul intent over the millennia of lifetimes is. Perhaps you were owed an experience, a lesson, because you held guilt from a past incarnation. If in the past you had been an Inquisitor, would it not undo this guilt by being in a concentration camp, lifetimes later? Wouldn't it allow your soul to experience both sides of the equation? Forgiveness can help stop this circle. If you hold no guilt, resentment, anger, pain, no negative emotions toward anything in your life and just accept that there is a purpose that you do not know yet, and that the purpose is not to punish or hurt you, the cycle stops and you are living outside the illusions of fear, guilt and pain."

"I was talking with Lydia, the psychic, earlier today," Ariana informed the group. "Somehow this subject came up. She told me a parable that I think fits this. When Jesus decided to come to Earth to save humanity, he chose his 12 best friends to accompany him, the apostles. Right before they were to leave to begin their incarnation on Earth, Jesus asked for the one who loved him the most to step forward. Judas stepped forward and Jesus said, 'Thank you Judas for loving me enough to betray me, because without your betrayal, none of the rest of what must happen will happen.' In other words, we all chose our Judases and without them, our lives would not proceed as they need to."

"Wow, that's heavy," Teja said.

"But true. So if you can see those people in your life that have caused you pain as those the soul chose because of their great love for you, then maybe it will be easier to forgive the person even if you can't forgive the behavior," Matthew added. "Okay, back to the story. The sweat lodge was attended by both men and women. It is a series of cleansing prayers, chants, and stories in a superheated room. I've just made a complex ritual very simple, but that's really all you need to know right now. You sweat then submerge yourself in an ice cold stream. It really was very purifying.

After the ceremony, I was sent to walk up the mountain until I found the place where the land would accept me. All I had with me was a blanket, a flannel shirt, and this jacket," Matthew said, pointing to the brown leather jacket hanging over the back of the chair. "It took me all day to find this place. It was at the very top of the hill overlooking the town. I found it right at sundown and got to watch a beautiful sunset as well as the rising of the full moon. I made a seat for myself then said a prayer to the Great Spirit, my ancestors, and totem animals, and sat down to await their answer. The first thing I saw was a fantastic silver wolf. He was beautiful. As I was looking for him to give me an indication of what came next, I felt something else. I looked, but saw nothing. When I turned back to the wolf, he was gone—and who I think was the Great Spirit—was standing where the wolf had been. He was holding a rattle and had a white bird. I think it was a Raven, but they're not white. This unusual bird was perched on his hand. I thought I had displeased him because I found myself in the middle of a dust devil. My mouth, eyes, and nose filled with dust and debris, choking me. About the time I thought I would be buried by the dust, the storm stopped and I found myself in a void, no sound or sight. I began to feel a deep despair over this new abandonment. I felt completely lost and hopeless. After what seemed like forever, I heard a slithering sound but could still see nothing. A voice talked to me. It sounded like a snake. It said I lived in the darkness of my past and in that place The Light could not get in. It said that was why the Dark could take me so easily. It said if I desired punishment, then it would punish me. I felt a deep pain in my left thigh and knew it had bitten me. I became feverish, hot then cold. My leg hurt so badly I was in agony. My leg would no longer hold my weight so I fell in a pile on the ground. It felt extremely swollen and the pain from my leg throbbed constantly. I also had such a bad pain in my head I could no longer lift it or think straight. I decided it would be better to die. I gave up. That was when Tara came and saved me. She brought The Light and with it made sense out of nonsense. She challenged me to be the person she knew me to be."

Matthew smiled at Tara. "How could I possibly refuse her? The pain and The Darkness disappeared and with it, all the illusions. I was well and whole and ready to be the warrior not the victim. The anger and guilt that had poisoned my body and mind were gone and my soul was again completely my own. The hawk and the wolf walk with me now and I walk the path chosen by my ancestors.

When I returned to Lame Deer there was a celebration of my success and I was given my new name by my people. Now you have the whole story."

"Oh no we don't," Teja objected. "What is your new name?"

"Ovana'xaetano notaxe. It means peaceful warrior."

Chapter 30

Tara's house was decorated with fall wreaths of multi-colored leaves, pine cones, and little red berries in preparation for the Thanksgiving feast. There were small pumpkins and gourds adorning beautiful glass bowls and candles of various sizes and colors throughout the living and dining rooms. She set the table with a white linen tablecloth and orange and gold napkins. She even used her abuela's china and real silver setting. A fire in her fireplace added the final touch to a perfect atmosphere for the celebration.

True to her word, Wendy had brought a 26-pound turkey from her parent's farm as well as fresh herbs, squash, sweet potatoes, and greens. Having never cooked greens, Tara gave that job to Teja who promptly enlisted her gram to instruct her. The sweet potatoes were given to Ariana, and Leesie worked her magic on the squash. Not wanting to leave the men out of the fun, Tara assigned them to mashing potatoes and grilling the corn on the cob. She created the salad, dressing, roasted the turkey and ordered her abuela, Teja's gram, and Zach's mother, Julie, to enjoy some wine and just relax by the fire.

Diablo, dressed in an orange and gold collar, helped by keeping everyone entertained and curling between the cooks' legs. Later, he would join in the feast with his own personal helping of turkey giblets.

"It's great how well they're getting along," Teja said to Tara as she nodded to the three women sitting and talking in front of the fire. "It's as though they've known each other for years instead of minutes."

"Were you expecting something else?" Tara asked.

"Well, the way things have been going over the past several weeks, who knows?"

"I knew," Leesie said. "Judging by you two and Zach, how could they not be great peeps?"

"You are very lucky to have your grandmothers with you still," Ariana said wistfully. "I really miss my oma. Every year on my birthday, she would sing "Happy Birthday" to me and bake me my favorite dessert, plum kugen. I really miss her this time of year."

"Is your birthday in November?" Wendy asked. "I can't believe I don't even know my roommate's birthday."

"It's no big deal," Ariana said, embarrassed.

"Whoa, girl. Are you cray-cray," Leesie argued, "That's the day you were sent here to help save this planet. It's probably the biggest deal ever! Cough it up, when's the big day and how old are you going to be?"

"Yeah, sista, tell us," Teja joined in.

"It's December eighth and I'll be nineteen."

"We've got to figure out some wonderful celebration for this momentous event," Wendy said. "Anyone got any ideas?"

"Let's not do this with Ariana here," Tara suggested, "that way we can come up with something special and surprise her."

Ariana said, "Come on you guys, don't do this. You'll embarrass me. I'm really not used to having people fuss over my birthday."

"Let's just ignore that crazy voice in the corner," Tara said. "Get over it, Chiquita, we've stopped listening to you."

"Well, just promise me you won't tell Zach. I don't want him to think he owes me something. Okay?"

"Still not listening," said Teja.

"We need to write down everyone's birthdays so we can celebrate all of us," suggested Leesie. "As the official group secretary I will record them all and send them out to everyone. Ariana, December 8, Leesie, March 3 and I'll be 16. Tara what's yours?"

"June 22, I'll be 18 this year."

"That is a big one. Your turn Teja," said Leesie.

"Can't you tell by my big mouth? I'm a Gemini. On June 3, I'll be 19."

"Your turn, Wendy," Leesie said.

"I'm another Sagittarius. My birthday is December 19 and I'll be 19, too."

"I'll be back," Leesie announced. "Gotta get the guys."

"I sure hope she doesn't tell Zach my birthday's coming up," Ariana worried.

"Give it up, girl. You know she will," Teja said.

Almost immediately Zach came into the kitchen and said, "When were you going to tell me I only have eleven days till your birthday?"

"How about never," Ariana answered. "I really don't like people making a big deal of it. I'm not used to that."

"Well I'm afraid it's time to get used to it. You're now part of a big family that likes to celebrate everything," Zach declared.

Interrupting, Leesie came in and announced, "Matthew's birthday is November 20, we missed it cause he was at his namee'me's in Lame Deer and he's now 19. There seems to be an age theme here. Andrew's is Jan 31, also 19, and Zach's is March 26, and again, 19. Do you think we should do something to celebrate Matt's birthday today?"

"I'll put candles on the pumpkin pie and we'll sing "Happy Birthday." I don't know what else we can do," Tara said.

The other girls thought hard about any alternatives, but all agreed there was really nothing else they could do on such short notice.

"The corn's done," Andrew yelled. "When do we eat?"

The men came into the kitchen to argue over the best way to carve the turkey as the women carried trays laden with food into the dining room. Eventually, the turkey got carved by Teja who was sick of the arguing and too hungry to wait to see who won. When everything was placed on the table, Tara lit the candles and turned down the lights, giving the room an intimate glow.

"Before we sit down I would like us all to join hands around the table and say a prayer for the blessing of this new group of friends who are fast becoming my true family," Tara suggested.

After they chose their seats and joined hands, Tara began, "Great Spirit, Jesus, God, the Source and our Creator, we thank you for this bounty you have set before us, not only the bounty of food but also the bounty of love, friendship, and happiness that we share. We ask for your help and your strength to walk our individual and our shared paths and to succeed in this mighty endeavor you have set before us."

They sat down. Leesie suggested they each say something for which they were grateful. She began, "I am grateful for the friendships I have made this year and the wonderful brain I was given."

Going around the table clockwise, Ariana was next. "I am grateful for moving to Arizona and beginning my new life with my new friends and with Zach."

Zach said, "I am grateful for having the best mom and the best girlfriend in the world and for having such a beautiful world to enjoy and for Matt being back."

Zach's mother Julie offered, "I am grateful to be here today with both my boys, Zach and Matthew, and that they are both so happy."

"I am so grateful that my Tara has finally found people who love her as much as I do and who she feels so comfortable with," Tara's Abuela said.

Tara squeezed her abuela's hand and replied, "I am so, so grateful to finally feel accepted as I am by so many wonderful friends and also for finding a real purpose."

"I am grateful for the help I received this week from all the people who I now understand love me. I love you all with an open heart. I am grateful to have banished the old Matthew and to have accepted the warrior Matthew."

"I am grateful to be living on campus and not having to take a bus every day and all the other stuff you guys have already said," Teja joined in.

Teja's gram added, "I am grateful to Jesus and to Teja's friends that they have helped her to accept her gifts without fear and to have blessed her with the knowledge of who her father really was."

When it was Wendy's turn, she said, "I am so grateful for everything these last few months have given me: a new identity, friendships, abilities, happiness, and Andrew."

Andrew kissed Wendy's hand and said, "Same for me and especially the part about having Wendy in my life. And I am especially grateful for all this great food that's getting cold, so let's eat!"

"We have something to add, right girls?" Tara declared as the girls stood and sang "Happy Birthday" to Matthew.

Chapter 31

The sky was bright blue with only a wisp of clouds. Dust motes swirled in the sunlight dancing to a tune only they could hear. If you listened closely, you could hear a variety of bird songs mixing with tunes playing in someone's dorm room. Every now and then the shrill sound of a ringing cell phone, and the occasional loud voice, disturbed the tranquility of the scene.

Wendy had spread a large, colorful quilt on the ground. It was handmade. Great care had been taken to pick the perfect swatches of cloth used to create the complex design. The colors were various shades of lavender, green, yellow, and blue accented by a small amount of beige. The pattern was called Starry Nights, an appropriate name as the design included an eight-point star that appeared to explode with dizzying color against a galaxy-black background and brilliant tumbling block shapes. It was beautiful.

"Are we really gonna sit on that?" asked Teja.

Wendy looked perturbed, "Why, what's wrong with it?"

"It's way too beautiful to throw down on the grass just to sit our butts on," said Teja.

"You really think so?" Wendy asked, obviously pleased by the comment.

"I agree," Tara said. "It's really beautiful. It had to cost a lot of money. I've seen quilts displayed at the fair with blue ribbons that weren't one-tenth this nice."

Wendy was blushing bright red.

"OMG," Leesie exclaimed, "you made it, didn't you?"

"I made it my junior year as a 4-H project," Wendy admitted. "And it did win first place."

"Wow, it's really wonderful," Tara said, "but Teja's right. I'd feel really bad sitting on it on the damp grass."

"It's washable and I can make more," Wendy objected. "Why

shouldn't we be sitting on something beautiful? We're beautiful, the day is awesome, and life is good."

"Okay, as long as you're sure," Teja said, plopping herself down and lying back.

Running her hand over the quilt Leesie said, "It really is absolutely awesome. How fast can you make one?"

"Why?" asked Wendy.

"It would be a beautiful present to give Ariana for her birthday, is all," Leesie said.

"I can't make one that fast, but I have a better one I've been working on for Christmas for her. We'll have to come up with something else for her birthday."

"I'm stumped," Tara said. "Beside the new hair style, there's nothing she seems to need or want. Even clothes aren't really a big deal to her. Does she wear any jewelry besides her crystal?"

"Not that I've seen," Wendy said. "And all she sleeps in are yoga pants and a T-shirt."

"We could always get her a Victoria's Secret gift certificate," Teja suggested.

"We need to do better than that," Leesie objected, "That seems so impersonal. Anyway, shouldn't that be Zach's job?"

"She's probably got a point," Wendy admitted. "I wish we knew of something special from her planet that we could get her."

"And how the hell, girl, do you think we could go about doing that?" Teja asked.

"I may have the answer to that," Tara replied. "I like to paint. Maybe if we combine our minds in a meditation and ask the Elders, they might show us something from there she'd love."

"That's fab," Leesie whooped, "I love it. When do we try it?"

"I'd need some paper to draw on so I don't forget what we learn," Tara said.

"I've got some I brought for class. Here," Wendy said, handing her notebook to Tara.

"How do we do this?" Teja asked.

Wendy suggested, "I think we should hold hands, close our eyes, surround ourselves with white light, and just begin to breathe deeply. Then we can each think about the Elders. As soon as one of us makes contact, we can ask them to help us."

"Do we stay sitting or should we stand?" Leesie wondered.

Tara answered, "If I'm going to draw, I think it would be easier for me if I'm sitting. Okay?"

The girls all agreed and sat in a circle facing each other.

"Whoops, forgot something," Wendy said. "Let's put our crystals in front of us. Anyone got an extra one to put in the middle of the circle?"

"I'm prepared. I've got a pocket full. Can't be too careful, right ladies?" Leesie said pulling out a handful of crystals. "Let's surround the circle, too. Up with that?"

They placed the crystals behind them forming a circle of protection. Each girl then placed their personal crystal in their lap. Leesie put her biggest crystal in the center. The crystals sparkled with light and threw colors everywhere.

"Wow, that's sweet! Our world is filled with rainbows," Leesie exclaimed.

"Ready?" Wendy asked, "Okay, let's close our eyes and breathe."

Soon their breathing was in unison as each girl adjusted her energy to match her sister's. As their energy grew, the crystals began to glow, surrounding the group with a shield of protection and light. It was as though they had captured the sunlight. The circle grew warm and their breathing slowed as each girl sent out their plea to the Elders. Their request was heard instantly. All together, the girls found themselves standing on a rugged cliff overlooking a sea alive with energy. The sky was a soft violet and in the distance was a city that seemed to shine like crystals. The leaves on the trees looked more like soft downy feathers than leaves and were multiple shades of greens. The tree trunks grew like thin knobby appendages to a height of about 12 feet, branching into two forks. At the apex of the forks, the leaves grew horizontally, forming a canopy around the trunk. Within this canopy lived a small, rodent-like creature with big eyes, chirping like a bird. Conveniently, the animal kept the tree's foliage pruned. The sea below created a spray of water as it hit the side of the cliff. The drops appeared more like ice crystals than water, and where they fell, a spotted plant that looked like a mushroom grew.

The sky was obscured by a cloud formation and there were two suns in the sky, one much smaller than the other. Neither one however, put out the amount of sunlight that the girls were used to on Earth. Consequently, the light was dim, much like at twilight. *No wonder everyone's eyes are large, even the rodent's,* thought the girls in unison.

We have a mind link, thought Tara, and all the girls agreed.

Why don't each of us look in different directions? thought Wendy. *That way Tara will have a panoramic view from which to choose the scene for her painting.*

No, this is the view Ariana loves, the sea calls to her and she stands here often, they all heard and knew the Elders had shared that thought.

Okay, thank you, Tara thought. *I have my painting.*

"Whoa, dude," exclaimed Leesie as they found themselves back on Earth, their mind link dissolved. "That was absolutely fabulous!"

"Do you think you can paint that in a week?" Wendy asked.

"No problem," answered Tara.

"We'd better put the crystals away," Leesie said suddenly. "We've got an audience."

Standing on the periphery of their circle was a lanky, pleasant looking stranger. He was holding up his bicycle and watching the girls.

"Wow, that was amazing," he declared.

"What was?" Teja challenged him gruffly.

Smiling, he said, "Didn't mean to piss you off, but you had a multi-colored circle that vibrated all around you like some Star Wars force field and each of you had this outrageous look of awe on your faces. Couldn't help but stop and watch. Oh, I'm Josh."

"Well, Josh, the show's over now so you can go to class or wherever you were going," Teja said curtly.

"What were you doing?"

Tara replied before Teja could say something mean, "We were just meditating. What you probably saw was the crystals reflecting the bright sunlight and mistook it for that force field thing."

"No," he said, "I know what I saw. The crystals were reflecting the sunlight, too, but this was completely different. Are you girls Wiccan or something?"

"No, we are just trying to learn mindful meditation. I'm really not sure what you saw," Tara responded sweetly.

"I'd love to join you next time if it's not just for girls."

"Sorry," Teja answered quickly, "this was just a one-time thing, right girls?"

Disappointed, Josh replied, "Okay, I get it, I'm not wanted here. You know, I've been looking all over this campus for somewhere I could grow my spirituality other than traditional religious groups, but every time I think I've found someone to ask, I get dissed. Very disheartening."

"Wait a minute," Leesie said. "We're not mean girls, you just freaked us a little with your story about that force field thing. Here, write your name and cell number for me," she said, handing him Wendy's pad of paper, "We are trying to get a group together. If we ever do, I'll call you. I'm Leesie."

Josh took the pad, wrote down his name and number and with a dazzling smile, bowed deeply to Leesie and said, "Thank you, Leesie. It's been a pleasure to meet you." Getting on his bike, he rode away.

"WTF did you just do?" Teja chided her. "You don't know that dude from squat and you invited him into our group?"

"I did not invite him into the group," Leesie defended herself, "but if we're going to get the work done, we are going to have to bring in other people. Right?"

"Yeah, it's just hard not knowing if it could be The Darkness masquerading as a nice looking guy trying to fool us or something," Teja said.

"I didn't give him our numbers, only took his. No harm, no foul," Leesie added.

"It's done now," Tara said. "I wish we had his last name, though, then we could google him."

"We do," Leesie said, brandishing the pad. "He wrote it down too. If he was dangerous would he have done that?"

"Probably not," admitted Teja.

"It still doesn't matter," Wendy said. "He doesn't know who we are. I want to talk about what he saw. Do you think just anyone would have seen the force field we constructed, or would he have to be psychic?"

"Good question," Leesie said. "I would guess that he's got some ability because if it had been that blatantly apparent, wouldn't other peeps have stopped to look, too?"

"How will we ever know?" Tara asked, "You know what students are like. They're hurrying to class, talking on the phones, texting, listening to music, or walking in groups talking to one another. Who really spends time looking at what anyone else is doing?"

"Something drew his attention," Leesie pointed out.

"Yeah, how many times have you seen four foxy women just sitting out in the sunlight with their eyes closed?" Teja asked. "If I was a dude, I'd have noticed."

"I guess you've got a point," Leesie acquiesced. "Oh, well, I've got to go to class. We can talk about it later with everyone else."

"Sounds good to me," Teja said.

"I've got to get to class, too," Wendy said, getting up and shooing the other girls off her quilt so she could fold it and put it in her backpack.

Tara waved her fingers at the group, "We'll talk later. Meanwhile I'll start work on the painting. Toodles."

Chapter 32

Where am I? Matthew thought as he looked around at the landscape. He thought he was back on the mountain where he had experienced his vision quest, but it wasn't quite the same. He was still overlooking a town, but the hill had beautiful green grass and all the trees, not just the furs, were green with new leaves. There were bright yellow, orange, and white wild flowers growing around him and he could hear the sound of the wind as it gently blew through the trees. The sun was warm on his face and arms and he realized he was wearing only jeans, no shirt or shoes. He wiggled his bare toes in the soft grass and felt the cool loam beneath it. The smell of the forest and growing things flooded his nostrils.

Okay, I think I'm back on my hill in Lame Deer, but why am I back? Matthew turned in a circle looking around, trying to find a sign. His wolf lay near him and his hawk flew overhead. *Maybe if I send my consciousness into the hawk I can see more and understand why I've been brought back here.* He closed his eyes and concentrated on his hawk while asking the bird if he might join with him on his flight. Abruptly, Matthew began to see the world completely differently. Everything was astonishingly clear and vibrant. He could see the smallest movement below him and sense the motion of the air. He had done it—entered the hawk and was now seeing and feeling things like the bird did. Even though the sun was bright, the air up here was cold and much thinner. It was the cold air hitting the warm that caused the air currents that the bird effortlessly rode upon. Through the hawk's eyes, Matthew could see for miles. But still, there appeared no obvious sign of why he was called here. *Maybe it was just to connect more thoroughly with my animals and learn to use my abilities with them,* he thought. But then he realized there was more.

Open your mind, he heard as he found himself once again in his own body.

After shielding himself even more thoroughly, Matthew began to breathe deeply and tried to empty his mind. No luck. He kept thinking, *stop thinking, empty my mind.* He was getting frustrated. He knew that would not help, in fact it would hurt his ability to succeed. He felt himself sit down and was glad to discover the seat he had made the last time he was here was his seat now. It felt familiar and helped calm him. He concentrated on relaxing. He thought about making his muscles go slack. He allowed himself to feel his head relax, starting with his scalp, then his forehead and eyes, next his cheeks and jaw. He began to feel warmth and a tingling in his neck and he relaxed it. He relaxed his shoulders, arms, and back. Still breathing deeply, the warmth covered his chest and his breathing slowed as his chest and back relaxed completely. The warmth spread to his groin and butt, down both legs to his feet. Now his entire body felt very relaxed, warm and comfortable. He felt his grounding cord, a connection to the planet that keeps one linked to Earth's energy and through which negativity can be eliminated, extend deep into the earth, anchoring him to his planet. A brilliant blue color appeared in his mind and he allowed his consciousness to concentrate on the color blue. The color blue became his entire focus. Nothing else existed but the color blue.

Where are you needed today? he heard the voice in his head ask and without feeling a need to answer, Matthew knew his help was needed in Israel. He could hear the earth screaming and realized a massive oil spill had drenched a nature reserve. The spill would have disastrous results for that part of the planet. Matthew filled the area with cleansing energy and love. Feeling that part of the planet as whole, he stopped. He realized much more needed to be done, but for now, that was all he knew to do.

Next, Matthew felt himself in Afghanistan, Africa, and other countries where people were fighting and being wounded, where people were starving, where people were dying of terrible diseases, where people were suffering. In each place he filled the earth and the minds of all those people who lived or fought there with love and God's energy. He sent healing to the planet. His focus was on the feeling of calm, not chaos.

You must do this with your group daily, said the voice. *You must perceive the planet as whole, just as you are now whole. See her, Gaia, Earth, Terra healed and filled with the energy of love. Visualize all the beautiful places on your planet and hold these visions always. Focus on the good on Earth, not on what is wrong. Remember—what you focus on grows. It is just as though you are watering and feeding plants. If you give them water and food, they grow large and strong. Thoughts are like plants. They grow large and stronger when fed. Watch what you are feeding them. It is a habit to see fearful, antagonistic, malignant things everywhere. At an early age you were told of dangers throughout your environment. As infants you were told there was danger in many things. As you grew a bit older, you were told that other people could hurt you so you must stay away from strangers. As teens everything became dangerous: the internet, driving, being with the opposite sex, almost everything else. Adults are warned of inclement weather, affairs, lack of funds, alcohol, cholesterol, cancer, their children going bad, as well as loss of their jobs. The aged are fearful of broken bones, ill health, loss of hearing and eye sight, reduction of their freedom, and finally, death. There is no time in your existence upon Earth that you are as bombarded with goodness and love and peace as with the negative. It then becomes almost natural to be a negative thinker. That is why the group must work to help one another to change these habits. Daily meditation is only a beginning. What do you want to grow? Remember it is not about getting rid of darkness, it's about bringing The Light back in. This is a daily ritual. All of you must cleanse your thoughts of the negative programming you live with and absorb every day. As your powers increase, so will your abilities at feeding the world energies. If you want to help the planet, you must have control of your thoughts. Unless constantly vigilant, the negative will again gain a foothold and what you are trying to do will be lost.*

Matthew awakened. He was sitting at his desk. Had he been sleeping? He wasn't sure what had just happened, but he knew he had gotten a very important message that he had to deliver to the group. He went to his computer and typed everything he remembered. *Should I send an email or call a meeting?* he wondered. He looked at the clock on his computer and saw that it was already 3:50. Zach should be home in about 15 minutes. Should he wait to talk to him or send it and contact the rest so they could meet for dinner to talk? He decided he would send what he had written along with a note that asked everyone to meet at the Chuckbox. A good burger sounded like a great way to reenergize. He sent the email. Within seconds his phone buzzed with a text from Tara which read, "I second that suggestion."

Before Zach got back from class, Matthew had heard from everyone. They decided to get together at 5:00 for dinner and some serious conversation. When Zach got to the dorm room, Andrew and Matthew informed him of what had been decided.

"I had plans for tonight. I'm on a very tough schedule here. Ariana's birthday is only days away and I can't figure out what to get her. I am seriously freaked," Zach confided.

"Dude, this is really important," Matthew said. "I wouldn't call a meeting on a whim."

"Sorry. I'm really feeling like a complete duster here. How can I not know what to give my lady for her birthday? A little help here, guys."

"Candy's always nice," Andrew said.

"That's for Valentine's Day," Zach said, exasperated. "She's not used to getting presents except from her grandmother who died nine years ago. Her parents just give her money. I've got to get her something great."

"Why don't you ask the girls?" Matthew suggested.

"Duh, you don't think I have?" Zach asked. "I even asked my mom. No one has any ideas!"

"I'm really sorry that you're feeling so desperate, but believe me this is more important. Afterward, if you want, I'll go with you to Tempe Marketplace and see what we can come up with. Deal?" Matthew asked.

"Deal," Zach agreed.

"Let's play some Xbox while we wait for 5:00," suggested Andrew.

"Sounds good, maybe it will get Zach's mind off gifts," Matthew agreed. "How about the new Walking Dead?"

The three men lost themselves in killing zombies for the next hour, Zach totally forgetting about Ariana's birthday.

Chapter 33

The Chuckbox was a favorite of both students and Tempe residents alike, partially because of its rustic, laid-back atmosphere. Seated at a long picnic table with their burgers and fries, the eight friends ate quietly waiting for Matthew to tell everyone why he had called this meeting.

"I had an interesting experience right before I texted everyone," Matthew began. "Did everyone but Zach read it?" They all acknowledged having read the message. Ariana passed her phone to Zach so that he would be filled in on the email as well.

"If you hadn't called the meeting," Tara admitted, "I would have. I've been having these weird, like, walking dreams. It's as though I'm walking through other places on the planet but I'm really just walking to class. It's hard to explain, but to say the least, it's really difficult to stay focused on the here and now while it's happening. I find myself so engrossed in what I'm seeing that I'm completely unconscious of what's really happening around me. Sometimes several minutes go by and I realize I've just been standing in one spot watching. I'm sure if anyone sees me doing it, they'll think I'm stoned or something."

"What are you seeing?" asked Ariana.

"Usually events like battles, or areas that are being polluted, or children crying. Things that are going on somewhere in the world. It's as though I have astral projected and am standing there listening and observing what's happening."

"That's very similar to what happened with me. I think the Elders or perhaps The Great Spirit are taking you to places that need you to send love and cleansing and healing energy," Matthew explained. "You are an artist and designer which makes you a visual person. As an empath, Ariana may feel what's happening. You Tara, however, may see things."

"That makes sense to me," Ariana concurred. "If I'm going to see something, the Elders bring me a dream."

"Speaking of dreams and our abilities," Zach said, "I had a doozy the other night. With so much going on, I forgot to tell anyone till our conversation reminded me."

Zach told the group his dream about Atlantis but didn't speculate about what he thought it meant.

"You obviously had a dream about your past life and the destruction, but do you think that the Atlantians and the Lemurians were the Greek and Roman Gods from history?" Matthew wondered.

"Why stop with Greek and Roman Gods?" Leesie inquired. "Why couldn't aliens have done that in every culture?"

"While we're all doing show and tell," Wendy announced, "I have my own story to tell. In my private session with the therapist, some really wonderful stuff happened. I wanted to tell everyone but I'm afraid you will all be mad at what I did."

"What did you do?" asked Ariana.

"I told her about Matthew's situation."

Matthew looked at Wendy. He didn't seem upset. She continued, "I told the therapist about Matt because I was afraid I was going to be the next one The Darkness took over."

"Snoodle, you have no anger. Why would you ever think you would be next?" Andrew asked, taking Wendy's hand.

Wendy gave Andrew a half smile and continued. "When I was eleven, my three-year-old brother was killed suddenly. I've always blamed myself. I've been riddled with guilt because I felt it was my fault. My mother had drummed into me that I was older so I had to take care of him. That day I was feeling particularly resentful of always having to be responsible for him. I ignored him and went about my own business. While I was in the barn working with my horse, he wandered out of the house and down to the pasture. We had a really mean gelding out there. Somehow my brother Peter got kicked in the head. Three days later, he died."

Wendy began crying. She pulled herself together and continued her story. "I didn't even find him until he was cold," she said, becoming hysterical.

Ariana sent love and calm to Wendy. Those closest to her, Andrew and Teja, reached out and held her.

When Wendy was composed she resumed her story. "I hated myself and nothing and no one could convince me it wasn't my fault. I wanted to die and trade places with Peter. He was so young and sweet. That's why I began cutting and abusing myself. That's why I became so angry and self-destructive. When Ariana adjusted my energy, it helped tremendously, but I still couldn't shake the guilt and shame. When The Darkness got to Matthew, who I always considered to be way stronger than me, it scared the shit out of me. At my session I opened up to the therapist about Matthew to explain why I thought The Darkness would go after me next. Here's the big thing—she's one of us. She knows why we are here, what we're doing, and she also knows the Elders."

"How do you know that?" Leesie asked.

"Because she told me. She said she had been waiting for us to come together and it was her path—she actually said 'path'—to help us," Wendy exclaimed. "She was surprised that the Elders had not told her about Matthew. She said 'Elders,' I didn't."

"That's wonderful news, but I wish you had told us about how you were feeling. I wish you had trusted us enough," said Ariana. "We can't keep these things to ourselves. It is too important for each of us to know the vulnerabilities of the others so that we can be alert to any help needed. I am glad you told the therapist, though, and found out that she's here to help us because we can use all the help we can get. This is just another example of the things we all have to work on. Each of us have skeletons in our closets, otherwise we wouldn't have been in group. It's time to stop being ashamed of the past so that we can all be stronger now and in the future. We can only do that by trusting one another completely and sharing what's bothering us even if we think it's too awful, unimportant, or whiney."

"How are you feeling now?" Matthew asked. "Do you have a handle on your guilt?"

"I'm still working on it," Wendy admitted. "But I think it's better."

"Well, I'm willing to help anyway I can," Matthew offered.

Teja hugged Wendy again and said, "You know you can count on any of us if you go into a rough patch."

"Yeah, I know and now I will ask for help," Wendy decided. "Before I was too afraid of being rejected to let any of you know what had happened."

"Wow, we have a lot to think about: this new spin on ancient history, the therapist being one of us," Tara pondered. "And we have to figure out how we are going to work on our negative thinking and speaking."

"I don't know why everyone's surprised about our therapist," Leesie reminded the group. "Lydia told us she was here to help. Remember?"

"Yes, but hearing it from a psychic and having it confirmed are two very different things," Andrew answered.

Zach looked contemplative. "So, how do we move forward now? I really want to know what we can do to rid ourselves of negativity."

"That's a hard one, but I think if we can get our heads around the idea that everything is happening for a reason, even if we can't discern what the reason is, and that if we don't know the reason we can't determine whether anything is really positive or negative, that may help," Tara responded.

"Yeah, like the Adam Walsh thing," Andrew said. "What if Adam's soul decided that it needed to be the one to draw attention to child abductions so that this country would finally band together to do something about it? Definitely the way that came about was sad and horrible, especially for the family, but the end result was extremely positive. Now police from all over have a national database of DNA, fingerprints, lost children's pictures, all kinds of things that were not available before Adam's death. There are criminal and child molester data banks, too."

Matthew agreed, "If the murderer was Adam's Judas, the person that helped his soul complete its mission, then he was doing exactly what he was meant to do."

"Wow, so that means if I were to get, let's say, raped, my soul wanted me to have that experience? So hating the perpetrator would be stupid?" Teja asked angrily.

"That's exactly what I mean," Matthew replied. "Just because your soul intended you to have that experience doesn't mean it wants you to react in any particular way. You have choices, remember? You can move forward and in moving forward, become strong and maybe help others to become strong, too. But what happens if because of that experience you grow mean or paranoid or bitter, like I did, and that you do nothing to help yourself move on? Instead of growing, you will probably get ill, either mentally or physically, or both. If you hold a piece of the rapist's anger inside of you, you are allowing it to destroy you again, just like I did with my anger. This means the perpetrator wins. The only way to get over violence is to stop dwelling on it. I'm not saying it won't take time and counseling and that it's not hard as hell, but in the end, it's the only thing that you can do if you want to live well instead of just surviving. Otherwise, it's just like being raped endlessly."

"I get it," Teja said, "but doing it seems impossible."

"It is possible, though," Tara replied. "I have read about several people who have forgiven the murderers of their spouses, parents, or children."

Leesie added, "I've read about people who have forgiven their torturers. They are usually very religious, but every one of them said that they didn't want to keep living the pain. They had to move on and forgiveness was the only way."

Wendy still seemed irate. "But what about babies that are abused, tortured, and killed. At that early age, what can the soul possibly learn?"

"In that case I don't think it's the child's soul. The lesson is for the family and society at large," Ariana speculated.

"But it's the baby going through all that pain," cried Wendy.

"I think the soul within that infant has chosen that path, just as the beings that incarnate as food animals choose theirs. Their paths are for the greater good. Their sacrifice is made to help our world or for the people involved to learn and hopefully grow in ways that would be impossible otherwise," Ariana suggested.

"I'm not sure I can stomach that," Teja admitted. "It seems so cruel."

"Less cruel than thinking God is punishing the infant for the parent's sins or believing it's just fate," Leesie replied.

"Unfortunately, as the world is now, humanity seems to have forgotten how to learn through good things," Matthew said. "Isn't that part of what we are here to change?"

"If we can't even get it, then it seems like a monumental task," Wendy moaned.

"That's just it," Ariana said, "We **don't** have to get it. We have to dwell on what is right in the world, not what is wrong. You know, I read a quote online the other day that keeps coming to mind. Let me see if I can find it again. I saved it." Pulling out her phone Ariana said, "Here it is, 'Some believe it is only great power that can hold evil in check, but that is not what I have found. I found that it is small everyday deeds of ordinary folk that keep the darkness at bay—small acts of kindness and love.' That's all we need to concentrate on, the small acts of goodness. Through those we drill holes in the Dark."

Teja nodded her head and said, "I've got a wonderful one from my man Dr. King, 'Returning hate for hate only multiplies hate, adding deeper darkness to a night already devoid of stars. Darkness cannot drive out darkness, only light can do that. Hate cannot drive out hate, only love can do that.' "

"Well if everyone is going to add a quote, I'll give you my favorite," Leesie said. " 'Giving up on a goal because of a setback is like slashing your other three tires because you got a flat.' "

"So how are we going to do this?" Zach asked.

Matthew spoke up, "By working together, correcting, trusting, and helping each other and, here's my favorite quote, 'taking it one day at a time.' "

Chapter 34

"You sure you don't need a ride home?" Ariana asked Tara.

"No thanks, I've got some things I need to do before going home. Also, to tell the truth, since you and Wendy moved back to the dorm, it's kind of lonely at home," Tara admitted.

"You sure there's nothing we can do or anything you need?" asked Ariana.

"Nope. Just have to go get some school stuff and some kitty treats. Diablo misses you too, so I need to help him feel better. You guys go be alone for a while."

"I'm just going home to study. Big econ test tomorrow and it's my weakest subject. Zach is doing something with Matt anyway, so if you need anything let me know."

Tara gave Ariana a dazzling smile, "I'm good. Maybe I'll go buy myself something wonderful to make me feel good, too. A Tara treat. Yup, that sounds killer."

"Okay, have fun then," Ariana said as she turned back to the car and the rest of her friends, "Everyone move over. Where do you expect me to sit, on the hood?"

"I'd invite you to sit back here on my lap," Matthew said, "but Zach would get mad at me and since we just got close again, I don't want to mess that up."

"I'll share Matt's lap with Teja and you can have the seat," Leesie said scooting over.

"Everyone in now," Zach said as he pulled away from the curb and headed back to the dorms.

Reaching Manzanita, Zach parked out front and walked Ariana to her door. Holding her close he whispered, "I'll miss you. Are you sure you'll be okay all alone until Wendy comes back?"

"I'm a big girl. I think I can handle it for a few hours. Go have fun with Matthew."

Zach gave Ariana a deep, long kiss then, wiggling his eyebrows, said "Something to think about while we're apart."

"Hmm, I think we need to do that again just to make sure."

The kiss was sweet and filled with all the love they felt for each other. "That one I won't forget," Ariana said, fanning herself with her hand. "Maybe I won't let you go."

Zach smiled back suggestively, "Maybe we can talk Wendy into staying at Andrew's tonight and I can come back and sleep here?"

"Yeah, I'm sure Andrew's roommate would just love that. Anyway, I don't trust myself in a bed alone with you. Go, don't keep everyone waiting," Ariana ordered.

Shutting her door, Ariana realized she would miss him. *How stupid are you? You'll see him tomorrow,* she chided herself. She walked to her desk, sat down, and tried to study. The room was entirely too quiet. She realized she hadn't been completely alone for weeks and it felt weird. She now understood why Tara didn't want to go back to her virtually empty apartment. The cat provided some company, but it wasn't like having a friend to talk to. She leaned back in her chair and closed her eyes. She let her mind wander over the past three months. Ariana marveled at how dramatically her life had changed. Leaving her family home where she had never felt wanted and traveling to Arizona where she not only found where she belonged but had made close friendships, discovering she was from Meria, learning her path, connecting with Zach—all felt like miracles—but she knew all of it, even being born an Abrams, was part of a greater plan. In only three months she had lived more than she had ever thought possible and learned more about life and the world than she could have conceived of even in her wildest imagination. Thinking about what the next few years would bring was almost incomprehensible.

Ariana thought about the topics the group had discussed earlier and wondered if she could learn to be forgiving enough, to live as they had been advised to. She still held negative feelings toward her family and her past. *That's what I'll do,* she thought. *I'll work on forgiveness of those in my past I feel angry toward. First, I'll make a list.* Opening a new file in Word, Ariana began to type her list: 1) Father, 2) Mother, 3) Sister, 4) Brother, 5) Gloria, 6) Girls in the neighborhood, 7) Girls at school.

That's it I think. Not as big a list as some, but still some work to do, Ariana realized. She got up and changed into her yoga pants and T-shirt, knowing that she needed to be comfortable to meditate and determining that was probably the best way to begin her forgiveness routine.

Sitting on the bed in a crossed-leg position, Ariana got as comfortable as possible then began to breathe deeply. Her usual method was to begin to count down from ten to one, but this time she decided to do what Matthew told them he had done to clear his mind. She relaxed her head and opened her crown chakra, the energy center located at the top of her head. Next, she opened her third eye chakra located in the middle of the forehead and relaxed her face and jaw. Then she relaxed her shoulders and opened her heart chakra by thinking about Zach's love. Opening her solar plexus and sacral chakras, she relaxed her chest and abdomen. Lastly, she relaxed her rear and let this relaxation flow down her legs to her feet and into the ground while simultaneously opening her root chakra and sending her grounding cord into the planet. Her hands, which were lying palms up on her knees, began to tingle as the minor chakras in her palms opened. Her body felt completely relaxed. Now it was time to relax her mind. She focused all her attention on the color violet, the color of the crown chakra. Violet vibrated to a very high octave and Ariana adjusted her energy so that they vibrated in harmony. When she felt she had coordinated her vibration and the vibration of the color violet, she allowed herself to just feel violet. Nothing else entered her thoughts as she flowed on the current of violet. The current felt as though it was taking her upward. As she flowed upward, the feeling of absolute love penetrated the deep calm. An unnoticed sigh escaped Ariana's mouth as she completely surrendered to this feeling of total love and calm.

Ariana had no consciousness of how long she floated on these currents, but eventually she became aware that a person was moving toward her. It was her father. Filled as she was with absolute love, she held no judgment as she entered his mind and relived his memories. She saw him as a small boy deeply craving the love and acceptance of his father. But instead of love, the little boy received physical, emotional, and mental abuse. No matter how hard he tried, the boy never pleased his father. Even his mother seemed occupied with so many other things that she had no time for this boy, her oldest son. As he aged, his family seemed to expect him to fulfill their desires and have none of his own. He was to become an attorney even though he desperately wanted to be an architect. When he fell in love with Ariana's mother, Ariana's father's father disowned him and refused to accept either of them in the family home. The new bride and groom moved from Boston to Indianapolis and Ariana's father never saw or spoke to his father again. When his father finally died, his mother had nowhere to go, her two other children not wanting her for their own reasons. So Ariana's father took her in. When his mother and Ariana grew close, her father was eaten up with jealousy. Throughout his childhood he had felt unwanted and unloved by his parents. After he was disinherited, he began to take his hurt and pain out on his family, his father's anger having taken pieces of his soul and filled it with anger instead.

As Ariana watched these scenes, tears began flowing from her eyes. She realized she was feeling her father's pain. She was the child that wanted love and got violence, she was the man that never pleased his father, the man who chose the wrong woman, the man who had finally been completely rejected when he was disinherited. Even his own mother preferred Ariana to him. The pain was almost unendurable. At least Ariana had Oma the first 10 years of her life. Her father had no one. How could she hate him now that she had felt his life and his pain? Immediately, she felt a deep release as her soul claimed one of the pieces it had lost.

Ariana did this same exercise with everyone on her list. Gloria, the neighborhood kids and her classmates were easy. They were all just immature, scared kids desirous of acceptance by their peers.

Ariana's sister and brother were as much victims of their dysfunctional family as she was. In different ways certainly, but each had felt the pain and hurt that was part of being an Abrams.

Finally, Ariana became her mother and allowed herself to feel the loss of leaving her family for a man who ended up blaming her for all the choices he felt were mistakes and always showing her his loathing instead of love. She felt how caged her mother felt because she had left home without getting an education and was at the mercy of her husband's financial charity. Having no money of her own, she learned to scrimp on the household budget just to buy presents for the kids on holidays. Her father didn't believe in God, so he didn't believe in holidays. She felt completely overwhelmed with having to single-handedly raise three children, keep an immaculate home, and always prepare gourmet meals for her husband's pleasure. He was OCD about cleanliness and if there was anything out of place, or the children weren't perfect, she would get beaten. She was a slave not a wife. If she tried to leave, she feared he would either kill her or take the children away from her. She couldn't bear the idea of her kids being raised solely by him. So she stayed, becoming more bitter and sad with each passing day.

How could Ariana hate her? Her mother hated herself so much there was no more room for anyone else's hate.

Seeing her family, not as family but as unique people with their own painful pasts, their own self-loathing and inner-demons, allowed Ariana to understand that none of what had happened in her life was done to make her suffer, but because they didn't know another way. They had been treated so disrespectfully they didn't know how to respect and value anyone else. None of this was about her. It was about them and their own self-hatred being projected on the people in their lives. Feeling unlovable, they pushed away anyone who could give them the kindness and love they felt they did not deserve. Their lives were self-destructing and the anger that caused was what produced the hateful, angry behavior toward others. The same thing had almost happened to Matthew.

With a deep sigh and a lightness of soul that Ariana had never felt before, she was released. There were no more negative threads holding her to her past. She was truly free!

Ariana opened her eyes and with a big smile, she began to study.

Chapter 35

After Tara left the group, she decided to do her shopping along Mill Avenue. The street held dozens of shops, some chains, but most were small, local ones. Tara thought she might find something different at one of the shops. She knew she could get the cat treats at Safeway and her paint at the art shop. She hoped to find something unique for herself at one of the local shops. She just didn't feel like going home to her condo yet.

Tara was surprised that she missed having roommates so much. She had never thought of herself as the roommate type and had been dreading living in a dorm. When her abuela bought her the condo, she felt saved. Now, here she was, missing having someone to live with. It was really weird. She thought she had gotten used to being a loner. Being transgender meant that she probably wouldn't marry, especially if she didn't have the surgery to make her a complete woman. Even if she did, there aren't many men who would want a 'manufactured' woman. She could lie and just not mention it, but that wasn't her style. She prided herself on her honesty. She had spent way too long pretending to be a normal male for her family. She could no longer live dishonestly. It took too much out of her.

Tara was in the parking lot of the Safeway when one of her visions hit. Transposed over the parking lot was dusty grassland like you might see in a documentary about Africa. Huddled together were hundreds of young girls. All of them were barefoot and wearing long head coverings. Standing above them were men holding rifles, many wearing some kind of camouflage uniform. They were screaming at the girls. Several of the girls were holding each other and crying. There was a feeling of desperation as well as utter fear. *What do I do?* Tara thought, feeling desperate herself. Sending love and positive energy seemed pointless. Suddenly she had an idea—she sent bravery to the girls. She also sent a vision of where the girls were to the people who were trying to find them. As soon as she completed her thought, the vision vanished.

Tara had no idea how long she had been in the vision, but it had been light when she started and now the streetlights and the parking lot lights were on and it was almost completely dark. She walked into the grocery to buy cat treats. She still felt not quite in the here and now. She also had an odd feeling of being watched. Shaking her head in order to clear the last of the sensations from her vision, and hoping that would stop this feeling of being watched, she proceeded with her mission. As she entered the light of the store, Tara looked around, but everything looked perfectly ordinary. *Wow, now I'm becoming paranoid,* she thought.

After buying Diablo's treats, Tara went to the art store on University. She loved to browse there, looking at the different colors of paint, the various brushes, watercolors, and all the other objects employed by artists. She was so lost in thought about whether the painting for Ariana would look better in acrylics, oils, or water color that she didn't notice the two men watching her.

Tara chose several colors of acrylic paints and some new brushes then headed to the counter. As she rounded a corner, she almost collided with the two males that had followed her into the store.

"Hey, chica, where you goin' so fast?" the thin, black-haired one asked.

"Excuse me, please, I've got to pay for these."

The man didn't move. The other shorter and stouter one moved closer.

"You too good to talk to us, bonita?"

"I'm really in a hurry, so will you two please let me by," she said more loudly.

"These guys bothering you, miss?" one of the clerks asked, coming down the aisle.

"No, I think they're just leaving now and I'm coming up front to pay," Tara answered the clerk.

"Okay, gentlemen, if you're not buying anything maybe you should go ahead and leave," the clerk said. "Come on up front and we'll get you taken care of," he said to Tara.

Tara and the clerk walked up front together and watched as the two men left the store.

"Sorry about that," the clerk apologized to Tara.

"There's nothing you need to be sorry for," she answered. "You're being a perfect gentleman."

"Are you alone?" the clerk asked, obviously concerned. "I'm a little worried that those guys might hang around. Do you want me to call the campus police?"

"I don't live far and there are lots of people out walking. I think I'll be safe, but thanks for worrying."

Tara picked up her purchases and left the store. Looking around, she didn't see the men anywhere. *Good,* she thought, *we scared them away so I'll just continue shopping.*

After two hours of aimlessly walking from store to store, looking for something to make her feel better, Tara gave up. She didn't need anything. She saw nothing she wanted or that screamed 'take me home.' Tara was tired and the cat food and paint were feeling very heavy after more than two hours of lugging them around. It was only a short walk to her condo if she got off the main street and walked through the parking lots behind the stores instead. She was so tired she decided to take the shorter route through the parking lot. As she walked out of the bright lights of the shops, bars, and restaurants that lined both sides of Mill Avenue she realized how dark and secluded it was back here. Mill Avenue was very well lit, but in the parking lot at the back of the stores there were few lights. The sky was cloudy and there was no moon. Tara was beginning to feel uncomfortable. She increased the speed of her walk. *I hope I don't have one of my visions now,* she worried and walked faster. She couldn't shake a feeling in the pit of her stomach that something was very wrong, but she didn't want to stop and look around.

When she got within a half block of her condo, Tara released the breath she had been holding. *Fool,* she thought. *You're scaring yourself for nothing.*

She rarely entered her condo through the front door, preferring to enter through the kitchen door that opened into the public garage. That way she avoided tracking dirt onto her beautiful Navaho rugs. When she got to her kitchen door, she discovered getting her keys and holding the bags was an impossible task. Bending over to put the bags on the concrete, she found her keys in her purse and stood upright again to place the key in the lock. As the key slid into the lock, an arm came from nowhere and grabbed her around the neck, pulling her backward. Tara found herself standing against someone, his arm around her neck, strangling her.

"What's wrong puta, you still don't want to talk to us?" a voice spoke in her ear. He pushed Tara forward, smashing her head against her door. He began groping her chest. "The bitch ain't got no pechos," he said to another man.

"Who gives a shit about the top," said the second voice. "Bend her over and we'll take the bitch backward."

Grabbing Tara around the waist and smashing her head against the door again, the first attacker bent Tara forward, pulling down her pants and panties.

"Hey, what the hell is this," he screamed as he put his hand between her legs. "This bitch got huevos!"

"What ya mean?" asked the second man. "Oh shit, you're right. It's a dude."

The attackers threw Tara to the ground and began to kick her. With each blow of their feet they became angrier as though Tara's inability to fight back was taunting them. Tara felt a rib break as the taller of the attackers gave her a vicious kick. The other attacker kicked Tara mercilessly between her legs screaming, "We'll make a girl out of you one way or another, you faggot bitch!"

The last thing Tara remembered before passing out was excruciating pain when her jaw was broken and the taste of blood as she swallowed two of her teeth.

When Tara awakened there was a strange man bending over her. She tried to scream but couldn't open her mouth. Tears were streaming from her swollen eyes and she could barely see. Through her panic she heard him asking her where she hurt and if she was all right. She passed out before she could answer.

Tara woke again as she was being lifted onto a gurney and into an ambulance. One of the EMTs was a woman, and as she was strapping her in, asked Tara if she had been raped. Tara tried to shake her head no, but with that slight movement the world began to spin and she started to vomit. *Oh God, help me,* she screamed in her mind. *Please God, don't let me vomit. I can't open my jaw and I'll drown in my own vomit.* Instantaneously, she calmed. Trying to breathe as deeply as she could through her shattered nose, she sent a message to the group, *Send me your energy, PLEASE!* Numb from the pain, Tara slipped again into unconsciousness.

Chapter 36

"Something's wrong," Matthew alerted Zach who was looking at pretty pastel blue tops, shopping for Ariana's birthday gift.

"What do you mean?" Zach asked, clearly disturbed.

"I'm not sure but I'm feeling really scared. I think something's happened to Tara. That's the only thing that makes sense. Let me see if I can reach her."

Zach watched as Matthew closed his eyes and breathed slowly, trying to open their mind link.

Unexpectedly, Matthew began to moan and then scream as though he were in great pain. Everyone in the store turned to look as Matthew grabbed his head and began retching. Zach grabbed Matthew's arm and pulled him out the door of the shop and onto a bench.

"Matt, what's wrong?" Zach asked, now very frightened. "Talk to me."

Matthew continued to hold his head and moan. Zach felt desperate. Taking out his phone, he called Ariana.

"Babe, where's Tara?" Zach asked when Ariana answered.

"I don't know. When we left her she said she was going shopping, but that was hours ago. She should be home by now. Did you call her at home?" Ariana asked. "Why, what's going on?"

"I'll call you right back," Zach said as he disconnected and dialed Tara's number. There was no answer and now Matthew was vomiting for real. His eyes were glazed over and he seemed to be somewhere else. *Shit,* Zach thought, *do I take him to the hospital, dorm, student health center? What do I do?* He called Ariana back.

"What's going on, Zach? What's the noise I'm hearing in the background?" Ariana said immediately.

"Matthew's going crazy. We were just standing in a store one minute and the next he says that he thinks something has happened to Tara. Then he tried to mind link, started screaming and moaning, now he's vomiting. What do I do?"

"First, breathe," Ariana advised. "You need to have a clear head. Take him to the car and head back here to pick me up. While you're coming to get me, I'll try to reach everyone else, okay?"

"You don't think I should take him to the hospital or something?"

"No, just get him here. I'll talk to you when you get here," Ariana said hanging up. She sent texts to Andrew and Wendy telling them to get to the dorm immediately. Then she called Leesie.

"Wassup?" Leesie answered.

"Leesie, did Tara give you her abuela's telephone number?" Ariana inquired. She tried her best to remain calm.

"Yeah, why?"

"Because Matt thinks something is wrong with Tara and she's not answering her phone. I thought maybe her grandmother might know where she is."

"Oh, crap, I'm sorry, just hang on a sec," Leesie said as she scrambled to get the phone number. "Okay, it's 602-405-5142."

"Thanks, now you and Teja get over here ASAP."

"Already on the way," Leesie replied.

Ariana looked at the phone number. She knew something horrible was wrong. She could feel it. She didn't want to talk to Tara's grandmother and confirm her fears. Her heart was racing and her stomach felt as though she might vomit. Ariana took some deep breaths and dialed the number. The phone rang and rang then went to voice mail. Ariana hadn't even considered what she would do if no one answered. She left a message to please call her as soon as possible and then sat staring at her phone. *What do we do next? If we can't get a hold of her grandmother, what next?* she thought. *We don't even know Tara's real name. She certainly wasn't Tara at birth.* Ariana began to feel desperation and fear and realized it was clouding her ability to think. *I've gotta get a grip!* She calmed herself by quickly entering her place of greatest calm. She opened her crown, third eye, and heart chakras and reached out with love to Tara. Instantaneously she was hit with a wave of pain so intense it almost knocked her off the chair. *It's not my pain,* she reminded herself. *I release this.* The pain left her. Ariana sent her energy of healing white light to Tara. She felt Tara seize the energy like a thirsty man would gulp water. *Where are you?* she thought and instantly she understood that Tara was at the hospital.

Ariana's phone rang. "Hello," she answered.

"Ariana, this is Maria Gonzales, Tara's grandmother. You and your group must come at once to Tempe St Luke's Hospital. Tara has been badly hurt. They say she might die," her grandmother sobbed uncontrollably.

"Maria, what name is she under?" Ariana asked.

"Oh," her grandmother said, "of course they would not recognize the name Tara. Her given name is Tomas. Tomas Herrera. I am still in the emergency waiting room, but they are taking her to surgery now and then ICU. I will wait for you in the ER waiting room, okay?"

"Yes, yes, that will be good," Ariana agreed. "The others are on their way. We should be there within half an hour."

"Please hurry," Grandma Gonzales begged as she began sobbing again.

The rest of the group arrived almost simultaneously several minutes later, Leesie in the lead. Matthew looked as though he could barely walk and Zach seemed to be holding his friend up.

"Did you reach her abuela and did she know where she is?" Leesie asked hysterically. "Matthew looks like he's dying and I'm freaking."

"Yes, I've reached her and she's waiting for us, so let's head for the car and I'll tell everyone what I know," Ariana said as she maneuvered the group out the door.

When they reached the car there was none of the usual bantering about who sat where, they just piled in.

"Okay, where are we going?" Zach asked as he started his car.

"Just drive straight south on Mill," Ariana answered.

Zach looked at her questioningly and raised his eyebrow. She heard him in her head wondering why she wasn't saying where exactly they were going. In the same manner she replied that she was trying to keep everyone, especially Matthew, calm. She was sending out calming energy in waves. She felt Matthew beginning to relax a little as he came back fully to alertness.

"Thanks, Ariana, I can feel what you are doing and I appreciate it," Matthew whispered to her.

"Ariana, what are you not telling us?" Wendy asked.

"As long as everyone remains calm, I'll tell you," Ariana replied, adding more soothing energy to the interior of the car. When everyone agreed, she continued. "Something bad happened to Tara tonight, I don't know what, but she's in surgery right now."

Matthew moaned and tears began streaming down his face. Ariana put her arm around his shoulder as Teja, Leesie, and Wendy tried to embrace him as best they could from the backseat. Ariana saw the tears on everyone's faces and felt the love the group was sending to both Matthew and Tara.

"Let's send her healing. It's just like sending love, but instead of surrounding someone in the energy," Ariana explained, "you see the energy being absorbed and used to heal every cell. Then you see the person whole and healthy. Just keep the vision of Tara laughing and as beautiful as always."

Arriving at the hospital emergency entrance, they rushed into the waiting room and found Tara's grandmother talking with an Asian man in green scrubs.

"This is Dr. Verma. He is the emergency physician that has been working on Tara," Maria told the group. "These are Tara's other family."

"When will her parents arrive?" the doctor asked Maria, barely acknowledging the others. "We cannot do all that needs to be done without their permission as she is not yet of age. She needs surgery immediately. That we can do with your permission, because it is life threatening, but some of the other things that might be necessary would be up to the family."

"You have my permission. What are you waiting for?" Maria replied frustrated.

The doctor asked Maria again, "When will the parents arrive?"

"At least another two hours. They are in California and must fly here."

"She is in extremely critical condition. We are not even sure she will make it through surgery. I hope they get here soon," the doctor said as he walked away.

Ariana asked, "What's going on, Maria?"

Maria's eyes were red from crying and her face so puffy she was almost unrecognizable as the beautiful grandmother they had gotten to know at their Thanksgiving celebration. Beginning to cry again, she looked at the group, contained herself, and said, "Tara has multiple injuries. There is bleeding into her brain. She has a collapsed lung and a ruptured spleen. There is extensive damage to her genitals and various broken bones. Because she is a minor, they will do only what is necessary to keep her alive. They will do nothing for her face or genitals. That is considered cosmetic and will be up to the parents as she is not of legal age and I am not her legal guardian. I feel so helpless. There is nothing more I can do and if she dies, I will not have told her today that I love her."

The group looked horror stricken and helpless. Matthew started gasping and collapsed to the floor. Around them they could hear people rushing and a speaker blaring "Code Red in emergency room 2." Everywhere there was chaos.

Only adding to the noise, Leesie started crying hysterically. "What will we do without Tara?" she wailed.

"Stop it," ordered Ariana. "It's time for us to do our work and put everything in the hands of the Source. Breathe! All of you, breathe deeply. Form a circle holding hands. You, too, Maria. Now begin sending God's love, White Light, and healing energy to Tara. See and feel her absorbing this energy. Release all fear and doubt. We know The Light can do anything. If the Source created us, it can fix us. Become The Light and shine brilliantly. Allow the energy of the Source to emanate throughout this place, healing and uplifting everything it touches."

They filled the hospital with love. They sent their consciousness to every corner of the building, filling it with light and healing. The whole area appeared to glow. They increased the vibration of the energy and released it to do what it will, knowing that everything would happen exactly as it should.

After several minutes Ariana spoke, "We release our sister Tara into your hands, God, knowing whatever happens is perfect in every way."

The Ariana Series

Book 3

Fighting Darkness

Chapter 1

"Code Red Room 2, Code Red," blared the speakers in the Emergency Room. Instantly, ER doctors and nurses surged toward Room 2. There was controlled chaos everywhere. Ariana and her group of friends knew what Code Red meant. Someone was dying. Matthew collapsed in the nearest chair holding his head and moaning, tears falling down his cheeks. Maria, Tara's abuela, panicked. She knew her beloved grandchild was in this place, but she didn't yet know where. Ariana rushed to Maria's side. She helped Tara's frightened grandmother to the seat next to Matthew, hoping to calm her. Everything was so confusing. Ariana had to force herself to look at her friends, to see how they were responding. By the looks on their faces it was obvious they were conflicted. None of them wanted anything bad to happen to anyone else, but thinking that Tara could be dying was too much. Everyone but Zach and Matthew huddled together in the middle of the waiting room. Zach struggled with Matthew, trying to get him to talk.

What do I do now? It's been hours since we've heard anything new. How do I help my friends cope? Ariana wondered. She felt overwhelmed, frustrated, and responsible. *They trusted me and I let them down. I was warned Tara might be in danger and I let her down. What kind of leader am I?* Ariana tortured herself with the thought that her failure had been the cause of whatever happened to Tara.

The feeling of a hand on her shoulder relieved Ariana from her anguished thoughts. She looked up to find Zach standing next to her. She had been so distracted she hadn't heard him approach or even felt his energy. This was very disturbing. Ariana had to remain alert in case there was some sort of danger out there, a possible threat to all of them.

"Ariana, do you think we should try to do some more healing or something?" Matthew asked.

"Yeah," exclaimed Teja, "I can't just stand here feeling helpless. Let's do something!"

Leesie reached for Teja's hand and said, "It will be all right. Tara's strong and young. That always helps people get well."

Teja pulled her hand away. She did not want to be soothed.

"How the hell do you know that she'll be okay?" Teja screamed. "We can't see her. We don't even know what happened to her. I hate this shit!"

"Getting mad at each other will only bring negative energy," Ariana responded. "We have to be strong and positive. We all know what happens with thoughts, they produce an effect. Negative thoughts do not produce solutions, they only cause fear. Negative thoughts can also bring The Darkness. I don't think any of us wants Tara to have to fight that, too."

"How the hell are we supposed to think positive thoughts? You heard the doctor, **she's critical!**" Teja persisted.

"Maria, do you know what happened to Tara?" Zach asked, hoping that more information might help them to know what to do somehow.

Maria shook her head and said, "I only know that a man in her condominium complex found her in the garage unconscious."

"Common, let's do what we did for Matthew, surround her with our love and send that along with our healing energy," Andrew suggested. "It helped Matthew even when he was traveling to a different state. Won't it help Tara, too? At least it will help us feel like we're doing something rather than bitching at each other."

"That's a wonderful idea," Ariana said, grateful that someone had suggested a positive action for the group to undertake. "Matthew, are you up for this?" When he stood up and walked to the group Ariana said, "Let's form a circle again, holding hands, and begin to build the positive energy of love, our love, and the Source's love, along with the healing energy."

"I cannot join with you," Maria said. "I must go to the chapel and pray to the Virgin for her help. With both our prayers to God, he will answer." Getting up from her chair, Maria patted Ariana's hand, smiled to the group and headed down the hallway to the nurse's station to ask for directions to the chapel.

"Boy, is that some strong lady," said Teja.

"Her faith makes her strong. We must be as strong in ours," Matthew declared.

The friends formed a circle, each person holding the hand of their neighbor as they began their deep breathing and relaxation rituals.

When Ariana could see the fully formed bubble of protection the group had visualized, she began, "See Tara as she was when we saw her earlier this evening: vibrant, healthy, and smiling. Hold that vision of her while you add to it a vision of intense blue energy. See Tara absorbing this wonderful healing energy. See her breathing in the energy and see her aura began to glow with vitality and strength. Allow yourself to fully accept that Tara is well, happy, and whole. Now, think of the love you feel for her. Attempt to magnify that love by feeling the love that is the Source. See her absorbing this beautiful energy, too. Keep sending both energies, maintaining the positive vision of her. Do not allow any doubt to enter your minds. She **is** perfectly healed and healthy, and this is already true!"

For fifteen minutes, the group stood together, sending the energy Ariana described. The waiting room grew warm and appeared to glow as the energy grew. Ariana sent some of it throughout the hospital, hoping to help anyone else that needed it. She knew that the seven friends were sending enough energy to heal everyone in the vicinity.

Ariana thought hard for Matthew to open his eyes and look in her direction. *Did Tara accept the energy?* Ariana thought. Matthew shook his head no. Ariana closed her eyes. She felt pain, desperation. *Why can't we reach her?*

"I'd like to say a prayer to Great Spirit if it's okay with everyone," Matthew said. When the group all agreed, he began. "Great Spirit, please walk beside me through this day. Clear the heavy air with the lightness of Your Presence. Guide my hands and steady my heart that I may give comfort when I cannot give hope, that I may give relief when I do not have a cure, and that I may radiate your healing peace when the limits of science, time, and the human body are overwhelmed. Guide your healing to Tara and help her accept your love and healing grace."

Teja still looking dejected said, "I know that's all we can do, but it feels like nothing. I feel completely helpless. This sucks!"

"I understand how you feel, Teja," Matthew interjected. "It would be easy to get depressed, frustrated, or angry, but remember—thoughts are alive and create an effect. We must keep thinking that what we are doing is working. We don't want to increase the negativity and bring The

Darkness to us. Instead, we need to raise The Light."

"That's really easy to say, but a lot harder to do," Wendy said, holding tight to Andrew. "I'm really scared. What do we do without Tara?"

"Tara isn't gone," Ariana said forcefully, "and I don't want to give that thought any power. We absolutely must deal only with those things that we know to be true, not what we fear. Remember, we are all working to become The Light and I believe the first step is to constantly remind ourselves that God holds all the power and that whatever happens today is happening because it is what needs to happen. We have been living in an abstract kind of reality—thinking we are here to save the world but not really feeling it. It was all just sort of a concept. Because the world is still functioning enough—it doesn't create as much fear and doubt as when it's less abstract—like what's going on with Tara. But we must treat this in almost the same way. It is selfish to think about what will happen to us. We'll keep going no matter who is working with us or who isn't. It's that simple, but it's not necessary to dwell on. The only thing we need to know is that is she is still alive and that if we really believe it, we **can** help her."

"Tara was always the strong, positive one. It's hard to think of her hurt," Leesie replied.

"She's still the strong, powerful one," Zach said. "Nothing's changed that. When you're sick or hurt your basic self doesn't get sick or hurt. Tara's basic self is a survivor. That's what we need to focus on."

"You're right," Leesie admitted, "but it's hard when you don't know what's happening or even what happened."

"Does anyone know what happened to her?" Andrew asked. "Was she hit by a car, or what?"

"You heard what Maria said. I don't think anyone knows," Ariana responded.

"I wonder if anyone called the police," Leesie said.

"If they did, wouldn't they be here?" asked Andrew.

"Maybe there's an officer in with her. I'm going to walk down the hall and see if I can find her room. The rest of you stay here and wait for Maria to come back," suggested Matthew as he started walking down the hallway, trying to look like he knew where he was going and what he was doing even though he still looked as though he needed to be in bed being taken care of himself.

It really doesn't matter what happened, Ariana thought. *I guess it's just our way of coping. If we know what happened, then we think we can hold on to the hope that there is something concrete we can do so we don't feel so helpless. Humanity is so weird.*

The remaining friends all waited quietly, sitting in the uncomfortable plastic chairs that were the only seats available in the waiting room. The walls were painted a pale green and there was industrial green carpet on the floor. The room looked as though it hadn't been remodeled since the 1960's. This wasn't surprising. The hospital itself was very small and not often used. The larger, newer hospitals drew most of the top doctors and also most of the patients. Ariana was surprised this hospital was still open, but she also knew it was the closet one. Tara must have been found in a very critical state otherwise she would have been taken somewhere else.

Everyone was so nervous, it seemed like Matthew was gone for hours. Finally, he reappeared.

"Did you see her?" Leesie asked.

"Sort of," Matthew replied. "She is covered with bandages, tubes, and wires."

"Did you find anything out?" inquired Ariana.

Matthew stood before his friends, looking for the right words to tell them what he had learned. Finally he said, "There is an officer in Tara's room. They want to talk to her as soon as she wakes up. The police think she was beaten by someone in the condo garage. I guess that's the door she usually enters by. Aside from that, they know nothing."

"Why would anyone want to hurt her?" Wendy exclaimed.

"You don't think The Darkness did it, do you?" Teja wondered.

Ariana answered before Matthew, "I doubt it was The Darkness itself setting out to attack her, but the world is filled with darkness and people who are letting it affect them. Watch the news—there are terrible things happening everywhere. We can't get paranoid and think that there's something waiting around every corner to get us. That's giving The Darkness power over us and we don't want that."

"I am so confused," admitted Wendy. "Is The Darkness after us or is it just the way the world is right now?"

"Both," Matthew answered. "When we are working with The Light attempting to dispel The Darkness, it will use what is already within us to fight. It will use our fear, self-doubt, anger, and whatever other negative energy we contain to drive us apart. What it won't do is beat us up. We can draw people to us however, who have filled themselves with darkness, and they can hurt us, but that is not The Dark itself. That could happen whether we are working in The Light or not."

Leesie interjected, "Yeah, I remember reading an article about serial killers and serial rapists. The FBI sent profilers to interview every serial killer and rapist they had in prison so that they would be better able to understand them. One of the things they asked was how they picked their victims. Many said that they just knew—the victim seemed to put out an energy that drew them. Maybe their aura appeared punishing or fearful and that was what they were reacting to without realizing it."

Teja was appalled, "That's not Tara. She is stronger and prouder than anyone."

"Just saying," Leesie said, hurt by Teja's tone. "It's what I read, not what I am accusing Tara of or anything."

"We don't know what happened to her, so it's impossible to come up with why it happened," Ariana reminded them. "We'll have to wait until she tells us, just like the police are waiting."

"Okay, but what do we do now?" Andrew asked.

"We wait and think positive thoughts," Matthew replied. "Unless someone has a better suggestion."

Turning and speaking almost under her breath, Teja mumbled, "Bullshit!"

Ariana spoke, "Teja, I know you're feeling helpless, all of us are, but being negative only makes us all worse off. Tara needs us to remain positive and hopeful. I know it's really, really hard, but it's also necessary. I realize that this is probably harder for you because of how you lost your Dad. Death isn't easy to understand, especially violent death, but we don't need to understand something in order to find a way through it. Don't get me wrong, I'm not saying that Tara's going to die; you know as much as I do about that. But I am saying that how you are acting will pull us apart. That's not what any of us wants or needs right now. We must find strength from each other. Remember, that's where our power lies."

"I'm sorry," Teja mumbled. "I'm used to taking action, not sitting around."

"Yeah, me too," admitted Andrew. "I'm a fighter, but there's nothing here to fight. Gets kinda hard just standing around."

A bustle of activity and voices brought their attention to the hallway where several people, including Tara's Abuela, stood arguing.

"We cannot stand out in the hall disturbing the whole hospital," Maria stated. "Let's go into the waiting room to discuss this."

"There's nothing to discuss," a loud female voice declared. "We are taking him home as soon as he can be moved."

"But this is her home," Maria argued.

"Stop calling him her," an irate male voice screamed. "Tomas is my son. He needs to be home with his family. If he had remained with us, none of this would have happened."

Maria lost her temper and stated powerfully, "This is where Tara felt at home. This is where she found acceptance, friends, and love. Not with you. We don't know what happened. How could you possibly know it would not have happened in California?"

"I've heard enough, Mother," Tara's father said menacingly. "You have no say in this matter. Tomas is 17 and we are his legal guardians, not you. He comes home as soon as we can take him."

Doctor Verma interjected, "Let's go into the waiting room to discuss the options."

"Can't we see him?" Tara's mother asked.

"We would prefer if you wait until after surgery," Dr. Verma answered, maneuvering them into the waiting room. "Tomas has bleeding into his brain and several broken bones, including his jaw and orbital bone. These need to be repaired immediately. We may have already waited too long. Please sign the surgery permission papers so that we can begin."

The family looked shocked. Immediately their anger was replaced with fear.

"We had no idea it was that serious. Maria only told us that Tomas had been in an accident. What happened to him?" Mr. Herrera asked.

"We are not sure," the doctor said. "What I am sure of, however, is that we must get him into surgery now."

"Of course, of course. Where is your paperwork?" Mr. Herrera asked.

"Follow me," answered Doctor Verma.

Turning to the group, Maria said, "Elicia and Conchita, these are Tomas' friends."

The two women turned toward the group.

Ariana walked forward and extended her hand to the oldest woman, "I am happy to meet you both. My name is Ariana."

"Do you know what happened to my son?" Tara's mother, Elicia, asked.

Ariana shook her head and replied, "I'm sorry, but I don't think anyone knows. Tara was found in her garage injured and was brought here. Let me introduce the others to you both." Pointing at each person in turn, Ariana said, "This is Zach, Wendy, Andrew, Teja, Matthew, and Leesie. We have all gotten very close to Tara, um I mean Tomas, and love her very much."

"But you do not know my son. You know the creature he pretends to be," Mrs. Herrera replied.

"The person we know is wonderful and so much more than a gender," Matthew said softly.

The other female glared at him. "You don't know what this 'wonderful person' has put my family through! You couldn't possibly understand the embarrassment he has caused all of us."

Teja rose to her feet, seething with anger, but before she could speak, Ariana took her hand and squeezed. Turning to the family Ariana said, "You are right, we could never know how Tara made her family feel. We can only know how she makes us feel and how we see her. She makes each of us feel special and loved and we see her as one of the strongest, most beautiful women we know." Turning back to the group Ariana said, "It is time for us to go. Maria, please let us know if anything changes or if there is anything we can do."

The group gave Maria a hug and walked out of the hospital.

"Why did you stop me from telling those skanky bitches what for?" Teja asked, sounding very annoyed.

"Because we want to see Tara again, and if we seriously piss them off, that won't happen," Ariana answered.

"What would have been the point anyway?" Zach asked. "It wouldn't have changed their minds about her and only made them hostile toward us."

"Anyways," Leesie said, "there was nothing more we could do there and maybe we can come up with something tomorrow. It's already after midnight. Let's go home."

Chapter 2

Teja was quiet, but inside, she was steaming mad. She knew the others expected her to take this lying down, but that just wasn't her way. She was going to find out what the hell happened to Tara and kick some ass. Let the others step back from their responsibilities. *This is really messed up! It's time for action, not talking and meditating!* Teja thought as she felt her anger increase.

So what the heck do I do? She began to pace every inch of her dorm room, her nervous energy building as she contemplated her options. *I could try to retrace Tara's steps and see if anyone knows anything, but then what?* Her feelings of helplessness grew. When her dad died, Teja was too young to do anything. Throughout the years that followed, she suffered because of it. Now that Teja knew what really happened to her father, she still could do nothing. Too much time had passed. Her anger grew stronger as she thought about how often she had allowed herself to be helpless. She had some totally awesome abilities now, but what good were they if she couldn't use them for payback?

Teja wished Leesie was home so that they could do some brain storming, but Leesie was out somewhere Christmas shopping with her mother. *I guess it's up to me,* she thought bitterly. *What good is a polarity when they're not around when you need one?*

Pacing only made her feel trapped so she finally sat down. Taking a deep breath, she tried to calm herself so that she could think more clearly. After calming her mind, an idea came to her almost immediately. If time didn't exist, and the astral body could go from realm to realm, why couldn't it go into the past? Isn't that what Zach had done when he went into a past life? She didn't need to go back that far. She only needed to go back to last night, to Tara's condo.

Closing her eyes, Teja let her mind wander to Tara's condo. She saw the outside of the condo clearly. Focusing all of her energy, she willed her consciousness to stay in this place, but to go backward in time until Tara approached her home. *There she is!* Teja could see Tara, packages in her hands, walking toward the condo. Tara didn't go to the front door as Teja expected, but instead, she entered the parking garage. Teja noticed two men appear out of the shadows. They were following her. She didn't like the look of them. Running to follow Tara, Teja found her standing at what must be her condo's back door. Tara was fumbling in her purse.

"No!" Teja screamed. *"Run!"*

But of course Tara couldn't hear her. She tried to grab Tara and turn her around as the men drew within arm's reach, her hand shot right through Tara as another hand, a physical one, grabbed Tara from behind, ramming her head against the door. *You mother,* Teja screamed in her mind as she tried to pull the man off her friend. Having no physical form meant that everything she tried failed. Instead, she had to impotently watch what the men did to her friend. Teja thought she felt helpless before, but watching this was almost unbearable.

Fight dammit, she screamed at Tara, but Tara never once resisted the onslaught of blows and kicks. Hearing the noise of someone approaching, the men stopped their vicious assault and ran. Teja saw a stranger run to Tara and ask her if she was all right, but she was so damaged all she could do was gurgle. The man dialed 911 and stayed with Tara, holding her hand and talking softly to her until the paramedics arrived. He even cleaned up after they left.

How can some people be so mean while others are so kind? Teja thought. *I guess that's what this world amounts to—those people who care about others and those who care only about themselves.*

Teja heard a voice in her mind say, *Now you understand. When people live in fear, many become selfish, and The Darkness convinces them that their narcissistic desires are more important than the wants or the needs of the whole. These people begin to categorize others into groups: those they hate and those they blame for what is wrong with their lives and their world. This hatred grows and often becomes an ideology. Through rationalization, this ideology becomes a truth and a mandate to purify all those that don't fit in or are different from the 'group wisdom.' Many of these groups justify these violent tenets as religious mandates. Most of these people destroy due to fear masked as rage. They are bullies who are too afraid to look at their lives and take responsibility for their personal failures. Instead, they band together into twos or threes or thousands and take their misplaced fears and turn them into rage that now gives them the illusion of power. To continue to feel powerful, they become destructive. Unfortunately, with this new power also come new fears. So once started, this cycle is never ending.*

Another distinctly different voice spoke to Teja, *Does not your Holy Book speak of 'an eye for an eye'? If you lie down and allow this atrocity then you are no better than the beasts that hurt your sister. You have abandoned her and told her she had no worth to you. Do you want to continue the behaviors from your past, moving on, and accepting what has been done to those you say you love instead of fighting for them? Or will you become like your mother, blaming the person that was wronged instead of showing love? Do you love your friend and your father? You have powers now; use them.*

How? Teja thought.

Think of the creatures that have done this to Tara. Order your consciousness to their residences and enter their sleep. Torture their dreams. Convince them that they are being punished by God and that the only way they can be purged of this wrong is to kill the other. Convince each the fault was that of the other and that they are blameless. Pit one against his partner until their violence and fear escalates and they destroy themselves.

No Teja, do not listen! the other voice pleaded, but Teja was beyond listening. Now she had a plan. She would cause the two to hurt each other as badly as they hurt Tara. She felt power surge within her. She no longer felt helpless. Now she was drunk on the new feeling of righteousness and power. She was the dominant one. The men who hurt Tara would learn what it is like to anger this goddess!

Teja focused all her attention on the man that had first grabbed Tara. She saw him, smelled him, felt her hand on his skin. Suddenly she found herself in a small, dirty apartment in South Phoenix. The man was sitting on his bed with his head in his hands. *Shit,* Teja thought, *I just wanted to influence his dreams. Now what?*

She stood in the small apartment surveying this stranger's domain, a studio apartment with a tiny kitchenette. A bed, a big-screen TV, two torn, fake leather chairs, and a small table that held a game console were the only contents. Empty beer bottles and food cartons were scattered throughout the room, the smell of stale beer, cigarettes, and body odor permeating it. *Yuck!* Teja thought.

Turning back to the man on the bed, Teja contemplated her options. First, she stood right in front of him, wiggled her arms and screamed. Nothing happened. Next, she tried reaching out to touch him. She was not physical so nothing happened. *What do I do now?* Teja thought again.

Try going into his mind and planting thoughts, she heard plainly in her own mind.

Yeah, if I can hear the Elders talk to me in my mind, why couldn't I do the same thing? Breathing deeply, Teja opened her consciousness and her shields as she focused on being this person before her. She willed herself to become this man. Momentarily she thought nothing had happened, but then she was overwhelmed with such grief, regret, remorse, and sadness that she involuntarily retreated. *WTF!*

Scared but still determined, Teja, tried again. This time she expected to feel harsh feelings. She did not pull back; she listened and felt. The man was going over in his mind what had happened that night. He had seen Tara coming out of the grocery. He thought she was amazingly beautiful and graceful. He liked this more boyish type of girl, not those big-assed ones with those mucho grande chi chis either. His friend, Frank, suggested that they try to catch up with her and talk to her. When she went into a store, they followed her, watching her awhile. Seeing Tara through his eyes was really weird for Teja, but she kept watching the memory. He finally got the nerve to approach her, and in his very inept way, attempted to start a conversation with her. Yet she rejected him like every other beautiful girl had done his whole life. That made him angry, and when the clerk threw them out of the store, the anger grew. *Who did the bitch think she was?* he wondered. Frank added to the anger by laughing at him for always wanting what he couldn't have. At that point, he decided he would have her no matter what. He'd show her who she could piss off.

The men continued to follow Tara when she left the store, and waited as she browsed other stores, watching her movements. With each new store, the man's anger and resolve grew. There was no way he was going to let her get away with rejecting him. Once he took her and showed her what a man he really was, she would be his, and he'd show that smart-ass Frank, too. He knew his luck had changed when she started walking behind the stores where it was dark. Even Frank commented on how she must really want someone to rape her if she was going to be stupid enough to walk through this deserted part of town instead of on the busy sidewalks. They followed Tara at a distance, waiting for a good chance to run at her. Secretly, the man was afraid she could outrun them. He had put on some weight recently and wasn't the fastest runner to begin with. When she walked into the garage, he knew they had her. They rushed her from behind.

The bitch never knew what hit her, and later she wouldn't be able to identify them to the police. He felt really smart at that moment. But when he felt her up and there was nothing there, he became confused, and when he felt her package he became enraged. He felt horrified that he had been so aroused by a person that turned out to be a boy. That horror turned into extreme barbarism. All he wanted to do was smash the bastard, destroy his pretty face and body and make him ugly. His mind was no longer thinking. Consequences never entered his mind. All he cared about was eradicating the source of his humiliation.

Now, hours later, he was tormented. What had he done? He had beaten to death a young boy just because he and his friend had thought the boy was a girl. He had thought of raping this person because she had rejected him and then beat him because he wasn't what he thought he was. *What's wrong with me?* he wondered. The man agonized over what he'd done, what could happen and whether he was now doomed to Hell. His life had been hard already, but now, how could he possibly go on? He was horrified that he would go to jail or be put to death, but at the same time, he felt that was exactly what he deserved. *What happened to me? I was never violent before, never really a bad guy. What happened to me?*

The fear, self-loathing, and guilt were too much for Teja. She left the man's body and then sent her consciousness home. She, too, was feeling guilt ridden. What she had been thinking about doing to that tortured man could never equal what he was doing to himself. She had hated him when what she should have hated was the act he had performed. Hatred had almost made her become him: an emotional, anger-driven, violent loser. How could she judge him when she was really no better? Teja realized this is how The Darkness works; it takes a spark, anger or fear, for example, and fans it into a forest fire. The hotter it burns, the more out of control the person becomes until all logic, knowledge, and repercussions are sent so far underground they don't even reach the conscious mind. The Elders had been there trying to warn her, but they did not ignite the passion or lust that The Darkness had. Teja had chosen what her emotions wanted, revenge, instead of what her spiritual self knew to be right. If she had almost become The Darkness, what must she and her friends do to help others to understand how easy it is to get lost in the dark?

Chapter 3

The next day, Ariana received a message from Maria that Tara was out of surgery. But there was no change in Tara's condition. Ariana texted the group with the update and asked them to come to her room after classes. She expected that everyone would be there by five.

Ariana was glad to have some time alone. She had decided to skip her first class. She needed to think, meditate, talk to the Elders, and figure out what to do next. She was supposed to be the one of the leaders of this group and that meant she had no time to screw up and leave everyone to brood. She had to make a plan and give each member of the group something concrete to do.

Making herself comfortable on her bed, Ariana started her breathing and count down. Before she spoke to the Elders, she needed to go to her place of relaxation and compose herself, formulating the questions she would ask them.

She found herself standing on a rocky shore, looking out toward a vast sea. The sky was purple, orange, and pink. It looked somewhat like an Arizona sunset but the purple sky was much more intense. *Maybe that's why I feel so at home in Arizona, it reminds me of home,* Ariana thought. The sea was also a dark purple and filled with energy. It was as though it powered the entire planet. Ariana allowed herself to breathe in this familiar, intense power. The more she absorbed, the calmer she became. She held her arms to her side, reaching outward. She felt the planet feed her. *This is what a healthy planet feels like,* she thought. Filling herself to capacity with the fuel that was her planetary lifeblood, she concentrated on how the planet responded to her and how it felt in its completeness. She wanted to remember these feelings so that she could work to transfer this wholeness to her adopted planet, Terra.

Ariana didn't need to turn around to know that the Elders were standing behind her. She had felt the energy shift. She turned to acknowledge them, and for the first time since she was reborn on Terra, she saw her home city. It was a series of glistening spirals reaching high into the sky. *They're made of crystals*, she thought. This astonished her, but she quickly realized this was why she had an almost supernatural affinity to the mineral.

"Yes, that is where the energy of this planet is centered, in the crystals," the fourth Elder stated. "They are the bedrock of this planet and the greatest deposits lie beneath our sea. That is why we seeded Terra with them, to energize her in the beginning before she was completely solid."

The second Elder continued, "The crystals on Terra used to be much stronger and even the untrained ear could hear their song. The resonance can be changed by singing the right note with the voice or by using a specialized musical instrument. However, when the Pleiadeans arrived on Terra with their crystals, the harmonics of Terra's crystals were changed. The Pleiadeans inadvertently did this by the experiments they were doing on the crystals from their home planet. As their crystals gained power, the crystals we seeded became corrupted which caused a severe disruption to the electromagnetic field of Terra. The disruption created the first planetary disaster of a magnitude so strong that it almost destroyed that entire world. Many of the creatures that existed then were wiped out, never to repopulate. Almost the entire human race was also destroyed, and those that were not, became very primitive again."

"Some of our people remained on Terra to observe our experiments. You were one of those people. Your soul has held the guilt of its failure for millennia," the first Elder stated.

"The entity that you know as Zach did survive. You warned him and he warned his peers and his superiors, but they chose not to listen. Even so, he has also held this guilt and still does," the third Elder resumed. "That is why he recognized you and needed to assist you."

"Because he felt guilty?" Ariana asked morosely.

The third Elder responded, "No, because he had grown to love you."

Ariana was quiet. She hadn't expected that. Zach seemed to be interested in her from almost the beginning, but she assumed it was guilt over having let her down in that past life. Now she knew it was because their souls had been waiting to reunite in order to fix what had gone wrong then and to complete what they had only just begun together.

"Why didn't we set things right then?" Ariana inquired.

"Because you did not survive."

So that's why he's always been so protective of me, Ariana thought. "Let me see if I understand this. We are together to help the planet, to pay back some wrongs done to it in the past. We are also together to complete the love bond that we started then."

"Yes, but these things are unimportant. That is the ego that needs a positive justification to do its work. The soul knows what must be done and looks for nothing from the ego but to gather experiences for growth," Elder number one reminded her.

"You must understand that the truth of all beings is that we are linked. There is no separation in any of the worlds or in any lifetimes. The idea of separateness is part of the illusion the ego creates in order to achieve its ends often at the expense of others, the planet, wildlife, and the future. On Terra, as in the Pleiades, this is even more prevalent. Somehow those planet's cultures adopted the belief that the individual's needs take precedence over the needs of the many. That is how some people can become ruthless with power. People must be made to realize that we are one entity; what we give, we also receive. This knowledge can improve life on Terra. The other fallacy that allows the ego to continue these habits is the belief in time. Time breeds the fable that either there is always more of it to complete something or that there is so little left that nothing matters anyway. These were not our concepts. As you have seen here, we recognize this connection and work as one mind with one idea: to make life better for all living things. When one is happy, all are happy. That includes the planet itself as it, too, is alive and a vital source of our continued happiness and existence. Terra is being exploited and destroyed without regard to the end result. This is pure ego on the part of humanity, placing its needs above the planet it needs for survival. On Terra, there are even those that are happiest when others are sad," Elder two explained.

Elder three continued, "There are those still surviving on Terra that are of the original seed and they recognize the truth. They understand the connection of all things and how that connection works toward the healthy growth of life on Terra. However, their numbers are greatly diminished and many of the young do not want to learn the truths. Instead, they want to be like the rest of the world. They reject the information and the knowledge held by their Elders."

"Who are these others?" Ariana asked.

"The Native people of the tribes," Elder four answered. "There are many tribes that know of this connection even when the un-awakened don't. Their tribal structure and adherence to the ways of nature help them to know not to over use their resources. It is this over use that eventually causes destruction and loss of the very thing that is necessary for survival. The rest of humanity does not seem to understand that or care. With the belief in time comes the illusion that there is always more time to correct the current problems. Many of the tribal people understand that time is a white man's self-deception and are working to sound the alarm of Terra's current situation. They have always been aware of what they call the 'Star People': those of us that attempt to help Terra. You must link with these tribal Elders."

Elder one added, "Native peoples understand that the dimensions are not separate either. Mankind adapted the convention of linear thought which goes with the illusion of time. The belief that following known cycles or step-by-step progression where a response to a step must be elicited before another step is taken creates a type of blindness. Humankind has become blind to options that cannot be explained readily or are not repeatable. Consequently, they are incapable of considering the possibility that the dimensions overlap and that you can traverse these other realities. Linear thinking creates limits. If one cannot perceive of a thing, then when that thing is directly before them, they will deny its existence. This causes humanity to constantly repeat the same mistakes. That paradigm of existence creates limiting beliefs and fear. Feeling powerless, man finds his power through aggression and condemnation."

"Native people throughout your world understand these things and also recognize that the only limits on humanity are those they have set for themselves. Before mankind invented the airplane and proved flight was possible, no one flew, even though one of your ancients, Leonardo De Vinci, proved flight was possible. However, once the concept of flight was accepted it took but a very short time for man to conceive of space flight and to then fly into space. For thousands of years, flight was inconceivable and within 55 of your years, man had invented rocket flight," said Elder two.

Elder one continued, "We know you are here about the disturbing events that have recently occurred. You want an explanation as to why this event occurred and what to do now. Is that correct?"

Ariana nodded her head yes.

"Contrary to what your group may believe, we do not know all things. We know the history of Terra and our responsibility to her, thus we know what you must do. Our planet has a different history which taught us different lessons and helped us develop different skills. We can help the group learn these skills and also explain what we have observed about Terra, but we cannot tell the future. We understand The Darkness because we have had our own history with it and recognize what you must do in order to fight it. We cannot, however, tell whether you will be successful. We can speculate as to why this situation has occurred with Tara, but it will be speculation based on our experience, not necessarily the truth. We would rather you get that information directly from Tara."

"How can we do that?" Ariana exclaimed, frustrated.

"You are thinking linearly again. You have boxed yourself into false beliefs instead of exploring other options," Elder two said calmly. "You must understand that what you call the 'Other Side' is a different dimension. If Teja can talk to entities there, why can't she seek out the dimension that Tara's soul resides in now and talk with her?"

Ariana was astounded. Why hadn't she even considered that? Had she adapted so thoroughly to the limited thinking on Earth that she had lost the ability to think outside the box? *That's what I have to do to lead this group, help them to reprogram their limited thinking*. It seemed so obvious now.

"That is one thing that must be done," Elder three agreed. "But all of you must also continue your learning so that you can develop more of your abilities. Additionally, the group must speak their pain and confusion to the therapist. We think this should be done with the Therapist as soon as possible so that The Darkness does not feel the pulling apart within the group and cause it to implode."

"I understand," Ariana replied. "Is there anything else we need to know?"

"That which you adhere to, time, is growing short. As long as Terrains believe in this thing, it will affect everyone on Terra and you, too, will be limited by that belief. Begin looking for the others. They will come to you in many ways. Don't discount them or turn them away."

Ariana opened her eyes feeling relieved and energized. Now that she had a direction, she knew they would be okay. Before she left for class, she took the Elder's advice and called the therapist. The therapist knew the group's schedules and she and Ariana set up a time to meet with her the next day at noon. She did the same thing with Lydia, setting up an appointment for Saturday at 11:30 in the morning.

Feeling like she was finally moving forward and taking charge again, Ariana left for her economics class.

Chapter 4

Ariana got back to her room before the others arrived. She typed out everything the Elders told her that morning and added the two appointments she made. Spending some time straightening the already clean room allowed her mind to plan the evening. Realizing that everyone would be hungry, Ariana ordered buffalo and barbecue wings, chicken quesadillas, and nachos to be delivered to her room at five p.m.

Having completed her tasks, Ariana sat on the bed and began to meditate, sending healing and love to Tara. Ariana felt Tara right away and took comfort in the fact that even though she was still in a coma, she was alive and felt all right. Ariana realized how odd this was. She wanted to know why she was feeling this way. Instantly she felt safety and peace emanating from Tara's energy. It felt full of white light and contentment. Ariana had no feelings of pain or distress and understood that Tara's body was being protected by her guides and a solid shield of pure energy. Tara was safe, Ariana was sure of it. Sending the power of happiness and understanding, Ariana withdrew her energy from the hospital room.

Rising from her bed, she opened her door. She knew Andrew and Wendy were just getting off the elevator. She realized that somehow, her ability to feel energy and identify the source of the energy had increased tenfold. Until just that moment, she never thought she would be able to feel the energy of a person while they were still in the elevator or know who they were. She was elated, but also confused. As far as she knew, she had done nothing to increase this ability. She made a mental note to ask the others if they were feeling increases in their abilities, too, and ask Matthew if he knew what was happening.

"Hey, girl," Ariana said giving Wendy a hug. "I missed you last night. I'm not used to sleeping alone anymore. You guys okay?"

"Sorry, I should have stayed here last night I guess," Wendy said, sounding guilty.

"No, that's not what I meant," Ariana protested. "I just meant that I missed you. I like having you as my roommate, but I understand needing the comfort of your man when you're upset. If Zach hadn't had to stay with Matt I would have wanted to be with him, too." Looking at Andrew she asked again, "I'm glad your roommate decided to stay somewhere else last night so that you would have the privacy you needed to decompress. And because I don't believe in coincidences, I think the Universe wanted you together, too. Are you guys okay?"

"Probably better than yesterday," Andrew answered, "but still freaked."

Wendy sat on her bed and picked up the teddy bear Andrew had won for her at the state fair. "It's hard not to want to cry or get depressed," she said.

"Why would you not cry?" Ariana asked, confused.

"I don't want to give up on Tara or give the Dark any reason to come and get me."

Ariana thought a moment before answering, "I don't think crying would be like giving up on Tara. I think crying is a natural response to a sad event; it's cleansing. I also don't think it would draw The Darkness unless you were thinking about getting revenge or something."

Andrew piped in, "That's what I tried to tell her too, but she seems to think that crying makes you weak or something."

"Wendy, isn't that what you did when your brother died, held it all in until you became self-destructive?" Ariana reminded her. "Don't do that again. There was nothing any of us could have done, and we don't know why Tara's soul wanted this to happen. Until we do, we need to take care of ourselves and the group so we have extra energy to send to her."

"Jeez, you're right again," Wendy agreed, "I keep retreating back to old negative behaviors. How do I stop doing that?"

"I think it is something we'll fight as long as we are alive. Human instincts that have become habitual are really hard to shake. We all develop defense mechanisms, some helpful, some harmful. Working to recognize them allows you to stop the negative ones when you are going in that direction," said Ariana.

"Before I got involved with this group, I never let anyone really know me. I played the happy-go-lucky big, dumb jock. But now I am comfortable with letting you guys realize I am not always happy and I'm not dumb. It was easier for me to stay in the background that way. That's the reason I started in group therapy, to allow myself to be real around other people," Andrew confessed.

Andrew's admission really surprised Ariana. She realized she **had** thought of him as a big, dumb teddy bear. Feeling immensely guilty, Ariana asked, "But why did you want to hide?"

"When I was young I stuttered badly. It was both hard and painful to speak. When I started kindergarten, I had a teacher that thought forcing me to stand in front of the class and recite poems would help me stop stuttering. It was excruciating. The other kids were vicious. They constantly attacked me as though I was an injured antelope and they were all lions. The taunting didn't quit until the fifth grade. At that point I had a growth spurt. I was significantly taller and heavier than everyone else in my class. They left me alone then. We moved when I started high school. I barely stuttered by that time thanks to lots of speech therapy and, believe it or not, choir."

"Choir?" Wendy and Ariana asked almost simultaneously. "You were in choir?" Wendy pursued.

"Yeah, choir!" Andrew defended. "Do you know that when you sing you don't stutter? Anyway, high school was when I became the big, dumb jock. My size had some advantages and if I played dumb, people didn't listen when I talked. They just assumed I had nothing valuable to say. It worked for me. I could watch, listen, and learn an awful lot about other humans," Andrew explained.

Ariana realized that Andrew was right. Even she had underestimated him and didn't look to Andrew for wisdom. She vowed she would never take anyone at face value again.

"Wow! I don't think that I've ever heard you say that much before. You have taught me a lot right now and I hope you will feel good about sharing your wisdom with everyone from now on. Andrew, promise me you'll jump my shit if I ever underestimate anyone again," Ariana stated. "One last question, though, why did you decide to come clean with me now?"

"Didn't Matthew say that we needed to be completely transparent with one another? I'm ready to show the group who I really am."

"Isn't he wonderful?" Wendy asked adoringly as she got up and hugged him. "He's smart, sweet, and cute. How'd I get so lucky?"

"Because that describes you, too," Ariana said to Wendy.

"You guys talking about me again?" Zach asked from the doorway where he stood with Matthew, Leesie, and Teja.

Looking embarrassed Andrew asked, "How long has everyone been standing there?"

"Pretty much for the whole thing, dude. I always wondered how you got into therapy group. You never seemed very weird to me. Good to know you are," Zach answered with a smile.

"Come here, big guy. I want a hug," Leesie said. "Sorry I'm always hitting you. I just always thought you were like the Hulk, strong and brave. You must be a pretty good actor to have all of us fooled. Congrats."

"Okay, it's done. You all know my story, so let's get to something important. Where's the food?" Andrew asked, back to his normal self.

Leesie, Teja, and Wendy all hit him on the arm and Ariana felt herself becoming very hopeful again.

"Not to be an echo or anything," Zach said, "but when are we going to eat?"

"What time is it?" Ariana asked.

"4:56," Leesie announced.

"Can everyone wait four minutes?" asked Ariana. "Otherwise, you'll have to raid Wendy's stash of Oreos."

"Oreos!" Teja screamed. "No holding out on your friends. Where are they?"

"No way, no one gets my Oreos. I'll become violent," Wendy warned.

"Hey, let's use our psychic abilities and see if we can find them," Andrew suggested.

"Bunny! You're a traitor," Wendy exclaimed.

"When it comes to food, I have no loyalty," Andrew admitted.

"Feel the room and see what feels like food," Leesie suggested. "Hey, Ariana, do Oreos have an aura?"

Before she could answer, an unfamiliar voice at the door asked, "Did someone here order wings?"

Wendy ran to the delivery boy and giving him a big hug, announced, "You're my hero! You saved my Oreos."

The young man smiled and playing along, answered, "Although it has always been my fondest dream to save a beautiful damsel in distress, I'm kinda weighted down with all this food. Can I put it somewhere?"

The guys jumped forward taking the bags of food as Ariana paid the bill. His work completed, the delivery boy turned to leave but then he turned back to Ariana and asked, "I heard what the girl was taking about, using your psychic abilities to find things. Do you guys know how to do that stuff?"

Remembering what the Elders had said about finding others to join with them, Ariana replied, "We've been working on developing some abilities. Why? Are you psychic?"

"Honestly, I don't know, but I've been having some pretty weird stuff happening in the last year or so. Some have been way cool, while others have really creeped me out."

"I can understand that," admitted Ariana. "That's why we came together. If you're interested, leave me your name and a phone number or e-mail and I'll let you know next time we get together."

While Ariana went looking for paper and a pen to have him write the information she had requested, Leesie walked over to the boy. "Hi, I'm Leesie. I heard what you said. I'm trying to learn numerology so will you please put your full name as it appears on your birth certificate and your birth date? I promise I'll put together a chart for you and even explain it."

"Wow, that would be killer," the boy exclaimed. "Could you show me how you do it?"

"Sure," Leesie said, blushing slightly. "I guess we could get together sometime and I'll show you."

"Do you all go to ASU?"

"Yup," Leesie responded. "Do you go here, too?"

Looking slightly embarrassed the boy responded, "Nah, it's just my Mom and me and we can't afford it. I am taking some classes at Glendale Community, though."

"That's good. Did you go to high school in Tempe?"

"No, I went to Independence in Glendale. You're a freshman?" he asked, looking directly at Leesie.

"Actually, I'm a sophomore," she replied.

"Wow, you don't look old enough to even be in college, much less be a sophomore."

"I skipped a lot of grades. I'm sixteen," Leesie admitted.

"That's really wicked. I wish I had those kinda of brains. I'm having trouble with algebra right now."

"I could help you with that, too. Math is like my ace."

Ariana returned with the paper and pen and handed them to the delivery boy. She looked questioningly at Leesie. Ignoring Ariana, Leesie walked over to the rest of the group who were busy divvying up the food.

"Hey Leesie! My name's Jason. Give me a call when you finish my chart. Okay?"

"Sure thing," Leesie said with a big smile as she headed to the food before everyone else decimated it.

Chapter 5

After eating, Ariana began the discussion. "Hopefully everyone read what I sent earlier, right?" When everyone acknowledged they had, she continued. "First I want to talk about contacting Tara. Matthew, do you think you can do that or would you rather wait until we talk to Lydia, the psychic, on Saturday?"

"I've been thinking about that since I got your e-mail. I think I can do it, after all I astral projected to Tara once before, but because her health is so tenuous right now, I don't think it would be a good idea. Let's wait till we talk to your psychic," Matthew advised.

"But what do we do for her until then?" Wendy asked. "We can't just ignore the fact that she's hurting."

"We won't," Ariana assured Wendy. "We'll keep sending love, energy, and healing. Every time we think of Tara we'll see her whole, healthy, and the wonderful person she always was. If you let yourself be negative, you will do harm. We do what we can and we accept that it's working without doubt."

"Has anyone heard from Maria today?" Teja asked. "My Gram wants to help out if she can and I think Maria could use someone her age around for support. What do you think?"

"I think we should call Maria and see what's happening and tell her your Grandmother would like to come over and be with her," Matthew suggested.

When they finally reached Maria, Ariana could tell she had been crying again. Alarmed, Ariana asked, "Maria are you all right? Has anything new happened?"

"Tara is still in a coma," Maria answered, sniffling. "The doctors say it is a good sign that she has made it past 24 hours."

"Why have you been crying?"

"They are taking her away from me," Maria moaned.

"Who is?" asked Ariana.

"My son, her father," Maria answered. "He says that it is my fault Tara is like this. He says that if she had stayed in California where she belonged and got this stupid idea of being a woman out of her head, she would have been fine. He will no longer talk to me. I can't stop this terrible thing. As soon as the doctors say Tara can travel, they will be taking her back."

Ariana was appalled. "You know that what they said was BS don't you? She loves you and she loves living in her condo and going to ASU. She told us that for the first time in her life she was really, truly happy. That was your doing, Maria. You got her away from them because you knew if she stayed she would be either miserable or dead. Believe me, you saved her by bringing her here, and even if they do take her, as soon as she's well she'll come back. I know it."

"Do you really think so?"

"Tara's strong, she's brave, and she's happy here. She'll be back and we'll all be waiting," assured Ariana.

"Then I will go back with her to make sure my stupid son does nothing to prevent it and to make sure she is treated right," Maria decided. "Will your group do me a favor? Will you take care of her condominium and Diablo? You can use it for your meetings, and if any of you want to stay there you are welcome to. You'll need to come to the hospital to get the key though. I don't want to leave her."

"Has anyone checked on Diablo today?" Ariana asked, concerned for the cat's welfare.

Maria answered, "A neighbor has a key. Her name is Susan and she lives next to Tara. She checked on Diablo today but she said she couldn't find him. She left food and water and promised to check later."

"Thank you, Maria. We want to go over and see if we can find and comfort him. I'll be at the hospital shortly to get the key."

"It will be good to see you again," Maria said and hung up.

Wendy looked stricken. "Poor Diablo. I'm sure he's totally messed up. We've gotta get there, like now!"

"You didn't mention my gram," Teja reminded Ariana.

"Oh, sorry. I'll do it when we see her. I agree with Wendy, we should get going. We don't all need to go; I think that would freak her parents out. Zach and I can run over and get the key while you guys wait at the condo," Ariana recommended.

"Sounds good," Andrew agreed, putting his arms around Wendy to comfort her.

"Wait about twenty minutes," Zach suggested, "then head for the condo. Hopefully that will give us enough time to get the key and meet you there."

"Matthew, is there anything else you want us to do?" Ariana asked.

Shaking his head no, Matthew answered, "I can't think of anything right now. I'll phone you if I think of something."

"Are we really going to live at Tara's?" Teja asked. "I'm not sure how I feel about taking over her beautiful home without her there."

"We can't bring Diablo to the dorm, and we can't leave him alone, so we really have no other choice," Wendy pointed out.

"We don't have to decide this right now do we?" Zach asked. "Maria is waiting for us. Can't we discuss it after we get the key?"

"I hope this doesn't make me sound too creeposaurus, but couldn't we use our abilities, like Zach and my place psychometry, to find out what happened to Tara?" Andrew wondered.

"Wow, that's a really good idea," Leesie exclaimed. "At least we'd be doing something useful."

"What do we do with the information if we get any?" Matthew asked.

Leesie answered immediately, "We tell the police."

"You really think they'd listen to us?" Wendy asked.

"Don't you watch TV? There are a bunch of shows where psychics help police. They're not made-up shows either, they're reality TV," said Leesie.

"Yeah, like that's real," Teja scoffed. Leesie glared at her. *I can't let them know I've already done exactly that, they will all be mad at me for taking such a risk. But I do want them to learn what I've learned,* thought Teja.

"Are the psychics a bunch of teenage college students?" Wendy asked.

"Well, no, but WTF. If we discover some valid information that's more than they have now. We have to try. Right, Ariana?" said Teja.

"If you're comfortable trying, I don't see a problem. But I'm not sure what the police will think, but I'll bet they'd be skeptical. Who knows? Maybe they'll surprise me and have an open mind," Ariana responded.

Leaving the rest of the group still debating, Ariana and Zach headed to the hospital.

"How do you feel about using your ability with place psychometry to sense the situation at Tara's place?" Ariana asked Zach. She was concerned about how he might be affected if he picked up something really bad. "Because we are polarities you have probably gained some of my empathic ability. It could be really painful for you to feel what Tara went through." Ariana explained.

"I know, but if Matt can handle it, I can," Zach declared. "We need to know. What if it was The Darkness and now it has developed some way to physically hurt us?"

"It isn't something like Satan, Zach. That's your old religious programming talking. It is just negative energy. It has no power of its own. Don't give it your fear."

"Yeah, but what if?"

"Then we deal with that, too."

Chapter 6

When they arrived at the hospital, Ariana realized she and Zach had no idea where Tara was. They certainly wouldn't keep her in the Emergency Room. Tara had required surgery, so was she on a surgical floor? Was she on a floor specializing in neurology because of the bleeding in her brain? Or was she on an orthopedic floor because of all her broken bones? Ariana wasn't even sure the hospital staff would tell her where Tara was because she wasn't family.

"Zach, I don't know where to start looking for her," Ariana admitted.

"We'll try the information desk first, and if they won't tell us, then we'll call Maria and ask her where she is," Zach responded.

Maria was waiting by the front desk.

"How'd you know we were here?" Ariana asked.

"I've been down here since shortly after we talked," Maria said. "I cannot take it, being in that waiting room with them. Tara is in ICU and they only allow one relative in at a time and only for a few minutes. My family is suspicious of me so they rarely let me go in. I think they worry that if she wakes I will convince her to stay here with me."

"You wouldn't have to convince her," Ariana assured her.

"I think you're right, but I would never say that to them. Here are Tara's keys. I know she wouldn't mind you staying at the condo especially so that Diablo is not alone. Taking care of him is not too much of an imposition, is it?"

"Never," Ariana instantly replied. "I know Wendy will be excited about spending time with him. They have quite a bond."

"Tara told me that Wendy can speak with the animals. It is a wonderful gift, no?"

Ariana replied truthfully, "I wish it was one of mine. Is there anything we can do for you? Anything you need? Teja's grandmother would like to spend some time here with you if you would be okay with that. She asked Teja to ask you."

Maria smiled for the first time, "I would like that. She is a good woman and we have grown close since Thanksgiving. Please tell her I am in the second floor waiting room most of the time. Tell her she can also call me."

"Will do. Is there anything else you need?"

"No, you go now and check on Diablo. That will be one worry gone, and if Tara awakens, I can set her mind at ease, too."

Walking back to the car Ariana texted Teja to have her Gram drop by the hospital. Maria seemed delighted by the idea. Ariana knew that Maria needed someone her age to talk to, and someone who would understand the tension between herself and her family. Pearl, Teja's gram, had been battling with Teja's mother for years. The two women had a lot in common.

As Zach and Ariana drove down Mill Avenue, Ariana found herself speculating on what could have happened to Tara. The idea that she was hit by a car so near her condo made no sense. People couldn't speed through that area; it was too tight and small. And why would the driver take off? His car would have been badly damaged and would have been noticed by other residents eventually. No, Tara had been mugged. Ariana wasn't sure why, but it had to be that. This theory, however, did not account for the severity of the beating. If a mugger wanted her purse or something, wouldn't they just grab it and run? Ariana was at a complete loss as to how to explain the entire situation. She could find logical answers, but they just didn't fit the whole picture. Ariana felt very frustrated. Would they ever know?

"What do you think happened?" Ariana eventually asked Zach.

"I have no idea, and truthfully, I haven't even thought about it. I've been too busy worrying about Matthew and you to think about much else. Why, do you think you know?"

"No," admitted Ariana. "I can't think of one single thing that makes real sense."

"So are you now open to the idea that it was The Darkness?"

"No, that makes the least sense to me. If it has no real power of its own, it can't manifest. And if it can't manifest it can't create physical injury. Yes, through manipulation it might be able to convince someone to harm themselves, but Tara was much too strong for that. I also think that she really likes herself. Since living with Maria, starting college, and getting involved with us, I believe she feels she had found her place and that we completely accept her. Even though she has been through hell about being transgender, it has not prevented her from having real faith in God. She would never try to kill herself."

"How do we know that the Dark can't take a physical form? Just because the Elders claim that it can't doesn't mean it's true. At the séance it bit you for God's sake!"

"It didn't bite me. There were no marks, remember. It found my fears and caused me to believe they were happening. It did nothing physical. I think if it could, The Darkness would have manifested physically then. That would have been the end of our group. I'm sure of it. We almost lost Andrew that night and what happened then is nothing compared to what happened to Tara," Ariana declared.

"Okay, you don't need to lecture me. I get it. But sometimes my religious training kicks in and I have some doubts," said Zach.

"I'm sorry I didn't realize I was lecturing. I just get really passionate at times. I also did not want that thought to enter the minds of any of the others. I'm afraid that if they thought what happened to Tara could happen to them, we'd lose some of them," admitted Ariana.

"Then how do you feel about us psychically trying to find out?"

"I'm not thrilled, but there's no way Leesie can be stopped now. I'll just have to deal with whatever happens and assume if we get some negative information we were meant to for some reason."

"Have you tried asking the Elders?"

"Didn't you read the e-mail I sent?"

"Yeah, but you could have left something out if you thought it was more than we could handle," Zach replied.

A bit shocked Ariana answered, "I wouldn't do that and I'm disturbed that you think I would."

"I know how protective you are of this group and how responsible you feel for us. I wasn't saying you were a liar or anything, just that you try to keep everyone secure by taking everything on yourself."

"Well, I don't lie. If they had told me, I would have let you know at least," she said defending herself.

"Should we be fighting right before we join the rest of the group?" Zach asked as he parked the car.

"Is that what we're doing? Yeah, I guess you're right. I didn't like what you said and I'm feeling a bit pissed off right now. I guess I'd better let it go before we go into that garage."

Zach leaned toward her. He smiled his crooked smile and wiggled his eyebrows suggestively. "Well, there's one good thing about fights, the make-up kiss. I'm sorry if I made you unhappy. I really didn't mean to or suggest that you lie. Forgive me?"

"How can I refuse those puppy dog eyes?"

They kissed gently then more passionately. *Wow!* Thought Ariana. *There's definitely something good about a fight now and then if it ends like this.*

After one last kiss, they got out of the car and walked across the street to Tara's condo.

Chapter 7

Standing on the sidewalk in front of Tara's condo, every person in the group felt disheartened. Ariana knew they were thinking about the last time they had been here and what a wonderful day that had been. "I know it's hard," Ariana began, "but we need to be thinking about the good stuff, like how wonderful Thanksgiving was and how happy we all were. If we keep thinking about our sadness it won't accomplish anything. Let's go in and look for Diablo."

"He's waiting for me right inside the door," Wendy informed the group. "Poor guy is really upset. He knows something has happened to Tara, he heard it, but couldn't do anything. He's really wigging out!"

They opened the door and Diablo immediately leaped into Wendy's arms. He was shaking and meowing in a very odd way. The group crowded around him, surrounding him with calm. Eventually the whimper subsided, but his feelings of fear and sadness seemed to remain.

"How are we all picking up the cat's feelings?" Leesie asked. "Are we picking them up through Wendy or what?"

"I think that as the group gets closer we are absorbing each other's gifts," speculated Matthew.

"Wow! Is that neat or what?" Leesie exclaimed. "So we should all pick up vibes from the garage then?"

"Let's deal with one thing at a time, Leesie," Ariana suggested. "We should take care of Diablo, find out what he knows and help him to feel better before we even think about anything else. Wendy, can you get him to tell you anything?"

"Give me some time to sooth him first, okay? Check to see if he's got food and water, please," Wendy ordered.

Leesie and Teja went to the kitchen. There was a full bowl of dry food and a half bowl of water.

"I wonder where she keeps the food and the litter box?" said Teja.

"The food's in the cabinet under the sink. There's some wet food, too. It's in the cabinet next to it. The litter box is in Tara's bathroom. I guess we should check that too," Ariana said from the doorway.

"Lucky for us you lived here for a week. You know where everything is," Teja commented. "I'll go check the litter box. I'm used to kitties."

"Okay, I think he's calmed down enough to understand," Wendy announced loudly, drawing the girls back into the living room. When they were all seated Wendy asked, "What do you want to know?"

"What he heard would probably be all he can tell us," replied Matthew.

Wendy quietly listened to the cat as she held and petted him to keep him calm. Finally, she said, "Diablo told me he could hear Tara as she approached the side door so he was standing there waiting for her like he was when we came in today. He heard a loud thump and a grunt that he thought was her. He heard two male voices and lots more loud pounding sounds along with grunts and cries. The only sounds he recognized were Tara's. He's sure he doesn't know either of the men."

"Two guys, that doesn't make sense," Wendy said. "Why would two guys beat her up?"

"Maybe they saw a lone woman and thought they could rob her," suggested Zach. "Do we know if anything was stolen?"

"Maria didn't say anything about a mugging, so maybe she didn't know," Ariana stated. "I suspect the only people that do are the police and maybe the guy that found her."

"Does anyone remember if she was carrying a purse when we saw her last?" Matthew asked.

No one remembered.

"Does anyone remember the name of the neighbor that was asked to feed the cat?" asked Ariana.

"Why?" Teja wondered.

"Because maybe she knows who found Tara and can tell us."

"I don't remember her name, but Maria said she lived next door. Because Tara's condo is on the end, there's only one person who lives next door. We can check the mailbox for her name, or we can just knock on her door," suggested Leesie.

"I'm always amazed at that brain of yours. It's a great idea, but I think I should do it. If all of us are standing there, it could be intimidating," Ariana responded.

"She probably won't be home yet," said Zach. "It's only 3:00. I doubt she'd be home this early."

"What now?" Teja asked.

Andrew answered, "We go out to the spot where it happened and see if we can feel the guys and get a description of them."

"Great idea," Leesie exclaimed.

"Wait, I have some thoughts about this," said Ariana. "It's obvious that we are developing each other's gifts. A few of us are empaths. That means we feel things not only mentally but physically. I've got to warn you, it can hurt really, really bad. Shield yourself well, and if you don't think you can handle it, don't go out there. Okay?"

Teja looked at Leesie. "Are you sure you want to do this? As your polarity, I will probably pick up what you're getting even if I'm not out there. I'm not real sure I can handle it."

"I won't go if it will hurt you," Leesie offered.

"But you would if I hadn't said anything, right?"

"Yes, I'd like to feel like I was really doing something that could help," Leesie answered.

Closing her eyes and taking a deep breath Teja said, "I can do this. I want to help, too."

"I guess we're going to do this then," Ariana declared. Remembering the prayer Lydia said at the channeling, she began, "Let's form a circle to raise our protections and say a prayer." When they were all in a circle clasping hands Matthew continued. "Feel a warmth enter your left palm. It is a tingling warm energy entering your left palm. Allow this feeling, this sensation, to grow in intensity and strength. Fill your entire palm with this glowing ball of God's White Light energy. Imagine your palm so full that it must begin to fill your entire body with healing, protective energy. You are so full of the energy that it must escape through your right hand thus connecting us in an unbroken circle of God's love, healing, and protection. Continue to build the energy so that it fills the building, especially the garage. Send it out into the world so that all that it touches is filled with God's love and the planet receives this wonderful healing."

"Wow, feel the heat in the room," Andrew remarked.

"That's the energy," said Ariana.

Leesie smiled and opened her eyes. Extending her arms into the air she declared, "I feel wonderful. I felt completely connected to everyone in this room, including Diablo. That was awesome. I feel so amped!"

"I could feel the energy as it entered, built, and moved through me. It was really wonderful, sorta relaxing. I think I'm ready now," Teja announced.

They all felt the circle had worked and that it was time to continue. Wendy told Diablo what they were going to do and the group walked out the back door together.

There were dark splotches everywhere: on the walls, on the pavement, and on the door. It was Tara's blood. Breathing deeply, Ariana placed her hand over one sizable splotch while Andrew prowled the space. Zach stood with his eyes closed absorbing the energy. Teja, Leesie, and Wendy joined hands and stood over an area that looked like the spot where Tara had lain. Matthew was overwhelmed with the pain and fear that filled him as soon as he walked out the back door. He was working very hard not to alert the group. He needed them to pick up relevant facts and he was afraid that if he drew their attention they would only feel what he was feeling. He also sensed that most of the others could not tolerate the intensity of the pain this energy was causing him. When he couldn't stand it any longer, he went back into the condo. *Thank God the others didn't notice,* he thought. He didn't want to disturb what they were doing, but mostly he didn't want to appear weak. He knew that was stupid and part of the old Matthew, but for right now, he succumbed to the weakness and went back into the condo.

"Hey, man, you all right?" Zach asked. He had seen Matthew reenter the condo and he came in to check on him.

Matthew decided to answer honestly. "Just feeling a bit overwhelmed. All Tara's pain, both physically and mentally, are coming through."

"I can imagine," admitted Zach. "I could barely stand it out there myself. Did you get anything we could use?"

"Not really. Just a lot of physical sensations and emotional turmoil."

They heard the rest of the group as they entered the kitchen on their way to the living room. They were all uncharacteristically quiet. Even Leesie wasn't being her usual boisterous self. *They must all be feeling overwhelmed,* thought Zach.

Ariana was the first to enter the room. She looked drained, almost as bad as she had looked after the séance. Zach went to her. Putting his arm around her shoulders, he began to send her energy. She soaked it up.

"It must have been really bad if it drained you that much," he whispered.

"I dropped my shields for a moment to see if I could pick up more. Bad mistake," she confessed.

"Let's all sit down and try to re-energize ourselves," Zach suggested to the group. "It looks like this took a lot out of everybody."

After several minutes Matthew asked, "What did everyone get?"

No one answered.

"Well, did anyone get anything?" Leesie asked. "Come on, I know this is hard, but we've got to do it. Someone talk!"

"Okay, okay, I hope this doesn't sound apeshit or anything," Teja said, "but I think Tara was talking to me out there."

"Well, tell us what you think she said," Leesie demanded.

Teja seemed hesitant but continued, "She told me she appreciated that we are trying to find out what happened, but it isn't relevant. All the attackers did is what her soul needed them to do."

"What the hell does that mean?" Matthew said angrily. "Wait, I'm sorry. I didn't mean to sound angry. I'm filled with Tara's pain and it's hard to keep my self-control."

"I'd rather you didn't keep your self-control, bottling up your anger like you did last time. You know what happened when you did that," Ariana countered.

"Yeah, you're right," Matthew agreed. "But WTF, Teja! Do you know what she meant?"

"I think I do," she said. "I think Tara meant that in order to help us in the best way possible, her soul determined she could do more if she wasn't physical."

"What kind of horse poop is that?" exclaimed Wendy. "And if that's true, why would her soul want there to be so much violence?"

"Hey," Leesie exclaimed, jumping to the rescue of her polarity, "Don't kill the messenger. She's just reporting what she thinks she heard. At least she's saying something."

Embarrassed, both Wendy and Matthew apologized to Teja.

"Do you guys remember the parable about Jesus and his disciples?"

Ariana asked the group. "Wouldn't that sort of apply here? If Tara's soul did want her to work from a different realm, couldn't it have arranged all this?"

Zach spoke up, "Yes, but Wendy's right. Why would it have done it so violently?"

"For us to learn a lesson." Ariana offered.

"What do you mean?" Matthew asked. The whole group was thinking the same question.

Ariana answered, "Will we get negative, morose, and vindictive like the war vet you ran into? If we do, we are almost begging The Darkness to come in. Or do we work to understand that everything happens for a reason? Even if we don't understand the reason and it may not make sense to us now, we must continue to be The Light and accept our challenge of continuing the work."

"That still sounds too much like a punishing God," Andrew claimed.

Ariana continued, "Tara said nothing about God. God loves everything and everyone. The energy of love does not recognize good and bad; those are just our perceptions. It wasn't God that allowed the attack to happen. Our souls see our lives as a play, an opportunity to gain experience for our souls and for God. It was Tara's soul that directed and wrote this particular play."

"Wow, all that's too much for my tired little brain," said Wendy.

"Yes, it does take work to stop thinking that things are allowed to happen to us for no good reason. It is easier to believe that God is punishing you for something. But we all know Tara. Do any of us think she deserved what she got? I don't know about you, but that wouldn't be a God I could worship," Matthew declared.

"Okay, not to sound pushy here, but did anyone else get anything?" Leesie asked.

"Not that it really matters now, but I saw the two guys. I can describe them," Andrew answered.

"Me, too," declared Zach.

"It should still matter, shouldn't it? Just because Tara's soul wanted this to happen doesn't mean these guys shouldn't be punished," Leesie reminded the group.

"I don't think Tara wants that," Teja said. "She seemed to want us to leave it alone. Maybe they're already being punished in some way anyway," she said, thinking about her visit to one of the men.

"Oh, okay I guess, but I'd still like to know just in case we need the info later," Leesie said.

"I felt everything that happened to her. It was a terrible experience. She didn't black out until she was in the ambulance. She is the bravest person I know," Matthew said tearing up.

Leesie offered, "I think I saw and felt the man that found her. He saw the guys running away, that's why he came over to Tara's door. He called the ambulance, then the police and waited with her trying to help her till everyone got here. He is really a nice guy. We should find him just so we can thank him."

"Wendy, did you get anything?" Ariana asked.

"No, I think I was too afraid to," she admitted. "What you said about feeling her pain before we came out here convinced me I shouldn't even try. I hope that was okay."

Ariana touched Wendy's arm and stated, "Of course that's okay. That's why I warned everyone. I'm glad you chose to take care of yourself." Looking around at the group, she took a deep breath then continued, "I know why they did it. It was as though I was in their minds." She put her head in her hands and breathed deeply again. "They saw Tara as she was walking to some shop. They thought she was hot. They were hoping to score. They spoke to her at an art store, but she was dismissive which really made them angry. The clerk threw them out of the store. That made them even angrier. They decided they would follow her and rape her. The thoughts in their heads and their conversation with each other were horrible. They didn't see her as a person, only a piece of meat to devour. They followed her home and attacked her in the garage. They hadn't intended to beat her, but when they realized she was not a biological female they became enraged. Homophobic, all they could think to do was to destroy her beauty. They did not want to be attracted to her. Once they started the beating, years of rage came out. Tara didn't even try to fight back. It was horrible. Eventually, their anger spent, they fled."

"OMG," Wendy exclaimed. The rest of the group was quiet, trying to absorb what they were just told.

"It was because she's transgender?" Zach questioned, shocked that this could be the cause of such a brutal attack.

Ariana shook her head yes and said, "It's not just Tara. It's happened everywhere to thousands of gay, lesbian, and transgender people throughout history. Anything humanity doesn't understand, or thinks is different, is often destroyed. Certainly there was and still is hated. It seems to be human nature to have to have someone or something to hate and demonize."

"I'm still conflicted. Are you sure we shouldn't do something more?" Leesie asked. "Maybe we should give this information to the police. But If we do, they'll probably tell Tara's parents and it will confirm everything they believe. It will also hurt Maria."

Wendy answered, "I don't think we should. It sounds to me like Tara doesn't want us to and I agree with Leesie, it would do more harm than good."

"But they might do it again if they're not caught," objected Andrew.

"I don't think so," Teja said. "I think the experience has not only soured their relationship, but also traumatized them. I would really be surprised if they did anything violent again."

"How could you possibly know that?" asked Andrew.

"Maybe because Tara can tell and she spoke directly to her," Leesie said, defending her polarity again.

"Then we agree to keep quiet?" Matthew clarified.

The group all seemed to agree this was the best strategy for now. Even Diablo was quiet. He was sitting in a corner of the room purring and appeared to be staring at the wall.

"What the heck is Diablo staring at?" Teja asked.

"Tara," was Wendy's reply.

Chapter 8

"Hi Lydia," Ariana said as they walked into the foyer of her home for their appointment. "In case you don't remember because you were kinda out of your body last time we were all here, let me introduce you to the group. Pointing to each member as she spoke, Ariana continued, "This is Leesie, Teja, Wendy, Andrew, Zach, and Matthew

"Welcome," she said as she put down the small squirmy dog she was holding. "That's Sammy. He won't bother us, but I would advise against leaving your purses open, he's a thief."

"Sammy," Leesie squealed, "that's the name of my old dog, too, but he was a Beagle. He died a little over a year ago, but he's still with me, just differently now."

Sammy couldn't take his eyes off Wendy. He walked toward her, sniffing, and then began to leap high into the air as though he had just been reunited with a long-lost friend.

"I see you can talk to animals," Lydia said matter-of-factly.

"You can tell that by how the dog's acting?" Andrew asked.

"No, I know because of what's happening in her aura," Lydia explained.

Wendy bent to pick up the excited dog. Rising, she looked at Lydia and asked, "My aura changes? How?"

The cute, small dog settled comfortably in her arms, staring at her with adoring eyes.

"Two things happen: your aura expands and extends toward the animal instead of retracting as most people's auras do when confronted with an unknown animal. Secondly, the two auras merge harmoniously," Lydia explained. "and yes, the way he acted is a dead giveaway, but now we need to get to what you are all here for. I don't usually see people on Sundays but I felt a strong need to work with the group right away," Lydia continued. "There are extremely unsettled conditions happening throughout the world. Time is short and if you have any chance of turning the tide of negative energy that is fueling these conditions you must start soon.

Many people are experiencing an awakening, an activation of sorts. Some grow and handle this energy and these new abilities well, others become insane. That, and the erratic planetary energy we are experiencing, are creating extreme violence, especially among the young. As the energy becomes more erratic, the insanity, anger, and fear grow, only feeding the negative energy. Thus, a circular pattern is being created that will destroy this planet and all the lives on her. We are all entwined. We need the planet's energy and she needs ours. We feed each other. As she becomes more polluted and ill, so does humanity."

The group was trying to absorb all that they had just heard. Finally, Zach said, "That's really overwhelming. I know that each of us has been told this before, but somehow hearing a stranger say it is more alarming. I'm really afraid that I'm not capable of doing what needs to be done."

Lydia responded, "If you succeed or not is less important than each of you keeping the commitment that your soul made. Whatever happens, have no guilt as long as you have tried. You are not responsible for the outcome; that responsibility belongs to the **entire** human race. Commitment and responsibility seem to be areas that current humans don't understand. They don't really care about what others do unless it directly impacts their life. It's easy for us to rationalize that our own commitment is finished because no one else seems to care. But that is not true. Until your soul feels complete, you are not done with the work your soul intended for you in this lifetime. Rationalizing otherwise only creates more trauma and lessons for you to learn and can cause other people to rationalize their responsibility toward you."

"Lydia, we would like you to teach us. There are so many things we don't know or understand. I know you can't help us with everything, but whatever you are willing to do would really help move us forward," Ariana said.

"What I said about commitment also applies to me, too. My soul committed to help the planet, and I believe you have been sent my way in order for us to complete this task. I will work with all of you. First, however, I need to know what abilities each of you have discovered you possess, and how much you already know. The last part I expect you to tell me as I teach. If you already know what I am teaching you, tell me and we'll work forward from there. Okay? I will also need a promise from each of you that you will come to class at least once a week, prepared to work."

"Because we keep hearing that time is short," Matthew stated, "would it be possible to do an entire weekend, from like 9:00 to 6 or something? Or would that be too taxing for you?"

Lydia answered, "I think if we took breaks it would be possible. I'm not sure that you will learn everything in a weekend, but it's worth trying."

"Lydia, I understand that you feel you must do this for us, but I also know that this is how you make your living. We are asking for a great deal of your time. I insist that we pay you. This is non-negotiable, otherwise I will not attend," proclaimed Ariana.

"I agree," said Matthew as the others nodded.

Lydia was touched that these young people were so considerate and caring that they would even think about her and her finances. Knowing that they were only the conduits for God's loving abundance, she accepted their generosity. She knew that since they were giving with no expectations they would be paid back by the Universe ten-fold. That was a spiritual law she had seen manifest consistently.

Taking seats in the living room rather than Lydia's small office, Leesie began the reading, "We need to understand what happened to our friend Tara."

"Lydia, our friend Tara was brutally beaten three days ago by men that wanted to rape her. She is in a coma. Yesterday we went to where the attack took place. We were attempting to find out what happened and who did it. Each of us picked up pieces of the incident. Teja was actually able to talk to Tara's spirit. It told her we should stop trying to find out who did it because her soul had decided that she needed to work with us from a different realm. We were actually told that the men who attacked her were only doing her soul a favor. We are having a difficult time coming to grips with this information. Why would her soul desire this? Why did she have to be so badly tortured?" Ariana questioned.

Lydia, her eyes closed, was silent for several minutes. Eventually she opened them and appeared to be staring over Ariana's shoulder. "She's here. She has a beautiful, vibrant energy. She is healing, but her soul wants her body to rest so it is keeping it in a coma. But Tara's energy has been very busy. Oh, she wants to thank Wendy for helping Diablo feel better."

"Can you ask her why the hell her soul hurt her so bad?" Teja demanded.

Lydia laughed and said, "You, girl, will have to work on your temper. She wants me to tell all of you that her soul determined she needed to be working in the other dimensions so that the healing of the planet can be complete. It chose the way that it did for several reasons. First, Tara explained to me that although she thought she had worked through all her anger and guilt, she had not, and it was holding back her effectiveness. This event cleansed her of all of it because she now completely understands forgiveness. She understands that everything happens exactly in a way that creates the most opportunity, not the other way around. Before the attack, she had been moving through different realms and going to many places observing situations she could do nothing about. This left her feeling both uncomfortable and frustrated. Now she can walk between the dimensions and make positive changes because she understands what those souls have been through. Additionally, it had to be done this way in order for each of you to understand forgiveness and to see how everything has a purpose, even if you don't understand that purpose until later."

"Okay, I'm officially confused. What are different realms and dimensions?" Wendy wondered.

"There are different realms of existence, for instance this is a physical realm. There are also nonphysical ones like what is commonly called the Other Side. When Tara speaks of other dimensions, she is also talking about the other existences that overlay ours. Again, most people understand the concept of the Other Side as not being in this dimension, but there are many other dimensions, too. String theory addresses this if you need to understand the physics. Between our dimension and the Other Side is an area that often overlaps our own. That area is inhabited by egos that left this realm in a tragic way. Many have unfinished business over here that keeps them from even seeing The Light. They are so busy being angry, scared, or guilty that they remain in this limbo until they forgive themselves or another."

"Who are these egos?" Andrew asked.

"Usually victims of a tragedy, murder victims or their perpetrators, victims whose families won't let them go, sudden deaths that don't want to accept that they are dead, and suicides," Lydia answered.

"Purgatory," Zach said. "The Catholic Church is right. Before you can go to Heaven you must spend time there to be absolved by Jesus when he returns."

"This has nothing to do with God. The Source does not punish or even consider good or bad as a reality. You must realize that those terms mean different things in different times and places. If we were discussing these things in the 15th century, we would be burned as heretics. Questioning accepted doctrine was considered not only bad but sinful. Accepting what you were told completely without question was considered the right thing to do. Now we think encouraging free thought is good and controlling thought and speech, like Islamic extremists are attempting to do, for example, is bad. See what I mean? It is the ego that judges both before or after death whether something feels good or bad. The ego is in control until reunited with the soul and is within The Light, the Source. This doesn't always occur if the ego feels unfinished. It may decide to reside in a dimension of darkness, forgetting that the Other Side exists. Or at this point, the ego may be too ashamed to enter The Light. This happens often and those with abilities can observe these egos. They are often called ghosts, spirits, spooks or shades."

"Do they have the power to affect us?" Leesie inquired.

"Not often. Occasionally a child or pubescent teen can empower and energize one of these spirits. Then the family will experience hauntings. The type of ego the spirit was in life will determine whether the spirit acts hostile or not. There are some extremely negative beings over there, but they are not supernatural beings like demons or devils, but egos that were very negative in life as well. When I say negative I mean angry, violent, and aggressive. Often they were rapists, murderers or warriors. Now that Tara can walk within the dimensions, not just between them, she can help these egos go to The Light. This is very important work. Their negativity is also causing disruption to Earth right now."

Ariana said thoughtfully, "So her experience made her more understanding of their plight and her forgiveness can show them how to forgive themselves?"

"Yes," replied Lydia.

"Can't the bad guys hurt her, too?" worried Leesie.

"They are not physical. They can't do harm," Lydia answered.

"Then how do they make things fly through the air and grope women when they are doing hauntings?" Teja responded.

"By using your energy against you. That is why it is often a child or pubescent teen that draws them. Their energy is not controlled. It can be erratic, thus easier to use," replied Lydia. "Tara's soul and ego must have felt they could be more useful helping souls to the Other Side from that realm than from here. Had she been having any odd occurrences?"

"Yes, many," Ariana stated, "When Matthew was in trouble she easily entered the realm his mind had created and helped him make it back to us. She also claimed that recently she had been having visions that seemed to take over her consciousness. She thought they were visions of places on Earth, but could she have been wrong?"

"It could have been a little of both," Lydia assured her. "For instance, if someone experiences a violent death and refuses to release the experience, they may continue having the experience over and over again until they let go and go to The Light. She may have picked up the experience and thought she was seeing something that was happening at that moment. Or she could have been actually seeing a present moment. Have you ever gone somewhere, like maybe Pearl Harbor, and felt what happened there?'

"We have," Andrew blurted out as he pointed at Zach.

"It's much the same thing. Coming upon a place where something terrible has happened may cause someone truly gifted to have the experience or witness it."

"But is she okay there and will she come back to us?" Matthew asked.

"As to whether she will return to you, that is up to her soul and how well you do in your work. Is she okay? By the look of her smile, she is wonderful. She feels that she is doing what she was meant to do, help lost souls."

"Lydia," Leesie said as she handed over a sheet of paper. "Here is a list of our names, what our abilities are, and what we have been studying and doing. Is there anything we need to do to get ready for the class? Anything we need to bring?"

"No, but thank you Leesie. I am Pisces with Cancer rising; we like to take care of people so I will have food here for all of us. As far as what you can do to prepare, maybe write down questions about anything metaphysical you don't understand or would like to learn," suggested Lydia. "Oh, and Matthew, just because your polarity is not physical doesn't mean that you are no longer polarities. You, too, are a spirit walker so go to her when you sleep. Just be sure you are well protected."

Chapter 9

The week had raced by as even the professors were getting into the holiday spirit. Winter break was only a little over a week away and none of the students were in the mood to go to classes, much less study. The weather was beautiful with a slightly cool bite in the air. All the stores and trees along Mill Avenue were decked out in sparkling lights. The sound of Christmas music filled the air. People were naturally affable in this University environment, but the holiday season seemed to bring out even more joy and friendliness than before.

The residents of Manzanita Hall had started decorating their rooms and hallways right after Halloween. They succeeded in creating a glittering, festive environment. The excitement was infectious. While waiting for Ariana to arrive home from class, Wendy busily adorned a small artificial tree she had purchased. She was excited to see how Ariana would respond to her eclectic decorating. There were strings of colored LED lights around both windows and doorways. Hanging from the lights were crystals. The small tree was hung with pretty red and gold ornaments and interspersed among the lights were more crystals. The room was filled with rainbows. Diablo, who Wendy had snuck into the dorm, was batting at the sparkling display of colors that covered the walls, ceiling, and floor. The room was filled with color and positive energy. It glowed.

Wendy wanted to get the room perfect before they went to Lydia's for class tomorrow. She thought it would raise their energy when coming home from working so hard and long on Saturday and Sunday. But the truth was, Wendy loved the Christmas season and everything about it. Her family had always decorated like crazy. Even when she was in the worst of her depression, she loved to watch the lights and look at all the beautiful houses decorated for the holidays.

She was so completely lost in her decorating frenzy she didn't even hear the knock on the door. She was startled when she heard the male voice that accompanied the second knock. "Hello. Is there anyone home?" the voice asked.

I wonder who that is; she thought as she walked to the door and opened it. On the other side of the doorway stood a young, reasonably attractive male who was vaguely familiar. *Where do I know him from?* she wondered. *Maybe he lives on this floor somewhere and that's why he looks kinda familiar.*

"Hi, I'm Jason. I was here a few days ago delivering wings. Remember? I saved your Oreos," the boy said.

"Yeah, I guess I remember. Didn't we pay you enough or something?"

"Sorry, I'm not here about that. There was this cute, little girl here with you guys that said she would do some numerology on my name and stuff. I was wondering if she'd gotten it done yet and this was the only way I knew to maybe get in touch with her," he explained.

"Leesie, are you talking about Leesie? Real short and looks kind of like a hobbit but with tiny feet?"

"Yeah, that sounds right."

Wendy was becoming a little uncomfortable. She didn't remember anything about numerology that day, but she had been pretty busy when the food arrived. *What do I do with this guy,* she worried. Finally, she decided to be safe. "She doesn't live here. Why don't you give me your phone number or something and when I see her I'll remind her."

"Okay," Jason said obviously disappointed. "I need something to write on though."

Wendy went to get some paper and as she was looking for her notebook she heard Ariana open the door.

"Oh, hi Jason. Is there something we can do for you?"

Knowing that Ariana knew him made Wendy feel considerably better and she replied for him, "He's here looking for Leesie."

"She told me she'd do some numerology on me, but I didn't know how to get in touch with her," he explained. "But to be completely truthful, what I heard last time I was here has kept me thinking. I need to talk to someone about what's been happening to me, but I don't know who. I have been really having a hard time with some of the things that have been happening to me for the last 13 months. I thought I was going crazy, so I began to do some research on line. I didn't find much that was real helpful, but it did start me thinking that maybe I had some psychic abilities or something. I heard you guys talking about your own psychic work. I'm hoping maybe one of you can help me figure out if it is psychic stuff that's going on with me or if I'm just going crazy."

"Why don't you come inside and sit down. I really don't want everyone in the dorm to know what we're doing. At least not now," Ariana explained as she entered the room holding the door for Jason. It was only then she noticed all the work that Wendy had done. "Whoa, Wendy! You've been busy. It's beautiful, but there's so much energy in here with all these beautiful crystals we'll never be able to sleep!"

Blushing, Wendy admitted, "Oh, I didn't even think about that. Maybe I should take them down."

"I think we can handle about half. Maybe if you use the ones on the tree, and leave one on each strand of lights, that will do it," Ariana stated just as Diablo darted toward a glistening reflection. "What's Diablo doing here? Won't we get in trouble if we're caught with him in our room?"

"He was really freaked out when I went to feed him today. He begged me not to leave him alone. No one saw me bring him in and he's been really quiet. If we're careful, I don't think there will be a problem before winter break and then you'll be staying at Tara's anyway," Wendy pleaded.

Forgetting Jason was in the room Ariana replied, "Sometimes your ability to talk to animals is more trouble than it's worth. But if you are sure he'll be really good, I'll chance it.

"He promised me," Wendy answered.

"Wow! You can talk to animals. That is way cool. You guys are awesome. I'm so glad I found you," Jason exclaimed. "I've been praying for help and look, here you are! You could have ordered pizza that night and I would never have met you. Then I probably would have gone crazy."

"Please sit down," Ariana asked him again. "Tell us what has been happening to you."

Jason sat in the desk chair and began. "About a year or so ago I began to have these really freaky dreams that were very dark and scary. It was as though I was observing some kind of catastrophe. The land was scorched and broken and bodies of both humans and animals lay everywhere, bloated and stinking. The first time I dreamed this I rationalized that it was because I watched *World War Z* that night. That wasn't the last time I had the dream, though. The next time there was more detail and I saw more places. Now the dreams reminded me of *Mad Max*. I like movies," he said, explaining his references. "There were lots of very violent people roaming what was left of the planet, doing even more destruction. The world had gone completely crazy. It was as though everyone had become violent. Suddenly, after several months of these kinds of dreams, they stopped. I was really glad and chalked it up to too many violent movies and video games.

Unfortunately, about five months ago the dreams started again, but they were different. I still had some apocalyptic dreams but now I was also having dreams about horrible events like plane crashes, shootings, terrorism; all kinds of tragic events. I know lots of people have dreams like that, but what was really creepy was that mine came true. Within a week of having one of those dreams the event would happen. That started making me worry that the others would eventually happen too. I was so freaked I stopped sleeping; I was too afraid I would dream. I even began to wonder if I was creating these horrible events. I was successful not sleeping for about 10 days, but one day I fell asleep on my delivery route. I just missed hitting a kid. That did it; I knew I had to start sleeping again. I was really f'd up. That's when I started praying. I know that sounds really petty, only praying when you need something, but I was desperate and it worked. That's when I found you guys. I wasn't even supposed to be working that night. I was doing a favor for someone. I believe that God answered my prayer."

"He's precognitive," Wendy said. "Look how Diablo is reacting to him."

Ariana had been so entranced listening to Jason's dialogue she hadn't even realized that Diablo had climbed into his lap and was happily purring. Diablo was very selective with his affection; if he didn't think you belonged with the group and weren't a good person, he wouldn't go near you. He rarely sat on someone's lap. She had only seen him do that with Wendy and Tara. He didn't even do it with her.

"I think you're right Wendy. Jason, do you know what being precognitive is?"

"Yeah, I came across it in my research, but I don't think that really is me," he replied.

"Then you know that precognition is the ability, with no apparent cues, to predict something that has not happened. Were any of your dreams about anything you had exposure to? Like the plane crashes or shootings, were they in Arizona or did you know anyone who lived in the areas they happened?" Ariana asked.

"Well, no," he admitted, "but the news reporting after the events led me to believe that somehow my mind was just playing the odds."

"I'm confused," Wendy said. "What do you mean 'playing the odds'?"

Jason turned to Wendy and replied, "You know, somewhere within the next week a plane will crash, violence will happen, and so will terrorism."

"How specific were your dreams, how much detail did you dream?" asked Ariana. "Did you know where the events happened? Did you know what group of terrorists would attack or how many people were in the plane, the terrain it crashed in, things like that?"

"I draw. I really want to work for Marvel someday, so I drew what I saw. I have a notebook filled with the drawings," he informed the girls.

"Okay, so how accurate are the drawings?"

Looking down as though he was embarrassed he replied, "Spot on."

"Well, that seems to be the answer," Wendy said. "You're precognitive whether you want to be or not." She extended her right hand to shake his and said, "Welcome to the Weirdxotics."

Chapter 10

The rest of the group gathered in Ariana and Wendy's room in preparation for the long drive to Lydia's. Ariana introduced Jason to the group. After telling them his history, she asked if he should come to the classes with them. She had already broached the subject with him prior to the others getting there. Jason was excited about the possibility of not only having some of his questions answered, but also learning to handle his precognition and maybe developing more skills. The general opinion of the group was that he might as well come along. If he belonged, he'd stay. If not, Lydia would recognize that he wasn't meant to be a part of their group and would probably tell them.

Leesie was ecstatic that the boy she had taken an instant liking to might become one of the group. She had completed his numerology and it had intrigued her. He seemed to be exclusively seven and nine; both were considered spiritual numbers. The seven often meant some sort of brilliance, while the nine, meaning endings, could indicate an old soul working on putting an end to a series of lives. She also liked that he was only two years older than her. *Maybe he'll be the first boy I fall for,* she thought.

Leesie and Jason were sitting close together on Wendy's bed as she explained his numerology to him. Diablo refused to get off his lap and was purring so loudly that Leesie nearly had to shout to be heard. "Remember, this is just a brief summary of your numbers. I would have to do a lot more work to find out potential timing of events in your life. Essentially, you are mostly seven; your destiny, reality number, and personality numbers are all seven. Your heart's desire and birth path numbers are nine. I would read from this that you are an old soul that is back in this lifetime to work on spirituality. It's not only because you have triple sevens, the number of spirituality, but also because that is the only number you are missing in your name. The numbers not present in our names indicate our karmic lessons."

"Sorry to cut you short, but we've got to get going," Zach said to Leesie. Turning to Jason he asked, "I'm going to assume that because you are a delivery driver you have a car, right?"

"Yes, why?"

"Because since we all got together eons ago I've been the only one with a car. Putting eight people in my Mustang is a pain and a half."

"I can help some. I have a truck that will hold three in the front and maybe four if we pushed really hard," Jason said with a smile.

"Do you mind driving to Glendale?"

"No. Just tell me where we're going and I'll meet you there."

Leesie piped up, "It's somewhere near Camelback and 71st Ave."

"OMG, that proves this isn't any accident," he exclaimed, "I live at 75th Ave and Missouri."

"You don't mind driving us over there, then back here to Tempe, then back home?" Wendy asked, impressed with Jason's generosity.

"I might need a little help with gas money, but otherwise, no sweat," he replied.

"I'll ride with Jason," offered Leesie.

"Me, too," said Teja. "She is my polarity after all."

"What's a polarity?" Jason whispered to Leesie.

"I'll tell you in the car. Teja and I will fill you in on what's been going on with the group."

The rest of the group rode with Zach. None of them were used to having so much space in his small car.

"It looks like our little girl is growing up," Matthew said.

Ariana smiled broadly. "Did you see her aura when she saw him? She lit up the room."

"You guys can see auras without trying?" Andrew asked. "When does that particular trick rub off on the rest of us?"

Color began rising up Wendy's neck to her face as she admitted, "I already can."

"When did that happen?" Andrew asked. "And why didn't you tell me?"

"Sorry, it just started. All of a sudden I noticed that everything had colors surrounding them. Actually, it can get a little distracting at times."

"Well, I'd like some of that distraction, too."

"Don't worry," said Ariana, "I'll bet now that Wendy can, you'll be able to see them soon. Zach is rapidly picking up my abilities."

"He can do it too?" Andrew asked, sounding disheartened.

"Sweet Baboo," Wendy soothed, "I am sure there are plenty of things you can do that the rest of us will have to learn."

"Let's change the subject. What do you think we're in for this weekend?" Zach questioned.

"Hopefully a good time," Andrew answered with a smile.

Quietly Matthew asked, "Do you think Tara will be there with us?"

"I'll bet she will be," Wendy assured him. "That is, if she's not too busy doing her work in the other dimensions."

"She was there the last time we saw Lydia. I'm sure she knows about this weekend so she'll be there," Ariana proclaimed.

Zach looked over at Matthew and asked, "Can't you feel her or are you still blocking?"

"I think she's blocking me. I can't seem to reach her. I have a feeling she's doing that on purpose so I won't feel any pain she might be in. She is my polarity after all, and that's what I did to her when I was really hurting."

Ariana replied, "You know I think you're right, but I also think we can convince her to stop if you are sure you can handle knowing what's going on with her."

"I want to know. I want to be able to help her if she needs me to," he confided.

"You can't rescue her, Matthew. You know that, don't you?" said Ariana.

"Yes, I know. But I still think I can help, like she helped me."

Zach looked at his friend and said, "Are you sure you won't punish yourself if you're wrong. Sorry, man, but that's been your MO."

"Polarities are strongest when combined. Even though we are on different planes right now, Lydia said the planes overlap. Can't I help from over here if I know what she's working on? For instance, let's say someone over there is stuck because someone in the family won't let go. I can work on the family from this side while she's working from her side."

"Maybe," Ariana said doubtfully. "I guess we can ask Lydia."

Wendy shook her head and exclaimed, "Boy, we have so much to learn! Do you think a weekend is enough?"

"No, but I do think we'll get enough for now," Ariana declared.

"Wow, maybe we shouldn't let that dude drive anyone we care about," Zach said when they got to Lydia's and found Jason and the girls had gotten there first. "He must have flown to get here."

"Maybe he knows short cuts," Andrew offered. "After all, he lives around here somewhere."

"Everyone ready?" Matthew asked, "Cause here we go."

Chapter 11

"Welcome," Lydia said from the open door. "Is everyone ready to learn? Oh, someone new. Hi, I'm Lydia and you are?"

"Hi, ma'am, I'm Jason. Um, not that I want to invade your privacy, but do you have a son?"

"Yes, I do. He's away at college."

"Yeah, I think I know him. He was a couple years ahead of me at Independence, but I think I was over here once. We were on the football team together his senior year."

"Then you probably have been here. This was the football team's hangout for a while."

"I didn't know you had a son," Leesie stated.

Lydia smiled, and cupping Leesie's chin in her hands replied, "Oh, little one, there's a lot you don't know about me. Maybe by the time this weekend is over you will. Let's get started then. There's water, tea, and coffee in the kitchen if anyone's thirsty. We'll also be taking regular breaks."

Looking around the living room, Wendy asked, "Where's Sammy?"

"I put him out back for a while. He can be a little disruptive. Don't worry; I'll bring him in later. Okay, everyone take a seat, please but if you have your polarity with you, separate."

"Why?" asked Andrew, not wanting to be separated from Wendy.

Lydia smiled when she answered, "Because sometimes polarities get dependent on one another, and at other times they can get competitive. I'd like to prevent both scenarios. Don't worry Andrew," she said with a smile, "you'll get her back soon."

When everyone was seated comfortably in the living room, Lydia surveyed the room. Ariana was sure she was looking at everyone's aura. Eventually Lydia commented, "Let me see if I can pick out who's who within your group. I have a slight advantage as I have read for Ariana and know she is one of your leaders. The gentleman in the blue shirt with the dark hair, you are her polarity and also her heart bond."

"Yup, that's me. I'm Zach," he said, flashing his signature smirk.

"She knows your name, dufus," Teja reminded him. "She was introduced to everyone during our reading, but she doesn't know who our polarities are or what all everyone can do."

Lydia continued as though Teja hadn't spoken, "The blond gentleman next to you is the co-leader and Tara's polarity. She is directly behind you and to your left".

Ariana could see the tears in his eyes even from where she was sitting.

"Why can't I contact her anymore? Oh, I'm Matthew."

"She seeks to protect you because she is still worried you might be fragile, but she will soon find out that she is wrong and your connection will be rebuilt. You too can walk between the realms so you will be the liaison to this world for her. The experience of your ordeal on the mountain and the way she helped you through it has prepared the two of you for this. Moving right along, the woman to your right is the group's medium. She has a police officer to her right. Your father?" Lydia asked.

"I'm Teja, and yes, that's my dad."

"Your polarity is the young, talkative one sitting next to Ariana."

"That's me," announced Leesie, "and my name is Leesie. "But you didn't say what I do."

"You are the glue, the memory, the chronicler, and the energizer. You will develop all the abilities, but your greatest contributions to the group are the things I mentioned first. Next to you is Jason. Because his aura does not yet fully blend with the group, he's new and doesn't yet have a place, but he has extreme precognitive abilities that are being activated. The larger gentleman is a sensitive, although you don't fully realize it yet. Your emotions are highly tuned to the environment and any disruption to energy will be keenly felt by you. Although you may appear placid on the outside, unless you learn to shield better, this energy turmoil could damage your health. And finally, there is your polarity, the group's animal whisperer. What a wonderful group this is."

"How did you do that?" Wendy asked.

"By observing not only your aura, but also the group aura, and noticing the people and things from the other planes that surround you."

"You can see the other planes?" Matthew asked.

"And so can you. The difference is I accept what I see without question or doubt. You and most humans block out what doesn't make obvious sense or rationalize what you see. 'Oh, I just have floaters in my eyes' or 'It's a trick of the light,' for example. That's what happens when one becomes civilized and acculturated. It causes you to want to fit in so you begin to accept what others tell you and ignore what is right in front of you. Some of us didn't get as civilized as others. It is a long-accepted belief in our culture that in extreme situations, paranormal experiences can happen. Society acknowledges the existence of angels or God helping. Soldiers tell of miraculous things occurring that save them and even their entire regiment. Hitler had one of these experiences in WW I which fostered his lifelong interest in the supernatural. Mothers sense when their children are in danger, and many of us have experienced Déjà vu. Within our culture these things are acceptable. But once you tell people that this is possible all the time, not just in moments of danger, all kinds of taboos are threatened. What humans don't understand they fear. Fear of these abilities will alter them. Either the abilities will be misinterpreted or they will be pushed so far inside that you will believe they aren't present at all. If someone is known to have abilities or seen as able to do something extraordinary that others cannot do or is consider impossible, then the gifted person will be ostracized, feared or at least discouraged from using it. No one in our society wants to be ostracized, so most people stop using what abilities they have and eventually forget they have them.

In my case, I came from a very violent upbringing. My survival sense was honed by this violence, causing me to hyper develop my psychic abilities. My abilities kept me alive. I believe that is also true for you, Ariana. For Teja and Jason, however, the opposite is true. Both of you initially responded to your abilities with fear and in your case Teja, you rejected it for years because of the condemnation you were getting. Right?"

Teja nodded.

"Truthfully," Jason said, "This stuff still scares the crap out of me. Oh sorry," he said, embarrassed.

Lydia laughed. "If crap was the worst word I ever heard, or even said, I would be eternally embarrassed. I can understand your fear, Jason. This just kind of showed up one day, am I right? You had no prior abilities before what, about a year ago?"

"Yeah, I just started having these horrible dreams. Never anything nice, just bad things," he agreed.

"If what you were getting was nice, you wouldn't have paid attention to them. Most people start this way with disturbing visions because those carry a stronger charge and are not easy to forget or rationalize. People rarely notice precognitive information that is pleasant. Your soul and guides wanted you to pay attention. That is why the dreams were so vivid and disturbing. It looks like it worked. What I'm going to do this weekend is introduce you to some new abilities, new ways to look at what you can do. We'll try to unlock whatever else is lurking inside and answer whatever questions you might have. This is not a competition. You will be great in some things and not so great in others. No one here will be great at everything. I've been doing this stuff since I was six and I'm 66 now and I can't do everything. Get over yourself. Allow that you might look like a fool part of the time and a champion at other times. Great, you're human. Everyone got it?"

Lydia had clearly captured her audience's attention. She continued, "Okay, first I'm going to explain some types of abilities. Clairvoyance is the ability to see or sense things that are not apparent in normal ways; when the phone rings you know it's your aunt that's calling or that your boyfriend is at the movies with your best friend. Have you ever walked into a room and all of a sudden you get a weird feeling? Maybe you sense something very sad has happened there? That's called clairsentience. Next there are precognitives; they literally see the events playing out in front of them, either in a dream or vision. Both of these types may taste, smell, and hear what they are getting, too.

There are lots of clinical terms for what we do, but here's how I break it down: empaths are those of us that feel what we get. We pick up other's emotions. This can include how another person physically feels. If the person has pain, the empath may actually feel pain. Through this means we can also access the potential for future events. I am not saying that these future predictions are set in stone; we are all given free will and thereby have the ability to change future events. What the empath feels is the potential for the future event to occur.

Then there are mediums, both conscious and unconscious. They receive information directly from souls or egos that are residing on other planes.

I think all psychic ability fits into these definitions, and I also feel that most of us combine them. I am basically an empath; I feel things including colors, landscapes, and emotions. Occasionally, however, I do see things, especially spirits. Those of you that have come to a channeling also know that I am a medium. When I channel Equinoxx, I am an unconscious medium. But I can also be a conscious medium and that is what I am for the most part when doing séances."

Teja raised her hand. After Lydia acknowledged her she said, "When I was doing our séance Ariana's grandmother came through. They tell me I spoke German and my voice changed completely. I don't remember any of it and I don't know any German."

"You are an unconscious channel and quite a good one it appears. It is rare that a medium can speak another language. Equinoxx tells me that they will take words out of my mind so that they can speak English. Consequently, if there are no German words in my brain they could not speak German."

Ariana asked, "I speak German and it was my oma. Could she have taken the words from my mind?"

Lydia thought about the question for a moment before answering. It appeared as though she was listening to something in her head. Finally, she responded, "I'm being told by my guides and by Equinoxx that what you say is possible especially because you all are so linked."

"You can just go quiet and they talk to you?" asked Jason.

"It's really easy if you learn to listen," Lydia answered. "That's something we will be working on. Your guides, higher consciousness, what we call the soul, and loved ones are always there working with us. If we took a moment to listen we'd know it. Most of us race through life barely seeing what's around us in the physical world much less paying attention to what is unseen. We only allow ourselves to listen when we are in great need. That is why they used disturbing dreams to get your attention, Jason."

"Good to know. Maybe if I start listening I can sleep better at night."

Lydia asked, "Does everyone in the group know which of these psychic skills you favor to get information?"

Leesie raised her hand and asked, "What about numerology,

astrology, Tarot, crystals; all those things you see psychics using? How do these things fit into the categories?"

"I call the things you mentioned tools," Lydia explained. "They are used to focus your attention so that you are open to extrasensory input. I also believe that you can be a good astrologer and numerologist without psychic ability; they are sciences after all. But I think that if you use both the science and your abilities you will get better information. An astrology chart is a map that shows potential, your psychic abilities can clarify whether your client will act on the potential or not and in what way. If you are more comfortable using a tool, use it.

Now back to the original questions, who knows which of these approaches they use most naturally?"

"I am an empath. I am attuned to energy; I feel it. I can see and hear it too, but I think I feel things first," Ariana said.

"Me too," Andrew claimed.

"I hear. I seem to be more comfortable listening. Is that more clairvoyant?" Wendy wondered.

"Yes, I think it is. Instead of seeing, you hear. Have you ever seen anything?" Lydia asked.

"Sometimes the animals show me things and I can see them," she admitted.

"Definitely clairvoyance then."

"You know what I am," Jason added. "But I have also felt things. Like there have been times when I've been on a delivery and I know the person who is paying me is very sick or mean or in emotional pain."

"Remember I said that I combine all three? It sounds like you do, too. Matthew?"

"I combine everything plus I can enter my spirit animal and see the world through its eyes. Also, I can travel to other realms."

"Shamanic abilities are often inherited as well as taught. Your grandfather has prepared you for your role well. You can do things I can't do. I would ask you to teach this to your group starting with Wendy as it will be very easy for her to merge her energy with the animals," Lydia suggested. "Teja?"

"All the above; I see, hear, and feel. I've seen ghosts forever and I've heard them talk to me. I feel pain, too, but didn't realize I was picking up other people," she answered.

"Matthew, Teja has been walking the realms, too. Work with her on this. Leesie, how do you perceive?"

"I'm not sure. I think about everything constantly and analyze everything. Because of that I think I try to rationalize, like you said before. Then I doubt what I'm getting and give up. Sometimes I just feel things, like feeling that something was off with Matthew before he went ballistic on us, but I don't know if I really felt it or whether I saw it in his aura. I'm so confused," she pouted.

"It sounds to me like you are doing both, but because you are so used to using your intellect for everything, you are applying logic to what isn't logical. Psychic ability cannot really be analyzed. There is a quantum physics theory that states if you observe an experiment you will alter the result. In the same way, if you try to understand how you are getting the information and what you think it means, you might just begin to doubt what you get or be so busy analyzing that you miss what you are getting entirely. Years ago, I asked for a world prediction. This was unusual for me because I don't like seeing something I can do nothing about. What the guides showed me was a large mountain with an 'H' on it exploding into activity, lava and ash destroying the surrounding area. I heard, 'Oh no, a dormant volcano has erupted creating lots of damage.' Here is what I wrote as my prediction, 'An inactive volcano in Hawaii will erupt causing lots of property damage.' I analyzed what I saw and interpreted the H as Hawaii which caused the prediction to be completely inaccurate because I applied logic instead of just writing down exactly what I got. The volcano was actually Mount Saint Helens."

"This is really tricky stuff," Andrew said.

"Not if you apply certain rules. Rule one: only say what you get. Rule 2: don't hold back anything you get. Rule 3: don't try to read for yourself. Rule 4: you are not responsible for what happens, you are only the messenger. We've talked about Rule 1; don't embellish the information, just state what you know, no more.

Regarding Rule 2, not withholding information, let's say you get something and assume the other person can't handle it so you don't tell them. What if the person has been waiting to see if you mention it and it is one of their tests of your ability? You have now failed because you made an assumption based on your own fears, prejudices, or misconceptions.

I learned Rule 3, not reading for myself, the hard way. Years ago I read Tarot cards. I was reading for my fiancé, which is as bad an idea as reading for yourself because you will be very prominent in his or her reading. I interpreted the cards then I wrote down the lay of the cards and my interpretation. Months later when I became aware of a massive deception, I went over my interpretation of the cards. The truth had been right there, but because I couldn't deal with what I saw, I didn't allow myself to see it. What if you had seen what would happen to Tara? Would you have tried to prevent it or would you have misinterpreted it? Because it was supposed to happen, you would have probably missed it altogether.

Rule 4 goes back to Rule 3. If you did see something and either tried to stop it and failed, or misinterpreted it, **it is not your fault**. You have zero control over what the soul intends for anyone, and because they have freewill, they will do as they choose even when warned. I did a reading several years ago where I saw a potential rape. I felt that it was completely avoidable and because I tell my clients everything I get, I warned her. She didn't want to hear it. She wouldn't let me tell her the circumstances so that she could avoid it, either. She said she wasn't interested and only wanted information about her career and potential success. This was not the only thing she refused information on. She didn't want to hear anything about her family, potential husband or her health, so I released the information with a blessing. About six months later she called me. The rape had just happened, and she was blaming me and wanting to know what she was supposed to do now. As I forget my readings, I could offer her nothing. I only remember this because she called me at 1:30 in the morning."

"And you didn't feel guilty at all?" Wendy asked.

"When I first started this work, I would have. But with years comes wisdom and I realized that even when I warn people not to do something, like marry the person they think they love, they will do as they want anyway. Later they come back and tell me how right I was. For some reason, they needed the lesson. I can't take responsibility for those people the information saved any more than I can accept the guilt for those that didn't listen. I don't want to be anyone's guru or savior. That's an ego path that only creates disaster for those that choose to walk it.

This is a good time to take a break. Use the restroom if you need to and get something to eat and drink. I'll be putting out some fresh fruit and cookies. Mingle, talk with one another, and if you have any questions, come talk to me."

Chapter 12

The group adjourned to the kitchen to fill their stomachs as full as their brains. Andrew piled his plate high with assorted cookies. Wendy stole a chocolate chip cookie from his plate as he slapped her hand and protested her theft.

"What kind of boyfriend are you?" she complained.

"A hungry one," he answered honestly.

Ariana stood back and watched her friends banter back and forth. She felt full of overwhelming love. *How did I get this lucky?* she wondered as Zach walked over to her.

"It's great being a part of such a diverse and exceptional group of people, isn't it?"

Ariana put her arm around his waist and asked, "Is mind reading one of your new abilities?"

"Only with you I think. That mind link thing. Also, you look so happy standing here, looking around at everyone. It wasn't hard to figure out."

"No using your left brain," Lydia said from behind them. They hadn't even realized she was standing there. "It's possible to modulate your energy to blend in with the environment," she explained. "Get something to eat. Working in the nonphysical realm can cause us to forget to fuel our bodies."

Ariana and Zach went to the treat table and began to pick out fuel for themselves. Zach chose cookies while Ariana, always mindful of gaining weight, chose grapes and apple slices. Matthew and Teja were in the corner of the kitchen talking. Ariana found herself being drawn in their direction.

"Can you see her?" Matthew asked.

"Only sometimes," Teja replied. "Like right now, she's over by the fridge watching what's going on."

"I wish she'd open up to me again. I really miss her and our connection."

"Maybe she realizes that and is afraid of the responsibility you are placing on her," offered Ariana.

Matthew seemed disturbed by her comment. "What do you mean exactly?"

"I mean that you're special to her and only newly resurrected yourself from a pretty horrific take over. Maybe she's concerned that because of her, you could be really hurt again. You do accept guilt pretty easily."

Teja responded, "Matt I think she's right. You have to grow stronger so that no matter what happens with Tara, you'll be okay. Until she believes that, she won't open the link."

"Can you work on letting go of your needs and concentrate on putting your energy into the work you are doing?" Lydia asked as she approached the small group. "Will you live up to your name, Peaceful Warrior, and allow those that assisted you on your quest to lead you now? You don't always need to lead or be in control. This is Tara's quest, not yours. Support her as she did you."

"You're like a ghost," Zach said. "It's as though you're showing up out of the ethers and reading everyone's minds!"

Lydia laughed, "No, Zach. That's not it exactly. I can read auras and feel energy. It's not hard to know what's going on if you learn to listen and see with more than your eyes." Turning toward Matthew she continued, "Well Matthew, are you as strong and loving as your polarity?"

Matthew thought, then answered, "I think with some help from my friends and some education from you, I can learn to be."

"Great! I hate it when someone says, 'I'll try.' That's a setup for failure. You either do it or you don't," Lydia stated.

"Did I hear Yoda over there?" Leesie asked.

"You're too young to know who Yoda was," Andrew chided her.

"Hey, I have older sisters and brothers and also parents that are sci-fi nerds. I spent the last seven years of my life going to LepreCon and Comic Con."

"Wow, lucky duck," exclaimed Jason, "I've always wanted to go but couldn't afford it."

"Holy cow, they're made for each other," Andrew joked.

As Leesie stood turning bright red, her mouth hanging open, Andrew continued, "Paybacks a bear isn't it? That's for all the arm hitting."

Jason took Leesie's arm and said in reply, "I think we make a good match, too."

"Whoa, dude, you can't have my girl Leesie," Teja announced grabbing Leesie's other arm, "She's my polarity and I don't want to lose her."

"Oh, sorry," he said, dropping Leesie's arm. "I didn't know you were a couple."

"No, no," Leesie exclaimed, "you've got it all wrong. We're not together that way. She's my polarity and my roommate."

"What's a polarity again?" Jason asked, still confused. "You promised to tell me on the way over but you didn't."

While Leesie and Teja explained polarities to Jason, the rest of the group went back to their seats. Ariana decided she would try to locate Tara. Unfocusing her eyes, she scanned the room looking for unusual energy. Instead of seeing misty, blurred or foggy energy, she saw Tara! She appeared almost as clear as she had the last time they were together. Her energy seemed to waver slightly. But still, the outline was so clear she almost looked like a hologram. *Maybe that's where the science fiction idea for holograms came from; someone who could see spirits thought of it.*

Tara was also focused on Ariana. *Please help Matthew understand.*

I will, promised Ariana.

"Okay everyone, come take your seat or we'll never get through today," Lydia called to her students. When they were settled, she began. "I was listening in to some of the conversations and I noticed something I think needs clarifying. I have the impression all of you believe that polarities consist of only two people. This is not correct. Polarities can also contain three people, especially if the original polarity consists of the same sex. I call these connections triangles; the two on the bottom supporting the most powerful of the three. The higher consciousness I channel, Equinoxx, has another concept called 'circles within circles.' You have already formed a circle with your group, but soon others who are part of their own circles will join with your circle. The original group will stay united, but you will also interact with the other circles, usually individually. I am noticing that Zach, Matthew, and Ariana form a triangle now, and Leesie, Jason, and Teja are forming their own as well. I suspect there is still one more to enter your group. He or she will connect with Andrew and Wendy."

"I'm not sure I want someone else with us," Andrew admitted as Wendy shook her head in agreement.

"Then you won't. Freewill, remember?" Lydia answered. "Now, let's try some hands-on work to see if you can determine how you pick things up and whether you can do it in multiple ways. In front of me are a number of envelopes and boxes. They are all numbered. I want each of you to number your paper one through 20. I will pass out the envelopes and boxes. You will attempt to determine as much about what they contain as you can. Write down everything you get. If you get 'hot,' put that down. If you hear, taste or smell something, write it down. Do the same with feelings or pictures. There's no time limit and no particular way to do it. When you're done with the item, hand it back to me and I'll give it to someone else. Pay attention to how you are getting the information. If you draw a blank, move on. You can come back to it later or just leave it alone. Any questions? Okay, pick one to start."

After all the items had been distributed, Lydia began watching the body language and auras of each student, attempting to see who was trying to use logic and who was allowing their inner knowing to take precedence. After almost an hour, everyone had finished.

"Did anyone notice anything about how their inner knowing functions? Did you try to use logic instead of just letting whatever came into your mind flow? Did you start feeling like you were being tested, thus putting pressure on yourself to perform? Did you feel uncomfortable?"

Leesie tentatively raised her hand. "I know I was getting in my own way. I am naturally competitive. I come from a big family of geniuses, so I felt real pressure to get something. I'm sure I was trying to use my logical mind as I was thinking about what would fit in the envelopes and what you might put in there. But occasionally I got a really strong impression and I did just go with that."

"Psychometry is one of my abilities," said Zach, "But it applies more to places. I started to use logic at first too, but worked really hard to stop it. That made me question everything I got. I wrote it all down though. It really surprised me how hard this was."

Ariana was worried that if she confessed she found the exercise easy the others would feel jealous or defeated. She decided not to comment.

Matthew spoke up, "I found this really easy. I don't know if I'm right or anything, but I guess I didn't think it was important enough to worry about so I just wrote down anything I picked up."

"Yeah, me too," Wendy agreed. "I decided to treat this like a game and just let whatever wanted to come out, come out."

"Places are usually my thing, too, but I guess I must of been picking up my polarity because I did the exact same thing," admitted Andrew.

"I think I cheated," Teja confessed, "I kinda asked for my dad's and Tara's help and I heard their answers in my brain and wrote them down. I can't wait to see if that worked."

Lydia responded, "Teja, you didn't cheat. You drew upon all of your abilities. That's what everyone needs to do. When I read for people, I use my guides and my client's guides and deceased loved ones to get the information I need."

"Whew! That makes me feel better," Teja exclaimed.

"This stuff is really new to me and I haven't had anyone else to work with, so I just wrote down everything that popped into my head or anything I felt in my body," Jason remarked.

"Ariana, would you like to share anything?" Lydia asked.

Oh shit, Ariana thought, *I guess I'm going to have to speak after all.* Taking a deep breath she replied, "This was really easy for me. My Oma played games like this with me growing up so I guess I had a leg-up on everyone else."

"Okay, let's take a look at what was in the packages and what you got," Lydia suggested. "Envelope number one is a $100 bill."

"OMG," Jason said amazed, "I was dead on. Yippee!"

"Excellent. Anyone else?"

"I got the color green and paper," Leesie answered, "but I could have been using logic on the last part."

"Or maybe you weren't," Lydia answered.

"I kept seeing myself shopping," Teja said. "Does that fit?"

"You need money to shop," said Lydia. "How did those of you that thought it was easy do?"

"Surprisingly, not as good as Jason," Matthew admitted. "I got the number 100 but not that it was money. I thought you had written 100 on a piece of paper. There's that logical brain again."

Ariana replied, "I knew it was money. No amount though."

"I got money, too, but I thought it was a ten," Andrew remarked.

The rest of the group looked uncomfortable because they felt they had done poorly, but Lydia reminded them that they were just starting and that some things might be harder than others to pick up.

"Number two is a picture of a horse running in a meadow."

"Whoopee," screamed Wendy, "now it's my turn. Is the horse a bay with three white stockings and are there mountains?"

Lydia turned the picture around confirming that Wendy was exactly right. "Because you're an animal whisperer I would imagine that animals will be easier for you. How'd everyone else do?"

Everyone acknowledged that they got pieces of the picture. Some got the landscape, others the colors. Ariana knew it was a horse because she got a distinct feeling of freedom which she had only experienced with her horse.

"Number three?"

"I'm not hungry, but my mouth started to water," Teja said. "I also heard a jingle in my head, 'Have it your way.' "

Zach was surprised by what Teja shared, "Me too. I got really hungry and smelled meat cooking on a grill. I felt as though I was in a really busy place, like a fast food restaurant, and I could hear the sounds of people talking."

"It's a hamburger," Andrew agreed. "I could taste it."

Lydia turned the picture around and showed the group that it was an advertisement for Burger King. Displayed prominently was a Whopper.

Everyone was impressed with how well the three friends had done.

Number four was a small box that looked like it could hold a ring.

"That one was hard for me," Zach admitted. "I kept wanting to believe it was a ring, but it made me very uncomfortable."

"I didn't want to touch it," Teja admitted, "but then my dad said to me, 'It isn't guns that kill people, its people.' It's too small to be a gun, so is it a bullet?"

Everyone in the group felt uncomfortable with the box except Wendy. When the object in the box did turn out to be a bullet, it was decided that the reason she wasn't uncomfortable was because she came from a family of hunters and that she had hunted. Bullets weren't foreign to her nor did she think of them as things that were used to harm people.

As the rest of the mystery items were revealed, Ariana was the only one to get them all correct. The rest of the group had mixed results. The funniest one of the day was when Zach answered, 'a throbbing penetrating object' to an ad for a fragrance showing a man and woman in a suggestive embrace. He knew the group would never stop teasing him over that one.

It was time for lunch and everyone agreed that even though they had eaten quite a bit at break and all they had been doing since then was sitting, they all felt ravenous. Lydia assured them this was normal. "When you expend that much energy, even psychic energy, it drains you. Aside from sleeping, eating will help you recharge. Unfortunately, that's how I put on a few extra pounds," she teased.

Chapter 13

Lydia had prepared a sumptuous lunch of cold cuts, breads, fruit, raw veggies and dip, chips, and a great tasting chocolate cake for dessert. With full stomachs, the group returned again to the living room to continue their class.

"I'm sure you're all probably a bit sleepy and relaxed after lunch, so now is a good time to try a meditative technique. I assume you meditate." Everyone answered in the affirmative, except Josh. "That's okay, Josh, it is actually very easy. Just listen to my voice and do what I tell you. Now, everyone get yourselves seated in a comfortable position. I prefer feet flat on the floor, palms on knees facing upward and back straight. Close your eyes and breathe deeply in and out, slowly concentrating all of your attention on your breath. Imagine that you are inhaling relaxation, exhaling all stress. Surround yourself with God's White Light of protection and send down into the Earth a silver grounding cord. With the cord firmly planted into the Earth, feel your crown chakra at the top of your head beginning to open slowly. See white light energy entering your body through this opening and cleansing all negativity, pain, illness, and fear out of your body and down the grounding cord. Feel a ball of golden light in the center of your being filling you with health, calm, peace, and centering. Take another deep breath and release and relax even more. Breathing and relaxing, just continue to breathe and relax. You are safe.

Bring your awareness to your forehead and allow your forehead to relax and your third eye to open gently. Relax your face, scalp, and the entirety of your head. Breathing in……..and out….…..in…….and……..out, relax and feel your consciousness going deeper and deeper within. Feel warmth at your throat chakra and allow your throat chakra to open relaxing your throat, neck, shoulders, and arms. Breathe. Relax and let this warm energy fill your chest opening your heart chakra. Relaxing your chest and all the muscles of your back, let yourself go deeper and deeper within. Feel your solar plexus chakra open and allow your belly to relax, and as that area relaxes, feel your sacral chakra open, too. Breathe and go deeper. Opening your root chakra, which is located at the very base of your spine, allow your pelvis, legs, and feet to relax. Now you are 10 times deeper or 100 times deeper if you so desire, completely relaxed and at peace."

Lydia was quiet for a minute observing the group to be sure everyone was deeply meditating. Finally she continued. "Breathing deeply and at peace, begin to see a very old forest directly before you. It is beautiful, ancient. The trees are so tall they almost block out the sun. You are calm and want to go into the forest and absorb the peace and beauty of this marvelous place. As you walk deeper into the forest, notice that it becomes cooler and that there is now dampness in the air. Looking down, you realize that you are walking on a path that curves through the underbrush and tall trees. The light is subdued, coming in streaks through the trees. It is very beautiful. There are Aspens with their papery white trunks, Firs with their needle-like leaves as well as Ferns and tall Pines with massive pinecones hanging from their branches. You can hear the scuttling sounds of the small creatures that inhabit this place and you may even notice squirrels high up in the trees. Bird songs fill the air. Breathe in the fresh fragrant air. Touch the leaves and feel the ancient energy the trees emit. Allow yourself to sense the life force in everything around you. Remember, even rocks are alive. They just exist at a much lower vibration. See if you can decipher the energy of all the creatures around you including plants, animals, and the Earth herself."

Lydia paused again, letting the group attempt to feel the different energies. "Now continue walking until you find yourself in a beautiful meadow. Feel the soft grass under your feet and smell the wildflowers. The trees tower all around the meadow and to one side is a glistening pool of water. Walk to this alluring pond. Notice how the light sparkles on the still water. Dip your hand into it and absorb the healing that is imbued within this pure fluid. Drink some and taste its crisp, clear refreshing flavor. Feel it healing your body all the way into the cellular level. Sit with your feet in the water and allow it to continue to heal and relax your energy, balancing it with the energy of the planet. As you are relaxing, allow your awareness to observe the surrounding area. Look for shifts in the energy that surrounds you. Without using your eyes, observe your surroundings. Attune yourself to the energy of this place so that you can instantly observe changes and ascertain whether this energy enhances or decreases yours. When energy is taken or decreased by the actions of another, it is felt as negative. Feel this area protected with your light and God's White Light. Sit and enjoy. When next you hear my voice, an hour of time will have passed at this level of the mind."

Lydia became quiet again as she watched the group meditate. She was not planning to keep them here for an hour. She intended to wait only fifteen minutes. Lydia had come to understand that time does not really exist and that her students would in fact accept that they had been there an hour.

After fifteen minutes had elapsed, Lydia began again, "It's time to come back to this time and this place. You can return to your healing pool anytime you come to this level of the mind, this place of absolute relaxation. I am going to count from one to five, and when I reach the number five, you will be wide awake, feeling wonderful, alert, relaxed, and healed. One. Breathe deeply again and start perceiving a cool breeze caressing your face and a tingling in your fingers and toes as they begin to awaken. Two, three. Feel your body and mind as they begin to become more alert. Four. When I reach the number five you will be back in this room wide awake feeling fine. Five. Wide awake now and back with me."

The group came back all at the same time, stretching and smiling at one another.

"That was a wonderful meditation," Matthew complimented Lydia. "I felt Tara. She was with me there and I felt her energy. She really felt good. I don't think I'll be worrying as much now. Thank you so much."

"It wasn't me," said Lydia. "It was Tara's choice to make her energy known to you."

"Well I'm grateful no matter how it happened."

"How about the rest of you?" asked Lydia.

"It was fabulous. I talked to plants," Wendy exclaimed. "First I was talking to all the animals then when you said to feel the different energies, I felt the plants and tried to talk to them and I did! They're really not much for conversation, but I could tell they were content and didn't need anything. Wow!"

"Wendy, you're getting ahead of us," Lydia said, a huge smile on her face. "That's one of the exercises we'll be doing tomorrow."

"Whoops," Wendy said, smiling even more broadly.

"That pool was wonderful. I wanted to submerge in it," Zach said. "I've had back problems most of my life from scoliosis and just drinking and putting my feet in it took it away. I feel better than I have in years. I also felt the energies of the plants and animals. I could tell what was animal, vegetable, or mineral. That's something I've never realized before, that the energy is different."

"Yeah," Leesie commented. "I never really felt energy before. I could see auras which are energy, right? But I never felt it. I could feel everything. It was way cool!"

Determining that everyone had felt the energy to some degree or other, Lydia moved into the next phase of her class. "If no one needs to take a break, then I think we should move to the next exercise. You all realize now that everything has energy and that individual energy vibrates at its own rate. Rock vibrates almost imperceptibly, while rodents vibrate very rapidly. Perhaps it has to do with length of life span; small animals live short lives while stone continues almost forever. I can see auras around objects that have never had life. I believe that is because the person who created it and anyone who touches it put a bit of their energy there. This next exercise should stretch your ability to recognize and find different energies.

I have hidden some things in this room. I will tell you what they are, and without moving from your seats, you will find them, and then write down the location. Do nothing to help the others, okay? Here's your list: a cactus, a vitamin pill, an egg, a gerbil, a worm, a cricket, a leather wallet, and another $100 bill. Did everyone get that? Then begin."

Lydia was curious to see how each of the group would approach this task. She quietly sat and watched their process, purposely avoiding looking at the hiding places of any of the objects. She also didn't tell them that this was one area with which she had real trouble personally. She could get impressions of where something was, but rarely a clear vision. Her students seemed to take to this task quickly.

"Okay, where's the cactus?" asked Lydia.

All eight people replied, "On the window sill in your office." This was the right answer.

Next, she asked about the vitamin. They all agreed it was in the couch, but there was debate as to exactly where. Lydia fished out the pill from under the middle cushion of the couch. The egg seemed too easy as all of them immediately felt it was behind the stereo. The gerbil provided more of a challenge. Everyone but Wendy used their left brains and assumed they were looking for a gerbil in a cage. Wendy knew better.

"You spoke to her, didn't you Wendy?" Lydia asked. "Please tell the group what they did wrong."

Wendy was embarrassed but obeyed Lydia's request, "You all thought Lizzie was in a cage. That's logical thinking. You couldn't imagine her roaming free. That's why you couldn't find her. She's been tooling around in her ball this whole time," Wendy called to the gerbil. Right away, a clear ball came into view from under the coffee table. Within the ball was a small brown rodent.

"Lizzie?" Leesie asked.

Lydia explained, "Lizzie is my son's gerbil. He named her after a high school sweetheart. I hope you learned something from this exercise about how easy it is to mess things up by going left brain. Where is everything else?"

The group tried hard to listen to Lydia's suggestion, but because they were all working too hard not to use their logical minds, almost everyone missed that the worm was in the potted plant where it belonged. The leather wallet, and the $100 bill which it contained, was much easier than the cricket. Everyone knew the wallet was in Lydia's sweater pocket. What almost no one seemed to consider, however, was that the cricket didn't need to be a live insect. Only two of the group allowed their imagination to accept that it could be a resin sculpture of Jiminy Cricket which sat on a top shelf of the étagère.

"I hope everyone learned something about their processing of psychic data," Lydia said. "Now I want you to work on energy. I know that all of you have already become considerably accomplished in that area, but there may be more to learn. Please split into pairs, but not polarities."

Ariana and Matthew paired up. Teja and Jason, Wendy and Leesie, Zach and Andrew, were the other teams.

"Now I want one of you to designate yourself as 'A' the other 'B.' A's raise your hands."

Ariana, Jason, Wendy, and Andrew raised their hands. "No A first letter in your group Wendy?" Lydia teased. "Okay, so obviously the rest of you are B's. Those of you that are B's please begin to think a thought, any kind of thought. Fill your mind with this thought. Now A's watch their energy, their auras. What are the colors in it and how far or close is it to their bodies? Is it smooth, bumpy, sharp? Can you feel it or hear it? Do you see anything within it? Open your shields and surround your partner with your energy. Are you getting anything else?" Lydia let the group do what she asked for several minutes before she enquired. "Anyone want to discuss what happened?"

Ariana was awed. Matthew had never been this open with her. When they first met, she had inadvertently invaded his inner space and he shut her out immediately. This time he exposed everything to her without fear or distrust. It made her feel wonderful.

"Matthew was thinking about Zach and what a good guy he is and how happy he is for us," Ariana shared. Matthew smiled broadly and she continued. "Tara's aura has combined with his, adding stability and deep reasoning abilities to all that Matthew already had. It is weird to observe how the two auras swirl together creating almost a third aura. His aura also contains the energy of wolf and hawk which are his spirit animals. I can feel his mee'me', his grandfather, in there as well. The 'music' that comes from the blending of all these things is amazing. I wish I was musical so that I could play it for everyone. I can't tell if it is smooth or what because it extends so far from his body I can't see the edges. I'm an empath, I mostly feel things, so I don't see anything but the colors in there. I want to learn to see the things I feel. When I extended my aura to encompass Matt, I felt that it blended in with the other auras instead of just encompassing his. Oh, and I heard the music change. Wow!"

"Okay, Matthew," Lydia said. "When Ariana blended her aura with yours, what did you see, feel, and hear?"

"At first I felt her tentativeness. I threw her out once before. This exercise let me feel her true self, her complete raw self. It let me understand her absolutely. I realized that even though she had been hurt in the past, she has somehow forgiven everyone, even me. She is absolutely authentic; she doesn't know how to lie. If she has any weakness it is that she takes complete responsibility for everyone and everything which makes her vulnerable. That is a fault that The Darkness can abuse. Her aura is a rich violet and gold and contains her Elders, her

Oma, and her crystal which feels like a living thing with its own aura that reinforces all the good that is Ariana. Her music is rich and high pitched like wind chimes."

"Wendy?"

"Leesie's aura is a bright yellowish-orange and sings like a bird. She has so much energy it was hard for me to absorb it at first. It was almost like I stepped into a crystal. Her energy extends way outward and appears to have fingers. It was touching everyone and everything in the room, fearlessly. I could tell that she has an almost compulsive need to know everything. Her aura contains a yellow striped cat and a beagle."

"OMG, that's my Sammy and Apricot," Leesie exclaimed. "Okay, what I got from Wendy was killer. Her aura is pink and blue and filled with so much loving energy. She will be a fab mom someday. Her music is gentle and sweet, kinda hard to describe. She still keeps her aura kinda close except where it seems to reach out to touch Andrew's. There's a young kid and an older man and woman as well as a horse and a dog and cat in there. Oh, and a cow with big brown eyes."

Andrew seemed to be struggling a little but eventually began, "This dude is way deeper than I thought he was. His aura felt good to me, as if we are kindred spirits in some way. He's a protector just like me. Like Ariana, he takes his responsibilities for the group real seriously. I feel ancient guilt like he screwed up in the past and hasn't forgiven himself. That's definitely a place The Darkness can attack. Looking at the aura was weird because it contained so much color. I could see the blending with Ariana, her colors swirled within his natural blue, but there was also some fuchsia. That's a color I never figured would be in a dude's aura. It is smooth, but contains one hole. I don't know what that's all about."

"The hole indicates a deep pain or loss that has not been forgiven," Lydia told the group. Smiling, she added. "And fuchsia can be a sign of sexual frustration."

Zach turned as red as Leesie's shirt. Acting as though he had heard nothing, he began to describe Andrew's aura. "Well, the big dude there is a pussycat. He is nurturing and I think romantic. He does have the need to protect, but not like a warrior, more like a good dad. His aura is yellow with some blue and white. It is perfectly smooth and extends quite a distance from his body. He doesn't hold it back. There's a young man, his brother maybe, in there. He has a mind almost as curious as Leesie's because when I'm in there I want to discover everything possible. His music is deep and calming."

"I guess it's my turn, but remember this is all pretty new to me. I've studied everything I could find, but this is actually the first time I've gotten to work with other people," Jason advised, "so here goes. First off, Teja has a police officer, a grandmother, maybe a mother in there. She acts all defensive on the outside, but her pinkish and blue aura shows me that she's really sweet and caring, just afraid to show it. I'm sure she's got a killer creative mind. When I'm in her energy, I seem to notice things differently. It's really hard to explain. There are places where her aura pulls in and others where it's a little prickly, but that could be 'cause she doesn't know me very well yet and felt uncomfortable. I think she's a private person until she really knows and trusts you. Trust doesn't come easily to her because of some past stuff, so that's something that needs work. Her music is upbeat with a medium pitch. If I had my guitar I think I could play it."

"Wow, that's actually good," Teja announced. "I thought I was keeping you out. I'm glad I didn't, because when I reached into you I was really impressed. Talk about creative energy. How many musical instruments do you play? Your aura's song is awesome with really complex rhythms. I used to sing so I'd love to sit down and do some jamming with you some time. The color of your aura is bright turquoise with lotsa gold and white. Even though you've been through some really tough times, you're an upbeat, caring person. You didn't shut down or become a victim like a lot of us did. Your mom and some man are in your aura and it extends outward way far. I think the best way to describe what I felt is playful."

"Everyone did amazingly well," Lydia said. "Now let's see how you do with manipulating energy. Let's work on some hands-on healing. Anyone here with past health issues like broken bones or anything?"

Wendy raised her hand.

"Okay, Wendy come here and sit on this chair. Don't tell us what has happened to you physically," Lydia instructed. "One by one, I want each student to come up and run your hands over her aura. If it's way out, you can just run your hands slightly above her body. See if you can feel any cold or warm spots. Or you might feel areas that feel devoid of energy or are hyper-energized. If you're really good at this and are an empath, you might feel the old pain and know what it was from. Everyone got this?"

Teja jumped up to try first. She stood in front of Wendy and began to trace the outline of her body with her hands, starting at the top of her head. In some areas she stopped as though she was thinking, then she would continue. Finally, she looked at Lydia and said, "Okay, what now?"

"Write down what you thought until everyone else gets their chance."

Each of the group stepped up and did pretty much what Teja had done, some stopping longer in places, others going more rapidly.

"First," Lydia said, "did you notice how you picked up the information you got? Did you actually feel the pain, or did you feel warmth, cold, or tingling. What alerted you to a problem in a certain area?"

Everyone in the group acknowledged they felt energy changes in different parts of Wendy's body. Some of the group felt the energy as more intense and others felt a complete lack of energy. Many of them felt the lack of energy as cold and while the others felt heat at the place that needed healing.

"Next, what did you get? Let's start with Teja and end with Andrew because that was the order you all chose."

"Well," Teja began. "In certain places my palms began to tingle. It felt kinda like when a body part has fallen asleep and is starting to wake up. Those were the places I stopped. Then I tried to see if I could feel what had happened in those places and whether it was past or present. I think in the past Wendy hurt her head, neck, and broke her left arm."

"Wendy, don't comment until everyone's done, please. Matthew?"

"I felt heat in certain places like the energy was still healing things. I also felt what Teja said, but I think there's some slight damage in her lower back and left hip, too."

Lydia continued around the room with each person adding their own take on what was going on with Wendy and how they were receiving the information. Finally, it was Ariana's turn.

"Because I'm an empath, I felt things," Ariana said. "I also think I saw why the issues happened. I think Wendy was thrown by a horse a couple of years ago. She suffered a mild concussion, broken arm, and minor injuries to her neck, back, and hip. Because of that, I think she still suffers from headaches. She also has allergies that make the headaches worse."

"It is obvious that you were trained on Meria to be a healer," Lydia claimed. "I've seen healers here that were not that comprehensive. The rest of you, please don't compare yourselves to Ariana. Wendy tell us about your body."

"You were all right. I was thrown from my horse just about two years ago and hurt all those places you mentioned. I do have seasonal allergies and get awful headaches, especially once a month. I think they're migraines and would really love to be rid of them forever," Wendy pleaded.

"You will get your wish. We are going to work to heal those things that are still lingering. You can do this singularly, but today we will do it together. Come stand around Wendy again. Some healers put their hand into the aura but never touch the person, others touch the body where the energy needs adjustment. Do what makes you the most comfortable. Each of you pick a different spot on the body that needs work. Do not accept the injuries into you own bodies. Triple shield and use God's energy to balance hers not your own. You will be the conduit only. Now either use the aura or her body and adjust the energy so that it harmonizes again with the rest of the body's energy. Listen and feel the energy until you sense it is in balance. Then stop and go wash your hands at the kitchen sink."

After everyone returned to the room, Lydia asked Wendy, "Well, how do you feel."

"Absolutely fabulous!"

"Wonderful. We still have one last exercise, however, then you can all go home and rest. Make sure you eat a good dinner tonight and a good breakfast tomorrow because working with energy can be exhausting for some folks. Who wants to be the first guinea pig?"

"Me! Pick me!" Leesie called out.

After spreading a soft alpaca rug on the floor, Lydia nodded for Leesie to come over and lie down on her stomach.

"Does everyone know what chakras are?" Lydia asked.

Jason answered, "Aren't they like energy centers in the body?"

"You're correct Jason. Chakra in Sanskrit means wheel. These energy centers spin, balancing the body by letting energy flow from one part of the body to another. To be healed, the chakras must be in alignment and spinning correctly. They are represented by placement, color, and sound. The first chakra is the root and is located at the base of the spine. It is connected to survival and grounding. It grounds us to the planet and the physical world. If you had a traumatic childhood, this may be out of balance. The color red is associated with this chakra.

The second chakra is called the spleen because it is located just below the naval. It is orange and helps with creativity and sexual and reproductive matters. Blockage can manifest as emotional problems and sexual guilt and dysfunction.

The solar plexus is the third chakra and is located below the diaphragm. It is yellow and represents emotions and personal power. If it is blocked, you can become a victim or a victimizer.

The heart chakra is next. This is the fourth chakra and represents love and caring. If it is blocked there can be heart problems and a lack of compassion. It can also manifest as belief that you are unlovable.

The fifth chakra is the throat which represents communication and speaking your truth. It is blue and can cause throat problems if you are not stating your emotions properly or are lying.

The third eye is the sixth chakra. It is in the middle of the forehead. It has to do with psychic abilities and imagination. It is indigo.

Finally, the crown chakra is at the top of your head. It is the soft spot babies have. This chakra connects you to messages, healing, bliss, higher consciousness, and all things of God. It is purple.

To do healings through the chakras, you can either use a pendulum or feel with your hands. This is a pendulum," said Lydia, as she held up an object that had a crystal on one end and a pretty stone on the other. They were connected with a chain similar to a chain worn with a pendent.

"I have plenty here if you would like to experience what working with one is like. Now, all of us need to sit on the floor surrounding Leesie. Lessie, lie down with your head pointing north. I will sit in front of her crown chakra and Ariana will be at her feet. The rest of you position yourselves on each side of her body. Place your hand over the area of a chakra and see if you can feel the energy within the chakra you have chosen."

The group did as instructed, each concentrating on the energy, or lack of energy, emanating from Leesie's chakras.

"Now I'll show you how to use the pendulum. I am right handed so I hold it in my dominant hand. Hold it over her chakra while keeping your arm and hand as still as possible. If the chakra is open, the pendulum should begin to move. If it doesn't, or does anything but rotate clockwise, it is either closed or off balance." The pendulum began moving slowly at first, then more rapidly as it built up momentum. "Does everyone understand how to use the pendulums? Okay, anybody want to try one?"

"I would," Wendy said while taking a pendulum with a pink crystal point and a beautiful multicolored cabochon on the other end. "But first, can I ask you why the crystals are different colors?"

"Different minerals have different vibrations and are said to work with different things. The pink one you have there is a rose quartz which has to do with unconditional love and the heart chakra. It has a soft feminine energy and is said to nourish, comfort, and heal."

"What is the pretty stone on the other end?"

"That's a piece of glass. It's called dichroic glass and is a space age material that both reflects and refracts light. It is a process of fusing glass in a kiln that creates the cabochon and the various colors. I work in glass, so I created those."

"Wow, you really are into a lot of different things," Wendy declared.

"When you open psychically, you begin using lots more of your brain. I think it makes you more creative. Okay, ready to see if her throat chakra is open?"

The pendulum swung just like before. It did the same thing for each of them until they got to the solar plexus and spleen chakras where it refused to move.

"Does anyone feel any energy in those chakras? Use your hands and see if you feel anything," suggested Lydia. There was no energy felt in either of them. "Okay, now that you have learned to diagnose a problem, let's work on clearing them and get them moving well again. I will talk everyone, including you Leesie, through the process. Put the pendulums down and rub your hands together briskly—not you Leesie—then place them back over the chakras. I'll be putting my hands over her crown and

Ariana is going to put her hands over the minor chakras at the bottom of her feet." When everyone complied, Lydia continued. "Begin to feel the energy build in your bodies everyone. Leesie, are you feeling the heat from our energy in your chakras?" Leesie nodded yes. "Good. Can you feel the heat building in your crown chakra? Good. Now I want you to perceive the energies building in your crown chakra. Allow yourself to feel this force descending down your body building in strength as it goes. Keep it moving stronger and stronger Leesie. Get ready to flush this energy out the bottom of your feet—NOW! Did you feel it come out, Ariana?"

"Wow, yeah. Boy, was that strong!"

"Don't move yet, Leesie. Okay, you that are sitting near the chakras that were out of balance, use the pendulums and see if they are still closed."

"Holy cow! Look at it go," Jason exclaimed, as the pendulum began to spin clockwise.

"They're both open again," announced Matthew.

"Not necessarily. We need to check the ones that were working well. Sometimes if you forcefully open one, another will close. Wendy and Andrew, check yours as I can tell mine is fine," Lydia instructed.

"Good here," Wendy replied.

"I'm good here too," answered Andrew.

"Wonderful," Lydia said. "You can sit up now Leesie, but take it slow. Sometimes people get a little dizzy."

After Leesie was up and appeared solid, Lydia asked her how she was feeling. "I feel fabulicious," she declared happily. "But why were those two chakras blocked?"

"I think I know," Ariana said. "You are still young and sexually inexperienced and you are a mathematical, literal person who prides herself on using logic instead of emotions and never worries about anything. Those chakras have to do with sexuality and emotions."

"Sounds like a very accurate conclusion," Lydia replied. "It's time for you to go eat, rest, and sleep well. I'll see everyone tomorrow."

Chapter 14

Dinner was Italian food in a restaurant on Central Ave. The building looked like it had been built in the early 1900s as a warehouse. It was still rustic with an eclectic mix of furnishings and decorations. The group settled into a large round table in the back. They had a room all to themselves which suited them fine as they had a lot to talk about.

"What did you guys think of the class?" Leesie asked between mouthfuls of spaghetti with meatballs.

Andrew grunted and said with a mouth full of lasagna, "Pretty killer."

"I learned a lot today," Wendy said, "and I feel wonderful. I think you people really healed me. That says a lot because since it happened, I've been going from one doctor to the next about my neck and headaches. All they wanted to do was give me drugs which didn't really help."

"I know what you mean," Zach said. "I've had really bad back pain all my life. My spine is curved the wrong way. Doctors told me that there wasn't much that could be done so I've been living on Excedrin and other pain relievers pretty much forever. That healing pool took the pain away better than the pills did. I know I'll have to use it in my meditations daily, but that's better than always being in pain."

"It wouldn't have worked if you hadn't wanted it to," Ariana claimed. "Some people need their pain for various reasons like attention, love, or punishment. It could also be from a past life and that becomes very complex to get rid of. You'd have to forgive yourself for that lifetime. Do you think that's what your back is about, Zach? Your past life guilt?"

The question seemed to make Zach angry. "Are you implying that I'm making up my scoliosis?"

"Not at all," Ariana denied. "I'm just wondering if it is a reminder of the guilt you never released. I'm also suggesting that when you completely release it, maybe the pain will decrease, that's all."

Zach was still not ready to let go of the anger. He replied, "What makes you such an expert on healing?"

"Remember when the Elders said I would begin to remember my training? Well, during the lessons today, a bunch of memories came flooding back. They were memories of how to heal and memories of what happened on my planet."

"I wondered why you were so quiet all afternoon. I just thought you were being polite or something," Wendy said.

Matthew asked, "What did you learn?"

"On my planet, before the fall, everyone could manifest. We needed nothing, because when we did, we created it with our minds. Many of my people became bored and restless. We had stopped terraforming after the disaster on Earth and so there was little to occupy our intelligence. I'm sure you've heard the quote, 'Idle minds are the Devil's playground.' Some of my people started lobbying to begin terraforming again, but this time they were determined to be prepared to fight anyone who tried to enter our space. They suggested that we put our energies into militarizing for the purposes of protecting what we created. The memory of the losses suffered on Earth was still painful in everyone's minds. This caused fear to take root on Meria for the first time in our memory. Some people suggested that the Pleiadians might be a threat, that they might come to Meria and do what they did on Earth—enslave the people and ultimately destroy our planet.

Now The Darkness had a new place to infect and it did its job so well that people began to close down to one another and take sides. There were those that wanted to protect Meria from potential invasions and those that believed this was only paranoia. The hawks won out over the doves and Meria began to create and stockpile armaments. Some of the hawks even suggested that perhaps we should thwart the potential at its home base—that we should attack the Pleiadians before they came at us. This suggestion created a rift between my people that kept festering with any suggestion made by either side. The negative rhetoric and disharmony grew to the point that even the planet was reacting to the negativity, much like Earth is now. Eventually a group of fanatics who were convinced that our planet would be better off if it was purged of the dissident faction began a systematic destruction of the electromagnetic grid of the planet. Many of you have seen the result. My planet was splintered. Landmasses broke into pieces and the beautiful sea that we depended on for our energy was poisoned with the radioactive debris left over from the processing of armaments. The people became ill with diseases that no one had ever seen before. No cures could be found partially because of our poisoned planet and partially because the life energy we received from our sea was gone. Our population was diminished by more than three quarters and those that were left were either sterile or the infants that were born were so badly deformed they died at birth, their mothers dying during childbirth. It has taken more than a thousand years to be almost back to where we started. I say almost back because my people still cannot reproduce naturally and they do not have even half of the healing and psychic abilities they once did.

You asked once how we eradicated The Darkness from our planet. I believe we did it by nearly dying out. We had to band together and help one another in order to survive. As the population grew older, my race knew they would have to fight for their existence. Science and metaphysics began working together. No longer capable of manifestation through thought, they learned to produce what they needed scientifically. We learned to create life. All children are created artificially and nurtured and loved deeply. There is no talk of negativity or fear. Over the many generations since the fall, we lost the memories of fear and negativity because they were not only unnecessary for survival, they were contrary to survival. Except for the Elders, almost no one knows of the fall, or if they do, it is a general knowledge of having to start over.

When the Elders sent me here to help, it was partially due to the fact that I had died here once and understood this world, but also because recently a few of us have the original DNA that was lost during the fall. We have the ability to do what others on Meria can't. That enables us to be effective here helping you. It means my people have the opportunity to be as they once were, able to procreate and have our own children."

"Why would they risk you then?" Wendy asked.

"Because we are the source of the original DNA for you too, so that if we need to, we can help you begin again."

"Wow! I sure hope we won't need you. I mean to start again, we already need you to help stop the problems on our planet," Leesie said. "Any info from the Elders on how things are going?"

"No," Ariana admitted.

"Well, I have some from the native tribes. I've been doing lots of research and think that some of it is killer." Looking around at the group Leesie said, "Oh, did we want to talk more about the class or do you guys what to hear this?"

"Go ahead Leesie, we can talk about the class tomorrow when we're finished," Matthew answered for the group.

"Well, you know that white bird you saw in your vision quest? You said you thought it was a raven but it couldn't be because it was white. There is a story among the native people of how the raven came to be black. The story says that when God created Earth he created a white raven to appreciate the wonders of his creation. The raven soared in the heavens from cloud to cloud, collecting snowflakes on his wings. Soon he wanted to go below and appreciate the planet. God created a white buffalo to carry the bird so that his feet never needed to touch the ground. These two creations were spirit mates; the buffalo provided a place for raven to rest and raven showed all the buffalo where the best grazing lands were. It was a good arrangement. God then created the brown man and told him that everything he saw was his to use and take care of except the White Raven and White Buffalo. All other buffalo were theirs to eat. They praised God and kept his covenant.

Eventually new humans with white skin came to these lands. They did not praise God or care for the Earth. They were thoughtless, caring only for themselves and killing many animals. White Raven went to God and told him of these humans. On that very day, the white men saw the White Buffalo, and not keeping God's covenant, killed him and many of his brown brothers. They took only a small bit of meat from the White Buffalo, leaving the rest to rot in the sun. When the Creator saw this, he became very sad and angry. He cried and cried for many days, causing the planet to flood. With no White Buffalo to carry him, the Raven grew tired and landed in the mud. His white feathers were covered in the wet dirt, turning them black. Stuck in the mud, the water began to rise. The bird became afraid he would drown. He saw an old man and his family floating in the water in a canoe. He called to them and they came and brought him into the boat, saving his life. They were kind to him and listened to his story of the White Buffalo and God's sadness. This old man told the bird that the Creator had chosen him to go throughout the world looking for anything good to save. He had found very little. The Creator had also told the man that in the future there would be much good and much evil, and at that time, God would have to cleanse the world again. The Creator also told him that from this moment onward he would create only black Ravens, to remind all peoples of the evil that man can create. However, at a time in the future when the Earth is filled with evil, the Creator will again send His White Raven. This time the White Raven will not turn black or be soiled, but will remain forever the color The Creator had given him in the beginning. Humanity will see White Raven and this Raven will give a message to many nations and to all who will listen to him about The Creator. This Raven will be giving a warning to all, of bad times that are coming. White Raven will again have the soft, white back of his spirit mate to rest on, and everyone should listen to his warning which will be: 'Return to the Creator, give Him songs of praise. Burn fires that will let their smokes rise up to Him as a pleasing smell. Put away your evil ways and desires, putting The Creator as the Way to follow, so He will be pleased with us.' I found this story called *The Legend of the White Raven* on the web.

Okay, you're probably all wondering what this has to do with anything, so here's the punchline: a female white buffalo who was not an albino was born in 1994 and white ravens have been seen on Vancouver Island British Columbia."

"That is weird," Zach said.

"The native people believe they are here to warn us that if we don't start caring for the planet and living in harmony, the end is near," Leesie reiterated. "Additionally, I found something else that's really weird. In 1996, for ten days in June on the Yankton Sioux Reservation, tribal leaders from around the globe and hundreds of native and Euro-American listeners gathered to reveal centuries of extraterrestrial contact. It was called the Star Knowledge Conference and Sun Dance. Shamans from all over the world gathered together. These leaders were seeing signs that had been predicted by ancient prophecies. They agreed the time had come for them to speak openly about their most closely held oral traditions. These beliefs include their origin story—that they came from the stars. They discussed the influence Star People visitors had on the formation of their culture, their spiritual beliefs and ceremonies, and the imminent return of the Star Nations. Many of the leaders claim they continue to speak with the Star People, still. They also claim that all the spiritual avatars, Jesus, Buddha, Mohammed, and White Buffalo Woman were actually Star People. The Native leaders believe there are seven different galaxies represented on Earth, and that each Native American tribe is actually originally from the Stars.

The people at the conference discussed the many changes our Earth is facing: fires, earthquakes, floods, a world drought. The electrical grid that supplies power to the United States is in desperate need of repair and is at risk of a full failure. Our cities cannot function without power.

There are four omens that predict a massive change. The first, second, and third are the births of three white buffalo calves. The fourth is the actual return of the Star People to Earth.

There's a lot more information that you can read if you want; I printed it out. The only thing that seemed wrong with the predictions by the Shamans was the dates. But maybe things have been happening that we don't know about. It's obvious that there are aliens living among us. Our dear Ariana is one. Why couldn't there be lots more?"

Matthew added, "My grandfather mentioned that we were what he called 'original people' and that Ariana would fit right in. I guess that was him telling me we were alien DNA."

Ariana spoke up, "What I'm hearing that is disturbing to me is that since the '90s, native tribes from all over the world have been giving warnings to us to pay attention to what we are doing to the planet. If they've been virtually ignored for years, how are we going to get through to everyone?"

"I think they've been talking to the wrong people," Leesie suggested. "They talk to governments and their own people, but no one has thought to talk to us. I don't mean us literally, I mean teens. We don't have a financial interest in keeping things as they are like most governments and businesses. We are still open-minded and ready for something new, especially new challenges. We are not set in our ways. We still believe in the possibilities for success in most things. Most of us are still looking to the future for wonderful things to happen, while many adults are already defeated and negative. Even though most of us in this group have had pretty shitty things go on in our lives, we are still hopeful, right? We're not giving up trying to find something better. How many adults do you see doing that? Yes, I'm aware that they don't have as much free time as we do, and that a lot of them are too tired or apathetic to get involved with much other than work and families, so it's up to us to lead the way. If we spark the kids, maybe the adults will come around. Remember the hippies of the '60s? They shook up the world pretty good. I think by using social media to promote our great cause, our survival, we can do much better."

Chapter 15

The group of friends gathered on Sunday at Denny's to make sure they were well fueled for the lengthy class ahead. Between the usual bantering, Jason showed them some sketches he had made for a proposed website called www.Becomingthelights.com.

"I think that if we have a really great web presence including Facebook, Twitter, Instagram, and Snapchat, for example, we can reach kids from everywhere. What do you guys think?" Jason asked.

"We discussed YouTube, too, but none of us has much expertise with making videos," Leesie answered.

"It can't be that hard. Most people have phones that do great video. We'll just have to figure it out or find someone willing to help," he replied.

"Oh yeah. We'll just stand in the quad and yell help, right?" Teja grumbled.

"It looks like one of us isn't at her best in the morning," remarked Andrew.

Teja looked at him disdainfully and mouthed the words, "Bite me." The group broke into laughter.

"Is she always this grumpy in the morning?" Wendy asked Leesie. "Makes me glad I'm rooming with Ariana."

"I slept really terrible last night," Teja defended herself. "I just kept seeing our planet in the same condition Ariana's was. It was horrible. I don't know if success is possible, but I know failure is way too horrible to consider."

"That's why we need to concentrate on everything we can do," offered Jason.

"Look at these drawings," Leesie said. "Jason's got some awesome ideas and some truly killer talent."

"Look at you two. You're like twins or something. Maybe he's your real polarity and I was only holding his place," Teja complained.

Ariana felt that it was time to intervene in the discussion, "Remember Teja, polarities are not the same; they are the balance. I think you three have formed a triangle."

Zach asked, "That thing Lydia mentioned yesterday? Can you explain it a little more? I'm not sure I completely understand."

"The two that are alike form the base and the one that is the polarity to both of them is at the top point of the triangle. The two at the bottom are similar but not exactly alike, and the third balances both. The energy moves between the three entities. The triangle symbol represents three concepts. The first is body, mind, and spirit. The second, sky, earth, water. And finally, the trinity. These are the lower realms in Sacred Geometry. The triangle also represents the number three in numerology. The square, for instance, represents stability and the four points of the compass, while the circle represents unity, wholeness, and completion. All possible geometric shapes have meanings and correspond to aspects of the planet."

"What the heck is Sacred Geometry?" Teja asked.

"It is an ancient science that explores and explains the energy patterns that create and unify all things and reveals the precise way that the energy of Creation organizes itself. On every scale, every natural pattern of growth or movement conforms inevitably to one or more geometric shapes," Matthew explained.

"Wow, really neat, something mathematical for me to learn. That's really killer," Leesie exclaimed.

"See, we are different," Jason said with a smile. "Math is not one of my favorite or best subjects."

Wendy looked a little chagrined when she asked, "Is there no end to this metaphysical stuff we have to learn?"

"Actually, there probably is no end," Matthew agreed. "But we aren't here to become alchemists or wizards or great sages, we are here to help defeat The Darkness. We don't really need any special training to do that. We just all need to be more like Leesie and Jason—excited by life and consistently optimistic."

"What's that quote from the Bible about being like children?" Andrew asked.

"Lots of quotes," Teja replied, "but I think you mean, 'Truly I tell you, unless you change and become like little children, you will never enter the Kingdom of Heaven.' Is that the one?"

"Yeah, sounds right," Andrew stated. "So, let me paraphrase; you must be innocent and open in order to even recognize Heaven."

"Okay," conceded Teja, "it could be something like that, I guess. So, you're saying as we grow older, we become jaded and bitter?"

"Don't we?"

She thought about it for a while then agreed, "Yeah, I guess we sorta do, don't we? We become jaded and bored needing new everything every 10 minutes. So how do we stop it?"

Ariana chimed in, "By continuing to see the beauty and wonder in this world. By understanding that yes, there are terrible things occurring, but there are equally wonderful things. Then dwell on the wonderful ones not the terrible ones. Allow yourself to be grateful for what you have, not what you want or think you are owed. If everything is an illusion, why don't we all work on the illusion that the world is peaceful, happy, healthy, creative, and filled with helpful, loving people?"

"We could also emulate the animals. Give a cat a box or bag and they're happy for hours. Little kids are like that too. I used to love to watch my brother, Peter, play with a stick and make it a magic wand, a sword, or a gun. Everything had possibilities. He could watch a bug for hours," Wendy offered. "I think remaining playful is healthy."

"Do you think that education has helped to jade us?" Zach asked. "The history of humanity is one war after another, filled with viciousness and horrible inhumanity. You could really get depressed and pessimistic. Perhaps ignorance is bliss."

"I think learning about the past can help us understand what has worked and what hasn't, if we want to pay attention," Leesie replied. "If anything is bad about education now, it's that instead of teaching people to think and use their creativity, the focus is based on passing tests which is little more than having a good memory."

"My mom's an elementary teacher," Andrew said. "She told me that modern public education is more about socializing kids than educating them, making us all fit in and function together and alike."

"I bet private schools don't do that," Teja stated.

"West Point does," Leesie said smiling.

"See what just happened?" Ariana pointed out. "We were talking about a somber subject and Leesie injected humor. Did you feel the energy lighten? Laughter is a wonderful gift from the Source. It changes the energy immediately to something buoyant and light. When we're feeling down or uncomfortable, let's make a pledge that one of us will do something ridiculous to make us laugh."

"I'll do it," Leesie volunteered. "I like being a clown."

"Thanks, Leesie, but I think we should all loosen up and work on being clowns. I know it's something I need to do. I've really never developed my sense of humor, so I think it's time. Do I have an amen ladies and gentlemen?" Ariana asked, raising her hand for a high five.

Chapter 16

"Looks like everyone made it back," Lydia said after they had seated themselves in the living room. "Any comments about yesterday?"

"We decided we would wait to talk about it until after we had completed the weekend," Matthew told her.

"All right then, I guess you're all ready to get started. I know yesterday I said we would be working on feeling plant energy, but after thinking about how far everyone is already where energy is concerned, I decided it wasn't necessary. So today I'd like to start working on the unseen realms that are relevant to us. You must understand that there are many dimensions that we on the physical plane of existence have no connection with. I'm not going to discuss those. You might hear people talking about them, but I would argue that we have enough to deal with on this dimension and those directly connected with this one. I think dealing with other dimensions turns our focus away from dealing with this reality. Also, please understand that I am using the words realms, planes, and dimensions interchangeably.

I want to talk with you about spirit guides, but before I do, I want to tell you what I know about reincarnation. Does everyone understand the basic concepts of reincarnation?"

Jason spoke up, "I've heard people talking about good and bad karma and about living more than once, but I really don't have an understanding about any of it."

"Thank you, Jason, for speaking up. Reincarnation is the concept or belief that our soul is on this plane to learn and grow and eventually return to a pure place of nirvana, the state of perfect happiness and peace described in Buddhism where there is release from all forms of suffering. To put it more succinctly, it's when the soul stays with the Source and no longer is reborn.

Many people have a hard time understanding that their existence in their current life is different than their existence in their past lives. Our souls create different egos for each life. Think of your ego in a particular life as an actor in a play written by the soul. The ego's past and present behavior in each individual life will create consequences that will be dealt with either in that life or another. The behaviors in the life of each ego can be good or bad. Each life creates different abilities and memories.

So, if your soul had experienced being a doctor or nurse in a past life, the current ego may have certain abilities that have bled over from a past life into this one. Just as those abilities have been carried over, so too are many lessons—what many refer to as karma. According to Equinoxx, negative karma is established by unresolved guilt, while positive karma is established for past positive deeds that are done with no thought of return—when you give with an open hand. For instance, perhaps in one life you were very wealthy, selfish, and mean with your wealth. The soul can decide to create another life with a new ego, giving that ego the opportunity to experience lack, or, it can again make life easy, but hope that the new ego will change the prior behavior. Whatever happens will provide new opportunities for the soul to learn and grow and bring more learning to the Source. Understand, the soul does not care whether the ego is experiencing something as good or bad; it is only looking for the experience. The Source does not recognize good or bad; everything is perfect because the Source is pure love. It is the ego that decides how it chooses to feel about an event. How often have you had an experience that you perceived as devastating but with time you saw why the event happened and realized the good that came from it? The soul and the Source have the full perspective of all the previous lifetimes and also the future ones. Remember, there is no time. Consequently, the Source and our higher selves understand how minuscule the event really is in the scheme of the entirety of existence and everything that is happening within that existence.

Is this too complex?" Lydia asked. "Is everyone still following me?"

"We've discussed these concepts before and got into a heated debate about things like child abuse, rape, stuff like that," Leesie remembered.

"Yes, that happens often. Because we live in an absolute reality and have no true understanding of the long-term meaning of events as they unfold, many people get hung up feeling that what they see is unfair. Believe me—the Source does not want you punished, hurt, or sad. It did not create a world full of beauty and wonderful things to forbid you from enjoying them. That sounds more demonic than godlike to me. Because this world believes in punishment and karma, we have punishment and karma, but it is as much a part of the illusion as lack is. There is enough food on this planet to properly feed everyone all the time. But because of many things, including greed, fear, and belief in lack, many people on this planet starve. Look at all the food Americans throw away daily."

"Are you saying karma doesn't really exist?" Ariana asked, confused.

"I am saying that karma exists here because we all believe in it in one form or another. We accept its existence, prove its existence, so it exists. Somehow, we have bought into the concept that we must be punished. So, some people believe the punishment comes by 'what goes around comes around.' Others believe you will get your punishment in Hell, and some others believe that Earth is Hell. Equinoxx tells us all you need to do to get rid of negative karma is to release the guilt. Determine that you will not do the same thing in the same way again and let go. We are all human which means we are all imperfect. Mistakes happen. Sometimes what you feel guilty for isn't even something you did, but instead something that was done to you. If you retain this guilt, you will develop karma, even if you were not the perpetrator. That is why forgiveness is so important. You are not forgiving the act, you are releasing the guilt and hatred and thus letting go of karma. If enough people believed in forgiveness and released the need for punishment, I believe negative karma would vanish.

As the world evolves, so do beliefs. In the past, you were a heretic if you believed the Earth revolved around the sun. It was also widely believed the Earth was flat so you would fall off if you tried to circumnavigate the globe. More recently—women, African Americans, and Jews—were considered defective and inferior and in some cases evil. Most of us now see these beliefs as silly though some still hold these opinions. Even 'scientific facts' evolve. All of classical physics, including Newtonian physics, was eventually superseded by relativistic physics and quantum physics. Who knows what will be disproven in the future.

Any other discussion on this? You don't have to believe any of it, but you need a base understanding of reincarnation to understand what I believe about guides. Okay?"

Everyone acknowledged that they understood, so Lydia continued, "I believe that your guides are individuals you have known well in past lives. They are chosen before your birth to help you with lessons and achievements in this life. Each of them represents certain areas or things you are working on or need to begin to work on, for instance, creativity. Let's say that you have a more literal nature, very mathematical and left brained. However, your soul intends that you develop a talent in the arts. This guide will encourage and help you in that endeavor.

Or maybe your path has to do with remembering a past life in which you knew about herbs, flower essences, and healing. There will be a guide to help you succeed in a career as a naturopath. There is no limit on the number of guides one may have, but you will have at least a male and a female. Your guides will come and go as you need them. If you are to learn about lack when you are young, and then riches when you are older, as you grow into your success you will have a different guide. You may have several at the same time or just two or three. The guides are like your best friends. They want you to succeed, but ultimately, they will follow your direction. Each of us also has a Master Guide. This is your spiritual teacher and will rarely answer questions, but instead, will teach you by making you find the answers. Your Master Guide will answer questions with a question. They will give you questions or show you where to look, but they will not tell you what to do. Do not pray to your guides; they are not deities. Have conversations with them, ask for assistance, but make sure you listen when they answer.

One of the most asked spiritual questions I get is, 'How do I contact my guides?' It is really easy: either think or verbally ask a question then **listen to the answer**. Just trust that you are hearing them. For a few months, keep a journal of their answers. Eventually you will recognize the distinctive way they communicate. If you are thinking about something, trying to figure out a problem, for example, and out of the blue you hear in your mind something completely different like, 'It's time to go check on the dog,' that's your guides. There may be nothing wrong with your dog. They may be trying to distract you so that you can come back to the problem later with a fresh mind or your dog may actually need you. Sometimes it could be a warning. Years ago, I was getting ready to leave my house when I heard clearly in my mind, 'Today is the day the nurse is going to call about your son.' When I heard it, I realized that for weeks, whenever I left the house, I would hear, 'I wonder if today is the day the nurse will call about Nathan.' Nathan is my son and he was six at the time. I never consciously realized I was hearing the earlier thought until the day I heard, 'Today is the day.' I decided to wait, and while I waited, I heard the guides tell me that the nurse would exaggerate the injury and Nathan was really all right. The phone rang, it was the hysterical nurse telling me he had fallen, and I'm quoting now, 'cut open his eye.' Because I had been warned, I asked her if it was the eyeball or the skin by the eye. She said it was his face and he was bleeding horribly. I picked him up from school and all that was necessary for the doctor to do was put three stitches in his cheek. I have no idea how she became a school nurse, but the point is, if they hadn't prepared me, I would have been away from home or would have become hysterical myself. Oh," Lydia said with a smile, "there once was a time when we didn't have cell phones!"

The group of friends chuckled. "Hard to imagine!" Leesie cracked.

"Sometimes guides will communicate in stranger ways. That's usually because you have not been listening. They may speak to you in a dream, through a friend, or the media. Or it can be something weirder. A friend may be talking to you about something in their life and you realize they are saying something that is an answer for you. Same with the media. Often I have the TV on in the background and I'm really not paying attention to it, but a sentence will pierce my consciousness. I may be completely unaware of anything else that has been said, but somehow, a particular statement will grab my attention and I'll realize it is the answer to something I've been wondering about. One of the stranger ways my guides contact me if I'm being obtuse is literally making something fall on my head. Many years ago, I went to the library to get a book for my late husband. The librarian directed me to the stacks. I grabbed the book he wanted and a paperback fell on my head. Its title was the answer to a question I had been wondering about for over a month.

My favorite way to work with my guides is through meditation, using a pendulum, or a technique I learned in a Silva Method course, putting my thumb and first two fingers together as a sign I am communicating with them and need an immediate answer.

When I meditate, they are always there, and will often direct my meditations. I use the pendulum for other kinds of guide contact. For instance, if I am concerned about whether some food in the refrigerator has spoiled, I will use the pendulum as a tool of contact for 'yes' or 'no' answers. I have used it to find lost people, to tell me what direction to go when driving, and basic 'yes and no' answers when I'm not hearing the guides. Any questions yet?"

"Ariana's Elders talk to us a lot. They just show up in our meditations and things, but they're not guides, are they? And can guides be kids?" Leesie asked.

"The Elders are helpers and, in a way, they are guiding you. But they haven't been with you since birth, your guides have. Yes, guides can be children, animals, cartoon creatures, deities, angels, just about anything. Because they are energy, they will take any form they think will make you most comfortable. Some may even be living," answered Lydia.

"Okay," Zach said, "You've completely lost me there. I thought guides were always angels."

"That's a common misconception," Lydia claimed. "Humanity has such a fragile ego, many reject the idea that spiritual helpers can be on an equal footing with those in the physical realm. Yet our guides are just on a different dimension where there is more information. For many humans, that is too hard to accept. Consequently, many people think that to be worthy of listening to, guides must be 'superior beings' or angels of some sort.

The guides understand your soul intent and want to help you have the life the soul has planned for you. And they want it to be as easy as possible for you. That is a really good reason to listen to them. It's like having a best friend that is very psychic and knows all the potentials and wants you to succeed. Why wouldn't you want to listen? Unfortunately, humans want to feel special. Many like to imagine they were Cleopatra, Caesar, a king or queen, Mary Magdalene, or one of the disciples in a past life, and that they have one or several archangels as guides. Equinoxx has a saying, 'In God's eyes, there is nothing greater or lesser than you.' "

"Okay, I get it, but I don't know what you mean by cartoon creatures and even living guides," Andrew admitted.

"I have had clients that had guides appear as Mickey and Minnie Mouse, Marilyn Monroe, John Kennedy, Jesus, and unicorns. Every one of them had a fascination for whatever they were seeing. One woman collected everything unicorn. One was an old movie buff, and the woman who had Jesus as a guide was a devout, ultra-religious Catholic," Lydia told the group.

"As to guides that are alive, sometimes you meet a person that has a deep impact on your life but they are in your life for only a very short time. These may be guides. I have had two experiences like that. One was a male that taught me how to meditate. He was very important to my growth and very dear to me for about eight months. Years later, after my husband died, I was lost. Remembering how this person helped me through another difficult period, I looked him up. When we met again after having been apart for 21 years, I couldn't relate to him at all. He had come into my life to help me in the past and teach me some valuable tools, but he had remained as he was and I had grown past him. Our work together was done when it ended 21 years before. I've never seen him again.

Even a pet can be your guide. I'm sure any of you who have had a pet know that there are some that just seem wiser, more aware. Let's say you are learning lessons about unqualified love, who better to teach it than a pet?"

"My horse kept me alive," Ariana remembered. "She always seemed to know how to make me feel better. When I needed to laugh, she would nuzzle my entire body, looking for her treat even when she knew that it was always in my back pocket. She'd wait until she had me laughing before she would finally take it. When I needed affection, she would put her head on my shoulder and give me kisses on my face, and when I needed to feel free and alive, she would run like the wind. Before I left for college, I had to sell her. It was here that I met all these wonderful friends. My horse completed her purpose with me and has gone on to another needy, young girl."

"Yeah, I had someone in my life when I was younger. He was few years older than me and he helped me to understand how to deal with the bullies that were messing with my brother and me," Andrew said. "He helped both of us to feel good about ourselves and to find the areas where we could excel. As soon as I started high school and got on the football team, he moved away. Once I was on the team no one tried to cause problems for either of us. They even let him be on the team even though they didn't play him. Everything good that happened to us when we were older was because of the stuff he taught us. I've thought about him a lot but have no idea what ever happened to him."

When no one else spoke up Lydia asked, "Anyone ready for a break and some food?"

"You don't have to ask twice," Andrew declared, moving toward the kitchen.

Chapter 17

"Did everyone get enough to eat?" Lydia asked after they came back into the living room.

"You spoil us," Jason said as he rubbed his stomach.

"One of the things that people with strong Cancer in their astrology charts like to do is feed people. Cancer is the nurturing sign of the Zodiac. Yes, Leesie?" Lydia said when she noticed Leesie's hand waving in the air.

"Are we going to be learning astrology today, too?"

Lydia laughed, "I couldn't teach astrology in one day. You might be able to learn it in an afternoon because you were once an Alchemist, but my astrology classes are eight weeks long and cover only the rudimentary basics in that first eight weeks. Sorry.

In these classes, I'd like to focus on what I think your group needs to understand in order to do the work you are committed to, so we're going to continue talking about the other realms, especially the realm that I feel is inhabited by what I call 'The Lost.' If someone dies badly, murder, suicide, tragic accident possibly, or if one has taken the life of another and died unresolved, unable to forgive themselves, then there is a place between what is usually called Heaven, which I call the Other Side, and Earth. It is this place where those egos go. It is not God that has created this place; it is the ego itself that has, or in some cases, a religious belief that has been accepted completely by the ego. Just as the ego will see the Other Side the way they expect it to be, perhaps with Jesus and pearly gates or a beautiful garden filled with their loved ones, those who find this place in-between have created what's there; another illusion. If one has a strong religious background and feels unworthy of Heaven, or is especially guilty or angry, or don't realize they are dead, they will not recognize The Light and will stay in this place that isn't Earth or the Other Side or Hell. Hell does not exist either, but if an ego believes that it does, and believes it will go there, it creates Hell in this place—the Lost Realm. This is where ghosts or discarnate spirits reside. That realm overlaps ours partially because those egos are still so connected to and often focused on this plane. That is where Tara is right now. Sometimes people in a coma can go there. It can be a kind of holding place for the ego until their body is healthy again. Rarely does the person realize they are there or interact with others that are also lost there. Those that can interact are spirit walkers or people that can walk between the realms. This is not the only dimension that these spirit walkers can investigate, as many native shamans have shown us. Both Matthew and Tara were born with this ability, but it can be learned as well. Any questions about this?"

"It's like purgatory?" Matthew asked.

"Yes, sort of. But understand that it is not God or Jesus that condemns egos to be there. It is the ego not wanting to let go of this plane and their leftover business that keeps them there. Occasionally, the family will be responsible," Lydia responded. "When a child dies, this is often the case. The grief-stricken parents hold on so tightly, the child feels guilty and will not leave. Their spirit remains in that realm to feel close to the family until it can see The Light and accept that it belongs on the Other Side, not there. This is also more likely in the case of sudden deaths. The family has had no preparation and both they and the ego of the loved one may feel there is unfinished business and not release. That is yet another reason forgiveness is so important."

"Oh my God," Wendy exclaimed, "does that mean my brother was in limbo all this time?"

"Yes, Wendy. Until you connected with the group and found your way, he didn't leave. Now he is with his grandparents and wants you to know how happy he is."

"But I tortured him for over seven years!"

"Quit it, Wendy," Lydia said sternly. "Threads on the Other Side feel our feelings. Peter is happy. Do you want him to feel your pain and guilt? Remember what I said about karma—it is guilt that is unresolved. Peter does not want to establish negative karma with you. What you did was done out of ignorance. You would not have done it had you known the effect it was having on him. Instead of wallowing in this self-centered guilt, be responsible now and show him how happy you are that he is on the Other Side. Can you be the loving sister he needs you to be?"

Drying her eyes, Wendy gave a determined nod.

"What exactly are threads?" Matthew asked.

"Well, we've discussed souls and egos; I hope all of you understand the difference. Threads are like memories. The soul, as the writer of the play, conceives of egos who act out their parts in the play. The soul learns significantly from the ego, and in absorbing this information, it also absorbs the personality of the ego. These combined with the memories is the thread. Consequently, no ego that ever lived is gone. That is how we can access deceased beings on the Other Side."

"But how does one of these threads still have emotions?" asked Andrew.

"The longer an ego exists on the Other Side, the less emotional they become and the less attached to things and people on this plane. When one first gets over there, there is a period of contemplation where the ego looks over their life and evaluates what was learned. Part of accessing information is also to feel what the people around them felt about their actions and how the people still on Earth are feeling now. Eventually the ego that has passed will understand that the current feelings really have little to do with them but instead are the loved-ones' ego learning whatever lessons their soul has chosen. Then those feelings will not disturb the ego that has passed. Unfortunately, Peter isn't at that place yet, so Wendy must watch her thoughts and emotions. Got it?"

Lydia continued, "Some of these lost egos interact with our world. Remember I said these two realms overlap. One result of that is hauntings. I've noticed that more people are aware of emotions that linger on a place. It can be a house, school, park, anywhere where a tragedy occurred. This could be a form of psychometry or a spirit manifesting its unhappiness. Many people have told me they get depressed going to certain places. When I investigate the places in person, I often find that something has occurred there. Equinoxx claims that the dimensions are thinning. But I also think more people are being activated which causes them to become more empathic to their environment and what's around them. More people are becoming sensitive to the other planes of existence and don't realize it. They just find themselves having erratic mood swings and worry that there's something wrong with them. Those people that are already emotionally off balance can be thrown over the deep end. That is why there are so many people doing horrendous things that are so out of character.

I have worked with many hauntings, sudden deaths, and spirits that have not been released. It is called rescue work. When a plane crash happens, or some catastrophe occurs, there will be many egos that can become lost. Those of us that have metaphysical practices will often go to those scenes in our meditations and work to take as many to the Other Side as possible. Ridding a property of a haunting involves going there to ascertain who is doing the haunting and what they want. Working to help the ego leave and go to the Other Side is the next step, but if they won't go, a much greater amount of work is required."

"Like what?" Leesie asked.

"It would depend on the being doing the haunting, and the situation of the residents, but the first step is always the same: using protections which usually involve sea salt, white candles, sage, and prayers.

The hardest thing to do is help release an ego. Usually that means working with the family member who is holding on. If the family won't let go, then the ego may not leave. This is particularly true with small children. In that case, I must work to convince whoever is holding on that they are doing harm, and then teach them to let go. I'm not always successful with that and it saddens me.

Tara is working to release souls in limbo by helping them understand that they are dead, by helping them to forgive themselves or others, or by showing those that are being held on to that they will not lose or further hurt their loved one by going to God and feeling good. Their imbalances are bleeding over and increasing both The Darkness and the planetary imbalance. We can help Tara do her work from here. I'm going to show you through a meditation how to go about this. Remember, anything you may see in this other realm is purely an illusion. After this class is finished today I would suggest that you download the movie *What Dreams May Come*. This is the closest Hollywood has come to describing both the Other Side and the Lost Realm. Now get comfortable again and close your eyes."

Lydia began her technique to initiate meditation through relaxation and counted down from 10 to one. When she saw that everyone was in a deep meditative state she continued. "Feel your group mind link and connect each of you to the other. When you feel this deep connection, send this energy outward and include Tara in the link."

Lydia waited until she could see the group's energy expand by one more then continued, "Tara will act as your guide to the lost realm. Let the mind link take you there. Become familiar so you will be able to help her often by going back again when you meditate so that you can continue the work over there. You might even want to pick an ego that is lost to help. When you hear my voice again you will come back to me fully, remembering your experiences, and knowing your way back to that other realm when you choose in the future to return." Lydia quietly watched the meditating group.

After fifteen minutes, Lydia began, "Come back to this time and this place but remain in a deep state of meditation. We are going to go searching for the students that have gone missing in Mexico and take the dead to the Other Side. Allow your consciousness to travel to Iguala Guerrera, Mexico. Visualize a green and forested area. Don't worry— your consciousness will know where to go. As soon as you get to the area, allow yourself to feel the energy. Where the energy is greatly disrupted you will find the deceased students. When you find them, begin to tell them they are gone and it is time to go to The Light. You will see a brilliant white light, don't go into it yourself, but direct them to walk in. Tell them that Jesus is waiting and so are the relatives they previously lost. Tell them that they can do more for their families by going to God. Convince them that they are blessed and loved by God and he is waiting. Keep seeing them walking into The Light until The Light vanishes."

Lydia waited, when she thought that they had as much time as it should take if the students were really listening to them, she concluded, "You have done all you can. It is time to come back to me, to this time and place, and to your bodies. I will be counting from one to five. When I reach the number five, you will be wide awake, feeling fine, so much better than before." When she finished the count, she asked if any of them wanted to share their experiences.

Wendy was the first to speak, "The place I went with Tara was desolate and very bleak. The light was dim and there was a man all hunched in on himself, crying and rocking. Lying at his feet was a dead woman. He kept begging her to forgive him—promising her he would never hit her again, telling her he never meant to hurt her—but she made him so mad sometimes. Standing above the body of the girl was the girl's spirit. She had such a confused look on her face. I decided to start with her. I told her she was dead and needed to pass over now. She kept looking at the man as though she couldn't hear me. So, I went to the man and told him that he had to forgive himself so that the woman could go to Heaven. He looked at me and asked if he was in Hell. I told him that he was in a self-inflicted Hell and that when he forgave himself, both he and the woman could leave. But as long as he continued to create the place he was in, she would remain with him. I asked him if he wanted to continue to hurt her. He started crying again, wracking sobs. He said he never wanted to hurt her but sometimes he was so frustrated and angry he hit out without thinking. I asked him if he had wanted her dead. He seemed very shocked at my question and answered that no, he had loved her. I asked him if he loved her enough to forgive himself and leave this place or was he really a coward using his guilt to keep them both trapped? That seemed to really wake him up. He looked at her beaten body, then at me, and begged me to help him. Just as he said that, a brilliant and beautiful light appeared behind him. I could see that the woman had turned toward it. I told him to turn around and walk into it. He turned, but hesitated at first before shaking his head resolutely and walking into it. She followed him almost at a run. As soon as they were gone, the desolate environment vanished and was flooded with light. It was really awesome."

"Wow, I had a completely different experience," Leesie offered. "I was in a beautiful bedroom that had a lavender canopy bed and stuffed animals everywhere. There was a young girl, about seven or eight, in a corner playing with a Barbie. The Barbie didn't look anything like the ones I used to play with and there was a record player sitting on a dresser. I'd never seen a record player for real before and her clothing was not like what any kid would wear now, so I made the assumption she had been there quite a while. Probably since before I was born, like the '50s or something. She was emaciated looking, with dark circles under her eyes, and she had a bald head. I figured she had died of cancer. I sat down in front of her and asked about her Barbie. We played and talked a little, then I asked her why she was there. She told me she was waiting for her mommy because her mommy told her not to leave. She said her mommy and daddy had been crying and her mommy had begged her to stay so she stayed. I assumed her parents were probably dead, but because I wasn't sure, I asked her if she had any pets. I told her about my cat and dog and she told me she had a wonderful dog named Patches that she missed very much. In my mind, I called to her guides and to Patches, asking them to come help. A beautiful glistening white tunnel appeared. There was a cute little puppy at the tunnel's entrance. It barked, and the little girl called his name. I asked her if she wanted to play with him and she said yes, but she had to stay here and wait for her mommy. I told her I would wait and bring her mommy to her when she showed up. I also said that I didn't think her mom would mind if she wanted to play with Patches. After all, she had been such a good girl for waiting. She looked at me with the sweetest blue eyes and asked me if I was sure. I told her I was positive. She went to the dog and he led her into The Light. She and the dog vanished. I've never felt so good about anything, ever."

"Wow! People can stay even after the people that were holding them back are dead?" Wendy asked, horrified thinking about how long her brother could have been stuck.

"Remember, Wendy, there is no time, so the ego is stuck at the point its physical existence ended on this plane. Nothing changes for them. Even though we perceive time continuing, they don't. Consequently, some have been there for centuries," said Lydia.

"I went to a concentration camp," Zach said. "There was barbed wire and barracks and what I think was a crematorium. There were wisps of what looked like people—I think they're called specters—everywhere. But they were very insubstantial, like memories or something. There was a woman sitting on a bunk in one of the barracks. She was just staring. I walked over to her and ask her what her name was. She told me it was Esther. I asked her what she was doing there. I told her the camp had been evacuated 50 years ago and she didn't need to remain anymore. She said she knew everyone else was gone, but this was where she had last seen her children before they were led into the crematorium and she couldn't leave knowing they had died and she hadn't. I told her that she was dead, too. She didn't believe me. It took a lot of convincing to prove to her that she wasn't alive and hadn't been for a very long time. I finally convinced her by showing her the town and how much it had changed. I showed her a calendar in the bank in the town and helped her to see the camp as the deteriorated place it really was. I convinced her that she could again be with her family if she just walked into The Light. She practically ran in. That poor woman had been living her nightmare for over 50 years."

"Again, remember there is no time. In limbo, it is especially clear. The egos stuck there still exist in the memories of their lives whether they lived in 1942 or 1742," Lydia explained again. "To them it is still whatever century they lived and died in."

Matthew admitted, "I was just so glad to be with Tara again I almost didn't do what you asked us to do. I found a group of Apaches whose burial grounds had been disturbed and their bones scattered. They believed they could not leave until all their bones were back in their burial places. I tried really hard to get them to go, but they wouldn't, so I told them that my grandfather and I would look into it. I didn't know what else I could do."

"The egos still have freewill so if they don't want to leave, there really is little you can do," Lydia assured him.

"I want to talk about those poor college kids in Mexico. They were kidnapped by the police and sold to a gang of thugs. The males were immediately killed, but some of the women are still alive. Isn't there anything we can do?" Andrew asked, obviously feeling helpless. "I helped a lot of them to go to The Light, but many wanted to wait until their friends were either saved or could go with them. I really feel terrible knowing that those girls are probably being raped and tortured. How do you stand it when you know something and can't really do much about it?"

"That's why I don't like getting world predictions. They are almost impossible to change and make me feel very helpless," Lydia confided. "The good police in Mexico are aware that the gang has the girls. They are doing everything they can to find them. All we can do is keep sending strength to them and if we get an idea of where they are alert the authorities."

"Well, that's something at least," Andrew remarked. "Do you think if we really worked at it, the group could find them?"

Yes," Lydia said, "I'm sure of it. Did any of the rest of you see where they might be?"

"They are in a compound about 20 miles from where they found the last bodies," Ariana claimed.

"Yeah, I saw that, too," Zach replied. "The place was a dirty cream color with razor wire fencing and an iron gate. Right?"

"Yup," Ariana said.

"It has large dogs patrolling it and the bad police know exactly where it is because they're part of the gang," added Jason.

"I was talking to some of the hostages," Teja said. "They're too scared to do anything. They watched the gang kill their friends. I tried to reassure them that there were many people looking for them, but they are now afraid of the police, too. They feel hopeless."

"You actually were able to talk to living people?" Lydia asked, astounded.

"Yeah, why?" Teja responded.

"That is amazing. Only the most advanced mediums and spirit walkers can be seen, much less heard. You have developed a really amazing ability with many uses."

Teja answered Lydia, "But it just seemed so natural and easy. I thought at first that I was talking with dead people like I did when I was with Tara in the lost realm, but somehow, I figured out they were still alive. I modulated my vibration to a frequency more compatible to theirs and they could see and hear me. I think they thought I was some kind of angel but were confused by my skin color. Aren't angels all depicted as white?"

"Yes," answered Zach, "at least the ones they had pictures of in my church."

"I think I gave them some hope because if I was an angel and I was helping them, then they may believe God will save them."

"This gives me something to think about and do a little research on. Sounds like a good time to break for lunch," Lydia declared.

Chapter 18

"Did anyone come up with any questions during lunch?" asked Lydia.

"Yeah, what did you find out about Teja?" Leesie asked.

"I did a Google search and could find very few references to what you did, Teja. I am at a loss to explain it. It is widely held that each plane functions on different frequencies and it is believed that being in the astral state resonates differently than the physical state of being. That is why it is believed to be impossible to be seen and communicate and many doubt the few people that claimed to have succeeded. What convinces me you did is your description as to how you did it. You said you modulated your energy to theirs. I believe that you succeeded in being in two places at once. I read an account of a woman who was both at work and in court arguing a speeding ticket. People at her work swore they saw and worked with her all day while the court had video proof that she was there arguing her case. That seems to me like what you did; astral projected then materialized in both places."

"Is that as amazing as it sounds?" Ariana asked. "And does that mean that we all may be able to do it eventually? It seems as though we each are gaining the abilities of the others."

"Because I am as much a novice to this as you are, I really have no answer other than we will have to wait and see."

Leesie raised her hand, and when she was acknowledged asked, "If we were successful with helping those in the lost realm, why is Tara feeling like she needs to remain there?"

"The imbalance of energy is much greater there than here, but their energy is now bleeding into our plane rapidly. Each week their impact seems to be increasing. If you have any hope of success here, there will need to be people working over there, too. Tara is not only saving as many as she can, she is also recruiting those she's helped so they can help change the vibration and rescue others. On that level, each ego is separate. They are completely focused on themselves and their memories of this plane. Tara is making them aware that they are not alone. It is making a huge difference."

"Do we need to help her?" Andrew asked.

"In your meditations, include what rescues you can," Lydia suggested. "Have all of you continued to send healing to the planet, and love and peace to everything on it?"

They all confirmed that they had.

"Okay, now we are going to work on remote viewing. Does anyone know what that is?"

"*Men Who Talk To Goats*, right? That movie with George Clooney," Leesie declared.

"Well, the Hollywood version at least," replied Lydia. "Remote viewing is using the unconscious mind to gain direct knowledge about inaccessible targets like people, places, things, or events in the past, present, or future. It was actually developed by the CIA and military during the Cold War as a technique to infiltrate usually inaccessible places like the Kremlin in an attempt to gather information.

A remote viewing session begins with a 'cue' or question that sets up what you are looking for. Perhaps the cue words would be a map of nuclear facilities in Russia. These cues may consist of anything from the world's next catastrophic event to locating lost car keys. To quote from a site called *Learn RV*, "In remote viewing theory, everything in the universe exists as a pattern of information within the collective unconscious, or what is sometimes referred to as the 'Matrix.' Remote viewing simply allows you to tap into this phenomenon and to transfer a particular pattern to your conscious awareness."

"So are you saying you can send your consciousness or astral project?" inquired Zach.

Lydia replied, "Whichever way works best for you, either will work. Again, according to the site on RV, to get started, remote viewing is structured as a set of formal stages which correspond to progressively deeper levels of awareness the viewer goes through as they gain greater contact with the object. This is done singularly. A typical description of these stages is as follows:

Stage 1. Perception of basic, overall nature of the site or target like 'land,' 'structure,' 'water,' 'event.'

Stage 2. Basic sensory perceptions like tastes, sounds, colors, qualities of light, textures, and temperatures.

Stage 3. Perception of the site's or targets dimensional qualities, i.e., height, breadth, width, depth, angularity, curvature, density, etc. Sketching of viewer perceptions is an important aspect of this stage.

Stage 4. Perception of increasingly complex and abstract perceptions about the site or target.

Stage 5. Asking your inner consciousness questions which allows details of the target in greater detail.

Stage 6. Allows further sketching and three-dimensional modeling or sculpting of aspects of the site or target, while acquiring further qualitative information.

Extended Remote Viewing takes longer; that's why it is called extended. In it, a viewer relaxes on a bed, or other comfortable support, and tries to reach a deep meditative state. If possible, the room is darkened and soundproofed.

As the viewer reaches the edge of consciousness, a second person in the room, the monitor, begins the session with directions to the viewer to access the desired target. Once the viewer can describe elements of the correct target, the monitor quietly poses questions about the target. These questions may request details, purpose, appearance, construction, activities, or other target-related information. The monitor records or writes down the answers the viewer provides. After the session, the viewer makes additional notes about what was perceived, along with appropriate sketches or drawings.

The question I put to the group is—which way would you like to do this? Alone or split-up into four pairs? Do you want to try an extended viewing?"

Ariana responded, "I think we should do pairs, but not as polarities."

"Why that way?" Matthew asked.

"Polarities are connected. Through that connection, it is easy to pick up information without really trying. Even if we try to hide the information, or don't have any real information, it is possible that our polarity would still see what we thought the target was and be swayed by what they think we know," she explained.

"So how would we do it then?" inquired Wendy.

"For now, how about one man and one woman, but no polarities," suggested Ariana. "Like maybe Jason and Wendy, Teja and Zach, Matthew and Leesie, and Andrew and me."

Before the group began debating the merits of Ariana's idea, Lydia took over. "Split into those pairs. Andrew and Ariana remain in this room. Jason and Wendy go into my office. Zach and Teja you may use my bedroom, first door on the left upstairs. Matthew and Leesie you may go into my significant other's work room, first room on the right upstairs.

This is what you are to do: I have a list of three places, persons, or things. You are to focus your inner consciousness on them one at a time and project yourself to where each one may be. Finish number one and then go on to number two and so on. The monitor will not only tell you what each of these things is, but will also ask questions and record your answers. After you verbally complete each one, draw a picture of what you saw. You don't need to draw a masterpiece, just an approximation. After the first person is completely finished, the person who will become the new monitor is to come into the kitchen and receive a new list for the next viewer. Is everyone clear?"

"So, we're going to take turns either finding an object, going to a place, or finding a person. One is the viewer and one the monitor. The monitor is a helper and the viewer is doing the actual remote viewing which will be given both in writing and in drawing, right?" Matthew asked.

"That's it in a nutshell. Okay, here are the first three. Monitors, do not show the viewer what the items are. Tell the viewer only the item they need to know before moving on to the next item. Complete one before going onto the next. I don't want the viewer to become confused as to which one they are working on."

With the lists passed to each monitor, the group split up and Lydia went into the kitchen to wait for the next monitors to come get their list.

It took the first group 45 minutes to finish and the others completed within fifteen minutes. In another hour, the entire group was back in their seats in the living room.

"While we wait," Lydia began, "I would like to hear what each of you thought of the experience without any of you saying what you received from the viewing itself."

"What are we waiting for?" Leesie asked.

"Is your numerological default the inquirer?" Lydia asked with a laugh. "You'll see soon enough. Why don't you tell us how your experience was as a viewer."

"I think I was better as a monitor," Lessie confided. "Maybe 'cause I am so good at asking questions. For some reason, I had a hard time sending my consciousness out while I was just lying there. I don't sleep well either, and it felt too much like trying to relax to go to sleep. When I was young, I was severely asthmatic. Between the drugs they gave me and my own manic nature, I'm not good at just laying still."

"Don't let her fool you," Matthew said, "she actually did quite well. I had a really fun time with this. I have extended my consciousness so that I can fly with my spirit hawk and run with my wolf, but going walking just to see what I could find, see, and experience, was really quite awesome. I can't wait to see how I did."

"This felt a lot like when I went to talk to the students, except this time no one could see or hear me. I think because I'm a medium it's easy for me to leave my body. I agree with Matthew, it was awesome," Teja declared.

Jason looked a bit sullen. This was unusual for him. Lydia asked, "Did you have a problem or did you encounter something disturbing?"

"I'm really new at all this and I usually get information only in dreams and have no control over anything then, so it was really hard for me to just release and go walk about. I kept worrying that I'd get lost or something or that I'd do better if I was asleep. Every time I got out, I would come flying back. I guess that was fear."

"There is such a thing as lucid dreaming," Lydia informed Jason. "That's where you train yourself to become aware you are dreaming and then you have the power to take control over the dream. Native people teach it to their very young children so that they will become brave and feel in control."

"My grandfather taught me how to do it because I often had nightmares. It really isn't hard Jason. I'll teach you," Matthew offered. "And maybe when you get that mastered, it will be easier for you to do this."

"Thanks man," Jason said enthusiastically, "I really appreciate it."

"Ariana, you're being quite quiet. Did something disturb you?"

"While I was out, I kept feeling as though I was being pulled into other dimensions, almost like parallel worlds. I had to really fight to stay on this plane. I also had to put up really strong shields which somewhat hampered what I was doing, but I think I succeeded."

"From what I see with you, you are a healer," Lydia said. "Many on other planes are still in both physical and mental pain. Because you are also an empath, you are feeling their pull. You did well to increase your shielding."

"At first it was hard for me, too," Wendy admitted, "but I just got myself into a quick meditative state and from that point, it was really easy. I'm hoping I wasn't kidding myself."

"Stop that, Wendy," Andrew chided. "There's no reason for you to act like that. I know you did really well. Okay, my turn. I think I've been doing something like this for a while now without realizing it. I've always thought that I had an ability to sense places, but I think over the last few months I can do more than that. I think I'm traveling outside a lot. I love it because I feel so limitless out there."

It was Zach's turn, "I know how Andrew felt. Everything seems so much more intense; the colors, sounds, and smells seem so real. I really didn't want to come back either. That kinda bothers me. I can see how it could become addicting."

"There are lots of things that can feel really good, helping people, either those that are alive or dead, astral travel, and meditation, to name a few. I've had clients that meditated several hours a day. Anything can become addicting, but that is where your spirituality must take over. You are in a physical body because your soul wants you to learn physical lessons. Escaping into non-physical realms is not the soul's intent and you all know what happens when the ego tries to do its own thing; the soul pulls it back, often painfully."

The door opened and a distinguished looking, older man walked in.

"Everybody, this is my significant other, Brad. He's the one responsible for everything you did just now. I didn't want any knowledge about what was being done so that I would not give you any cues. He will tell you how you did. Who wants to begin?" Lydia asked.

"Me, me, me," Leesie squealed, "I drew him! One of the things I do is draw. I'm actually drawing a comic book and I saw him sitting on a bench in a park playing with your little dog. Here's what I drew."

Brad looked at the picture of himself and complimented Leesie on how well she drew and how accurate the picture was.

"I saw you, too, but it seemed like it was much earlier, like in the morning or something. You were putting a bronze of an elephant or a guy in a tree. I was really confused which it was. I know that sounds really weird," Wendy declared. "This is what I drew. Unfortunately, I don't have the skill that Leesie has." Her picture was a stick figure of a man climbing a tree with something in his hand.

"This is what I put in the tree," Brad said, as he held up a bronze sculpture of the Indian God Ganesh, a man with the head of an elephant.

"OMG, that's too cool," exclaimed Andrew. "I saw that and drew a picture of it. You were in the park at Bethany and 59th Avenue, right?"

"That's right."

"Why didn't Leesie pick up the statue?" Wendy asked.

Matthew answered Wendy's question. "She didn't see it, I did. Remember, we didn't all have the same things to see because we were given things to find. That was mine. Here's my drawing," he said as he showed the group a picture of a man carrying the statue and looking up into the tree."

"Zach or Teja, what did you see?" Lydia asked.

"Here's my drawing," responded Teja. The drawing showed a man looking up into a tree at an indistinguishable shape. "I couldn't figure out what it was. I knew it was metal, and it was about twelve inches by seven inches, but that's it."

Ariana decided that she should go next, "I had the same scene Leesie did except I must have seen it later. I saw you walking the dog around a small lake with ducks. At times the dog would start to enter the lake then stop at the edge of the bank. One of the ducks got very aggressive with him and scared him badly enough that you picked him up. The park was very nice, but not very big. It was mostly Weeping Willow trees and water. You had the place pretty much to yourself and you both felt very content. I could feel the cool breeze and smell the scent of the lake. There were times I felt I was seeing everything through the dog's eyes. It was interesting looking up at everything. I was also amazed at how smart he is. He knew you had his treats in your pants pocket and he was trying to figure a way to get them. I enjoyed this experience a lot."

"Nothing to report," Jason said. "Like I said, I kept coming back. I did have the sense that there was a man and a dog somewhere, but that's it."

"Actually, that wasn't nothing," Lydia said. "You got two of the objects: Brad and Sammy."

Zach spoke, "I first saw a car. I think it was a Kia Soul, light colored. Then I saw a man driving and a little furry dog riding in the backseat. I don't think he knew where he wanted to go. Oh, there was that statue on the floor, too. Finally, he turned into a parking lot of a Circle K, went in, and bought some water. When he came out, he saw the park across the street. He drove over there, got the dog out, and started walking, carrying the statue. Eventually, he picked a small tree, an Acacia tree, climbed it and put the statue up there. I thought that was kinda weird. Then he went walking with the dog."

"Holy shit! How'd you do that?" Leesie asked.

Zach shrugged, "I don't know. I just put myself in the car with Brad."

"Well kids, I'm very impressed. Everyone seems to have mastered remote viewing," complimented Brad.

"Yes," Lydia agreed, "these are no ordinary kids. Each of them has distinct abilities, and together, they really are amazing."

Chapter 19

After taking a short break, the group was ready for the final exercise of the day and the final class of the weekend.

"I'm afraid this next meditation is going to be a bit intense, however, it is essential if you are going to proceed with your path. Begin your relaxation ritual. When you are at your deepest level of consciousness, let your head fall to your chest."

Lydia waited and observed each of her students closely before she lifted the heavy shielding that surrounded the house. During dinner she had entered this portion of the house and removed all the crystals and placed them in the backyard. This room was now barely protected.

When she believed everyone was ready, Lydia began, "Take a deep breath and allow your consciousness to become completely open to my voice. Listen closely and do everything I say. Within each of you is at least one extreme fear. It is buried quite deeply, but it can be unearthed. To be truly whole and gain the full extent of your abilities, you must find this fear and face it, eliminating it forever. I am going to count down from ten to one and when I reach the number one you will be in a place or a time that you first encountered this fear. Every part of you will believe that you are there, facing your fear. You must conquer it, you have no choice in this.

Let's begin. Ten, allow yourself to go deeper than you have ever gone; deeper and deeper into the depth of your psyche. Nine, eight, going even deeper. Seven, six, five, when we reach the number one you will be in that place and time experiencing the event or events that created this fear. Four, three, two, when I say the next number you will be facing the worst situation, the worst fear of any lifetime. You must conquer this fear now or it will kill you later. Your body is frozen and cannot react to anything you see and the only way you can rid yourself of this fear is with the strength of your will and consciousness. ONE!"

From the outside, every member of the group looked placid, but

Lydia knew otherwise. She knew that each of them was facing one of the hardest fights of their young lives.

Lydia also knew, however, that every human being has pushed down their most painful events, those that are just too hard to deal with at the time. Some of these events are sad or uncomfortable. But for this set of students, she knew that the events that they had not faced were the truly terrible ones. Each of them had developed the defense mechanism of denial. This is the most popular one for human beings. It is commonly described as the refusal to accept reality or fact, acting as if a painful event, thought, or feeling does not exist. Denial is considered one of the most primitive of the defense mechanisms because it begins in early childhood. Many people use denial in their everyday lives to avoid dealing with painful feelings or areas of their life they don't wish to take a close look at. Lydia knew each of her students had a hole in their center that contained a fear so intense they had spent most of their years in denial and avoidance. It was time for them to fill the hole with strength and face the reality of this fear.

Ariana found herself back in a lifetime she had lived when Earth was new. She looked out through the eyes of her former self, through Ariadney's eyes. She saw beautiful vistas filled with brilliant green grasses and trees, azure blue water, the riot of colors that were the flowers and vegetation, and finally, all manner of exquisite animals. Her heart filled with Ariadney's joy and love. She had spent more time here than she had lived on Meria. She watched this planet go from a molten state to this exceptional paradise. With its diversity of creatures and plant life and its warm bright sun, she thought she might even prefer it to her home planet.

Breathing in the cool, moist air, she decided to walk to her home. As she reached her enclosure, she became aware of a disturbance in the energy. She heard animals scatter and noticed the air change. Looking toward the area of the disturbance she noticed that the atmosphere seemed to part. A spacecraft materialized from the rift. It was not a ship she was familiar with; it was not her people returning. She was concerned that the indigenous population would observe this phenomena and panic. It had been her habit to keep herself separate from the people of this planet in order to observe but not alter their progression. They were still fairly primitive compared to her people. She did not want to alter their development. This new arrival, however, was bound to change who they would become. The thought disturbed her, but it was her job to observe, nothing more.

The scene seemed to shift and Ariana knew a great deal of time had passed. The beautiful planet's energy seemed off. She also noticed that there were no dragons in the sky and no unicorns grazing with the deer in the meadow. In fact, there were no animals to be seen. Ariana again felt herself enter Ariadney's mind. She felt panic. Ariadney began to run down the hill toward the village. She hid in the adjacent forest so she could observe without being seen. There was a man dressed in white robes talking to a group of humans who lay flat, face down on the ground before him. Ariana did not recognize the man, but she felt sure that Ariadney did.

"You have angered us," the man said. "That is why the animals have fled and your crops are dying. You must work harder. We need more of the crystals to put things right. Without the crystals, we will be displeased and you will starve."

One of the prostrate forms lifted his head and pleaded with the man, "Please help us. Our children starve, the land shakes which frightens us, and we find no more stones. We beg you."

"Enough! Either we receive the amount we have asked for, or your homes will be destroyed and you will starve. Bring me your women."

Three young girls that looked no older than thirteen were brought before the man. He looked them over, nodded his head, and began to walk toward the mountain with the girls following him.

As Ariana watched, she realized she could feel Ariadney's emotions as well as her own. At times it was disconcerting not knowing whose emotions she was feeling, but at this moment, both of them were filled with deep fear.

The young girls followed the man until they came to a compound of square buildings, the largest of which reminded Ariana of pictures she'd seen of temples to the gods in both Greece and Rome. They were by far the largest and most elaborate structures Ariana had seen on the planet. Even her doppelganger, Ariadney, seemed impressed as well as dismayed. Ariana was very disturbed and worried about what would happen to these girls and also to the planet. Ariana sensed Ariadney's anger and guilt with herself for not taking action sooner. Determined to correct that, Ariadney vowed she would make protecting the planet her mission.

She headed back in the direction they had come. Ariana was becoming uncomfortable with the amount of anger and fear she felt from Ariadney. It was almost crippling, but still they ran on. Finally, they approached an area deep in the forest. She saw a small building. Ariana knew they were looking for someone. She saw a man walk out of the building. She knew he was the source of the intense anger she felt. The anger bordered on hatred. She felt herself shake as emotions of betrayal and heartache rushed through her body.

"Ares!" Ariadney screamed.

The handsome man turned toward the voice. When he saw Ariadney, he smiled, obviously happy to see her.

"You've done nothing to stop what is happening here!" she screamed. "They are stealing the young women, the animals are vanishing, and the plates within the planet are shifting. You are destroying my world!"

Ares walked toward her, obviously confused. In a gentle voice he asked, "What are you speaking of Ariadney? Women vanishing, the planet being destroyed? What do you mean?"

"I have just witnessed your friend Hephaestus. He told the villagers that they are not bringing enough crystals to him and they will be punished if they do not do better. When he left, he took with him three younglings no more than thirteen sun revolutions."

Ares looked greatly disturbed and Ariana could feel Ariadney's hope. Perhaps she was wrong, maybe there had been a misinterpretation.

Ares was thinking the same thing. He hoped Ariadney was mistaken. He listened as she described what took her to the village in the first place and he asked questions about what she had seen and heard. When she was through with her rendition of events, he felt only worry.

"Take me to your equipment," he ordered.

They walked to each of her seismometers. He looked closely at the results. He agreed with Ariadney's concern that the planet's crust was breaking up and then rubbing together. His concern deepened.

"I hadn't realized it was increasing in velocity and strength at this rapid pace. I spoke to our leader many revolutions of this moon ago. He promised to talk to the other researchers to confirm the data and take appropriate steps. I will talk with him again," Ares promised.

"It is too late. You have waited too long. This planet is undone now. What this data shows is an extinction event occurring. The animals have already departed in search of safety, but they will find none," Ariadney cried. Her whole being was wracked with grief and guilt. "This is my fault. I trusted you when you told me not to go to your people. I trusted that you cared as much about Terra as I do. I believed your words instead of my own knowing. This is my failure."

He reached for her, needing to hold and reassure her, but she pulled away.

"I will fix this," he promised again.

Turning back to him one last time, her heart breaking for the love and the trust she had once had for him, she said, "There is no more to be done. You must leave. This planet has less than three moon revolutions left."

She walked back toward her home to prepare her mourning ritual.

Ares ran to her, "Where are you going? We must talk to the leader together. If you are right, you will come with us. I will not leave you here."

"Leave me," she said, the pain she and now also Ariana were feeling was so excruciating that Ariana did not think she could stand it. "I will not leave this place. I will do my job and record everything as it happens so that my existence will still have had a purpose."

"I will not leave you. I cannot conceive of being anywhere without you. You have become my reason to continue. Without you there is nothing."

"If you truly feel what your words claim, then you must continue," Ariadney pleaded. "You must stop your people from this terrible destruction you bring to beautiful worlds. Give my life meaning. Stop this horror. Make your people see their responsibility to the greater good and to the balance of the Universe. You and your people are not all there is. Everything that exists is important. Without the lowest plant or insect in any world, the balance of all the worlds is compromised. Teach all your people the greatness and beauty of all life so that if they still chose to destroy it, they will realize what they do. Now leave me."

Ariadney walked away. Ariana watched Ares and felt his pain, too. He felt hopeless and lost. He knew he could not change Ariadney's mind.

He was tortured by what was about to happen on this beautiful, lush planet. Everything would die. Ariadney would die. He screamed into the quiet afternoon and collapsed onto the ground.

Ariadney kept walking even though her heart and her mind wanted to rush to him and ease his pain. She wanted to spend forever in his embrace, but she knew this was not possible. **She had failed.** She had allowed her love for him to cloud her awareness of what his people were like. She knew that their energy was not of creation but destruction. Ariadney had not wanted to allow her knowledge to taint her love. She had been alone so long and when they had connected, it was total. There was nothing else but him in her consciousness. She had been selfish and now this planet would pay the ultimate price, extinction.

When Ariadney heard the airship leave, she knew the time was close. Ariana felt the screams and tears of Ariadney. The explosion came just minutes after the ship left. The blast from the giant crystal decimated the village and the surrounding terrain. Ariana watched Ariadney die. She shared every feeling: guilt, doubt, recrimination, hatred, and grief.

It was too much for Ariana. Paralyzing fear gripped her. *That could be me. If I make another mistake, this will again be the result. I cannot stand that.* Her thoughts were screaming at her. She felt nothing but fear, deep gnawing fear accompanied by doubt. *There's no way I can do this. I know I'll fail.* She began to cry deep, tormented, defeated sobs.

You're right Ariana. You failed last time and you were well trained then. Now you have no real training. All you have is your arrogance. How can you possibly defeat that which is endemic to this world? These people love their excuses for failure. Many actually enjoy their fear, anger, and chaos. Others relish the pain of others. How can you possibly offer them anything?

Ariana knew it was The Darkness talking to her. She wanted to tell it to go away, but it was making sense. How could she possibly defeat something when so many people seemed to want it? She was nothing, just a nineteen-year-old girl with a few deluded friends. She could still feel the agony of failure and loss that she felt through Ariadney. She couldn't imagine feeling that again. She didn't want to feel that again. *Maybe I should just give up. I can't stand another failure, especially one that involves letting down the group or being let down by Zach. What am I doing?* She thought, fear gripping her. Feeling the complete hopelessness of her life as Ariadney, Ariana allowed herself to drop into a deep, depressive hole. She felt engulfed within the dark, soundlessness of the hole. *Matthew,* she thought. *He, too, was in this hole of despair. What had Tara said to him? Oh, I can't remember. Help me guides and Elders. Help me!* Suddenly Ariana remembered. Tara made Matthew aware that his dark experience was just an illusion. Tara reminded him that the poison he thought he felt in his body was really the poison from his past. He had to forgive himself to be free. Ariana realized what she must do is believe in herself.

"You'll fail, just like you failed us. You never belonged in our family. You are an untalented, fat, hopeless misfit. You belong nowhere, not in our family, not in school, not on this planet. You aren't even one of us. Why should we ever listen to you?" her father's voice asked.

At that moment, Ariana decided she would never be intimidated by The Darkness again.

You f'd up this time, she screamed in her mind. *I've forgiven my father and know that what he said or says is coming from his own pain and desperation. It has no effect on me anymore.*

Now she was just plain mad. *I will no longer think of myself as a misfit or untalented. I have talents I haven't even discovered yet. People will listen to me because what I am telling them is fact. We have no more time. We must work for change or the change we don't want, the disasters we are closing our eyes to, will happen. This time I fight. I'm not going to wait for anyone to fight for me. I'm not going to just wait to die. If I fail, it will not be for lack of trying. I will not allow fear or guilt to stop me. Giving up is the real failure. I will allow the fear, because it will show me where to focus to help others, but I will not give in to it.*

Darkness, you have no sway over me anymore. I might still have fear at times, but now I will use it to motivate me, not make me feel helpless. I AM THE LIGHT IN THE DARKNESS! You cannot win this time.

Suddenly pain seared through her head as though she had been struck by lightning. Ariana screamed. It was the worst pain she had ever felt. A voice sliced through her torment, *I can hurt you. If I, with my superior mind, can cause this pain in you, imagine what I can do to Zach.*

Ariana felt panic build within her. What if The Darkness could hurt

Zach like this? She could not stand to see the man she loved hurting. The risk of brain damage seemed so real. Through the fog of her pain Ariana heard a voice full of love and comfort. Tara was with her! *It's just an illusion again, dear Ariana. The pain is not real. You scared it by that great show of power. Remember, it can't stand The Light. It functions and grows through fear and pain. Don't give it any.* Ariana knew Tara was right. She focused all her attention on Zach and their kisses and immediately she felt the energy of their love and the profound sexual energy they shared. Her body began to glow with the heat of this energy and she felt an intense, survival energy build in her root chakra. Ariana found herself unlocking this dormant energy at the base of her spine. Flowing upward throughout her spine, her kundalini energy was unlocking her chakras. When it reached the heart chakra, it transmuted to love. Climbing to her crown chakra, Ariana felt herself bathed in the love and white light of the Source. As though she was plugged into the consciousness of All There Is, she knew completely that everything was perfect. It was not just a philosophical concept. She felt herself knowing on the deepest levels of her being that everything was and always will be absolutely perfect. Opening her eyes, Ariana found herself back in Lydia's living room, her body and her mind wide awake. She had never felt better and more sure of her power.

<h1 style="text-align:center">Chapter 20</h1>

Matthew was having a wonderful conversation with Tara. Having released all his deepest fears and angers through his vision quest, the only thing he was still at all emotional about was what had happened to Tara. He wasn't angry about what happened to her, especially because she seemed happy at the result, yet Matthew was disturbed that she had suffered such violence. He decided that to rid himself of these troubling feelings, he would need to talk with her. He willed his consciousness back to the place of limbo and found her waiting for him, their mind link having alerted her to his feelings.

"I've missed you so much. I still don't understand why you wouldn't talk to me or why any of this needed to happen, but I am working hard on not allowing any of this to bring back the old Matthew."

Tara smiled her beautiful smile and responded, "I never intended on hurting you by closing off. I had a lot to absorb and understand. I didn't want you to pick up anything from me before I understood everything myself."

"The old Matthew would have felt as though you were rejecting and abandoning me, and I must admit, it was hard not to think that way. But I know you would never hurt anyone, so I had to learn to be patient and trust. If I'm being too pushy today, and you're still not ready, just tell me."

"I think I'm ready to share what I've figured out. When we were all working so hard to rid ourselves of anything that The Darkness could use, it brought up a lot of things from my past that I thought I had dealt with but hadn't. We are more polarity than anyone knew. All of us have demons. I led you all to believe that I had mastered mine, but I had only repressed them. Do you know many trans teens attempt suicide? The guilt and shame and hatred we feel is overwhelming. I thought about it, but I believe in God too much. When I got involved with the group it only strengthened that belief. But even though I believe that God is complete love without judgment, I kept judging myself as bad and weird. I felt like I was a horrible person for putting my family through so much. It's not easy living in a small Latino community with your only boy child wanting to be a girl. I definitely flaunted it too, especially at school. It got so bad that people in the neighborhood stopped coming to my parents' restaurant. They moved us to a mixed area to escape— somewhere that no one knew us. I never even thought about what all this was doing to my sister. All I thought about was myself and what I was going through. Once I really looked at my actions, the guilt became overwhelming as I realized the harm my selfishness had created in people's lives.

Watching what you and the others in our group were going through, I realized I had to become authentic, but now I wasn't sure what the authentic me was. I began to allow the guilt to eat at me and it was making me feel unworthy to be part of the group and the important mission we had to perform.

Being around all of you, and finally having friends that seemed to accept and care about me, brought all of this to my consciousness. I had to become the real me. But now I wasn't sure what that meant. I began to allow the guilt to eat at me and it was making me feel unworthy to be part of the group and the important mission we had to perform.

I had been agonizing over whether to begin reassignment surgery when I went with the group to hear Equinoxx. EQ suggested that I consider leaving my body as it is. At the time, that really upset me because I thought they were telling me that my parents had been right, that I was only being selfish. I felt condemned to a life of being half a person. I know now that I misinterpreted their meaning. I also know that the guilt I was feeling about taking the final step, and forever severing the ties with my family, made me hear it wrong.

Now I know why they suggested I not undergo the surgery. Beside the health risks and the huge amounts of potentially dangerous hormones I would have to take, the surgery would not make me any more of a woman than I already am. I now understand that my body is only a necessary device to live in a physical world—it is not me. Every ounce of my energy is female. This is true no matter what my body looks like. I understand now why Equinoxx made the suggestion they did. I can keep my body intact so that I can show others that gender has nothing to do with genitalia and femininity is not something that only women possess. Even the dictionary got that wrong. I have decided that I will be a bridge between the sexes, between masculinity and femininity. I understand now that humanity is neither completely masculine or feminine; we contain both male and female hormones and traits of both sexes. There are strong, aggressive women and nurturing, gentle men. It isn't nature that decides how we will act—it is society training us to our roles. In some people however, this training fails. It failed with me because society was basing my role on my genitals, not my mind or my heart. I didn't figure this out on my own; this knowledge only became known to me during my time in the Lost Realm.

When I first entered that realm, it was because my guides left me there. They told me it was up to me whether I returned to the group and fulfilled my commitment or remained there where I could continue punishing myself through guilt and self-loathing. They helped me understand how I brought the violence to myself as a punishment for my perceived 'sins.' As a devoted believer in God, I would never commit suicide, but I saw clearly how I set up this attack. I left my death in God's hands. I refused the clerk's advice to call someone about the two men that accosted me at the art store. I walked home through dark alleyways even though I felt I was being watched. I chose to enter through the condo's garage, my hands full of packages and my keys deep in my purse. I had never done anything that stupid before. I see now how I chose this pain and violence to purge my guilt. I have finally taken a stand and decided who I want to be. I am a survivor. I decided to fight at any cost for my survival. I am now committed to my position within the group and also to myself. It doesn't matter what my body looks like. It's who I am that matters. I am Tara, and Tara is one hell of a woman."

Matthew was shocked. He knew that we create everything in our world by the choices we make, but this horror? He just didn't want to believe that the sweet, gentle being in front of him could have created and actually wanted this violence. "I wish you had talked to me about all this. Maybe I could have helped you like you helped me."

"None of this was conscious, and if the guides hadn't deposited me in the Lost Realm, I might not have realized how much I hated myself and thought I needed to be punished. I was raised Catholic after all, and Catholicism is all about suffering and punishment. Right?" she said, teasing Matthew. "It's obvious to me now that I chose for all this to happen. I know how to be safe and I chose to act carelessly. I guess I was committing suicide my way."

Matthew thought about what Tara had said and realized how many ways our choices affect our lives. She was right. Her choices had been careless; she had even refused the offer of a ride home.

"I made a lot of bad choices that night, too many to be an accident. I unconsciously needed to experience the attack in order to understand how much I want to live. I'm making new choices now. I'm choosing to help here until it's time to return to my body. I'm choosing to release my guilt and relish the fact that I am unique and that uniqueness is not an affront to God and shouldn't embarrass or demean my family. If they chose to turn their backs on me, then they may, but I will always love them and be there if they need me. That's my choice. I can absolutely say that I love myself exactly as I am, a beautiful, vibrant, feminine being."

Matthew and Tara's conversation was suddenly interrupted. They both knew something was very wrong. Someone needed them badly. Sending their consciousness to each member of their group, they felt Zach. He was the one in trouble. Matthew began to panic. He had never even considered that the one fear he had not dealt with was the fear of losing Zach. Matthew felt Tara's calming energy surround him.

"Panicking is not what he needs," Tara reminded Matthew. "He needs our calm and our strength. You know how to rid yourself of fear, you've already done it. Do it again now and then let's go show Zach how to rid himself of his."

Matthew calmed himself then began to think about this new fear. He knew that what Zach was feeling was an illusion. He was safe in Lydia's living room. But that was not the real issue. Matthew needed to understand how he would cope if anything really happened to Zach.

"Play it out," Tara suggested. "Play out your worst fear and allow yourself to see what you would do."

Matthew saw Zach lying dead in a coffin. Looking at Zach's lifeless body, he allowed all the pain to surface. Tears began to fall down his cheeks as he felt the excruciating pain of the loss of his true brother, Zach. He saw Zach's mother. She was just a shell of her vibrant self. He felt her pain, too. He sensed the love of the rest of the Weirdxotics and he perceived their pain and grief. As he focused on this sad scene, he realized something. One of the reasons he had grown so close to Zach was because for a long time, Zach was the only friend he had, the only one who had really known him. But now he had the others in the group. They would console and uplift each other. He also knew that he would never really lose Zach. As long as he could walk between the realms he could meet and speak with Zach just as he had been doing with Tara. He realized that the loss of a person was also an illusion. Many in the physical realm think the loss is permanent, but they do not understand the way the Universe and energy works. Matthew understood completely; he would not grieve the loss of Zach's physical body. Instead, he would be happy that Zach was set free to exist in all the dimensions, realms, and planes.

"I understand," Matthew announced to Tara. "I will not fear loss ever again because loss is just part of the illusion. Everyone's physical body will die eventually but our energy continues forever, and if we really understand that, then we would know that we will continue together in many more lifetimes and many other planes. Let's get the others and go help Zach."

"I must stay here, Matthew," Tara said. "I am limited to where I may go while my body is healing. I must be ready at the instant I am called back. If I was helping with Zach I would be tempted to stay if called, then I might never come back. Do you understand?

Matthew nodded and said, "I understand. Conserve and grow your energy and heal that body as rapidly as you can because I miss hugging you. Anyway, there are seven of us to go to Zach. We can take care of this."

Matthew focused his energy on the group and sent out the call to find Zach. He felt the mind link that connected them all. He knew everyone understood exactly what Zach was experiencing. As one mind, they went to Zach.

Chapter 21

When Zach found himself on Atlantis, he wasn't surprised. He knew that his greatest fear was losing everything he loved because of his inability to take the proper action. He understood that his life in Atlantis was just one of many roles his soul had played. He knew his current life was distinct from the previous ones, yet he still believed that the events that took place during that difficult life were somehow his fault.

Knowing how horrendous the failure was then only made him more scared and insecure about succeeding now. He did not want to be the cause of billions of deaths, then or now. He couldn't stand to think about causing pain or destruction to anyone he loved. He had felt helpless as a child, watching his father hurt his mother and his siblings. As a small child, he could do nothing. Now he felt almost crippled by the fear that he would once again fail to act, but the consequences would be on a much larger scale.

He had worked hard in therapy to get rid of the hatred he felt for his father. He thought he had accomplished that well enough, but he still felt the pain of being helpless. As a child there was nothing he could do when his father's actions brought ruin to his family and so much pain to his mother. He understood, at least mentally, that his father had a disease, a gambling addiction that he couldn't seem to kick. Understanding something mentally, however, did not stop the emotional repercussions. He felt the shame, anger, and embarrassment that came from watching an addict undo every good thing that anyone in the family accomplished.

His father lost several businesses, stole from employers and even from his own children. Eventually, Zach's mother was forced to go to work just to make sure the children were fed. When he stole the food right out of his children's mouths, she divorced him. By that time, it was only the two of them left in the home—the other children ran as soon as they were grown. Zach and his mother moved into a small, two-bedroom apartment, and between the money each of them made, survived. When

Matthew moved in it helped them even more. Because his father had died, Matthew received Social Security benefits he contributed to the household. Even with three people helping out, it was still difficult at times.

Zach could not imagine life without the people he loved. When he thought of his Atlantian life, knowing that someone he loved and an entire planet died because of his ineptitude, Zach was rendered nearly immobile. The fear overtook him and dissolved any confidence he had.

Overlooking the decimation of what had been a vibrant, amazing planet, Zach felt tears begin to flow down his cheeks. He began walking through the ruins, attempting to recognize anything. There were still small areas of pristine beauty among the devastation, making the horror only more poignant. Reaching the top of a pile of debris, he looked down on a small patch of ground that was scorched but still somewhat intact. He walked toward the area, not really knowing exactly why.

When he reached the edge of the small clearing surrounded by burned and broken trees, he noticed the remains of a modest building. He both lost his breath and felt a painful jab of emotion in his gut when he realized where he was. *This is where Ariadney lived and where she stayed to die.* Pulling away the remains of the structure, Zach discovered the decimated body of a woman. Reaching out his shaking hand, he turned the body over. He couldn't believe what he was seeing. This wasn't Ariadney. It was Ariana. He started looking around the charred room and realized it was filled with bodies. Turning over one after the other, he identified all the Weirdoxtics, his mother, his brothers and sister, Lydia the therapist, and even people that were so destroyed he couldn't recognize them. Everywhere there were corpses. He realized this wasn't Atlantis after all. This was what was left of Earth. Again he had failed and now he was totally alone. Everyone he loved was dead. His home was destroyed and it was all his fault. He fell to his knees and began to scream. Tears poured from his eyes, his body quaked with sobs, and his screams echoed through the destroyed world. He crawled to the body of Ariana and held and rocked her rotting corpse, begging her to forgive him. He ran his hands through the beautiful hair he had loved so much, falling from her skull as his hands touched it. Covering her lifeless face with his tears, he felt the total desolation of this loss.

"Take me, too," he begged to no one. "I can't stand this!" *I cannot live with this guilt and pain,* he thought as he sobbed even harder.

He ran outside, screaming into the night, "You did it, you mothers! You let it happen. You destroyed what could have been saved. All you had to do was fight. All you had to do was become The Light!"

Having spent all his energy screaming, he collapsed to the ground. His body curled into a fetal position, he gave up and began waiting, hoping that death would come soon.

This is how the group found him. Even though Zach's body was at Lydia's, his essence was here. Matthew knew that he could remain at this desolate place forever, severing all connection to his physical body if he chose to. The group had to do something now, immediately, if they had any chance of bringing him back. Matthew conveyed these thoughts through the mind link to the rest of the group. *What do we do?* screamed many voices in his head. Matthew thought about what Tara had done to help him get out of his illusion. She had come and supported him and talked to him logically. Matthew asked the rest of the group to support him so that he could reach out to Zach. With their added energy, he materialized his image and stood next to Zach.

"Zach, you know this is only an illusion."

"It's an illusion," Zach said, "or it's a precognition of what's to come. I messed up bad once before. I can't stand for it to happen again."

"But you're giving up before you even try!"

"Come on, Matthew, what are the odds that we will succeed? There are only a few of us and millions of them."

"You don't know how many of 'us' there are. We know there are at least 13 of us now. A couple of months ago we didn't have anyone but the two of us. Are you just going to give up and leave Ariana, me, and the group to shoulder all the responsibility? I thought you were stronger, braver, and more committed than that. What happened to the guy that I thought was so together? The guy I wished I was for so many years."

"You really wanted to be me?"

"Yeah," Matthew admitted. "But dude, I'm ashamed of you now, cowering here in this place, giving up. What's with this shit?"

"Look at this," Zach said, waving his arms around. "This is what's going to happen, Matt. How are we going to stop it? It's totally impossible and you know it!"

Matthew looked at Zach with distain, "Sure it's possible that this will be the outcome, but I'd much rather know that I tried then to spend eternity here knowing that I was a quitter who let all his friends mourn him and all that he could have been. What about Ariana? Do you know what it's like to lose your polarity? No, you don't, because you're the one who's shoving her away. Well, let me tell you man, its gut wrenching. It's a much greater loss than a death because you are a part of each other. You're melded down to the DNA; even your thoughts are connected. Having that connection severed is impossible to get over. It might kill Ariana. Then we'd lose both of you because your choice was a selfish one. God, Zach, you make me so mad. What I'd give to have Tara back as she was," Matthew said, tears flowing down his face.

"How do I stop being afraid?" Zach asked, feeling cowed by Matthew's words and emotions.

"By leaning on us, and trusting that whatever we accomplish will be enough to make a difference. That's all any of us can do. Zach, my friend, are you ready to come back to us? Please."

"No."

"Well then, I guess you're more like your Dad than your mom."

"What the hell do you mean by that?"

"Your Dad was a quitter. He escaped from his responsibility into gambling. Whenever things got rough, he just gave up and destroyed everything good around him. He pushed away the people that loved him and instead wallowed in his guilt and shame. Your Mom, on the other hand, stood by as long as she could, but when it became evident there was nothing else to do, she moved on. She took you, and even though she knew it would be hard, she walked away and she made it work, because unlike your Dad, she's a fighter. You're willing to lay down and give up before we've even begun to fight. Just because of your guilt and shame you're willing to throw away everyone who loves you. So who are you most like? Your father or your mother?"

"Shit!" Zach realized how true Matthew's words were.

"So, who you gonna be? A loser or a winner?"

"I don't want to be like my dad."

"Then you'd better come back with me."

"Yeah, I guess so. Matt, was this what your vision quest was like?"

"Yeah, sort of, if you throw in freezing cold, hunger, rattlesnake venom, wolves, and an old man with a white raven and a hawk,"

Matthew answered with a grin.

"I guess I should consider myself lucky. All I had to deal with were the corpses of my friends and loved ones. Oh, and how do we get out of here?"

"Click your heels together and say, 'There's no place like home.' "

Chapter 22

Back in Lydia's living room, Zach admitted to Lydia and the group, "That was really tough for me. I didn't realize that I was a quitter. I've never faced anything that hard before. The thought that I could once again cause the destruction of this beautiful place and the people I love made me want to just say 'forget it' and lie down."

"That's exactly what fear does," Lydia answered. "It is the mind destroyer. It takes away one's ability to perceive options and makes us either give up or ignore the object of our fear. That is why people can deny the obvious climate changes.

Within all of us is the desire to escape, especially to escape those things that create fear. So we keep quiet when we see injustice. Way back when I was your age, a woman was beaten and murdered in the courtyard of an apartment building in New York City. The beating, rape, and stabbing took over 30 minutes and the woman was screaming loudly for her life. The assailant ran off three separate times when apartment lights were turned on, but returned when no one did anything to stop him. Eventually, when it was obvious that the woman was dead and the man would not be returning, someone finally called the police. It was discovered that 38 people witnessed the entire event from their apartment windows and no one called the police because they were afraid to become involved.

Fear can take the humanity out of humans. We watch atrocities happen then deny that we knew what the Nazi's did in World War II, or what Pol Pot did in Cambodia, for example.

Fear also creates apathy by convincing us that one person can do nothing. But history has shown us that one person can change the world. Look at what Buddha, Moses, Gandhi, and Martin Luther King accomplished. Those are a few very public examples, but there are so many other voices that are never made public that start people around them thinking new thoughts, and those thoughts create wondrous change.

Becoming people that dare to be different and unique is the first step to overcoming fear. The second step is to face the fears you are aware of and overcome them while working to find the new ones that will inevitably crop up. The third step is to understand that bravery isn't overcoming fear, it's moving ahead even when you are scared stiff," declared Lydia.

"Some of the Native tribes teach their young children to awaken during nightmares and face the thing that is scaring them in the dream, and then bring that awareness into their waking state to be challenged there also," Matthew recounted. "It's a type of lucid dreaming, like what you mentioned to Jason, allowing yourself to be aware that you are dreaming during the dream. But it doesn't just stop when the dream does. They use the experience to understand fears so that they can be dealt with on all levels of consciousness. I think most people don't even know how much fear rules their lives."

"I know that was definitely true for me," Ariana confided to the group. "I spent most of my life hiding. I even walked with my head down and my long hair covering my face. I think I believed, maybe not consciously, that if I was invisible, no one could hurt me. That invisibility kept me from facing my fears and also kept me very lonely and sad."

"The way I dressed kept people away from me, and if that didn't work, I was so negative no one could stand to be near me," Wendy agreed. "I was so afraid that if people found out my secret—that I killed my brother—then they would hate me. The truth was that I hated myself so much no one else could possibly compete."

Matthew said, "I don't have to tell all of you how much fear affected my life. It ruined every close relationship I had. Until Zach realized my secret, I lived in terror that someone would. Then, when I left my Mom, I lived in terror that someone would send her to jail or she'd kill herself and it would be all my fault. I even feared that when people found out my secret they would think that I was evil or that they would reject me as a dirty thing not worth knowing. My entire life was full of fear that later turned to anger."

"You kids have already gotten through the first and second hurdles, now you just have to believe in your bravery and keep moving forward. The past is no longer a burden for any of you. You have all faced it.

You've also faced your deepest fears and mastered those. You all have exceptional abilities and those abilities will activate new fears or perhaps uncover old ones. Now you have each other and the immense strength your difficult pasts give you. Never allow doubt—another word for fear—to linger very long in your minds. Express it, discuss it, and move forward together," Lydia suggested.

"I know we can do it," Andrew claimed. "We've all shared our deepest selves with each other and no one rejected anyone, it just made us love each other more."

"Anyway, now with the mind link, it will be impossible to hide anything from each other," Teja reminded the group.

"Eeeek," Leesie exclaimed, "You all will know what I'm thinking and feeling—no privacy? I'm not sure I like that."

Lydia laughed, "I think the mind link will only be for serious work together or if anyone needs rescuing, not for invading anyone's privacy."

"What could you possibly have to hide?" Teja scoffed.

Leesie glanced ever so briefly at Jason and everyone noticed. Turning red she commanded, "Get out of my mind!" The sound of laughter was a welcome conclusion to a difficult day.

<h1 style="text-align:center">Chapter 23</h1>

Teja, Jason, and Leesie were sitting on the dormitory lawn, basking in the warm sunshine, sharing lunch and discussing the weekend.

"So, what were you scared of?" Leesie asked Jason. "I know that I'm being nosy, but I had to wait a whole night to ask. I was really bummed that everyone wanted to go home and rest before discussing what happened to them. I was pumped because I won and wanted to brag a little."

"You won what?" Teja asked. "If you mean you beat your fear, I think we all did. Wasn't that the idea?"

"No, I meant I won because I had no fears. I'd already worked on all of them and conquered them, so there was nothing to face," Leesie said, a smug smile on her face.

"Not me," admitted Jason. "I had a lot of things to work on. I didn't understand 'til Sunday how much my mom means to me and how scared I was of losing her. I know that probably sounds wimpy, but it's the truth. We've been through so much together and she's always been my champion. It was hard to face the idea that she could die. I know she will someday, but no one thinks it could be right now."

"So what did you do to get over it?" Teja asked.

"Well, knowing about Tara helped. I realized that no one ever really leaves you. You may not be able to hug them, but you can still talk with them if you learn how to be open to their way of communicating. I went to talk to Tara and she explained that talking to someone on the Other Side is no different than talking to someone in the limbo realm. We just do the same things to open and listen."

"Okay Teja, your turn," Leesie directed, pushy as ever.

With a roll of her eyes, Teja said, "I realized when Tara was hurt that I hated feeling helpless. Right after we left the hospital, I almost did something horrible in order to stop feeling that way. When things happen, I want to dive in and do something, anything. What I had to do to rid myself of the fear of helplessness was to learn to surrender. I don't mean giving up, but understanding that there is nothing more that can be done. Surrendering is actually empowering. When you can really let go and allow the Universe to do whatever it feels is best, you are open to new possibilities or new situations to focus on."

"Wow, that's really deep girl," Leesie stated. "I wondered why you felt so much mellower."

"Hi there. Is this group still closed?" a voice behind them asked.

Everyone turned around and discovered Josh on his bicycle.

"Is that bike stuck to your body?" Leesie asked smiling. "And this isn't a closed anything. Just three friends enjoying good conversation and a beautiful day between classes. Have a sit."

Josh looked at Teja suspiciously, "Are you cool with this?" he asked.

"Whatever," she replied.

Jason nodded at Josh and said, "Hey, I'm Jason."

"I'm Josh. You're the first guy I've seen with the girls."

"Been seeing them often?" Jason asked suspiciously.

"Not really, but when I do, it's usually right in this same spot. Is there something magical here?"

"No, it's just pretty and is a great location between classes," Leesie answered. "How come you seem to be here a lot?"

"It's on my way to my apartment. I like to cut through here so I don't have to ride in traffic. Where are the rest of the girls?"

"Here and there," Teja replied tersely.

"Sorry if I pissed you off," Josh said to Teja, "but it seems like I do that every time we meet. Do I smell or something?"

Teja was brought up short by his question. Why was she so nasty to him? He really didn't do anything except stop to talk. He'd always been polite. *What is my problem?* she wondered.

"Maybe you two had a really bad past life?" Leesie suggested.

"Hum, could be I guess. But how do we work through it now so we can all be friendly?" Josh asked.

Leesie answered again, "Why don't we just get to know each other?"

"I'm game if it's all right with everyone else," Josh answered, looking at Teja.

"Why not?" she answered.

"Let's start easy. What's your major?" asked Leesie.

"I'm sorta weird. I have a double major that's light years apart. I practically had to enroll as two people to get them to let me do them. One's quantum physics and the other is computer science."

"Not as weird as some people may think. They both need logic and precision," Leesie responded. "It would have been weirder if it had been a social science major and quantum physics."

Josh was impressed with Leesie's knowledge. "What's your major?"

"I used to know, but now I'm not sure," Leesie admitted. "A lot has changed in my life which has also changed my priorities. I may be changing majors soon. Maybe I'll try psychology and environmental science."

Jason said, "Well, you both lost me. I'm still in community college trying to do well enough to get here. I have no idea what I want to major in. 'One day at a time' is my motto."

"And you?" Josh addressed Teja.

"I also used to think I knew, but now I'm with Leesie. New priorities mean new goals. Maybe I should look at poli sci. What do you think, the first black woman president?"

"I'd vote for you," Leesie declared, "but I'm sure glad you aren't running soon. I can't vote yet."

"How old are you?" Josh asked.

"I'm almost 16, just 3 more months."

"You look really young but I would never have figured you for fifteen. No wonder you understood what I meant with my two majors. You must be one smart girl."

Blushing, Leesie said, "So I'm told. But tell us some juicy stuff about you."

"I'm nineteen. I'll be twenty in August. I'm a Leo. My family lives in California, but I really love the desert. I'm an only child who always wanted a sister. My best friend is Ralph, my Golden Retriever. My family likes to travel and I've seen most of the world. I've spent the last six years exploring metaphysics and spirituality. I think I've got some abilities and I want to explore them. I tried some groups in California but felt uncomfortable with them. I've had a heck of a time finding anything on campus. I always thought Arizona was like a psychic mecca with Sedona and everything, but I haven't found anything that felt real to me yet until I saw that girl out here meditating and then you girls out here that one day. I just felt drawn to all of you. I really wish the other girl hadn't been afraid of me because I think she had some awesome abilities."

"Other girl?" Teja asked.

"Yeah, a good-looking brunette. I watched her meditating out here for forty-five minutes without her moving at all. Her aura, the lights around her, was amazing. I tried to talk to her, but she brushed me off and ran away. I got the feeling that I'd scared her somehow."

"You don't know her name, do you?"

"Yeah, I remember it because of that singer. It's Ariana."

Chapter 24

Matthew, Zach, Ariana, Wendy, and Andrew were lounging in the dorm room shared by the two girls. Diablo lay snoring on Wendy's lap, convincing Ariana that Tara was not present today. When her spirit was present the cat reacted. At first he would seem uncomfortable, not hissing or anything, but staring in a direction and backing off. After Wendy explained to him why he couldn't smell Tara, he seemed to become excited about having her around. When she was present, he would jump up from his resting place and run to a spot in the room and stand there staring at nothing, purring loudly. Although Ariana could not see Tara, she imagined that Tara was talking to him as she had while she was on this plane of existence.

Today had been a great day so far. The weather was glorious as usual, classes had been easy as it seemed everyone, even the professors were thinking about Christmas break, not school. It also seemed that the group had completely forgotten about Ariana's birthday which made her glad. She hated having a fuss made over her. She wasn't used to it and it embarrassed her, though she was kind of hurt that Zach hadn't said anything.

As usual, her parents called early that morning. Her father said she would be receiving a check. Her brother sent a text and her sister sent an e-card. No one said a thing about coming home for break. That was her real birthday present, being able to stay in Arizona for Christmas with the people she thought of as her actual family.

She was more than happy to spend her birthday with her friends, just hanging out and talking about their plans for the weekend.

"Anyone had any visits from The Darkness?" Matthew asked.

"No, I think we are in a mellow period with Christmas and all. Seems to happen every year. People start thinking about being kinder to one another and by January first, it's gone again," commented Zach.

"Yeah," Wendy agreed, "so wouldn't this be a good time to try to get the word out about the difference between positive and negative energy and The Light?"

"Wasn't that mostly Leesie's job?" Andrew asked. "But I don't think we'll get a lot from her right now. Hasn't anyone noticed that the baby of the family is in love?"

"What?" Ariana asked, surprised.

"She can't seem to stay away from Jason. They're joined at the hip. Poor Teja is like a third wheel or something. You haven't noticed?" Wendy asked.

The three others shook their heads no, looks of amazement on their faces.

"Oh, God," Zach said, "does that mean we need to have 'the talk' with her?"

"I'm feeling especially dense today," Ariana admitted, "but I'm lost now. What talk?"

Matthew started laughing, "The sex, STDs, and birth control talk."

Ariana blushed bright red and admitted, "Well, I'll leave that talk to you guys. I'll just listen in because I'm sure I need some education on those subjects myself."

As if by magic, there was a knock on the door and Leesie came into the room. "What talk?" she said. "Who are we talking to and about what?"

"Later," Ariana said as she watched Jason, Teja, and a new guy that looked vaguely familiar, walk into the room. "What are you guys doing here?"

"Now I'm hurt," Teja announced dramatically. "Can't your friends drop over to say 'whasup?' Oh, and we brought a new enrollee. Josh, this is Matthew, Zach, Ariana, Wendy, and Andrew."

"Hey," Josh said. "Nice seeing you again, Ariana."

"The grass the day I was meditating, right?" she asked. "I was pretty rude to you that day. It was the beginning of our awakening and I was sort of paranoid about everything. Sorry."

"That's cool. These guys explained what you all are up to and I'm in, if no one objects. For several years, I've been looking to connect with something like what you're doing. I became obsessed with everything spiritual when I was twelve. There was lots of information on the internet, and lots of groups recruiting on there, too, but nothing that really resonated with me. When I first saw you, Ariana, I was fascinated. I couldn't take my eyes off you. You stood perfectly still for over 45 minutes, surrounded by the most amazing array of lights and energy. That still freaks me. I had never seen that before. Even the Sai Baba couldn't do it."

"You've been to India?" Matthew asked.

"Yeah, I've traveled quite a bit looking for the illusive 'it.' I've been to India, Bali, Tibet, Stonehenge, Machu Picchu, and even Sedona, only to find it on the lawn at ASU," Josh chuckled.

"My Cheyenne grandfather says, positive energy is everywhere if it is within you. Otherwise, it is nowhere," Matthew replied.

"Native American spirituality is my next adventure, but I was waiting till the summer," Josh said. "I went through the gauntlet as I worked to find the 'it.' Every group that wanted me didn't seem to fit, and then each of you rejected me. Somehow, I knew I needed to hook up with you guys. If I'd been a different person, being rejected over and over again by you girls might have discouraged me. But I knew there was a reason I was at ASU. I understood that reason when I first saw you, Ariana, and later the group of girls when you were glowing! Then today I accidently met up with these three. I knew trying to become a part of your group was worth fighting for, so I never gave up. And today these three actually let me in and invited me to the party!"

Ariana looked a bit spooked. "What party?" she asked.

Before Josh could answer Leesie jumped in, "Oh, I'm sure that was just a figure of speech or something. Right, Josh?"

A confused Josh agreed, "Yeah, just a figure of speech."

Wendy stood and announced, "I'm out of Diablo food. Does anyone want to go with me to Tara's to get it? This cat does love him some food."

"I'll go," Andrew said. "Why don't we make it a convoy and then stop on Mill and get some dinner?"

"Sounds good to me," Zach replied. "This cat does love him some food, too, and is pretty hungry. Just saying."

Ariana was suspicious that something was up. But when everyone else said they had other things they needed to get done and they'd see everyone in the next day or so, she decided it had just been her imagination.

"Let's get going then," Ariana suggested. "If the guys are hungry, we don't want to have them get mean or anything."

"I've got to touch up my makeup," Wendy declared. "It'll only take a minute. Chill guys."

Andrew groaned. "She's always worried about how she looks since Tara gave her that makeover. I sort of liked the old Wendy better at times. She wasn't as girlie."

Ariana sat down and settled in, knowing this would take a while. Andrew was right. Wendy had gotten a lot more girlie since Tara cut her hair and showed her how to put on makeup and dress to fit her figure.

"While we're waiting, let's decide where we want to eat," Ariana suggested.

"You want to go to the Mexican place we went to the first night we all went out?" Zach asked. "That could be kinda romantic. This time I promise not to try to burn your mouth too badly."

"Okay, as long as you promise that this won't be another 'trial by fire,' " she said laughing. "You know, when I think about that night, it feels like years ago. The girl I was then isn't even familiar anymore."

"You are a lot stronger and psychically smarter now, that's for sure," Matthew agreed. "Time is really an interesting illusion. When you're waiting for something it takes forever, but when you're remembering something, it often feels like ages ago. In our case, that night was only two months ago, almost exactly."

"That **is** weird," Zach agreed. "Look at how much has happened and how close we've all become in such a short time. I feel as though I know this group better than anyone else in my life, including my family, and I feel closer to all of you, too."

"That's probably because we have a purpose," Andrew suggested. "Our goal is massive and if we didn't really know each other or trust each other, we would probably fail."

"What do you guys think of Josh?" Ariana asked.

"I'm impressed with his travels," Matthew responded, "but I can't make a determination about him yet. His aura looked good. I couldn't detect any obvious lying from watching it."

"What did he mean that he met you before?" Zach asked Ariana.

"Oh, a little jealous, are we?" she replied with a smirk. "It was just at the beginning of all this. Matthew, remember the day we went looking for crystals? I think I mentioned him to you. He creeped me out a little then, because I opened my eyes from this wonderful meditation to find him, a stranger, staring at me. He was kinda surrounded by shadows so I wondered if he had been sent by The Darkness. I brushed him off and left pretty abruptly."

"Yeah, I sorta remember. That was the first few days after Zach and I decided to watch out for you girls. You called me that day because you felt there were malevolent shadows all around you. Right?"

"Yes, and there were. That was one of the reasons I bought crystals for everyone. So see Zach, nothing to worry about."

"Okay everyone," Wendy said as she exited the bathroom. "How do I look?"

"Perfect." Andrew replied, "But can we go eat now? I'm starving."

"When aren't you?" Wendy asked, rolling her eyes. "We have to go to Tara's condo first, remember?"

"Oh, come on, can't we go after we eat?"

"No," Wendy replied as she grabbed her purse and walked out the door.

Chapter 25

The evening was just as beautiful as the day had been. The temperature had dropped. Ariana was grateful she brought a jacket. It was a little ratty, but really comfortable. Besides memories and pictures, her old denim jacket was the only thing she had left that reminded her of her horse. She always wore it riding because it was comfortable and easy to clean, but chic it wasn't.

The five friends decided to walk. The night was splendidly clear and cool, so it seemed like the perfect thing to do.

Ariana and Zach walked holding hands, as had become their custom, while Andrew had his arm around Wendy's waist. Matthew walked between the two couples, alone. Ariana worried that he might be missing Tara so she reached her hand out and grasped his. Wendy, walking on Matthew's other side, noticed what she had done and followed suit. They were taking up the entire sidewalk but no one was left out. *This is what a loving family feels like,* Ariana thought, overcome with love for her friends. She was feeling so good she felt like skipping and humming and just being joyful.

Zach squeezed her hand. "You seem like you're in a good mood."

"Yeah, I am. For right now, nothing could be better than this: wonderful friends, a beautiful night, and a sky sparkling with stars. Isn't life wonderful?"

"I'm hurt," Zach teased. "What about also having the greatest boyfriend any girl could want?"

Laughing, Ariana replied, "Oh, but that goes without saying. How could I resist those puppy dog eyes?"

"We're here!" Wendy announced loudly.

"I think everyone can see that, Wendy," Ariana chided her. "The whole condo complex knows we're here now."

"Whoops, sorry," Wendy said more quietly as she put the key in the door.

As soon as the door swung open, Ariana was engulfed in bright light accompanied by the loud refrain of "Surprise!" as her friends jumped from behind the couch and chairs. The room was decorated with purple balloons and there were gift wrapped packages piled on the coffee table. On an easel in the middle of the room was the most beautiful painting Ariana had ever seen. The sky in the painting was pink and purple, a naked black tree stood in the foreground, and a sea and two suns were in the background. Tears streamed down Ariana's face as she realized the painting was of Meria, her home.

Leesie looked stricken. "We thought you'd like it. Tara didn't have the chance to finish it. We know it's actually more purple and there are creatures and more rocks, but she ran out of some of the paint colors and, well, you know. I'm sorry if it makes you sad."

"I love it. It's absolutely perfect. The tears are because now I'll be able to see my planet every day, not just in my meditations. Thank you, guys," Ariana said. "This is the best thing anyone has ever done for me."

"Oh, you're not getting off that easily," Zach exclaimed. "There are lots more presents, food, ice cream, and cake!"

"You thought we'd forgotten, didn't you?" Wendy said, very proud that the surprise had been a success.

"Actually, I did think you all had forgotten. Truthfully, I was sort of glad because I wasn't sure how I'd react. But this is so neat! I think I could get used to being pampered."

"Enough BS, let's eat!" said Matthew.

"Do we want to open presents first?" Teja asked.

Almost in unison the males in the room screamed, "Hell, no!"

The women looked disgusted but acquiesced to the guy's demands.

Ariana was amazed at the spread. Her friends had been busy as it was obvious that the food was homemade, not store bought.

"Who did all this work?" she asked her friends.

"We all shared the responsibility. I hope you like pork chops, sweet potatoes, and some of Teja's Gram's greens. We also have fruit salad, decadent chocolate cake, and three kinds of gelato. Yum," Leesie replied.

Bright plastic dishes and cups adorned the table. The utensils were Tara's. The wall was covered by a poster announcing *Happy Birthday!* and there were purple balloons everywhere.

When everyone was seated Teja asked, "Anyone care if I say a prayer?" When no one objected she began, "Dear Lord, Universe, Great Spirit or whatever, we thank you so much for bringing Ariana to our world and allowing us to help her on her path. Thank you for bringing us all together and help us to always remember that all we can do is our best. The end result is out of our hands. Thank you for this wonderful food, event, friends, planet, and life. Amen."

Ariana heard a pop and realized that someone had opened a bottle of Champaign. "Oh, my," she exclaimed. "I've never had alcohol before."

"Well, you aren't having it now either," Andrew said, "its non-alcoholic. It's the thought that counts, right?"

When the drink had been poured into everyone's glasses, Wendy asked, "Who wants to make a toast?"

"Me," Zach announced. Holding his glass high he said, "To the most wonderful woman I'm lucky to love and to the person who will lead us to our success at saving the world."

"My turn," Leesie declared. "To the woman that changed my life and gave it purpose. I am so glad I met you."

Acknowledging Leesie's toast, Wendy offered her own, "To my roomy that saved my life, also gave me a purpose, helped me start loving myself, and brought Andrew into my life."

"Ariana, you were the impetus to all of our growth. Without you being the hub to our spokes, we would all still be trying to figure out our lives. Whether we succeed with this grand plan or not, we are all better people for having you as our friend," Matthew declared.

"I guess it's my turn," Andrew claimed. "I'm not one for speeches, but thank you Ariana for helping me find more happiness than I ever thought possible."

"Amen, and there's nothing I can add to all that except I love you, sista," said Teja.

"I'm new here, but thank you for accepting me and helping me grow," Jason added.

Josh looked concerned. "I feel like an interloper in a large family. All I can say is that I'm hoping one day all of you will feel like I not only belong to this great group, but that I really have something valuable to contribute."

This time, before Andrew could say it, Wendy yelled, "Let's eat!"

Chapter 26

Now that the party was over, Ariana was thinking about what an unbelievable birthday it had been. Wendy had made her the most beautiful quilt in the colors of Meria, Teja bought her some fabulous perfume, Leesie and Jason put a really great music playlist on her iPhone, Andrew bought her a gift certificate to a local clothing store, Matthew made her a suede medicine bag, and Jason had given her a gift certificate to the Wing Stop. After leaving the condo, she and Zach drove to South Mountain to park at their spot.

"I had a heck of a time figuring out what to get you, so I really hope you like what I decided on," he said, handing Ariana a large box, carefully wrapped in purple paper.

When she took it from him, she noticed it was heavy. She looked quizzically in his direction.

"Open it and you'll find out," he chided her.

She felt uncomfortable tearing into the beautifully wrapped present. It was obvious he had taken a lot of care and creativity wrapping it, so she began opening it slowly, hoping not to damage the wrapping paper.

"For God's sake," he exclaimed, "open it!"

Before he could grab it and tear it open himself, Ariana ripped the paper and opened the box. She was very surprised by what it contained. Reaching in, she pulled out a brown, butter leather jacket. It was beautiful and must have been very costly. Ariana looked at him shocked beyond words. Finally, she said, "This had to cost you a few hundred dollars. You can't afford that."

"Well, I had help. My mom and Matthew wanted to contribute, and I actually got a really good deal because it's last year's style. Put it on."

The jacket fit perfectly and was even more comfortable then her denim one. It was so soft, even the inside of the pockets were soft because they were made of suede. She purred with delight. Though her parents had money, they would never have let her buy a jacket this luxurious. She put her hands in the pockets to feel the softness and discovered something wrapped in tissue paper. Pulling it out she turned to Zach and asked, "What's this?"

"I don't know," he lied, his eyes twinkling. "Why don't you unwrap it and see?"

Inside the lavender tissue paper was a pendent in the shape of a heart. There were tiny diamonds in the heart that twinkled even in the low light.

"Oh, Zach, it's beautiful. But all this is way too extravagant."

"I know you wear your crystal all the time, but this is on a shorter chain and shouldn't cause a problem. That is my gift to you, no one helped pay for it."

"Your gift to me is being in my life and loving me," she reminded him. "You have been the kindest, sweetest man. Now you're way too generous, too. You're really making me learn the lesson of accepting graciously. I've never had such a wonderful birthday."

"I love you, Ariana. I want to see you laugh and feel loved. I want you to wear the necklace and jacket so that I can see how beautiful you look in something I provided. You deserve wonderful things."

She began to cry deep sobs. Zach was shocked.

"Are you all right? What did I do?"

It took Ariana a moment to calm herself before she could reply. "I never expected to be loved by anyone, especially a good-looking, sweet person like you. I thought I would go through life alone, hopefully working a career that was fulfilling, but never having a family and probably having few friends. Now everything is like a fantasy. If it's an illusion it's one I'm afraid to lose. Zach, I know you really love me and so do my friends, but you all are counting on me as a leader. You expect me to make us successful. And really, that scares the shit out of me."

Zach knew Ariana was truly scared. Ariana rarely cussed, ever. He had to find a way to convince her that this was not all her responsibility. It was everyone's—not just their group's—but everyone's on the planet.

"It is not about you succeeding or failing or losing anything. It's about everyone, especially people outside our group, wanting things to change. All we can do is inform and show the way and hope others will pick up the banner and run with it. We are lights in the darkness, but we are not The Light. We can offer suggestions and set examples, all of us in the group, not just you. We cannot force the people of this planet to want change and be willing to fight for it. We are not the first on this planet to try to change the world. The others failed because nothing has changed yet. We can only do our best, nothing more. Maybe you and Matt are thought of as the leaders now, but if we are mind linked, then we all will have equal abilities and soon there will be no leaders." Zach cupped Ariana's face in his hands. "Ariana, whether you believe it or not, you're not getting rid of me, no matter what happens."

Snuggling close to him, she replied, "Just hold me for a while, okay?"

"Gladly," he said as he pulled her to him, his arms around her waist, her back tight against his front. She began to relax against him, leaning completely into him. He loved when they sat this way. It made him feel like he was protecting her. He breathed in her scent, so fruity and clean. Sighing deeply, he felt complete contentment and hoped that Ariana did too.

After several minutes she whispered, "Thank you Zach, for just holding me, and not trying to talk or solve things. What you said earlier is right, it's not all on me, but often I feel like it is. It's my thing to deal with and I will, but for now, this feels wonderful."

They sat together, watching the stars. Zach thought about how lucky he was as Ariana marveled at the beauty of this planet. From their view at the top of the mountain they could see Phoenix and the surrounding cities spread out in a beautiful grid of colored lights. It was hard to believe that anything could be wrong with the world. Ariana wanted this night to remain fixed in time, just she and Zach together, bonded in love and calm forever. She was glad that for right now, there was no one else to think about and no responsibilities, only the two of them, lost in time, surrounded by a protective bubble of love and happiness. She savored every moment.

A deep knowing was rising within her. She knew this contentment would be short lived.

Chapter 27

Ariana awoke with a start. At first, she didn't know where she was, or what had awakened her. Then she remembered the dream. She was riding in a small plane talking with the pilot and looking forward to reaching their destination. They had big plans for the evening and a corporate event to attend the next day. They were discussing strategy. The plane seemed to skid in the air, then there was a bump followed by a strange noise. She could see smoke and the instrument panel was going crazy. She felt herself panic as the plane lurched into free fall. Her body was wracked with pain as the plane crashed into a house. She was awake now, but still could not stop her body from shaking. The dream had felt so real.

She looked at her bedside clock. The time was exactly 6:45 in the morning. Ariana wasn't sure why she felt compelled to, but she made sure to write the time down. She wanted to stop thinking about the dream, so even though it was too early for class, she decided to get ready and head to the cafeteria for breakfast.

As she got out of bed she noticed that Wendy was tossing her head and whimpering in her sleep. *Should I wake her?* she thought as she stood watching. The whimpering grew louder. Suddenly, there was a scream.

"No!"

"Wendy, wake up. You're having a bad dream."

Wendy sat up suddenly and stared at Ariana as though she didn't recognize her.

"Ariana," she finally acknowledged, "how'd you know I needed to wake up?"

"You were whimpering and seemed in distress. You even screamed. I just wanted to make sure you were all right."

"I was in distress," she admitted. "I was having the worst dream ever and I couldn't wake up. I was burning and I had to watch my kids die. It was horrible!"

"It must have been one of those nights. I had an awful nightmare, too."

Ariana's phone buzzed.

"Who's calling this early?" Wendy wondered out loud.

"I'll put it on speaker," Ariana said as she answered. "Hello."

"Ariana, this is Leesie. Teja and I just had the weirdest experience that we need to talk to you about. It really freaked us out. Do you have time to listen?"

"Sure. I'm on speaker. Wendy is listening, too. If that's cool, go ahead."

"I just woke up from having a really terribad dream. I watched an airplane crash into three houses and burst into flames. I could hear people screaming and there was nothing I could do. But here's the megaweird of it—Teja had the same dream!"

"What kind of plane?" Ariana asked.

"What? Why does that matter? It was small. I don't know planes."

"Was it a small commercial plane, a small personal plane, or what?"

"I don't know. It was small, like for no more than 10 people small. Why?

"Because I dreamt I was in a plane that crashed into a house."

"Wait, wait," Wendy exclaimed. "The dream you just woke me from, the one where I watched my kids and myself die in a fire, might have been the house the plane crashed into. I was in the bathroom getting the kids dressed. I heard a very weird sound followed by a crash, a big explosion, then fire. It could have been a plane crashing."

"I think you're right, Wendy," Teja answered. "In my dream, I watched the plane crash and then I was on the second floor of a burning house helping a mom and two kids go to the Other Side."

"What's going on?" Leesie whined. "Is it The Darkness playing with us again?"

"It's the mind link, I think," Ariana replied. "Isn't Jason precognitive through dreams?"

"Yes," Leesie said hesitantly, "he told us he's seen some things in the past, but I don't think they were this clear."

"He wasn't as strong before. By linking with us and taking Lydia's classes, I think his powers have increased," Ariana surmised.

"Does that mean all of us got this dream in some way or another?" Wendy asked.

"I don't know," Ariana admitted. "Let's call the guys and find out. After we've reached each of them, let's have a group call. I'll call Zach and Matthew. Wendy, you call Andrew. Leesie, call Jason. Anyone know how to get ahold of Josh?"

"Teja and I do," Leesie said. "We'll call him. Do we find out if they had a dream or wait until we're all connected?"

"Let's just get everyone on a group chat."

"Laters," Leesie said as she hung up.

Ten minutes later they were all connected. "Well," Ariana said, "you guys are probably wondering why we are doing this at 7:15 in the morning. We girls have a question for you guys. How was your sleep last night?"

Zach was the first to answer, "Terrible for both Matt and me. We both had some awful dreams."

"It's been a long time since I had one of my 'special' dreams," Jason said, "but last night I had the most vivid, intense one yet."

"Me, too," Andrew replied. "I had a clear, very disturbing nightmare. My first one since I was a child."

"Tell me what you dreamt about," said Ariana.

Almost simultaneously they replied, "A plane crash and a fire."

"All of you saw a plane crash?"

"No, I saw a house on fire. Somehow, I knew there was a woman and two kids inside. I wanted to run in and save them, but Tara was with me and she told me it was too late, that it was her job now," Matthew stated sadly.

"I was flying the plane that fell from the sky. We fell onto three houses, but one suffered the most damage," Zach said, obviously disturbed by what he had witnessed.

"I was observing from a distance," Andrew said.

Josh agreed, "Me too. I was around the block, and when I heard the explosion, I ran there but it was too late to do anything."

"I was there from the beginning. I watched the three people board the plane. They were on their way to a corporate event. One of the men owned the company. I watched what happened to them. Then suddenly, I was in the house with the woman. They didn't die right away. I hope

Tara is successful at taking them to the Other Side. No one was responsible for what happened, it was truly an accident," Jason told the group.

"Why did we all dream this? Can we stop the crash from happening?" Wendy asked, obviously affected by what they had all seen.

Jason answered first, "From past experience, I would say no. Usually the event happens within hours. Although I know the plane took off from South Carolina, I don't know where it was going, the flight numbers, or the people's names. No one would take that kind of information seriously. Now you know why this kind of experience has always left me feeling helpless."

"I think it has already happened, probably around the time we dreamed it," Matthew said. "Remember, Tara told me it was too late to help them. I'm going to assume that meant they were already dead or about to be. Jason, I understand why you felt helpless in the past but now we all have the tools to help situations like this by helping the people involved go to The Light instead of getting stuck in limbo."

"I'll look," Josh offered.

"Aren't you talking on your computer?" Leesie asked.

"One of them," Josh replied as he pulled back and displayed the room he was in. One wall was covered in computers and very large monitors.

"Whoa dude, you're one serious computer geek," Andrew commented.

"Yeah, that and spirituality are my major passions. I kind of inherited my love of computers, though. My dad's Daniel Rogan."

"**The** Daniel Rogan?" Leesie asked astonished.

"Who's Daniel Rogan?" Teja asked.

"He invented a computer program language that revolutionized the way computers work. He was only 24 when he became one of the world's youngest self-made millionaires," Leesie answered. "No wonder you got to travel all over the world and back. Aren't your family philanthropists?"

"Yeah, they're part of Buffet's Giving Pledge."

"What's that?" Andrew asked.

The Giving Pledge is a commitment by the world's wealthiest individuals and families to dedicate the majority of their wealth to philanthropy."

"How much is the majority?" Matthew asked.

"In my family's case, 80%. They also followed Warren's lead in that they will leave no inheritance to their children. They will pay for my schooling, and some of my living expenses, but they expect me to make my own way in the world. They also do not interfere in my life. If I want to be a dishwasher or a monk, they believe it's up to me."

"How did you pay for all that computer equipment?" quizzed Teja.

"Some of my father's abilities rubbed off on me. About three years ago me and a friend wrote a program that was bought by a company. We both made a bit of money. That's what I've been living on and how I've been able to spend a year traveling and trying to find myself."

"Well people, I think we've found our tech person," Ariana announced.

"Yeah. Bless you Josh, now it's not all on me," Leesie said, sounding relieved.

"I found it," Josh announced. "It just came on CNN. I'll quote the article, "A pilot, also CEO of a research firm, who survived a similar mishap in 2010, was among six people killed in Litchfield on Monday when a twin-engine plane crashed into a subdivision. Marie Randall and her son, Cole, 3, and her daughter, Devon, an infant, were found in the second-floor bathroom of one of the houses struck by the plane, said Pete Sperrling, public information officer for Litchfield County Fire and Rescue."

"Wow," Andrew said.

"Does it say what time it happened?" Ariana asked.

"The impact happened at 6:44 this morning."

"I woke up from my dream at 6:45," she stated almost woodenly.

"Looks like we were seeing it as it happened," Josh agreed.

"But why?" Wendy asked. "If there was nothing we could do and Tara was already there helping, why did we get the information?"

"Maybe Tara wouldn't have been there if we hadn't been," Matthew suggested.

"I don't think that's it," Jason said. "I think it has more to do with our developing mind link. I also think that eventually we will get things we can do something about."

"I don't like this," Teja complained. "I hate feeling helpless!"

"Maybe that's part of it," Zach replied. "We need to be witnesses and understand that we are not totally responsible for another soul's choices. Maybe this is about us understanding what we can and cannot do and what we are really responsible for. I know that both Ariana and I have been driving ourselves crazy thinking about what if we fail. Maybe this is to show us that some things just have to happen."

"Yeah," Andrew said. "Maybe it's like Wendy's brother's soul choosing to die so that she would come to group and get together with the rest of us."

"What?" Wendy asked. "Explain."

"Well, you were a pretty together kid before it happened, right? You had friends, 4-H, goals, and a really good family life. You wouldn't have needed group therapy. Without group, we would never have met."

"He's right," Matthew said. "Each of us was damaged because of events in our lives. That damage made us stronger than most people, but it also caused all of us to seek help. That's what caused us to meet and come together. We were alike because we all felt weird and messed up and that made us want to find something greater than ourselves. It's really interesting how if you release the emotions attached to the past you can see how the past sets-up the now."

"So you're saying that this horrible crash had a purpose—that we needed to be a part of it to understand that things happen?" Leesie asked horrified.

"Not quite," Matthew answered. "We had to witness it for that reason, but there was a greater purpose for those that are left behind and those that were there to witness. I can't imagine what that is, it's not my lesson, but I'm sure bad things do not happen randomly. I **know** they happen for a purpose, even if I don't know yet what that purpose is."

"Bad things happen constantly. I'm not sure I could take this every night," Teja announced.

"It was never every night for me," Jason assured her.

"But who knows what may happen now?" Leesie replied.

"Are we going to worry about it and let The Darkness sniff out our fear, or are we going to make a plan?" Zach asked.

No one answered him, because no one knew where to go from here.

Finally, Ariana reminded everyone that they needed to go to class and suggested that they each think, meditate, and perhaps come up with some kind of plan to discuss in the next few days.

Chapter 28

After classes, Ariana came back to her room. She wanted to be alone to think and to meditate. It had been a long time since she had been completely alone. She was either with the group, Zach, or Wendy. She breathed in the quiet of the empty room. Ariana enjoyed having a roommate, but she found that she also missed her alone time. Sitting on her bed, she absorbed the positive energy that filled the room. All the laughter, closeness and love, not to mention all the crystals Wendy had decorated with, had penetrated the walls and furniture, and when she opened herself to it, she felt herself relax.

It was time to meditate and talk with the Elders. She felt lost, and she knew the group was looking desperately for guidance. Right now, she had none to give. Ariana hoped the Elders would have the answers she was seeking.

She did her relaxation count down and found herself back on Meria, but this time she was in the Grand Chamber. Standing before her were not just the usual three Elders, but the entire Council of Nine. Some of these Elders were so ancient they remembered the Dark Times because they had lived them.

"You are disturbed."

No beating around the bush, Ariana thought. "Yes, Mother, we are all disturbed and I don't know what to tell the group to help them feel better. Why did we need to witness what happened without being able to do anything?"

"Because those that survived need your attention. You must help them to see that there was no fault in this. They will be angry and want to take that anger and focus it somewhere. That negative energy can spark violence. There was another child in that family, an important child. This child has the potential of using this trauma to do something meaningful for the planet or he can choose to become bitter and lost. Which way he goes will depend largely on how the remaining parent handles his grief.

If he withdraws from the child, or treats the child angrily, he will do irreparable damage and the child will be lost."

"How can we possibly do anything to cause the father to respond in a positive way toward this child? How can we begin to help him understand why this horrible thing happened to his family when we don't understand?"

"All the events that happen in life are not random, they happen in order for the ego to have the opportunity to make choices. Whatever is chosen then creates paths that contain more choices and all those choices create growth and learning. If one chooses one path, it will create choices completely different than if another path had been chosen. Do you understand this?"

"I think so."

"The different paths have different consequences and different end results. One path may create harmony and success, another pain and unhappiness. Ariana, you understand that humans have guidance from the spirit realm?"

"Yes, we call them guides," she answered. "As I was growing up, I talked with them when I was scared and lonely."

"No, you talked with us. We supported your learning and your growth. We helped you to develop empathy and we helped you come into some of your abilities while you were growing. Guides do not do this thing for the humans."

"What do guides do then? I'm really confused."

"Guides are the messengers of the soul. They are chosen by the soul before the ego is birthed. These beings are there to act as celestial best friends and advisors. They understand what the soul intent for that lifetime is and which will be the best path to reach this intent. They work to help direct the ego onto that path and keep it there. However, as you well know, humans have free will and if they choose to disregard their guides, and most do, that is understood, even though as we said before, the path may then be harder. But when humans listen and follow the guide's advice, life is usually easier and flows more perfectly. Most humans mistakenly think that all guides are in spirit. This is not true. Many guides are physical. These are the friends, mentors, teachers, pets—the beings that make an important impact on a person's life—then leave. They were there for a brief moment, but their impact will remain for the entirety of the ego's life on Terra. Your group is to be the guides for the child that was left behind."

"Wait a minute," Ariana cried, "we don't live anywhere near there. It's practically the other side of the planet!"

"Now you are thinking three dimensionally. Did we not appear to you physically when you were young?"

"I guess sometimes, but not often," she admitted.

"Did not Matthew accomplish this same feat even before he was as energized as he is now?"

"Yes."

"You can do that, too. One of you can go to the father and comfort him, first as non-physical, then eventually perhaps appearing physically. The boy, however, must see whoever will take on the task of being his guide. That is a huge commitment, so it must not be taken lightly."

Ariana was still puzzled, "But where are his guides?"

"This child, although only twelve years of age, is part of your group. That is why it must be one of you. He will be developing right along with the group, but he will not have the obvious connections to know what is happening."

"Does this sort of thing happen often?"

"Throughout the planetary history, you will find recorded accounts of angelic beings coming to guide humanity. Because in the past people were very superstitious, it had to be in this way that guides contacted and helped humanity. Just as your Matthew appeared within a light, so did those beings. Humanity thought they were angels. That was good because it did not create fear and those humans would accept the teachings, often going on to teach others. That is how you must appear to the father, as angelic."

"What? Why me? Why can't Tara do it or couldn't she talk to the wife and have her do it?"

"What do you fear, Ariana?"

"That I'll fail," she replied immediately.

"What do you fear?" the Elder asked again.

"I just told you!"

"What do you fear?" they asked again.

Ariana was frustrated. What did they want from her? She told them that she couldn't bear the idea of failing. Why wouldn't they believe her?

Is that really why? She wondered. She searched deep inside and understood suddenly that was only one of the reasons. She realized the real reason was that she knew she would have to embrace the father's immense pain to truly understand and empathize with him. It was hard enough to bear witness to what had happened to his family, but to feel all the horrible emotions that come with grief would be overwhelming for her.

She gasped, "I can't do it."

"Yes you can, and you will," was their response. "You will help this man to heal."

"How do I keep the pain away?"

"You don't," the Elder replied. "Feeling the pain means that you are empathically linked to this man. With this link there is no judgement, only love. In this way you will be as the Source is—pure love. As humanity grows into consciousness, they too will realize the empathic connection to all things, and that realization will bring about worldly enlightenment. Your group witnesses events in order to help the aggrieved and grow the empathic link. This link will help create the 100th monkey effect. When humanity cares, understands, and loves more than it fears, the dark will be forever eradicated. You are the forerunners of this cycle of caring, so if you cannot conquer your fears, then Terra is doomed."

Ariana felt herself awaken from her deep meditation with a jerk. Nothing in her room had changed—it was still filled with loving energy. But she felt cold and scared. With each new growth, the feeling of responsibility became more overwhelming.

"Quit thinking that you are alone," she heard the Elders say in her head. "You have hundreds of thousands of people growing aware. As they become more activated they will become more desirous of helping create the change. All you need to do is begin the process."

Even though Ariana did not necessarily feel more confident and assured knowing that everything was not on her shoulders alone, she knew she had no choice but to move forward. She could not let her personal fears call to The Darkness and destroy all the good they had already begun.

She typed out an e-mail to the group explaining why they had witnessed the tragic event and where they must go from here.

No more fear and doubt, she pledged to herself. *We can do this! We have to.*

Chapter 29

Jason had never talked to the group about what happened to his Dad. For that matter, he had never talked to anyone about it. He wasn't sure why. Maybe he wasn't over it. He was only twelve when his father died suddenly in a car accident. One moment he was trying to get Katie Alan to pay attention to him in choir practice and the next minute his world as he knew it came to an end.

His Dad had been his soccer coach, scout leader, golf teacher, and best friend. Jason didn't know how he got through those first few days. He only remembered the excruciating pain and confusion. How could his strong, vibrant father be dead? His family had gone camping with a group of friends just the weekend before. There had been over thirty people in the group. His dad cooked breakfast and dinner both days for everyone. He helped them all set up and tear down and even chopped wood for the huge campfire. He was so strong, healthy and young. How could he die?

Day after day Jason walked around in a gray fog of disbelief. He kept waiting for his father to walk through the door and tell him it was all a joke. Sometimes he even thought he saw him walking up ahead or in the grocery store, but when he ran to the person, it was always someone else. And again, Jason felt the devastation of loss.

Around his mother he acted as though everything was fine. She was little more than a zombie at first anyway, so she couldn't see the lie. He had to feed her and dress her half the time as she dissolved into a deep depression. Eventually she coped with the loss by running from the pain, going from one romance to another. Now she pretended everything was fine, thinking that he wouldn't see the lie. From the moment his father died he felt as though he lost his mother, too.

His father's death created a severe lack of money for the family. There was no life insurance and only his mother's meager salary and the small amount he got from Social Security Survivors Benefits to support them. He did odd jobs in the neighborhood to help out and as soon as he could, he got a job. He still felt somehow responsible for his Mom—that was until this past weekend at Lydia's. Now he wasn't sure what he felt. That made him sad because he knew that both of them had coped in the only way they knew how, and in doing so, had somehow pushed each other away.

The day Jason found out his father was dead he stopped being a kid. Children live in a magical world where nothing really bad ever happens. All you need to feel safe is to run home to mommy. But on August 29th, 2009, Jason became a man. He stopped believing the world was safe. He no longer found safety or even solace through his mother.

When he received Ariana's e-mail explaining why they witnessed the plane crash, Jason knew this was the reason he had become precognitive. He had to act as the guide for this other twelve year old who was experiencing the same hell he had six years ago. Jason knew his empathy for this child would allow him to convince the now motherless boy that he understood his pain and could help. A thought flickered in his mind, *Perhaps this experience will help me understand more deeply my own pain and confusion.*

Jason wanted to talk to his guides or Ariana's Elders before he told the group about his own life and why he felt it was necessary for him to fill this role. He needed their guidance so that he could better understand why this was so important to him and the possible consequences if he messed up. He was so new to all this. Until very recently, he'd never even meditated, much less communicated with his guides. Jason realized he was scared, but he was also determined. He knew he needed to do this for both the boy and himself.

Sitting on the floor of his bedroom he prepared to meditate by breathing deeply and trying to relax his body. His shoulders were always tight, so he began by feeling them loosen up. He remembered to surround himself with God's White Light of protection and mentally called to his guides. Nothing happened so he continued to breathe deeply and relax. Relaxing his back, neck, and arms, followed by his butt, legs, and feet, he finally allowed his concentration to focus on calm. Jason focused his attention on this feeling of calm and envisioned himself on a small catamaran in the middle of a placid, aqua blue lake. He felt himself lying on the deck looking up and watching geese as they flew over a cloudless, periwinkle sky. He could never remember feeling this content before.

"Hello, Jason." It was a voice he never expected to hear again.

Sitting next to him was his father, looking exactly as he had the last time Jason saw him. *This can't be real*, he thought.

"I am here, but real? Well, that depends on what you think real is," his father responded to his thought.

"But you're dead and have been for over six years."

"Yes, I am dead, but I am not gone. Only my body is. My energy continues. Isn't that what you spent the weekend learning?" his father asked.

"I get what you're saying, but if you could do this all along—come back and talk to me—why didn't you? I needed you so many times, but you just weren't f'ing there! Mom fell apart. She was useless. I felt like she was purposely running from me. I had no one, nothing, and I didn't know what to do. I was so scared and angry. Why did you die? Why did you leave us?"

"We all die when our allotted time is up. There's no way out of that. That's one of the things that are nonnegotiable. The soul choses and there's no free will there. I knew you were angry and scared, so was your mother. She wasn't running from you. She was running from the pain and all the staggering responsibility and problems. She never wanted to be a single mom and didn't know what a teenage boy needed. She knew how much you loved me. She and I often talked about how if we separated, you would never want to live with her. She knew you wished it had been her that died, not me. She wished that herself. She loves you very much and has spent every day since I died scared that you would be next. I can't tell you how to feel, but please try to understand that I would never have caused this pain for either of you if I could have prevented it. Both your mother and I love you very much.

There are lots of reasons why I didn't come to you sooner. I wasn't ready. When you die, there is a period of reflection. Not only must you review all that you did and didn't do while you were alive, you must feel what those you left behind are feeling. Your pain was too much for me. I'm a coward. Feeling your raw, intense emotions was crippling. I understood that even if I did come to you, you weren't ready to understand or believe that it was really me, so I waited. I watched you growing and evolving, and I continued to wait. You have grown in so many wonderful ways and I am very proud of the man you have become. But you have never really dealt with my death. I was frightened that if I came to you, I would do you more harm than good."

"Why now then?" Jason exploded. He was still not ready to forgive.

"Because now it is time for you to guide another young boy and you cannot do this until you are resolved within yourself. Guides must be impartial. They must guide, not lead. They must love you enough to allow you your own path. They can nudge, suggest, teach, answer, and encourage, but they may not alter the ego's freewill. The hardest thing for a parent to do is allow their child to grow in their own way. To watch the child stumble or fall or choose a path of misery is exactly what a good parent must do without interfering or judging. Through their child's struggles the parent learns and grows, too. A parent cannot alter a child's path—they can only advise and teach. Being a guide is much like being a parent. You will learn and grow and fear and cry over the choices this child makes, but you will not be able to alter his path. I came to help you come to terms with your loss so that you will not project your feelings onto him. This is an important child. Guide him well and he will be very significant to your group."

"How?"

"That's not part of my story so I don't know the details. I was told to tell you that, and that's all I know."

"Told by who?"

"His guides."

"Are you one of my guides?"

"No, I'm your father. My connection runs too deep to be a guide. I couldn't be impartial. Loved ones have more constraints even than guides, otherwise we will continue to develop karma. Most parents are meddlers. They want to run their children's lives, so we aren't allowed to act as guides," Jason's father said with a sad smile.

"Can you at least tell me why Mom and I had to go through this? Why'd you have to die?"

"Look at you, Jason. You are strong, responsible, caring, and loving. The man you have become is amazing. Would you be that same man if I hadn't died? We can never know for sure, but I don't think so. Every person is an accumulation of their experiences, decisions, and the results of those decisions. All the scars you carry define who you are.

With different scars, you might have chosen a different path. I kinda like the path you're on now. You will make a difference."

"But how do I help this other kid? I'm scared."

"I can't answer that question. All I can say is that I love you and I am always with you. It's time for me to go now. You can do this. Oh, and Jason, please be kind to your mother."

Chapter 30

"We need to discuss where we go from here and who's going to be the boy's guide," Ariana said to the group who had gathered at Tara's condo. "Winter break starts the end of next week, and for those of us who will still be here, it's a good time to brainstorm on how to proceed next. I know we'll be busy with finals, so let's start deciding things now."

"Who's staying in town?" Andrew asked.

"Well, Wendy, Jason, Leesie, and Teja live here. Matthew, Ariana, and I plan to stay in town so that only leaves Josh, and you, Andrew," Zach said.

Leesie raised her hand tentatively, and looking slightly embarrassed, replied, "I won't be here part of the time either. My family owns a second home in the White Mountains and we go there to ski during winter break."

"I have to go home for Christmas, or wherever my parents are at that time, but it won't be the entire three weeks," Josh said.

"I'm only going home for a week. I don't want to leave my foxy lady alone too long. Can't take a chance on losing her," Andrew answered, lovingly squeezing Wendy in a one-armed embrace, his other arm supporting the hand that was busy helping him eat the Christmas cookies Teja and Leesie baked for the gathering.

A look of concern on her face, Lessie asked, "What are you three doing for Christmas?"

"We'll think of something," Matthew assured her. "No worries."

"Well, you can come to my house for Christmas dinner," Wendy offered.

Ariana smiled lovingly at her considerate roommate. "Even though I was raised Jewish, I know that Christmas is family time." Looking at the group she continued, "You guys are my family, so I want to spend my time with you, and if only Zach and Matthew are available, then we'll have our own Yule celebration."

"I've got an idea," Leesie declared enthusiastically. "Why don't we have our own celebration on New Year's Eve? We can celebrate both holidays at the same time. Ring in the New Year with presents!"

"I'll only do group presents if we have to make them ourselves," Teja replied. "Some of us aren't rolling in money."

Ariana agreed, "Making something special for each other is a wonderful suggestion. You will be filling the present you make with your own wonderful energy and loving thoughts. I think it's a perfect idea."

The rest of the group was in complete agreement. Ariana and Matthew explained that if they meditated on each member of the group while trying to figure out what to create for them, perhaps their guides would show them. That made the project another psychic exercise.

"Are we avoiding talking about the crash?" Jason asked.

The group looked surprised, but realized they probably had been avoiding the inevitable.

"Death is a really painful topic, but sudden, tragic death is the worst. I know this pain first hand. A little over six years ago that's how I lost my dad," Jason confided to the group.

Everyone quietly waited for him to continue.

Taking a deep breath, Jason explained, "I went to school as usual one morning and mid-way through chorus the principal came for me. The news crushed me. My Dad was my best friend and mentor. I loved him almost insanely, almost as though I knew he would be gone one day. I didn't even get to say goodbye because he always had to leave for work before I got up." Jason fought to hold back tears. Leesie went to him, putting her arms around him. She rocked him while suppressed tears flooded his eyes and steamed down his face. As he cried, the group surrounded him, holding him both physically and psychically. He cried until he had no more tears. Then he began again.

"I'm sorry. I guess I still have a lot of pain. I've never told anyone else before. I stayed away from the friends I had before my dad's death and I didn't allow myself to make new friends in case they asked where he was. Somehow it was as though sharing my pain would be the final thing that took my dad from me. My mom and I haven't even talked about it. But now I understand that this is the time for me to share and allow myself to become a true part of this family. I have to be the mentor for this kid. I understand what he's experiencing and what he'll face as the shock wears off. I need this for my own healing too, I think. I know it will hurt like hell and that I will experience my pain as well as his, but I can do this and even if you all say no, I'll do it on my own."

Leesie hadn't moved from his side. "It looks to me like this is Jason's job, why he was brought to us from the get go and why he has his abilities. Right?"

"I agree," Matthew said. "Has anyone else in the group lost a parent suddenly?"

Ariana seemed concerned, "Are you sure you can handle this? The pain of their feelings will be horrible. I'm afraid and I don't have the same pain you do, Jason."

"It's because I need to deal with my own terrible memories that I know I can do this," Jason replied. "I can't let another kid go through years and years of this pain alone. When I first found out about this psychic stuff I tried to reach my dad—nothing happened. I also tried to reach my guides—failed again. But yesterday my dad showed up, just sitting right there next to me on the floor. He told me I had to do this and that he and my guides would now help. He explained a whole lot of interesting stuff to me. I sent it all to your emails right before I got here today just in case I freaked and couldn't tell you guys about his death. That way you would come to me and ask and I'd have to open up. I guess that was a little wussy, but I knew I would have no choice after that. Oh, he said the reason we witnessed the kid's tragedy, besides me needing to help him, is because he's one of the group and he's here to do something special."

"Well, that makes things even more complicated. Are you sure you can be impartial enough to work with this kid," Andrew asked, "especially if you're not completely healed yet?"

"All I can do is try and also talk with each of you about what I'm doing," Jason replied. "If I feel myself falling apart I'll get your help."

"But by then it will be too late cause the kid will already be dependent on you," argued Andrew. "He's vulnerable now and couldn't take it if his guardian angel vanished too."

"Then I won't let it happen," Jason promised resolutely. "Matthew, because you can walk between the realms, will you work with me to keep me on track?"

Matthew thought about his answer, "Sure, man, I think you can do this. Actually, I think you have to, so I'll be there whenever you need me. Ariana what do you think?"

"I think he can do it," she replied. "I think that's one of the reasons he was led to us. The question is, can I? This is all so new to me. I've never been close to my father. He wasn't much of a role model. On Meria I had no father. How am I going to help this man be a good dad to his son?"

"Work with Jason," Matthew said. "His dad must have been stellar if he found it so hard to release the pain after his father's death."

Ariana turned to Jason, "Well, looks like we're going to need to help each other. Are you up for it?"

"Yup," Jason declared without hesitation.

The group spent the rest of the evening divvying up assignments, eating cookies, and planning New Year's Eve.

Chapter 31

Ariana and Jason sat out on the quad, lazily basking in the sun. Even though it was mid-December, the sun was warm and bright. They had decided to get together to make a plan about how they would approach this new assignment. If they needed to work together then it was important that they decide on a complimentary approach.

"Tell me about your father," Ariana said. "What did he do that was so wonderful?"

Jason was quiet for so long Ariana wondered if he had heard her. He appeared deep in thought. She decided he was remembering.

Eventually it was as though he woke up from a deep slumber. He smiled and answered her question. "My dad was awesome. He always seemed interested in me. He listened to everything I said, no matter how silly my conversations were. After all, how deep can a six year old be? I can't remember a time when he didn't take me seriously or encourage me to do anything I thought was important. Before he or Mom punished me for something, they would discuss with me why I did what I did and why they must give me a punishment. Even when I was as young as three, they let me give them input into my punishments. I never felt as though they were trying to hurt me. I also knew they were really looking out for me, not just trying to control me.

Dad was interested in everything I did. He learned soccer so that he could coach my team. He was my Cub and Boy Scout leader, he taught me about rockets, trains, and anything else that was neat and interesting. We'd play Xbox for hours as long as I also did something that took me outside or educated me. I always knew how much he loved me because he told me and showed me every day. We were always laughing and he was really affectionate and nurturing. He was also very giving. At Christmas, our house would be full of people. He would invite anyone who didn't have family to come and enjoy Christmas dinner with us. For anyone who couldn't come for dinner we would create fabulous desserts to share later. One year we made a huge gingerbread train that we filled with candy and took to the children's hospital. The following year he cooked Thanksgiving dinner for an entire homeless shelter. Another year we made about twelve different kinds of cheesecake and delivered them to all my friends' families. He was extremely creative, caring, and giving. Christmas was wonderful in our home.

My dad took care of everything. He couldn't let anyone or anything suffer. At one point we had 15 cats and 8 dogs because he didn't want them to be killed or left on the streets to starve. He gave away money as though we could live without it. All you needed was a good sob story. That's why we were in such bad shape when he died, because he always thought there would be more tomorrow. But one day, tomorrow didn't come."

"Wow, I can see why his loss was so hard for you. In your young eyes, he was bigger than life," Ariana said.

"Not just my eyes," Jason declared. "After he died, more than two hundred people came to our house to celebrate his life."

"So, what do I say to this kid's father? Any suggestions?"

"Yeah, I've been thinking about this. Is there a way to read the father and the son's minds so we can see how they're doing first?"

"I'm not sure, but I think there must be. Before you were with the group Matthew got himself into a pretty desperate state. We didn't know how to help him, but then Tara entered Matthews's illusion and saw what he was experiencing—like she was in his head watching his hallucination. If she could see that, I don't see why we can't do the same thing—sort of enter their minds and figure out what's going on with them, an advanced form of telepathy."

"How'd she do it?"

Ariana replied, "When I was working on forgiveness I concentrated really hard during a meditation on my dad. Suddenly, it was as though I could see things as he did. I began to experience his past and understood how he perceived it and how that created his current reality. It was very hard to hate him after that. I think that must be something like what she did. Why couldn't we do the same thing? First, we'll project ourselves to where they are and just observe them. As we watch them, we can concentrate very hard on who they are and how they're acting. I think the next step may just happen automatically. It's worth a try at least. You want to try it right now?"

"How do I know where they are?" Jason asked, worried he'd end up in some kind of permanent limbo.

"You don't need to know, you just need to get to your calm place in meditation, then think of them. At least that's what I did last time. Make sure you are very calm and feeling loved and loving. If you're scared, they might pick it up and be scared, too. I don't know that for certain, but if we can feel them it only makes sense that they can pick-up things from us too. Ready?"

"I'm going to have to really work on that calm thing, cause right now, I'm really, really scared," Jason admitted.

"Do you want me to go with you this first time?"

"Wow, can you? I do think having someone more experienced with me may help," Jason replied, genuinely relieved.

"It's worth a try. Let's face each other with our knees touching and holding hands."

When they were in position, Ariana continued, "Now let's breathe deeply while focusing on each other's eyes and surrounding ourselves with God's White Light of love and protection. Feel content and fill yourself with feelings of joy, love, and peace."

Both Jason and Ariana sighed as they felt the wonderful feelings engulf them. They closed their eyes simultaneously. "Now, from this calm place, think of the boy. A name isn't necessary. Just allow your essence to seek his."

Ariana could feel Jason straining to send himself in search of the boy. She remembered that at Lydia's he'd said that leaving his body was hard for him. *I guess I'll need to help,* she thought as she projected her consciousness into Jason's mind. She felt his body jerk as it perceived Ariana as an invasion. She sent calming, loving energy into his mind, and his body stopped its reaction. It had recognized her essence and his gatekeepers, the guides used for protection against intrusion, allowed her to be present.

Breathe deeply Jason, he heard Ariana say in his mind, *and relax. There really isn't anything to be frightened of. Your gatekeepers and your father are here protecting you and no harm will come to you, and you will cause no harm to the boy. Think with me now. Allow your thoughts to be only of him.* She felt a shift in Jason's energy from fearful to inquisitive. Her presence had calmed him and he was ready to do the work. She allowed her inner being to follow Jason's lead.

They were in a brightly lit room. There were people everywhere dressed in suits and dresses. The mood was somber. In the front of the room were three caskets, two small white ones, and a larger walnut one. Sitting next to each was a picture of a person. Ariana and Jason approached the caskets reverently knowing that there were also three spirits observing the occasion.

Where's Tara? Jason wondered.

Hush, Ariana thought as they walked to the egos.

Approaching the mother, Ariana thought about what they were hoping to do to help the boy and the woman's husband. Immediately she felt relief emanate from the female and decided to reach out to her. *Tell us about your family. We could use your guidance on how to approach them and help them.*

The woman gathered her two young ones close to her and shook her head yes.

Please tell me about your husband and son, Ariana thought.

Suddenly, Ariana felt like she was in a darkened movie theatre, the dead mother's memories playing on the screen. When she first began to observe the memories, it felt weird, as though she was living someone else's life. But the feeling changed from observer to participant. Like her experience thinking about her father, Ariana actually felt as though she was this woman. She perceived the deep love she had for her husband and the pride she felt in all her children especially her older one, Richard, who was named after his father. She realized that little Richard went by the initials RJ to differentiate him from his father. Ariana watched as the father and son interacted in a way she had never experienced in her family. Ariana was also made aware of the protective, loving nature of the young RJ. Even as a toddler he was a very sensitive, loving child who loved to cuddle. When the twins were born, a boy and a girl, he took his responsibility as the older brother quite seriously. Even though he was barely eight years old, RJ took wonderful care of his mother during her pregnancy with his younger siblings. Ariana could feel this mother's anguish, guilt, and pain at having left this wonderful son and husband behind to suffer so greatly. Ariana surrounded the trio with her aura of purple and gold light and assured them that in no way was any of this their fault. There was no way the events could have been prevented.

God is not punishing you. God does not want you to be in pain, Ariana communicated to the mother and children as they continued to be surrounded by the beautiful light. Ariana turned her focus to the loving White Light the pained souls needed to go to.

She communicated to the woman, *You must turn to The Light. Allow yourself to feel the love coming from this source. Once you enter The Light you will not only heal yourself but will be able to help your surviving family and friends. Staying in this in-between state will only continue to cause pain for your family left behind. Your children that are with you will suffer. You must not remain here.*

The woman seemed very confused and torn.

Ariana searched for an idea to convince the mother to cross over.

Why don't we see if we can make a deal with her? It was Jason speaking to her telepathically. *We can tell her we are here to help her son and husband, and if she remains, we will be unable to. We know she doesn't want to cause them anymore harm. We need to emphasize to her that they will not hear or see us if they are concentrating on her.*

How can we prove that?

Jason immediately replied, *We help the boy to have one moment of peace. That will show the mother that we really can help him.*

Oh, I get it. She instantly knew what Jason was proposing as their mind link allowed her to read his thoughts. *Let's go for it.*

Jason approached the woman and lovingly coerced the bargain—if he and Ariana could give either the father or the son one moment of peace, she would go to The Light. As soon as the bargain was struck, Tara appeared. Bathed in a golden light and back-lit by the most beautiful white light imaginable, they were awe struck. The light created a vibration of peace, love, and acceptance.

The group became aware that the people at the funeral had become quiet. The teenage boy and his father rose from the front row of seats and approached the three caskets.

It's now or never, Ariana communicated to Jason.

Holding hands, they approached the duo, extending their glowing auras and God's light of love and peace to surround the two family members. At first all Ariana could feel was their pain. Then, almost miraculously, she felt the young boy reach for his father's hand and say,

"They're not here, Dad. These are only caskets. They are safe and in a place filled with love. Don't let them look down and feel our sadness, instead let them feel all the love we hold in our hearts."

The father looked at his son and Ariana could hear his thoughts. He wondered how his son could be so old and so wise at only twelve. Ariana sent him a message, *He is an old soul who is here to make a difference. Help him. Be the loving, strong father and friend he will need over the coming months. Reach inside and trust that you are receiving help for your pain from the Divine Source of all love.* She could feel and hear the widowed father's thoughts and emotions. He was torn. A part of him was still angry, feeling that God had let him down. But deep below that feeling was a loving father and husband that needed to believe.

Ariana looked to where the three souls had stood and realized they had gone into The Light. Only Tara remained, her radiant smile directed at Jason and her. They had succeeded. They had taken the first step toward helping this family.

Chapter 32

Jason felt high all day. He should have been working to bring in some extra money, but after his wonderful success that morning, he was way too hyper to be driving around delivering chicken wings or working behind the counter. He hiked North Mountain and then sat in a ramada enjoying the spectacular views.

His growing hunger led him to the Hamburger Palace. He hadn't noticed that he was ravenous, but as he ate his burger, he realized nothing had ever tasted and smelled this good before. His food tasted amazing, like each of his taste buds had awakened. All the different flavors were distinct and individual, especially the tomato and lettuce. He had never really appreciated salads. His preference always had been meat and potatoes, but now he was enjoying the crunch and crispness of the lettuce. He realized how full of liquid this vegetable was as he enjoyed the earthiness of its flavor. The tomato was exquisite. He took it out of the bun and appreciated its various colors and textures. He realized the skin was a strong membrane that held the squishy pulp and seeds together. There were at least three distinct colors in this slice of tomato: the bright red of the skin, almost white of the pulp, and yellow-orange seeds. Why hadn't he notice these things before? Each of these components that made up this fruit was different, too. The skin was smooth and taut while the pulp was wet and flavorful. When he bit into a seed there was a distinctly different taste and texture. How could such a small fruit be so complex? How many other foods had he just gobbled down without appreciating how wonderful and diverse they were? He felt more alive than he ever had. Everything was more vibrantll the different colors stood out and vibrated, and he was sure he could feel the energy in everything. *How could I have lived in this world for so long and been oblivious to all these wonderful things?*

As Jason savored the rich tastes, he also felt the energy of the food as it entered his system and enriched him. He realized that until right now he had only been existing, one day flowing into the next. He had floated through life doing what needed to be done, but never really seeing or feeling the world around him. Even when his dad was alive, he still was blind to everything but his immediate interests. The world was just a place where you lived and did what needed to be done. Now he realized that the planet was a living, magnificent being, and that everything in it was also living, creating, and returning whatever it took. Just as water moves from the sky to the Earth and back in the hydrologic cycle, oxygen is also cycled through the environment. Plants are the beginning of this cycle because they "breathe" in carbon dioxide and "breathe" out oxygen. Animals, including humans, form the other half of this oxygen cycle, breathing in oxygen to break down carbohydrates into energy, a process called respiration. Carbon dioxide produced during respiration is breathed out by animals into the air, creating a continuous, interdependent circle of life. Without this interconnected system, life could not exist on Earth.

Jason now understood that he, like most everyone else on this wonderful planet, took all this unbelievable complexity for granted and it concerned him. *We ignore the link between us and everything else. That allows us to destroy everything. We think we are superior to the animals, plants, and water, when in reality, we are dependent on them. How in the hell did we become so blind and self-absorbed?*

Walking out of the restaurant, Jason was again overcome by his new senses. Why is everything so intense now? What changed?

Because you are now truly alive, he heard his guide say. This time hearing a guide did not amaze him because with all his new senses so acute it was understandable that hearing them would be easier, too. He realized what this guide was saying was true. Up until now, he was just pretending to be alive. He saw the world around him but it didn't stimulate him. But now his view of the world had gone from black and white to 3D Technicolor and it was glorious!

Jason's sense of smell was more acute, too. He thought he could decipher individual scents and feelings, like the slight moisture in the air. He knew this would allow him to know days in advance when rain was coming. *I'm like a lizard. I can smell where to find the water in this desert. How cool is that?*

The breeze on his skin tickled. *I've never noticed that before. It's like little fingers caressing the hair on my arms.*

The persistent Arizona sunshine also had a different quality. He fully comprehended that even with his eyes closed, he could sense the sunlight and tell what time of year it was, what time of day, and how much pollution there was blocking the light. He could feel his body absorbing the vitamin D and knew that he would be able to tell when his skin was at risk of sunburn, something he had never noticed before.

He knew his senses would tell him when things were wrong in his environment, too. *I'm a living seismometer. Why am I not overwhelmed with all this new stuff?*

Because you are now linked consciously with the planet. She is balancing you.

Realizing he was hearing more voices in his head, he was filled with awe, and decided to clarify who he was hearing. *Are you my guides or Ariana's Elders?*

Immediately he heard the answer: *I am your gatekeeper.*

Jason was astounded. Not only was he conversing with a guide, but now he had the opportunity to get to know his gatekeeper. *Why are you talking to me now when I tried so hard before and nothing happened?*

You were not ready. But now that you are linked with Ariana and her group, you are able to do the things they can do. You have grown from this association. Today you have also allowed yourself to detach from your physical body and become your true self, energy. This allows you to merge your energies with those that surround you because you can sense where your energy begins and ends.

Thrilled by this news, Jason realized he could really contribute to his new group of friends. *I wonder if there's more I can do now that I am beginning to understand energy?*

Yes, now that you recognize both the connection of all energy and where you can be separate from it if you choose, you can begin to manipulate the energy so that where it is depleted it can be strengthened and recharged.

Whoa dude! Jason had never considered he might have such power.

But be careful. It also means that until you can control this ability well, you can give too much or take in too much and harm your physical body. You must learn to control and modulate this flow or you will exhaust yourself and begin to drain others.

That thought stopped Jason in his tracks. Everything had happened so naturally, he hadn't thought about anything but what he was getting from this ability. *No wonder humanity has for so long just taken what it wanted. It's so easy to think only about yourself.*

His gatekeeper responded, *That which comes easily is rarely thought completely through. Abilities have been used without thinking of consequences, dangers, or responsibility for the entirety of the time man has existed on Earth. If you are to be a leader of the coming shift in consciousness, you must live your life from now on with a conscious understanding that you are not alone in the Universe and that everything you do, every act of free will, affects everything else. Always be aware of your actions and what is happening to your world because of your decisions. It has always been such, but now you need to be fully aware and committed to doing no harm.*

I know that I am doing harm when I drive my truck, but I live in a world and a place where I will not be able to do my job without it. My mom is dependent on my paycheck. How do I live in the world as it is with this new knowledge?

You acknowledge to your planet that you are aware of what you do and you attempt to compensate in other ways until the humans become conscious and develop new ways of living.

That sounds like a cop out.

Plant trees to atone for the damage your vehicle is causing. You must live in the world as it is but do what you can to mitigate the damage you are causing. You are not responsible for the damage others are causing. You are only responsible for yourself and helping others to become aware of what's happening to your world. You cannot do everything. After all, you are only human.

The day was still beautiful, bright and vibrant, but Jason now had a lot on his mind. Slipping into his old mindset, he began to feel oblivious to the wonders of energy and the beauty of this world. *It's easy to slip back into old behaviors,* he thought. *Sometimes being only human sucks!*

Chapter 33

"Hi, Ariana, this is Lydia. How are you and your group?"

"We're good. Is everything all right with you?" Ariana asked. It was a little unnerving to get a call from a psychic. She wondered why Lydia was contacting her.

"Sorry if I am disturbing you. I normally don't call clients because it often makes them wonder if I saw something about them and am checking on them. But I was instructed by Equinoxx to call. Please don't be alarmed. There's nothing to be afraid of. They just would like me to invite you and your group and a few of the regular participants to a private channeling on New Year's Eve. That is, if you don't have plans."

"Well, we were talking about having our Christmas celebration on New Year's Eve because we can't all get together on Christmas, but I'm sure we can come up with another plan. Is a special channeling like this normal?" Ariana inquired.

"Actually, not anymore. Years ago, there was a group of us that got together every Friday to work together with them on planetary healing and rescue work."

"Why do you think they want to do this again now?"

"I would be guessing, but I think maybe it's because time is getting shorter and they need to inform us of something," Lydia speculated.

"Couldn't they have just told you and passed a message through you?"

"Ariana, is there a reason you don't want to come?"

That question stopped Ariana in her tracks. Why was she being so difficult? She was sure the group would love to have the opportunity to ask Equinoxx more questions. Why was she fighting this so hard? Why was she being so disrespectful and unkind to Lydia, a person who had been wonderful to them?

"Lydia, I'm sorry. I have no idea what's happening. Maybe I'm scared. If that's it, I don't know why."

"A lot has happened in your life in a very short time. Change is hard no matter what, but also being activated to your psychic nature, learning your purpose, making friends for the first time, and meeting your soul mate is overwhelming no matter who you are or how old. You've accomplished all of this in less than three months. Every time you've been over here, you've been given more alarming information. It makes sense that you would be concerned at the prospect of some more life-changing information," offered Lydia. "Your soul is so old. Sometimes I forget that Ariana is so young."

Ariana was quiet, thinking about what Lydia suggested. Lydia waited patiently.

"You're right," Ariana admitted. "I've had so much to absorb and it's all so overwhelming. I can't really talk to the group about it because I feel as though they think I'm so far ahead of them, like I'm some kind of psychic guru when I'm really just me, a scared girl. I worry that I will disappoint them, fail everyone, and lose the only friendships I've ever known. I know how selfish that sounds when I should be thinking about the work that needs be done, but I've been making myself sick over all this. I thought I was past all this!"

"Ariana, no matter what your purpose and past training in other lives might be, and how much information and power you have received in this life, you are still human. Even Jesus doubted in the end when he asked God why he had forsaken him. Once your soul incarnates into an ego you must live with all things human and physical, which includes doubt, and at times, helplessness. Your soul was kind enough to send you help. I'm not just speaking of your group or the Elders, but also me and the therapist. We are all here to support you. Never feel as though you can't call me and just talk. I would consider it a blessing because I am learning from you, too. You need to understand that there are certain words that are worthless. One of those is the word 'should.' It's a guilt word and is an unnecessary, self-defeating way to think. Feelings and fears are just thoughts. You can surrender to them or talk them through. You can torture yourself or understand that it is normal to have doubts. If you don't let them hold you back, they will keep you humble and careful."

"I know all you're saying is true, but it just feels so overwhelming. Everyone expects me to know what to do about everything, and I feel like they also expect me to be up and positive all the time. Sometimes it's all just too much. Sometimes I'm scared."

"Everyone gets scared," Lydia responded. "And really honey, I would be worried about you if you weren't. We aren't talking about you kids winning a contest or something. We're talking about stopping the potential end of the world. I know that sounds dramatic, but that's the truth in a nutshell. So being scared is a good thing. It will keep you from getting cocky or arrogant. But again, I must remind you, now listen real close, **you are not alone.** You are here to help spread the word and help the others that are activated to understand what's happening and how to use those gifts to begin the consciousness shift. It will still be up to humanity to listen and begin to act. You are just the messengers and teachers."

"What is the consciousness shift?" Ariana asked.

"Let's let Equinoxx talk about that Friday, okay? Are you feeling any better?"

"How do I get over the feeling that the group is depending on me to be the strong, all-knowing, ever happy guru?"

"Well, if it were me, I would have a heart-to-heart talk with them and tell them how you feel. They may surprise you and tell you that it's all in your head, or if you're right, at least you'll be letting them know how you feel. And from there, I'm sure a solution can be found," Lydia answered.

"I know you're right again, but I don't want to let them down," Ariana argued.

"No, you don't want to take the chance of losing your friends. If they truly are your friends, telling them what you feel is doing them a service. If they aren't your friends, pretending to be someone you aren't won't hold the friendship together permanently because there's no real friendship anyway. Think about the people in your group. Do you really believe that any of them would abandon you because you were scared of all this responsibility?"

Ariana thought about the question. She absolutely knew that Zach and Matthew would understand. She was equally sure of Tara, Wendy, Leesie, and Andrew. The question marks in her mind were Teja, Jason, and Josh. Because of her fiery temper, Teja was always a wild card. Jason and Josh were too new to all of this for her to form a complete picture of how they might respond. She knew Jason depended on her knowledge to help him with the boy. Would her fear make him feel uncomfortable while working with her? Josh was so new she wasn't even sure they should trust him yet. Finally, she answered Lydia, "I think the majority of the group would understand."

"Who don't you trust and why?"

Embarrassed to admit that she didn't trust some of her group, Ariana hesitated in her reply. "Well, you know we have two new members, Jason and Josh. I haven't really gotten to know Josh at all and the first time I met him, he bothered me, but I can't really tell you why. That was early in our experience with The Darkness and that day was particularly scary for me. It might not have been him but the whole, unnerving day. I just don't know. Josh feels all right, but it usually takes me awhile to fully trust new people."

"Anyone else?"

God, it's hard trying to be evasive with a psychic.

Ariana decided to come clean. "I've become uncomfortable with Teja. She seems so angry and out of control sometimes."

Lydia chuckled and replied, "Kind of like your dad, right?"

"OMG," Ariana exclaimed, truly shocked by this revelation. "Yes, exactly like my father!"

"Isn't it wonderful how the Universe works? When we have something to work on and we can't really work on it with the person involved, a substitute is often provided. What a great opportunity for you to see and work on an area yet unresolved," Lydia suggested.

"But I thought I had forgiven my father!"

"Yes, I think you have, but that doesn't necessarily get rid of the post-traumatic stress that can be caused living with someone that angry and volatile. Working to help Teja find her peaceful center may help you learn to control your own volatility."

"Me, volatile?" Ariana asked, confused.

"Inside you are the remnants of growing up abused. Those remnants can be activated when the right circumstances occur. When they are activated you are no longer the clear-thinking girl you have forced yourself to become. Instead, you will become your father. The fact that you have not experienced this yet only means two things: you are great at controlling yourself, and you have never had the right circumstances occur. I know for sure that one day these circumstances will happen. So, isn't it wonderful that the Universe has provided you with the opportunity to address your issues through Teja? This will give you the tools you need when circumstances test you. There's a well-supported psychological theory that an abused child will very likely become an abusive adult. You now have the opportunity to prove psychology wrong."

"But what do I do to deal with Teja? I'm really lost here."

"First, reach inside yourself and find the little girl that still rages. That's the Ariana that's angry and wants to strike out. Once you quiet her, the adult will also be at peace. So, will I see you all at the private channeling?"

"I'll contact everyone. I'm sure there won't be a problem. If there is, I'll call you," Ariana said, still wondering how she was going to deal with her new dilemma.

Chapter 34

The talk with Lydia left Ariana completely dismayed. She knew the psychic was right, there was an angry, raging child within her. Even though Ariana now felt loved and accepted she knew that the child in her that never received affection or appreciation was still grieving and bitter. She had forgiven her father's deeds intellectually, but she knew there was still pain on some deeply emotional level, the child's level. *So how do I go about reaching her?*

She tried addressing the child in her mind. *Hello, little Ariana. I'm adult Ariana.* That just sounded ridiculous and completely unhelpful. *What do I do?*

Meditate and talk to her in her time, not this time, Ariana heard one of the Elders suggest.

Ariana thought about the suggestion. She knew that time was an illusion and all things were actually going on simultaneously. Could she really reverse time—or the illusion of time—and as an adult go talk to her child self? Three months ago she would have found this thought preposterous, but with all the phenomenal experiences she'd had recently, how could she think this could be impossible?

Making herself comfortable and banishing all doubt, she began her meditation ritual. This time, however, instead of telling herself that with each descending number she would go deeper within, she said that she would go backward in time. She wanted to go back to age five. For some reason she couldn't fully comprehend, she felt this would be the perfect time.

Number nine, going back to age fifteen. Number eight, going backward in time slowly to age twelve, visualize age twelve, be age twelve. Number seven, I allow myself to be age eleven. Six, I am age ten, I feel myself being age ten. Five, being age nine, laying in the grass and looking at the clouds I am age nine. Four, being age eight. Number three, I am now seven, I feel myself at age seven. Number two, I am six and starting school, I am so excited I am a big girl and getting to walk to school. Ariana could actually feel the excitement of going off to school for the first time. *Number one, I am now age five and sitting on the front porch watching the other kids head for school.*

Ariana could see herself sitting on the porch of the family's first home. She could also feel the five year old's envy and sadness as she watched the neighborhood kids laughing together while she sat alone.

As Ariana watched, the child entered the house and walked into the kitchen. She took paper and crayons off the table, sat on the floor and began drawing squiggly lines on the page.

"What are you making?" Ariana asked out loud.

When the child looked up it was obvious that she had been crying. She looked at Ariana with the biggest, most forlorn eyes and just whimpered. Ariana could decipher no words. *I guess she can't see me or hear me.*

Sitting in front of the child, she tried to send her feelings of love. She reached out her energy and had it firmly rebuffed. *Oh my gosh, she pushed me out!* Ariana tried again, this time more forcefully.

The child looked her in the eye and said, "No!"

Can you see me?

No answer came from the little girl who again began to make the odd little marks across the paper.

I won't hurt you. I want to be your friend. Why are you crying? Ariana thought to the child.

I was going to go to school, but they wouldn't let me, the child answered telepathically. *Nobody likes me, not even Mommy.*

Ariana could feel the pain and loneliness. *I like you. Will you play with me?*

I'm drawing. Can you draw?

Not near as well as you. What are you drawing?

Letters like sister. Who are you?

I'm a friend, Ariana replied.

No friends, the child thought, shaking her head. *Nobody likes me. Nobody will play with me. Mommy's too busy with brother and she won't let me go outside to play with the other little kids. She said to stay in here and be quiet or she'll put me in the basement with the monsters. I don't like the monsters so I stay at the top of the stairs by the door where they can't get me.*

Ariana was shocked almost senseless as the memories of the basement came flooding back to her. She remembered vividly the terror as she sat shivering on the top step of the hard, wooden stairs that led into the basement. Even in the daytime the basement was cold and dark. The small windows, she remembered two, were covered with grime that blocked much of the light. She remembered the noises, too. Sometimes they sounded like scurrying feet, other times there was a deep groaning, and at other times creaking and crunching. Her father told her that a monster lived in the basement and that the monster ate bad children. When her parents thought she had been bad they would whip her with a belt and push her into the basement. She would hurriedly run back up the stairs and huddle at the top. The first few times she banged on the door and pleaded, but no one came to rescue her. She eventually learned that no help would ever come, and that if she was very quiet the monster wouldn't find her. That was the first time Ariana remembered talking to her invisible friends.

You know there aren't really any monsters down there, don't you? Ariana reassured the child. *The noises are only mice, the furnace, and the creaky old house complaining. Anyway, if you are ever down there again, think of me and I'll come be with you.*

The child looked her in the eyes again, *You're beautiful. Are you an angel?*

.Then you can see me? Ariana said in awe.

Yes. You shine. Are you a rainbow? There are so many colors and there's a song, too. The child said as she started humming.

I am here to protect and love you. Ariana, you are beautiful, smart, and one day you will have lots of friends and people who love you.

Speaking, the child said, "No I'm not! My sister is pretty, not me. Mommy and Daddy said so. I'm fat."

You're talking out loud. Let's talk quietly. Come here and sit on my lap.

"Can I?" the child whispered, moving toward Ariana. When she reached her and sat down she began to giggle. "I'm falling right through you!"

Giggling with her, Ariana replied, *Looks like you did. Let's pretend that you are on my lap and I'm hugging you. Can you feel that?*

"Yes," the child whispered with a smile on her face and her eyes closed. "You smell really good."

What do I smell like?

"Like flowers and sunshine and clover," she said, her eyes still closed. "I love your hug."

Sweetie you need to listen to me. You can do things other people can't. They won't understand and will probably make fun of you. It's because they're afraid of what you can do that they can't. I'd tell you not to talk about any of it, but I know you will, so just don't let the other people hurt you. Your oma loves you and I love you, so that will have to be enough for now. Do you understand?

The tears began to flow again. "I don't like it here. I want to go home but don't know how," the child said through her tears.

You remember home?

"I 'member a place that was so pretty with lots of nice people who liked me. There was an ocean and stars and everything was this color," the child said, displaying a purple crayon. "I could hear songs there too, just like your song."

That's because I'm from home, too. That's why I'm here, so that you will know you are loved and also to help you understand that you are different. We will work on some of what you can do later, but for now, talk to Oma. She will help you.

"I have to stay here?" she said plaintively. "But I don't want to!"

Will it help you if I said I, or someone else that's a friend, will come anytime you need us?

"No."

Sweetie, it will have to. I can't stay, and I can't take you with me, but I'll be around you forever. Please trust me. If things get hard just think about me holding you. Think about how much Oma loves you. Now, just close your eyes and pretend I'm holding you again. Feel the love. Can you feel me stroking your pretty hair? Remember you are beautiful and worthy of the love that I feel and that Oma feels for you. Soon your life will become wonderful and you will do amazing things.

The child lifted her head and Ariana saw the tears again. She knew she felt that she was being abandoned. Ariana felt helpless. What could she do? What had her guides done? Suddenly a thought hit her like a pistol exploding near her ear. **She** was the guide. If she hadn't shown up today, would there ever have been a guide, someone else to help her through the hard times? She knew the answer was no. Because the adult-Ariana had done this, the child-Ariana would survive her life with her family. If she hadn't, it was likely her life would have proceeded quite differently. She had forgotten so much of her early life. She only retained bits and pieces before her first year of school. All these years she assumed the high fever she had the four days before her sixth birthday had caused her memory loss. Measles had almost killed her then. It wasn't her illness that wiped out her early memories. She had forgotten because she couldn't know that she would become her own guide. Is this why Lydia suggested she come here to nurture her child self?

Ariana don't cry. I am not abandoning you. During the summer, we will lie together in the sun, making the wisp of clouds vanish or seeing if any of them look like animals. We will read together and learn together and when you are lonely, I will whisper stories in your ear. When you are angry, we will go into the fields and the forest that will surround your new home and we will scream and howl our anger together. Eventually, you will be grown and go far away to a new place filled with blue skies, mountains, cactus, and lots of friends. I promise.

Promise me you won't believe the bad things your family says about you, Ariana continued, looking deep into the child's tear-filled eyes. *Those things aren't true. They don't understand you or know who you are, but when they do, they will be very proud of the things you do.*

"We will be in another house?" little Ariana said sounding elated.

Ariana laughed, thinking that in that entire diatribe, all she heard was there would be a new house.

Yes, honey. Oma will live with you and you'll have a pink room all to yourself.

"I don't like pink! I like blue!"

The petulant five year old was back and the tears were gone. *Was I ever really this strong willed?* That was another thing that vanished once she turned six. She couldn't even remember this version of herself.

"Who are you talking to?" they heard from the doorway.

"My friend," the child answered honestly.

Ariana sat staring at the woman her mother once was: young, slim, blond, and obviously angry.

"Get off the floor!" Mother screamed. "You are such a liar, always making up things."

"But Mommy, it's true. Don't you see her? See, she's sitting right here with me."

Walking rapidly toward her and grabbing her by the collar of her Winnie-the-Pooh T-shirt, she pulled little Ariana to her feet. Shaking her she screamed, "Don't you lie to me girl! Do you want to go into the basement?"

Little Ariana's eyes looked huge as she said, "No Mommy, I'm sorry. I'll be good. I promise."

"Then come with me and be quiet. I just got your brother to sleep and I don't want you to wake him up. Go to your room and take your nap."

"I'm not sleepy. Can't I just stay in here and draw? I promise I'll be quiet," the child pleaded.

"Get your ass to bed now. I'm not going to tell you again," her mother ordered.

With her head down, little Ariana began the short walk to the bedroom she shared with her brother. Reaching the doorway, she turned slightly and gave Ariana a small wave then continued the walk to her room, the ever-present tears shining in her eyes.

With little Ariana out of the room, Ariana stood and observed her mother who had seated herself in a chair. Instead of looking angry, she seemed exhausted and depressed. This was a side of her mother she'd never seen nor even contemplated. Ariana had always thought of her mother as put together and calm at all times, make-up and hair always perfect. This was a side of her mother she had forgotten, the years before her illness. Her youthful exterior, although attractive, also seemed cold. Now she was seeing the private side of her mother, the side she obviously didn't let anyone see. This woman was dejected, depressed, and exhausted. She just sat staring out into space.

Ariana began to think about what her mother's life must be like married to a perfectionist who was demanding, temperamental, and often cruel. He demanded that his home be impeccable, his meals exceptional and served on time, and that his wife wait on him and provide what he wanted instantly. His children had to be respectful, clean, and no bother. If they were in any way less than perfect, it was his wife's fault. His wife's grooming, clothing, hair color, and style were all selected by her father and if her mother didn't look fantastic at all times, then she would pay for it through his cruelty and derision. All this was expected of his wife without compliments or affection.

Wow, thought Ariana, *no wonder she was depressed and cold.* From this point on Ariana realized any anger she held for her mother was gone. How could she hate someone that was little more than a puppet, a defeated drone that lived to follow orders in hopes of receiving a crumb of affection from someone who probably didn't know how to love? Both her parents were products of their environments. They never thought about the fact that they both could make different choices. Because her mother had been an orphan she craved love, acceptance, and family. She chose to be comfortable with the semblance of those things instead of the reality. Her father had been rejected and abused by his father and mother. He thought that as long as he provided well for his family, he was being a good father and husband.

Thank you, Lydia for suggesting I do this, thought Ariana as she realized that now she truly felt free of the anger and resentments she had not even known were there.

Letting her consciousness return back to her room, Ariana realized that the memories from before her illness had returned. Now she could purge any left-over fears, angers, resentments, and lingering pain forever. She understood that forgetting was a tool the mind used to cope, another way to escape from pain. She didn't need it anymore.

Chapter 35

"Okay, what's the big surprise?" Leesie inquired as she walked into Tara's townhouse with Teja, Josh, and Jason. "Some of us need to be on our way out of town so we can be sure to make it back for the big channeling event on New Year's Eve. We don't have the luxury of lounging around during Christmas."

"You guys know as much as we do," Ariana claimed. "We got a call from Matthew last night to round everybody up and meet here at one today."

"Yeah, he wouldn't even tell me what the big surprise is," Zach added.

"Well, I hope he gets here soon, 'cause I have a plane to catch," Andrew reminded everyone.

Wendy clutched her boyfriend as though his trip home meant she'd lose him forever. He hugged her tightly and ruffling her short pixie cut hair stated lovingly, "Baby, I'm not going off to war. I'm only going home for five days. You'll be busy with your family, too. You probably won't even miss me."

"Won't miss you! I already miss you and you're not even gone yet," she exclaimed, her feelings hurt.

Kissing her on the forehead Andrew turned back to Ariana, "Got anything to eat?"

Ariana looked at Andrew in awe. "Do you ever stop eating? I wasn't expecting to entertain today, but I think I can come up with something. Let me look."

"I'll help," Wendy said jumping up from the couch. "I need to do something or I'll start crying. It's going to be hard knowing that all of us are going to be separated for a week. I'm so used to having everyone close all the time."

"Hey, we have the mind link thing, right?" Jason asked. "Can't we use that to keep in touch and also to practice what we've learned?"

Ariana thought about it a moment, "That's a great idea. It will be an especially good way to practice astral projection and some of the other techniques Lydia showed us. Oh everyone, don't forget that we have to be at Lydia's for the private channeling on New Year's Eve by 7 that evening, and because it is New Year's Eve, the traffic will probably be killer. We'll postpone our party to New Year's Day. Okay?"

Everyone was in agreement. Wendy and Ariana proceeded to the kitchen to prepare a snack.

"While I'm with my family," Josh said to the rest of the group, "I'll see if anyone has any feedback about what we're doing and if they have some suggestions about getting it all out there into the world."

Leesie smiled broadly, "Thanks, Josh. That takes a humongous load off me."

"Any suggestions as to what the rest of us should be doing?" asked Zach to no one in particular.

"Yeah," Josh answered, "enjoying your time off. My family rarely rests. I think we're all ADHD. Talking to them about our ideas would give their crazy energy some focus. Also, I'm the new one in this group. You guys have been doing the heavy lifting here for the last three months. It's my turn to prove my worth."

The girls returned with chips, cookies, and grapes. The group began to devour the snacks as they fell into their normal jokes and banter. They didn't even notice the kitchen door open until Diablo raced off his seat by the window and went streaking by them.

"Whoa, what was that about?" Andrew wondered.

"He's all excited. Someone's here. Oh my God! It's Tara!" Wendy shouted as she ran toward the kitchen. The rest of the group came rushing after her. Standing in the kitchen, while holding onto Matthew for support, was a still-battered Tara but glowing with her usual warmth and smile.

Without thinking, Lessie rushed to Tara and threw her arms around her dear friend. "How is this possible? Whoa girl, what's happened? How are you even here?"

"Sorry Leesie," Matthew said. "I'm glad you're happy to see her, but she's still a little fragile here. Can you try not hanging on her? Help me to get her into the living room."

A crimson-faced Leesie gently withdrew her embrace and helped

Matthew escort Tara to a chair while the others, still speechless, followed behind.

Ariana extended her energy to Tara not only to help her but also to scan her body. She was still bruised and quite a bit thinner, but all life-threatening injuries were completely healed. How was that possible?

You know how that's possible, the Elders reminded her. *She accepted the healing. It was time for her to return to this plane and help again.*

"Before the rest of you bombard her with questions, sit down," directed Matthew. Then turning to Tara, he asked, "Do you want to tell the story or do you want me to?"

"You go ahead," she answered. "It's as much your story as it is mine."

Matthew squeezed Tara's hand and began. "Like you Teja, I couldn't stand feeling helpless. I couldn't stand not being able to see Tara and only communicating psychically. One day I decided to go to the hospital and see if I could find anything out. When I got there no one was around. It must have been a shift change or something because there was only one nurse and she was at the desk. It was easy to sneak past her when her back was turned. I knew what room Tara was in because I could follow her energy pattern."

"What the hell is an energy pattern?" Teja interrupted.

Smiling calmly Tara answered, "It's your aura's song. Remember we discussed this before. Everyone's energy vibrates differently and those that are attuned to it can hear it."

"Okay, can I go on?" Matthew asked.

Looking embarrassed Teja said, "Yeah, go ahead. But you know I'm pissed you didn't tell any of us this shit earlier. We're a group and should be honest with each other. Work together and shit."

"I know you're angry, Teja," Tara replied, "but I asked him not to. I didn't want to disappoint anyone if we failed. Matthew wanted all of you to know. I stopped him."

"Oh," Teja said meekly. "Sorry. Go on Matthew."

"That first day I just stood there looking at her and sending energy and healing. I knew she knew I was there, but she didn't communicate. I assumed she was busy. I decided I would come back the next day. The second day was more intense. Tara had returned to her body and was overwhelmed with the pain. I took as much of it as I could so she wouldn't leave again and that seemed to work, at least for as long as I was there. From that point on I went back every day. Then I started to use all the healing energy you guys were sending, too. I could feel her getting better. It was as though I could feel her cells begin to mend. I watched the bruises began to fade and the stitches heal. Within a week, she opened her eyes. Her jaw was wired so she couldn't talk. Each day something else would mend. The doctors didn't understand and it took Maria and me screaming at them to get them to X-ray her hips and jaw. She was healed. Her parents had been trying to get me thrown out of the hospital but when they found out about the miraculous healing, they became distracted. Maria convinced everyone that the Virgin of Guadeloupe had answered her prayers. Tara and I think she really believed it, and maybe there's some truth to it. After all, prayer is a powerful healing tool. The healing became more rapid until now all that's left is some bruises, some weight loss, and getting some more strength back.

So you see, even though I didn't tell you what was happening, all of you were participating, too. Tara, do you want to tell them your story?"

"Well, Matthew actually told you the salient information, but I'll tell you what made me decide to come back. Before Matthew came to the hospital, I was content working in the Los Realm. It was easy for me and made me feel like I was accomplishing something. I'd given no thought to the fact that eventually I would either die and go to the Other Side or come back here. I guess I just didn't want to think about it because in both cases, I would have to return first to my body and experience all the pain and fear that is part of the human condition. But when Matthew showed up in the room with my physical body and poured all his love into it, it jerked me back to this plane, the physical one. **It hurt**. My first instinct was to flee again, but this time my soul wouldn't let me. It was time for me to decide where I belonged. Was I done or did I still have work to do here? Each day that Matthew returned he filled my body with his love and all of yours, too. Bodies respond to love and mine decided to heal almost before I realized that I had decided to live. The more love, light, and hope Matthew poured into me, the stronger I became and my will to live and to be Tara strengthened. I knew that I would hurt my family, but I must be me, and almost dying convinced me that being me is very important. I can help others on this plane because I am not confined to only this existence. I am not fully female or male, and I am alive but also connected to the realms of the dead. Only I can help those who walk in the shadows. Matthew understands, but by not having physically experienced all that I have, he will never fully connect as I can. Staying alive and being physical was my only choice. Once I allowed myself to delight in all the possibilities present in that choice, I began to heal at a supersonic pace. Because Abuela and Matthew convinced my family that Our Lady of Guadalupe saved me, and that she had a purpose for me, my family decided to leave me here to accomplish that mission. I am free and I feel wonderful," Tara finished, lighting the room with her magnificent smile.

Diablo, who had been sitting on Tara's lap the whole time, was ecstatic. He radiated the happiness the others felt. At the conclusion of Tara's story, he stood on his hind legs and began rubbing his face on her chin and neck, purring loudly as he kneaded her chest. His emotions filled the room with love.

"I'm feeling kinda awkward here. Tara, although I feel like I know you, I'm sure you have no idea who I am. Hi, I'm Josh."

"Hi, Josh. I do know you through the others and I am looking forward to knowing you better as we all work together to do what must be done," Tara replied.

"I need a group hug," Wendy said. "Is there any way to hug you without causing you pain?"

"I don't care. If we don't hug soon I'll wonder if coming back was worth it," Tara said with a big grin.

Chapter 36

After the rest of the group left, Ariana decided to quiz Tara on the knowledge she gleaned from being in the Lost Realm. She also wanted to know whether she learned anything about the Other Side. "Are you too tired to answer some questions?" she enquired of Tara.

"Actually, I'm not tired at all. I'm exhilarated by being home and surrounded by everyone's positive energy. It's my body that needs to get stronger. My energy is great. Being in a hospital is really hard. You are surrounded by death, pain, fear, and sorrow, and if you are at all in tune with energy, it can sometimes be overwhelming. I can't imagine what it must be like if you don't know you're sensitive and you work there or go there to visit frequently. If you don't know about protections you are vulnerable to all that horror. Ariana, that's another thing I learned by the experience. We can't just work on saving the planet. We must also educate people about what may be happening to them. There may be thousands out there feeling depressed, desperate, angry or afraid, not because those are their emotions but because they are picking up other peoples'. Some may think they are going crazy. I can see how this would be especially horrifying for children. If they told anyone they were hearing voices, seeing colors around people, or their moods were shifting often, I can see how they might be diagnosed as schizophrenic or bipolar. How many very psychic people are misdiagnosed right now?"

"I've been worrying so much about how we would accomplish our goal I didn't even think about looking outside our group and determining what was going on with other people. Even when Josh came to us and explained what was going on with him, I didn't think about how this could be happening with lots of people out there. All of this energy would certainly be creating chaos for them, too. How could I possibly be so blind and egotistical that I thought all this trauma and confusion were only happening to us? What's wrong with me that I am constantly missing what's right in front of me?" Ariana asked, feeling very angry with herself.

"If there's anything wrong with you Ariana, it's that you think you must understand and be on top of every situation," Tara answered lovingly. "Why do you think the Universe brought us all together? So you could take complete responsibility for everything? No, we are together so each of us can offer a different perspective and viewpoint, as well as sharing the responsibility for the tasks and the results. We each have different abilities and different information to bring to the group. No one but you expects you to know everything and to be responsible for all of us and the world, too."

Zach placed his arm protectively around Ariana, "That's my girl," he said warmly, "always thinking she is responsible for everything."

"Let's not get wrapped up in personalities, but instead let's try to figure out what we can do to help those people out there that are being activated and don't understand what's happening," suggested Matthew.

"It's not just those people who have been newly activated. It's also all the people with psychic abilities that have spent their lives denying their abilities. With the changes in energy, and the different realms overlapping more and more, their psychic abilities will become way too hard to ignore. I'm concerned about helping them to understand how to deal with this new information they have no logical way of defining," advised Tara.

"Overlapping?" Zach asked. "What do you mean exactly?"

"While I was on the lost realm I noticed there were times that it was very hard to distinguish whether I was on this realm or that one. It was as though they were blending into one another. I also noticed that the realm of time, which only exists here on this three-dimensional realm, was bleeding into that one. Many of the lost had started to understand that they had been there a very long time. They are able to observe this realm and understand that it's no longer the 50s or the 1800s, let's say. They see the changes that time has brought to this side and understand that it is no longer the same place as they remembered. When they consigned themselves to the Lost Realm, nothing changed from day to day. They remained in the period and the situation which caused them to deny themselves peace and happiness and believed they were still living the horror that had been their lives. However, in the short time I spent there, things began to change dramatically. Many of these spirits began to walk among you here. They were not solid forms, more like wisps of energy, but their energy was felt by many on this realm and your energy by them. Of course, this has happened in the past. Many people have seen ghosts. The difference now is that veil between these two worlds is becoming so thin at times that all of the beings over there can make themselves felt over here more strongly. This is adding to the chaos on both sides."

"Doesn't that make it easier to help them go to the Other Side?" Matthew asked.

"Just the opposite. It made many of them think they could go back to the Realm of the Living, at least partially. Some thought they could make amends, while others who were not so nice while living, wanted to continue to cause harm."

Zach was both confused and angry. "What the hell are their guides doing while all this shit is going on?"

"Zach, you are letting your religious training rule your thinking again," stated Ariana. "The guides can only suggest and try to help, but you must be willing to listen and follow. No one punishes or forces. Free will exists on all realms."

Tara added, "On the Lost Realm, the egos listen to nothing but their own guilt, shame, or anger. Once they choose that path the guides withdraw."

"So they are just abandoned?" Zach asked angrily.

"All they have to do is remember what they learned when they were alive about forgiveness and love and then The Light appears. God is never gone, but you must be willing to see," Tara reminded him. "God is not a being that passes judgement. That includes judging that these entities would be better off on the Other Side than there. We make that judgement even when we don't entirely understand the circumstances that brought these egos to this place. We chose to believe that we are wiser than God. This belief has brought heartache to this wonderful world. Do you understand?"

Zach thought about it then replied, "I guess, but sometimes it would be easier to believe some angel will swoop down and make everything all right."

"Yes," Matthew replied, "and that's exactly what some Light Workers still believe, that the mothership or their personal angels will rescue them. However, our freewill is still what creates our present and future. The beings that tried to help Terra for so long often did more harm than good. So now it's our turn to grab the white horse and become our own champions."

Always the pragmatist Ariana questioned, "So how do we help those people out there that don't understand what's happening?"

"I think it makes it even more essential to get the word out," responded Tara.

"But how? Those people that would read anything we put on the web are probably already interested in metaphysics. How do we reach those who aren't?" asked Zach.

"We don't post things only on metaphysical sites. We go to social commentary sites, mental illness sites, chronic pain sites, maybe even transgendered sites. We don't immediately jump into the information that we are heading toward Armageddon or that people are being activated, we talk about the issue that the page is about and then start making some suggestions about energy and stuff," Matthew offered.

With a twinkle in her eye Tara responded, "Or we can write a book."

"What?" Ariana asked, shocked.

"I had a lot of time to think once I came back to my body. It took my mind from the pain. Why couldn't we write a book, a novel, about a group of college kids coming together to help the world?"

"Like an autobiography?" Matthew asked.

"Yes and no. We would know that it was autobiographical, but no one else would need to know. Sometimes novels open minds which then turn into conversations. Maybe we could put together Facebook pages, blogs, podcasts, and webinars, with each of us taking the role of a character in the book. We would know that we were just being ourselves, but everyone else would think we were acting as the character. Kind of like what kids do when they go to see the Rocky Horror movies. I bet we'd have people writing us about their experiences. Then we could help them and even incorporate them into our group or help them to form their own development groups where ever they are."

"OMG! You've got it, Tara. I really, really think this could work," exclaimed Ariana.

Matthew asked, "So what do we call the book?"

Ariana answered immediately, "How about, *Be the Light*."

Chapter 37

After the conversation with his guides, Jason decided it was time to talk with his mother. He wanted her to know about everything that was going on in his life. He wanted to bring back the closeness he felt toward his family when he was a little boy. And he needed his mother's help to work with the young boy.

It was time for him to take responsibility for his own actions. He now had a greater perspective on what his mother had gone through when his father died. He realized he had done to her exactly what he thought she had done to him—closed her out. He resented her for being alive when the parent he preferred was dead. And although at first he acted like he cared about her, he kept his grief to himself and resisted all her attempts at communication and sharing.

As they each grieved in their own way, he found himself judging her and his resentment grew. He had never even considered how hard everything was for her. He had idolized his father, but his father had some serious flaws. When he died, he left them not only destitute but also in debt. His mother had to work two jobs to keep them afloat. She never complained and didn't file bankruptcy, instead she worked long hours and paid off all the debt. When he was old enough to get a job she never once asked for his help, and even after he was working, she never asked for money from him. He used his money to purchase his truck and clothes while she still paid the insurance, rent, and bought all the groceries. His new perspective of the world had not only opened his eyes to the beauty of everything, it also destroyed the veil of anger and selfishness that had occluded his vision of his mother. He needed to apologize and allow them to grow close again.

His mother hadn't arrived home from work yet. Jason dumped his books on the kitchen table. He looked around the small apartment and realized it didn't get clean all by itself. Being neat was not one of Jason's strong points. Long ago he and his mother agreed that she would not be responsible for cleaning his pigsty. He just kept his door closed. But the rest of the apartment, although sometimes a little messy, was always clean. He couldn't remember the last time he helped make it that way. Usually he just came home and left his stuff where ever it landed, but somehow it still ended up neatly put away in his room.

Wow, look how much I just take for granted, he thought. *Food just miraculously appears on the table, my clothes get cleaned and put in the closet, the rent, electricity, and water gets paid, and all I have to do is go to school and work a part-time job if I want to. How many other things in the world do I take for granted?*

Grabbing the vacuum cleaner, Jason decided it was time to take some responsibility. He vacuumed, mopped, started a load of laundry, and cleaned the bathroom. Surveying his work he realized how good he felt and decided he would go even further. When his father was alive the whole family would cook together. His father was a creative and wonderful cook and really enjoyed making meals for the family. When his mother was forced to add becoming the family cook to her duties, all Jason did was bitch. *God, was I mean to her! Everything she did I condemned. Why?* he wondered.

Grieving is a personal act.

Jason was shocked. He could hear his guide so clearly in his mind.

When one grieves, they become concerned only with their own pain and loss and can begin to resent anyone that tries to intrude. Because grief is so totally self-centered, thinking about how anyone else is feeling becomes unimportant. Many people become angry when they grieve. It is one of the many steps of loss. That anger can be extended toward the person who died, to God, or anyone who survived the death, including the person grieving. In your case your grief extended to your mother. Your anger made you see everything she did as wrong because she wasn't your father. Having an awareness of this process is good because now you can make a choice to remedy it. You can't change what has happened, and because it was a response to extreme pain and confusion, not a thought-out act of revenge, betrayal or hatred, you should not allow yourself to feel guilt. It was not a conscious choice. You have learned. Your eyes have opened so the lesson has been learned.

Jason felt wonderful. He had actually heard one of his guides clearly again. He decided to make something delicious for dinner. He looked at the clock on the wall: 3:30. He had plenty of time to go to the store and have dinner ready by 5:30, the time his mother usually came home.

Humming, he went back out to his truck and headed to the grocery store. He began thinking about what he would make for dinner. He hadn't cooked since he was twelve and then he was more a helper than a chef. If he asked, maybe his Dad would assist him from the Other Side.

Walking down the meat aisle he was hit with a thought, *Animals are living beings. Do I have a right to eat them?*

Again, Jason heard his guide's voice, *Food animals come to your realm in order to sacrifice for the good of the planet. Grazing animals are not just food for humans but also other animals. This is their purpose. As long as you appreciate their gift and acknowledge it, both of you are enriched by the interaction. The animal becomes part of you and you receive its energy. It is interesting to us on this realm that humans find fault with eating flesh of animals but do not find it disturbing to eat plants. All things on Terra are alive even if you cannot recognize it. Plants feel just like animals do. Humans are often disturbed to eat an animal but not a plant. Today you felt the aliveness of your tomato. You grew joyous eating it and absorbing its energies. This is how you must eat all things at all times, appreciating and relishing in the gift it is giving you. As you became aware earlier, life is a circle—you eat, you defecate, you fertilize both in life and in death.*

Even with this information, Jason decided he'd feel better eating pasta tonight. He decided to try his hand at fresh pesto pasta, garlic bread, and a wonderful field green salad that, of course, contained tomatoes.

Arriving back home he looked up a recipe for pesto pasta and began. He knew his dad was with him because he instinctively knew what to buy and how to prepare this dish. He put the ingredients into the small food processor, made the garlic butter and slathered it on the bread, placing it in the oven at 425 degrees. He looked at the clock, 5:15. He started the water to boil the pasta.

When the door opened at 5:33, Jason was ready. "Hi, Mom. Come on in and have a seat," he said, holding out a chair at the kitchen table."

A look of dismay then confusion appeared on her face. "Jason, what's up?" she asked, obviously disturbed.

"I've cleaned the house and cooked some dinner and now we're going to sit down and eat and talk," he replied.

Now Angie was really worried. "Is everything all right?"

Jason walked to his mother and put his arms around her. "Yes, Mom, everything's okay now. I know it hasn't been for the last many years, but my eyes got opened today and I want to talk with you. I want us to be like we used to be."

He could feel her tears as they wet his shirt, her body shaking. He held her and rocked her until the sobbing stopped.

She pulled back slightly and caressed his face, still fighting back her tears. "You are so like your father, Jason. You are a good man, and even if I haven't shown you, I am so very proud of you."

"I love you, Mom." Trying to lighten the mood he exclaimed, "But you gotta let me feed you or all this work will be ruined!"

After dinner, they cleaned the dishes together. Jason asked his mother to join him in their living room. "Mom, some pretty amazing things have started to happen in my life that I need to explain to you." He proceeded to tell her all about the group, his new-found abilities, and what he had realized that afternoon. "I know you might think I'm crazy or something, but it's all true and what has happened allowed me to get out of myself and clearly see all the things I've been doing to our relationship. I love you ,Mom. And I'm really sorry for judging you and blocking you from my life."

Taking both his hands in hers, Angie began to open up too. "I've missed our closeness. When your father died, I became a coward, just walking around like a zombie. Then I thought if I replaced him I would feel better. I don't blame you for shutting me out because you probably felt I was doing that to you. Somehow, through all of it, you turned out to be one hell of a man. I'm so proud of you."

"Are you freaked out about the psychic stuff?"

"Hardly. You never met my mom. Now I wish you had, but your father wasn't particularly enamored with her. She was a hippie who lived in a metaphysical commune in a small town in Indiana. Everyone there was either a healer or a psychic. Your grandmother was amazing at both."

"You grew up in a commune?" Jason asked. This was shocking news. Of all the things he had ever thought about his mother, this would never have entered his mind.

Angie laughed, "No, sweetie. I only lived there for two years and then I left to come to college here. I returned occasionally for visits. I took you father back with me right before we married, but everything about it seemed too eccentric for him. My mother told me not to marry him. She said he was a good man but the marriage would bring me sorrow. That really made him dislike her. I didn't realize she meant your father's death. I think she was afraid to tell me what she saw so she tried to scare me away from him. Even though she was right, and the relationship brought me sorrow, it also brought me joy and it created you."

"Why didn't you ever tell me about her?"

"She died shortly after you were born. There was no reason to talk about her especially because it made your father upset. So I just kept her in my heart. It never occurred to me that I might pass on her psychic gifts, but it appears as though I have."

"Oh my God, Mom! Are you psychic, too?"

Blushing, Angie admitted, "I do have some of her gifts. Even before we moved to Chesterfield Mom did readings for people out of our home. She used Tarot cards and she taught me how to read them. Occasionally she did séances and I helped. We were members of a Spiritualist church."

"What about your father? How'd he feel about all this stuff?"

"Remember I told you my mother was a hippie? Being a hippie meant believing in free love. There were lots of men before I was born and mom wasn't exactly sure which one was my father. It was okay though, she was a great mom."

Putting his arms around his mother and hugging her tightly, Jason felt wonderful. She wasn't freaked by who he was. She could even help. Maybe she, too, was meant to be part of the group.

"Mom, I want you to meet the group. I think you can help us and I think we can help you. I am so glad that you listened and confided in me. I feel like we're a family again."

"I'd love to meet your friends, though I'm not sure what I can do to help," Angie replied. "But whatever knowledge or abilities I possess, I'd love to begin using and sharing them again."

"We're supposed to go to a channeling soon, do you know what that is?"

"It's a New Age term for a séance?"

"Well, sort of, I guess. Will you come with us?"

"That depends. Who's doing the channeling? There are a lot of fakes, especially here in Arizona."

"She lives right down the street. We took some classes with her and I knew her son. She's really nice and I think she's authentic," Jason answered.

"Are you talking about Lydia?" Angie asked. "I've been going to her for readings and to talk with your dad after he died. She's great. If it's her, I'd love to go."

God, it's a small world, Jason thought.

And there are no accidents, added the voice in his head.

Chapter 38

The celebration of the season the four friends created was a wonderful, eclectic combination of Hanukah and Yule. Tara and Ariana spent hours decorating the condo with evergreen boughs, candles, a menorah, and a beautifully decorated Christmas tree. Matthew and Zach went to work stringing popcorn and berries, attaching ribbon on the cookie ornaments and putting the lights on the tree and around the house. They had present wrapping contests and sat in front of the fire every night relaxing, laughing, and talking until very early every morning.

Occasionally, through their mind link, they would receive glimpses of what the rest of the group was experiencing. They would send thoughts and feelings of their celebrations back. It was a wonderful and unique way of celebrating together. They could even feel Josh's exploits in the Philippines where he and his family were building a school and hospital in an especially damaged area of that country. Even though everyone was scattered throughout the world, these glimpses helped the group to feel connected to one another.

The two couples celebrated Christmas Eve at Tara's condo. They opened the presents that each of them had used their psychic abilities to choose for each other.

Ariana received a wonderful book from Matthew, *Illusions* by Richard Bach. Tara finished the painting of Ariana's home she had begun before the attack. Zach's present to Ariana was a weekend in Sedona for the two of them that they would use during Spring Break.

Tara received a turquoise necklace from Matthew and Ariana chipped in with Zach to purchase the matching Navaho turquoise and silver bracelet.

The girls combined their resources and bought the guys the latest Xbox and some new games which the four of them spent Christmas Eve enjoying.

"Hey everyone, we should go to bed," Tara announced at one in the morning. "We have to get up early tomorrow and cook and clean for our Christmas feast."

"When is everyone going to be here?" Zach asked.

"Around 3, so let's get some sleep."

⁂

Morning seemed to come too early for the group. Ariana slept in until ten, and when she went into the living room, both Zach and Matthew were still sound asleep. She heard noise coming from the kitchen and found Tara already cooking.

"Wow, how long have you been up?" Ariana asked.

"Since about seven, I think."

"I'm so sorry I slept in. Why did you get up so early?"

Tara started laughing. "Obviously you didn't let Diablo sleep with you. This is one spoiled kitty. He demands pets followed by food as soon as the sun comes through the curtains. He paws my face, kneads my chest, or chews on my ear until I get out of bed."

"He didn't do that to me. We had him at the dorm with us and he was a perfect gentleman."

"Maybe he was with you but if we ask Wendy, I'm sure she'd have a different story. This cat loves to eat," Tara claimed.

"What can I do to help?" Ariana asked.

"Well, you could go wake up the guys because breakfast is ready."

"You made breakfast, too?"

"Breakfast! Did I hear the word food?" Zach asked, entering the kitchen in his bare feet, pajama bottoms, and seriously mussed hair.

Rubbing sleep from his eyes, Matthew followed Zach into the kitchen looking as though he'd just stepped off the cover of a magazine, his hair perfect, a big smile on his face.

"Go sit down. I'll bring everything to the table. Ariana, can you help me, please?" Tara asked.

After breakfast, they split the tasks to ready the house for their company. Not only were they celebrating the holidays, they wanted to celebrate Tara's recovery. The guests arrived promptly at three. The grandmothers Maria and Pearl arrived with Teja. Tara's mother, father, and sister were also with them. Tara's family had never seen her condo. Tara gave them the grand tour and settled everyone in the living room while she returned to the cooking.

"How'd you get your family to come?" Ariana asked Tara.

"More than my healing is a miracle. They've decided to let me live my life on my own terms. Between my abuela, her priest friend, Teja's Grandmother Pearl, and the doctor at the hospital, they realized that cutting me off from the family was exactly like treating me as though I were dead. The possibility of my actual death woke them up. If everything goes well today maybe they'll grow to like me, not just love me," she said with a wistful smile. "Go into the living room and make sure the boys are behaving themselves. I don't need help right now."

Ariana returned to the living room and joined the conversation about Tara's paintings.

"I never realized he was so artistic," Mr. Herrera said.

Maria answered, "You've never bothered to get to know her, you've been too busy trying to make her into what you wanted her to be, not who she is. Not only did she do these paintings, she decorated the entire place herself. Our girl has much talent."

Conchita and Elicia were sitting on the couch talking with Matthew and Pearl. Diablo sat contentedly on Elicia's lap purring loudly. *He's being the ambassador,* Ariana thought. Just then the doorbell chimed. Jason stood in the doorway with a pretty brunette woman.

"Hey, Ariana," he said, "This is my mom."

The woman's smile seemed to illuminate the entire room. Ariana noticed how lovingly she looked at her son. Turning to Ariana she handed her a poinsettia plant and said, "Please, call me Angie. I am so pleased to meet you. Jason is happier now than he's been in six years and I'm sure your group is the reason. Thank you for that and also for inviting us to attend your Yule celebration."

"Oh, you didn't have to bring anything, but thank you. We're all so happy you two could come. Please come on in and let me introduce you to everyone," Ariana answered. She took them around and made the introductions, then left Jason with Zach to discuss the new game system and games.

"Come with me to the kitchen and I'll introduce you to our hostess, Tara," Ariana suggested to Angie. Ariana was usually reserved around new people but she felt an instant connection to Angie. Her aura was huge and beautiful with vibrant shades of lavender, violet, and blue.

Everything about her seemed genuine and open—she seemed to fit in.

Immediately on entering the kitchen Angie exclaimed, "Oh my, what is that wonderful smell? Hi, you must be Tara. I'm Angie, Jason's mom."

Just as Tara was about to speak, Pearl entered the room. "Angie is that you?" she said.

"Oh my God, Pearl? What are you doing here?" Angie exclaimed as she threw her arms around Pearl and gave her a big hug. "Did you bring your daughter and granddaughter with you?"

"My granddaughter is part of this group," Pearl announced proudly, "She finally came around and is using her abilities. My daughter is at church. Like usual, she'd rather be there instead of with her family. Are you using your abilities again, too? Is that why you're here?"

"You have abilities?" Ariana cut into the conversation to ask.

"Lordy, this woman is one very good psychic," Pearl announced, "but she gave it up when she became pregnant. She used to attend our Spiritualist Church, but we only see her occasionally now."

"You over estimate my abilities," Angie said. Turning to Ariana she added, "My husband didn't approve of my beliefs so when Jason was born I became a good wife and mother and left it behind. When Jason's father died I started going back to the Spiritualist church Pearl belongs to until my work schedule and my responsibilities got in the way."

"Jason never told us," Ariana replied.

"He didn't know until last week. He didn't want to say anything until after I met all of you."

"That's really wonderful," Tara said. "I wish my family was more spiritual instead of religious so they could understand everything I'm into, but I will have to be patient and take one step at a time."

"I think your family has come a long way in a short time, little girl. Be grateful they're here today celebrating your life instead of still condemning who you are," Pearl chastised her.

"Yes, you're right," Tara admitted. "Today is a day for gratitude and celebration. Why don't you three help me take the food to the table so we can eat."

The day was filled with joy, laughter, good food, and good friends. There was no talk of The Darkness, pain, fear or sadness. Everyone felt blessed and expressed their happiness openly. Even Tara's melancholy sister was animated and talkative and seemed to be fascinated with Matthew. Diablo and Matthew had completely won her over, and by the end of the evening, she began talking about the four friends coming to visit in California.

Tara's parents Conchita and Pablo were quiet but appeared to be more accepting, less negative. They were working very hard to understand and accept their son as he was now.

The most wonderful thing for Jason was how well his mother fit in with his friends. His friends treated her like she was one of them instead of someone's mother. She glowed and was friendly and vibrant. Her energy seemed to fill the room. *God,* he thought, *I really do love her.*

"Hey, Jason," Ariana said. He hadn't realized she was standing right next to him.

Startled, he replied, "Hi, Ariana. How ya doing?"

"Your mom is really great. You are so lucky."

"Yeah, I was just thinking that," he admitted. "She knows Lydia. Do you think the group would mind if my mom went with us to the private channeling?"

"I'm sure they wouldn't mind. Lydia said to bring the entire group and I think we have a new member, if you guys agree."

Jason's smile animated his whole face. "Way cool," he exclaimed.

"And in case you were wondering, I think Leesie will love her, too," Ariana assured him.

Embarrassed, Jason realized he **had** been wondering and now he felt relieved. *What a perfect Christmas,* he thought as he realized that for the first time in six years, he was completely happy.

Chapter 39

Yule was over, and the friends were together for the first time since Winter Break began. Tara's condo seemed very crowded with the whole gang filling the living room again. Ariana stood in the kitchen doorway watching the group interact. The energy in the room was immensely exuberant, almost hyper, because everyone was so happy to be together once again.

"It's really wonderful what we have here, isn't it?" Tara said from behind Ariana. "Just think, it was a few short months ago that we were all friendless and considered ourselves weird and unlovable. Now we all have a purpose. We believe in ourselves and we have created a family of uniquely gifted individuals. I feel so privileged to be part of this group!"

Turning to face her friend, Ariana put her arm around her. "Tara, I am so glad you decided to come back to us. I missed you so much, my friend. Your calm, gentle energy and keen mind are such a blessing to me. Somehow you always know exactly what to say to capture a moment or clarify a thought. I think I might really need your help and I didn't even know it till you came up behind me just now."

"You're worried about how to work with the young father who lost his whole family aren't you?" asked Tara. "You've seemed especially quiet these last few days and even today you felt distracted to me."

"Yes," admitted Ariana. "I'm not sure I can comprehend what he's feeling right now. I know nothing of his history or even how his marriage was. Did he love her? Was he a good father?"

Tara smiled and patted Ariana's arm, "You're complicating things. When your oma died what did your guides do? What did you need from them? It's that simple. Every human being needs the same things: to feel cared about and loved, to feel safe, and to have hope. Provide those things. If you can, then the only other guidance he needs is to understand how to deal with a very sensitive, psychic son. That one should be easy for you too. You have what your oma did for you and what you would have wanted from your family as a template."

"You know, often I think you should be the leader of this group. You have so much more wisdom than me," Ariana admitted.

"No thanks," Tara said, laughing and shaking her head vigorously. "I'll leave the tough stuff to you and Matthew. Anyway, I think it would be better for you to think that we will all contribute what we can, not that it's all on any one individual's shoulders. You take everything too personally for that. C'mon, let's join the chaos."

Josh was explaining what his family had been doing in the Philippines when Tara and Ariana joined the group. "It was just like people do here when they help build houses for Habitat for Humanity, except we were working on a school and hospital. Since the typhoon and floods, things there have been horrible. My mom and dad have been there working the whole time, so we all agreed to meet there for winter break. The people of the Philippines are really gentle and kind. They have so little. It's a pleasure helping them out."

"You know, when things were really rough for Mom and me, I found myself resenting the hell out of the rich. Pretty much all we hear about is the decadence of people with lots of money and not much about people like your family," Jason admitted.

"That's because most of the families that are working for good aren't looking for publicity," Josh stated. "Since Warren Buffett started the Giving Pledge, there are over 100 families that have committed to giving away at least 70 percent of their wealth to philanthropy. In addition to them there are people like Oprah Winfrey and Angelina Jolie that are doing what they can in their own way. It's easy to focus on the selfish media whores that splash their faces all over the media, but really, they are a very small minority. What I've discovered is most people are really wonderful and kind. There are more unsung heroes out there than villains. The problem is it's the villains that get the media's attention."

Teja snorted, "Ain't that the truth. All you gotta do to get your face plastered all over the television or newspapers is brutally kill enough people or have sex and put it on YouTube."

"That means any disenfranchised creepasaurus that is trying to become famous knows just what to do, while we are still trying to figure out how we're going to save the planet. That really does suck toes," Leesie exclaimed.

"Suck toes?" Teja said, laughing so hard diet soda flew out her nose. "Sista, where in the hell do you get your slang?"

Blushing profusely Leesie replied, "Well, I thought it was kinda dirty just to say sucks, so I just added my own take on it. Anyway, you looked pretty funny with pop flying out your nose."

"Okay, children," Tara said as she sprang to clean up the mess, "No fighting. We've got important things to discuss before we head to Lydia's, like what questions should we be asking?"

Ariana shook her head. "I really don't think we should ask anything. Equinoxx requested this private channeling. That says to me they have something they want to discuss."

"I agree with Ariana," Matthew stated. "Let's see what they need us to know first. I'm sure that will provide us with lots of questions to ask them."

Zach, who was seated between Ariana and Matthew added, "Anyway, remember it won't be just us there. It wouldn't be fair for us to monopolize the time with our questions unless Lydia or the woman that helps run the channelings tells us personal questions are okay. This may be completely different from the channeling we attended before."

Ariana turned to Jason and asked, "Is your mom going to be there, Jason? I really enjoyed her and think she belongs with us. I want everyone else to meet her, too."

"Yeah, she'll be there and so will Pearl. The only reason she's not with us right now is she thought we needed this time alone because we've been apart for a while. She and Pearl decided to go shopping and out to dinner together before the channeling. They may even be having dinner with Lydia. I think they've known her for a long time. It seems there's a lot I didn't know about my mom until recently."

"Like what?" Wendy inquired.

"Like she grew up in a spiritualist community and had a psychic, hippie mother."

"Whoa, dude, that's really extreme," Leesie exclaimed. "And I thought my family was different. Are you ever lucky!"

"No wonder you're psychic, man. That's really rad," Andrew agreed.

"So did anyone else discover anything really weird while we were apart?" Zach asked.

"Only that I missed all you creeps," Andrew laughed, hitting Zach on the arm for a change.

Wendy nodded her head in agreement and added, "Even though there were times I felt as though I was observing what everyone was doing, it wasn't the same as being together. The mind link is great, but it's more like watching something on TV rather than really having the experiences. I missed you guys, too."

"When we're together we can feel the energy of everyone and how that energy is harmonizing with each other in creating a group energy," Matthew suggested. "That energy nurtures and enhances all of us. That's why we are so good together."

"And why we all feel so much better when we are together," Ariana added. "Can you imagine what this planet will feel like when everyone in it is harmonized with the planet and all other life on her? I can, because that's what my planet is like. It's our job, I think, to help people on Terra to understand and begin the planetary link. I think that's what it will take to complete our mission here."

Leesie put her hand up for a high five and exclaimed, "Can I get an amen, ladies?"

Chapter 40

The night was beautiful, dark with no moon and lots of brilliant stars. Ariana loved the dark, it made her feel safe and calm as though she was wrapped in black velvet. Until she remembered her home planet, she spent many nights wondering why the night seemed so soothing. But now that she knew the light on her planet appeared to be shades of deep purple, she understood. This particular night, however, as Matthew, Zach, Tara, and she drove to Lydia's, Ariana wasn't feeling calm. She still found herself worried about what they would hear from Equinoxx. She realized the pace of the last couple of months had taken its toll on her. She was grateful for her new friends, especially Zach, but the responsibility was still overwhelming. How would this small band of teens possibly accomplish what they were tasked with?

Don't worry, Matthew whispered, the mind link allowing them to remain in contact. *This isn't only about you. We are in this together and we'll do what we can. No one is asking for more than that.*

"Yeah," Zach replied out loud. "Quit thinking it's all your deal. Just because our souls made some mistakes before doesn't mean this is completely our responsibility."

Ariana sighed, "You know what, this mind link isn't always awesome. Knowing that I can't have a private thought isn't particularly comfortable."

"It doesn't take the mind link to understand what's going on with you," Matthew offered. "Since we left the condo you've been especially quiet and deep in thought. We all know that you fill yourself with angst over what you perceive is all your responsibility. Get over it. It's time to move away from mistakes made in past lives, and even this life, and move ahead as though we're a team, no one person having all the responsibility, all the work, or all the glory either. If we fail it won't be because we didn't try our hardest. That's all that's required of us."

"I'm not even going to give failure a thought," Tara replied. "All we have to do is get the word out. There are others just like us out there that are waiting to be awakened. And just like a snowball rolling downhill, once started, gravity will do the rest."

"I'm curious as to why Equinoxx called this meeting, but I'm not afraid. I'm even a little excited," proclaimed Zach. "Everything has been speeding up. People are coming to us that have more abilities, resources, and information than we did when we first met. We haven't had to do anything for this to happen. Our abilities have been increasing with little to no effort. I'm convinced tonight will only enhance our knowledge and maybe even set us in the direction we need to be going next. Anyway, we're here, so we'll find out soon enough."

Pulling into the cul-de-sac the group was relieved to see that there was room for three cars: Jason's truck and Josh's new Jeep as well as Zach's Mustang.

Maybe it will only be us this evening, hoped Ariana.

Lydia opened the door immediately and ushered everyone inside. Angie and Pearl were seated in the kitchen. Sammie was running crazily throughout the house, ecstatic about something. "He's excited about having friends visit," Lydia explained. "The energy that's generated during our meetings always makes him feel hyper and happy. Let's all have a seat in the living room. You two also," she said to Angie and Pearl.

The living room was set up differently. Instead of rows of seats, as was the norm for the channelings, the chairs were in a circle. Ariana counted 20 chairs.

"Who else is expected tonight?" Wendy asked.

"Just some of the regulars from my monthly channeling," Lydia answered. "I'll introduce everyone when the others have all arrived. Please, pick your seats."

It didn't take long for everyone to show up and as soon as they were seated, Lydia began.

"Thank you everyone for choosing to spend New Year's Eve with Equinoxx and me. This channeling will be different than the ones you have previously participated in. Equinoxx would like to begin by discussing why they called us together, then you may ask questions about what they have said. The only personal questions, however, should be about what this information means to you and what, if any, your participation might be.

First, I would like everyone to become comfortable with each other. Now's the time to ask any questions you might have. When we are ready, I will ask them to come through. So let's just go around the circle and introduce ourselves."

Ariana was glad that the evening was starting off slowly and that she was getting an opportunity to put names to the faces she had seen once before. Elaine and Wendy 2 were here, and so was the German man, Bernie, and his lady, Victoria. An older gentleman named Joseph with a woman called Judy, and finally, a woman named Jo rounded out the group. Everyone must have been regulars because they all seemed to know each other well. They were all older. That created an interesting mix—her group of ten with no one over 19 and the rest of the people all over 50. There were twenty people present: half not fully adult and half senior citizens. She knew there had to be a reason for this peculiar mix and she was curious to see what it was.

"Does anyone have any questions?" Lydia asked.

"I don't have a question," Joseph answered, "but I do have something I need to ask about. I know that Equinoxx has an agenda for tonight, but I got this information channeled to me earlier this evening, and I need to know if it came from them. If it did, I think they would want me to let everyone know what I got. If it didn't come from them then I'd like to have feedback as to how accurate it may be. Is that okay with the group?"

Everyone agreed that it was, so Joseph began to read from his notes. "If you have any awareness of metaphysics or spirituality, you have heard about the Veils of Forgetfulness, the veils that keep you from remembering past lifetimes in your current lifetime on Earth. Seems logical and truthful when sitting in our current body and pondering such things. Yesterday, though, it came to me that that saying is just a metaphor, like so many other metaphysical and spiritual adages. I believe the true meaning is as follows: a veil is a layer of a past unresolved fear that we brought with us to re-examine this lifetime, or not. It is held in our subconscious mind where it remains in control until we are willing to spend the time to look inward as to why things in our current incarnation are not in harmony, are in discord, or in 'dis-ease.' These hidden fear-based beliefs came into existence in a previous life through either a direct experience or observation, or by taking on false beliefs of the mass consciousness. And when not resolved in that first formation they travel forward to the next incarnation, and the next, until they are examined and resolved. That is why some are so hard to change because they have been carried forward many lifetimes, building layer upon layer, thus increasing their density which makes them less penetrable.

As we remove the layers, more light, and by that I mean energy of God, is able to flow through us, for there is less in the way that would keep it stuck. Remember, we are all just energy, and energy needs to flow. When it doesn't, dis-ease, which causes disease, is created. So the veils that refer to our memory of the past are just layers of fears, fears based on the belief that we have done wrong and will be judged by a wrathful God. Many have taken on the belief that they are less than anyone or anything, including Prime Creator. In truth, what we have forgotten is that we, being the creation of the Prime Creator, are thus creators ourselves. And that all we have ever done at any time and in any situation was to create an experience for the knowing it imparts. There is no right or wrong, good or bad—everything just is. With that being said, there are no victims and nothing to judge, for we are all just having experiences.

There is nothing to be guilty about for guilt's root is fear. When you can know 100 percent in your heart who you really are—a piece of the Divine and a creator—the shrouds of fear will dissolve in the light that is ever present and always working to flow freely through every cell of your body, to sustain them in their natural state of Divine perfection. And when the last conscious being on Earth fully embraces their divinity and light, there will no longer be a need for this dense, lower dimensional playground, theatre, school called Planet Earth.

We need to recognize the existence of cycles. We all know that Mother Earth's vibration is being raised for her to survive mistreatment by humans. Creation created cycles and patterns to allow variety and variation in how we approach experiences and the degree of difficulty or ease in maneuvering through them. We have moved from the Piscean Era to the Age of Aquarius which brings us new, higher vibrational opportunities. Earth herself is leading the way and all who wish to remain with her must bring up their vibration to stay in sync with hers. It is a choice. Other arrangements have lovingly been made and are available to anyone not wanting to yet experience higher vibrational living. So as we began this dialogue, our veils of fear, their removal, is key to moving out of the old density into more light, the place Mother Earth has moved. No longer can veils or fears be carried forward or tolerated in the new light-filled existence. Illusions and fears must be shed."

After Joseph was finished reading his channeled material, the room was completely silent, everyone thinking about what they had just heard.

Eventually, Ariana spoke. "I am not familiar with the 'Veil of Forgetfulness' but our group has become aware of everything else you are speaking of. The planet's energy is changing and many of us are feeling the pull to raise our vibration. However, many other people don't know what is happening to them. That is increasing fear for many. It is as though there is a fight going on between The Light and The Darkness.

The more one accepts their power and becomes more powerful, the more we must also accept the responsibility for using our power. Energy can be either creator or destroyer. Fear has the ability to camouflage reality. It convinces humanity that they are powerless instead of creators. Fear makes The Light invisible. Consequently, we are working on helping humanity empower themselves, release fear and guilt, and accept The Light. I have wondered if remembering past lives enhances the empowerment or hinders it. I have come to the opinion that in some cases it will hinder growth because it seems to be a human trait to feel guilt for things you were not even responsible for. It is hard for humans to understand that the person in the past life was not them but instead it is an imaginary creation of the soul. It is an actor acting in a play the soul has created, just as we are now.

Additionally, it seems to be human nature to place blame instead of learning from an experience. So blaming oneself for something done in a past life complicates learning from the experience. It's hard to think about the idea that those who harm us are actually giving us our greatest gift because they are helping us grow, and for this, they develop negative karma. It's equally hard to contemplate that the who we are now is not responsible for any karma brought forth from past lives. It's difficult for us to accept that who we are now is not a reflection of our past lives and that the role we are playing in this life negates responsibility for any karma bought from those lives. Believe me, I know this is hard to understand. If those of us that are aware of what's happening are having trouble understanding these complex concepts, how are we possibly going to help ordinary people to understand?"

Chapter 41

"That sounds like the perfect segue to begin the channeling," Lydia said with a smile. "Feel free at the end of their message to ask any questions that you need answered. I don't want anyone leaving here confused, angry, afraid, or disheartened. Now give me a second as I release my ego and let them enter."

Unlike last time when it took several seconds for Equinoxx to come through, it seemed like the transition was immediate. Lydia's aura changed completely. It was radiant and flooded the entire room with violet and golden light. She seemed to sit straighter on the couch and her face changed dramatically. She was beaming. Even the energy in the room felt larger and warmer.

"Myama, we are grateful that you accepted our invitation," they began. "The time is growing short for you to complete your tasks. Some of you are aware of what we speak. Others of you are being activated to your purpose this night. But all of you are on this planet at this time to facilitate the enlightenment. There is a reason the word enlightenment contains the word light. All of you must be The Light. All of you must bring the knowledge of The Light to your world. There is no accident that the room contains both the old and the young, the beginning and the ending. Both groups are striving to understand your places in the Universe. The elderly, as they begin to recognize their own mortality, seek answers to their existence and place within the Universal order. As humans grow older they begin to search for The Light in many ways and ask serious questions about their legacy, what they will be leaving behind. The young are making the decisions that will impact their entire existence from this point on. That is why we need both groups. Together with the sick, the scared, the disenfranchised, you can reach so many more than any group can reach alone. All of you in the beginning felt alone and ached for unity. You didn't realize that what you sought was linkage. Some of you isolated, while others grew closer to the animal world. If you call to these others that are struggling just as you were, they will hear because they ache just as you did—to be seen, to be heard, to be loved. Age, race, nationality, religion, none of these are relevant, because in the end, everyone desires three things: love, security, and acknowledgment.

Every human is flawed. That is what creates their beauty. The trials that become the blessings create the faults within the crystals which allow them to shine more beautifully. It is the judgment of imperfection that tarnishes the beauty, not the flaws. Humanity judges, and in its judgement it often declares a situation as hopeless. Hopelessness like fear creates destruction. By bringing light to the fearful and hopeless, light being knowledge and truth, you can eradicate The Darkness.

None of you are special because you were awakened sooner. Everyone on Terra contains the original DNA which means everyone has the ability to use their psychic knowing. For those who are not using their psychic skills they must first believe in the possibility and then believe in themselves. There are many being activated just like you at this precise time. The entire human race has these skills. They have lain dormant because it was seen by the powerful ones on this planet, those that wanted to keep their power, as too dangerous. These abilities are now stirring. Announce this activation so it doesn't create fear. Bring others together to work on opening. When enough of you realize that The Darkness is **not** an outside force but an inner construct, you have the choice to banish it forever and banish the erroneous notion of polarities as well. With the belief in polarities—not as you have come to know the term as balance—but as the world sees them as differences/opposites, bad/good, ugly/beautiful, righteous/sinful, for example, this is what stirs the belief in darkness. If there is no good or bad, then darkness is just another shade of existence, just as night is no more evil than day.

It is important to understand that everything is perfect. Within your limited view you may not always know that, so humans find it easy to give up, judge, blame, and feel depressed and victimized. The scales are always in balance. What is given is always received. There is no one or nothing pulling strings to create chaos. **You** are the creators. Lose the need to know why and instead learn to trust in the process even if it isn't always apparent what the goal may be.

There are others out there working on their versions of the 100th

Monkey. Those that want devastation, destruction, and pain, as well as those who want to continue the status quo, to continue the illusion of darkness, fear, and helplessness. It serves their financial purposes. Knowledge and questioning will change this.

All of you must raise your voices. Bring to the other humans the knowledge of their power and the abilities that are being returned to them. Help them to understand that with this activation comes the knowledge of the linkage—everything and everyone is connected. What you do to all things directly effects the quality of your life and the lives of generations to come, and knowing this can significantly change how you relate to your planet, the poor, the lost, and all other beings that inhabit this plane and this place. Eventually there will be a mind link throughout Terra and a blending of all energy. But first, all of you must make sure that you are synchronized with your planet. She nurtures you, and without healthy energy from her, humanity will cease to exist."

"Equinoxx, are you saying there is no darkness?" Zach asked, obviously disturbed.

"That is exactly what we are saying. The concept of darkness and a punishing deity was brought to Terra right before the first destruction. These concepts were used by the destroyers in order to subjugate the human inhabitants of this world. With these concepts also came fear which infected all subsequent civilizations. Since that time, people who wanted power continued to perpetrate these beliefs on humanity. It is easy to get humans to follow, especially if you tell them they will receive a blessing or a punishment."

"Then all our religious leaders were liars?" questioned Zach as he grew more angry.

"No. The avatars you are thinking of, Jesus, Buddha, Moses, Mohammed, Krishna, and all the others, never propagated fear. Their message was one of love as well as instructions as to how man could live together well. What has been written down by man contains less truth than flawed memories and manipulations. What earthly religions often become is less about God and more about condemnation, more about evil and less about love, more about power and less about empowerment. The Source does not recognize anything but love. Everything else is a creation of man. When you live your life ever conscious of being loving there is no need for commandments or punishment.

We understand that being indoctrinated into religious beliefs at an early age makes what we are telling you difficult to hear or even believe. Telling children frightening stories in order to keep them in line is not God's way. Nor is it correct for you to believe that the Source would be on the side of one culture and against another. Isn't that what has been taught to man about wars? The crusaders believed absolutely that through their violent actions they were bringing God to the heathens. Unfortunately, those heathens believed their God was the one true deity and they fought as hard for their beliefs. No one was correct. The source has no desire to create anything but love, all else is an invention of man. It is important to examine the purpose behind what you are told. Often the reality of a situation is vastly different than what you have been led to believe. Ask the Native peoples.

What you are calling The Darkness is your own negative programming, self-hatred, judgement, and fear. We call this *living in the illusion.* When you are fearful or negative you project those things outward and draw like situations and people to you that reinforce these beliefs. You see others as a threat. If these things are compounded with religions that preach superiority, 'God is only on our side,' then it not only reinforces negative thought but also allows for one to feel justified in hating others. Believing in separation, whether it is through race, religion, nationality, political affiliation, gender, or whatever creates separation at the moment, increases humanity's feelings of insecurity and can increase the ability to rationalize and create destructive thinking and foster hopelessness instead of empowerment. When one accepts that God is all love and that everything is linked, then the illusion of separateness also disappears and you begin to understand that everything and everyone need each other. You begin to see how the linkage empowers you. For as you grow stronger, healthier, happier, and more secure, the negative illusion vanishes and there is no longer need for fear, anger, jealousy, hatred, or any of the negative emotions that eat at humanity. You see that there is enough of everything for everyone. The illusion of lack vanishes and you feel truly safe. The Source did not create a world filled with abundance in order to allow only the chosen to partake of the bounty. Humanity did that. The Source believes in you and your power. When you choose not to believe in yourself, you choose to believe in The Darkness, thus creating helplessness. When you feel helpless, you turn over your power to others, to beliefs, to fear, to cults, to governments, to whatever makes you give up the responsibility for your own twisted thinking and gives you the illusion of belonging.

It is time for humanity to claim their power and take the responsibility for what it has created and sustained. You are to be the voices. You must help the people of this planet to awaken and take back their blessings. All you can do is carry the torch. It is not possible for you to succeed alone nor is it expected. You will bring the information to as many of mankind as possible, but in the end whether Terra is destroyed again is up to everyone. You are living on a dying planet. Many know this now but feel helpless to change the course of events. Once you make them aware of their power and the illusion of helplessness, they have the freewill to come together or continue with the status quo. Humanity has the opportunity to heal their planet now, to come together in the linkage, to build unity through responsibility and caring, and to create a more perfect, stable world. It is their choice. You can work as one or be destroyed as before. Whatever your people choose, to the Source it will be perfect either way."

Epilogue

Now it's up to you. The books are fiction, but the information contained in them is not. The planet is in trouble. The changing energy and toxic nature of our environment, both physical and emotional, is creating an imbalance in the human nervous system as well as generating climate change. For generations our seas, oceans, and rivers have been poisoned. Those poisons have been absorbed into every corner of the world and into our food and air. The incidences of cancer have increased and are showing up in clusters throughout the world. These cancers are often traced back to harmful pollutants and toxic wastes that have been hidden from the general public. Probably the best examples are Three Mile Island and the case of Pacific Gas and Electric Company of California made famous by Julia Roberts in her role as Erin Brockovich, the woman who has now become an environmental activist.

The information about Native Elders extraterrestrial convocation is true and taken from an article by Richard Boylan, Ph.D. See: drboylan.com.

For many generations, the Hopi people have retained information about a coming apocalypse. On December 10, 1992, the Hopi Elders brought this knowledge to the General Assembly of the United Nations. You can easily search the internet and read what was said.

To this day their advice has gone unheeded.

And now, as this new compilation edition of *The Ariana Series* is going to press, the world faces the very real question of human habitability on our planet as the COVID-19 virus touches every corner of our world.

For over 30 years I have been a practicing spiritual teacher and metaphysician. In the past few years I have noticed that many of my clients seem to be spontaneously developing empathic abilities. Many have no idea what is happening and worry they are "going crazy." Several have experienced severe mood swings with suicidal thoughts. The majority of these people had no suicidal tendency prior to this "activation." It was at that time I realized many people throughout the world were redeveloping their natural psychic abilities. Many people had no idea they had them or what they were. Activation can cause significant mental and physical problems, including strange physical symptoms such as headaches, stomach aches, and extreme reactions to stress. That started me thinking. If adults were reacting to the energy so dramatically, what was it doing to teens who were at the height of their psychic abilities and whose hormones were often out of whack? Could that be part of the answer to school shootings? The teen years are very dramatic ones for most kids. If you add "psychic activation" to the mix I can see how difficult things could become. How do you discuss that you are hearing voices, have horrific dreams, or feeling other people's emotions and physical problems? What if you don't even know that you are picking up other people's emotions? What if telling anyone would cause you to be considered weird, evil, or insane?

After my first book, *Be the Light*, was released, I received an e-mail from a woman who told me her nine-year-old granddaughter had been placed in an institution with a diagnosis of schizophrenia. After reading the book she realized that her granddaughter had been seeing auras and talking with her guides. She sent a drawing her granddaughter had drawn showing her mother surrounded in beautiful colors with the caption, "When Mommy is happy." Her voices did not tell her to do anything horrible to herself or others, which is classic in schizophrenia, but instead were loving and supportive. How many other children and teens are being diagnosed as crazy and then medicated just because they are now using more of their minds and using them in new ways?

These thoughts are the motivation for *The Ariana Series*, to alert people to what is happening not only to our planet, but to themselves, and give some structure and suggestions as to how to work with the changes.

I also hope the books and the membership site my team and I have developed that is hosted on Facebook, *The Circle Led by Joan Scibienski*, will create a platform for discussion and empowerment, a place for those that are being activated to come and receive help and understanding as well as knowledge. We truly are creators with amazing powers. For too long we have let others control our destinies and beliefs about ourselves and our world. It is time to vanquish the illusion and take our power back. The world cannot change if those of us with vision don't fight for it.

Joan L. Scibienski, 2015
Revised April 2020

About the Author

Joan L. Scibienski is a professional intuitive consultant, numerologist, and astrologer working with thousands of clients throughout the world. She has lectured and taught classes on psychic development and spiritual topics in the U.S., Canada, and parts of Europe, as well as hosting her own television talk shows in Arizona. She holds degrees in nursing, psychology, and metaphysics.

She lives in Arizona with her soulmate Christopher, the ghost of her soul-puppy Sammie, and their new sweet puppy Cinnamon.

Be the Light, Becoming the Light, and Fighting Darkness are Scibienski's first novels. Through this series, she is attempting to educate the public, especially teens, on psychic phenomenon, spirituality, and helping our beautiful planet to survive.

Visit Scibienski's website at: intuitivedirections.net or join her on Facebook at Joan L. Scibienski, author.

Your feedback on the book is greatly appreciated. Please consider leaving a review on Amazon.com.

NOW YOU CAN BE PART OF A COMMUNITY LED BY JOAN

Joan and her team have developed a web-based membership site where Joan teaches classes on a variety of metaphysical topics, provides a monthly message that includes timely astrology information, hosts streamed events including Facebook Live and Zoom meetings, as well as providing access to the monthly Equinoxx channeling (yes, the same Equinoxx channeling that is described in *The Ariana Series*). In addition to the classroom website, there is also a Private Facebook group where members share a variety of ideas with each other as they work to shine **The Light on our beautiful planet!**

For more information, search:
"The Circle Led by Joan Scibienski" on Facebook.

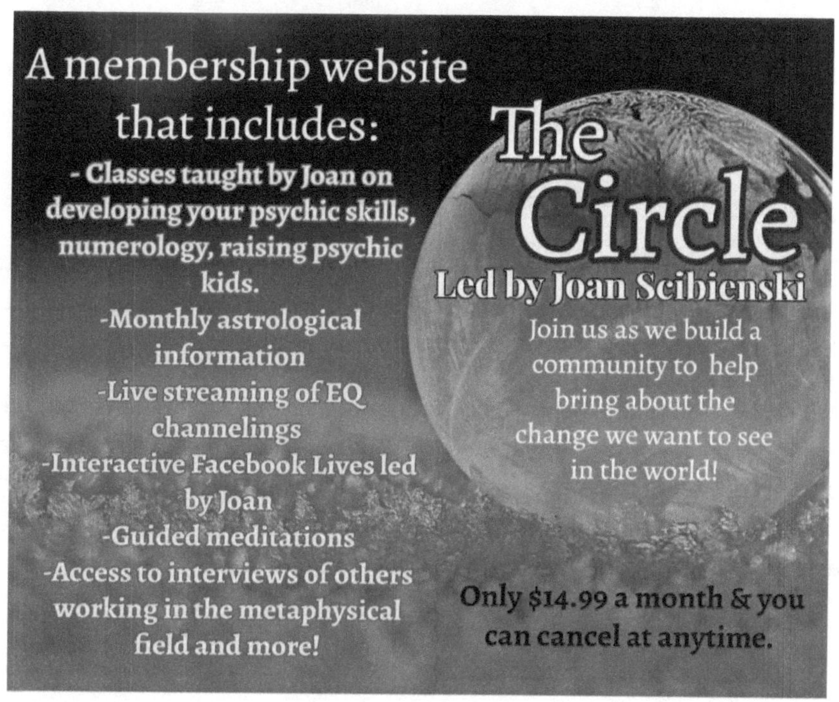

Being Psychic is Not A Gift. . .

Much like all our other senses, it is a survival tool we are all born with. In this workbook, basic metaphysical concepts and exercises are provided to teach you how to unlock your inner power.

This step-by-step approach filled with explanations and exercises can be used daily to solve problems, have a healthier body, protect yourself and your environment, contact your angels, guides, and loved ones, and help release fears and past hurts that keep you from having the happy life you deserve.

Available on Amazon and wherever books are sold.

Raising children is one of the most important things anyone can do. . .

Unfortunately, children don't come with a how-to manual. There are, however, some unique tools we can use to get a better understanding of what makes our children tick. Through the ancient science of numerology, the Universe has given us a map. This book will help you discover your child's basic tendencies, needs, and talents. It can also help you understand how to educate and discipline in ways that enhance these tendencies, helping to avoid bringing out the less desirable parts of your child's innate personality.

Available on Amazon and wherever books are sold.

Passion and Fairy Lore Come Together ~ Creating a Spelling Binding Series

An accident on a snowy road in the Sierra Nevada Mountains wipes away the memories of a beautiful, mysterious woman. Guilt-stricken that he could cause such pain, even by accident, the man who drove the truck that struck the woman is determined to help. He quickly realizes there is something special about her. She feels his strength and kindness. And despite that fact she knows nothing of her past, or if the man truly is who he says he is, she feels herself unmistakably drawn to him.

Her life is a mystery, yet her live is timeless. Can it continue once the awful truth is uncovered? Only the faeries know.

Available on Amazon and wherever books are sold.

www.ingramcontent.com/pod-product-compliance
Lightning Source LLC
Chambersburg PA
CBHW020224110726
47898CB00004B/1138